An Expensive Place to Die

Len Deighton was trained as an illustrator at the Royal College of Art in London. His writing career began with *The Ipcress File* which was a spectacular success and was made into a classic film starring Michael Caine.

Since then he has written many books of fiction and non-fiction. These include spy stories and war novels such as *Goodbye Mickey Mouse* and *Bomber* which the BBC recently made into a day-long radio drama in 'real time'. Last year Deighton's history of World War Two, *Blood, Tears and Folly*, was published to wide acclaim – Jack Higgins called it 'an absolute landmark'.

Three of his Bernard Samson stories – *Game*, *Set* and *Match* – were made into an internationally aired thirteen-hour television series. These were followed by *Hook*, *Line* and *Sinker*. He is at present working on the third Samson trilogy, *Faith*, *Hope* and *Charity*.

BY LEN DEIGHTON

FICTION

The Ipcress File
Horse Under Water
Funeral in Berlin
Billion-Dollar Brain
An Expensive Place to Die
Only When I Larf
Bomber
Declarations of War
Close-Up
Spy Story
Yesterday's Spy
Twinkle, Twinkle, Little Spy
SS-GB
XPD
Goodbye Mickey Mouse
Mamista
City of Gold
Violent Ward

THE SAMSON SERIES

Berlin Game
Mexico Set
London Match
Winter: A Berlin Family
1899–1945
Spy Hook
Spy Line
Spy Sinker
Faith
Hope

NON-FICTION

Fighter: The True Story of
the Battle of Britain
Blitzkrieg: From the Rise of
Hitler to the Fall of Dunkirk
Airshipwreck
ABC of French Food
Blood, Tears and Folly

LEN DEIGHTON

AN EXPENSIVE PLACE TO DIE

HarperCollins*Publishers*

HarperCollins*Publishers*
77–85 Fulham Palace Road,
Hammersmith, London W6 8JB

This paperback edition 1995
1 3 5 7 9 8 6 4 2

Previously published in paperback by Grafton 1977
Reprinted fourteen times

First published in Great Britain by
Jonathan Cape Ltd 1967

Copyright © Vico Patentverwertungs- und
Vermögensverwaltungs GMBH 1967

ISBN 0 586 02671 1

Set in Times

Printed in Great Britain by
Clays Ltd, St Ives plc

Do not disturb the President of the Republic
except in the case of world war.
Instructions for night duty officers
at the Élysée Palace

You should never beat a woman,
not even with a flower.
The Prophet Mohammed

Dying in Paris is a terribly expensive
business for a foreigner.
Oscar Wilde

The poem 'May' quoted on page 38 is from Twentieth Century Chinese Poetry, *translated by Kai-yu Hsu (copyright © Kai-yu Hsu 1963) and reprinted by permission of Doubleday & Co. Inc., New York*

1

The birds flew around for nothing but the hell of it. It was that sort of day: a trailer for the coming summer. Some birds flew in neat disciplined formations, some in ragged mobs, and higher, much higher, flew the loner who didn't like corporate decisions.

I turned away from the window. My visitor from the Embassy was still complaining.

'Paris lives in the past,' said the courier scornfully. 'Manet is at the opera and Degas at the ballet. Escoffier cooks while Eiffel builds, lyrics by Dumas, music by Offenbach. Oo-là-là our Paree is gay, monsieur, and our private rooms discreet, our coaches call at three, monsieur, and Schlieffen has no plans.'

'They're not all like that,' I said. Some birds hovered near the window deciding whether to eat the seed I'd scattered on the window-sill.

'All the ones I meet are,' said the courier. He too stopped looking across the humpty-backed rooftops, and as he turned away from the window he noticed a patch of white plaster on his sleeve. He brushed it petulantly as though Paris was trying to get at him. He pulled at his waistcoat – a natty affair with wide lapels – and then picked at the seat of the chair before sitting down. Now that he'd moved away from the window the birds returned, and began fighting over the seed that I had put there.

I pushed the coffee pot to him. 'Real coffee,' he said. 'The French seem to drink only instant coffee nowadays.' Thus reassured of my decorum he unlocked the briefcase that rested upon his knees. It was a large black case and

1

contained reams of reports. One of them he passed across to me.

'Read it while I'm here. I can't leave it.'

'It's secret?'

'No, our document copier has gone wrong and it's the only one I have.'

I read it. It was a 'stage report' of no importance. I passed it back. 'It's a lot of rubbish,' I said. 'I'm sorry you have to come all the way over here with this sort of junk.'

He shrugged. 'It gets me out of the office. Anyway it wouldn't do to have people like you in and out of the Embassy all the time.' He was new, this courier. They all started like him. Tough, beady-eyed young men anxious to prove how efficient they can be. Anxious too to demonstrate that Paris could have no attraction for them. A near-by clock chimed 2 P.M. and that disturbed the birds.

'Romantic,' he said. 'I don't know what's romantic about Paris except couples kissing on the street because the city's so overcrowded that they have nowhere else to go.' He finished his coffee. 'It's terribly good coffee,' he said. 'Dining out tonight?'

'Yes,' I said.

'With your artist friend Byrd?'

I gave him the sort of glance that Englishmen reserve for other Englishmen. He twitched with embarrassment. 'Look here,' he said, 'don't think for a moment . . . I mean . . . we don't have you . . . that is . . .'

'Don't start handing out indemnities,' I said. 'Of course I am under surveillance.'

'I remembered your saying that you always had dinner with Byrd the artist on Mondays. I noticed the Skira art book set aside on the table. I guessed you were returning it to him.'

'All good stuff,' I said. 'You should be doing my job.'

He smiled and shook his head. 'How I'd hate that,' he said. 'Dealing with the French all day; it's bad enough having to mix with them in the evening.'

'The French are all right,' I said.

'Did you keep the envelopes? I've brought the iodine in pot iodide.' I gave him all the envelopes that had come through the post during the previous week and he took his little bottle and painted the flaps carefully.

'Resealed with starch paste. Every damn letter. Someone here, must be. The landlady. Every damned letter. That's too thorough to be just nosiness. *Prenez garde.*' He put the envelopes, which had brown stains from the chemical reaction, into his case. 'Don't want to leave them around.'

'No,' I said. I yawned.

'I don't know what you do all day,' he said. 'Whatever do you find to do?'

'I do nothing all day except make coffee for people who wonder what I do all day.'

'Yes, well thanks for lunch. The old bitch does a good lunch even if she does steam your mail open.' He poured both of us more coffee. 'There's a new job for you.' He added the right amount of sugar, handed it to me and looked up. 'A man named Datt who comes here to Le Petit Légionnaire. The one that was sitting opposite us at lunch today.' There was a silence. I said:

'What do you want to know about him?'

'Nothing,' said the courier. 'We don't want to know anything about him, we want to give him a caseful of data.'

'Write his address on it and take it to the post office.'

He gave a pained little grimace. 'It's got to sound right when he gets it.'

'What is it?'

'It's a history of nuclear fall-out, starting from New Mexico right up to the last test. There are reports from

3

the Hiroshima hospital for bomb victims and various stuff about its effect upon cells and plant-life. It's too complex for me but you can read it through if your mind works that way.'

'What's the catch?'

'No catch.'

'What I need to know is how difficult it is to detect the phoney parts. One minute in the hands of an expert? Three months in the hands of a committee? I need to know how long the fuse is, if I'm the one that's planting the bomb.'

'There is no cause to believe it's anything other than genuine.' He pressed the lock on the case as though to test his claim.

'Well that's nice,' I said. 'Who does Datt send it to?'

'Not my part of the script, old boy. I'm just the errand boy, you know. I give the case to you, you give it to Datt, making sure he doesn't know where it came from. Pretend you are working for CIA if you like. You are a clean new boy, it should be straightforward.'

He drummed his fingers to indicate that he must leave.

'What am I expected to do with your bundle of papers – leave it on his plate one lunchtime?'

'Don't fret, that's being taken care of. Datt will know that you have the documents, he'll contact you and ask for them. Your job is just to let him have them . . . reluctantly.'

'Was I planted in this place six months ago just to do this job?'

He shrugged, and put the leather case on the table.

'Is it that important?' I asked. He walked to the door without replying. He opened the door suddenly and seemed disappointed that there was no one crouching outside.

'Terribly good coffee,' he said. 'But then it always is.' From downstairs I could hear the pop music on the radio.

4

It stopped. There was a fanfare and a jingle advertising shampoo.

'This is your floating favourite, Radio Janine,' said the announcer. It was a wonderful day to be working on one of the pirate radio ships: the sun warm, and three miles of calm blue sea that entitled you to duty-free cigarettes and whisky. I added it to the long list of jobs that were better than mine. I heard the lower door slam as the courier left. Then I washed up the coffee cups, gave Joe some fresh water and cuttlefish bone for his beak, picked up the documents and went downstairs for a drink.

2

Le Petit Légionnaire ('*cuisine faite par le patron*') was a plastic-trimmed barn glittering with mirrors, bottles and pin-tables. The regular lunchtime customers were local businessmen, clerks from a near-by hotel, two German girls who worked for a translation agency, a couple of musicians who slept late every day, two artists and the man named Datt to whom I was to offer the nuclear fall-out findings. The food was good. It was cooked by my landlord who was known throughout the neighbourhood as *la voix* – a disembodied voice that bellowed up the lift shaft without the aid of a loudspeaker system. *La voix* – so the stories went – once had his own restaurant in Boul. Mich. which during the war was a meeting place for members of the Front National.[1] He almost got a certificate signed by General Eisenhower but when his political past became clearer to the Americans he got his restaurant declared out of bounds and searched by the MPs every week for a year instead.

La voix did not like orders for *steck bien cuit, charcuterie* as a main dish or half-portions of anything at all. Regular customers got larger meals. Regular customers also got linen napkins but were expected to make them last all the week. But now lunch was over. From the back of the café I could hear the shrill voice of my landlady and the soft voice of Monsieur Datt who was saying, 'You might be making a mistake, you'll pay one hundred and ten thousand francs in Avenue Henri Martin and never see it come back.'

[1] Politically mixed but communist-dominated underground anti-Nazi organization.

'I'll take a chance on that,' said my landlord. 'Have a little more cognac.'

M. Datt spoke again. It was a low careful voice that measured each word carefully, 'Be content, my friend. Don't search for the sudden flashy gain that will cripple your neighbour. Enjoy the smaller rewards that build imperceptibly towards success.'

I stopped eavesdropping and moved on past the bar to my usual table outside. The light haze that so often prefaces a very hot Paris day had disappeared. Now it was a scorcher. The sky was the colour of well-washed *bleu de travail*. Across it were tiny wisps of cirrus. The heat bit deep into the concrete of the city and outside the grocers' fruit and vegetables were piled beautifully in their wooden racks, adding their aroma to the scent of a summer day. The waiter with the withered hand sank a secret cold lager, and old men sat outside on the *terrasse* warming their cold bones. Dogs cocked their legs jauntily and young girls wore loose cotton dresses and very little make-up and fastened their hair with elastic bands.

A young man propped his *moto* carefully against the wall of the public baths across the road. He reached an aerosol can of red paint from the pannier, shook it and wrote '*lisez l'Humanite nouvelle*' across the wall with a gentle hiss of compressed air. He glanced over his shoulder, then added a large hammer and sickle. He went back to his *moto* and sat astride it surveying the sign. A thick red dribble ran down from the capital H. He went back to the wall and dabbed at the excess paint with a piece of rag. He looked around, but no one shouted to him, so he carefully added the accent to the *e* before wrapping the can into the rag and stowing it away. He kicked the starter, there was a puff of light-blue smoke and the sudden burp of the two-stroke motor as he roared away towards the Boulevard.

I sat down and waved to old Jean for my usual Suze.

The pin-table glittered with pop-art-style illuminations and click-clicked and buzzed as the perfect metal spheres touched the contacts and made the numbers spin. The mirrored interior lied about the dimensions of the café and portrayed the sunlit street deep in its dark interior. I opened the case of documents, smoked, read, drank and watched the life of the *quartier*. I read ninety-three pages and almost understood by the time the rush-hour traffic began to thicken. I hid the documents in my room. It was time to visit Byrd.

I lived in the seventeenth arrondissement. The modernization project that had swept up the Avenue Neuilly and was extending the smart side of Paris to the west had by-passed the dingy Quartier des Ternes. I walked as far as the Avenue de la Grande Armée. The Arc was astraddle the Étoile and the traffic was desperate to get there. Thousands of red lights twinkled like bloodshot stars in the warm mist of the exhaust fumes. It was a fine Paris evening, Gauloises and garlic sat lightly on the air, and the cars and people were moving with the subdued hysteria that the French call *élan*.

I remembered my conversation with the man from the British Embassy. He seemed upset today, I thought complacently. I didn't mind upsetting him. Didn't mind upsetting all of them, come to that. No cause to believe it's anything other than genuine. I snorted loudly enough to attract attention. What a fool London must think I am. And that stuff about Byrd. How did they know I'd be dining with him tonight? Byrd, I thought, art books from Skira, what a lot of cock. I hardly knew Byrd, even though he was English and did lunch in Le Petit Légionnaire. Last Monday I dined with him but I'd told no one that I was dining with him again tonight. I'm a professional. I wouldn't tell my mother where I keep the fuse wire.

3

The light was just beginning to go as I walked through the street market to Byrd's place. The building was grey and peeling, but so were all the others in the street. So, in fact, were almost all the others in Paris. I pressed the latch. Inside the dark entrance a twenty-five-watt bulb threw a glimmer of light across several dozen tiny hutches with mail slots. Some of the hutches were marked with grimy business cards, others had names scrawled across them in ball-point writing. Down the hall there were thick ropes of wiring connected to twenty or more wooden boxes. Tracing a wiring fault would have proved a remarkable problem. Through a door at the far end there was a courtyard. It was cobbled, grey and shiny with water that dripped from somewhere overhead. It was a desolate yard of a type that I had always associated with the British prison system. The concierge was standing in the courtyard as though daring me to complain about it. If mutiny came, then that courtyard would be its starting place. At the top of a narrow creaking staircase was Byrd's studio. It was chaos. Not the sort of chaos that results from an explosion, but the kind that takes years to achieve. Spend five years hiding things, losing things and propping broken things up, then give it two years for the dust to settle thickly and you've got Byrd's studio. The only really clean thing was the gigantic window through which a sunset warmed the whole place with rosy light. There were books everywhere, and bowls of hardened plaster, buckets of dirty water, easels carrying large half-completed canvases. On the battered sofa were the two posh English Sunday papers still pristine and unread. A huge enamel-topped table that Byrd used as a palette was sticky with patches of colour, and across one wall was a fifteen-foot-high hardboard construction upon which Byrd was painting a mural. I walked straight in – the door was always open.

'You're dead,' called Byrd loudly. He was high on a ladder working on a figure near the top of the fifteen-foot-high painting.

'I keep forgetting I'm dead,' said the model. She was nude and stretched awkwardly across a box.

'Just keep your right foot still,' Byrd called to her. 'You can move your arms.'

The nude girl stretched her arms with a grateful moan of pleasure.

'Is that okay?' she asked.

'You've moved the knee a little, it's tricky . . . Oh well, perhaps we'll call that a day.' He stopped painting. 'Get dressed, Annie.' She was a tall girl of about twenty-five. Dark, good-looking, but not beautiful. 'Can I have a shower?' she asked.

'The water's not too warm, I'm afraid,' said Byrd, 'but try it, it may have improved.'

The girl pulled a threadbare man's dressing-gown around her shoulders and slid her feet into a pair of silk slippers. Byrd climbed very slowly down from the ladder on which he was perched. There was a smell of linseed oil and turpentine. He rubbed at the handful of brushes with a rag. The large painting was nearly completed. It was difficult to put a name to the style; perhaps Kokoschka or Soutine came nearest to it but this was more polished, though less alive, than either. Byrd tapped the scaffolding against which the ladder was propped.

'I built that. Not bad, eh? Couldn't get one like it anywhere in Paris, not anywhere. Are you a do-it-yourself man?'

'I'm a let-someone-else-do-it man.'

'Really,' said Byrd and nodded gravely. 'Eight o'clock already, is it?'

'Nearly half past,' I said.

'I need a pipe of tobacco.' He threw the brushes into a floral-patterned chamber-pot in which stood another hundred. 'Sherry?' He untied the strings that prevented his trouser bottoms smudging the huge painting, and looked back towards the mural, hardly able to drag himself away from it. 'The light started to go an hour back. I'll have to repaint that section tomorrow.' He took the glass from an oil lamp, lit the wick carefully and adjusted the flame. 'A fine light these oil lamps give. A fine silky light.' He poured two glasses of dry sherry, removed a huge Shetland sweater and eased himself into a battered chair. In the neck of his check-patterned shirt he arranged a silk scarf, then began to sift through his tobacco pouch as though he'd lost something in there.

It was hard to guess Byrd's age except that he was in the middle fifties. He had plenty of hair and it was showing no sign of grey. His skin was fair and so tight across his face that you could see the muscles that ran from cheekbone to jaw. His ears were tiny and set high, his eyes were bright, active and black, and he stared at you when he spoke to prove how earnest he was. Had I not known that he was a regular naval officer until taking up painting eight years ago I might have guessed him to be a mechanic who had bought his own garage. When he had carefully primed his pipe he lit it with slow care. It wasn't until then that he spoke again.

'Go to England at all?'

'Not often,' I said.

'Nor me. I need more baccy; next time you go you might bear that in mind.'

'Yes,' I said.

'This brand,' he held a packet for me to see. 'Don't seem to have it here in France. Only stuff I like.'

He had a stiff, quarter-deck manner that kept his elbows at his waist and his chin in his neck. He used words like 'roadster' that revealed how long it was since he had lived in England.

'I'm going to ask you to leave early tonight,' he said. 'Heavy day tomorrow.' He called to the model, 'Early start tomorrow, Annie.'

'Very well,' she called back.

'We'll call dinner off if you like.' I offered.

'No need to do that. Looking forward to it to tell the truth.' Byrd scratched the side of his nose.

'Do you know Monsieur Datt?' I asked. 'He lunches at the Petit Légionnaire. Big-built man with white hair.'

'No,' he said. He sniffed. He knew every nuance of the sniff. This one was light in weight and almost inaudible. I dropped the subject of the man from the Avenue Foch.

Byrd had asked another painter to join us for dinner. He arrived about nine thirty. Jean-Paul Pascal was a handsome muscular young man with a narrow pelvis who easily adapted himself to the cowboy look that the French admire. His tall rangy figure contrasted sharply with the stocky blunt rigidity of Byrd. His skin was tanned, his teeth perfect. He was expensively dressed in a light-blue suit and a tie with designs embroidered on it. He removed his dark glasses and put them in his pocket.

'An English friend of Monsieur Byrd,' Jean-Paul repeated as he took my hand and shook it. 'Enchanted.' His handshake was gentle and diffident as though he was ashamed to look so much like a film star.

'Jean-Paul speaks no English,' said Byrd.

'It is too complicated,' said Jean-Paul. 'I speak a little but I do not understand what you say in reply.'

'Precisely,' said Byrd. 'That's the whole idea of English. Foreigners can communicate information to us but Englishmen can still talk together without an outsider being able to comprehend.' His face was stern, then he smiled primly. 'Jean-Paul's a good fellow just the same: a painter.' He turned to him. 'Busy day, Jean?'

'Busy, but I didn't get much done.'

'Must keep at at, my boy. You'll never be a great painter unless you learn to apply yourself.'

'Oh but one must find oneself. Proceed at one's own speed,' said Jean-Paul.

'Your speed is too slow,' Byrd pronounced, and handed Jean-Paul a glass of sherry without having asked him what he wanted. Jean turned to me, anxious to explain his apparent laziness. 'It is difficult to begin a painting – it's a statement – once the mark is made one has to relate all later brush-strokes to it.'

'Nonsense,' said Byrd. 'Simplest thing in the world to begin, tricky though pleasurable to proceed with, but difficult – dammed difficult – to end.'

'Like a love affair,' I said. Jean laughed. Byrd flushed and scratched the side of his nose.

'Ah. Work and women don't mix. Womanizing and loose living is attractive at the time, but middle age finds women left sans beauty, and men sans skills; result misery. Ask your friend Monsieur Datt about that.'

'Are you a friend of Datt?' Jean-Paul asked.

'I hardly know him,' I said. 'I was asking Byrd about him.'

'Don't ask too many questions,' said Jean. 'He is a man of great influence; Count of Périgord it is said, an ancient family, a powerful man. A dangerous man. He is a doctor and a psychiatrist. They say he uses LSD a great deal. His clinic is as expensive as any in Paris, but he gives the most scandalous parties there too.'

'What's that?' said Byrd. 'Explain.'

'One hears stories,' said Jean. He smiled in embarrassment and wanted to say no more, but Byrd made an impatient movement with his hand, so he continued. 'Stories of gambling parties, of highly placed men who

13

have got into financial trouble and found themselves . . .' he paused '. . . in the bath.'

'Does that mean dead?'

'It means "in trouble", idiom,' explained Byrd to me in English.

'One or two important men took their own lives,' said Jean. 'Some said they were in debt.'

'Damned fools,' said Byrd. 'That's the sort of fellows in charge of things today, no stamina, no fibre; and that fellow Datt is a party to it, eh? Just as I thought. Oh well, chaps won't be told today. Experience better bought than taught they say. One more sherry and we'll go to dinner. What say to La Coupole? It's one of the few places still open where we don't have to reserve.'

Annie the model reappeared in a simple green shirt-waist dress. She kissed Jean-Paul in a familiar way and said good evening to each of us.

'Early in the morning,' Byrd said as he paid her. She nodded and smiled.

'An attractive girl,' Jean-Paul said after she had gone.

'Yes,' I said.

'Poor child,' said Byrd. 'It's a hard town for a young girl without money.'

I'd noticed her expensive crocodile handbag and Charles Jourdan shoes, but I didn't comment.

'Want to go to an art show opening Friday? Free champagne.' Jean-Paul produced half a dozen gold-printed invitations, gave one to me and put one on Byrd's easel.

'Yes, we'll go to that,' said Byrd; he was pleased to be organizing us. 'Are you in your fine motor, Jean?' Byrd asked.

Jean nodded.

Jean's car was a white Mercedes convertible. We drove down the Champs with the roof down. We wined and dined well and Jean-Paul plagued us with questions like do the Americans drink Coca-Cola because it's good for their livers.

It was nearly one A.M. when Jean dropped Byrd at the studio. He insisted upon driving me back to my room over Le Petit Légionnaire. 'I am especially glad you came tonight,' he said. 'Byrd thinks that he is the only serious painter in Paris, but there are many of us who work equally hard in our own way.'

'Being in the navy,' I said, 'is probably not the best of training for a painter.'

'There is no training for a painter. No more than there is training for life. A man makes as profound a statement as he is able. Byrd is a sincere man with a thirst for knowledge of painting and an aptitude for its skills. Already his work is attracting serious interest here in Paris and a reputation in Paris will carry you anywhere in the world.'

I sat there for a moment nodding, then I opened the door of the Mercedes and got out. 'Thanks for the ride.'

Jean-Paul leaned across the seat, offered me his card and shook my hand. 'Phone me,' he said, and – without letting go of my hand – added, 'If you want to go to the house in the Avenue Foch I can arrange that too. I'm not sure I can recommend it, but if you have money to lose I'll introduce you. I am a close friend of the Count; last week I took the Prince of Besacoron there – he is another very good friend of mine.'

'Thanks,' I said, taking the card. He stabbed the accelerator and the motor growled. He winked and said, 'But no recriminations afterward.'

'No,' I agreed. The Mercedes slid forward.

I watched the white car turn on to the Avenue with enough momentum to make the tyres howl. The Petit Légionnaire was closed. I let myself in by the side entrance. Datt and my landlord were still sitting at the same table as they had been that afternoon. They were still playing Monopoly. Datt was reading from his Community Chest card, '*Allez en prison. Avancez tout droit en prison. Ne passez pas par la case "Départ". Ne recevez pas Frs 20.000.*' My landlord laughed, so did M. Datt.

'What will your patients say?' said my landlord.

'They are very understanding,' said Datt; he seemed to take the whole game seriously. Perhaps he got more out of it that way.

I tiptoed upstairs. I could see right across Paris. Through the dark city the red neon arteries of the tourist industry flowed from Pigalle through Montmartre to Boul. Mich., Paris's great self-inflicted wound.

Joe chirped. I read Jean's card. '"Jean-Paul Pascal, artist painter". And good friend to princes,' I said. Joe nodded.

4

Two nights later I was invited to join the Monopoly game. I bought hotels in rue Lecourbe and paid rent at the Gare du Nord. Old Datt pedantically handled the toy money and told us why we went broke.

When only Datt remained solvent he pushed back his chair and nodded sagely as he replaced the pieces of wood and paper in the box. If you were buying old men, then Datt would have come in a box marked White, Large and Bald. Behind his tinted spectacles his eyes were moist and his lips soft and dark like a girl's, or perhaps they only seemed dark against the clear white skin of his face. His head was a shiny dome and his white hair soft and wispy like mist around a mountain top. He didn't smile much, but he was a genial man, although a little fussy in his mannerisms as people of either sex become when they live alone.

Madame Tastevin had, upon her insolvency, departed to the kitchen to prepare supper.

I offered my cigarettes to Datt and to my landlord. Tastevin took one, but Datt declined with a theatrical gesture. 'There seems no sense in it,' he proclaimed, and again did that movement of the hand that looked like he was blessing a multitude at Benares. His voice was an upper-class voice, not because of his vocabulary or because he got his conjugations right but because he sang his words in the style of the Comédie Française, stressing a word musically and then dropping the rest of the sentence like a half-smoked Gauloise. 'No sense in it,' he repeated.

17

'Pleasure,' said Tastevin, puffing away. 'Not sense.' His voice was like a rusty lawn-mower.

'The pursuit of pleasure,' said Datt, 'is a pitfall-studded route.' He removed the rimless spectacles and looked up at me blinking.

'You speak from experience?' I asked.

'I've done everything,' said Datt. 'Some things twice. I've lived in eight different countries in four continents. I've been a beggar and I've been a thief. I've been happy and sad, rich and poor, master and manservant.'

'And the secret of happiness,' mocked Tastevin, 'is to refrain from smoking?'

'The secret of happiness,' Datt corrected, 'is to refrain from wishing to.'

'If that's the way you feel,' said Tastevin, 'why do you come to my restaurant almost every day?'

At that moment Madame Tastevin came in with a tray holding a coffee jug and plates of cold chicken and terrine of hare.

'There's your reason for not smoking,' said Datt. 'I would never let tobacco mar the taste of the food here.' Madame Tastevin purred with delight. 'I sometimes think my life is too perfect. I enjoy my work and never wish to do less of it, and I eat your wonderful food. What a perfect life.'

'That's self-indulgent,' said Tastevin.

'Perhaps it is – so what? Isn't your life self-indulgent? You could make far more money working in one of the three-star restaurants but you spend your life running this small one – one might almost say for your friends.'

'I suppose that's true,' said Tastevin. 'I enjoy cooking, and my customers appreciate my work I think.'

'Quite so. You are a sensible man. It's madness to go every day to work at something you do not enjoy.'

'But suppose,' asked Madame Tastevin, 'that such a

job brought us a lot of money that would enable him to retire and then do as he wishes?'

'Madame,' said Datt. His voice took on that portentous, melodious quality that narrators on arty French films employ. 'Madame Tastevin,' he said again, 'there is a cave in Kashmir – Amarnath cave – the most sacred spot on earth to a worshipper of the Hindu god Siva. The pilgrims who journey there are old; sometimes sick too. Many of them die on the high passes, their tiny tents swept away by the sudden rainstorms. Their relatives do not weep. To them this does not matter; even the arrival – which must always be on a night of full moon – is not more vital than the journey. Many know they will never arrive. It is the journey that is holy, and so it is to Existentialists: life is more important than death. Whatever they do, men are too anxious to get to the end. The sex act, eating a fine meal, playing golf, there is a temptation to rush, gobble or run. That is foolish, for one should move at a relaxed pace through life doing the work one enjoys instead of chasing ambition helter-skelter, pursuing one's ultimate death.'

Tastevin nodded sagely and I stopped gobbling the cold chicken. Datt tucked a napkin in his collar and savoured a little terrine, pursing his lips and remarking on the salt content. When he had finished he turned to me. 'You have a telephone, I believe,' he said, and without waiting for my reply was already on his feet and moving towards the door.

'By all means use it,' I told him and by a burst of speed was able to get upstairs before him. Joey blinked in the sudden electric light. Datt dialled a number and said 'Hello, I am at the Petit Légionnaire and I am ready for the car in about five minutes.' He hung up. Datt came over to where I was standing with Joey. 'It's my belief,' said Datt, 'that you are making inquiries about me.'

I didn't answer.

'It would be a fruitless task.'

'Why?'

'Because no matter what you discover it will not harm me.'

'The art of Zen in clandestine behaviour?'

Datt smiled. 'The art of Zen in having influential friends,' he said.

I didn't answer him. I pushed open the shutters and there was Paris. Warm streets, a policeman, two lovers, four cats, fifty dented *deux-chevaux* cars and a pavement full of garbage bins. The life of Paris centres on its streets; its inhabitants sit at the windows gazing down upon people as they buy, sell, thieve, drive, fight, eat, chat, posture, cheat or merely stand looking, upon the streets of Paris. Its violence too centres upon the streets and outside the public baths the previous night M. Picard, who owned the laundry, was robbed and knifed. He died twitching his own blood into ugly splashes that could still be seen upon the torn election posters flapping from the ancient shutters.

A black Daimler came down the road and stopped with a tiny squeak.

'Thank you for the use of your telephone,' said Datt. At the door he turned. 'Next week I should like to talk with you again,' he said. 'You must tell me what you are curious about.'

'Any time,' I agreed. 'Tomorrow if you wish.'

Datt shook his head. 'Next week will be soon enough.'

'As you wish.'

'Yes,' said Datt. He walked out without saying good night.

After Datt left Joey took a brief swing. I checked that the documents were still in their hiding-place. Perhaps I should have given them to Datt a few minutes before, but I looked forward to seeing him again next week. 'It seems to me, Joe,' I said, 'that we are the only people in town who don't have powerful friends.' I put the cover on him before he could answer.

5

Faubourg St Honoré, seven thirty P.M. Friday. The tiny art gallery was bursting at the seams. Champagne, free champagne, was spilling over high suede boots and broken sandals. I had spent twenty-five minutes prising triangular pieces of smoked salmon away from circular pieces of toast, which is not a rewarding experience for a fully grown human male. Byrd was talking to Jean-Paul and rapping at one of the abstract panels. I edged towards them, but a young woman with green eye-shadow grabbed my arm. 'Where's the artist?' she asked. 'Someone's interested in "Creature who fears the machine" and I don't know if it's one hundred thousand francs or fifty.' I turned to her but she had grabbed someone else already. Most of my champagne was lost by the time I got to Byrd and Jean-Paul.

'There's some terrible people here,' said Jean-Paul.

'As long as they don't start playing that dashed rock-and-roll music again,' said Byrd.

'Were they doing that?' I asked.

Byrd nodded. 'Can't stand it. Sorry and all that, but can't stand it.'

The woman with green eye-shadow waved across a sea of shoulders, then cupped her mouth and yelled to me. 'They have broken one of the gold chairs,' she said. 'Does it matter?'

I couldn't stand her being so worried. 'Don't worry,' I called. She nodded and smiled in relief.

'What's going on?' said Jean-Paul. 'Do you own this gallery?'

'Give me time,' I said, 'and maybe I'll give you a one-man show.'

Jean-Paul smiled to show that he knew it was a joke, but Byrd looked up suddenly. 'Look here, Jean-Paul,' he said severely, 'a one-man show would be fatal for you right now. You are in no way prepared. You need time, my boy, time. Walk before you run.' Byrd turned to me. 'Walk before you run, that's right, isn't it?'

'No,' I said. 'Any mother will tell you that most kids can run before they can walk; it's walking that's difficult.'

Jean-Paul winked at me and said, 'I must decline, but thank you anyway.'

Byrd said, 'He's not ready. You gallery chappies will just have to wait. Don't rush these young artists. It's not fair. Not fair to them.'

I was just going to straighten things out when a short thickset Frenchman with a Légion d'Honneur in his buttonhole came up and began to talk to Byrd.

'Let me introduce you,' said Byrd. He wouldn't tolerate informality. 'This is Chief Inspector Loiseau. Policeman. I went through a lot of the war with his brother.'

We shook hands, and then Loiseau shook hands with Jean-Paul, although neither of them showed a great deal of enthusiasm for the ritual.

The French, more particularly the men, have developed a characteristic mouth that enables them to deal with their language. The English use their pointed and dexterous tongues, and their mouths become pinched and close. The French use their lips and a Frenchman's mouth becomes loose and his lips jut forward. The cheeks sink a little to help this and a French face takes on a lean look, back-sloping like an old-fashioned coal-scuttle. Loiseau had just such a face.

'What's a policeman doing at an art show?' asked Byrd.

'We policemen are not uncultured oafs,' said Loiseau

with a smile. 'In our off-duty hours we have even been known to drink alcohol.'

'You are never off duty,' said Byrd. 'What is it? Expecting someone to make off with the champagne buckets?' Loiseau smiled slyly. A waiter nearly passed us with a tray of champagne.

'One might ask what you are doing here?' said Loiseau to Byrd. 'I wouldn't think this was your sort of art.' He tapped one of the large panels. It was a highly finished nude, contorted in pose, the skin shiny as though made from polished plastic. In the background there were strange pieces of surrealism, most of them with obvious Freudian connotations.

'The snake and the egg are well drawn,' said Byrd. 'The girl's a damn poor show though.'

'The foot is out of drawing,' said Jean-Paul. 'It's not well observed.'

'A girl that could do that would have to be a cripple,' said Byrd.

Still more people crowded into the room and we were being pushed closer and closer to the wall.

Loiseau smiled. 'But a *poule* that could get into that position would earn a fortune on the rue Godot de Mauroy,' said the Chief Inspector.

Loiseau spoke just like any police officer. You can easily recognize them by their speech, to which a lifetime of giving evidence imparts a special clarity. The facts are arranged before the conclusions just like a written report, and certain important words – bus route numbers and road names – are given emphasis so that even young constables can remember them.

Byrd turned back to Jean-Paul: he was anxious to discuss the painting. 'You've got to hand it to him though, the *trompe l'œil* technique is superb, the tiny brushwork. Look at the way the Coca-Cola bottle is done.'

'He's copied that from a photo,' said Jean-Paul. Byrd bent down for a close look.

'Damn me! The rotten little swine!' said Byrd. 'It *is* a bloody photo. It's stuck on. Look at that!' He picked at the corner of the bottle and then appealed to the people around him. 'Look at that, it's been cut from a coloured advert.' He applied himself to other parts of the painting. 'The typewriter too, and the girl . . .'

'Stop picking at that nipple,' said the woman with green eye-shadow. 'If you touch the paintings once more you'll be asked to leave.' She turned to me. 'How can you stand there and let them do it? If the artist saw them he'd go mad.'

'Gone mad already,' said Byrd curtly. 'Thinking chaps are going to pay money for bits cut out of picture books.'

'It's quite legitimate,' said Jean-Paul. 'It's an *objet trouvé* . . .'

'Rot,' said Byrd. 'An *objet trouvé* is a piece of driftwood or a fine stone – it's something in which an artist has found and seen otherwise unnoticed beauty. How can an advert be found? How can you find an advert – the damned things are pushed under your noses every way you look, more's the pity.'

'But the artist must have freedom to . . .'

'Artist?' snorted Byrd. 'Damned fraud. Damned rotten little swine.'

A man in evening dress with three ballpoint pens in his breast pocket turned round. 'I haven't noticed you decline any champagne,' he said to Byrd. He used the intimate *tu*. Although it was a common form of address among the young arty set, his use of it to Byrd was offensive.

'What I had,' interrupted Jean-Paul – he paused before delivering the insult – 'was Sauternes with Alka Seltzer.'

The man in the dinner suit leaned across to grab at

him, but Chief Inspector Loiseau interposed himself and got a slight blow on the arm.

'A thousand apologies, Chief Inspector,' said the man in the dinner suit.

'Nothing,' said Loiseau. 'I should have looked where I was going.'

Jean-Paul was pushing Byrd towards the door, but they were moving very slowly. The man in the dinner suit leaned across to the woman with the green eye-shadow and said loudly, 'They mean no harm, they are drunk, but make sure they leave immediately.' He looked back towards Loiseau to see if his profound understanding of human nature was registering. '*He's* with them,' the woman said, nodding at me. 'I thought he was from the insurance company when he first came.' I heard Byrd say, 'I will not take it back; he's a rotten little swine.'

'Perhaps,' said dinner-jacket tactfully, 'you would be kind enough to make sure that your friends come to no harm in the street.'

I said, 'If they get out of here in one piece they can take their own chances in the street.'

'Since you can't take a hint,' said dinner-jacket, 'let me make it clear . . .'

'He's with me,' said Loiseau.

The man shied. 'Chief Inspector,' said dinner-jacket, 'I am desolated.'

'We are leaving anyway,' said Loiseau, nodding to me. Dinner-jacket smiled and turned back to the woman with green eye-shadow.

'You go where you like,' I said. 'I'm staying right here.'

Dinner-jacket swivelled back like a glove puppet.

Loiseau put a hand on my arm. 'I thought you wanted to talk about getting your *carte de séjour* from the Prefecture.'

25

'I'm having no trouble getting my *carte de séjour*,' I said.

'Exactly,' said Loiseau and moved through the crowd towards the door. I followed.

Near the entrance there was a table containing a book of newspaper clippings and catalogues. The woman with green eye-shadow called to us. She offered Loiseau her hand and then reached out to me. She held the wrist limp as women do when they half expect a man to kiss the back of their hand. 'Please sign the visitors' book,' she said.

Loiseau bent over the book and wrote in neat neurotic writing 'Claude Loiseau'; under comments he wrote 'stimulating'. The woman swivelled the book to me. I wrote my name and under comments I wrote what I always write when I don't know what to say – 'uncompromising'.

The woman nodded. 'And your address,' she said.

I was about to point out that no one else had written their address in the book, but when a shapely young woman asks for my address I'm not the man to be secretive. I wrote it: 'c/o Petit Légionnaire, rue St Ferdinand, 17ième.'

The woman smiled to Loiseau in a familiar way. She said, 'I know the Chief Inspector's address: Criminal Investigation Department, Sûreté Nationale, rue des Saussaies.'[1]

---

[1] France has a particularly complex police system. The Sûreté Nationale is the police system for all France that operates directly for the Minister of the Interior in the Ministry at rue des Saussaies. At Quai des Orfèvres there is the Prefecture which does the same job for Paris. There is also the Gendarmerie – recognized by their khaki coats in summer – who police the whole of France under the orders of the Army Ministry and are, in effect, soldiers. As well as this there are special groups – Gardes Mobiles and CRS (Compagnie Républicaine de Sécurité) companies – which are highly mobile and have violent striking power. Loiseau worked for the first-named, the Sûreté

26

Loiseau's office had that cramped, melancholy atmosphere that policemen relish. There were two small silver pots for the shooting team that Loiseau had led to victory in 1959 and several group photos – one showed Loiseau in army uniform standing in front of a tank. Loiseau brought a large M 1950 automatic from his waist and put it into a drawer. 'I'm going to get something smaller,' he said. 'This is ruining my suits.' He locked the drawer carefully and then went through the other drawers of his desk, riffling through the contents and slamming them closed until he laid a dossier on his blotter.

'This is your dossier,' said Loiseau. He held up a print of the photo that appears on my *carte de séjour*. '"Occupation,"' he read, '"travel agency director".' He looked up at me and I nodded. 'That's a good job?'

'It suits me,' I said.

'It would suit me', said Loiseau. 'Eight hundred new francs each week and you spend most of your time amusing yourself.'

'There's a revived interest in leisure,' I said.

'I hadn't noticed any decline among the people who work for me.' He pushed his Gauloises towards me. We lit up and looked at each other. Loiseau was about fifty years old. Short muscular body with big shoulders. His face was pitted with tiny scars and part of his left ear was missing. His hair was pure white and very short. He had plenty of energy but not so much that he was prepared to waste any. He hung his jacket on his chair back and rolled up his shirtsleeves very neatly. He didn't look like a policeman now, more like a paratroop colonel planning a coup.

Nationale, who as well as all standard police work also attend to counter-espionage, economic espionage (unions and potential strikes etc.), frontier policing and gaming. The sixty CRS units are also controlled by one of the directorates (Public Security) of the Sûreté Nationale.

'You are making inquiries about Monsieur Datt's clinic on the Avenue Foch.'

'Everyone keeps telling me that.'

'Who for?'

I said, 'I don't know about that place, and I don't want to know about it.'

'I'm treating you like an adult,' said Loiseau. 'If you prefer to be treated like a spotty-faced j.v. then we can do that too.'

'What's the question again?'

'I'd like to know who you are working for. However, it would take a couple of hours in the hen cage to get that out of you. So for the time being I'll tell you this: I am interested in that house and I don't want you to even come downwind of it. Stay well away. Tell whoever you are working for that the house in Avenue Foch is going to remain a little secret of Chief Inspector Loiseau.' He paused, wondering how much more to tell me. 'There are powerful interests involved. Violent groups are engaged in a struggle for criminal power.'

'Why do you tell me that?'

'I thought that you should know.' He gave a Gallic shrug.

'Why?'

'Don't you understand? These men are dangerous.'

'Then why aren't you dragging them into your office instead of me?'

'Oh, they are too clever for us. Also they have well-placed friends who protect them. It's only when the friends fail that they resort to . . . coercion, blackmail, killing even. But always skilfully.'

'They say it's better to know the judge than to know the law.'

'Who says that?'

'I heard it somewhere.'

'You're an eavesdropper,' said Loiseau.

'I am,' I said. 'And a damned good one.'

'It sounds as though you like it,' said Loiseau grimly.

'It's my favourite indoor sport. Dynamic and yet sedentary; a game of skill with an element of chance. No season, no special equipment . . .'

'Don't be so clever,' he said sadly. 'This is a political matter. Do you know what that means?'

'No. I don't know what that means.'

'It means that you might well spend one morning next week being lifted out of some quiet backwater of the St Martin canal and travelling down to the Medico-Legal Institute[2] where the boys in butchers' aprons and rubber boots live. They'll take an inventory of what they find in your pockets, send your clothes to the Poor Law Administration Office, put a numbered armband on you, freeze you to eight degrees centigrade and put you in a rack with two other foolish lads. The superintendent will phone me and I'll have to go along and identify you. I'll hate doing that because at this time of year there are clouds of flies as large as bats and a smell that reaches to Austerlitz Station.' He paused. 'And we won't even investigate the affair. Be sure you understand.'

I said, 'I understand all right. I've become an expert at recognizing threats no matter how veiled they are. But before you give a couple of cops tape measures and labels and maps of the St Martin canal, make sure you choose men that your department doesn't find indispensable.'

'Alas, you have misunderstood,' said Loiseau's mouth, but his eyes didn't say that. He stared. 'We'll leave it like that, but . . .'

'Just leave it like that,' I interrupted. 'You tell your cops to carry the capes with the lead-shot hems and I'll wear my water-wings.'

---

[2] An old building on a prison site adjacent to Mazas Square near Austerlitz Station. It is used as a mortuary.

Loiseau allowed his face to become as friendly as it could become.

'I don't know where you fit into Monsieur Datt's clinic, but until I do know I'll be watching you very closely. If it's a political affair, then let the political departments request information. There's no point in us being at each other's throat. Agreed?'

'Agreed.'

'In the next few few days you might be in contact with people who claim to be acting for me. Don't believe them. Anything you want to know, come back to me directly. I'm 22.22.[3] If you can't reach me here then this office will know where I am. Tell the operator that "*Un sourire est différent d'un rire*".'

'Agreed,' I said. The French still use those silly code words that are impossible to use if you are being overheard.

'One last thing,' said Loiseau. 'I can see that no advice, however well meant, can register with you, so let me add that, should you tackle these men and come off best . . .' he looked up to be sure that I was listening, '. . . then I will personally guarantee that you'll *manger les haricots* for five years.'

'Charged with . . .?'

'Giving Chief Inspector Loiseau trouble beyond his normal duties.'

'You might be going further than your authority permits,' I said, trying to give the impression that I too might have important friends.

Loiseau smiled. 'Of course I am. I have gained my present powerful position by always taking ten per cent more authority than I am given.' He lifted the phone and jangled the receiver rest so that its bell tinkled in the outer office. It must have been a prearranged signal

---

[3] Senior police officers in France are assigned their own private lines.

because his assistant came quickly. Loiseau nodded to indicate the meeting was over.

'Goodbye,' he said. 'It was good to see you again.'

'Again?'

'NATO conference on falsification of cargo manifests, held in Bonn, April 1956. You represented BAOR, if I remember rightly.'

'You talk in endless riddles,' I said. 'I've never been in Bonn.'

'You are a glib fellow,' said Loiseau. 'Another ten minutes and you'd convince me I'd never been there.' He turned to the assistant who was waiting to conduct me downstairs. 'Count the fire extinguishers after he's left,' said Loiseau. 'And on no account shake hands with him; you might find yourself being thrown into the Faubourg St Honoré.'

Loiseau's assistant took me down to the door. He was a spotty-faced boy with circular metal-framed spectacles that bit deep into his features like pennies that had grown into the trunk of a tree. 'Goodbye,' I said as I left him, and gave him a brief smile. He looked through me, nodding to the policeman on sentry who eased the machine gun on his shoulder. Abandoning the *entente cordiale* I walked towards the Faubourg St Honoré looking for a taxi. From the gratings in the road there came the sound of a Métro train, its clatter muffled by four huddled *clochards* anxious for the warmth of the sour subterranean air. One of them came half-awake, troubled by a bad dream. He yelled and then mumbled.

On the corner an E-type was parked. As I turned the corner the headlights flashed and it moved towards me. I stood well back as the door swung open. A woman's voice said, 'Jump in.'

'Not right now,' I said.

6

Maria Chauvet was thirty-two years old. She had kept her looks, her gentleness, her figure, her sexual optimism, her respect for men's cleverness, her domestication. She had lost her girlhood friends, her shyness, her literary aspirations, her obsession with clothes and her husband. It was a fair swop, she decided. Time had given her a greater measure of independence. She looked around the art gallery without seeing even one person that she really desired to see again. And yet they were her people: the ones she had known since her early twenties, the people who shared her tastes in cinema, travel, sport and books. Now she no longer wished to hear their opinions about the things she enjoyed and she only slightly wished to hear their opinions about the things she hated. The paintings here were awful, they didn't even show a childish exuberance; they were old, jaded and sad. She hated things that were too real. Ageing was real; as things grew older they became more real, and although age wasn't something she dreaded she didn't want to hurry in that direction.

Maria hoped that Loiseau wasn't going to be violent with the Englishman that he had taken away. Ten years ago she would have said something to Loiseau, but now she had learned discretion, and discretion had become more and more vital in Paris. So had violence, come to that. Maria concentrated on what the artist was saying to her. '. . . the relationships between the spirit of man and the material things with which he surrounds himself . . .'

Maria had a slight feeling of claustrophobia; she also had a headache. She should take an aspirin, and yet she didn't, even though she knew it would relieve the pain. As a child she had complained of pain and her mother had said that a woman's life is accompanied by constant pain. That's what it's like to be a woman, her mother had said, to know an ache or a pain all day, every day. Her mother had found some sort of stoic satisfaction in that statement, but the prospect had terrified Maria. It still terrified her and she was determined to disbelieve it. She tried to disregard all pains, as though by acknowledging them she might confess her feminine frailty. She wouldn't take an aspirin.

She thought of her ten-year-old son. He was living with her mother in Flanders. It was not good for the child to spend a lot of time with elderly people. It was just a temporary measure and yet all the time he was there she felt vaguely guilty about going out to dinner or the cinema, or even evenings like this.

'Take that painting near the door,' said the artist. '"Holocaust quo vadis?" There you have the vulture that represents the ethereal and . . .'

Maria had had enough of him. He was a ridiculous fool; she decided to leave. The crowd had become more static now and that always increased her claustrophobia, as did people in the Métro standing motionless. She looked at his flabby face and his eyes, greedy and scavenging for admiration among this crowd who admired only themselves. 'I'm going now,' she said. 'I'm sure the show will be a big success.'

'Wait a moment,' he called, but she had timed her escape to coincide with a gap in the crush and she was through the emergency exit, across the *cour* and away. He didn't follow her. He probably already had his eye on some other woman who could become interested in art for a couple of weeks.

Maria loved her car, not sinfully, but proudly. She looked after it and drove it well. It wasn't far to the rue des Saussaies. She positioned the car by the side of the Ministry of the Interior. That was the exit they used at night. She hoped Loiseau wouldn't keep him there too long. This area near the Élysée Palace was alive with patrols and huge Berliot buses, full of armed cops, the motors running all night in spite of the price of petrol. They wouldn't do anything to her, of course, but their presence made her uncomfortable. She looked at her wristwatch. Fifteen minutes the Englishman had been there. Now, the sentry was looking back into the court-yard. This must be him. She flashed the headlights of the E-type. Exactly on time; just as Loiseau had told her.

7

The woman laughed. It was a pleasant musical laugh. She said, 'Not in an E-type. Surely no whore solicits from an E-type. Is it a girl's car?' It was the woman from the art gallery.

'Where I come from,' I said, 'they call them hair-dressers' cars.'

She laughed. I had a feeling that she had enjoyed my mistaking her for one of the motorized prostitutes that prowled this district. I got in alongside her and she drove past the Ministry of the Interior and out on to the Malesherbes. She said,

'I hope Loiseau didn't give you a bad time.'

'My resident's card was out of date.'

'Poof!' she scoffed. 'Do you think I'm a fool? You'd be at the Prefecture if that was the case, not the Ministry of the Interior.'

'So what do *you* think he wanted?'

She wrinkled her nose. 'Who can tell? Jean-Paul said you'd been asking questions about the clinic on the Avenue Foch.'

'Suppose I told you I wish I'd never heard of the Avenue Foch?'

She put her foot down and I watched the speedometer spin. There was a screech of tyres as she turned on to the Boulevard Haussmann. 'I'd believe you,' she said. 'I wish I'd never heard of it.'

I studied her. She was no longer a girl – perhaps about thirty – dark hair and dark eyes; carefully applied make-up; her clothes were like the car, not brand-new but of good quality. Something in her relaxed manner told me that she had been married and something in her overt friendliness told me she no longer was. She came into the Étoile without losing speed and entered the whirl of traffic effortlessly. She flashed the lights at a taxi that was on a collision course and he sheered away. In the Avenue Foch she turned into a driveway. The gates opened.

'Here we are,' she said. 'Let's take a look.'

The house was large and stood back in its own piece of ground. At dusk the French shutter themselves tightly against the night. This gaunt house was no exception.

Near to, the cracks in the plaster showed like wrinkles in a face carelessly made-up. The traffic was pounding down the Avenue Foch but that was over the garden wall and far away.

'So this is the house on the Avenue Foch,' I said.

'Yes,' said the girl.

The big gates closed behind us. A man with a flashlight came out of the shadows. He had a small mongrel dog on a chain.

'Go ahead,' said the man. He waved an arm without exerting himself. I guessed that the man was a one-time cop. They are the only people who can stand motionless without loitering. The dog was a German Shepherd in disguise.

We drove down a concrete ramp into a large underground garage. There were about twenty cars there of various expensive foreign makes: Ford GTs, Ferraris, a Bentley convertible. A man standing near the lift called, 'Leave the keys in.'

Maria slipped off her soft driving shoes and put on a pair of evening shoes. 'Stay close,' she said quietly.

I patted her gently. 'That's close enough,' she said.

When we got out of the lift on the ground floor, everything seemed red plush and cut glass – *un décor maison-fin-de-siècle* – and all of it was tinkling: the

36

laughter, the medals, the ice cubes, the coins, the chandeliers. The main lighting came from ornate gas lamps with pink glass shades; there were huge mirrors and Chinese vases on plinths. Girls in long evening dresses were seated decorously on the wide sweep of the staircase, and in an alcove a barman was pouring drinks as fast as he could work. It was a very fancy affair; it dididn't have the Republican Guard in polished helmets lining the staircase with drawn sabres, but you had the feeling that they'd wanted to come.

Maria leaned across and took two glasses of champagne and some biscuits heaped with caviare. One of the men said, 'Haven't seen you for ages.' Maria nodded without much regret. The man said, 'You should have been in there tonight. One of them was nearly killed. He's hurt; badly hurt.'

Maria nodded. Behind me I heard a woman say, 'He must have been in agony. He wouldn't have screamed like that unless he had been in agony.'

'They always do that, it doesn't mean a thing.'

'I can tell a real scream from a fake one,' said the woman.

'How?'

'A real scream has no music, it slurs, it . . . screeches. It's ugly.'

"The cuisine,' said a voice behind me, 'can be superb; the very finely sliced smoked pork served hot, cold citrus fruits divided in half, bowls of strange hot grains with cream upon it. And those large eggs that they have here in Europe, skilfully fried crisp on the outside and yet the yolk remains almost raw. Sometimes smoked fish of various kinds.' I turned to face them. The speaker was a middle-aged Chinese in evening dress. He had been speaking to a fellow countryman and as he caught my eye he said, 'I am explaining to my colleague the fine Anglo-Saxon breakfast that I always enjoy so much.'

'This is Monsieur Kuang-t'ien,' said Maria, introducing us.

'And you, Maria, are exquisite this evening,' said M. Kuang-t'ien. He spoke a few lines of soft Mandarin.

'What's that?' asked Maria.

'It is a poem by Shao Hsŭn-mei, a poet and essayist who admired very much the poets of the West. Your dress reminded me of it.'

'Say it in French,' said Maria.

'It is indelicate, in parts.' He smiled apologetically and began to recite softly.

> 'Ah, lusty May is again burning,
> A sin is born of a virgin's kiss;
> Sweet tears tempt me, always tempt me
> To feel between her breasts with my lips.
>
> Here life is as eternal as death,
> As the trembling happiness on a wedding night;
> If she is not a rose, a rose all white,
> Then she must be redder than the red of blood.'

Maria laughed. 'I thought you were going to say "she must be redder than the Chinese People's Republic".'

'Ah. Is not possible,' said M. Kuang-t'ien, and laughed gently.

Maria steered me away from the two Chinese. 'We'll see you later,' she called over her shoulder. 'He gives me the creeps,' she whispered.

'Why?'

'"Sweet tears", "if she isn't white she'll be red with blood", death "between breasts".' She shook away the thought of it. 'He has a sick sadistic streak in him that frightens me.'

A man came pushing through the crowd. 'Who's your friend?' he asked Maria.

'An Englishman,' said Maria. 'An old friend,' she added untruthfully.

'He looks all right,' said the man approvingly. 'But I wished to see you in those high patent shoes.' He made a clicking sound and laughed, but Maria didn't. All around us the guests were talking excitedly and drinking. 'Excellent,' said a voice I recognized. It was M. Datt. He smiled at Maria. Datt was dressed in a dark jacket, striped trousers and black tie. He looked remarkably calm; unlike so many of his guests, his brow was not flushed nor his collar wrinkled. 'Are you going in?' he asked Maria. He looked at his pocket watch. 'They will begin in two minutes.'

'I don't think so,' said Maria.

'Of course you are,' said Datt. 'You know you will enjoy it.'

'Not tonight,' said Maria.

'Nonsense,' said Datt gently. 'Three more bouts. One of them is a gigantic Negro. A splendid figure of a man with gigantic hands.'

Datt lifted one of his own hands to demonstrate, but his eyes watched Maria very closely. She became agitated under his gaze and I felt her grip my hand tightly as though in fear. A buzzer sounded and people finished their drinks and moved towards the rear door.

Datt put his hands on our shoulders and moved us the way the crowd went. As we reached the large double doors I saw into the salon. A wrestling ring was set up in the centre and around it were folding chairs formed up in rows. The salon itself was a magnificent room with golden caryatids, a decorated ceiling, enormous mirrors, fine tapestry and a rich red carpet. As the spectators settled the chandeliers began to dim. The atmosphere was expectant.

'Take a seat, Maria,' said Datt. 'It will be a fine fight; lots of blood.' Maria's palm was moist in mine.

'Don't be awful,' said Maria, but she let go of my hand and moved towards the seats.

'Sit with Jean-Paul,' said Datt. 'I want to speak with your friend.'

Maria's hand trembled. I looked around and saw Jean-Paul for the first time. He was seated alone. 'Go with Jean-Paul,' said Datt gently.

Jean-Paul saw us, he smiled. 'I'll sit with Jean-Paul,' said Maria to me.

'Agreed,' I said. By the time she was seated, the first two wrestlers were circling each other. One was an Algerian I would guess, the other had bright dyed yellow hair. The man with straw hair lunged forward. The Algerian slid to one side, caught him on the hip and butted him heavily with the top of his head. The crack of head meeting chin was followed by the sharp intake of breath by the audience. On the far side of the room there was a nervous titter of laughter. The mirrored walls showed the wrestlers repeated all around the room. The central light threw heavy shadows under their chins and buttocks, and their legs, painted dark with shadow, emerged into the light as they circled again looking for an opening. Hanging in each corner of the room there was a TV camera linked by landline to monitor screens some distance away. The screens were showing the recorded image.

It was evident that the monitor screens were playing recordings, for the pictures were not clear and the action on the screen took place a few seconds later than the actual fighting. Because of this time-lag between recording and playing back the audience were able to swing their eyes to the monitors each time there was an attack and see it take place again on the screen.

'Come upstairs,' said Datt.

'Very well.' There was a crash; they were on the mat and the fair man was in a leg lock. His face was contorted. Datt spoke without turning to look. 'This fighting is

40

rehearsed. The fair-haired man will win after being nearly throttled in the final round.'

I followed him up the magnificent staircase to the first floor. There was a locked door. Clinic. Private. He unlocked the door and ushered me through. An old woman was standing in the corner. I wondered if I was interrupting one of Datt's interminable games of Monopoly.

'You were to come next week,' said Datt.

'Yes he was,' said the old woman. She smoothed her apron over her hips like a self-conscious maidservant.

'Next week would have been better,' said Datt.

'That's true. Next week – without the party – would have been better,' she agreed.

I said, 'Why is everyone speaking in the past tense?'

The door opened and two young men came in. They were wearing blue jeans and matching shirts. One of them was unshaven.

'What's going on now?' I asked.

'The footmen,' said Datt. 'Jules on the left. Albert on the right. They are here to see fair play. Right?' They nodded without smiling. Datt turned to me. 'Just lie down on the couch.'

'No.'

'What?'

'I said no I won't lie down on the couch.'

Datt tutted. He was a little put out. There wasn't any mockery or sadism in the tutting. 'There are four of us here,' he explained. 'We are not asking you to do anything unreasonable, are we? Please lie down on the couch.'

I backed towards the side table. Jules came at me and Albert was edging around to my left side. I came back until the edge of the table was biting my right hip so I knew exactly how my body was placed in relation to it. I watched their feet. You can tell a lot about a man from the way he places his feet. You can tell the training he

41

has had, whether he will lunge or punch from a stationary position, whether he will pull you or try to provoke you into a forward movement. Jules was still coming on. His hands were flat and extended. About twenty hours of gymnasium karate. Albert had the old *course d'échalotte* look about him. He was used to handling heavyweight, over-confident drunks. Well, he'd find out what I was; yes, I thought: a heavyweight, over-confident drunk. Heavyweight Albert was coming on like a train. A boxer; look at his feet. A crafty boxer who would give you all the fouls; the butts, kidney jabs and back of the head stuff, but he fancied himself as a jab-and-move-around artist. I'd be surprised to see him aim a kick in the groin with any skill. I brought my hands suddenly into sparring position. Yes, his chin tucked in and he danced his weight around on the balls of his feet. 'Fancy your chances, Albert?' I jeered. His eyes narrowed. I wanted him angry. 'Come on soft boy,' I said. 'Bite on a piece of bare knuckle.'

I saw the cunning little Jules out of the corner of my eye. He was smiling. He was coming too, smooth and cool inch by inch, hands flat and trembling for the killer cut.

I made a slight movement to keep them going. If they once relaxed, stood up straight and began to think, they could eat me up.

Heavyweight Albert's hands were moving, foot forward for balance, right hand low and ready for a body punch while Jules chopped at my neck. That was the theory. Surprise for Albert: my metal heelpiece going into his instep. You were expecting a punch in the buffet or a kick in the groin, Albert, so you were surprised when a terrifying pain hit your instep. Difficult for the balancing too. Albert leaned forward to console his poor hurt foot. Second surprise for Albert: under-swung flat hand on the nose; nasty. Jules is coming, cursing Albert for forcing his hand. Jules is forced to meet me head down. I felt the edge of the table against my hip. Jules thinks I'm going to lean into him. Surprise for Jules: I lean back just as he's getting ready to give me a hand edge on the corner of the neck. Second surprise for Jules: I do lean in after all and give him a fine glass paperweight on the earhole at a range of about eighteen inches. The paperweight seems none the worse for it. Now's the chance to make a big mistake. Don't pick up the paperweight. Don't pick up the paperweight. Don't pick up the paperweight. I didn't pick it up. Go for Datt, he's standing he's mobile and he's the one who is mentally the driving force in the room.

Down Datt. He's an old man but don't underrate him. He's large and weighty and he's been around. What's more he'll use anything available; the old maidservant is careful, discriminating, basically not aggressive. Go for Datt. Albert is rolling over and may come up to one side of my range of vision. Jules is motionless. Datt is moving around the desk; so it will have to be a missile. An inkstand, too heavy. A pen-set will fly apart. A vase: unwieldy. An ashtray. I picked it up, Datt was still moving, very slowly now, watching me carefully, his mouth open and white hair disarrayed as though he had been in the scuffle. The ashtray is heavy and perfect. Careful, you don't want to kill him. 'Wait,' Datt says hoarsely. I waited. I waited about ten seconds, just long enough for the woman to come behind me with a candlestick. She was basically not aggressive, the maidservant. I was only unconscious thirty minutes, they told me.

8

I was saying 'You are not basically aggressive' as I regained consciousness.

'No,' said the woman as though it was a grave short-coming. 'It is true.' I couldn't see either of them from where I was full length on my back. She switched the tape recorder on. There was the sudden intimate sound of a girl sobbing. 'I want it recording,' she said, but the sound of the girl became hysterical and she began to scream as though someone was torturing her. 'Switch that damn thing off,' Datt called. It was strange to see him disturbed, he was usually so calm. She turned the volume control the wrong way and the sound of the screams went right through my head and made the floor vibrate.

'The other way,' screamed Datt. The sound abated, but the tape was still revolving and the sound could just be heard; the girl was sobbing again. The desperate sound was made even more helpless by its diminished volume, like someone abandoned or locked out.

'What is it?' asked the maidservant. She shuddered but seemed reluctant to switch off; finally she did so and the reels clicked to a standstill.

'What's it sound like?' said Datt. 'It's a girl sobbing and screaming.'

'My God,' said the maidservant.

'Calm down,' said Datt. 'It's for amateur theatricals. It's just for amateur theatricals,' he said to me.

'I didn't ask you,' I said.

'Well, I'm telling you.' The servant woman turned the reel over and rethreaded it. I felt fully conscious now and

I sat up so that I could see across the room. The girl Maria was standing by the door, she had her shoes in her hand and a man's raincoat over her shoulders. She was staring blankly at the wall and looking miserable. There was a boy sitting near the gas fire. He was smoking a small cheroot, biting at the end which had become frayed like a rope end, so that each time he pulled it out of his mouth he twisted his face up to find the segments of leaf and discharge them on the tongue-tip. Datt and the old maidservant had dressed up in those old-fashioned-looking French medical gowns with high buttoned collars. Datt was very close to me and did a patent-medicine commercial while sorting through a trayful of instruments.

'Has he had the LSD?' asked Datt.

'Yes,' said the maid. 'It should start working soon.'

'You will answer any questions we ask,' said Datt to me.

I knew he was right: a well-used barbiturate could nullify all my years of training and experience and make me as co-operatively garrulous as a tiny child. What the LSD would do was anyone's guess.

What a way to be defeated and laid bare. I shuddered, Datt patted my arm.

The old woman was assisting him. 'The Amytal,' said Datt, 'the ampoule, and the syringe.'

She broke the ampoule and filled the syringe. 'We must work fast,' said Datt. 'It will be useless in thirty minutes; it has a short life. Bring him forward, Jules, so that she can block the vein. Dab of alcohol, Jules, no need to be inhuman.'

I felt hot breath on the back of my neck as Jules laughed dutifully at Datt's little joke.

'Block the vein now,' said Datt. She used the arm muscle to compress the vein of the forearm and waited a moment while the veins rose. I watched the process with interest, the colours of the skin and the metal were shiny and unnaturally bright. Datt took the syringe and the old woman said, 'The small vein on the back of the hand. If it clots we've still got plenty of patent ones left.'

'A good thought,' said Datt. He did a triple jab under the skin and searched for the vein, dragging at the plunger until the blood spurted back a rich gusher of red into the glass hypodermic. 'Off,' said Datt. 'Off or he'll bruise. It's important to avoid that.'

She released the arm vein and Datt stared at his watch, putting the drug into the vein at a steady one cc per minute.

'He'll feel a great release in a moment, an orgastic response. Have the Megimide ready. I want him responding for at least fifteen minutes.'

M. Datt looked up at me. 'Who are you?' he asked in French. 'Where are you, what day is it?'

I laughed. His damned needle was going into someone else's arm, that was the only funny thing about it. I laughed again. I wanted to be absolutely sure about the arm. I watched the thing carefully. There was the needle in that patch of white skin but the arm didn't fit on to my shoulder. Fancy him jabbing someone else. I was laughing more now so that Jules steadied me. I must have been jostling whoever was getting the injection because Datt had trouble holding the needle in.

'Have the Megimide and the cylinder ready,' said M. Datt, who had hairs – white hairs – in his nostrils. 'Can't be too careful. Maria, quickly, come closer, we'll need you now, bring the boy closer; he'll be the witness if we need one.' M. Datt dropped something into the white enamel tray with a tremendous noise. I couldn't see Maria now, but I smelled the perfume – I'd bet it was *Ma Griffe*, heavy and exotic, oh boy! It's orange-coloured that smell. Orange-coloured with a sort of silky touch to it. 'That's good,' said M. Datt, and I heard Maria say

46

orange-coloured too. Everyone knows, I thought, everyone knows the colour of *Ma Griffe* perfume.

The huge glass orange fractured into a million prisms, each one a brilliant, like the Sainte Chapelle at high noon, and I slid through the coruscating light as a punt slides along a sleepy bywater, the white cloud low and the colours gleaming and rippling musically under me.

I looked at M. Datt's face and I was frightened. His nose had grown enormous, not just large but enormous, larger than any nose could possibly be. I was frightened by what I saw because I knew that M. Datt's face was the same as it had always been, and that it was my awareness that had distorted. Yet even knowing that the terrible disfigurement had happened inside my mind, not on M. Datt's face, did not change the image; M. Datt's nose had grown to a gigantic size.

'What day is it?' Maria was asking. I told her. 'It's just a gabble,' she said. 'Too fast to really understand.' I listened but I could hear no one gabbling. Her eyes were soft and unblinking. She asked me my age, my date of birth and a lot of personal questions. I told her as much, and more, than she asked. The scar on my knee and the day my uncle planted the pennies in the tall tree. I wanted her to know everything about me. 'When we die,' my grandmother told me, 'we shall all go to Heaven,' she surveyed her world, 'for surely this is Hell?' 'Old Mr Gardner had athlete's foot, whose was the other foot?' Recitation: 'Let me like a soldier fall . . .'

'A desire,' said M. Datt's voice, 'to externalize, to confide.'

'Yes,' I agreed.

'I'll bring him up with the Megimide if he goes too far,' said M. Datt. 'He's fine like that. Fine response. Fine response.'

Maria repeated everything I said, as though Datt could not hear it himself. She said each thing not once but twice. I said it, then she said it, then she said it again differently; sometimes very differently so that I corrected her, but she was indifferent to my corrections and spoke in that fine voice she had; a round reed-clear voice full of song and sorrow like an oboe at night.

Now and again there was the voice of Datt deep and distant, perhaps from the next room. They seemed to think and speak so slowly. I answered Maria leisurely but it was ages before the next question came. I tired of the long pauses eventually. I filled the gaps telling them anecdotes and interesting stuff I'd read. I felt I'd known Maria for years and I remember saying 'transference', and Maria said it too, and Datt seemed very pleased. I found it was quite easy to compose my answers in poetry – not all of it rhymed, mind you – but I phrased it carefully. I could squeeze those damned words like putty and hand them to Maria, but sometimes she dropped them on to the marble floor. They fell noiselessly, but the shadows of them reverberated around the distant walls and furniture. I laughed again, and wondered whose bare arm I was staring at. Mind you, that wrist was mine, I recognized the watch. Who'd torn that shirt? Maria kept saying something over and over, a question perhaps. Damned shirt cost me £3.10s and now they'd torn it. The torn fabric was exquisite, detailed and jewel-like. Datt's voice said, 'He's going now: it's very short duration, that's the trouble with it.'

Maria said, 'Something about a shirt, I can't understand, it's so fast.'

'No matter,' said Datt. 'You've done a good job. Thank God you were here.'

I wondered why they were speaking in a foreign language. I had told them everything. I had betrayed my employers, my country, my department. They had opened me like a cheap watch, prodded the main spring and laughed at its simple construction. I had failed and failure closed over me like a darkroom blind coming down.

Dark. Maria's voice said, 'He's gone,' and I went, a white seagull gliding through black sky, while beneath me the even darker sea was welcoming and still. And deep, and deep and deep.

9

Maria looked down at the Englishman. He was contorted and twitching, a pathetic sight. She felt inclined to cuddle him close. So it was as easy as that to discover a man's most secret thoughts – a chemical reaction – extraordinary. He'd laid his soul bare to her under the influence of the Amytal and LSD, and now, in some odd way, she felt responsible – guilty almost – about his well-being. He shivered and she pulled the coat over him and tucked it around his neck. Looking around the damp walls of the dungeon she was in, she shivered too. She produced a compact and made basic changes to her make-up: the dramatic eye-shadow that suited last night would look terrible in the cold light of dawn. Like a cat, licking and washing in moments of anguish or distress. She removed all the make-up with a ball of cotton-wool, erasing the green eyes and deep red lips. She looked at herself and pulled that pursed face that she did only when she looked in a mirror. She looked awful without make-up, like a Dutch peasant; her jaw was beginning to go. She followed the jawbone with her finger, seeking out that tiny niche halfway along the line of it. That's where the face goes, that niche becomes a gap and suddenly the chin and the jawbone separate and you have the face of an old woman.

She applied the moisture cream, the lightest of powder and the most natural of lipstick colours. The Englishman stirred and shivered; this time the shiver moved his whole body. He would become conscious soon. She hurried with her make-up, he mustn't see her like this. She felt a strange physical thing about the Englishman. Had she spent over thirty years not understanding what physical attraction was? She had always thought that beauty and physical attraction were the same thing, but now she was unsure. This man was heavy and not young – late thirties, she'd guess – and his body was thick and uncared for. Jean-Paul was the epitome of masculine beauty: young, slim, careful about his weight and his hips, artfully tanned – all over, she remembered – particular about his hairdresser, ostentatious with his gold wristwatch and fine rings, his linen, precise and starched and white, like his smile.

Look at the Englishman: ill-fitting clothes rumpled and torn, plump face, hair moth-eaten, skin pale; look at that leather wristwatch strap and his terrible old-fashioned shoes – so English. Lace-up shoes. She remembered the lace-up shoes she had as a child. She hated them, it was the first manifestation of her claustrophobia, her hatred of those shoes. Although she hadn't recognized it as such. Her mother tied the laces in knots, tight and restrictive. Maria had been extra careful with her son, he never wore laced shoes. Oh God, the Englishman was shaking like an epileptic now. She held his arms and smelled the ether and the sweat as she came close to him.

He would come awake quickly and completely. Men always did, they could snap awake and be speaking on the phone as though they had been up for hours. Man the hunter, she supposed, alert for danger; but they made no allowances. So many terrible rows with men began because she came awake slowly. The weight of his body excited her, she let it fall against her so that she took the weight of it. He's a big ugly man, she thought. She said 'ugly' again and that word attracted her, so did 'big' and so did 'man'. She said 'big ugly man' aloud.

I awoke but the nightmare continued. I was in the sort of dungeon that Walt Disney dreams up, and the woman

51

was there saying 'Big ugly man' over and over. Thanks a lot, I thought, flattery will get you nowhere. I was shivering, and I came awake carefully; the woman was hugging me close, I must have been cold because I could feel the warmth of her. I'll settle for this, I thought, but if the girl starts to fade I'll close my eyes again, I need a dream.

It was a dungeon, that was the crazy thing. 'It really is a dungeon,' I said.

'Yes,' said Maria, 'it is.'

'What are *you* doing here then?' I said. I could accept the idea of me being in a dungeon.

'I'm taking you back,' she said. 'I tried to lift you out to the car but you were too heavy. How heavy are you?'

'Never mind how heavy I am,' I said. 'What's been going on?'

'Datt was questioning you,' she said. 'We can leave now.'

'I'll show you who's leaving,' I said, deciding to seek out Datt and finish off the ashtray exercise. I jumped off the hard bench to push open the heavy door of the dungeon. It was as though I was descending a non-existent staircase and by the time I reached the door I was on the wet ground, my legs twitching uselessly and unable to bear my weight.

'I didn't think you'd get even this far,' said Maria, coming across to me. I took her arm gratefully and helped myself upright by clawing at the door fixtures. Step by difficult step we inched through the cellar, past the rack, pincers and thumbscrews and the cold fireplace with the branding irons scattered around it. 'Who lives here?' I asked. 'Frankenstein?'

'Hush,' said Maria. 'Keep your strength for walking.'

'I had a terrible dream,' I said. It had been a dream of terrible betrayal and impending doom.

'I know,' said Maria. 'Don't think about it.'

The dawn sky was pale as though the leeches of my night had grown fat upon its blood. 'Dawns should be red,' I said to Maria.

'You don't look so good yourself,' she said, and helped me into the car.

She drove a couple of blocks from the house and parked under the trees amid the dead motor cars that litter the city. She switched the heater on and the warm air suffused my limbs.

'Do you live alone?' she asked.

'What's that, a proposal?'

'You aren't fit enough to be left alone.'

'Agreed,' I said. I couldn't shake off the coma of fear and Maria's voice came to me as I had heard it in the nightmare.

'I'll take you to my place, it's not far away,' she said.

'That's okay,' I said. 'I'm sure its worth a detour.'

'It's worth a journey. Three-star food and drink,' she said. 'How about a *croque monsieur* and a baby?'[1]

'The *croque monsieur* would be welcome,' I agreed.

'But having the baby together might well be the best part,' she said.

She didn't smile, she kicked the accelerator and the power surged through the car like the blood through my reviving limbs. She watched the road, flashing the lights at each intersection and flipping the needle around the clock at the clear stretches. She loved the car, caressing the wheel and agog with admiration for it; and like a clever lover she coaxed it into effortless perfomance. She came down the Champs for speed and along the north side of the Seine before cutting up through Les Halles. The last of the smart set had abandoned their onion soup and now the lorries were being unloaded. The *fortes* were working like looters, stacking the crates of vegetables

[1] baby: a small whisky.

53

and boxes of fish. The lorry-drivers had left their cabs to patronize the brothels that crowd the streets around the Square des Innocents. Tiny yellow doorways were full of painted whores and arguing men in *bleu de travail*. Maria drove carefully through the narrow streets.

'You've seen this district before?' she asked.

'No,' I said, because I had a feeling that she wanted me to say that. I had a feeling that she got some strange titillation from bringing me this way to her home. 'Ten new francs,' she said, nodding towards two girls standing outside a dingy café. 'Perhaps seven if you argued.'

'The two?'

'Maybe twelve if you wanted the two. More for an exhibition.'

She turned to me. 'You are shocked.'

'I'm only shocked that you want me to be shocked,' I said.

She bit her lip and turned on to the Sebastopol and speeded out of the district. It was three minutes before she spoke again. 'You are good for me,' she said.

I wasn't sure she was right but I didn't argue.

That early in the morning the street in which Maria lived was little different from any other street in Paris; the shutters were slammed tight and not a glint of glass or ruffle of curtain was visible anywhere. The walls were colourless and expressionless as though every house in the street was mourning a family death. The ancient crumbling streets of Paris were distinguished socially only by the motor cars parked along the gutters. Here the R4s, corrugated *deux chevaux* and dented Dauphines were outnumbered by shiny new Jags, Buicks and Mercs.

Inside, the carpets were deep, the hangings lush, the fittings shiny and the chairs soft. And there was that symbol of status and influence: a phone. I bathed in hot perfumed water and sipped aromatic broth, I was tucked into crisp sheets, my memories faded and I slept a long dreamless sleep.

When I awoke the radio was playing Françoise Hardy in the next room and Maria was sitting on the bed. She looked at me as I stirred. She had changed into a pink cotton dress and was wearing little or no make-up. Her hair was loose and combed to a simple parting in that messy way that takes a couple of hours of hairdressing expertise. Her face was kind but had the sort of wrinkles that come when you have smiled cynically about ten million times. Her mouth was small and slightly open like a doll, or like a woman expecting a kiss.

'What time is it?' I asked.

'It's past midnight,' she said. 'You've slept the clock round.'

'Get this bed on the road. What's wrong, have we run out of feathers?'

'We ran out of bedclothes; they are all around you.'

'Fill her up with bedclothes mister and if we forget to check the electric blanket you get a bolster free.'

'I'm busy making coffee. I've no time to play your games.'

She made coffee and brought it. She waited for me to ask questions and then she answered deftly, telling me as much as she wished without seeming evasive.

'I had a nightmare and awoke in a medieval dungeon.'

'You did,' said Maria.

'You'd better tell me all about it,' I said.

'Datt was terrified that you were spying on him. He said you have documents he wants. He said you had been making inquiries so he had to know.'

'What did he do to me?'

'He injected you with Amytal and LSD (it's the LSD that takes time to wear off). I questioned you. Then you went into a deep sleep and awoke in the cellars of the house. I brought you here.'

55

'What did I say?'

'Don't worry. None of those people speak English. I'm the only one that does. Your secrets are safe with me. Datt usually thinks of everything, but he was disconcerted when you babbled away in English. I translated.'

So that was why I'd heard her say everything twice. 'What did I say?'

'Relax. It didn't interest me but I satisfied Datt.'

I said, 'And don't think I don't appreciate it, but why should you do that for me?'

'Datt is a hateful man. I would never help him, and anyway, I took you to that house, I felt responsible for you.'

'And . . . ?'

'If I had told him what you really said he would have undoubtedly used amphetamine on you, to discover more and more. Amphetamine is dangerous stuff, horrible. I wouldn't have enjoyed watching that.'

'Thanks,' I said. I reached towards her, took her hand, and she lay down on the bed at my side. She did it without suspicion or arch looks, it was a friendly, rather than a sexual gesture. She lit a cigarette and gave me the packet and matches. 'Light it yourself,' she said. 'It will give you something to do with your hands.'

'What did I say?' I asked casually. 'What did I say that you didn't translate into French for Datt?'

'Nothing,' Maria said immediately. 'Not because you said nothing, but because I didn't hear it. Understand? I'm not interested in what you are or how you earn your living. If you are doing something that's illegal or dangerous, that's your worry. Just for the moment I feel a little responsible for you, but I've nearly worked off that feeling. Tomorrow you can start telling your own lies and I'm sure you will do it remarkably well.'

'Is that a brush-off?'

She turned to me. 'No,' she said. She leaned over and kissed me.

'You smell delicious,' I said. 'What is it you're wearing?'

'Agony,' she said. 'It's an expensive perfume, but there are few humans not attracted to it.'

I tried to decide whether she was geeing me up, but I couldn't tell. She wasn't the sort of girl who'd help you by smiling, either.

She got off the bed and smoothed her dress over her hips.

'Do you like this dress?' she asked.

'It's great,' I said.

'What sort of clothes do you like to see women in?'

'Aprons,' I said. 'Fingers a-shine with those marks you get from handling hot dishes.'

'Yes, I can imagine,' she said. She stubbed out her cigarette.

'I'll help you if you want help but don't ask too much, and remember that I am involved with these people and I have only one passport and it's French.'

I wondered if that was a hint about what I'd revealed under the drugs, but I said nothing.

She looked at her wristwatch. 'It's very late,' she said. She looked at me quizzically. 'There's only one bed and I need my sleep.' I had been thinking of having a cigarette but I replaced them on the side table. I moved aside. 'Share the bed,' I invited, 'but I can't guarantee sleep.'

'Don't pull the Jean-Paul lover-boy stuff,' she said, 'it's not your style.' She grabbed at the cotton dress and pulled it over her head.

'What is my style?' I asked irritably.

'Check with me in the morning,' she said, and put the light out. She left only the radio on.

10

I stayed in Maria's flat but the next afternoon Maria went
back to my rooms to feed Joey. She got back before the
storm. She came in blowing on her hands and complaining
of the cold.

'Did you change the water and put the cuttlefish bone
in?' I asked.

'Yes,' she said.

'It's good for his beak,' I said.

'I know,' she said. She stood by the window looking
out over the fast-darkening boulevard. 'It's primitive,'
she said without turning away from the window. 'The sky
gets dark and the wind begins to lift hats and boxes and
finally dustbin lids, and you start to think this is the way
the world will end.'

'I think politicians have other plans for ending the
world,' I said.

'The rain is beginning. Huge spots, like rain for giants.
Imagine being an ant hit by a . . .'

The phone rang. '. . . raindrop like that.' Maria finished
the sentence hurriedly and picked up the phone.

She picked it up as though it was a gun that might
explode by accident. 'Yes,' she said suspiciously. 'He's
here.' She listened, nodding, and saying 'yes'. 'The walk
will do him good,' she said. 'We'll be there in about an
hour.' She pulled an agonized face at me. 'Yes,' she said
to the phone again. 'Well you must just whisper to him
and then I won't hear your little secrets, will I?' There
was a little gabble of electronic indignation, then Maria
said, 'We'll get ready now or we'll be late,' and firmly
replaced the receiver. 'Byrd,' she said. 'Your countryman

58

Mr Martin Langley Byrd craves a word with you at the Café Blanc.' The noise of rain was like a vast crowd applauding frantically.

'Byrd,' I explained, 'is the man who was with me at the art gallery. The art people think a lot of him.'

'So he was telling me,' said Maria.

'Oh, he's all right,' I said. 'An ex-naval officer who becomes a bohemian is bound to be a little odd.'

'Jean-Paul likes him,' said Maria, as though it was the epitome of accolades. I climbed into my newly washed underwear and wrinkled suit. Maria discovered a tiny mauve razor and I shaved millimetre by millimetre and swamped the cuts with cologne. We left Maria's just as the rain shower ended. The concierge was picking up the potted plants that had been standing on the pavement.

'You are not taking a raincoat?' she asked Maria.

'No,' said Maria.

'Perhaps you'll only be out for a few minutes,' said the concierge. She pushed her glasses against the bridge of her nose and peered at me.

'Perhaps,' said Maria, and took my arm to walk away.

'It will rain again,' called the concierge.

'Yes,' said Maria.

'Heavily,' called the concierge. She picked up another pot and prodded the earth in it.

Summer rain is cleaner than winter rain. Winter rain strikes hard upon the granite, but summer rain is sibilant soft upon the leaves. This rainstorm pounced hastily like an inexperienced lover, and then as suddenly was gone. The leaves drooped wistfully and the air gleamed with green reflections. It's easy to forgive the summer rain; like first love, white lies or blarney, there's no malignity in it.

Byrd and Jean-Paul were already seated at the café. Jean-Paul was as immaculate as a shop-window dummy but Byrd was excited and dishevelled. His hair was awry and his eyebrows almost non-existent, as though he'd been too near a water-heater blow-back. They had chosen a seat near the side screens and Byrd was wagging a finger and talking excitedly. Jean-Paul waved to us and folded his ear with his fingers. Maria laughed. Byrd was wondering if Jean-Paul was making a joke against him, but deciding he wasn't, continued to speak.

'Simplicity annoys them,' Byrd said. 'It's just a rectangle, one of them complained, as though that was a criterion of art. Success annoys them. Even though I make almost no money out of my painting, that doesn't prevent the critics who feel my work is bad from treating it like an indecent assault, as though I have deliberately chosen to do bad work in order to be obnoxious. They have no kindness, no compassion, you see, that's why they call them critics – originally the word meant a captious fool; if they had compassion they would show it.'

'How?' asked Maria.

'By painting. That's what a painting is, a statement of love. Art is love, stricture is hate. It's obvious, surely. You see, a critic is a man who admires painters (he wants to be one) but cares little for paintings (which is why he isn't one). A painter, on the other hand, admires paintings, but doesn't like painters.' Byrd, having settled that problem, waved to a waiter. 'Four grands crèmes and some matches,' he ordered.

'I want black coffee,' said Maria.

'I prefer black too,' said Jean-Paul.

Byrd looked at me and made a little noise with his lips. 'You want black coffee?'

'White will suit me,' I said. He nodded an appreciation of a fellow countryman's loyalty. 'Two crèmes – grands crèmes – and two small blacks,' he ordered. The waiter arranged the beer mats, picked up some ancient checks and tore them in half. When he had gone Byrd leaned towards me. 'I'm glad,' he said – he looked around to see that the other two did not hear. They were talking to each other – 'I'm glad you drink white coffee. It's not good for the nerves, too much of this very strong stuff.' He lowered his voice still more. 'That's why they are all so argumentative,' he said in a whisper. When the coffees came Byrd arranged them on the table, apportioned the sugar, then took the check.

'Let me pay,' said Jean-Paul. 'It was my invitation.'

'Not on your life,' said Byrd. 'Leave this to me, Jean-Paul. I know how to handle this sort of thing, it's my part of the ship.'

Maria and I looked at each other without expression. Jean-Paul was watching closely to discover our relationship.

Byrd relished the snobbery of certain French phrases. Whenever he changed from speaking French into English I knew it was solely because he intended to introduce a long slab of French into his speech and give a knowing nod and slant his face significantly, as if we two were the only people in the world who understood the French language.

'Your inquiries about this house,' said Byrd. He raised his forefinger. 'Jean-Paul has remarkable news.'

'What's that?' I asked.

'Seems, my dear fellow, that there's something of a mystery about your friend Datt and that house.'

'He's not a friend of mine,' I said.

'Quite quite,' said Byrd testily. 'The damned place is a brothel, what's more . . .'

'It's not a brothel,' said Jean-Paul as though he had explained this before. 'It's a *maison de passe*. It's a house that people go to when they already have a girl with them.'

'Orgies,' said Byrd. 'They have orgies there. Frightful

61

goings on Jean-Paul tells me, drugs called LSD, pornographic films, sexual displays . . .'

Jean-Paul took over the narrative. 'There are facilities for every manner of perversion. They have hidden cameras there and even a great mock torture-chamber where they put on shows . . .'

'For masochists,' said Byrd. 'Chaps who are abnormal, you see.'

'Of course he sees,' said Jean-Paul. 'Anyone who lives in Paris knows how widespread are such parties and exhibitions.'

'*I* didn't know,' said Byrd. Jean-Paul said nothing. Maria offered her cigarettes around and said to Jean-Paul, 'Where did Pierre's horse come in yesterday?'

'A friend of theirs with a horse,' Byrd said to me.

'Yes,' I said.

'Nowhere,' said Jean-Paul.

'Then I lost my hundred nouveaux,' said Maria.

'Foolish,' said Byrd to me. He nodded.

'My fault,' said Jean-Paul.

'That's right,' said Maria. 'I didn't give it a second look until you said it was a certainty.'

Byrd gave another of his conspiratorial glances over the shoulder.

'You,' he pointed to me as though he had just met me on a footpath in the jungle, 'work for the German magazine *Stern*.'

'I work for several German magazines,' I admitted. 'But not so loud, I don't declare all of it for tax.'

'You can rely upon me,' said Byrd. 'Mum's the word.'

'Mum's the word,' I said. I relished Byrd's archaic vocabulary.

'You see,' said Byrd, 'when Jean-Paul told me this fascinating stuff about the house on Avenue Foch I said that you would probably be able to advance him a little of the ready if you got a story out of it.'

'I might,' I agreed.

'My word,' said Byrd, 'what with your salary from the travel agency and writing pieces for magazines you must be minting it. Absolutely minting it, eh?'

'I do all right,' I admitted.

'All right, I should think you do. I don't know where you stack it all if you are not declaring it for tax. What do you do, hide it under your bed?'

'To tell you the truth,' I said, 'I've sewn it into the seat of my armchair.'

Byrd laughed. 'Old Tastevin will be after you, tearing his furniture.'

'It was his idea,' I joked, and Byrd laughed again, for Tastevin had a reputation for being a skinflint.

'Get you in there with a camera,' mused Byrd. 'Be a wonderful story. What's more it would be a public service. Paris is rotten to the core you see. It's time it was given a shaking up.'

'It's an idea,' I agreed.

'Would a thousand quid be too much?' he asked.

'Much too much,' I said.

Byrd nodded. 'I thought it might be. A hundred more like it eh?'

'If it's a good story with pictures I could get five hundred pounds out of it. I'd pay fifty for an introduction and guided tour with co-operation, but the last time I was there I was persona non grata.'

'Precisely, old chap,' said Byrd. 'You were man-handled, I gather, by that fellow Datt. All a mistake, wasn't it?'

'It was from my point of view,' I said. 'I don't know how Monsieur Datt feels about it.'

'He probably feels *désolé*,' said Byrd. I smiled at the idea.

'But really,' said Byrd, 'Jean-Paul knows all about it. He could arrange for you to do your story, but meanwhile mum's the word, eh? Say nothing to anyone about any aspect. Are we of one mind?'

'Are you kidding me?' I said. 'Why would Datt agree to expose his own activities?'

'You don't understand the French, my boy.'

'So everyone keeps telling me.'

'But really. This house is owned and controlled by the Ministry of the Interior. They use it as a check and control on foreigners – especially diplomats – blackmail you might almost say. Bad business, shocking people, eh? Well they are. Some other French johnnies in government service – Loiseau is one – would like to see it closed down. Now do you see, my dear chap, now do you see?'

'Yes,' I said. 'But what's in it for you?'

'Don't be offensive, old boy,' said Byrd. 'You asked me about the house. Jean-Paul is in urgent need of the ready; ergo, I arrange for you to make a mutually beneficial pact.' He nodded. 'Suppose we say fifty on account, and another thirty if it gets into print?'

A huge tourist bus crawled along the boulevard, the neon light flashing and dribbling down its glasswork. Inside, the tourists sat still and anxious, crouching close to their loudspeakers and staring at the wicked city.

'Okay,' I said. I was amazed that he was such an efficient bargain-maker.

'In any magazine anywhere,' Byrd continued. 'With ten per cent of any subsequent syndication.'

I smiled. Byrd said, 'Ah, you didn't expect me to be adept at bargaining, did you?'

'No,' I said.

'You've a lot to learn about me. Waiter,' he called. 'Four kirs.' He turned to Jean-Paul and Maria. 'We have concluded an agreement. A small celebration is now indicated.'

The white wine and cassis came. 'You will pay,' Byrd said to me, 'and take it out of our down payment.'

64

'Will we have a contract?' asked Jean-Paul.

'Certainly not,' said Byrd. 'An Englishman's word is his bond. Surely you know that, Jean-Paul. The whole essence of a contract is that it's mutually beneficial. If it isn't, no paper in the world will save you. Besides,' he whispered to me in English, 'give him a piece of paper like that and he'll be showing everyone; he's like that. And that's the last thing you want, eh?'

'That's right,' I said. That's right, I thought. My employment on a German magazine was a piece of fiction that the office in London had invented for the rare times when they had to instruct me by mail. No one could have known about it unless they had been reading my mail. If Loiseau had said it, I wouldn't have been surprised, but Byrd . . . !

Byrd began to explain the theory of pigment to Jean-Paul in the shrill voice that he adopted whenever he talked art. I bought them another kir before Maria and I left to walk back to her place.

We picked our way through the dense traffic on the boulevard.

'I don't know how you can be so patient with them,' Maria said. 'That pompous Englishman Byrd and Jean-Paul holding his handkerchief to protect his suit from wine stains.'

'I don't know them well enough to dislike them,' I explained.

'Then don't believe a word they say,' said Maria.

'Men were deceivers ever.'

'You are a fool,' said Maria. 'I'm not talking about amours, I'm talking about the house on Avenue Foch; Byrd and Jean-Paul are two of Datt's closest friends. Thick as thieves.'

'Are they?' I said. From the far side of the boulevard I looked back. The wiry little Byrd – as volatile as when we'd joined him – was still explaining the theory of pigment to Jean-Paul.

'*Comédiens*,' Maria pronounced. The word for 'actor' also means a phoney or impostor. I stood there a few minutes, looking. The big Café Blanc was the only brightly lit place on the whole tree-lined boulevard. The white coats of the waiters gleamed as they danced among the tables laden with coffee pots, *citron pressé* and soda siphons. The customers were also active, they waved their hands, nodded heads, called to waiters and to each other. They waved ten-franc notes and jangled coins. At least four of them kissed. It was as though the wide dark boulevard was a hushed auditorium, respecting and attentive, watching the drama unfold on the stage-like *terrasse* of the Café Blanc. Byrd leaned close to Jean-Paul. Jean-Paul laughed.

11

We walked and talked and forgot the time. 'Your place,' I said finally to Maria. 'You have central heating, the sink is firmly fixed to the wall, you don't share the w.c. with eight other people and there are gramophone records I haven't even read the labels on yet. Let's go to your place.'

'Very well,' she said, 'since you are so flattering about its advantages.' I kissed her ear gently. She said, 'But suppose the landlord throws you out?'

'Are you having an affair with your landlord?'

She smiled and gave me a forceful blow that many French women conveniently believe is a sign of affection.

'I'm not washing any more shirts,' she said. 'We'll take a cab to your place and pick up some linen.'

We bargained with three taxi-drivers, exchanging their directional preferences with ours; finally one of them weakened and agreed to take us to the Petit Légionnaire.

I let myself into my room with Maria just behind me. Joey chirped politely when I switched on the light.

'My God,' said Maria, 'someone's turned you over.'

I picked up a heap of shirts that had landed in the fireplace.

'Yes,' I said. Everything from the drawers and cupboards had been tipped on to the floor. Letters and cheque stubs were scattered across the sofa and quite a few things were broken. I let the armful of shirts fall to the floor again, I didn't know where to begin on it. Maria was more methodical, she began to sort through the clothes, folding them and putting trousers and jackets on

67

the hangers. I picked up the phone and dialled the number Loiseau had given me.

'*Un sourire est différent d'un rire,*' I said. France is one place where the romance of espionage will never be lost, I thought. Loiseau said 'Hello.'

'Have you turned my place over, Loiseau?' I said.

'Are you finding the natives hostile?' Loiseau asked.

'Just answer the question,' I said.

'Why don't you answer mine?' said Loiseau.

'It's my jeton,' I said. 'If you want answers you buy your own call.'

'If my boys had done it you wouldn't have noticed.'

'Don't get blasé. Loiseau. The last time your boys did it – five weeks back – I did notice. Tell 'em if they must smoke, to open the windows; that cheap pipe tobacco makes the canary's eyes water.'

'But they are very tidy,' said Loiseau. 'They wouldn't make a mess. If it's a mess you are complaining of.'

'I'm not complaining about anything,' I said. 'I'm just trying to get a straight answer to a simple question.'

'It's too much to ask of a policeman,' said Loiseau. 'But if there is anything damaged I'd send the bill to Datt.'

'If anything gets damaged it's likely to be Datt,' I said.

'You shouldn't have said that to me,' said Loiseau. 'It was indiscreet, but *bonne chance* anyway.'

'Thanks,' I said and hung up.

'So it wasn't Loiseau?' said Maria, who had been listening.

'What makes you think that?' I asked.

She shrugged. 'The mess here. The police would have been careful. Besides, if Loiseau admitted that the police have searched your home other times why should he deny that they did it this time?'

'Your guess is as good as mine,' I said. 'Perhaps Loiseau did it to set me at Datt's throat.'

68

'So you were deliberately indiscreet to let him think he'd succeeded?'

'Perhaps.' I looked into the torn seat of the armchair. The horse-hair stuffing had been ripped out and the case of documents that the courier had given me had disappeared. 'Gone,' said Maria.

'Yes,' I said. 'Perhaps you did translate my confession correctly after all.'

'It was an obvious place to look. In any case I was not the only person to know your "secret": this evening you told Byrd that you kept your money there.'

'That's true, but was there time for anyone to act on that?'

'It was two hours ago,' said Maria. 'He could have phoned. There was plenty of time.'

We began to sort out the mess. Fifteen minutes passed, then the phone rang. It was Jean-Paul.

'I'm glad to catch you at home,' he said. 'Are you alone?'

I held a finger up to my lips to caution Maria. 'Yes,' I said. 'I'm alone. What is it?'

'There's something I wanted to tell you without Byrd hearing.'

'Go ahead.'

'Firstly. I have good connections in the underworld and the police. I am certain that you can expect a burglary within a day or so. Anything you treasure should be put into a bank vault for the time being.'

'You're too late,' I said. 'They were here.'

'What a fool I am. I should have told you earlier this evening. It might have been in time.'

'No matter,' I said. 'There was nothing here of value except the typewriter.' I decided to solidify the freelance-writer image a little. 'That's the only essential thing. What else did you want to tell me?'

'Well that policeman, Loiseau, is a friend of Byrd.'

'I know,' I said. 'Byrd was in the war with Loiseau's brother.'

'Right,' said Jean-Paul. 'Now Inspector Loiseau was asking Byrd about you earlier today. Byrd told Inspector Loiseau that . . .'

'Well, come on.'

'He told him you are a spy. A spy for the West Germans.'

'Well that's good family entertainment. Can I get invisible ink and cameras at a trade discount?'

'You don't know how serious such a remark can be in France today. Loiseau is forced to take notice of such a remark no matter how ridiculous it may seem. And it's impossible for you to *prove* that it's not true.'

'Well thanks for telling me,' I said. 'What do you suggest I do about it?'

'There is nothing you can do for the moment,' said Jean-Paul. 'But I shall try to find out anything else Byrd says of you, and remember that I have very influential friends among the police. Don't trust Maria whatever you do.'

Maria's ear went even closer to the receiver. 'Why's that?' I asked. Jean-Paul chuckled maliciously. 'She's Loiseau's ex-wife, that's why. She too is on the payroll of the Sûreté.'

'Thanks,' I said. 'See you in court.'

Jean-Paul laughed at that remark – or perhaps he was still laughing at the one before.

12

Maria applied her make-up with unhurried precision. She was by no means a cosmetics addict but this morning she was having lunch with Chief Inspector Loiseau. When you had lunch with an ex-husband you made quite sure that he realized what he had lost. The pale-gold English wool suit that she had bought in London. He'd always thought her a muddle-headed fool so she'd be as slick and businesslike as possible. And the new plain-front shoes; no jewellery. She finished the eyeliner and the mascara and began to apply the eye-shadow. Not too much; she had been wearing much too much the other evening at the art gallery. You have a perfect genius, she told herself severely, for getting yourself involved in situations where you are a minor factor instead of a major factor. She smudged the eye-shadow, cursed softly, removed it and began again. Will the Englishman appreciate the risk you are taking? Why not tell M. Datt the truth of what the Englishman said? The Englishman is interested only in his work, as Loiseau was interested only in *his* work. Loiseau's love-making was efficient, just as his working day was. How can a woman compete with a man's work? Work is abstract and intangible, hypnotic and lustful; a woman is no match for it. She remembered the nights she had tried to fight Loiseau's work, to win him away from the police and its interminable paperwork and its relentless demands upon their time together. She remembered the last bitter argument about it. Loiseau had kissed her passionately in a way he had never done before and they had made love and she had clung to him, crying silently in the sudden release of tension, for at that moment she knew that they would separate and divorce, and she had been right.

Loiseau still owned a part of her, that's why she had to keep seeing him. At first they had been arranging details of the legal separation, custody of the boy, then agreements about the house. Then Loiseau had asked her to do small tasks for the police department. She knew that he could not face the idea of losing her completely. They had become dispassionate and sincere, for she no longer feared losing him; they were like brother and sister now, and yet . . . she sighed. Perhaps it all could have been different; Loiseau still had an insolent confidence that made her pleased, almost proud, to be with him. He was a man, and that said everything there was to say about him. Men were unreasonable. Her work for the Sûreté had become quite important. She was pleased with the chance to show Loiseau how efficient and businesslike she could be, but Loiseau would never acknowledge it. Men were unreasonable. All men. She remembered a certain sexual mannerism of his, and smiled. All men set tasks and situations in which anything a woman thinks, says, or does will be wrong. Men demand that women should be inventive, shameless whores, and then reject them for not being motherly enough. They want them attract their men friends and then they get jealous about it.

She powdered her lipstick to darken it and then pursed her lips and gave her face one final intent glare. Her eyes were good, the pupils were soft and the whites gleaming. She went to meet her ex-husband.

13

Loiseau had been smoking too much and not getting enough sleep. He kept putting a finger around his metal wristwatch band; Maria remembered how she had dreaded those nervous mannerisms that always preceded a row. He gave her coffee and remembered the amount of sugar she liked. He remarked on her suit and her hair and liked the plain-fronted shoes. She knew that sooner or later he would mention the Englishman.

'Those same people have always fascinated you,' he said. 'You are a gold-digger for brains, Maria. You are drawn irresistibly to men who think only of their work.'

'Men like you,' said Maria. Loiseau nodded.

He said, 'He'll just bring you trouble, that Englishman.'

'I'm not interested in him,' said Maria.

'Don't lie to me,' said Loiseau cheerfully. 'Reports from seven hundred policemen go across this desk each week. I also get reports from informers and your concierge is one of them.'

'The bitch.'

'It's the system,' said Loiseau. 'We have to fight the criminal with his own weapons.'

'Datt gave him an injection of something to question him.'

'I know,' said Loiseau.

'It was awful,' said Maria.

'Yes, I've seen it done.'

'It's like a torture. A filthy business.'

'Don't lecture me,' said Loiseau. 'I don't like Amytal injections and I don't like Monsieur Datt or that clinic, but there's nothing I can do about it.' He sighed. 'You know that, Maria.' But Maria didn't answer. 'That house is safe from even my wide powers.' He smiled as if the idea of him endangering anything was absurd. 'You deliberately translated the Englishman's confession incorrectly, Maria,' Loiseau accused her.

Maria said nothing. Loiseau said, 'You told Monsieur Datt that the Englishman is working under my orders. Be careful what you say or do with these people. They are dangerous – all of them are dangerous; your flashy boy-friend is the most dangerous of all.'

'Jean-Paul you mean?'

'The playboy of the Buttes Chaumont,' said Loiseau sarcastically.

'Don't keep calling him my boy-friend,' said Maria.

'Come come, I know all about you,' said Loiseau, using a phrase and a manner that he employed in interrogations. 'You can't resist these flashy little boys and the older you get the more vulnerable you become to them.' Maria was determined not to show anger. She knew that Loiseau was watching her closely and she felt her cheeks flushing in embarrassment and anger.

'He wants to work for me,' said Loiseau.

'He likes to feel important,' explained Maria, 'as a child does.'

'You amaze me,' said Loiseau, taking care to be unamazed. He stared at her in a way that a Frenchman stares at a pretty girl on the street. She knew that he fancied her sexually and it comforted her, not to frustrate him, but because to be able to interest him was an important part of their new relationship. She felt that in some ways this new feeling she had for him was more important than their marriage had been, for now they were friends, and friendship is less infirm and less fragile than love.

'You mustn't harm Jean-Paul because of me,' said Maria.

'I'm not interested in Drugstore cowboys,' said Loiseau. 'At least not until they are caught doing something illegal.'

Maria took out her cigarettes and lit one as slowly as she knew how. She felt all the old angers welling up inside her. This was the Loiseau she had divorced; this stern, unyielding man who thought that Jean-Paul was an effeminate gigolo merely because he took himself less seriously than Loiseau ever could. Loiseau had crushed her, had reduced her to a piece of furniture, to a dossier – the dossier on Maria; and now the dossier was passed over to someone else and Loiseau thought the man concerned would not handle it as competently as he himself had done. Long ago Loiseau had produced a cold feeling in her and now she felt it again. This same icy scorn was poured upon anyone who smiled or relaxed; self-indulgent, complacent, idle – these were Loiseau's words for anyone without his self-flagellant attitude to work. Even the natural functions of her body seemed something against the law when she was near Loiseau. She remembered the lengths she went to to conceal the time of her periods in case he should call her to account for them, as though they were the mark of some ancient sin.

She looked up at him. He was still talking about Jean-Paul. How much had she missed – a word, a sentence, a lifetime? She didn't care. Suddenly the room seemed cramped and the old claustrophobic feeling that made her unable to lock the bathroom door – in spite of Loiseau's rages about it – made this room unbearably small. She wanted to leave.

'I'll open the door,' she said. 'I don't want the smoke to bother you.'

'Sit down,' he said. 'Sit down and relax.'

She felt she must open the door.

'Your boy-friend Jean-Paul is a nasty little casserole,'[1] said Loiseau, 'and you might just as well face up to it. You accuse me of prying into other people's lives: well perhaps that's true, but do you know what I see in those lives? I see things that shock and appal me. That Jean-Paul. What is he but a toe-rag for Datt, running around like a filthy little pimp. He is the sort of man that makes me ashamed of being a Frenchman. He sits all day in the Drugstore and the other places that attract the foreigners. He holds a foreign newspaper pretending that he is reading it – although he speaks hardly a word of any foreign language – hoping to get into conversation with some pretty little girl secretary or better still a foreign girl who can speak French. Isn't that a pathetic thing to see in the heart of the most civilized city in the world? This lout sitting there chewing Hollywood chewing-gum and looking at the pictures in *Playboy*. Speak to him about religion and he will tell you how he despises the Catholic Church. Yet every Sunday when he's sitting there with his hamburger looking so *transatlantique*, he's just come from Mass. He prefers foreign girls because he's ashamed of the fact that his father is a metal-worker in a junk yard and foreign girls are less likely to notice his coarse manners and phoney voice.'

Maria had spent years hoping to make Loiseau jealous and now, years after their divorce had been finalized, she had succeeded. For some reason the success brought her no pleasure. It was not in keeping with Loiseau's calm, cold, logical manner. Jealousy was weakness, and Loiseau had very few weaknesses.

Maria knew that she must open the door or faint. Although she knew this slight dizziness was claustrophobia she put out the half-smoked cigarette in the hope that it would make her feel better. She stubbed it

[1] Informer.

out viciously. It made her feel better for about two minutes. Loiseau's voice droned on. How she hated this office. The pictures of Loiseau's life, photos of him in the army: slimmer and handsome, smiling at the photographer as if to say 'This is the best time of our lives, no wives, no responsibility.' The office actually smelled of Loiseau's work; she remembered that brown card that wrapped the dossiers and the smell of the old files that had come up from the cellars after goodness knows how many years. They smelled of stale vinegar. It must have been something in the paper, or perhaps the fingerprint ink.

'He's a nasty piece of work, Maria,' said Loiseau. 'I'd even go so far as to say evil. He took three young German girls out to that damned cottage he has near Barbizon. He was with a couple of his so-called artist friends. They raped those girls, Maria, but I couldn't get them to give evidence. He's an evil fellow; we have too many like him in Paris.'

Maria shrugged, 'The girls should not have gone there, they should have known what to expect. Girl tourists – they only come here to be raped; they think it's romantic to be raped in Paris.'

'Two of these girls were sixteen years old, Maria, they were children; the other only eighteen. They'd asked your boy-friend the way to their hotel and he offered them a lift there. Is this what has happened to our great and beautiful city, that a stranger can't ask the way without risking assault?'

Outside the weather was cold. It was summer and yet the wind had an icy edge. Winter arrives earlier each year, thought Maria. Thirty-two years old, it's August again but already the leaves die, fall and are discarded by the wind. Once August was hot midsummer, now August was the beginning of autumn. Soon all the seasons would merge, spring would not arrive and she would know the menopausal womb-winter that is half-life.

'Yes,' said Maria. 'That's what has happened.' She shivered.

14

It was two days later when I saw M. Datt again. The courier was due to arrive any moment. He would probably be grumbling and asking for my report about the house on the Avenue Foch. It was a hard grey morning, a slight haze promising a scorching hot afternoon. In the Petit Légionnaire there was a pause in the business of the day, the last *petit déjeuner* had been served but it was still too early for lunch. Half a dozen customers were reading their newspapers or staring across the street watching the drivers argue about parking space. M. Datt and both the Tastevins were at their usual table, which was dotted with coffee pots, cups and tiny glasses of Calvados. Two taxi-drivers played 'ping-foot', swivelling the tiny wooden footballers to smack the ball across the green felt cabinet. M. Datt called to me as I came down for breakfast.

'This is terribly late for a young man to wake,' he called jovially. 'Come and sit with us.' I sat down, wondering why M. Datt had suddenly become so friendly. Behind me the 'ping-foot' players made a sudden volley. There was a clatter as the ball dropped through the goal-mouth and a mock cheer of triumph.

'I owe you an apology,' said M. Datt. 'I wanted to wait a few days before delivering it so that you would find it in yourself to forgive me.'

'That humble hat doesn't fit,' I said. 'Go a size larger.'

M. Datt opened his mouth and rocked gently. 'You have a fine sense of humour,' he proclaimed once he had got himself under control.

'Thanks,' I said. 'You are quite a joker yourself.'

M. Datt's mouth puckered into a smile like a carelessly

ironed shirt-collar. 'Oh I see what you mean,' he said suddenly and laughed. 'Ha-ha-ha,' he laughed. Madame Tastevin had spread the Monopoly board by now and dealt us the property cards to speed up the game. The courier was due to arrive, but getting closer to M. Datt was the way the book would do it.

'Hotels on Lecourbe and Belleville,' said Madame Tastevin.

'That's what you always do,' said M. Datt. 'Why don't you buy railway stations instead?'

We threw the dice and the little wooden discs went trotting around the board, paying their rents and going to prison and taking their chances just like humans. 'A voyage of destruction,' Madame Tastevin said it was.

'That's what all life is,' said M. Datt. 'We start to die on the day we are born.'

My chance card said '*Faites des réparations dans toutes vos maisons*' and I had to pay 2,500 francs on each of my houses. It almost knocked me out of the game but I scraped by. As I finished settling up I saw the courier cross the *terrasse*. It was the same man who had come last time. He took it very slow and stayed close to the wall. A coffee crème and a slow appraisal of the customers before contacting me. Professional. Sift the tails off and duck from trouble. He saw me but gave no sign of doing so.

'More coffee for all of us,' said Madame Tastevin. She watched the two waiters laying the tables for lunch, and now she called out to them, 'That glass is smeary', 'Use the pink napkins, save the white ones for evening', 'Be sure there is enough terrine today. I'll be angry if we run short.' The waiters were keen that Madame shouldn't get angry, they moved anxiously, patting the cloths and making microscopic adjustments to the placing of the cutlery. The taxi-drivers decided upon another game and there was a rattle of wooden balls as the coin went into the slot.

The courier had brought out a copy of *L'Express* and was reading it and sipping abstractedly at his coffee. Perhaps he'll go away, I thought, perhaps I won't have to listen to his endless official instructions. Madame Tastevin was in dire straits, she mortgaged three of her properties. On the cover of *L'Express* there was a picture of the American Ambassador to France shaking hands with a film star at a festival.

M. Datt said, 'Can I smell a terrine cooking? What a good smell.'

Madame nodded and smiled. 'When I was a girl all Paris was alive with smells; oil paint and horse sweat, dung and leaky gas lamps and everywhere the smell of superb French cooking. Ah!' She threw the dice and moved. 'Now,' she said, 'it smells of diesel, synthetic garlic, hamburgers and money.'

M. Datt said, 'Your dice.'

'Okay,' I told him. 'But I must go upstairs in a moment. I have so much work to do.' I said it loud enough to encourage the courier to order a second coffee.

Landing on the Boul des Capucines destroyed Madame Tastevin.

'I'm a scientist,' said M. Datt, picking up the pieces of Madame Tastevin's bankruptcy. 'The scientific method is inevitable and true.'

'True to what?' I asked. 'True to scientists, true to history, true to fate, true to what?'

'True to itself,' said Datt.

'The most evasive truth of all,' I said.

M. Datt turned to me, studied my face and wet his lips before beginning to talk. 'We have begun in a bad . . . a silly way.' Jean-Paul came into the café – he had been having lunch there every day lately. He waved airily to us and bought cigarettes at the counter.

81

'But there are certain things that I don't understand,' Datt continued. 'What are you doing carrying a case-load of atomic secrets?'

'And what are you doing stealing it?'

Jean-Paul came across to the table, looked at both of us and sat down.

'Retrieving,' said Datt. 'I retrieved it for you.'

'Then let's ask Jean-Paul to remove his gloves,' I said.

Jean-Paul watched M. Datt anxiously. 'He knows,' said M. Datt. 'Admit it, Jean-Paul.'

'On account,' I explained to Jean-Paul, 'of how we began in a bad and silly way.'

'I said that,' said M. Datt to Jean-Paul. 'I said we had started in a bad and silly way and now we want to handle things differently.'

I leaned across and peeled back the wrist of Jean-Paul's cotton gloves. The flesh was stained violet with 'nin'.[1]

'Such an embarrassment for the boy,' said M. Datt, smiling. Jean-Paul glowered at him.

'Do you want to buy the documents?' I asked.

M. Datt shrugged. 'Perhaps. I will give you ten thousand new francs, but if you want more than that I would not be interested.'

'I'll need double that,' I said.

'And if I decline?'

'You won't get every second sheet, which I removed and deposited elsewhere.'

'You are no fool,' said M. Datt. 'To tell you the truth the documents were so easy to get from you that I suspected their authenticity. I'm glad to find you are no fool.'

---

[1] Ninhydrine: a colour reagent, reddish-black powder. Hands become violet because of amino acid in the skin. It takes three days before it comes off. Washing makes it worse.

'There are more documents,' I said. 'A higher percentage will be Xerox copies but you probably won't mind that. The first batch had a high proportion of originals to persuade you of their authenticity, but it's too risky to do that regularly.'

'Whom do you work for?'

'Never mind who I work for. Do you want them or not?'

M. Datt nodded, smiled grimly and said, 'Agreed, my friend. Agreed.' He waved an arm and called for coffee. 'It's just curiosity. Not that your documents are anything like my scientific interests. I shall use them merely to stimulate my mind. Then they will be destroyed. You can have them back . . .' The courier finished his coffee and then went upstairs, trying to look as though he was going no farther than the toilets on the first floor.

I blew my nose noisily and then lit a cigarette. 'I don't care what you do with them, monsieur. My fingerprints are not on the documents and there is no way to connect them with me; do as you wish with them. I don't know if these documents connect with your work. I don't even know what your work is.'

'My present work is scientific,' explained Datt. 'I run my clinic to investigate the patterns of human behaviour. I could make much more money elsewhere, my qualifications are good. I am an analyst. I am still a good doctor. I could lecture on several different subjects: upon oriental art, Buddhism or even Marxist theory. I am considered an authority on Existentialism and especially upon Existentialist psychology; but the work I am doing now is the work by which I will be known. The idea of being remembered after death becomes important as one gets old.' He threw the dice and moved past Départ. 'Give me my twenty thousand francs,' he said.

'What do you do at this clinic?' I peeled off the toy

83

money and passed it to him. He counted it and stacked it up.

'People are blinded by the sexual nature of my work. They fail to see it in its true light. They think only of the sex activity.' He sighed. 'It's natural, I suppose. My work is important merely because people cannot consider the subject objectively. I can; so I am one of the few men who can control such a project.'

'You analyse the sexual activity?'

'Yes,' said Datt. 'No one does anything they do not wish to do. We do employ girls but most of the people who go to the house go there as couples, and they leave in couples. I'll buy two more houses.'

'The same couples?'

'Not always,' said Datt. 'But that is not necessarily a thing to be deplored. People are mentally in bondage, and their sexual activity is the cipher which can help to explain their problems. You're not collecting your rent.' He pushed it over to me.

'You are sure that you are not rationalizing the ownership of a whorehouse?'

'Come along there now and see,' said Datt. 'It is only a matter of time before you land upon my hotels in the Avenue de la République.' He shuffled his property cards together. 'And then you are no more.'

'You mean the clinic is operating at noon?'

'The human animal,' said Datt, 'is unique in that its sexual cycle continues unabated from puberty to death.' He folded up the Monopoly board.

It was getting hotter now, the sort of day that gives rheumatism a jolt and expands the Eiffel Tower six inches. 'Wait a moment,' I said to Datt. 'I'll go up and shave. Five minutes?'

'Very well,' said Datt. 'But there's no real need to shave, you won't be asked to participate.' He smiled.

84

I hurried upstairs, the courier was waiting inside my room. 'They bought it?'

'Yes,' I said. I repeated my conversation with M. Datt.

'You've done well,' he said.

'Are you running me?' I lathered my face carefully and began shaving.

'No. Is that where they took it from, where the stuffing is leaking out?'

'Yes. Then who is?'

'You know I can't answer that. You shouldn't even ask me. Clever of them to think of looking there.'

'I told them where it was. I've never asked before,' I said, 'but whoever is running me seems to know what these people do even before I know. It's someone close, someone I know. Don't keep poking at it. It's only roughly stitched back.'

'That at least is wrong,' said the courier. 'It's no one you know or have ever met. How did you know who took the case?'

'You're lying. I told you not to keep poking at it. Nin; it colours your flesh. Jean-Paul's hands were bright with it.'

'What colour?'

'You'll be finding out,' I said. 'There's plenty of nin still in there.'

'Very funny.'

'Well who told you to poke your stubby peasant fingers into my stuffing?' I said. 'Stop messing about and listen carefully. Datt is taking me to the clinic, follow me there.'

'Very well,' said the courier without enthusiasm. He wiped his hands on a large handkerchief.

'Make sure I'm out again within the hour.'

'What am I supposed to do if you are not out within the hour?' he asked.

'I'm damned if I know,' I said. They never ask questions

like that in films. 'Surely you have some sort of emergency procedure arranged?'

'No,' said the courier. He spoke very quietly. 'I'm afraid I haven't. I just do the reports and pop them into the London dip mail secret tray. Sometimes it takes three days.'

'Well this could be an emergency,' I said. 'Something should have been arranged beforehand.' I rinsed off the last of the soap and parted my hair and straightened my tie.

'I'll follow you anyway,' said the courier encouragingly. 'It's a fine morning for a walk.'

'Good,' I said. I had a feeling that if it had been raining he would have stayed in the café. I dabbed some lotion on my face and then went downstairs to M. Datt. Upon the great bundle of play-money he had left the waiter's tip: one franc.

Summer was here again; the pavement was hot, the streets were dusty and the traffic cops were in white jackets and dark glasses. Already the tourists were everywhere, in two styles: beards, paper parcels and bleached jeans, or straw hats, cameras and cotton jackets. They were sitting on benches complaining loudly. 'So he explained that it was one hundred new francs or it would be ten thousand old francs, and I said, "Gracious me I sure can understand why you people had that revolution."'

Another tourist said, 'But you don't speak the language.'

A man replied, 'I don't have to speak the language to know what that waiter meant.'

As we walked I turned to watch them and caught sight of the courier strolling along about thirty yards behind us.

'It will take me another five years to complete my

work,' said Datt. 'The human mind and the human body; remarkable mechanisms but often ill-matched.'

'Very interesting,' I said. Datt was easily encouraged.

'At present my researches are concerned with stimulating the registering of pain, or rather the excitement caused by someone pretending to have sudden physical pain. You perhaps remember that scream I had on the tape recorder. Such a sound can cause a remarkable mental change in a man if used in the right circumstances.'

'The right circumstances being that film-set-style torture chamber where I was dumped after treatment.'

'Exactly,' said Datt. 'You have hit it. Even if they can see that it's a recording and even if we tell them that the girl was an actress, even then the excitement they get from it is not noticeably lessened. Curious, isn't it?'

'Very,' I said.

The house on the Avenue Foch quivered in the heat of the morning. The trees before it moved sensuously as though anxious to savour the hot sun. The door was opened by a butler; we stepped inside the entrance hall. The marble was cold and the curve of the staircase twinkled where sunbeams prodded the rich colours of the carpeting. High above us the chandeliers clinked with the draught from the open door.

The only sound was a girl's scream. I recognized it as the tape-recording that Datt mentioned. The screams were momentarily louder as a door opened and closed again somewhere on the first floor beyond the top of the staircase.

'Who is up there?' said Datt as he handed his umbrella and hat to the butler.

'Monsieur Kuang-t'ien,' said the butler.

'A charming fellow,' said Datt. 'Major-domo of the Chinese Embassy here in Paris.'

Somewhere in the house a piano played Liszt, or perhaps it was a recording.

I looked towards the first floor. The screams continued, muffled by the door that had now closed again. Suddenly, moving noiselessly like a figure in a fantasy, a young girl ran along the first-floor balcony and came down the stairs, stumbling and clinging to the banister rail. She half-fell and half-ran, her mouth open in that sort of soundless scream that only nightmares produce. The girl was naked but her body was speckled with patches of bright wet blood. She must have been stabbed twenty, perhaps thirty times, and the blood had produced an intricate pattern of rivulets like a tight bodice of fine red lace. I remembered M. Kuang-t'ien's poem: 'If she is not a rose all white, then she must be redder than the red of blood.'

No one moved until Datt made a half-hearted attempt to grab her, but he was so slow that she avoided him effortlessly and ran through the door. I recognized her face now; it was the model that Byrd had painted, Annie.

'Get after her.' Datt called his staff into action with the calm precision of a liner captain pulling into a pier. 'Go upstairs, grab Kuang-t'ien, disarm him, clean the knife and hide it. Put him under guard, then phone the Press Officer at the Chinese Embassy. Don't tell him anything, but he must stay in his office until I call him to arrange a meeting. Albert, get on my personal phone and call the Ministry of the Interior. Tell them we'll need some CRS policemen here. I don't want the Police Municipale poking around too long. Jules, get my case and the drug box and have the transfusion apparatus ready; I'll take a look at the girl.' Datt turned, but stopped and said softly, 'And Byrd, get Byrd here immediately; send a car for him.'

He hurried after the footmen and butler who were running across the lawn after the bleeding girl. She glanced over her shoulder and gained fresh energy from the closeness of the pursuit. She grabbed at the gatepost and swung out on to the hot dusty pavement of the

Avenue Foch, her heart pumping the blood patches into shiny bulbous swellings that burst and dribbled into vertical stripes.

'Look!' I heard the voices of passers-by calling.

Someone else called 'Hello darling', and there was a laugh and a lot of wolf-whistles. They must have been the last thing the girl heard as she collapsed and died on the hot, dusty Parisian pavement under the trees in the Avenue Foch. A bewhiskered old crone carrying two *baguettes* came shuffling in her threadbare carpet-slippers. She pushed through the onlookers and leaned down close to the girl's head. 'Don't worry chérie, I'm a nurse,' she croaked. 'All your injuries are small and superficial.' She pushed the loaves of bread tighter under her armpit and tugged at her corset bottom. 'Just superficial,' she said again, 'so don't make so much fuss.' She turned very slowly and went shuffling off down the street muttering to herself.

There were ten or twelve people around her by the time I reached the body. The butler arrived and threw a car blanket over her. One of the bystanders said '*Tant pis*', and another said that the *jolie pépée* was well barricaded. His friend laughed.

A policeman is never far away in Paris and they came quickly, the blue-and-white corrugated van disgorging cops like a gambler fanning a deck of cards. Even before the van came to a halt the police were sorting through the bystanders, asking for papers, detaining some, prodding others away. The footmen had wrapped the girl's body in the blanket and began to heave the sagging bundle towards the gates of the house.

'Put it in the van,' said Datt. One of the policemen said, 'Take the body to the house.' The two men carrying the dead girl stood undecided.

'In the van,' said Datt.

'I get my orders from the Commissaire de Police,' said

the cop. 'We are on the radio now.' He nodded towards the van.

Datt was furious. He struck the policeman a blow on the arm. His voice was sibilant and salivatory. 'Can't you see that you are attracting attention, you fool? This is a political matter. The Ministry of the Interior are concerned. Put the body in the van. The radio will confirm my ruling.' The policeman was impressed by Datt's anger. Datt pointed at me. 'This is one of the officers working with Chief Inspector Loiseau of the Sûreté. Is that good enough for you?'

'Very well,' said the policeman. He nodded to the two men, who pushed the body on to the floor of the police van. They closed the door.

'Journalists may arrive,' said Datt to the policeman. 'Leave two of your men on guard here and make sure they know about article ten.'

'Yes,' said the policeman docilely.

'Which way are you going?' I asked the driver.

'The meat goes to the Medico-Legal,' he said.

'Ride me to the Avenue de Marigny,' I said. 'I'm going back to my office.'

By now the policeman in charge of the vehicle was browbeaten by Datt's fierce orders. He agreed to my riding in the van without a word of argument. At the corner of the Avenue de Marigny I stopped the van and got out. I needed a large brandy.

15

I expected the courier from the Embassy to contact me again that same day but he didn't return until the next morning. He put his document case on top of the wardrobe and sank into my best armchair.

He answered an unasked question. 'It's a whorehouse,' he pronounced. 'He calls it a clinic but it's more like a whorehouse.'

'Thanks for your help,' I said.

'Don't get snotty – you wouldn't want me telling you what to say in your reports.'

'That's true,' I admitted.

'Certainly it's true. It's a whorehouse that a lot of the Embassy people use. Not just our people – the Americans, etc., use it.'

I said, 'Straighten me up. Is this just a case of one of our Embassy people getting some dirty pictures back from Datt? Or something like that?'

The courier stared at me. 'I'm not allowed to talk about anything like that,' he said.

'Don't give me that stuff,' I said. 'They killed that girl yesterday.'

'In passion,' explained the courier. 'It was part of a kinky sex act.'

'I don't care if it was done as a publicity stunt,' I said. 'She's dead and I want as much information as I can get to avoid trouble. It's not just for my own skin; it's in the interests of the department that I avoid trouble.'

The courier said nothing, but I could see he was weakening.

I said, 'If I'm heading into that house again just to

recover some pictures of a secretary on the job, I'll come back and haunt you.'

'Give me some coffee,' said the courier, and I knew he had decided to tell me whatever he knew. I boiled the kettle and brewed up a pint of strong black coffee.

'Kuang-t'ien,' said the courier, 'the man who knifed the girl: do you know who he is?'

'Major-domo at the Chinese Embassy, Datt said.'

'That's his cover. His name is Kuang-t'ien, but he's one of the top five men in the Chinese nuclear programme.'

'He speaks damn good French.'

'Of course he does. He was trained at the Laboratoire Curie, here in Paris. So was his boss, Chien San-chiang, who is head of the Atomic Energy Institute in Peking.'

'You seem to know a lot about it,' I said.

'I was evaluating it this time last year.'

'Tell me more about this man who mixes his sex with switchblades.'

He pulled his coffee towards his and stirred it thoughtfully. Finally he began.

'Four years ago the U2 flights picked up the fourteen-acre gaseous diffusion plant taking hydro-electric power from the Yellow River not far from Lanchow. The experts had predicted that the Chinese would make their bombs as the Russians and French did, and as we did too: by producing plutonium in atomic reactors. But the Chinese didn't; our people have been close. I've seen the photos. Very close. That plant proves that they are betting all or nothing on hydrogen. They are going full steam ahead on their hydrogen research programme. By concentrating on the light elements generally and by pushing the megaton instead of the kiloton bomb they could be the leading nuclear power in eight or ten years if their hydrogen research pays off. This man Kuang-t'ien is their best authority on hydrogen. See what I mean?'

I poured more coffee and thought about it. The courier

got his case down and rummaged through it. 'When you left the clinic yesterday did you go in the police van?'

'Yes.'

'Um. I thought you might have. Good stunt that. Well, I hung around for a little while, then when I realized that you'd gone I came back here. I hoped you'd come back, too.'

'I had a drink,' I said. 'I put my mind in neutral for an hour.'

'That's unfortunate,' said the courier. 'Because while you were away you had a visitor. He asked for you at the counter, then hung around for nearly an hour, but when you didn't come back he took a cab to the Hotel Lotti.'

'What was he like?'

The courier smiled his mirthless smile and produced some ten-by-eight glossy pictures of a man drinking coffee in the afternoon sunlight. It wasn't a good-quality photograph. The man was about fifty, dressed in a light-weight suit with a narrow-brimmed felt hat. His tie had a small monogram that was unreadable and his cufflinks were large and ornate. He had large black sunglasses which in one photo he had removed to polish. When he drank coffee he raised his little finger high and pursed his lips.

'Ten out of ten,' I said. 'Good stuff: waiting till he took the glasses off. But you could use a better D and P man.'

'They are just rough prints,' said the courier. 'The negs are half-frame but they are quite good.'

'You are a regular secret agent,' I said admiringly. 'What did you do – shoot him in the ankle with the toe-cap gun, send out a signal to HQ on your tooth and play the whole thing back on your wristwatch?'

He rummaged through his papers again, then slapped a copy of *L'Express* upon the table top. Inside there was a photo of the US Ambassador greeting a group of American businessmen at Orly Airport. The courier looked up at me briefly.

'Fifty per cent of this group of Americans work – or did work – for the Atomic Energy Commission. Most of the remainder are experts on atomic energy or some allied subject. Bertram: nuclear physics at MIT. Bestbridge: radiation sickness of 1961. Waldo: fall-out experiments and work at the Hiroshima hospital. Hudson: hydrogen research – now he works for the US Army.' He marked Hudson's face with his nail. It was the man he'd photographed.

'Okay,' I said. 'What are you trying to prove?'

'Nothing. I'm just putting you in the picture. That's what you wanted, isn't it?'

'Yes,' I said. 'Thanks.'

'I'm just juxtaposing a hydrogen expert from Peking with a hydrogen expert from the Pentagon. I'm wondering why they are both in the same city at the same time and especially why they both cross your path. It's the sort of thing that makes me nervous.' He gulped down the rest of his coffee.

'You shouldn't drink too much of that strong black coffee,' I said. 'It'll be keeping you awake at night.'

The courier picked up his photos and copy of *L'Express*. 'I've got a system for getting to sleep,' he said. 'I count reports I've filed.'

'Watch resident agents jumping to conclusions,' I said.

'It's not soporific.' He got to his feet. 'I've left the most important thing until last,' he said.

'Have you?' I said, and wondered what was more important than the Chinese People's Republic preparing for nuclear warfare.

'The girl was ours.'

'What girl was whose?'

'The murdered girl was working for us, for the department.'

'A floater?'

'No. Permanent; warranty contract, the lot.'

'Poor kid,' I said. 'Was she pumping Kuang-t'ien?'

'It's nothing that's gone through the Embassy. They know nothing about her there.'

'But you knew?'

'Yes.'

'You are playing both ends.'

'Just like you.'

'Not at all. I'm just London. The jobs I do for the Embassy are just favours. I can decline if I want to. What do London want me to do about this girl?'

He said, 'She has an apartment on the left bank. Just check through her personal papers, her possessions. You know the sort of thing. It's a long shot but you might find something. These are her keys – the department held duplicates for emergencies – small one for mail box, large ones front door and apartment door.'

'You're crazy. The police were probably turning it over within thirty minutes of her death.'

'Of course they were. I've had the place under observation. That's why I waited a bit before telling you. London is pretty certain that no one – not Loiseau nor Datt nor anyone – knew that the girl worked for us. It's probable that they just made a routine search.'

'If the girl was a permanent she wouldn't leave anything lying around,' I said.

'Of course she wouldn't. But there may be one or two little things that could embarrass us all . . .' He looked around the grimy wallpaper of my room and pushed my ancient bedstead. It creaked.

'Even the most careful employee is tempted to have something close at hand.'

'That would be against orders.'

'Safety comes above orders,' he said. I shrugged my grudging agreement. 'That's right,' he said. 'Now you see why they want you to go. Go and probe around there as though it's your room and you've just been killed. You might find something where anyone else would fail. There's an insurance of about thirty thousand new francs if you find someone who you think should get it.' He wrote the address on a slip of paper and put it on the table. 'I'll be in touch,' he said. 'Thanks for the coffee, it was very good.'

'If I start serving instant coffee,' I said, 'perhaps I'll get a little less work.'

16

The dead girl's name was Annie Couzins. She was twenty-four and had lived in a new piece of speculative real estate not far from the Boul. Mich. The walls were close and the ceilings were low. What the accommodation agents described as a studio apartment was a cramped bed-sitting room. There were large cupboards containing a bath, a toilet and a clothes rack respectively. Most of the construction money had been devoted to an entrance hall lavished with plate glass, marble and bronze-coloured mirrors that made you look tanned and rested and slightly out of focus.

Had it been an old house or even a pretty one, then perhaps some memory of the dead girl would have remained there, but the room was empty, contemporary and pitiless. I examined the locks and hinges, probed the mattress and shoulder pads, rolled back the cheap carpet and put a knife blade between the floorboards. Nothing. Perfume, lingerie, bills, a postcard greeting from Nice, '. . . some of the swimsuits are divine . . .', a book of dreams, six copies of *Elle*, laddered stockings, six medium-price dresses, eight and a half pairs of shoes, a good English wool overcoat, an expensive transistor radio tuned to France Musique, tin of Nescafé, tin of powdered milk, saccharine, a damaged handbag containing spilled powder and a broken mirror, a new saucepan. Nothing to show what she was, had been, feared, dreamed of or wanted.

The bell rang. There was a girl standing there. She may have been twenty-five but it was difficult to say. Big cities leave a mark. The eyes of city-dwellers scrutinize

97

rather than see; they assess the value and the going-rate and try to separate the winners from the losers. That's what this girl tried to do.

'Are you from the police?' she asked.

'No. Are you?'

'I'm Monique. I live next door in apartment number eleven.'

'I'm Annie's cousin, Pierre.'

'You've got a funny accent. Are you a Belgian?' She gave a little giggle as though being a Belgian was the funniest thing that could happen to anyone.

'Half Belgian,' I lied amiably.

'I can usually tell. I'm very good with accents.'

'You certainly are,' I said admiringly. 'Not many people detect that I'm half Belgian.'

'Which half is Belgian?'

'The front half.'

She giggled again. 'Was your mother or your father Belgian, I mean.'

'Mother. Father was a Parisian with a bicycle.'

She tried to peer into the flat over my shoulder. 'I would invite you in for a cup of coffee,' I said, 'but I musn't disturb anything.'

'You're hinting. You want me to invite you for coffee.'

'Damned right I do.' I eased the door closed. 'I'll be there in five minutes.'

I turned back to cover up my searching. I gave a last look to the ugly cramped little room. It was the way I'd go one day. There would be someone from the department making sure that I hadn't left 'one or two little things that could embarrass us all'. Goodbye, Annie, I thought. I didn't know you but I know you now as well as anyone knows me. You won't retire to a little *tabac* in Nice and get a monthly cheque from some phoney insurance company. No, you can be resident agent in hell, Annie, and your bosses will be sending directives from Heaven telling you to clarify your reports and reduce your expenses.

I went to apartment number eleven. Her room was like Annie's: cheap gilt and film-star photos. A bath towel on the floor, ashtrays overflowing with red-marked butts, a plateful of garlic sausage that had curled up and died.

Monique had made the coffee by the time I got there. She'd poured boiling water on to milk powder and instant coffee and stirred it with a plastic spoon. She was a tough girl under the giggling exterior and she surveyed me carefully from behind fluttering eyelashes.

'I thought you were a burglar,' she said, 'then I thought you were the police.'

'And now?'

'You're Annie's cousin Pierre. You're anyone you want to be, from Charlemagne to Tin-Tin, it's no business of mine, and you can't hurt Annie.'

I took out my notecase and extracted a one-hundred-new-franc note. I put it on the low coffee table. She stared at me thinking it was some kind of sexual proposition.

'Did you ever work with Annie at the clinic?' I asked.

'No.'

I placed another note down and repeated the question.

'No,' she said.

I put down a third note and watched her carefully. When she again said no I leaned forward and took her hand roughly. 'Don't no me,' I said. 'You think I came here without finding out first?'

She stared at me angrily. I kept hold of her hand. 'Sometimes,' she said grudgingly.

'How many?'

'Ten, perhaps twelve.'

'That's better,' I said. I turned her hand over, pressed my fingers against the back of it to make her fingers open and slapped the three notes into her open palm. I let go of her and she leaned back out of reach, rubbing the back of her hand where I had held it. They were slim, bony hands with rosy knuckes that had known buckets of cold water and Marseilles soap. She didn't like her hands. She put them inside things and behind them and hid them under her folded arms.

'You bruised me,' she complained.

'Rub money on it.'

'Ten, perhaps twelve, times,' she admitted.

'Tell me about the place. What went on there?'

'You are from the police.'

'I'll do a deal with you, Monique. Slip *me* three hundred and I'll tell you all about what *I* do.'

She smiled grimly. 'Annie wanted an extra girl sometimes, just as a hostess . . . the money was useful.'

'Did Annie have plenty of money?'

'Plenty? I never knew anyone who had plenty. And even if they did it wouldn't go very far in this town. She didn't go to the bank in an armoured car if that's what you mean.' I didn't say anything.

Monique continued, 'She did all right but she was silly with it. She gave it to anyone who spun her a yarn. Her parents will miss her, so will Father Marconi; she was always giving to his collection for kids and missions and cripples. I told her over and over, she was silly with it. You're not Annie's cousin, but you throw too much money around to be the police.'

'The men you met there. You were told to ask them things and to remember what they said.'

'I didn't go to bed with them . . .'

'I don't care if you took *thé anglais* with them and dunked the *gâteau sec,* what were your instructions?' She hesitated, and I placed five more one-hundred-franc notes on the table but kept my fingers on them.

'Of course I made love to the men, just as Annie did, but they were all refined men. Men of taste and culture.'

'Sure they were,' I said. 'Men of real taste and culture.'

'It was done with tape recorders. There were two switches on the bedside lamps. I was told to get them talking about their work. So boring, men talking about their work, but are they ready to do it? My God they are.'

'Did you ever handle the tapes?'

'No, the recording machines were in some other part of the clinic.' She eyed the money.

'There's more to it than that. Annie did more than that.'

'Annie was a fool. Look where it got her. That's where it will get me if I talk too much.'

'I'm not interested in you,' I said. 'I'm only interested in Annie. What else did Annie do?'

'She substituted the tapes. She changed them. Sometimes she made her own recordings.'

'She took a machine into the house?'

'Yes. It one of those little ones, about four hundred new francs they cost. She had it in her handbag. I found it there once when I was looking for her lipstick to borrow.'

'What did Annie say about it?'

'Nothing. I never told her. And I never opened her handbag again either. It was her business, nothing to do with me.'

'The miniature recorder isn't in her flat now.'

'I didn't pinch it.'

'Then who do you think did?'

'I told her not once. I told her a thousand times.'

'What did you tell her?'

She pursed up her mouth in a gesture of contempt. 'What do you think I told her, M. Annie's cousin Pierre? I told her that to record conversations in such a house was a dangerous thing to do. In a house owned by people like those people.'

'People like what people?'

101

'In Paris one does not talk of such things, but it's said that the Ministry of the Interior or the SDECE[1] own the house to discover the indiscretions of foolish aliens.' She gave a tough little sob, but recovered herself quickly.

'You were fond of Annie?'

'I never got on well with women until I got to know her. I was broke when I met her, at least I was down to only ten francs. I had run away from home. I was in the laundry asking them to split the order because I didn't have enough to pay. The place where I lived had no running water. Annie lent me the money for the whole laundry bill – twenty francs – so that I had clean clothes while looking for a job. She gave me the first warm coat I ever had. She showed me how to put on my eyes. She listened to my stories and let me cry. She told me not to live the life that she had led, going from one man to another. She would have shared her last cigarette with a stranger. Yet she never asked me questions. Annie was an angel.'

'It certainly sounds like it.'

'Oh I know what you're thinking. You're thinking that Annie and I were a couple of Lesbians.'

'Some of my best lovers are Lesbians,' I said.

Monique smiled. I thought she was going to cry all over me, but she sniffed and smiled. 'I don't know if we were or not,' she said.

'Does it matter?'

'No, it doesn't matter. Anything would be better than to have stayed in the place I was born. My parents are still there; it's like living through a siege, besieged by the cost of necessities. They are careful how they use detergent, coffee is measured out. Rice, pasta and potatoes eke out tiny bits of meat. Bread is consumed, meat is revered and Kleenex tissues never afforded.

[1] Service de Documentation Extérieure et Contre-Espionage.

Unnecessary lights are switched off immediately, they put on a sweater instead of the heating. In the same building families crowd into single rooms, rats chew enormous holes in the woodwork – there's no food for them to chew on – and the w.c. is shared by three families and it usually doesn't flush. The people who live at the top of the house have to walk down two flights to use a cold water tap. And yet in this same city I get taken out to dinner in three-star restaurants where the bill for two dinners would keep my parents for a year. At the Ritz a man friend of mine paid nine francs a day to them for looking after his dog. That's just about half the pension my father gets for being blown up in the war. So when you people come snooping around here flashing your money and protecting the République Française's rocket programme, atomic plants, supersonic bombers and nuclear submarines or whatever it is you're protecting, don't expect too much from my patriotism.'

She bit her lip and glared at me, daring me to contradict her, but I didn't contradict. 'It's a lousy rotten town,' I agreed.

'And dangerous,' she said.

'Yes,' I said. 'Paris is all of those things.'

She laughed. 'Paris is like me, cousin Pierre; it's no longer young, and too dependent upon visitors who bring money. Paris is a woman with a little too much alcohol in her veins. She talks a little too loud and thinks she is young and gay. But she has smiled too often at strange men and the words "I love you" trip too easily from her tongue. The ensemble is chic and the paint is generously applied, but look closely and you'll see the cracks showing through.'

She got to her feet, groped along the bedside table for a match and lit her cigarette with a hand that trembled very slightly. She turned back to me. 'I saw the girls I knew taking advantage of offers that came from rich men they could never possibly love. I despised the girls and wondered how they could bring themselves to go to bed with such unattractive men. Well, now I know.' The smoke was getting in her eyes. 'It was fear. Fear of being a woman instead of a girl, a woman whose looks are slipping away rapidly, leaving her alone and unwanted in this vicious town.' She was crying now and I stepped closer to her and touched her arm. For a moment she seemed about to let her head fall upon my shoulder, but I felt her body tense and unyielding. I took a business card from my top pocket and put it on the bedside table next to a box of chocolates. She pulled away from me irritably. 'Just phone if you want to talk more,' I said.

'You're English,' she said suddenly. It must have been something in my accent or syntax. I nodded.

'It will be strictly business,' she said. 'Cash payments.'

'You don't have to be so tough on yourself,' I said. She said nothing.

'And thanks,' I said.

'Get stuffed,' said Monique.

17

First there came a small police van, its klaxon going. Co-operating with it was a blue-uniformed man on a motor-cycle. He kept his whistle in his mouth and blew repeatedly. Sometimes he was ahead of the van, sometimes behind it. He waved his right hand at the traffic as if by just the draught from it he could force the parked cars up on the pavement. The noise was deafening. The traffic ducked out of the way, some cars went willingly, some grudgingly, but after a couple of beeps on the whistle they crawled up on the stones, the pavement and over traffic islands like tortoises. Behind the van came the flying column: three long blue buses jammed with Garde Mobile men who stared at the cringing traffic with a bored look on their faces. At the rear of the column came a radio car. Loiseau watched them disappear down the Faubourg St Honoré. Soon the traffic began to move again. He turned away from the window and back to Maria. 'Dangerous,' pronounced Loiseau. 'He's playing a dangerous game. The girl is killed in his house, and Datt is pulling every political string he can find to prevent an investigation taking place. He'll regret it.' He got to his feet and walked across the room.

'Sit down, darling,' said Maria. 'You are just wasting calories in getting annoyed.'

'I'm not Datt's boy,' said Loiseau.

'And no one will imagine that you are,' said Maria. She wondered why Loiseau saw everything as a threat to his prestige.

'The girl is entitled to an investigation,' explained Loiseau. 'That's why I became a policeman. I believe in equality before the law. And now they are trying to tie my hands. It makes me furious.'

'Don't shout,' said Maria. 'What sort of effect do you imagine that has upon the people that work for you, hearing you shouting?'

'You are right,' said Loiseau. Maria loved him. It was when he capitulated so readily like that that she loved him so intensely. She wanted to care for him and advise him and make him the most successful policeman in the whole world. Maria said, 'You are the finest policeman in the whole world.'

He smiled. 'You mean with your help I could be.' Maria shook her head. 'Don't argue,' said Loiseau. 'I know the workings of your mind by now.'

Maria smiled too. He did know. That was the awful thing about their marriage. They knew each other too well. To know all is to forgive nothing.

'She was one of my girls,' said Loiseau. Maria was surprised. Of course Loiseau had girls, he was no monk, but it surprised her to hear him talk like that to her. 'One of them?' She deliberately made her voice mocking.

'Don't be so bloody arch, Maria. I can't stand you raising one eyebrow and adopting that patronizing tone. One of my girls.' He said it slowly to make it easy for her to understand. He was so pompous that Maria almost giggled. 'One of my girls, working for me as an informant.'

'Don't all the tarts do that?'

'She wasn't a tart, she was a highly intelligent girl giving us first-class information.'

'Admit it, darling,' Maria cooed, 'you were a tiny bit infatuated with her.' She raised an eyebrow quizzically.

'You stupid cow,' said Loiseau. "What's the good of treating you like an intelligent human.' Maria was shocked by the rusty-edged hatred that cut her. She had made a kind, almost loving remark. Of course the girl had fascinated Loiseau and had in turn been fascinated by him. The fact that it was true was proved by Loiseau's anger. But did his anger have to be so bitter? Did he have to wound her to know if blood flowed through her veins?

Maria got to her feet. 'I'll go,' she said. She remembered Loiseau once saying that Mozart was the only person who understood him. She had long since decided that that at least was true.

'You said you wanted to ask me something.'

'It doesn't matter.'

'Of course it matters. Sit down and tell me.'

She shook her head. 'Another time.'

'Do you have to treat me like a monster, just because I won't play your womanly games?'

'No,' she said.

There was no need for Maria to feel sorry for Loiseau. He didn't feel sorry for himself and seldom for anyone else. He had pulled the mechanism of their marriage apart and now looked at it as if it were a broken toy, wondering why it didn't work. Poor Loiseau. My poor, poor, darling Loiseau. I at least can build again, but you don't know what you did that killed us.

'You're crying, Maria. Forgive me. I'm so sorry.'

'I'm not crying and you're not sorry.' She smiled at him. 'Perhaps that's always been our problem.'

Loiseau shook his head but it wasn't a convincing denial.

Maria walked back towards the Faubourg St Honoré. Jean-Paul was at the wheel of her car.

'He made you cry,' said Jean-Paul. 'The rotten swine.'

'I made myself cry,' said Maria.

Jean-Paul put his arm around her and held her tight. It was all over between her and Jean-Paul, but feeling his arm around her was like a shot of cognac. She stopped feeling sorry for herself and studied her make-up.

'You look magnificent,' said Jean-Paul. 'I would like to take you away and make love to you.'

There was a time when that would have affected her, but she had long since decided that Jean-Paul seldom *wanted* to make love to anyone, although he did it often enough, heaven knows. But it was a good thing to hear when you have just argued with an ex-husband. She smiled at Jean-Paul and he took her hand in his large tanned one and turned it around like a bronze sculpture on a turntable. Then he released it and grabbed at the controls of the car. He wasn't as good a driver as Maria was, but she preferred to be his passenger rather than drive herself. She lolled back and pretended that Jean-Paul was the capable tanned he-man that he looked. She watched the pedestrians, and intercepted the envious glances. They were a perfect picture of modern Paris: the flashy automobile, Jean-Paul's relaxed good looks and expensive clothes, her own well-cared-for appearance – for she was as sexy now as she had ever been. She leaned her head close upon Jean-Paul's shoulder. She could smell his after-shave perfume and the rich animal smell of the leather seats. Jean-Paul changed gear as they roared across the Place de la Concorde. She felt his arm muscles ripple against her cheek.

'Did you ask him?' asked Jean-Paul.

'No,' she said. 'I couldn't. He wasn't in the right mood.'

'He's never in the right mood, Maria. And he's never going to be. Loiseau knows what you want to ask him and he precipitates situations so that you never will ask him.'

'Loiseau isn't like that,' said Maria. She had never thought of that. Loiseau was clever and subtle; perhaps it was true.

'Look,' said Jean-Paul, 'during the last year that house on the Avenue Foch has held exhibitions, orgies, with perversions, blue movies and everything, but has never

108

had any trouble from the police. Even when a girl dies there, there is still little or no trouble. Why? Because it has the protection of the French Government. Why does it have protection? Because the activities at the house are filmed and photographed for official dossiers.'

'I'm not sure you're right. Datt implies that, but I'm not sure.'

'Well I am sure,' said Jean-Paul. 'I'll bet you that those films and photos are in the possession of the Ministry of the Interior, Loiseau probably sees every one of them. They probably have a private showing once a week. Loiseau probably saw that film of you and me within twenty-four hours of its being taken.'

'Do you think so?' said Maria. A flash of fear rose inside her, radiating panic like a two-kilowatt electric fire. Jean-Paul's large cool hand gripped her shoulder. She wished he would grip her harder. She wanted him to hurt her so that her sins would be expiated and erased by the pain. She thought of Loiseau seeing the film in the company of other policemen. Please God it hadn't happened. Please please God. She thought she had agonized over every aspect of her foolishness, but this was a new and most terrible one.

'But why would they keep the films?' Maria asked, although she knew the answer.

'Datt selects the people who use that house. Datt is a psychiatrist, a genius . . .'

'. . . an evil genius.'

'Perhaps an evil genius,' said Jean-Paul objectively. 'Perhaps an evil genius, but by gathering a select circle of people – people of great influence, of prestige and diplomatic power – Datt can compile remarkable assessments and predictions about their behaviour in everything they do. Many major shifts of French Government policy have been decided by Datt's insights and analysis of sexual behaviour.'

'It's vile,' said Maria.

'It's the world in our time.'

'It's France in our time,' Maria corrected. 'Foul man.'

'He's not foul,' said Jean-Paul. 'He is not responsible for what those people do. He doesn't even encourage them. As far as Datt is concerned his guests could behave with impeccable decorum; he would be just as happy to record and analyse their attitudes.'

'*Voyeur.*'

'He's not even a *voyeur*. That's the odd thing. That's what makes him of such great importance to the Ministry. And that's why your ex-husband could do nothing to retrieve that film even if he wished to.'

'And what about you?' asked Maria casually.

'Be reasonable,' said Jean-Paul. 'It's true I do little jobs for Datt but I am not his *confidant*. I've no idea of what happens to the film . . .'

'They burn them sometimes,' Maria remembered. 'And often they are taken away by the people concerned.'

'You have never heard of duplicate prints?'

Maria's hopes sank. 'Why didn't you ask for that piece of film of us?'

'Because you said let them keep it. Let them show it every Friday night, you said.'

'I was drunk,' said Maria. 'It was a joke.'

'It's a joke for which we are both paying dearly.'

Maria snorted. 'You love the idea of people seeing the film. It's just the image you love to project. The great lover . . .' She bit her tongue. She had almost added that the film was his sole documentary proof of heterosexuality, but she closed her eyes. 'Loiseau could get the film back,' she said. She was sure, sure, sure that Loiseau hadn't seen that piece of film, but the memory of the fear remained.

'Loiseau *could* get it,' she said desperately, wanting Jean-Paul to agree on this one, very small point.

'But he won't,' said Jean-Paul. 'He won't because I'm involved and your ex-husband hates me with a deep and illogical loathing. The trouble is that I can understand why he does. I'm no good for you, Maria. You would probably have managed the whole thing excellently except that Loiseau is jealous of your relationship with me. Perhaps we should cease to see each other for a few months.'

'I'm sure we should.'

'But I couldn't bear it, Maria.'

'Why the hell not? We don't love each other. I am only a suitable companion and you have so many other women you'd never even notice my absence.' She despised herself even before she'd completed the sentence. Jean-Paul detected her motive immediately, of course, and responded.

'My darling little Maria.' He touched her leg lightly and sexlessly. 'You are different from the others. The others are just stupid little tarts that amuse me as decorations. They are not women. You are the only real woman I know. You are the woman I love, Maria.'

'Monsieur Datt himself,' said Maria, '*he* could get the film.' Jean-Paul pulled into the side of the road and double parked.

'We've played this game long enough, Maria,' he said.

'What game?' asked Maria. Behind them a taxi-driver swore bitterly as he realized they were not going to move.

'The how-much-you-hate-Datt game,' said Jean-Paul.

'I do hate him.'

'He's your father, Maria.'

'He's not my father, that's just a stupid story that he told you for some purpose of his own.'

'Then where is your father?'

'He was killed in 1940 in Bouillon, Belgium, during the fighting with the Germans. He was killed in an air raid.'

'He would have been about the same age as Datt.'

'So would a million men,' said Maria. 'It's such a stupid lie that it's not worth arguing about. Datt hoped I'd swallow that story but now even he no longer speaks of it. It's a stupid lie.'

Jean-Paul smiled uncertainly. 'Why?'

'Oh Jean-Paul. Why. You know how his evil little mind works. I was married to an important man in the Sûreté. Can't you see how convenient it would be to have me thinking he was my father? A sort of insurance, that's why.'

Jean-Paul was tired of this argument. 'Then he's not your father. But I still think you should co-operate.'

'Co-operate how?'

'Tell him a few snippets of information.'

'Could he get the film if it was really worth while?'

'I can ask him.' He smiled. 'Now you are being sensible, my love,' he said. Maria nodded as the car moved forward into the traffic. Jean-Paul planted a brief kiss on her forehead. A taxi-driver saw him do it and tooted a small illegal toot on the horn. Jean-Paul kissed Maria's forehead again a little more ardently. The great Arc de Triomphe loomed over them as they roared around the Étoile like soapsuds round the kitchen sink. A hundred tyres screamed an argument about centrifugal force, then they were into the Grande Armée. The traffic had stopped at the traffic lights. A man danced nimbly between the cars, collecting money and whipping newspapers from window to window like a fan dancer. As the traffic lights changed the cars slid forward. Maria opened her paper; the ink was still wet and it smudged under her thumb. 'American tourist disappears,' the headline said. There was a photograph of Hudson, the American hydrogen-research man. The newspaper said he was a frozen foods executive named Parks, which was the story the US Embassy had given out. Neither the face nor either name meant anything to Maria.

'Anything in the paper?' asked Jean-Paul. He was fighting a duel with a Mini-Cooper. 'No,' said Maria. She rubbed the newsprint on her thumb. 'There never is at this time of year. The English call it the silly season.'

18

Les Chiens is everything that delights the yeh yeh set. It's dark, hot, and squirming like a tin of live bait. The music is ear-splitting and the drink remarkably expensive even for Paris. I sat in a corner with Byrd.

'Not my sort of place at all,' Byrd said. 'But in a curious way I like it.'

A girl in gold crochet pyjamas squeezed past our table, leaned over and kissed my ear. 'Chéri,' she said. 'Long time no see,' and thereby exhausted her entire English vocabulary.

'Dash me,' said Byrd. 'You can see right through it, dash me.'

The girl patted Byrd's shoulder affectionately and moved on.

'You do have some remarkable friends,' said Byrd. He had ceased to criticize me and begun to regard me as a social curiosity well worth observing.

'A journalist must have contacts,' I explained.

'My goodness yes,' said Byrd.

The music stopped suddenly. Byrd mopped his face with a red silk handkerchief. 'It's like a stokehold,' he said. The club was strangely quiet.

'Were you an engineer officer?'

'I did gunnery school when I was on lieutenants' list. Finished a Commander; might have made Captain if there'd been a little war, Rear-Admiral if there'd been another big one. Didn't fancy waiting. Twenty-seven years of sea duty is enough. Right through the hostilities and out the other side, more ships than I care to remember.'

'You must miss it.'

'Never. Why should I? Running a ship is just like running a small factory; just as exciting at times and just as dull for the most part. Never miss it a bit. Never think about it, to tell you the truth.'

'Don't you miss the sea, or the movement, or the weather?'

'Good grief, laddie, you've got a nasty touch of the Joseph Conrads. Ships, especially cruisers, are large metal factories, rather prone to pitch in bad weather. Nothing good about that, old boy – damned inconvenient, that's the truth of it! The Navy was just a job of work for me, and it suited me fine. Nothing against the Navy mind, not at all, owe it an awful lot, no doubt of it, but it was just a job like any other; no magic to being a sailor.' There was a plonking sound as someone tapped the amplifier and put on another record. 'Painting is the only true magic,' said Byrd. 'Translating three dimensions into two – or if you are a master, four.' He nodded suddenly, the loud music started. The clientèle, who had been stiff and anxious during the silence, smiled and relaxed, for they no longer faced the strain of conversing together.

On a staircase a wedge of people were embracing and laughing like advertising photos. At the bar a couple of English photographers were talking in cockney and an English writer was explaining James Bond.

A waiter put four glasses full of ice cubes and a half-bottle of Johnnie Walker on the table before us. 'What's this?' I asked.

The waiter turned away without answering. Two Frenchmen at the bar began to argue with the English writer and a bar stool fell over. The noise wasn't loud enough for anyone to notice. On the dance floor a girl in a shiny plastic suit was swearing at a man who had burned a hole in it with his cigarette. I heard the English writer behind me say, 'But I have always immensely adored

115

violence. His violence is his humanity. Unless you understand that you understand nothing.' He wrinkled his nose and smiled. One of the Frenchmen replied, 'He suffers in translation.' The photographer was clicking his fingers in time to the music.

'Don't we all?' said the English writer, and looked around.

Byrd said, 'Shocking noise.'

'Don't listen,' I said.

'What?' said Byrd.

The English writer was saying '. . . a violent Everyman in a violent but humdrum . . .' he paused, 'but humdrum world.' He nodded agreement to himself. 'Let me remind you of Baudelaire. There's a sonnet that begins . . .'

'So this bird wants to get out of the car . . .' one of the photographers was saying.

'Speak a little more quietly,' said the English writer. 'I'm going to recite a sonnet.'

'Belt up,' said the photographer over his shoulder. 'This bird wanted to get out of the car . . .'

'Baudelaire,' said the writer. 'Violent, macabre and symbolic.'

'You leave bollicks out of this,' said the photographer, and his friend laughed. The writer put a hand on his shoulder and said, 'Look my friend . . .' The photographer planted a right jab into his solar plexus without spilling the drink he was holding. The writer folded up like a deckchair and hit the floor. A waiter grabbed towards the photographer but stumbled over the English writer's inert body.

'Look here,' said Byrd, and a passing waiter turned so fast that the half-bottle of whisky and the four glasses of ice were knocked over. Someone aimed a blow at the photographer's head. Byrd got to his feet saying quietly and reasonably, 'You spilled the drink on the floor. Dash me, you'd better pay for it. Only thing to do. Damned rowdies.' The waiter pushed Byrd violently and he fell back and disappeared among the densely packed dancers. Two or three people began to punch each other. A wild blow took me in the small of the back, but the attacker had moved on. I got both shoulder-blades rested against the nearest piece of wall and braced the sole of my right foot for leverage. One of the photographers came my way, but he kept going and wound up grappling with a waiter. There was a scuffle going on at the top of the staircase, and then violence travelled through the place like a flash flood. Everyone was punching everyone, girls were screaming and the music seemed to be even louder than before. A man hurried a girl along the corridor past me. 'It's those English that make the trouble,' he complained.

'Yes,' I said.

'You look English.'

'No, I'm Belgian,' I said. He hurried after the girl. When I got near the emergency exit a waiter was barring the way. Behind me the screaming, grunting and breaking noises continued unabated. Someone had switched the music to top volume.

'I'm coming through,' I said to the waiter.

'No,' he said. 'No one leaves.'

A small man moved quickly alongside me. I flinched away from what I expected would be a blow upon my shoulder but it was a pat of encouragement. The man stepped forward and felled the waiter with two nasty karate cuts. 'They are all damned rude,' he said, stepping over the prostrate waiter. 'Especially waiters. If they showed a little good manners their customers might behave better.'

'Yes,' I said.

'Come along,' said Byrd. 'Don't moon around. Stay close to the wall. Watch the rear. You!' he shouted to a man with a ripped evening suit who was trying to open the emergency doors. 'Pull the top bolt, man, ease the mortice at the same time. Don't hang around, don't want to have to disable too many of them, this is my painting hand.'

We emerged into a dark side-street. Maria's car was drawn up close to the exit. 'Get in,' she called.

'Were you inside?' I asked her.

She nodded. 'I was waiting for Jean-Paul.'

'Well, you two get along,' said Byrd.

'What about Jean-Paul?' Maria said to me.

'You two get along,' said Byrd. 'He'll be quite safe.'

'Can't we give you a lift?' asked Maria.

'I'd better go back and see if Jean-Paul is all right,' said Byrd.

'You'll get killed,' said Maria.

'Can't leave Jean-Paul in there,' explained Byrd. 'Close ranks, Jean-Paul's got to stop hanging around in these sort of places and get to bed early. The morning light is the only light to paint in. I wish I could make him understand that.'

Byrd hurried back towards the club. 'He'll get killed,' said Maria.

'I don't think so,' I said. We got into Maria's E-type.

Hurrying along the street came two men in raincoats and felt hats.

'They are from the PJ crime squad,' said Maria. One of the men signalled to her. She wound the window down. He leaned down and touched his hat in salute. 'I'm looking for Byrd,' he said to Maria.

'Why?' I asked, but Maria had already told them he was the man who had just left us.

'Police judiciaire. I'm arresting him for the murder of Annie Couzins,' he said. 'I've got sworn statements from witnesses.'

'Oh God,' said Maria. 'I'm sure he's not guilty, he's not the violent type.'

118

I looked back to the door but Byrd had disappeared inside. The two policemen followed. Maria revved the motor and we bumped off the pavement, skimmed past a *moto* and purred into the Boul. St Germain.

The sky was starry and the air was warm. The visitors had spread through Paris by now and they strolled around entranced, in love, jilted, gay, suicidal, inspired, bellicose, defeated; in clean cotton St Trop, wine-stained Shetland, bearded, bald, bespectacled, bronzed. Acned little girls in bumbag trousers, lithe Danes, fleshy Greeks, nouveau-riche communists, illiterate writers, would-be directors – Paris had them all that summer; and Paris can keep them.

'You didn't exactly inspire me with admiration,' said Maria.

'How was that?'

'You didn't exactly spring to the aid of the ladies.'

'I didn't exactly know which ones were ladies,' I said.

'All you did was to save your own skin.'

'It's the only one I've got left,' I explained. 'I used the others for lampshades.' The blow I'd had in my kidneys hurt like hell. I'm getting too old for that sort of thing.

'Your funny time is running out,' said Maria.

'Don't be aggressive,' I said. 'It's not the right mood for asking favours.'

'How did you know I was going to ask a favour?'.

'I can read the entrails, Maria. When you mistranslated my reactions to the injections that Datt gave me you were saving me up for something.'

'Do you think I was?' she smiled. 'Perhaps I just salvaged you to take home to bed with me.'

'No, it was more than that. You are having some sort of trouble with Datt and you think – probably wrongly – that I can do something about it.'

'What makes you think so?' The streets were quieter at the other end of St Germain. We passed the bomb-scarred façade of the War Ministry and raced a cab over

119

the river. The Place de la Concorde was a great concrete field, floodlit like a film set.

'There's something in the way you speak of him. Also that night when he injected me you always moved around to keep my body between you and him. I think you had already decided to use me as a bulwark against him.'

'Teach Yourself Psychiatry, volume three.'

'Volume five. The one with the Do-It-Yourself Brain Surgery Kit.'

'Loiseau wants to see you tonight. He said it's something you'll enjoy helping him with.'

'What's he doing – disembowelling himself?' I said.

She nodded. 'Avenue Foch. Meet him at the corner at midnight.' She pulled up outside the Café Blanc.

'Come and have coffee,' I suggested.

'No. I must get home,' she said. I got out of the car and she drove away. Jean-Paul was sitting on the terrace drinking a Coca-Cola. He waved and I walked over to him. 'Were you in Les Chiens this evening?' I asked.

'Haven't been there for a week,' he said. 'I was going tonight but I changed my mind.'

'There was a *bagarre*. Byrd was there.'

Jean-Paul pulled a face but didn't seem interested. I ordered a drink and sat down. Jean-Paul stared at me.

19

Jean-Paul stared at the Englishman and wondered why he had sought him out. It was more than a coincidence. Jean-Paul didn't trust him. He thought he had seen Maria's car in the traffic just before the Englishman sat down. What had they both been plotting? Jean-Paul knew that no woman could be trusted. They consumed one, devoured one, sapped one's strength and confidence and gave no reassurance in return. The very nature of women made them his . . . was 'enemy' too strong a word? He decided that 'enemy' wasn't too strong a word. They took away his manhood and yet demanded more and more physical love. 'Insatiable' was the only word for them. The other conclusion was not worth considering – that his sexual prowess was under par. No. Women were hot and lustful and, if he was truthful with himself, evil. His life was an endless struggle to quench the lustful fires of the women he met. And if he ever failed they would mock him and humiliate him. Women were waiting to humiliate him.

'Have you seen Maria lately?' Jean-Paul asked.

'A moment ago. She gave me a lift here.'

Jean-Paul smiled but did not comment. So that was it. At least the Englishman had not dared to lie to him. He must have read his eyes. He was in no mood to be trifled with.

'How's the painting going?' I asked. 'Were the critics kind to your friend's show the other day?'

'Critics,' said Jean-Paul, 'find it quite impossible to separate modern painting from teenage pregnancy, juvenile delinquency and the increase in crimes of violence.

121

They think that by supporting the dull repetitious, representational type of painting that is out of date and unoriginal, they are also supporting loyalty to the flag, discipline, a sense of fair play and responsible use of world supremacy.'

I grinned. 'And what about those people that like modern painting?'

'People who buy modern paintings are very often interested only in gaining admittance to the world of the young artists. They are often wealthy vulgarians who, terrified of being thought old and square, prove that they are both by falling prey to quick-witted opportunists who paint modern – very modern – paintings. Provided that they keep on buying pictures they will continue to be invited to bohemian parties.'

'There are no genuine painters?'

'Not many,' said Jean-Paul. 'Tell me, are English and American exactly the same language, exactly the same?'

'Yes,' I said. Jean-Paul looked at me. 'Maria is very taken with you.' I said nothing. 'I despise all women.'

'Why?'

'Because they despise each other. They treat each other with a cruelty that no man would inflict upon another man. They never have a woman friend who they can be sure won't betray them.'

'That sounds like a good reason for men to be kind to them,' I said.

Jean-Paul smiled. He felt sure it was not meant seriously.

'The police have arrested Byrd for murder,' I said.

Jean-Paul was not surprised. 'I have always thought of him as a killer.'

I was shocked.

'They all are,' said Jean-Paul. 'They are all killers for their work. Byrd, Loiseau, Datt, even you, my friend, are killers if work demands.'

'What are you talking about? Whom did Loiseau kill?'

'He killed Maria. Or do you think she was always like she is now – treacherous and confused, and constantly in fear of all of you?'

'But you are not a killer?'

'No,' said Jean-Paul. 'Whatever faults I have I am not a killer, unless you mean . . .' He paused before carefully pronouncing the English word, 'a "lady-killer"'

Jean-Paul smiled and put on his dark glasses.

20

I got to the Avenue Foch at midnight.

At the corner of a narrow alley behind the houses were
four shiny motor-cycles and four policemen in crash
helmets, goggles and short black leather coats. They
stood there impassively as only policemen stand, not
waiting for anything to happen, not glancing at their
watches or talking, just standing looking as though they
were the only people with a right to be there. Beyond the
policemen there was Loiseau's dark-green DS 19, and
behind that red barriers and floodlights marked the section of the road that was being evacuated. There were
more policemen standing near the barriers. I noticed that
they were not traffic policemen but young, tough-looking
cops with fidgety hands that continually tapped pistol
holsters, belts and batons to make sure that everything
was ready.

Inside the barriers twenty thick-shouldered men were
bent over road-rippers. The sound was deafening, like
machine-guns firing long bursts. The generator trucks
played a steady drone. Near to me the ripper operator
lifted the handles and prised the point into a sunsoft area
of tar. He fired a volley and the metal buried its point
deep, and with a sigh a chunk of paving fell back into the
excavated area. The operator ordered another man to
take over, and turned towards us mopping his sweaty
head with a blue handkerchief. Under the overalls he
wore a clean shirt and a silk tie. It was Loiseau.

'Hard work,' he said.

'You are going into the cellars?'

'Not the cellars of Datt's place,' Loiseau said to me.

124

'We're punching a hole in these cellars two doors away, then we'll mousehole through into Datt's cellars.'

'Why didn't you ask these people?' I pointed at the house behind which the roadwork was going on. 'Why not just ask them to let you through?'

'I don't work that way. As soon as I ask a favour I show my hand. I hate the idea of *you* knowing what we are doing. I may want to deny it tomorrow.' He mopped his brow again. 'In fact I'm damned sure I will be denying it tomorrow.' Behind him the road-ripper exploded into action and the chiselled dust shone golden in the beams of the big lights, like illustrations for a fairy story, but from the damp soil came that sour aroma of death and bacteria that clings around a bombarded city.

'Come along,' said Loiseau. We passed three huge Berliot buses full of policemen. Most were dozing with their képis pulled forward over their eyes; a couple were eating crusty sandwiches and a few were smoking. They didn't look at us as we passed by. They sat, muscles slack, eyes unseeing and minds unthinking, as experienced combat troops rest between battles.

Loiseau walked towards a fourth bus; the windows were of dark-blue glass and from its coachwork a thick cable curved towards the ground and snaked away into a manhole cover in the road. He ushered me up the steps past a sentry. Inside the bus was a brightly lit command centre. Two policemen sat operating radio and teleprinter links. At the back of the bus a large rack of MAT 49 sub-machine guns was guarded by a man who kept his silver-braided cap on to prove he was an officer.

Loiseau sat down behind a desk, produced a bottle of Calvados and two glasses. He poured a generous measure and pushed one across the desk to me. Loiseau sniffed at his own drink and sipped it tentatively. He drank a mouthful and turned to me. 'We hit some old *pavé* just under the surface. The city engineer's department didn't

125

know it was there. That's what slowed us down, otherwise we'd be into the cellars by now, all ready for you.'

'All ready for me,' I repeated.

'Yes,' said Loiseau. 'I want you to be the first into the house.'

'Why?'

'Lots of reasons. You know the layout there, you know what Datt looks like. You don't look too much like a cop – especially when you open your mouth – and you can look after yourself. And if something's going to happen to the first man in I'd rather it wasn't one of my boys. It takes a long time to train one of my boys.' He allowed himself a grim little smile.

'What's the real reason?'

Loiseau made a motion with the flattened hand. He dropped it between us like a shutter or screen. 'I want you to make a phone call from inside the house. A clear call for the police that the operator at the Prefecture will enter in the log. We'll be right behind you, of course, it's just a matter of keeping the record straight.'

'Crooked, you mean,' I said. 'It's just a matter of keeping the record crooked.'

'That depends where you are sitting,' said Loiseau.

'From where I'm sitting, I don't feel much inclined to upset the Prefecture. The *Renseignements généraux* are there in that building and they include dossiers on us foreigners. When I make that phone call it will be entered on to my file and next time I ask for my *carte de séjour* they will want to deport me for immoral acts and goodness knows what else. I'll never get another alien's permit.'

'Do what all other foreigners do,' said Loiseau. 'Take a second-class return ticket to Brussels every ninety days. There are foreigners who have lived here for twenty years who still do that rather than hang around for five hours at the Prefecture for a *carte de séjour*.' He held his flat hand

126

high as though shielding his eyes from the glare of the sun.

'Very funny,' I said.

'Don't worry,' Loiseau said. 'I couldn't risk your telling the whole Prefecture that the Sûreté had enlisted you for a job.' He smiled. 'Just do a good job for me and I'll make sure you have no trouble with the Prefecture.'

'Thanks,' I said. 'And what if there is someone waiting for me at the other side of the mousehole? What if I have one of Datt's guard dogs leap at my throat, jaws open wide? What happens then?'

Loiseau sucked his breath in mock terror. He paused. 'Then you get torn to pieces,' he said and laughed, and dropped his hand down abruptly like a guillotine.

'What do you expect to find there?' I asked. 'Here you are with dozens of cops and noise and lights – do you think they won't get nervous in the house?'

'You think they will?' Loiseau asked seriously.

'Some will,' I told him. 'At least a few of the most sophisticated ones will suspect that something's happening.'

'Sophisticated ones?'

'Come along, Loiseau,' I said irritably. 'There must be quite a lot of people close enough to your department to know the danger signals.'

He nodded and stared at me.

'So that's it,' I said. 'You were ordered to do it like this. Your department couldn't issue a warning to its associates but it could at least warn them by handling things noisily.'

'Darwin called it natural selection,' said Loiseau. 'The brightest ones will get away. You can probably guess my reaction, but at least I shall have the place closed down and may catch a few of the less imaginative clients. A little more Calvados.' He poured it.

I didn't agree to go, but Loiseau knew I would. The

wrong side of Loiseau could be a very uncomfortable place to reside in Paris.

It was another half-hour before they had broken into the cellars under the alley and then it took twenty minutes more to mousehole through into Datt's house. The final few demolitions had to be done brick by brick with a couple of men from a burglar-alarm company tapping around for wiring.

I had changed into police overalls before going through the final breakthrough. We were standing in the cellar of Datt's next-door neighbour under the temporary lights that Loiseau's men had slung out from the electric mains. The bare bulb was close to Loiseau's face, his skin was wrinkled and grey with brick dust through which little rivers of perspiration were shining bright pink.

'My assistant will be right behind you as far as you need cover. If the dogs go for you he will use the shotgun, but only if you are in real danger, for it will alert the whole house.'

Loiseau's assistant nodded at me. His circular spectacle lenses flashed in the light of the bare bulb and reflected in them I could see two tiny Loiseaus and a few hundred glinting bottles of wine that were stacked behind me. He broke the breach of the shotgun and checked the cartridges even though he had only loaded the gun five minutes before.

'Once you are into the house, give my assistant your overalls. Make sure you are unarmed and have no compromising papers on you, because once we come in you might well be taken into custody with the others and it's always possible that one of my more zealous officers might search you. So if there's anything in your pockets that would embarrass you . . .'

'There's a miniaturized radio transmitter inside my denture.'

'Get rid of it.'

'It was a joke.'

Loiseau grunted and said, 'The switchboard at the Prefecture is being held open from now on' – he checked his watch to be sure he was telling the truth – 'so you'll get through very quickly.'

'You told the Prefecture?' I asked. I knew that there was bitter rivalry between the two departments. It seemed unlikely that Loiseau would have confided in them.

'Let's say I have friends in the Signals Division,' said Loiseau. 'Your call will be monitored by us here in the command vehicle on our loop line.'[1]

'I understand,' I said.

'Final wall going now,' a voice called softly from the next cellar. Loiseau smacked me lightly on the back and I climbed through the small hole that his men had made in the wall. 'Take this,' he said. It was a silver pen, thick and clumsily made. 'It's a gas gun,' explained Loiseau. 'Use it at four metres or less but not closer than one, or it might damage the eyes. Pull the bolt back like this and let it go. The recess is the locking slot; that puts it on safety. But I don't think you'd better keep it on safety.'

'No,' I said, 'I'd hate it to be on safety.' I stepped into the cellar and picked my way upstairs.

The door at the top of the service flight was disguised as a piece of panelling. Loiseau's assistant followed me. He was supposed to have remained behind in the cellars but it wasn't my job to reinforce Loiseau's discipline. And anyway I could use a man with a shotgun.

I stepped out through the door.

One of my childhood books had a photo of a fly's eye magnified fifteen thousand times. The enormous glass chandelier looked like that eye, glinting and clinking and unwinking above the great formal staircase. I walked

---

[1] Paris police have their own telephone system independent of the public one.

across the mirror-like wooden floor feeling that the chandelier was watching me. I opened the tall gilded door and peered in. The wrestling ring had disappeared and so had the metal chairs; the salon was like the carefully arranged rooms of a museum: perfect yet lifeless. Every light in the place was shining bright, the mirrors repeated the nudes and nymphs of the gilded stucco and the painted panels.

I guessed that Loiseau's men were moving up through the mouseholed cellars but I didn't use the phone that was in the alcove in the hall. Instead I walked across the hall and up the stairs. The rooms that M. Datt used as offices – where I had been injected – were locked. I walked down the corridor trying the doors. They were all bedrooms. Most of them were unlocked; all of them were unoccupied. Most of the rooms were lavishly rococo with huge four-poster beds under brilliant silk canopies and four or five angled mirrors.

'You'd better phone,' said Loiseau's assistant.

'Once I phone the Prefecture will have this raid on record. I think we should find out a little more first.'

'I think . . .'

'Don't tell me what you think or I'll remind you that you're supposed to have stayed down behind the wainscoting.'

'Okay,' he said. We both tiptoed up the small staircase that joined the first floor to the second. Loiseau's men must be fretting by now. At the top of the flight of steps I put my head round the corner carefully. I put my head everywhere carefully, but I needn't have been so cautious, the house was empty. 'Get Loiseau up here,' I said.

Loiseau's men went all through the house, tapping panelling and trying to find secret doors. There were no documents or films. At first there seemed to be no secrets of any kind except that the whole place was a kind of

130

secret: the strange cells with the awful torture instruments, rooms made like lush train compartments or Rolls Royce cars, and all kinds of bizarre environments for sexual intercourse, even beds.

The peep-holes and the closed-circuit TV were all designed for M. Datt and his 'scientific methods'. I wondered what strange records he had amassed and where he had taken them, for M. Datt was nowhere to be found. Loiseau swore horribly. 'Someone,' he said, 'must have told Monsieur Datt that we were coming.'

Loiseau had been in the house about ten minutes when he called his assistant. He called long and loud from two floors above. When we arrived he was crouched over a black metal device rather like an Egyptian mummy. It was the size and very roughly the shape of a human body. Loiseau had put cotton gloves on and he touched the object briefly.

'The diagram of the Couzins girl,' he demanded from his assistant.

It was obtained from somewhere, a paper pattern of Annie Couzins's body marked in neat red ink to show the stab wounds, with the dimensions and depth written near each in tiny careful handwriting.

Loiseau opened the black metal case. 'That's it,' he said. 'Just what I thought.' Inside the case, which was just large enough to hold a person, knife points were positioned exactly as indicated on the police diagram. Loiseau gave a lot of orders and suddenly the room was full of men with tape-measures, white powder and camera equipment. Loiseau stood back out of their way. 'Iron maidens I think they call them,' he said. 'I seem to have read about them in some old schoolboy magazines.'

'What made her get into the damn thing?' I said.

'You are naïve,' said Loiseau. 'When I was a young officer we had so many deaths from knife wounds in brothels that we put a policeman on the door in each one. Every customer was searched. Any weapons he carried were chalked for identity. When the men left they got them back. I'll guarantee that not one got by that cop on the door but still the girls got stabbed, fatally sometimes.'

'How did it happen?'

'The girls – the prostitutes – smuggled them in. You'll never understand women.'

'No,' I said.

'Nor shall I,' said Loiseau.

21

Saturday was sunny, the light bouncing and sparkling as it does only in impressionist paintings and Paris. The boulevard had been fitted with wall-to-wall sunshine and out of it came the smell of good bread and black tobacco. Even Loiseau was smiling. He came galloping up my stairs at 8.30 A.M. I was surprised; he had never visited me before, at least not when I was at home.

'Don't knock, come in.' The radio was playing classical music from one of the pirate radio ships. I turned it off.

'I'm sorry,' said Loiseau.

'Everyone's at home to a policeman,' I said, 'in this country.'

'Don't be angry,' said Loiseau. 'I didn't know you would be in a silk dressing-gown, feeding your canary. It's very Noël Coward. If I described this scene as typically English, people would accuse me of exaggerating. You were talking to that canary,' said Loiseau. 'You were *talking* to it.'

'I try out all my jokes on Joe,' I said. 'But don't stand on ceremony, carry on ripping the place apart. What are you looking for this time?'

'I've said I'm sorry. What more can I do?'

'You could get out of my decrepit but very expensive apartment and stay out of my life. And you could stop putting your stubby peasant finger into my supply of coffee beans.'

'I was hoping you'd offer me some. You have this very light roast that is very rare in France.'

'I have a lot of things that are very rare in France.'

'Like the freedom to tell a policeman to "scram"?'

'Like that.'

'Well, don't exercise that freedom until we have had coffee together, even if you let me buy some downstairs.'

'Oh boy! Now I know you are on the tap. A cop is really on the make when he wants to pick up the bill for a cup of coffee.'

'I've had good news this morning.'

'They are restoring public executions.'

'On the contrary,' said Loiseau, letting my remark roll off him. 'There has been a small power struggle among the people from whom I take my orders and at present Datt's friends are on the losing side. I have been authorized to find Datt and his film collection by any means I think fit.'

'When does the armoured column leave? What's the plan – helicopters and flame-throwers and the one that burns brightest must have been carrying the tin of film?'

'You are too hard on the police methods in France. You think we could work with bobbies in pointed helmets carrying a wooden stick, but let me tell you, my friend, we wouldn't last two minutes with such methods. I remember the gangs when I was just a child – my father was a policeman – and most of all I remember Corsica. There were bandits; organized, armed and almost in control of the island. They murdered gendarmes with impunity. They killed policemen and boasted of it openly in the bars. Finally we had to get rough; we sent in a few platoons of the Republican Guard and waged a minor war. Rough, perhaps, but there was no other way. The entire income from all the Paris brothels was at stake. They fought and used every dirty trick they knew. It was war.'

'But you won the war.'

'It was the very last war we won,' Loiseau said bitterly. 'Since then we've fought in Lebanon, Syria, Indo-China,

Madagascar, Tunisia, Morocco, Suez and Algeria. Yes, that war in Corsica was the last one we won.'

'Okay. So much for your problems; how do I fit into your plans?'

'Just as I told you before; you are a foreigner and no one would think you were a policeman, you speak excellent French and you can look after yourself. What's more you would not be the sort of man who would reveal where your instructions came from, not even under pressure.'

'It sounds as though you think Datt still has a kick or two left in him.'

'They have a kick or two left in them even when they are suspended in space with a rope around the neck. I never underestimate the people I'm dealing with, because they are usually killers when it comes to the finale. Any time I overlook that, it will be one of my policemen who takes the bullet in the head, not me. So I don't overlook it, which means I have a tough, loyal, confident body of men under my command.'

'Okay,' I said. 'So I locate Datt. What then?'

'We can't have another fiasco like last time. Now Datt will be more than ever prepared. I want all his records. I want them because they are a constant threat to a lot of people, including stupid people in the Government of my country. I want that film because I loathe blackmail and I loathe blackmailers – they are the filthiest section of the criminal cesspit.'

'But so far there's been no blackmail, has there?'

'I'm not standing around waiting for the obvious to happen. I want that stuff destroyed. I don't want to hear that it was destroyed. I want to destroy it myself.'

'Suppose I don't want anything to do with it?'

Loiseau splayed out his hands. 'One,' he said, grabbing one pudgy finger, 'you are already involved. Two,' he grabbed the next finger, 'you are employed by some sort of British government department from what I can understand. They will be very angry if you turn down this chance of seeing the outcome of this affair.'

I suppose my expression changed.

'Oh, it's my business to know these things,' said Loiseau. 'Three. Maria has decided that you are trustworthy and in spite of her occasional lapses I have great regard for her judgement. She is, after all, an employee of the Sûreté.'

Loiseau grabbed his fourth digit but said nothing. He smiled. In most people a smile or a laugh can be a sign of embarrassment, a plea to break the tension. Loiseau's smile was a calm, deliberate smile. 'You are waiting for me to threaten you with what will happen if you don't help. me.' He shrugged and smiled again. 'Then you would turn my previous words about blackmail upon me and feel at ease in declining to help. But I won't. You are free to do as you wish in this matter. I am a very unthreatening type.'

'For a cop,' I said.

'Yes,' agreed Loiseau, 'a very unthreatening type for a cop.' It was true.

'Okay,' I said after a long pause. 'But don't mistake my motives. Just to keep the record straight, I'm very fond of Maria.'

'Can you really believe that would annoy me? You are so incredibly Victorian in these matters: so determined to play the game and keep a stiff upper lip aand have the record straight. We do not do things that way in France; another man's wife is fair game for all. Smoothness of tongue and nimbleness of foot are the trump cards; nobleness of mind is the joker.'

'I prefer my way.'

Loiseau looked at me and smiled his slow, nerveless smile. 'So do I,' he said.

'Loiseau,' I said, watching him carefully, 'this clinic of Datt's: is it run by your Ministry?'

'Don't *you* start that too. He's got half Paris thinking he's running that place for us.' The coffee was still hot. Loiseau got a bowl out of the cupboard and poured himself some. 'He's not connected with us,' said Loiseau. 'He's a criminal, a criminal with good connections but still just a criminal.'

'Loiseau,' I said, 'you can't hold Byrd for the murder of the girl.'

'Why not?'

'Because he didn't do it, that's why not. I was at the clinic that day. I stood in the hall and watched the girl run through and die. I heard Datt say, "Get Byrd here." It was a frame-up.'

Loiseau reached for his hat. 'Good coffee,' he said.

'It was a frame-up. Byrd is innocent.'

'So you say. But suppose Byrd had done the murder and Datt said that just for you to overhear? Suppose I told you that we know that Byrd was there? That would put this fellow Kuang in the clear, eh?'

'It might,' I said, 'if I heard Byrd admit it. Will you arrange for me to see Byrd? That's my condition for helping you.' I expected Loiseau to protest but he nodded. 'Agreed,' he said. 'I don't know why you worry about him. He's a criminal type if ever I saw one.' I didn't answer because I had a nasty idea that Loiseau was right.

'Very well,' said Loiseau. 'The bird market at eleven A.M. tomorrow.'

'It's Sunday tomorrow,' I said.

'All the better, the Palais de Justice is quieter on Sunday.' He smiled again. 'Good coffee.'

'That's what they all say,' I said.

22

A considerable portion of that large island in the Seine is occupied by the law in one shape or another. There's the Prefecture and the courts, Municipal and Judicial police offices, cells for remand prisoners and a police canteen. On a weekday the stairs are crammed with black-gowned lawyers clutching plastic briefcases and scurrying like disturbed cockroaches. But on Sunday the Palais de Justice is silent. The prisoners sleep late and the offices are empty. The only movement is the thin stream of tourists who respectfully peer at the high vaulting of the Sainte Chapelle, clicking and wondering at its unparalleled beauty. Outside in the Place Louis Lépine a few hundred caged birds twitter in the sunshine and in the trees are wild birds attracted by the spilled seed and commotion. There are sprigs of millet, cuttlebone and bright new wooden cages, bells to ring, swings to swing on and mirrors to peck at. Old men run their shrivelled hands through the seeds, sniff them, discuss them and hold them up to the light as though they were fine vintage Burgundies.

The bird market was busy by the time I got there to meet Loiseau. I parked the car opposite the gates of the Palais de Justice and strolled through the market. The clock was striking eleven with a dull dented sound. Loiseau was standing in front of some cages marked '*Caille reproductrice*'. He waved as he saw me. 'Just a moment,' he said. He picked up a box marked 'vitamine phospate'. He read the label: '*Biscuits pour oiseaux*'. 'I'll have that too,' said Loiseau.

The woman behind the table said, 'The *mélange saxon* is very good, it's the most expensive, but it's the best.'

'Just half a litre,' said Loiseau.

She weighed the seed, wrapped it carefully and tied the package. Loiseau said, 'I didn't see him.'

'Why?' I walked with him through the market.

'He's been moved. I can't find out who authorized the move or where he's gone to. The clerk in the records office said Lyon but that can't be true.' Loiseau stopped in front of an old pram full of green millet.

'Why?'

Loiseau didn't answer immediately. He picked up a sprig of millet and sniffed at it. 'He's been moved. Some top-level instructions. Perhaps they intend to bring him before some *juge d'instruction* who will do as he's told. Or maybe they'll keep him out of the way while they finish the *enquêtes officieuses*.'[1]

'You don't think they've moved him away to get him quietly sentenced?'

Loiseau waved to the old woman behind the stall. She shuffled slowly towards us.

'I talk to you like an adult,' Loiseau said. 'You don't really expect me to answer that, do you? A sprig.' He turned and stared at me. 'Better make it two sprigs,' he

---

[1] Under French Law the Prefect of Paris Police can arrest, interrogate, inquire, search, confiscate letters in the post, without any other authority than his own. His only obligation is to inform the Public Prosecutor and bring the prisoner before a magistrate within twenty-four hours. Note that the magistrate is part of the law machine and not a separate functionary as he is in Britain.

When he is brought before the magistrate – *juge d'instruction* – the police explain that the man is *suspected* and the magistrate directs the building up of evidence. (In Britain, of course, the man is not brought before a magistrate until after the police have built up their case.)

Inquiries prior to the appearance before a *juge d'instruction* are called *enquêtes officieuses* (informal inquiries). In law the latter give no power to search or demand statements but in practice few citizens argue about this technicality when faced with the police.

139

said to the woman. 'My friend's canary wasn't looking so healthy last time I saw it.'

'Joe's all right,' I said. 'You leave him alone.'

'Suit yourself,' said Loiseau. 'But if he gets much thinner he'll be climbing out between the bars of that cage.'

I let him have the last word. He paid for the millet and walked between the cliffs of new empty cages, trying the bars and tapping the wooden panels. There were caged birds of all kinds in the market. They were given seed, millet, water and cuttlefish bone for their beaks. Their claws were kept trimmed and they were safe from all birds of prey. But it was the birds in the trees that were singing.

23

I got back to my apartment about twelve o'clock. At
twelve thirty-five the phone rang. It was Monique,
Annie's neighbour. 'You'd better come quickly,' she said.
'Why?'
'I'm not allowed to say on the phone. There's a fellow
sitting here. He won't tell me anything much. He was
asking for Annie, he won't tell me anything. Will you
come now?'
'Okay,' I said.

24

It was lunchtime. Monique was wearing an ostrich-feather-trimmed négligé when she opened the door. 'The English have got off the boat,' she said and giggled. 'You'd better come in, the old girl will be straining her earholes to hear, if we stand here talking.' She opened the door and showed me into the cramped room. There was bamboo furniture and tables, a plastic-topped dressing-table with four swivel mirrors and lots of perfume and cosmetic garnishes. The bed was unmade and a candlewick bedspread had been rolled up under the pillows. A copy of *Salut les Copains* was in sections and arranged around the deep warm indentation. She went across to the windows and pushed the shutters. They opened with a loud clatter. The sunlight streamed into the room and made everything look dusty. On the table there was a piece of pink wrapping paper; she took a hard-boiled egg from it, rapped open the shell and bit into it.

'I hate summer,' she said. 'Pimples and parks and open cars that make your hair tangled and rotten cold food that looks like left-overs. And the sun trying to make you feel guilty about being indoors. I like being indoors. I like being in bed; it's no sin, is it, being in bed?'

'Just give me the chance to find out. Where is he?'

'I hate summer.'

'So shake hands with Père Noël,' I offered. 'Where is he?'

'I'm taking a shower. You sit down and wait. You are all questions.'

'Yes,' I said. 'Questions.'

142

'I don't know how you think of all these questions. You must be clever.'

'I am,' I said.

'Honestly, I wouldn't know where to start. The only questions I ever ask are "Are you married?" and "What will you do if I get pregnant?" Even then I never get told the truth.'

'That's the trouble with questions. You'd better stick to answers.'

'Oh, I know all the answers.'

'Then you must have been asked all the questions.'

'I have,' she agreed.

She slipped out of the négligé and stood naked for one millionth of a second before disappearing into the bathroom. The look in her eyes was mocking and not a little cruel.

There was a lot of splashing and ohh-ing from the bathroom until she finally reappeared in a cotton dress and canvas tennis shoes, no stockings.

'Water was cold,' she said briefly. She walked right through the room and opened her front door. I watched her lean over the balustrade.

'The water's stone cold, you stupid cow,' she shrieked down the stair-well. From somewhere below the voice of the old harridan said, 'It's not supposed to supply ten people for each apartment, you filthy little whore.'

'I have something men want, not like you, you old hag.'

'And you give it to them,' the harridan cackled back. 'The more the merrier.'

'Poof!' shouted Monique, and narrowing her eyes and aiming carefully she spat over the stair-well. The harridan must have anticipated it, for I heard her cackle triumphantly.

Monique returned to me. 'How am I expected to keep clean when the water is cold? Always cold.'

143

'Did Annie complain about the water?'

'Ceaselessly, but she didn't have the manner that brings results. I get angry. If she doesn't give me hot water I shall drive her into her grave, the dried-up old bitch. I'm leaving here anyway,' she said.

'Where are you going?' I asked.

'I'm moving in with my regular. Montmartre. It's an awful district, but it's larger than this, and anyway he wants me.'

'What's he do for a living?'

'He does the clubs, he's – don't laugh – he's a conjurer. It's a clever trick he does: he takes a singing canary in a large cage and makes it disappear. It looks fantastic. Do you know how he does it?'

'No.'

'The cage folds up. That's easy, it's a trick cage. But the bird gets crushed. Then when he makes it reappear it's just another canary that looks the same. It's an easy trick really, it's just that no one in the audience suspects that he would kill the bird each time in order to do the trick.'

'But you guessed.'

'Yes. I guessed the first time I saw it done. He thought I was clever to guess but as I said, "How much does a canary cost? Three francs, four at the very most." It's clever though, isn't it, you've got to admit it's clever.'

'It's clever,' I said, 'but I like canaries better than I like conjurers.'

'Silly.' Monique laughed disbelievingly. ' "The incredible Count Szell" he calls himself.'

'So you'll be a countess?'

'It's his stage name, silly.' She picked up a pot of face cream. 'I'll just be another stupid woman who lives with a married man.'

She rubbed cream into her face.

'Where is he?' I finally asked. 'Where's this fellow that

you said was sitting here?' I was prepared to hear that she'd invented the whole thing.

'In the café on the corner. He'll be all right there. He's reading his American newspapers. He's all right.'

'I'll go and talk to him.'

'Wait for me.' She wiped the cream away with a tissue and turned and smiled. 'Am I all right?'

'You're all right,' I told her.

25

The café was on the Boul. Mich., the very heart of the left bank. Outside in the bright sun sat the students; hirsute and earnest, they have come from Munich and Los Angeles sure that Hemingway and Lautrec are still alive and that some day in some left bank café they will find them. But all they ever find are other young men who look exactly like themselves, and it's with this sad discovery that they finally return to Bavaria or California and become salesmen or executives. Meanwhile here they sat in the hot seat of culture, where businessmen became poets, poets became alcoholics, alcoholics became philosophers and philosophers realized how much better it was to be businessmen.

Hudson. I've got a good memory for faces. I saw Hudson as soon as we turned the corner. He was sitting alone at a café table holding his paper in front of his face while studying the patrons with interest. I called to him.

'Jack Percival,' I called. 'What a great surprise.'

The American hydrogen research man looked surprised, but he played along very well for an amateur. We sat down with him. My back hurt from the rough-house in the discothèque. It took a long time to get served because the rear of the café was full of men with tightly wadded newspapers trying to pick themselves a winner instead of eating. Finally I got the waiter's attention. 'Three grands crèmes,' I said. Hudson said nothing else until the coffees arrived.

'What about this young lady?' Hudson asked. He dropped sugar cubes into his coffee as though he was suffering from shock. 'Can I talk?'

'Sure,' I said. 'There are no secrets between Monique and me.' I leaned across to her and lowered my voice. 'This is very confidential, Monique,' I said. She nodded and looked pleased. 'There is a small plastic bead company with its offices in Grenoble. Some of the holders of ordinary shares have sold their holdings out to a company that this gentleman and I more or less control. Now at the next shareholders' meeting we shall . . .'

'Give over,' said Monique. 'I can't stand business talk.'

'Well run along then,' I said, granting her her freedom with an understanding smile.

'Could you buy me some cigarettes?' she asked.

I got two packets from the waiter and wrapped a hundred-franc note round them. She trotted off down the street with them like a dog with a nice juicy bone.

'It's not about your bead factory,' he said.

'There is no bead factory,' I explained.

'Oh!' He laughed nervously. 'I was supposed to have contacted Annie Couzins,' he said.

'She's dead.'

'I found that out for myself.'

'From Monique?'

'You are T. Davis?' he asked suddenly.

'With bells on,' I said and passed my resident's card to him.

An untidy man with a constantly smiling face walked from table to table winding up toys and putting them on the tables. He put them down everywhere until each table had its twitching mechanical figures bouncing through the knives, table mats and ashtrays. Hudson picked up the convulsive little violin player. 'What's this for?'

'It's on sale,' I said.

He nodded and put it down. 'Everything is,' he said.

He returned my resident's card to me.

'It looks all right,' he agreed. 'Anyway I can't go back to the Embassy, they told me that most expressly, so I'll

147

have to put myself in your hands. I'm out of my depth to tell you the truth.'

'Go ahead.'

'I'm an authority on hydrogen bombs and I know quite a bit about all the work on the nuclear programme. My instructions are to put certain information about fall-out dangers at the disposal of a Monsieur Datt. I understand he is connected with the Red Chinese Government.'

'And why are you to do this?'

'I thought you'd know. It's such a mess. That poor girl being dead. Such a tragedy. I did meet her once. So young, such a tragic business. I thought they would have told you all about it. You were the only other name they gave me, apart from her I mean. I'm acting on US Government orders, of course.'

'Why would the US Government want you to give away fall-out data?' I asked him. He sat back in the cane chair till it creaked like elderly arthritic joints. He pulled an ashtray near him.

'It all began with the Bikini Atoll nuclear tests,' he began. 'The Atomic Energy Commission were taking a lot of criticism about the dangers of fall-out, the biological result upon wildlife and plants. The AEC needed those tests and did a lot of follow-through testing on the sites, trying to prove that the dangers were not anything like as great as many alarmists were saying. I have to tell you that those alarmists were damn nearly right. A dirty bomb of about twenty-five megatons would put down about 15,000 square miles of lethal radio-activity. To survive that, you would have to stay underground for months, some say even a year or more.

'Now if we were involved in a war with Red China, and I dread the thought of such a thing, then we would have to use the nuclear fall-out as a weapon, because only ten per cent of the Chinese population live in large – quarter-million size – towns. In the USA more than half the population live in the large towns. China with its dispersed population can only be knocked out by fall-out . . .' He paused. 'But knocked out it can be. Our experts say that about half a billion people live on one-fifth of China's land area. The prevailing wind is westerly. Four hundred bombs would kill fifty million by direct heat-blast effect, one hundred million would be seriously injured though they wouldn't need hospitalization, but three hundred and fifty million would die by windborne fall-out.

'The AEC minimized the fall-out effects in their follow-through reports on the tests (Bikini, etc.). Now the more militant of the Chinese soldier-scientists are using the US reports to prove that China can survive a nuclear war. We couldn't withdraw those reports, or say that they were untrue – not even slightly untrue – so I'm here to leak the correct information to the Chinese scientists. The whole operation began nearly eight months ago. It took a long time getting this girl Annie Couzins into position.'

'In the clinic near to Datt.'

'Exactly. The original plan was that she should intro-duce me to this man Datt and say I was an American scientist with a conscience.'

'That's a piece of CIA thinking if ever I heard one?'

'You think it's an extinct species?'

'It doesn't matter what I think, but it's not a line that Datt will buy easily.'

'If you are going to start changing the plan now . . .'

'The plan changed when the girl was killed. It's a mess; the only way I can handle it is my way.'

'Very well,' said Hudson. He sat silent for a moment.

Behind me a man with a rucksack said, 'Florence. We hated Florence.'

'We hated Trieste,' said a girl.

'Yes,' said the man with the rucksack, 'my friend hated Trieste last year.'

'My contact here doesn't know why you are in Paris,' I said suddenly. I tried to throw Hudson, but he took it calmly.

'I hope he doesn't,' said Hudson. 'It's all supposed to be top secret. I hated to come to you about it but I've no other contact here.'

'You're at the Lotti Hotel.'

'How did you know?'

'It's stamped across your *Tribune* in big blue letters.'

He nodded. I said, 'You'll go to the Hotel Ministère right away. Don't get your baggage from the Lotti. Buy a toothbrush or whatever you want on the way back now.' I expected to encounter opposition to this idea but Hudson welcomed the game.

'I get you,' he said. 'What name shall I use?'

'Let's make it Potter,' I said. He nodded. 'Be ready to move out at a moment's notice. And Hudson, don't telephone or write any letters; you know what I mean. Because I could become awfully suspicious of you.'

'Yes,' he said.

'I'll put you in a cab,' I said, getting up to leave.

'Do that, their Métro drives me crazy.'

I walked up the street with him towards the cab-rank. Suddenly he dived into an optician's. I followed.

'Ask him if I can look at some spectacles,' he said.

'Show him some spectacles,' I told the optician. He put a case full of tortoiseshell frames on the counter.

'He'll need a test,' said the optician. 'Unless he has his prescription he'll need a test.'

'You'll need a test or a prescription,' I told Hudson.

He had sorted out a frame he liked. 'Plain glass,' he demanded.

'What would I keep plain glass around for?' said the optician.

'What would he keep plain glass for?' I said to Hudson.

'The weakest possible, then,' said Hudson.

'The weakest possible,' I said to the optician. He fixed the lenses in in a moment or so. Hudson put the glasses on and we resumed our walk towards the taxi. He peered around him myopically and was a little unsteady.

'Disguise,' said Hudson.

'I thought perhaps it was,' I said.

'I would have made a good spy,' said Hudson. 'I've often thought that.'

'Yes,' I said. 'Well, there's your cab. I'll be in touch. Check out of the Lotti into the Ministère. I've written the name down on my card, they know me there. Try not to attract attention. Stay inside.'

'Where's the cab?' said Hudson.

'If you'll take off those bloody glasses,' I said, 'you might be able to see.'

26

I went round to Maria's in a hurry. When she opened the door she was wearing riding breeches and a roll-neck pullover. 'I was about to go out,' she said.

'I need to see Datt,' I said.

'Why do you tell me that?'

I pushed past her and closed the door behind us. 'Where is he?'

She gave me a twitchy little ironical smile while she thought of something crushing to say. I grabbed her arm and let my fingertips bite. 'Don't fool with me, Maria. I'm not in the mood. Believe me I would hit you.'

'I've no doubt about it.'

'You told Datt about Loiseau's raid on the place in the Avenue Foch. You have no loyalties, no allegiance, none to the Sûreté, none to Loiseau. You just give away information as though it was toys out of a bran tub.'

'I thought you were going to say I gave it away as I did my sexual favours,' she smiled again.

'Perhaps I was.'

'Did you remember that I kept your secret without giving it away? No one knows what you truly said when Datt gave you the injection.'

'No one knows yet. I suspect that you are saving it up for something special.'

She swung her hand at me but I moved out of range. She stood for a moment, her face twitching with fury.

'You ungrateful bastard,' she said. 'You're the first real bastard I've ever met.'

I nodded. 'There's not many of us around. Ungrateful

for what?' I asked her. 'Ungrateful for your loyalty? Was that what your motive was: loyalty?'

'Perhaps you're right,' she admitted quietly. 'I have no loyalty to anyone. A woman on her own becomes awfully hard. Datt is the only one who understands that. Somehow I didn't want Loiseau to arrest him.' She looked up. 'For that and many reasons.'

'Tell me one of the other reasons.'

'Datt is a senior man in the SDECE, and that's one reason. If Loiseau clashed with him, Loiseau could only lose.'

'Why do you think Datt is an SDECE man?'

'Many people know. Loiseau won't believe it but it's true.'

'Loiseau won't believe it because he has got too much sense. I've checked up on Datt. He's never had anything to do with any French intelligence unit. But he knew how useful it was to let people think so.'

She shrugged. 'I know it's true,' she said. 'Datt works for the SDECE.'

I took her shoulders. 'Look, Maria. Can't you get it through your head that he's a phoney? He has no psychiatry diploma, has never been anything to do with the French Government except that he pulls strings among his friends and persuades even people like you who work for the Sûreté that he's a highly placed agent of SDEGE.'

'And what do you want?' she asked.

'I want you to help me find Datt.'

'Help,' she said. 'That's a new attitude. You come bursting in here making your demands. If you'd come in here asking for help I might have been more sympathetic. What is it you want with Datt?'

'I want Kuang; he killed the girl at the clinic that day. I want to find him.'

'It's not your job to find him.'

153

'You are right. It's Loiseau's job, but he is holding Byrd for it and he'll keep on holding him.'

'Loiseau wouldn't hold an innocent man. Poof, you don't know what a fuss he makes about the sanctity of the law and that sort of thing.'

'I am a British agent,' I said. 'You know that already so I'm not telling you anything new. Byrd is too.'

'Are you sure?'

'No, I'm not. I'd be the last person to be told anyway. He's not someone whom I would contact officially. It's just my guess. I think Loiseau has been instructed to hold Byrd for the murder – with or without evidence – so Byrd is doomed unless I push Kuang right into Loiseau's arms.'

Maria nodded.

'Your mother lives in Flanders. Datt will be at his house near by, right?' Maria nodded. 'I want you to take an American out to your mother's house and wait there till I phone.'

'She hasn't got a phone.'

'Now, now, Maria,' I said. 'I checked up on your mother: she has a phone. Also I phoned my people here in Paris. They will be bringing some papers to your mother's house. They'll be needed for crossing the border. No matter what I say don't come over to Datt's without them.'

Maria nodded. 'I'll help. I'll help you pin that awful Kuang. I hate him.'

'And Datt, do you hate him too?'

She looked at me searchingly. 'Sometimes, but in a different way,' she said. 'You see, I'm his illegitimate daughter. Perhaps you checked up on that too?'

27

The road was straight. It cared nothing for geography, geology or history. The oil-slicked highway dared children and divided neighbours. It speared small villages through their hearts and laid them open. It was logical that it should be so straight, and yet it was obsessive too. Carefully lettered signs – the names of villages and the times of Holy Mass – and then the dusty clutter of houses flicked past with seldom any sign of life. At Le Chateau I turned off the main road and picked my way through the small country roads. I saw the sign Plaisir ahead and slowed. This was the place I wanted.

The main street of the village was like something out of Zane Grey, heavy with the dust of passing vehicles. None of them stopped. The street was wide enough for four lanes of cars, but there was very little traffic. Plaisir was on the main road to nowhere. Perhaps a traveller who had taken the wrong road at St Quentin might pass through Plaisir trying to get back on the Paris–Brussels road. Some years back when they were building the autoroute, heavy lorries had passed through, but none of them had stopped at Plaisir.

Today it was hot; scorching hot. Four mangy dogs had scavenged enough food and now were asleep in the centre of the roadway. Every house was shuttered tight, grey and dusty in the cruel biting midday light that gave them only a narrow rim of shadow.

I stopped the car near to a petrol pump, an ancient, handle-operated instrument bolted uncertainly on to a concrete pillar. I got out and thumped upon the garage doors, but there was no response. The only other vehicle in sight was an old tractor parked a few yards ahead. On the other side of the street a horse stood, tethered to a piece of rusty farm machinery, flicking its tail against the flies. I touched the engine of the tractor: it was still warm. I hammered the garage doors again, but the only movement was the horse's tail. I walked down the silent street, the stones hot against my shoes. One of the dogs, its left ear missing, scratched itself awake and crawled into the shade of the tractor. It growled dutifully at me as I passed, then subsided into sleep. A cat's eyes peered through a window full of aspidistra plants. Above the window, faintly discernible in the weathered woodwork, I read the word 'café'. The door was stiff and opened noisily. I went in.

There were half a dozen people standing at the bar. They weren't talking and I had the feeling that they had been watching me since I left the car. They stared at me.

'A red wine,' I said. The old woman behind the bar looked at me without blinking. She didn't move.

'And a cheese sandwich,' I added. She gave it another minute before slowly reaching for a wine bottle, rinsing a glass and pouring me a drink, all without moving her feet. I turned around to face the room. The men were mostly farm workers, their boots heavy with soil and their faces engraved with ancient dirt. In the corner a table was occupied by three men in suits and white shirts. Although it was long past lunchtime they had napkins tucked into their collars and were putting forkfuls of cheese into their mouths, honing their knives across the bread chunks and pouring draughts of red wine into their throats after it. They continued to eat. They were the only people in the room not looking at me except for a muscular man seated at the back of the room, his feet propped upon a chair, placing the cards of his patience game with quiet confidence. I watched him peel each card loose from the pack, stare at it with the superior impartiality of a computer and place it face up on the marble table-top. I watched him play for a minute or so, but he didn't look up.

It was a dark room; the only light entering it filtered through the jungle of plants in the window. On the marble-topped tables there were drip-mats advertising aperitifs; the mats had been used many times. The bar was brown with varnish and above the rows of bottles was an old clock that had ticked its last at 3.37 on some long-forgotten day. There were old calendars on the walls, a broken chair had been piled neatly under the window and the floor-boards squealed with each change of weight. In spite of the heat of the day three men had drawn their chairs close to a dead stove in the centre of the room. The body of the stove had cracked, and from it cold ash had spilled on to the floor. One of the men tapped his pipe against the stove. More ash poured out like the sands of time.

'I'm looking for Monsieur Datt,' I said to the whole room. 'Which is his house?'

There was not even a change of expression. Outside I heard the sudden yelp of a frightened dog. From the corner came the regular click of playing cards striking the marble. There was no other sound.

I said, 'I have important news for him. I know he lives somewhere in the village.' I moved my eyes from face to face searching for a flicker of comprehension; there was none. Outside the dogs began to fight. It was a ragged, vicious sound: low growls and sudden shrieks of pain.

'This is Plaisir?' I asked. There was no answer. I turned to the woman behind the bar. 'Is this the village of Plaisir?' She half smiled.

'Another carafe of red,' called one of the men in white shirts.

The woman behind the bar reached for a litre bottle of wine, poured a carafe of it and pushed it down the

157

counter. The man who had asked for it walked across to the counter, his napkin stuck in his collar, a fork still in his hand. He seized the carafe by the neck and returned to his seat. He poured a glass of wine for himself and took a large gulp. With the wine still in his mouth he leaned back in his chair, raised his eyes to mine and let the wine trickle into his throat. The dogs began fighting again.

'They are getting vicious,' said the man. 'Perhaps we should do away with one of them.'

'Do away with them all,' I said. He nodded.

I finished my drink. 'Three francs,' said the woman.

'What about a cheese sandwich?'

'We sell only wine.'

I put three new francs on the counter-top. The man finished his patience game and collected the dog-eared cards together. He drank his glass of red wine and carried the empty glass and the greasy pack of cards to the counter. He put them both down and laid two twenty-old-franc pieces on top, then he wiped his hands on the front of his work jacket and stared at me for a moment. His eyes were quick and alert. He turned towards the door.

'Are you going to tell me how to get to Monsieur Datt's house?' I asked the woman again.

'We only sell wine,' she said, scooping up the coins. I walked out into the hot midday sun. The man who had been playing patience walked slowly across to the tractor. He was a tall man, better nourished and more alert than the local inhabitants, perhaps thirty years old, walking like a horseman. When he reached the petrol pump, he whistled softly. The door opened immediately and an attendant came out.

'Ten litres.'

The attendant nodded. He inserted the nozzle of the pump into the tank of the tractor, unlocked the handle and then rocked it to pump the spirit out. I watched them close to, but neither looked round. When the needle read ten litres, he stopped pumping and replaced the nozzle. 'See you tomorrow,' said the tall man. He did not pay. He threw a leg over the tractor seat and started the motor. There was an ear-splitting racket as it started. He let in the clutch too quickly and the big wheels slid in the dust for an instant before biting into the *pavé* and roaring away, leaving a trail of blue smoke. The one-eared dog awoke again as the sound and the hot sun hit it and went bounding up the road barking and snapping at the tractor wheels. That awoke the other dogs and they, too, began to bark. The tall man leaned over his saddle like an apache scout and caught the dog under its only ear with a wooden stick. It sang a descant of pain and retired from the chase. The other dogs too lost heart, their energy sapped by the heat. The barking ended raggedly.

'I'm thinking of driving to the Datt house,' I said to the pump attendant. He stared after the tractor. 'He'll never learn,' he said. The dog limped back into the shade of the petrol pump. The attendant turned to face me. 'Some dogs are like that,' he said. 'They never learn.'

'If I drive to the Datt house I'll need twenty litres of the best.'

'Only one kind,' said the man.

'I'll need twenty litres *if* you'll be kind enough to direct me to the Datt place.'

'You'd better fill her up,' said the man. He raised his eyes to mine for the first time. 'You're going to need to come back, aren't you?'

'Right,' I said. 'And check the oil and water.' I took a ten-franc note from my pocket. 'That's for you,' I said. 'For your trouble.'

'I'll look at the battery too,' he said.

'I'll commend you to the tourist board,' I said. He nodded. He took the pump nozzle and filled the tank, he

159

opened up the rad cap with a cloth and then rubbed the battery. 'Everything's okay,' he said. I paid him for the petrol.

'Are you going to check the tyres?'

He kicked one of them. 'They'll do you. It's only down the road. Last house before the church. They are waiting for you.'

'Thanks,' I said, trying not to look surprised. Down the long straight road I watched the bus come, trailed by a cloud of dust. It stopped in the street outside the café. The customers came out to watch. The driver climbed on to the roof of the bus and got some boxes and cases down. One woman had a live chicken, another a birdcage. They straightened their clothes and stretched their limbs.

'More visitors,' I said.

He stared at me and we both looked towards the bus. The passengers finished stretching themselves and got back aboard again. The bus drove away, leaving just four boxes and a birdcage in the street. I glanced towards the café and there was a movement of eyes. It may have been the cat watching the fluttering of the caged bird; it was that sort of cat.

28

The house was the last one in the street, if you call endless railings and walls a street. I stopped outside the gates; there was no name or bell pull. Beyond the house a small child attending two tethered goats stared at me for a moment and ran away. Near to the house was a copse and half concealed in it a large grey square concrete block: one of the Wehrmacht's indestructible contributions to European architecture.

A nimble little woman rushed to the gates and tugged them open. The house was tall and narrow and not particularly beautiful, but it was artfully placed in about twenty acres of ground. To the right, the kitchen garden sloped down to two large glasshouses. Beyond the house there was a tiny park where statues hid behind trees like grey stone children playing tag, and in between, there were orderly rows of fruit trees and an enclosure where laundry could just be glimpsed flapping in the breeze.

I drove slowly past a grimy swimming pool where a beach ball and some ice-cream wrappers floated. Tiny flies flickered close to the surface of the water. Around the rim of the pool there was some garden furniture: armchairs, stools and a table with a torn parasol. The woman puffed along with me. I recognized her now as the woman who had injected me. I parked in a paved yard, and she opened the side door of the house and ushered me through a large airy kitchen. She snapped a gas tap *en passant*, flipped open a drawer, dragged out a white apron and tied it around her without slowing her walk. The floor of the main hall was stone flags, the walls were white-washed and upon them were a few swords, shields and ancient banners. There was little furniture: an oak chest, some forbidding chairs, and tables bearing large vases full of freshly-cut flowers. Opening off the hall there was a billiard room. The lights were on and the brightly coloured balls lay transfixed upon the green baize like a pop-art tableau.

The little woman hurried ahead of me opening doors, waving me through, sorting amongst a bundle of large keys, locking each door and then darting around me and hurrying on ahead. Finally, she showed me into the lounge. It was soft and florid after the stark austerity of the rest of the house. There were four sofas with huge floral patterns, plants, knick-knacks, antique cases full of antique plates. Silver-framed photos, a couple of bizarre modern paintings in primary colours and a kidney-shaped bar trimmed in golden tin and plastic. Behind the bar were bottles of drink and arranged along the bar-top some bar-tender's implements: strainers, shakers and ice-buckets.

'I'm delighted to see you,' said Monsieur Datt.

'That's good.'

He smiled engagingly. 'How did you find me?'

'A little bird told me.'

'Damn those birds,' said Datt, still smiling. 'But no matter, the shooting season begins soon, doesn't it?'

'You could be right.'

'Why not sit down and let me get you a drink. It's damned hot, I've never known such weather.'

'Don't get ideas,' I said. 'My boys will come on in if I disappear for too long.'

'Such crude ideas you have. And yet I suppose the very vulgarity of your mind is its dynamic. But have no fear, you'll not have drugged food or any of that nonsense. On the contrary, I hope to prove to you how very wrong your whole notion of me is.' He reached towards a bevy of cut-glass decanters. 'What about Scotch whisky?'

'Nothing,' I said. 'Nothing at all.'

'You're right.' He walked across to the window. I followed him.

'Nothing,' he said. 'Nothing at all. We are both ascetics.'

'Speak for yourself,' I said. 'I like a bit of self-indulgence now and again.'

The windows overlooked a courtyard, its ivy-covered walls punctuated by the strict geometry of white shutters. There was a dovecote and white doves marched and counter-marched across the cobbles.

There was a hoot at the gate, then into the courtyard drove a large Citroën ambulance. 'Clinique de Paradis' it said along the side under the big red cross. It was very dusty as though it had made a long journey. Out of the driver's seat climbed Jean-Paul; he tooted the horn.

'It's my ambulance,' said Datt.

'Yes,' I said, 'Jean-Paul driving.'

'He's a good boy,' said Datt.

'Let me tell you what I want,' I said hurriedly.

Datt made a movement with his hand. 'I know why you are here. There is no need to explain anything.' He eased himself back into his armchair.

'How do you know I've not come to kill you?' I asked.

'My dear man. There is no question of violence, for many reasons.'

'For instance?'

'Firstly you are not a man to use gratuitous violence. You would only employ violent means when you could see the course of action that the violence made available to you. Secondly, we are evenly matched, you and I. Weight for weight we are evenly matched.'

'So are a swordfish and an angler, but one is sitting strapped into an armchair and the other is being dragged through the ocean with a hook in his mouth.'

'Which am I?'

'That's what I am here to discover.'

'Then begin, sir.'

'Get Kuang.'

'What do you mean?'

'I mean get Kuang. K.U.A.N.G. Get him here.'

Datt changed his mind about the drink; he poured himself a glass of wine and sipped it. 'I won't deny he's here,' he said finally.

'Then why not get him?'

He pressed a buzzer and the maid came in. 'Get Monsieur Kuang,' he said.

The old woman went away quietly and came back with Kuang. He was wearing grey flannel trousers, open-neck shirt and a pair of dirty white tennis shoes. He poured himself a large Perrier water from the bar and sat down in an armchair with his feet sprawled sideways over the arm. 'Well?' he said to me.

'I'm bringing you an American hydrogen expert to talk to.'

Kuang seemed unsurprised. 'Petty, Barnes, Bertram or Hudson?'

'Hudson.'

'Excellent, he's a top man.'

'I don't like it,' said Datt.

'You don't have to like it,' I said. 'If Kuang and Hudson want to talk a little it's nothing to do with you.' I turned to Kuang. 'How long will you want with him?'

'Two hours,' said Kuang. 'Three at the most, less if he has written stuff with him.'

'I believe he will have,' I said. 'He's all prepared.'

'I don't like it,' Datt complained.

'Be quiet,' said Kuang. He turned to me. 'Are you working for the Americans?'

'No,' I said. 'I'm acting for them, just this one operation.'

Kuang nodded. 'That makes sense; they wouldn't want to expose one of their regular men.'

I bit my lip in anger. Hudson had, of course, been acting on American instructions, not on his own initiative. It was a plan to expose me so that the CIA could keep their own men covered. Clever bastards. Well, I'd grin and bear it and try to get something out of it.

'That's right,' I agreed.

'So you are not bargaining?'

'I'm not getting paid,' I said, 'if that's what you mean.'

'How much do you want?' asked Kuang wearily. 'But don't get big ideas.'

'We'll sort it out after you've seen Hudson.'

'A most remarkable display of faith,' said Kuang. 'Did Datt pay you for the incomplete set of documents you let us have?'

'No,' I said.

'Now that our cards are on the table I take it you don't really want payment.'

'That's right,' I said.

'Good,' said Kuang. He hooked his legs off the arm of the chair and reached for some ice from the silver bucket. Before pouring himself a whisky he pushed the telephone across to me.

Maria was waiting near the phone when I called her. 'Bring Hudson here,' I said. 'You know the way.'

'Yes,' said Maria. 'I know the way.'

29

Kuang went out to get ready for Hudson. I sat down again in a hard chair. Datt noticed me wince.

'You have a pain in the spine?'

'Yes,' I said. 'I did it in a discothèque.'

'Those modern dances are too strenuous for me,' said Datt.

'This one was too strenuous for me,' I said. 'My partner had brass knuckles.'

Datt knelt down at my feet, took off my shoe and probed at my heel with his powerful fingers. He felt my ankle bone and tut-tutted as though it had been designed all wrong. Suddenly he plunged his fingers hard into my heel. 'Ahh,' he said, but the word was drowned by my shout of pain. Kuang opened the door and looked at us.

'Are you all right?' Kuang asked.

'He's got a muscular contraction,' said Datt. 'It's acupuncture,' he explained to me. 'I'll soon get rid of that pain in your back.'

'Ouch,' I said. 'Don't do it if it's going to make me lame for life.'

Kuang retreated back to his room. Datt inspected my foot again and pronounced it ready.

'It should get rid of your pain,' he said. 'Rest for half an hour in the chair.'

'It is a bit better,' I admitted.

'Don't be surprised,' said Datt, 'the Chinese have practised these arts for centuries; it is a simple matter, a muscular pain.'

'You practise acupuncture?' I asked.

'Not really, but I have always been interested,' said

Datt. 'The body and the mind. The interaction of two opposing forces: body and mind, emotion and reason, the duality of nature. My ambition has always been to discover something new about man himself.' He settled back into his chair. 'You are *simple*. I do not say that as a criticism but rather in admiration. Simplicity is the most sought-after quality in both art and nature, but your simplicity encourages you to see the world around you in black-and-white terms. You do not approve of my inquiry into human thoughts and actions. Your puritan origin, your Anglo-Saxon breeding make it sinful to inquire too deeply into ourselves.'

'But you don't inquire into yourself, you inquire into other people.'

He leaned back and smiled. 'My dear man, the reason I collect information, compile dossiers and films and recordings and probe the personal secrets of a wide range of important men, is twofold. Primarily because important men control the fate of the world and I like to feel that in my small way I influence such men. Secondly, I have devoted my life to the study of mankind. I love people; I have no illusions about them, it's true, but that makes it much easier to love them. I am ceaselessly amazed and devoted to the strange convoluted workings of their devious minds, their rationalizations and the predictability of their weaknesses and failings. That's why I became so interested in the sexual aspect of my studies. At one time I thought I understood my friends best when I watched them gambling: their avarice, kindness, and fear were so much in evidence when they gambled. I was a young man at the time. I lived in Hanoi and I saw the same men every day in the same clubs. I liked them enormously. It's important that you believe that.' He looked up at me.

I shrugged. 'I believe it.'

'I liked them very much and I wished to understand them better. For me, gambling could never hold any fascination: dull, repetitive and trivial. But it did unleash the deepest emotions. I got more from seeing their reactions to the game than from playing. So I began to keep dossiers on all my friends. There was no malign intent; on the contrary, it was expressly in order to understand and like them better that I did it.'

'And did you like them better?'

'In some ways. There were disillusions, of course, but a man's failings are so much more attractive than his successes – any woman will tell you that. Soon it occurred to me that alcohol was providing more information to the dossiers than gambling. Gambling showed me the hostilities and fears, but drink showed me the weaknesses. It was when a man felt sorry for himself that one saw the gaps in the armour. See how a man gets drunk and you will know him – I have told so many young girls that: see your man getting drunk and you will know him. Does he want to pull the blankets over his head or go out into the street and start a riot? Does he want to be caressed or to commit rape? Does he find everything humorous, or threatening? Does he feel the world is secretly mocking him, or does he throw his arms around a stranger's shoulders and shout that he loves everyone?'

'Yes. It's a good indication.'

'But there were even better ways to reach deep into the subconscious, and now I wanted not only to understand people but also to try planting ideas into their heads. If only I could have a man with the frailty and vulnerability of drunkenness but without the blurriness and loss of memory that drink brought, then I would have a chance of really improving my dossiers. How I envied the women who had access to my friends in their most vulnerable – post-coital *triste* – condition. Sex, I decided, was the key to man's drives and post-sex was his most vulnerable state. That's how my methods evolved.'

I relaxed now that Datt had become totally involved in

his story. I suppose he had been sitting out here in this house, inactive and musing about his life and what had led to this moment of supreme power that he was now enjoying so much. He was unstoppable, as so many reserved men are once explanations start burbling out of them.

'Eight hundred dossiers I have now, and many of them are analyses that a psychiatrist would be proud of.'

'Are you qualified to practise psychiatry?' I asked.

'Is anyone qualified to practise it?'

'No,' I said.

'Precisely,' said Datt. 'Well, I am a little better able than most men. I know what can be done, because I have done it. Done it eight hundred times. Without a staff it would never have developed at the same rate. Perhaps the quality would have been higher had I done it all myself, but the girls were a vital part of the operation.'

'The girls actually compiled the dossiers?'

'Maria might have been able to if she'd worked with me longer. The girl that died – Annie Couzins – was intelligent enough, but she was not temperamentally suited to the work. At one time I would work only with girls with qualifications in law or engineering or accountancy, but to find girls thus qualified and also sexually alluring is difficult. I wanted girls who would understand. With the more stupid girls I had to use recording machines, but the girls who understood produced the real results.'

'The girls didn't hide the fact that they understood?'

'At first. I thought – as you do now – that men would be afraid and suspicious of a woman who was clever, but they aren't, you see. On the contrary, men like clever women. Why does a husband complain "my wife doesn't understand me" when he goes running off with another woman? Why, because what he needs isn't sex, it's someone to talk to.'

'Can't he talk to the people he works with?'

'He can, but he's frightened of them. The people he works with are after his job, on the watch for weakness.'

'Just as your girls are.'

'Exactly, but he does not understand that.'

'Eventually he does, surely?'

'By then he no longer cares – the therapeutic aspect of the relationship is clear to him.'

'You blackmail him into co-operating?'

Datt shrugged. 'I might have done had it ever proved necessary, but it never has. By the time a man has been studied by me and the girls for six months he needs us.'

'I don't understand.'

'You don't understand,' said Datt patiently, 'because you persist in regarding me as some malign monster feeding on the blood of my victims.' Datt held up his hands. 'What I did for these men was helpful to them. I worked day and night, endless sessions to help them understand themselves: their motives, their aspirations, their weaknesses and strengths. The girls too were intelligent enough to be helpful, and reassuring. All the people that I have studied become better personalities.'

'Will become,' I corrected. 'That's the promise you hold out to them.'

'In some cases, not all.'

'But you have tried to increase their dependency upon you. You have used your skills to make these people *think* they need you.'

'You are splitting hairs. All psychiatrists must do that. That's what the word "transference" means.'

'But you have a hold over them. These films and records: they demonstrate the type of power you want.'

'They demonstrate nothing. The films, etc. are nothing to me. I am a scientist, not a blackmailer. I have merely used the sexual activities of my patients as a short cut to understanding the sort of disorders they are likely to have. A man reveals so much when he is in bed with a woman; it's this important element of *release*. It's common to all the activities of the subject. He finds release in talking to me, which gives him freedom in his sexual appetites. Greater and more varied sexual activity releases in turn a need to talk at greater length.'

'So he talks to you.'

'Of course he does. He grows more and more free, and more and more confident.'

'But you are the only person he can boast to.'

'Not boast exactly, talk. He wishes to share this new, stronger, better life that he has created.'

'That you have created for him.'

'Some subjects have been kind enough to say that they lived at only ten per cent of their potential until they came to my clinic.' M. Datt smiled complacently. 'It's vital and important work showing men the power they have within their own minds if they merely take courage enough to use it.'

'You sound like one of those small ads from the back pages of skin magazines. The sort that's sandwiched between acne cream and peeping-tom binoculars.'

'*Honi soit qui mal y pense.* I know what I am doing.'

I said, 'I really believe you do, but I don't *like* it.'

'Mind you,' he said urgently, 'don't think for one moment I'm a Freudian. I'm not. Everyone thinks I'm a Freudian because of this emphasis on sex. I'm not.'

'You'll publish your results?' I asked.

'The conclusions possibly, but not the case histories.'

'It's the case histories that are the important factor,' I said.

'To some people,' said Datt. 'That's why I have to guard them so carefully!'

'Loiseau tried to get them.'

'But he was a few minutes too late.' Datt poured himself another small glass of wine, measured its clarity

171

and drank a little. 'Many men covet my dossiers but I guard them carefully. This whole neighbourhood is under surveillance. I knew about you as soon as you stopped for fuel in the village.'

The old woman knocked discreetly and entered. 'A car with Paris plates – it sounds like Madame Loiseau – coming through the village.'

Datt nodded. 'Tell Robert I want the Belgian plates on the ambulance and the documents must be ready. Jean-Paul can help him. No, on second thoughts don't tell Jean-Paul to help him. I believe they don't get along too well.' The old woman said nothing. 'Yes, well that's all.'

Datt walked across to the window and as he did so there was the sound of tyres crunching on the gravel.

'It's Maria's car,' said Datt.

'And your backyard Mafia didn't stop it?'

'They are not there to stop people,' explained Datt. 'They are not collecting entrance money, they are there for my protection.'

'Did Kuang tell you that?' I said. 'Perhaps those guards are there to stop you getting out.'

'Poof,' said Datt, but I knew I had planted a seed in his mind. 'I wish she'd brought the boy with her.'

I said, 'It's Kuang who's in charge. He didn't ask you before agreeing to my bringing Hudson here.'

'We have our areas of authority,' said Datt. 'Everything concerning data of a technical kind – of the kind that Hudson can provide – is Kuang's province.' Suddenly he flushed with anger. 'Why should I explain such things to you?'

'I thought you were explaining them to yourself,' I said.

Datt changed the subject abruptly. 'Do you think Maria told Loiseau where I am?'

'I'm sure she didn't,' I said. 'She has a lot of explaining

to do the next time she sees Loiseau. She has to explain why she warned you about his raid on the clinic.'

'That's true,' said Datt. 'A clever man, Loiseau. At one time I thought you were his assistant.'

'And now?'

'Now I think you are his victim, or soon will be.'

I said nothing. Datt said, 'Whoever you work for, you run alone. Loiseau has no reason to like you. He's jealous of your success with Maria – she adores you, of course. Loiseau pretends he's after me, but you are his real enemy. Loiseau is in trouble with his department, he might have decided that you could be the scapegoat. He visited me a couple of weeks ago, wanted me to sign a document concerning you. A tissue of lies, but cleverly riddled with half-truths that could prove bad for you. It needed only my signature. I refused.'

'Why didn't you sign?'

M. Datt sat down opposite me and looked me straight in the eye. 'Not because I like you particularly. I hardly know you. It was because I had given you that injection when I first suspected that you were an *agent provocateur* sent by Loiseau. If I treat a person he becomes my patient. I become responsible for him. It is my proud boast that if one of my patients committed even a murder he could come to me and tell me; in confidence. That's my relationship with Kuang. I must have that sort of relationship with my patients – Loiseau refuses to understand that. I must have it.' He stood up suddenly and said, 'A drink – and now I insist. What shall it be?'

The door opened and Maria came in, followed by Hudson and Jean-Paul. Maria was smiling, but her eyes were narrow and tense. Her old roll-neck pullover and riding breeches were stained with mud and wine. She looked tough and elegant and rich. She came into the room quietly and aware, like a cat sniffing, and moving stealthily, on the watch for the slightest sign of things

173

hostile or alien. She handed me the packet of documents: three passports, one for me, one for Hudson, one for Kuang. There were some other papers inside, money and some cards and envelopes that would prove I was someone else. I put them in my pocket without looking at them.

'I wish you'd brought the boy,' said M. Datt to Maria. She didn't answer. 'What will you drink, my good friends? An aperitif perhaps?' He called to the woman in the white apron, 'We shall be seven to dinner but Mr Hudson and Mr Kuang will dine separately in the library. And take Mr Hudson into the library now,' he added. 'Mr Kuang is waiting there.'

'And leave the door ajar,' I said affably.

'And leave the door ajar,' said M. Datt.

Hudson smiled and gripped his briefcase tight under his arm. He looked at Maria and Jean-Paul, nodded and withdrew without answering. I got up and walked across to the window, wondering if the woman in the white apron was sitting in at dinner with us, but then I saw the dented tractor parked close behind Maria's car. The tractor driver was here. With all that room to spare the tractor needn't have boxed both cars tight against the wall.

30

'Read the greatest thinkers of the eighteenth century,'
M. Datt was saying, 'and you'll understand what the
Frenchman still thinks about women.' The soup course
was finished and the little woman – dressed now in a
maid's formal uniform – collected the dishes. 'Don't stack
them,' M. Datt whispered loudly to her. 'That's how they
get broken. Make two journeys; a well-trained maid
never stacks plates.' He poured a glass of white wine for
each of us. 'Diderot thought they were merely courtesans,
Montesquieu said they were pretty children. For Rous-
seau they existed only as an adjunct to man's pleasure
and for Voltaire they didn't exist at all.' He pulled the
side of smoked salmon towards him and sharpened the
long knife.

Jean-Paul smiled knowingly. He was more nervous
than usual. He patted the white starched cuff that artfully
revealed the Cartier watch and fingered the small disc of
adhesive plaster that covered a razor nick on his chin.

Maria said, 'France is a land where men command and
women obey. "Elle me plaît" is the greatest compliment
a woman can expect from men; they mean she obeys.
How can anyone call Paris a woman's city? Only a
prostitute can have a serious career there. It took two
world wars to give Frenchwomen the vote.'

Datt nodded. He removed the bones and the salmon's
smoke-hard surface with two long sweeps of the knife.
He brushed oil over the fish and began to slice it, serving
Maria first. Maria smiled at him.

Just as an expensive suit wrinkles in a different way
from a cheap one, so did the wrinkles in Maria's face add

to her beauty rather than detract from it. I stared at her, trying to understand her better. Was she treacherous, or was she exploited, or was she, like most of us, both?

'It's all very well for you, Maria,' said Jean-Paul. 'You are a woman with wealth, position, intelligence,' he pause, 'and beauty . . .'

'I'm glad you added beauty,' she said, still smiling.

Jean-Paul looked towards M. Datt and me. 'That illustrates my point. Even Maria would sooner have beauty than brains. When I was eighteen – ten years ago – I wanted to give the women I loved the things I wanted for myself: respect, admiration, good food, conversation, wit and even knowledge. But women despise those things. Passion is what they want, intensity of emotion. The same trite words of admiration repeated over and over again. They don't want good food – women have poor palates – and witty conversation worries them. What's worse it diverts attention away from them. Women want men who are masterful enough to give them confidence, but not cunning enough to outwit them. They want men with plenty of faults so that they can forgive them. They want men who have trouble with the little things in life; women excel at little things. They remember little things too; there is no occasion in their lives, from confirmation to eightieth birthday, when they can't recall every stitch they wore.' He looked accusingly at Maria.

Maria laughed. 'That part of your tirade at least is true.'

M. Datt said, 'What did you wear at your confirmation?'

'White silk, high-waisted dress, plain-front white silk shoes and cotton gloves that I hated.' She reeled it off.

'Very good,' said M. Datt and laughed. 'Although I must say, Jean-Paul, you are far too hard on women. Take that girl Annie who worked for me. Her academic standards were tremendous . . .'

'Of course,' said Maria, 'women leaving university have such trouble getting a job that anyone enlightened enough to employ them is able to demand very high qualifications.'

'Exactly,' said M. Datt. 'Most of the girls I've ever used in my research were brilliant. What's more they were deeply involved in the research tasks. Just imagine that the situation had required men employees to involve themselves sexually with patients. In spite of paying lip-service to promiscuity men would have given me all sorts of puritanical reasons why they couldn't do it. These girls understood that it was a vital part of their relationship with patients. One girl was a mathematical genius and yet such beauty. Truly remarkable.'

Jean-Paul said, 'Where is this mathematical genius now? I would dearly appreciate her advice. Perhaps I could improve my technique with women.'

'You couldn't,' said Maria. She spoke clinically, with no emotion showing. 'Your technique is all too perfect. You flatter women to saturation point when you first meet them. Then, when you decide the time is right, you begin to undermine their confidence in themselves. You point out their shortcomings rather cleverly and sympath-etically until they think that you must be the only man who would deign to be with them. You destroy women by erosion because you hate them.'

'No,' Jean-Paul said. 'I love women. I love all women too much to reject so many by marrying one.' He laughed.

'Jean-Paul feels it is his duty to make himself available to every girl from fifteen to fifty,' said Maria quietly.

'Then you'll soon be outside my range of activity,' said Jean-Paul.

The candles had burned low and now their light came through the straw-coloured wine and shone golden on face and ceiling.

Maria sipped at her wine. No one spoke. She placed

the glass on the table and then brought her eyes up to Jean-Paul's. 'I'm sorry for you, Jean-Paul,' she said.

The maid brought the fish course to the table and served it: *sole Dieppoise,* the sauce dense with shrimps and speckled with parsley and mushroom, the bland smell of the fish echoed by the hot butter. The maid retired, conscious that her presence had interrupted the conversation. Maria drank a little more wine and as she put the glass down she looked at Jean-Paul.

He didn't smile. When she spoke her voice was mellow and any trace of bitterness had been removed by the pause.

'When I say I'm sorry for you, Jean-Paul, with your endless succession of lovers, you may laugh at me. But let me tell you this: the shortness of your relationships with women is due to a lack of flexibility in you. You are not able to adapt, change, improve, enjoy new things each day. Your demands are constant and growing narrower. Everyone else must adapt to you, never the other way about.

'Marriages break up for this same reason – my marriage did and it was at least half my fault: two people become so set in their ways that they become vegetables. The antithesis of this feeling is to be in love. I fell in love with you, Jean-Paul. Being in love is to drink in new ideas, new feelings, smells, tastes, new dances – even the air seems to be different in flavour. That's why infidelity is such a shock. A wife set in the dull, lifeless pattern of marriage is suddenly liberated by love, and her husband is terrified to see the change take place, for just as I felt ten years younger, so I saw my husband as ten years older.'

Jean-Paul said, 'And that's how you now see me?'

'Exactly. It's laughable how I once worried that you were younger than me. You're not younger than me at all. You are an old fogey. Now I no longer love you I can see that. You are an old fogey of twenty-eight and I am a young girl of thiry-two.'

'You bitch.'

'My poor little one. Don't be angry. Think of what I tell you. Open your mind. Open your mind and you will discover what you want so much: how to be eternally a young man.'

Jean-Paul looked at her. He wasn't as angry as I would have expected. 'Perhaps I am a shallow and vain fool,' he said. 'But when I met you, Maria, I truly loved you. It didn't last more than a week, but for me it was real. It was the only time in my life that I truly believed myself capable of something worthwhile. You were older than me but I liked that. I wanted you to show me the way out of the stupid labyrinth life I led. You are highly intelligent and you, I thought, could show me the solid good reasons for living. But you failed me, Maria. Like all women you are weak-willed and indecisive. You can be loyal only for a moment to whoever is near to you. You have never made one objective decision in your life. You have never really wanted to be strong and free. You have never done one decisive thing that you truly believed in. You are a puppet, Maria, with many puppeteers, and they quarrel over who shall operate you.' His final words were sharp and bitter and he stared hard at Datt.

'Children,' Datt admonished. 'Just as we were all getting along so well together.'

Jean-Paul smiled a tight, film-star smile. 'Turn off your charm,' he said to Datt. 'You always patronize me.'

'If I've done something to give offence . . .' said Datt. He didn't finish the sentence but looked around at his guests, raising his eyebrows to show how difficult it was to even imagine such a possibility.

'You think you can switch me on and off as you please,' said Jean-Paul. 'You think you can treat me like a child; well you can't. Without me you would be in big trouble now. If I had not brought you the information about Loiseau's raid upon your clinic you would be in prison now.'

'Perhaps,' said Datt, 'and perhaps not.'

'Oh I know what you want people to believe,' said Jean-Paul. 'I know you like people to think you are mixed up with the SDECE and secret departments of the Government, but we know better. I saved you. Twice. Once with Annie, once with Maria.'

'Maria saved me,' said Datt, 'if anyone did.'

'Your precious daughter,' said Jean-Paul, 'is good for only one thing.' He smiled. 'And what's more she hates you. She said you were foul and evil; that's how much she wanted to save you before I persuaded her to help.'

'Did you say that about me?' Datt asked Maria, and even as she was about to reply he held up his hand. 'No, don't answer. I have no right to ask you such a question. We all say things in anger that later we regret.' He smiled at Jean-Paul. 'Relax, my good friend, and have another glass of wine.'

Datt filled Jean-Paul's glass but Jean-Paul didn't pick it up. Datt pointed the neck of the bottle at it. 'Drink.' He picked up the glass and held it to Jean-Paul. 'Drink and say that these black thoughts are not your truly considered opinion of old Datt who has done so much for you.'

Jean-Paul brought the flat of his hand round in an angry sweeping gesture. Perhaps he didn't like to be told that he owed Datt anything. He sent the full glass flying across the room and swept the bottle out of Datt's hands. It slid across the table, felling the glasses like ninepins and flooding the cold blond liquid across the linen and cutlery. Datt stood up, awkwardly dabbing at his waistcoat with a table napkin. Jean-Paul stood up too. The only sound was of the wine, still chug-chugging out of the bottle.

'*Salaud!*' said Datt. 'You attack me in my own home!

You *casse-pieds*! You insult me in front of my guests and assault me when I offer you wine!' He dabbed at himself and threw the wet napkin across the table as a sign that the meal would not continue. The cutlery jangled mournfully. 'You will learn,' said Datt. 'You will learn here and now.'

Jean-Paul finally understood the hornet's nest he had aroused in Datt's brain. His face was set and defiant, but you didn't have to be an amateur psychologist to know that if he could set the clock back ten minutes he'd rewrite his script.

'Don't touch me,' Jean-Paul said. 'I have villainous friends just as you do, and my friends and I can destroy you, Datt. I know all about you, the girl Annie Couzins and why she had to be killed. There are a few things you don't know about that story. There are a few more things that the police would like to know too. Touch me, you fat old swine, and you'll die as surely as the girl did.' He looked around at us all. His forehead was moist with exertion and anxiety. He managed a grim smile. 'Just touch me, just you try . . . !'

Datt said nothing, nor did any one of us. Jean-Paul gabbled on until his steam ran out. 'You need me,' he finally said to Datt, but Datt didn't need him any more and there was no one in the room who didn't know it.

'Robert!' shouted Datt. I don't know if Robert was standing in the sideboard or in a crack in the floor, but he certainly came in fast. Robert was the tractor driver who had slapped the one-eared dog. He was as tall and broad as Jean-Paul but there the resemblance ended: Robert was teak against Jean-Paul's papier-mâché.

Right behind Robert was the woman in the white apron. Now that they were standing side by side you could see a family resemblance: Robert was clearly the woman's son. He walked forward and stood before Datt like a man waiting to be given a medal. The old woman

181

stood in the doorway with a 12-bore shotgun held steady in her fists. It was a battered old relic, the butt was scorched and stained and there was a patch of rust around the muzzle as though it had been propped in a puddle. It was just the sort of thing that might be kept around the hall of a country house for dealing with rats and rabbits: an ill-finished mass-production job without styling or finish. It wasn't at all the sort of gun I'd want to be shot with. That's why I remained very, very still.

Datt nodded towards me, and Robert moved in and brushed me lightly but efficiently. 'Nothing,' he said. Robert walked over to Jean-Paul. In Jean-Paul's suit he found a 6.35 Mauser automatic. He sniffed it and opened it, spilled the bullets out into his hand and passed the gun, magazine and bullets to Datt. Datt handled them as though they were some kind of virus. He reluctantly dropped them into his pocket.

'Take him away, Robert,' said Datt. 'He makes too much noise in here. I can't bear people shouting.' Robert nodded and turned upon Jean-Paul. He made a movement of his chin and a clicking noise of the sort that encourages horses. Jean-Paul buttoned his jacket carefully and walked to the door.

'We'll have the meat course now,' Datt said to the woman.

She smiled with more deference than humour and withdrew backwards, muzzle last.

'Take him out, Robert,' repeated Datt.

'Maybe you think you don't,' said Jean-Paul earnestly, 'but you'll find . . .' His words were lost as Robert pulled him gently through the door and closed it.

'What are you going to do to him?' asked Maria.

'Nothing, my dear,' said Datt. 'But he's become more and more tiresome. He must be taught a lesson. We must frighten him, it's for the good of all of us.'

'You're going to kill him,' said Maria.

'No, my dear.' He stood near the fireplace, and smiled reassuringly.

'You are, I can feel it in the atmosphere.'

Datt turned his back on us. He toyed with the clock on the mantelpiece. He found the key for it and began to wind it up. It was a noisy ratchet.

Maria turned to me. 'Are they going to kill him?' she asked.

'I think they are,' I said.

She went across to Datt and grabbed his arm. 'You mustn't,' she said. 'It's too horrible. Please don't. Please father, please don't, if you love me.' Datt put his arm around her paternally but said nothing.

'He's a wonderful person,' Maria said. She was speaking of Jean-Paul. 'He would never betray you. Tell him,' she asked me, 'he must not kill Jean-Paul.'

'You mustn't kill him,' I said.

'You must make it more convincing than that,' said Datt. He patted Maria. 'If our friend here can tell us a way to guarantee his silence, some other way, then perhaps I'll agree.'

He waited but I said nothing. 'Exactly,' said Datt.

'But I love him,' said Maria.

'That can make no difference,' said Datt. 'I'm not a plenipotentiary from God, I've got no halos or citations to distribute. He stands in the way – not of me but of what I believe in: he stands in the way because he is spiteful and stupid. I do believe, Maria, that even if it were you I'd still do the same.'

Maria stopped being a suppliant. She had that icy calm that women take on just before using their nails.

'I love him,' said Maria. That meant that he should never be punished for anything except infidelity. She looked at me. 'It's your fault for bringing me here.'

Datt heaved a sigh and left the room.

'And your fault that he's in danger,' she said.

'Okay,' I said, 'blame me if you want to. On my colour soul the stains don't show.'

'Can't you stop them?' she said.

'No,' I told her, 'it's not that sort of film.'

Her face contorted as though cigar smoke was getting in her eyes. It went squashy and she began to sob. She didn't cry. She didn't do that mascara-respecting display of grief that winkles tear-drops out of the eyes with the corner of a tiny lace handkerchief while watching the whole thing in a well-placed mirror. She sobbed and her face collapsed. The mouth sagged, and the flesh puckered and wrinkled like blow-torched paintwork. Ugly sight, and ugly sound.

'He'll die,' she said in a strange little voice.

I don't know what happened next. I don't know whether Maria began to move before the sound of the shot or after. Just as I don't know whether Jean-Paul had really lunged at Robert, as Robert later told us. But I was right behind Maria as she opened the door. A. 45 is a big pistol. The first shot had hit the dresser, ripping a hole in the carpentry and smashing half a dozen plates. They were still falling as the second shot fired. I heard Datt shouting about his plates and saw Jean-Paul spinning drunkenly like an exhausted whipping top. He fell against the dresser, supporting himself on his hand, and stared at me pop-eyed with hate and grimacing with pain, his cheeks bulging as though he was looking for a place to vomit. He grabbed at his white shirt and tugged it out of his trousers. He wrenched it so hard that the buttons popped and pinged away across the room. He had a great bundle of shirt in his hand now and he stuffed it into his mouth like a conjurer doing a trick called 'how to swallow my white shirt'. Or how to swallow my pink-dotted shirt. How to swallow my pink shirt, my red, and finally dark-red shirt. But he never did the trick. The cloth fell away from his mouth and his blood poured over his chin, painting his teeth pink and dribbling down his neck and ruining his shirt. He knelt upon the ground as if to pray but his face sank to the floor and he died without a word, his ear flat against the ground, as if listening for hoof-beats pursuing him to another world.

He was dead. It's difficult to wound a man with a .45. You either miss them or blow them in half.

The legacy the dead leave us are life-size effigies that only slightly resemble their former owners. Jean-Paul's bloody body only slightly resembled him: its thin lips pressed together and the small circular plaster just visible on the chin.

Robert was stupefied. He was staring at the gun in horror. I stepped over to him and grabbed the gun away from him. I said 'You should be ashamed,' and Datt repeated that.

The door opened suddenly and Hudson and Kuang stepped into the kitchen. They looked down at the body of Jean-Paul. He was a mess of blood and guts. No one spoke, they were waiting for me. I remembered that I was the one holding the gun. 'I'm taking Kuang and Hudson and I'm leaving,' I said. Through the open door to the hall I could see into the library, its table covered with their scientific documents: photos, maps and withered plants with large labels on them.

'Oh no you don't,' said Datt.

'I have to return Hudson intact because that's part of the deal. The information he's given Kuang has to be got back to the Chinese Government or else it wasn't much good delivering it. So I must take Kuang too.'

'I think he's right,' said Kuang. 'It makes sense, what he says.'

'How do you know what makes sense?' said Datt. 'I'm arranging your movements, not this fool; how can we trust him? He admits this task is for the Americans.'

'It makes sense,' said Kuang again. 'Hudson's information is genuine. I can tell: it fills out what I learnt from that incomplete set of papers you passed to me last week. If the Americans want me to have the information, then they must want it to be taken back home.'

'Can't you see that they might want to capture you for interrogation?' said Datt.

'Rubbish!' I interrupted. 'I could have arranged that at any time in Paris without risking Hudson out here in the middle of nowhere.'

'They are probably waiting down the road,' said Datt. 'You could be dead and buried in five minutes. Out here in the middle of the country no one would hear, no one would see the diggings.'

'I'll take that chance,' said Kuang. 'If he can get Hudson into France on false papers, he can get me out.'

I watched Hudson, fearful that he would say I'd done no such thing for him, but he nodded sagely and Kuang seemed reassured.

'Come with us,' said Hudson, and Kuang nodded agreement. The two scientists seemed to be the only ones in the room with any mutual trust.

I was reluctant to leave Maria but she just waved her hand and said she'd be all right. She couldn't take her eyes off Jean-Paul's body.

'Cover him, Robert,' said Datt.

Robert took a table-cloth from a drawer and covered the body. 'Go,' Maria called again to me, and then she began to sob. Datt put his arm around her and pulled her close. Hudson and Kuang collected their data together and then, still waving the gun around, I showed them out and followed.

As we went across the hall the old woman emerged carrying a heavily laden tray. She said, 'There's still the *poulet sauté chasseur*.'

'Vive le sport,' I said.

31

From the garage we took the camionette – a tiny grey corrugated-metal van – because the roads of France are full of them. I had to change gear constantly for the small motor, and the tiny headlights did no more than probe the hedgerows. It was a cold night and I envied the warm grim-faced occupants of the big Mercs and Citroëns that roared past us with just a tiny peep of the horn, to tell us they had done so.

Kuang seemed perfectly content to rely upon my skill to get him out of France. He leaned well back in the hard upright seat, folded his arms and closed his eyes as though performing some oriental contemplative ritual. Now and again he spoke. Usually it was a request for a cigarette.

The frontier was little more than a formality. The Paris office had done us proud: three good British passports – although the photo of Hudson was a bit dodgy – over twenty-five pounds in small notes (Belgian and French), and some bills and receipts to correspond to each passport. I breathed more easily after we were through. I'd done a deal with Loiseau so he'd guaranteed no trouble, but I still breathed more easily after we'd gone through.

Hudson lay flat upon some old blankets in the rear. Soon he began to snore. Kuang spoke.

'Are we going to an hotel or are you going to blow one of your agents to shelter me?'

'This is Belgium,' I said. 'Going to an hotel is like going to a police station.'

'What will happen to him?'

'The agent?' I hesitated. 'He'll be pensioned off. It's bad luck but he was the next due to be blown.'

'Age?'

'Yes,' I said.

'And you have someone better in the area?'

'You know we can't talk about that,' I said.

'I'm not interested professionally,' said Kuang. 'I'm a scientist. What the British do in France or Belgium is nothing to do with me, but if we are blowing this man I owe him his job.'

'You owe him nothing,' I said. 'What the hell do you think this is? He'll be blown because it's his job. Just as I'm conducting you because that's my job. I'm doing it as a favour. You owe no one anything, so forget it. As far as I'm concerned you are a parcel.'

Kuang inhaled deeply on his cigarette, then removed it from his mouth with his long delicate fingers and stubbed it into the ashtray. I imagined him killing Annie Couzins. Passion or politics? He rubbed the tobacco shreds from his fingertips like a pianist practising trills.

As we passed through the tightly shuttered villages the rough *pavé* hammered the suspension and bright-eyed cats glared into our lights and fled. One a little slower than the others had been squashed as flat as an ink blot. Each successive set of wheels contributed a new pattern to the little tragedy that morning would reveal.

I had the camionette going at its top speed. The needles were still and the loud noise of the motor held a constant note. Everything was unchanging except a brief fusillade of loose gravel or the sudden smell of tar or the beep of a faster car.

'We are near to Ypres,' said Kuang.

'This was the Ypres salient,' I said. Hudson asked for a cigarette. He must have been awake for some time. 'Ypres,' said Hudson as he lit the cigarette, 'was that the site of a World War One battle?'

'One of the biggest,' I said. 'There's scarcely an Englishman that didn't have a relative die here. Perhaps a piece of Britain died here too.'

Hudson looked out of the rear windows of the van. 'It's quite a place to die,' he said.

32

Across the Ypres salient the dawn sky was black and getting lower and blacker like a Bulldog Drummond ceiling. It's a grim region, like a vast ill-lit military depot that goes on for miles. Across country go the roads: narrow slabs of concrete not much wider than a garden path, and you have the feeling that to go off the edge is to go into bottomless mud. It's easy to go around in circles and even easier to imagine that you are. Every few yards there are the beady-eyed green-and-white notices that point the way to military cemeteries where regiments of Blanco-white headstones parade. Death pervades the topsoil but untidy little farms go on operating, planting their cabbages right up to 'Private of the West Riding – Known only to God'. The living cows and dead soldiers share the land and there are no quarrels. Now in the hedges evergreen plants were laden with tiny red berries as though the ground was sweating blood. I stopped the car. Ahead was Passchendaele, a gentle upward slope.

'Which way were your soldiers facing?' Kuang said.

'Up the slope,' I said. 'They advanced up the slope, sixty pounds on their backs and machine guns down their throats.'

Kuang opened the window and threw his cigarette butt on to the road. There was an icy gust of wind.

'It's cold,' said Kuang. 'When the wind drops it will rain.'

Hudson leaned close to the window again. 'Oh boy,' he said, 'trench warfare here,' and shook his head when no word came. 'For them it must have seemed like for ever.'

'For a lot of them it was for ever,' I said. 'They are still here.'

'In Hiroshima even more died,' said Kuang.

'I don't measure death by numbers,' I said.

'Then it's a pity you were so careful not to use your atom bomb on the Germans or Italians,' said Kuang.

I started the motor again to get some heat in the car, but Kuang got out and stamped around on the concrete roadway. He did not seem to mind the cold wind and rain. He picked up a chunk of the shiny, clay-heavy soil peculiar to this region, studied it and then broke it up and threw it aimlessly across the field of cabbages.

'Are we expecting to rendezvous with another car?' he asked.

'Yes,' I said.

'You must have been very confident that I would come with you.'

'Yes,' I said. 'I was. It was logical.'

Kuang nodded. 'Can I have another cigarette?' I gave him one.

'We're early,' complained Hudson. 'That's a sure way to attract attention.'

'Hudson fancies his chances as a secret agent,' I said to Kuang.

'I don't take to your sarcasm,' said Hudson.

'Well that's real old-fashioned bad luck, Hudson,' I said, 'because you are stuck with it.'

Grey clouds rushed across the salient. Here and there old windmills – static in spite of the wind – stood across the skyline, like crosses waiting for someone to be nailed upon them. Over the hill came a car with its head-lights on.

They were thirty minutes late. Two men in a Renault 16, a man and his son. They didn't introduce themselves, in fact they didn't seem keen to show their faces at all. The older man got out of the car and came across to me. He spat upon the road and cleared his throat.

'You two get into the other car. The American stays in this one. Don't speak to the boy.' He smiled and gave a short, croaky, mirthless laugh. 'In fact don't speak to me even. There's a large-scale map in the dashboard. Make sure that's what you want.' He gripped my arm as he said it. 'The boy will take the camionette and dump it somewhere near the Dutch border. The American stays in this car. Someone will meet them at the other end. It's all arranged.'

Hudson said to me, 'Going with you is one thing, but taking off into the blue with this kid is another. I think I can find my own way . . .'

'Don't think about it,' I told him. 'We just follow the directions on the label. Hold your nose and swallow.' Hudson nodded.

We got out of the car and the boy came across, slowly detouring around us as though his father had told him to keep his face averted. The Renault was nice and warm inside. I felt in the glove compartment and found not only a map but a pistol.

'No prints,' I called to the Fleming. 'Make sure there's nothing else, no sweet wrappers or handkerchiefs.'

'Yes,' said the man. 'And none of those special cigarettes that are made specially for me in one of those exclusive shops in Jermyn Street.' He smiled sarcastically. 'He knows all that.' His accent was so thick as to be almost unintelligible. I guessed that normally he spoke Flemish and the French was not natural to him. The man spat again in the roadway before climbing into the driver's seat alongside us. 'He's a good boy,' the man said. 'He knows what to do.' By the time he got the Renault started the camionette was out of sight.

I'd reached the worrying stage of the journey. 'Did you

take notes?' I asked Kuang suddenly. He looked at me without answering. 'Be sensible,' I said. 'I must know if you are carrying anything that would need to be destroyed. I know there's the box of stuff Hudson gave you.' I drummed upon it. 'Is there anything else?'

'A small notebook taped to my leg. It's a thin book. I could be searched and they would not find it.'

I nodded. It was something more to worry about.

The car moved at high speed over the narrow concrete lanes. Soon we turned on to the wider main road that led north to Ostend. We had left the over-fertilized salient behind us. The fearful names: Tyne Cot, St Julien, Poelcapelle, Westerhoek and Pilckem faded behind us as they had faded from memory, for fifty years had passed and the women who had wept for the countless dead were also dead. Time and TV, frozen food and transistor radios had healed the wounds and filled the places that once seemed unfillable.

'What's happening?' I said to the driver. He was the sort of man who had to be questioned or else he would offer no information.

'His people,' he jerked his head towards Kuang, 'want him in Ostend. Twenty-three hundred hours tonight at the harbour. I'll show you on the city plan.'

'Harbour? What's happening? Is he going aboard a boat tonight?'

'They don't tell me things like that,' said the man. 'I'm just conducting you to my place to see your case officer, then on to Ostend to see his case officer. It's all so bloody boring. My wife thinks I get paid because it's dangerous but I'm always telling her: I get paid because it's so bloody boring. Tired?' I nodded. 'We'll make good time, that's one advantage, there's not much traffic about at this time of morning. There's not much commercial traffic if you avoid the inter-city routes.'

'It's quiet,' I said. Now and again small flocks of birds

darted across the sky, their eyes seeking food in the hard morning light, their bodies weakened by the cold night air.

'Very few police,' said the man, 'The cars keep to the main roads. It will rain soon and the cyclists don't move much when it's raining. It'll be the first rain for two weeks.'

'Stop worrying,' I said. 'Your boy will be all right.'

'He knows what to do,' the man agreed.

33

The Fleming owned an hotel not far from Ostend. The car turned into a covered alley that led to a cobbled courtyard. A couple of hens squawked as we parked and a dog howled. 'It's difficult,' said the man, 'to do anything clandestine around here.'

He was a small broad man with a sallow skin that would always look dirty no matter what he did to it. The bridge of his nose was large and formed a straight line with his forehead, like the nose metal of a medieval helmet. His mouth was small and he held his lips tight to conceal his bad teeth. Around his mouth were scars of the sort that you get when thrown through a windscreen. He smiled to show me it was a joke rather than an apology, and the scars made a pattern around his mouth like a tightened hairnet.

The door from the side entrance of the hotel opened and a woman in a black dress and white apron stared at us.

'They have come,' said the man.

'So I see,' she said. 'No luggage?'

'No luggage,' said the man. She seemed to need some explanation, as though we were a man and girl trying to book a double room.

'They need to rest, *ma jolie môme*,' said the man. She was no one's pretty child, but the compliment appeased her for a moment.

'Room four,' she said.

'The police have been?'

'Yes,' she said.

'They won't be back until night,' said the man to us.

'Perhaps not then even. They check the book. It's for the taxes more than to find criminals.'

'Don't use all the hot water,' said the woman. We followed her through the yellow peeling side door into the hotel entrance hall. There was a counter made of carelessly painted hardboard and a rack with eight keys hanging from it. The lino had the large square pattern that's supposed to look like inlaid marble; it curled at the edges and something hot had indented a perfect circle near the door.

'Name?' said the woman grimly as though she was about to enter us in the register.

'Don't ask,' said the man. 'And they won't ask our name.' He smiled as though he had made a joke and looked anxiously at his wife, hoping that she would join in. She shrugged and reached behind her for the key. She put it down on the counter very gently so she could not be accused of anger.

'They'll need two keys, Sybil.'

She scowled at him. 'They'll pay for the rooms,' he said.

'We'll pay,' I said. Outside the rain began. It bombarded the window and rattled the door as though anxious to get in.

She slammed the second key down upon the counter. '*You* should have taken it and dumped it,' said the woman angrily. 'Rik could have driven these two back here.'

'This is the important stage,' said the man.

'You lazy pig,' said the woman. 'If the alarm is out for the car and Rik gets stopped driving it, then we'll see which is the important stage.'

The man didn't answer, nor did he look at me. He picked up the keys and led the way up the creaky staircase. 'Mind the handrail,' he said. 'It's not fixed properly yet.'

'Nothing is,' called the woman after us. 'The whole place is only half-built.'

He showed us into our rooms. They were cramped and rather sad, shining with yellow plastic and smelling of quick-drying paint. Through the wall I heard Kuang swish back the curtain, put his jacket on a hanger and hang it up. There was the sudden chug-chug of the water pipe as he filled the wash-basin. The man was still behind me, hanging on as if waiting for something. I put my finger to my eye and then pointed towards Kuang's room; the man nodded. 'I'll have the car ready by twenty-two hundred hours. Ostend isn't far from here.'

'Good,' I said. I hoped he would go but he stayed there.

'We used to live in Ostend,' he said. 'My wife would like to go back there. There was life there. The country is too quiet for her.' He fiddled with the broken bolt on the door. It had been painted over but not repaired. He held the pieces together, then let them swing apart.

I stared out of the window; it faced south-west, the way we had come. The rain continued and there were puddles in the roadway and the fields were muddy and windswept. Sudden gusts had knocked over the pots of flowers under the crucifix and the water running down the gutters was bright red with the soil it carried from somewhere out of sight.

'I couldn't let the boy bring you,' the man said. 'I'm conducting you. I couldn't let someone else do that, not even family.' He rubbed his face hard as if he hoped to stimulate his thought. 'The other was less important to the success of the job. This part is vital.' He looked out of the window. 'We needed this rain,' he said, anxious to have my agreement.

'You did right,' I said.

He nodded obsequiously, as if I'd given him a ten-pound tip, then smiled and backed towards the door. 'I know I did,' he said.

34

My case officer arrived about 11 A.M.; there were cooking smells. A large black Humber pulled into the courtyard and stopped. Byrd got out. 'Wait,' he said to the driver. Byrd was wearing a short Harris tweed overcoat and a matching cap. His boots were muddy and his trouser-bottoms tucked up to avoid being soiled. He clumped upstairs to my room, dismissing the Fleming with only a grunt.

'You're my case officer?'

'That's the ticket.' He took off his cap and put it on the bed. His hair stood up in a point. He lit his pipe. 'Damned good to see you,' he said. His eyes were bright and his mouth firm, like a brush salesman sizing up a prospect.

'You've been making a fool of me,' I complained.

'Come, come, trim your yards, old boy. No question of that. No question of that at all. Thought you did well actually. Loiseau said you put in quite a plea for me.' He smiled again briefly, caught sight of himself in the mirror over the wash-basin and pushed his disarranged hair into place.

'I told him you didn't kill the girl, if that's what you mean.'

'Ah well.' He looked embarrassed. 'Damned nice of you.' He took the pipe from his mouth and searched around his teeth with his tongue. 'Damned nice, but to tell you the truth, old boy, I did.'

I must have looked surprised.

'Shocking business of course, but she'd opened us right up. Every damned one of us. They got to her.'

'With money?'

'No, not money; a man.' He put the pipe into the ashtray. 'She was vulnerable to men. Jean-Paul had her eating out of his hand. That's why they aren't suited to this sort of work, bless them. Men were deceivers ever, eh? Gels get themselves involved, what? Still, who are we to complain about that, wouldn't want them any other way myself.'

I didn't speak, so Byrd went on.

'At first the whole plan was to frame Kuang as some sort of oriental Jack-the-Ripper. To give us a chance to hold him, talk to him, sentence him if necessary. But the plans changed. Plans often do, that's what gives us so much trouble, eh?'

'Jean-Paul won't give you any more trouble; he's dead.'

'So I hear.'

'Did you arrange that too?' I asked.

'Come, come, don't be bitter. Still, I know just how you feel. I muffed it, I'll admit. I intended it to be quick and clean and painless, but it's too late now to be sentimental or bitter.'

'Bitter,' I said. 'If you really killed the girl, how come you got out of prison?'

'Set-up job. French police. Gave me a chance to disappear, talk to the Belgians. Very co-operative. So they should be, with this damned boat these Chinese chappies have got anchored three miles out. Can't touch them legally, you see. Pirate radio station; think what it could do if the balloon went up. Doesn't bear thinking of.'

'No. I see. What will happen?'

'Government level now, old chap. Out of the hands of blokes like you and me.'

He went to the window and stared across the mud and cabbage stumps. White mist was rolling across the flat ground like a gas attack.

'Look at that light,' said Byrd. 'Look at it. It's positively ethereal and yet you could pick it up and rap it. Doesn't it make you ache to pick up a paintbrush?'

'No,' I said.

'Well it does me. First of all a painter is interested in form, that's all they talk about at first. But everything is the light falling on it – no light and there's no form, as I'm always saying; light's the only thing a painter should worry about. All the great painters knew that: Francesca, El Greco, Van Gogh.' He stopped looking at the mist and turned back towards me glowing with pleasure. 'Or Turner. Turner most of all, take Turner any day . . .' He stopped talking but he didn't stop looking at me. I asked him no question but he heard it just the same. 'Painting is my life,' he said. 'I'd do anything just to have enough money to go on painting. It consumes me. Perhaps you wouldn't understand what art can do to a person.'

'I think I'm just beginning to,' I said.

Byrd stared me out. 'Glad to hear it, old boy.' He took a brown envelope out of his case and put it on the table.

'You want me to take Kuang up to the ship?'

'Yes, stick to the plan. Kuang is here and we'd like him out on the boat. Datt will try to get on the boat, we'd like him here, but that's less important. Get Kuang to Ostend. Rendezvous with his case chappie – Major Chan – hand him over.'

'And the girl, Maria?'

'Datt's daughter – illegitimate – divided loyalties. Obsessed about these films of her and Jean-Paul. Do anything to get them back. Datt will use that factor, mark my words. He'll use her to transport the rest of his stuff.' He ripped open the brown envelope.

'And you'll try to stop her?'

'Not me, old boy. Not my part of the ship those dossiers, not yours either. Kuang to Ostend, forget everything else. Kuang out to the ship, then we'll give you a spot of leave.' He counted out some Belgian money and gave me a Belgian press card, an identity card, a letter of credit and two phone numbers to ring in case of trouble. 'Sign here,' he said. I signed the receipts.

'Loiseau's pigeon, those dossiers,' he said. 'Leave all that to him. Good fellow, Loiseau.'

Byrd kept moving like a flyweight in the first round. He picked up the receipts, blew on them and waved them to dry the ink.

'You used me, Byrd,' I said. 'You sent Hudson to me, complete with prefabricated hard-luck story. You didn't care about blowing a hole in me as long as the overall plan was okay.'

'London decided,' Byrd corrected me gently.

'All eight million of 'em?'

'Our department heads,' he said patiently. 'I personally opposed it.'

'All over the world people are personally opposing things they think are bad, but they do them anyway because a corporate decision can take the blame.'

Byrd had half turned towards the window to see the mist.

I said, 'The Nuremberg trials were held to decide that whether you work for Coca-Cola, Murder Inc. or the Wehrmacht General Staff, you remain responsible for your own actions.'

'I must have missed that part of the Nuremberg trials,' said Byrd unconcernedly. He put the receipts away in his wallet, picked up his hat and pipe and walked past me towards the door.

'Well let me jog your memory,' I said as he came level and I grabbed at his chest and tapped him gently with my right. It didn't hurt him but it spoiled his dignity and he backed away from me, smoothing his coat and pulling at the knot of his tie which had disappeared under his shirt collar.

Byrd had killed, perhaps many times. It leaves a

blemish in the eyeballs and Byrd had it. He passed his right hand round the back of his collar. I expected a throwing knife or a cheese-wire to come out, but he was merely straightening his shirt.

'You were too cynical,' said Byrd. 'I should have expected you to crack.' He stared at me. 'Cynics are disappointed romantics; they keep looking for someone to admire and can never find anyone. You'll grow out of it.'

'I don't want to grow out of it,' I said.

Byrd smiled grimly. He explored the skin where my hand had struck him. When he spoke it was through his fingers. 'Nor did any of us,' he said. He nodded and left.

35

I found it difficult to get to sleep after Byrd had gone and yet I was too comfortable to make a move. I listened to the articulated trucks speeding through the village: a crunch of changing gears as they reached the corner, a hiss of brakes at the crossroads, and an ascending note as they saw the road clear and accelerated. Lastly, there was a splash as they hit the puddle near the 'Drive carefully because of our children' sign. Every few minutes another came down the highway, a sinister alien force that never stopped and seemed not friendly towards the inhabitants. I looked at my watch. Five thirty. The hotel was still but the rain hit the window lightly. The wind seemed to have dropped but the fine rain continued relentlessly, like a long-distance runner just getting his second breath. I stayed awake for a long time thinking about them all. Suddenly I heard a soft footstep in the corridor. There was a pause and then I saw the door knob revolve silently. 'Are you asleep?' Kuang called softly. I wondered if my conversation with Byrd had awakened him, the walls were so thin. He came in.

'I would like a cigarette. I can't sleep. I have been downstairs but no one is about. There is no machine either.' I gave him a pack of Players. He opened it and lit one. He seemed in no hurry to go. 'I can't sleep,' he said. He sat down in the plastic-covered easy chair and watched the rain on the window. Across the shiny landscape nothing moved. We sat silent a long time, then I said, 'How did you first meet Datt?'

He seemed glad to talk. 'Vietnam, 1954. Vietnam was a mess in those days. The French *colons* were still there but they'd begun to realize the inevitability of losing. No matter how much practice they get the French are not good at losing. You British are skilled at losing. In India you showed that you knew a thing or two about the realities of compromise that the French will never learn. They knew they were going and they got more and more vicious, more and more demented. They were determined to leave nothing; not a hospital blanket nor a kind word.

'By the early 'fifties Vietnam was China's Spain. The issues were clear, and for us party members it was an honour to go there. It meant that the party thought highly of us. I had grown up in Paris. I speak perfect French. I could move about freely. I was working for an old man named de Bois. He was pure Vietnamese. Most party members had acquired Vietnamese names no matter what their origins, but de Bois couldn't bother with such niceties. That's the sort of man he was. A member since he was a child. Communist party adviser; purely political, nothing to do with the military. I was his secretary – it was something of an honour; he used me as a messenger boy. I'm a scientist, I haven't got the right sort of mind for soldiering, but it was an honour.

'Datt was living in a small town. I was told to contact him. We wanted to make contact with the Buddhists in that region. They were well organized and we were told at that time that they were sympathetic to us. Later the war became more defined (the Vietcong versus the Americans' puppets), but then the whole country was a mess of different factions, and we were trying to organize them. The only thing that they had in common was that they were anti-colonial – anti-French-colonial, that is: the French had done our work for us. Datt was a sort of soft-minded liberal, but he had influence with the Buddhists – he was something of a Buddhist scholar and they respected him for his learning – and more important, as far as we were concerned, he wasn't a Catholic.

'So I took my bicycle and cycled sixty kilometres to see Datt, but in the town it was not good to be seen with a rifle, so two miles from the town where Datt was to be found I stopped in a small village. It was so small, that village, that it had no name. Isn't it extraordinary that a village can be so small as to be without a name? I stopped and deposited my rifle with one of the young men of the village. He was one of us: a Communist, in so far as a man who lives in a village without a name can be a Communist. His sister was with him. A short girl – her skin bronze, almost red – she smiled constantly and hid behind her brother, peering out from behind him to study my features. Han Chinese[1] faces were uncommon around there then. I gave him the rifle – an old one left over from the Japanese invasion; I never did fire a shot from it. They both waved as I cycled away.

'I found Datt.

'He gave me cheroots and brandy and a long lecture on the history of democratic government. Then we found that we used to live near each other in Paris and we talked about that for a while. I wanted him to come back and see de Bois. It had been a long journey for me, but I knew Datt had an old car and that meant that if I could get him to return with me I'd get a ride back too. Besides I was tired of arguing with him, I wanted to let old de Bois have a go, they were more evenly matched. My training had been scientific, I wasn't much good at the sort of arguing that Datt was offering me.

'He came. We put the cycle in the back of his old Packard and drove west. It was a clear moonlit night and soon we came to the village that was too small even to have a name.

[1] A Chinese description to differentiate pure Chinese from various minority groups in China or even Vietnamese etc. Ninety-five per cent of China's population are Han Chinese.

'"I know this village," said Datt. "Sometimes I walk out as far as this. There are pheasants."

'I told him that walking this far from the town was dangerous. He smiled and said there could be no danger to a man of goodwill.

'I knew that something was wrong as soon as we stopped, for usually someone will run out and stare, if not smile. There was no sound. There was the usual smell of sour garbage and woodsmoke that all the villages have, but no sound. Even the stream was silent, and beyond the village the rice paddy shone in the moonlight like spilled milk. Not a dog, not a hen. Everyone had gone. There were only men from the Sûreté there. The rifle had been found; an informer, an enemy, the chief – who knows who found it. The smiling girl was there, dead, her nude body covered with the tiny burns that a lighted cigarette end can inflict. Two men beckoned Datt. He got out of the car. They didn't worry very much about me; they knocked me about with a pistol, but they kicked Datt. They kicked him and kicked him and kicked him. Then they rested and smoked Gauloises, and then they kicked him some more. They were both French, neither was more than twenty years old, and even then Datt wasn't young; but they kicked him mercilessly. He was screaming. I don't think they thought that either of us was Viet Minh. They'd waited for a few hours for someone to claim that rifle, and when we stopped near by they grabbed us. They didn't even want to know whether we'd come for the rifle. They kicked him and then they urinated over him and then they laughed and they lit more cigarettes and got into their Citroën car and drove away.

'I wasn't hurt much. I'd lived all my life with the wrong-coloured skin. I knew a few things about how to be kicked without getting hurt, but Datt didn't. I got him back in the car – he'd lost a lot of blood and he was a heavy man, even then he was heavy. "Which way do you want me to drive?" I said. There was a hospital back in the town and I would have taken him to it. Datt said, "Take me to Comrade de Bois." I'd said "comrade" all the time I'd spoken with Datt, but that was perhaps the first time Datt had used the word. A kick in the belly can show a man where his comrades are. Datt was badly hurt.'

'He seems to have recovered now,' I said, 'apart from the limp.'

'He's recovered now, apart from the limp,' said Kuang. 'And apart from the fact that he can have no relationships with women.'

Kuang examined me carefully and waited for me to answer.

'It explains a lot,' I said.

'Does it?' said Kuang said mockingly.

'No,' I said. 'What right does he have to identify thuggery with capitalism?' Kuang didn't answer. The ash was long on his cigarette and he walked across the room to tap it into the wash-basin. I said, 'Why should he feel free to probe and pry into the lives of people and put the results at your disposal?'

'You fool,' said Kuang. He leaned against the wash-basin smiling at me. 'My grandfather was born in 1878. In that year thirteen million Chinese died in the famine. My second brother was born in 1928. In that year five million Chinese people died in the famine. We lost twenty million dead in the Sino–Japanese war and the Long March meant the Nationalists killed two and a half million. But we are well over seven hundred million and increasing at the rate of fourteen or fifteen million a year. We are not a country or a party, we are a whole civilization, unified and moving forward at a speed that has never before been equalled in world history. Compare

our industrial growth with India's. We are unstoppable.'
I waited for him to go on, but he didn't.

'So what?' I said.

'So we don't need to set up clinics to study your foolishness and frailty. We are not interested in your minor psychological failings. Datt's amusing pastime is of no interest to my people.'

'Then why did you encourage him?'

'We have done no such thing. He financed the whole business himself. We have never aided him, or ordered him, nor have we taken from him any of his records. It doesn't interest us. He has been a good friend to us but no European can be very close to our problems.'

'You just used him to make trouble for us.'

'That I will admit. We didn't stop him making trouble. Why should we? Perhaps we have used him rather heartlessly, but a revolution must use everyone so.' He returned my pack of cigarettes.

'Keep the pack,' I said.

'You are very kind,' he said. 'There are ten left in it.'

'They won't go far among seven hundred million of you,' I said.

'That's true,' he said, and lit another.

36

I was awakened at nine thirty. It was *la patronne*. 'There is time for a bath and a meal,' she said. 'My husband prefers to leave early, sometimes the policeman calls in for a drink. It would be best if you were not here then.'

I supposed she noticed me look towards the other room. 'Your colleague is awake,' she said. 'The bathroom is at the end of the corridor. I have put soap there and there is plenty of hot water at this time of night.'

'Thanks,' I said. She went out without answering.

We ate most of the meal in silence. There was a plate of smoked ham, trout *meunière* and an open tart filled with rice pudding. The Fleming sat across the table and munched bread and drank a glass of wine to keep us company through the meal.

'I'm conducting tonight.'

'Good,' I said. Kuang nodded.

'You've no objection?' he asked me. He didn't want to show Kuang that I was senior man, so he put it as though it was a choice between friends.

'It will suit me,' I said. 'Me too,' said Kuang.

'I've got a couple of scarves for you, and two heavy woollen sweaters. We are meeting his case officer right on the quayside. You are probably going out by boat.'

'Not me,' I said. 'I'll be coming straight back.'

'No,' said the man. 'Operations were quite clear about that.' He rubbed his face in order to remember more clearly. 'You will come under his case officer, Major Chan, just as he takes orders from me at this moment.'

Kuang stared impassively. The man said, 'I suppose they'll need you if they run into a coastguard or fisheries protection vessel or something unexpected. It's just for territorial waters. You'll soon know if their case officer tries something.'

'That sounds like going into a refrigerator to check that the light goes out,' I said.

'They must have worked something out,' said the man. 'London must . . .' He stopped and rubbed his face again.

'It's okay,' I said. 'He knows we are London.'

'London seemed to think it's okay.'

'That's really put my mind at rest,' I said.

The man chuckled. 'Yes,' he said, 'yes,' and rubbed his face until his eye watered. 'I suppose I'm blown now,' he said.

'I'm afraid so,' I agreed. 'This will be the last job you'll do for us.'

He nodded. 'I'll miss the money,' he said sadly. 'Just when we could most do with it too.'

37

Maria kept thinking about Jean-Paul's death. It had thrown her off balance, and now she had to think lopsidedly, like a man carrying a heavy suitcase; she had to compensate constantly for the distress in her head.

'What a terrible waste,' she said loudly.

Ever since she was a little girl Maria had had the habit of speaking to herself. Many times she had been embarrassed by someone coming close to her and hearing her babbling on about her trivial troubles and wishes. Her mother had never minded. It doesn't matter, she had said, if you speak to yourself, it's what you say that matters. She tried to stand back and see herself in the present dilemma. Ridiculous, she pronounced, all her life had been something of a pantomime but driving a loaded ambulance across northern France was more than she could have bargained for even in her most imaginative moments. An ambulance loaded with eight hundred dossiers and sex films; it made her want to laugh, almost. Almost.

The road curved and she felt the wheels start to slide and corrected for it, but one of the boxes tumbled and brought another box down with it. She reached behind her and steadied the pile of tins. The metal boxes that were stacked along the neatly made bed jangled gently together, but none of them fell. She enjoyed driving, but there was no fun in thrashing this heavy old blood-wagon over the ill-kept back roads of northern France. She must avoid the main roads; she knew – almost instinctively – which ones would be patrolled. She knew the way the road patrols would obey Loiseau's order to intercept

Datt, Datt's dossiers, tapes and films, Maria, Kuang or the Englishman, or any permutation of those that they might come across. Her fingers groped along the dashboard for the third time. She switched on the wipers, cursed, switched them off, touched the choke and then the lighter. Somewhere there must be a switch that would extinguish that damned orange light that was reflecting the piled-up cases, boxes and tins in her windscreen. It was dangerous to drive with that reflection in the screen but she didn't want to stop. She could spare the time easily but she didn't want to stop. Didn't want to stop until she had completed the whole business. Then she could stop, then she could rest, then perhaps she could be reunited with Loiseau again. She shook her head. She wasn't at all sure she wanted to be reunited with Loiseau again. It was all very well thinking of him now in the abstract like this. Thinking of him surrounded by dirty dishes and with holes in his socks, thinking of him sad and lonely. But if she faced the grim truth he wasn't sad or lonely; he was self-contained, relentless and distressingly complacent about being alone. It was unnatural, but then so was being a policeman unnatural.

She remembered the first time she'd met Loiseau. A village in Périgord. She was wearing a terrible pink cotton dress that a friend had sold her. She went back there again years later. You hope that the ghost of him will accompany you there and that some witchcraft will reach out to him and he will come back to you and you will be madly in love, each with the other, as you were once before. But when you get there you are a stranger; the people, the waitress, the music, the dances, all of them are new and you are unremembered.

Heavy damned car; the suspension and steering were coarse like a lorry's. It had been ill treated, she imagined, the tyres were balding. When she entered the tiny villages the ambulance slid on the *pavé* stones. The villages were

212

old and grey with just one or two brightly painted signs advertising beer or *friture*. In one village there were bright flashes of a welding torch as the village smith worked late into the night. Behind her, Maria heard the toot, toot, toot of a fast car. She pulled over to the right and a blue Land-Rover roared past, flashing its headlights and tooting imperious thanks. The blue rooftop light flashed spookily over the dark landscape, then disappeared. Maria slowed down; she hadn't expected any police patrols on this road and she was suddenly aware of the beating of her heart. She reached for a cigarette in the deep soft pockets of her suede coat, but as she brought the packet up to her face they spilled across her lap. She rescued one and put it in her mouth. She was going slowly now, and only half her attention was on the road. The lighter flared and trembled, and as she doused the flame, more flames grew across the horizon. There were six or seven of them, small flaring pots like something marking an unknown warrior's tomb. The surface of the road was black and shiny like a deep lake, and yet it couldn't be water, for it hadn't rained for a week. She fancied that the water would swallow the ambulance up if she didn't stop. But she didn't stop. Her front wheels splashed. She imagined the black water closing above her, and shivered. It made her feel claustrophobic. She lowered the window and recoiled at the overwhelming smell of *vin rouge*. Beyond the flares there were lamps flaring and a line of headlights. Farther still were men around a small building that had been built across the road. She thought at first that it was a customs control hut, but then she saw that it wasn't a building at all. It was a huge wine tanker tipped on to its side and askew across the road, the wine gushing from the split seams. The front part of the vehicle hung over the ditch. Lights flashed behind shattered glass as men tried to extricate

213

the driver. She slowed up. A policeman beckoned her into the side of the road, nodding frantically.

'You made good time,' the policeman said. 'There's four dead and one injured. He's complaining, but I think he's only scratched.'

Another policeman hurried over. 'Back up against the car and we'll lift him in.'

At first Maria was going to drive off but she managed to calm down a little. She took a drag on the cigarette. 'There'll be another ambulance,' she said. She wanted to get that in before the real ambulance appeared.

'Why's that?' said the policeman. 'How many casualties did they say on the phone?'

'Six,' lied Maria.

'No,' said the policeman. 'Just one injured, four dead. The car driver injured, the four in the tanker died instantly. Two truck-drivers and two hitch-hikers.'

Alongside the road the policemen were placing shoes, a broken radio, maps, clothes and a canvas bag, all in an impeccably straight line.

Maria got out of the car. 'Let me see the hitch-hikers,' she said.

'Dead,' said the policeman. 'I know a dead 'un, believe me.'

'Let me see them,' said Maria. She looked up the dark road, fearful that the lights of an ambulance would appear.

The policeman walked over to a heap in the centre of the road. There from under a tarpaulin that police patrols carry especially for this purpose stuck four sets of feet. He lifted the edge of the tarpaulin. Maria stared down, ready to see the mangled remains of the Englishman and Kuang, but they were youths in beards and denim. One of them had a fixed grin across his face. She drew on the cigarette fiercely. 'I told you,' said the policeman. 'Dead.'

'I'll leave the injured man for the second ambulance,' said Maria.

'And have him ride with four stiffs? Not on your life,' said the policeman. 'You take him.' The red wine was still gurgling into the roadway and there was a sound of tearing metal as the hydraulic jacks tore the cab open to release the driver's body.

'Look,' said Maria desperately. 'It's my early shift. I can get away if I don't have to book a casualty in. The other ambulance won't mind.'

'You're a nice little darling,' said the policeman. 'You don't believe in work at all.'

'Please.' Maria fluttered her eyelids at him.

'No I wouldn't darling and that's a fact,' said the policeman. 'You are taking the injured one with you. The stiffs I won't insist upon and if you say there's another ambulance coming then I'll wait here. But not with the injured one I won't.' He handed her a little bundle. 'His personal effects. His passport's in there, don't lose it now.'

'No, I don't parle,' said a loud English voice. 'And let me down, I can toddle myself, thanks.'

The policeman who had tried to carry the boy released him and watched as he climbed carefully through the ambulance rear doors. The other policeman had entered the ambulance before him and cleared the tins off the bed. 'Full of junk,' said the policeman. He picked up a film tin and looked at it.

'It's hospital records,' said Maria. 'Patients transferred. Documents on film. I'm taking them to the other hospitals in the morning.'

The English tourist – a tall boy in a black woollen shirt and pink linen trousers – stretched full length on the bed. 'That's just the job,' he said appreciatively. The policeman locked the rear doors carefully. Maria heard him say, 'We'll leave the stiffs where they are. The other ambulance will find them. We'll get up to the road blocks. Everything is happening tonight. Accident, road blocks, contraband search and the next thing you know we'll be asked to do a couple of hours' extra duty.'

'Let the ambulance get away,' said the second policeman. 'We don't want her to report us leaving the scene before the second ambulance arrived.'

'That lazy bitch,' said the first policeman. He slammed his fist against the roof of the ambulance and called loudly, 'Right, off you go.'

Maria turned around in her seat and looked for the switch for the interior light. She found it and switched off the orange lamp. The policeman leered in through the window. 'Don't work too hard,' he said.

'Policeman,' said Maria. She said it as if it was a dirty word and the policeman flinched. He was surprised at the depth of her hatred.

He spoke softly and angrily. 'The trouble with you people from hospitals,' he said, 'you think you're the only normal people left alive.'

Maria could think of no answer. She drove forward. From behind her the voice of the Englishman said, 'I'm sorry to be causing you all this trouble.' He said it in English hoping that the tone of his voice would convey his meaning.

'It's all right,' said Maria.

'You speak English!' said the man. 'That's wonderful.'

'Is your leg hurting you?' She tried to make it as professional and clinical as she knew how.

'It's nothing. I did it running down the road to find a telephone. It's hilarious really: those four dead and me unscratched except for a strained knee running down the road.'

'Your car?'

'That's done for. Cheap car, Ford Anglia. Crankcase sticking through the rear axle the last I saw of it. Done for. It wasn't the lorry driver's fault. Poor sod. It wasn't my fault either, except that I was going too fast. I always drive too fast, everyone tells me that. But I couldn't have avoided this lot. He was right in the centre of the road. You do that in a heavy truck on these high camber roads. I don't blame him. I hope he doesn't blame me too much either.'

Maria didn't answer; she hoped he'd go to sleep so she could think about this new situation.

'Can you close the window?' he asked. She rolled it up a little, but kept it a trifle open. The tension of her claustrophobia returned and she knocked the window handle with her elbow, hoping to open it a little more without the boy's noticing.

'You were a bit sharp with the policeman,' said the boy. Maria grunted an affirmative.

'Why?' asked the boy. 'Don't you like policemen?'

'I married one.'

'Go on,' said the boy. He thought about it. 'I never got married. I lived with a girl for a couple of years . . .' He stopped.

'What happened?' said Maria. She didn't care. Her worries were all upon the road ahead. How many road blocks were out tonight? How thoroughly would they examine papers and cargoes?

'She chucked me,' said the boy.

'Chucked?'

'Rejected me. What about you?'

'I suppose mine chucked me,' said Maria.

'And you became an ambulance driver,' said the boy with the terrible simplicity of youth.

'Yes,' said Maria and laughed aloud.

'You all right?' asked the boy anxiously.

'I'm all right,' said Maria. 'But the nearest hospital that's any good is across the border in Belgium. You lie

217

back and groan and behave like an emergency when we get to the frontier. Understand?'

Maria deliberately drove eastward, cutting around the Forêt de St Michel through Watigny and Signy-le-Petit. She'd cross the border at Riezes.

'Suppose they are all closed down at the frontier?' asked the boy.

'Leave it with me,' said Maria. She cut back through a narrow lane, offering thanks that it hadn't begun to rain. In this part of the world the mud could be impassable after half an hour's rain.

'You certainly know your way around,' said the boy. 'Do you live near here?'

'My mother still does.'

'Not your father?'

'Yes, he does too,' said Maria. She laughed.

'Are you all right?' the boy asked again.

'You're the casualty,' said Maria. 'Lie down and sleep.'

'I'm sorry to be a bother,' said the boy.

Pardon me for breathing, thought Maria; the English were always apologizing.

38

Already the brief butterfly summer of the big hotels is almost gone. Some of the shutters are locked and the waiters are scanning the ads for winter resort jobs. The road snakes past the golf club and military hospital. Huge white dunes, shining in the moonlight like alabaster temples, lean against the grey Wehrmacht gun emplacements. Between the points of sand and the cubes of concrete nightjars swoop open-mouthed upon the moths and insects. The red glow of Ostend is nearer now and yellow trams rattle alongside the motor road and over the bridge by the Royal Yacht Club where white yachts – sails neatly rolled and tied – sleep bobbing on the grey water like seagulls.

'I'm sorry,' I said. 'I thought they would be earlier than this.'

'A policeman gets used to standing around,' Loiseau answered. He moved back across the cobbles and scrubby grass, stepping carefully over the rusty railway lines and around the shapeless debris and abandoned cables. When I was sure he was out of sight I walked back along the *quai*. Below me the sea made soft noises like a bathful of serpents, and the joints of four ancient fishing boats creaked. I walked over to Kuang. 'He's late,' I said. Kuang said nothing. Behind him, farther along the *quai*, a freighter was being loaded by a huge travelling crane. Light spilled across the waterfront from the spotlights on the cranes. Could their man have caught sight of Loiseau and been frightened away? It was fifteen minutes later than rendezvous. The standard control procedure was to wait only four minutes, then come back twenty-four hours later; but I hung on. Control procedures were invented by diligent men in clean shirts and warm offices. I stayed. Kuang seemed to notice the passage of time – or more accurately perhaps he revelled in it. He stood patiently. He hadn't stamped his feet, breathed into his hands or smoked a cigarette. When I neared him he didn't raise a quizzical eyebrow, remark about the cold or even look at his watch. He stared across the water, glanced at me to be sure I was not about to speak again, and then resumed his pose.

'We'll give him ten more minutes,' I said. Kuang looked at me. I walked back down the quayside.

The yellow headlight turned off the main road a trifle too fast and there was a crunch as the edge of an offside wing touched one of the oil drums piled outside the Fina station. The lights kept coming, main beams. Kuang was illuminated as bright as a snowman and there was only a couple of foot of space between him and the wire fence around the sand heap. Kuang leapt across the path of the car. His coat flapped across the headlight, momentarily eclipsing its beam. There was a scream as the brakes slammed on and the engine stalled. Suddenly it was quiet. The sea splashed greedily against the jetty. Kuang was sucking his thumb as I got down from the oil drum. It was an ambulance that had so nearly run us down.

Out of the ambulance stepped Maria.

'What's going on?' I said.

'I'm Major Chan,' said Maria.

'You are?' Kuang said. He obviously didn't believe her.

'You're Major Chan, case officer for Kuang here?' I said.

'For the purposes that we are all interested in, I am,' she said.

'What sort of answer is that?' I asked.

'Whatever sort of answer it is,' said Maria, 'it's going to have to do.'

'Very well,' I said. 'He's all yours.'

'I won't go with her,' said Kuang. 'She tried to run me down. You saw her.'

'I know her well enough to know that she could have tried a lot harder,' I said.

'You didn't show that sort of confidence a couple of minutes ago,' said Maria. 'Scrambling out of the way when you thought I was going to run *you* down.'

'What's confidence?' I said. 'Smiling as you fall off a cliff to prove that you've jumped?'

'That's what it is,' said Maria and she leaned forward and gave me a tiny kiss, but I refused to be placated. 'Where's your contact?'

'This is it,' said Maria, playing for time. I grabbed her arm and clutched it tight. 'Don't play for time,' I told her. 'You said you're the case officer. So take Kuang and start to run him.' She looked at me blankly. I shook her.

'They should be here,' she said. 'A boat.' She pointed along the jetty. We stared into the darkness. A small boat moved into the pool of light cast by the loading freighter. It turned towards us.

'They will want to load the boxes from the ambulance.'

'Hold it,' I told her. 'Take your payment first.'

'How did you know?'

'It's obvious, isn't it?' I said. 'You bring Datt's dossiers as far as this, using your ingenuity, your knowledge of police methods and routes, and if the worst comes to the worst you use your influence with your ex-husband. For what? In return Datt will give you your own dossier and film, etc. Am I right?'

'Yes,' she said.

'Then let them worry about loading.' The motor boat was closer now. It was a high-speed launch; four men in pea-jackets stood in the stern. They stared towards us

221

but didn't wave or call. As the boat got to the stone steps, one man jumped ashore. He took the rope and made it fast to a jetty ring. 'The boxes,' I called to them. 'Your papers are here.'

'Load first,' said the sailor who had jumped ashore.

'Give me the boxes,' I said. The sailors looked at me and at Kuang. One of the men in the boat made a motion with his hand and the others took two tin boxes, adorned with red seals, from the bottom of the boat and passed them to the first man, who carried them up the steps to us.

'Help me with the boxes,' said Maria to the Chinese sailor.

I still had hold of her arm. 'Get back into the ambulance and lock the doors from inside,' I said.

'You said I should start . . .'

I pushed her roughly towards the driver's door.

I didn't take my eyes off Maria but on the periphery of my vision to the right I could see a man edging along the side of the ambulance towards me. He kept one hand flat against the side of the vehicle, dabbing at the large scarlet cross as if testing to see if the paint was wet. I let him come to within arm's length and still without swivelling my head I flicked out my hands so that my fingertips lashed his face, causing him to blink and pull back. I leaned a few inches towards him while sweeping my hand back the way it had come, slapping him not very hard across the side of the cheek.

'Give over,' he shouted in English. 'What the hell are you on?'

· 'Get back in the ambulance,' Maria called to him. 'He's harmless,' she said. 'A motor accident on the road. That's how I got through the blocks so easily.'

'You said Ostend hospital,' said the boy.

'Stay out of this, sonny,' I said. 'You are in danger

even if you keep your mouth shut. Open it and you're dead.'

'I'm the case officer,' she insisted.

'You are what?' I said. I smiled one of my reassuring smiles, but I see now that to Maria it must have seemed like mockery. 'You are a child, Maria, you've no idea of what this is all about. Get into the ambulance,' I told her. 'Your ex-husband is waiting down the jetty. If you have this cart-load of documents with you when he arrests you things might go easier for you.'

'Did you hear him?' Maria said to the sailor and Kuang. 'Take the documents, and take me with you – he's betrayed us all to the police.' Her voice was quiet but the note of hysteria was only one modulation away.

The sailor remained impassive and Kuang didn't even look towards her.

'Did you hear him?' she said desperately. No one spoke. A rowboat was moving out around the far side of the Yacht Club. The flutter of dripping blades skidding upon the surface and the gasp of oars biting into the water was a lonely rhythm, like a woman's sobs, each followed by the sharp intake of breath.

I said, 'You don't know what it's all about. This man's job is to bring Kuang back to their ship. He's also instructed to take me. As well as that he'll try to take the documents. But he doesn't change plans because you shout news about Loiseau waiting to arrest you. In fact, that's a good reason for leaving right away because their big command is to stay out of trouble. This business doesn't work like that.'

I signalled Kuang to go down to the motor boat and the sailor steadied him on the slimy metal ladder. I punched Maria lightly on the arm. 'I'll knock you unconscious, Maria, if that's the way you insist I do it.' I smiled but I meant it.

'I can't face Loiseau. Not with that case I can't face

223

him.' She opened the driver's door and got into the seat. She would rather face Datt than Loiseau. She shivered. The boy said, 'I feel I'm making a lot of trouble for you. I'm sorry.'

'Just don't say you're sorry once again,' I heard Maria say.

'Get in,' I called to the sailor. 'The police will be here any moment. There's no time to load boxes.' He was at the foot of the ladder and I had my heavy shoes on. He shrugged and stepped into the boat. I untied the rope and someone started the motor. There was a bright flurry of water and the boat moved quickly, zigzagging through the water as the helmsman got the feel of the rudder.

At the end of the bridge there was a flashlight moving. I wondered if the whistles were going. I couldn't hear anything above the sound of the outboard motor. The flashlight was reflected suddenly in the driver's door of the ambulance. The boat lurched violently as we left the harbour and entered the open sea. I looked at the Chinese sailor at the helm. He didn't seem frightened, but then how would he look if he did? I looked back. The figures on the quay were tiny and indistinct. I looked at my watch: it was 2.10 A.M. The Incredible Count Szell had just killed another canary, they cost only three francs, four at the most.

39

Three miles out from Ostend the water was still and a layer of mist hugged it; a bleak bottomless cauldron of broth cooling in the cold morning air. Out of the mist appeared M. Datt's ship. It was a scruffy vessel of about 10,000 tons, an old cargo boat, its rear derrick broken. One of the bridge wings had been mangled in some long-forgotten mishap and the grey hull, scabby and peeling, had long brown rusty stains dribbling from the hawse pipes down the anchor fleets. It had been at anchor a long time out here in the Straits of Dover. The most unusual feature of the ship was a mainmast about three times taller than usual and the words 'Radio Janine' newly painted in ten-foot-high white letters along the hull.

The engines were silent, the ship still, but the current sucked around the draught figures on the stem and the anchor chain groaned as the ship tugged like a bored child upon its mother's hand. There was no movement on deck, but I saw a flash of glass from the wheelhouse as we came close. Bolted to the hull-side there was an ugly metal accommodation ladder, rather like a fire-escape. At water level the steps ended in a wide platform complete with stanchion and guest warp to which we made fast. M. Datt waved us aboard.

As we went up the metal stairs Datt called to us, 'Where are they?' No one answered, no one even looked up at him. 'Where are the packets of documents – my work? Where is it?'

'There's just me,' I said.

'I told you . . .' Datt shouted to one of the sailors.

'It was not possible,' Kuang told him. 'The police were right behind us. We were lucky to get away.'

'The dossiers were the important thing,' said Datt. 'Didn't you even wait for the girl?' No one spoke. 'Well didn't you?'

'The police almost certainly got her,' Kuang said. 'It was a close thing.'

'And my documents?' said Datt.

'These things happen,' said Kuang, showing little or no concern.

'Poor Maria,' said Datt. 'My daughter.'

'You care only about your dossiers,' said Kuang calmly. 'You do not care for the girl.'

'I care for you all,' said Datt. 'I care even for the Englishman here. I care for you all.'

'You are a fool,' said Kuang.

'I will report this when we are in Peking.'

'How can you?' asked Kuang. 'You will tell them that you gave the documents to the girl and put my safety into her hands because you were not brave enough to perform your duties as conducting officer. You let the girl masquerade as Major Chan while you made a quick getaway, alone and unencumbered. You gave her access to the code greeting and I can only guess what other secrets, and then you have the effrontery to complain that your stupid researches are not delivered safely to you aboard the ship here.' Kuang smiled.

Datt turned away from us and walked forward. Inside, the ship was in better condition and well lit. There was the constant hum of the generators and from some far part of the ship came the sound of a metal door slamming. He kicked a vent and smacked a deck light which miraculously lit. A man leaned over the bridge wing and looked down on us, but Datt waved him back to work. He walked up the lower bridge ladder and I followed him, but Kuang remained at the foot of it. 'I am hungry,'

Kuang said. 'I have heard enough. I'm going below to eat.'

'Very well,' said Datt without looking back. He opened the door of what had once been the captain's cabin and waved me to precede him. His cabin was warm and comfortable. The small bed was dented where someone had been lying. On the writing table there were a heap of papers, some envelopes, a tall pile of gramophone records and a vacuum flask. Datt opened a cupboard above the desk and reached down two cups. He poured hot coffee from the flask and then two brandies into tulip glasses. I put two heaps of sugar into my coffee and poured the brandy after it, then I downed the hot mixture and felt it doing wonders for my arteries.

Datt offered me his cigarettes. He said, 'A mistake. A silly mistake. Do you ever make silly mistakes?'

I said, 'It's one of my very few creative activities.' I waved away his cigarettes.

'Droll,' said Datt. 'I felt sure that Loiseau would not act against me. I had influence and a hold on his wife. I felt sure he wouldn't act against me.'

'Was that your sole reason for involving Maria?'

'To tell you the truth: yes.'

'Then I'm sorry you guessed wrong. It would have been better to have left Maria out of this.'

'My work was almost done. These things don't last for ever.' He brightened. 'But within a year we'll do the same operation again.'

I said, 'Another psychological investigation with hidden cameras and recorders, and available women for influential Western men? Another large house with all the trimmings in a fashionable part of Paris?'

Datt nodded. 'Or a fashionable part of Buenos Aires, or Tokyo, or Washington, or London.'

'I don't think you are a true Marxist at all,' I said. 'You merely relish the downfall of the West. A Marxist at least

227

comforts himself with the idea of the proletariat joining hands across national frontiers, but you Chinese Communists relish aggressive nationalism just at a time when the world was becoming mature enough to reject it.'

'I relish nothing. I just record,' said Datt. 'But it could be said that the things of Western Europe that you are most anxious to preserve are better served by supporting the real, uncompromising power of Chinese communism than by allowing the West to splinter into internecine warrior states. France, for example, is travelling very nicely down that path; what will she preserve in the West if her atom bombs are launched? We will conquer, we will preserve. Only we can create a truly world order based upon seven hundred million true believers.'

'That's really 1984,' I said. 'Your whole set-up is Orwellian.'

'Orwell,' said Datt, 'was a naïve simpleton. A middle-class weakling terrified by the realities of social revolution. He was a man of little talent and would have remained unknown had the reactionary press not seen in him a powerful weapon of propaganda. They made him a *guru*, a pundit, a seer. But their efforts will rebound upon them, for Orwell in the long run will be the greatest ally the Communist movement ever had. He warned the bourgeoisie to watch for militancy, organization, fanaticism and thought-planning, while all the time the seeds of their destruction are being sown by their own inadequacy, apathy, aimless violence and trivial titillation. Their destruction is in good hands: their own. The rebuilding will be ours. My own writings will be the basis of our control of Europe and America. Our control will rest upon the satisfaction of their own basest appetites. Eventually a new sort of European man will evolve.'

'History,' I said. 'That's always the alibi.'

'Progress is only possible if we learn from history.'

'Don't believe it. Progress is man's indifference to the lessons of history.'

'You are cynical as well as ignorant,' said Datt as though making a discovery. 'Get to know yourself, that's my advice. Get to know yourself.'

'I know enough awful people already,' I said.

'You feel sorry for the people who came to my clinic. That's because you really feel sorry for yourself. But these people do not deserve your sympathy. Rationalization is their destruction. Rationalization is the aspirin of mental health and, as with aspirin, an overdose can be fatal.

'They enslave themselves by dipping deeper and deeper into the tube of taboos. And yet each stage of their journey is described as greater freedom.' He laughed grimly. 'Permissiveness is slavery. But so has history always been. Your jaded, overfed section of the world is comparable to the ancient city states of the Middle East. Outside the gates the hard nomads waited their chance to plunder the rich, decadent city-dwellers. And in their turn the nomads would conquer, settle into the newly-conquered city and grow soft, and new hard eyes watched from the barren stony desert until their time was ripe. So the hard, strong, ambitious, idealistic peoples of China see the over-ripe conditions of Europe and the USA. They sniff the air and upon it floats the aroma of garbage cans overfilled, idle hands and warped minds seeking diversions bizarre and perverted, they smell violence, stemming not from hunger, but from boredom, they smell the corruption of government and the acrid flash of fascism. They sniff, my friend: you!'

I said nothing, and waited while Datt sipped at his coffee and brandy. He looked up. 'Take off your coat.'

'I'm not staying.'

'Not staying?' He chuckled. 'Where are you going?'

'Back to Ostend,' I said. 'And you are going with me.'

'More violence?' He raised his hands in mock surrender.

I shook my head. 'You know you've got to go back,' I said. 'Or are you going to leave all your dossiers back there on the quayside less than four miles away?'

'You'll give them to me?'

'I'm promising nothing,' I told him, 'but I know that you have to go back there. There is no alternative.' I poured myself more coffee and gestured to him with the pot. 'Yes,' he said absent-mindedly. 'More.'

'You are not the sort of man that leaves a part of himself behind. I know you, Monsieur Datt. You could bear to have your documents on the way to China and yourself in the hands of Loiseau, but the converse you cannot bear.'

'You expect me to go back there and give myself up to Loiseau?'

'I know you will,' I said. 'Or live the rest of your life regretting it. You will recall all your work and records and you will relive this moment a million times. Of course you must return with me. Loiseau is a human being and human activities are your speciality. You have friends in high places, it will be hard to convict you of any crime on the statute book . . .'

'That is very little protection in France.'

'Ostend is in Belgium,' I said. 'Belgium doesn't recognize Peking, Loiseau operates there only on sufferance. Loiseau too will be amenable to any debating skill you can muster. Loiseau fears a political scandal that would involve taking a man forcibly from a foreign country . . .'

'You are glib. Too glib,' said Datt. 'The risk remains too great.'

'Just as you wish,' I said. I drank the rest of my coffee and turned away from him.

'I'd be a fool to go back for the documents. Loiseau

can't touch me here.' He walked across to the barometer and tapped it. 'It's going up.' I said nothing.

He said, 'It was my idea to make my control centre a pirate radio boat. We are not open to inspection nor even under the jurisdiction of any government in the world. We are, in effect, a nation unto ourselves on this boat, just as all the other pirate radio ships are.'

'That's right,' I said. 'You're safe here.' I stood up. 'I should have said nothing,' I said. 'It is not my concern. My job is done.' I buttoned my coat tight and blessed the man from Ostend for providing the thick extra sweater.

'You despise me?' said Datt. There was an angry note in his voice.

I stepped towards him and took his hand in mine. 'I don't,' I said anxiously. 'Your judgement is as valid as mine. Better, for only you are in a position to evaluate your work and your freedom.' I gripped his hand tight in a stereotyped gesture of reassurance.

He said, 'My work is of immense value. A breakthrough you might almost say. Some of the studies seemed to have . . .' Now he was anxious to convince me of the importance of his work.

But I released his hand carefully. I nodded, smiled and turned away. 'I must go. I have brought Kuang here, my job is done. Perhaps one of your sailors would take me back to Ostend.'

Datt nodded. I turned away, tired of my game and wondering whether I really wanted to take this sick old man and deliver him to the mercies of the French Government. They say a man's resolution shows in the set of his shoulders. Perhaps Datt saw my indifference in mine. 'Wait,' he called. 'I will take you.'

'Good,' I said. 'It will give you time to think.'

Datt looked around the cabin feverishly. He wet his lips and smoothed his hair with the flat of his hand. He flicked through a bundle of papers, stuffed two of them in his pocket, and gathered up a few possessions.

They were strange things that Datt took with him: an engraved paperweight, a half-bottle of brandy, a cheap notebook and finally an old fountain pen which he inspected, wiped and carefully capped before pushing it into his waistcoat pocket. 'I'll take you back,' he said. 'Do you think Loiseau will let me just look through my stuff?'

'I can't answer for Loiseau,' I said. 'But I know he fought for months to get permission to raid your house on the Avenue Foch. He submitted report after report proving beyond all normal need that you were a threat to the security of France. Do you know what answer he got? They told him that you were an X., an *ancien X.* You were a Polytechnic man, one of the ruling class, the elite of France. You could *tutoyer* his Minister, call half the Cabinet *cher camarade*. You were a privileged person, inviolate and arrogant with him and his men. But he persisted, he showed them finally what you were, Monsieur Datt. And now perhaps he'll want them to pay their bill. I'd say Loiseau might see the advantage in letting a little of your poison into their bloodstream. He might decide to give them something to remember the next time they are about to obstruct him and lecture him, and ask him for the fiftieth time if he isn't mistaken. Permit you to retain the dossiers and tapes?' I smiled. 'He might well insist upon it.'

Datt nodded, cranked the handle of an ancient wall phone and spoke some rapid Chinese dialect into it. I noticed his large white fingers, like the roots of some plant that had never been exposed to sunlight.

He said, 'You are right, no doubt about it. I must be where my research is. I should never have parted company from it.'

He pottered about absent-mindedly. He picked up his

Monopoly board. 'You must reassure me on one thing,' he said. He put the board down again. 'The girl. You'll see that the girl's all right?'

'She'll be all right.'

'You'll attend to it? I've treated her badly.'

'Yes,' I said.

'I threatened her, you know. I threatened her about her file. About her pictures. I shouldn't have done that really but I cared for my work. It's not a crime, is it, caring about your work?'

'Depends upon the work.'

'Mind you,' said Datt, 'I have given her money. I gave her the car too.'

'It's easy to give away things you don't need,' I said. 'And rich people who give away money need to be quite sure they're not trying to buy something.'

'I've treated her badly.' He nodded to himself. 'And there's the boy, my grandson.'

I hurried down the iron steps. I wanted to get away from the boat before Kuang saw what was happening, and yet I doubt if Kuang would have stopped us; with Datt out of the way the only report going back would be Kuang's.

'You've done me a favour,' Datt pronounced as he started up the outboard motor.

'That's right,' I said.

40

The Englishman had told her to lock the ambulance door.
She tried to, but as her finger hovered over the catch, the
nausea of fear broke over her. She imagined just for a
moment the agony of being imprisoned. She shuddered
and pushed the thought aside. She tried again, but it was
no use, and while she was still trying to push the lock the
English boy with the injured knee leaned across her and
locked the door. She wound the window down, urgently
trying to still the claustrophobia. She leaned forward with
her eyes closed and pressed her head against the cold
windscreen. What had she done? It had seemed so right
when Datt had put it to her: if she took the main bulk of
the documents and tapes up to the rendezvous for him,
then he would be waiting there with her own film and
dossier. A fair exchange, he had said. She touched the
locks of the case that had come from the boat. She
supposed that her documents were inside, but suddenly
she didn't care. Fine rain beaded the windscreen with
little lenses. The motor boat was repeated a thousand
times upside down.

'Are you all right?' the boy asked. 'You don't look
well.'

She didn't answer.

'Look here,' he said, 'I wish you'd tell me what all this
is about. I know I've given you a lot of trouble and all
that, you see . . .'

'Stay here in the car,' Maria said. 'Don't touch anything
and don't let anyone else touch anything. Promise?'

'Very well. I promise.'

She unlocked the door with a sigh of relief and got out

into the cold salty air. The car was on the very brink of the waterside and she stepped carefully across the worn stones. Along the whole quayside men were appearing out of doorways and warehouse entrances. Not ordinary men but men in berets and anklets. They moved quietly and most of them were carrying automatic rifles. A group of them near to her stepped under the wharfside lights and she saw the glitter of the paratroop badges. Maria was frightened of the men. She stopped near the rear doors of the ambulance and looked back; the boy stared at her across the metal boxes and film tins. He smiled and nodded to reassure her that he wouldn't touch anything. Why did she care whether he touched anything? One man broke away from the group of paratroops near her. He was in civilian clothes, a thigh-length black leather coat and an old-fashioned trilby hat. He had taken only one step when she recognized Loiseau.

'Maria, is it you?'

'Yes, it's me.'

He hurried towards her, but when he was a pace away stopped. She had expected him to embrace her. She wanted to hang on to him and feel his hand slapping her awkwardly on the back, which was his inadequate attempt to staunch miseries of various kinds.

'There are a lot of people here,' she said. '*Bif?*'

'Yes, the army,' said Loiseau. 'A paratroop battalion. The Belgians gave me full co-operation.'

Maria resented that. It was his way of saying that she had never given him full co-operation. 'Just to take me into custody,' she said, 'a whole battalion of Belgian paratroops? You must have exaggerated.'

'There is a ship out there. There is no telling how many men are aboard. Datt might have decided to take the documents by force.'

He was anxious to justify himself, like a little boy

seeking an advance on his pocket money. She smiled and repeated, 'You must have exaggerated.'

'I did,' said Loiseau. He did not smile, for distorting truth was nothing to be proud of. But in this case he was anxious that there should be no mistakes. He would rather look a fool for over-preparation than be found inadequate. They stood there staring at each other for several minutes.

'The documents are in the ambulance?' Loiseau asked.

'Yes,' she said. 'The film of me is there too.'

'What about the tape of the Englishman? The questioning that you translated when he was drugged?'

'That's there too, it's a green tin; number B fourteen.' She touched his arm. 'What will you do with the Englishman's tape?' She could not ask about her own.

'Destroy it,' said Loiseau. 'Nothing has come of it, and I've no reason to harm him.'

'And that's part of your agreement with him,' she accused.

Loiseau nodded.

'And my tape?'

'I will destroy that too.'

'Doesn't that go against your principles? Isn't destruction of evidence the cardinal sin for a policeman?'

'There is no rule book that can be consulted in these matters whatever the Church and the politicians and the lawyers tell us. Police forces, governments and armies are just groups of men. Each man must do as his conscience dictates. A man doesn't obey without question or he's not a man any more.'

Maria gripped his arm with both hands, and pretended just for a moment that she would never have to let go.

'Lieutenant,' Loiseau called along the wharf. One of the paratroops slammed to attention and doubled along the waterfront. 'I'll have to take you into custody,' Loiseau said quietly to Maria.

'My documents are on the front seat of the ambulance,' she told him hurriedly before the lieutenant reached them.

'Lieutenant,' Loiseau said, 'I want you to take the boxes out of the ambulance and bring them along to the shed. By the way, you had better take an inventory of the tins and boxes; mark them with chalk. Keep an armed guard on the whole operation. There might be an attempt to recover them.'

The lieutenant saluted Loiseau warmly and gave Maria a passing glance of curiosity.

'Come along, Maria,' said Loiseau. He turned and walked towards the shed.

Maria patted her hair and followed him.

It was a wooden hut that had been put up for the duration of World War Two. A long, badly lit corridor ran the whole length of the hut, and the rest was divided into four small, uncomfortable offices. Maria repaired her make-up for the third time. She decided to do one eye at a time and get them really right.

'How much longer?' she asked. Her voice was distorted as she held her face taut to paint the line over her right eye.

'Another hour,' said Loiseau. There was a knock at the door and the paratroop lieutenant came in. He looked briefly at Maria and then saluted Loiseau.

'We're having a little trouble, sir, getting the boxes out of the ambulance.'

'Trouble?' said Loiseau.

'There's some madman with an injured leg. He's roaring and raging and punching the soldiers who are trying to unload the vehicle.'

'Can't you deal with it?'

'Of course I can deal with it,' said the paratroop officer.

237

Loiseau detected a note of irritation in his voice. 'It's just that I don't know who the little squirt is.'

'I picked him up on the road,' said Maria. 'He was injured in a road crash. I told him to look after the documents when I got out of the car. I didn't mean . . . he's nothing to do with . . . he's just a casualty.'

'Just a casualty,' Loiseau repeated to the lieutenant. The lieutenant smiled. 'Get him along to the hospital,' said Loiseau.

'The hospital,' repeated Maria. 'Everything in its proper place.'

'Very good sir,' said the lieutenant. He saluted with an extra display of energy to show that he disregarded the sarcasm of the woman. He gave the woman a disapproving look as he turned about and left.

'You have another convert,' said Maria. She chuckled as she surveyed her painted eye, twisting her face slightly so that the unpainted eye was not visible in the mirror. She tilted her head high to keep her chin line. She heard the soldiers piling the boxes in the corridor. 'I'm hungry,' she said after a while.

'I can send out,' said Loiseau. 'The soldiers have a lorry full of coffee and sausages and some awful fried things.'

'Coffee and sausage.'

'Go and get two sweet coffees and some sausage sandwiches,' Loiseau said to the young sentry.

'The corporal has gone for his coffee,' said the soldier.

'That's all right,' said Loiseau. 'I'll look after the boxes.'

'He'll look after the boxes,' Maria said flatly to the mirror.

The soldier looked at her, but Loiseau nodded and the soldier turned to get the coffee. 'You can leave your gun with me,' Loiseau said. 'You'll not be able to carry the coffee with that slung round your neck and I don't want guns left lying around in the corridor.'

'I'll manage the coffee and the gun,' said the soldier. He said it defiantly, then he slung the strap of the gun around his neck to prove it was possible. 'You're a good soldier,' said Loiseau.

'It won't take a moment,' said the soldier.

Loiseau swung around in the swivel chair, drummed his fingers on the rickety desk and then swivelled back the other way. He leaned close to the window. The condensation was heavy on it and he wiped a peephole clear so that he could see the waterfront. He had promised the Englishman that he would wait. He wished he hadn't: it spoiled his schedule and also it gave this awkward time of hanging about here with Maria. He couldn't have her held in the local police station, obviously she had to wait here with him; it was unavoidable, and yet it was a bad situation. He had been in no position to argue with the Englishman. The Englishman had offered him all the documents as well as the Red Chinese conducting officer. What's more he had said that if Loiseau would wait here he would bring Datt off the ship and deliver him to the quayside. Loiseau snorted. There was no good reason for Datt to leave the pirate radio ship. He was safe out there beyond the three-mile limit and he knew it. All the other pirate radio ships were out there and safe. Datt had only to tune in to other ships to confirm it.

'Have you got a cold?' Maria asked him, still inspecting her painted eye.

'No.'

'It sounds like it. Your nose is stuffed up. You know that's always the first sign with those colds you get. It's having the bedroom window open, I've told you about that hundreds of times.'

'And I wish you'd stop telling me.'

'Just as you like.' She scrubbed around in the tin of eye

239

black and spat into it. She had smudged the left eye and now she wiped it clean so that she looked curiously lop-sided: one eye dramatically painted and the other white and naked. 'I'm sorry,' she said. 'Really sorry.'

'It will be all right,' said Loiseau. 'Somehow I will find a way.'

'I love you,' she said.

'Perhaps.' His face was grey and his eyes deep sunk the way they always were when he had missed a lot of sleep.

They had occupied the same place in her mind, Loiseau and her father, but now she suddenly saw Loiseau as he really was. He was no superman, he was middle-aged and fallible and unrelaxingly hard upon himself. Maria put the eye-black tin down and walked across to the window near Loiseau.

'I love you,' she said again.

'I know you do,' said Loiseau. 'And I am a lucky man.'

'Please help me,' said Maria, and Loiseau was amazed, for he could never have imagined her asking for help, and Maria was amazed, for she could not imagine herself asking for help.

Loiseau put his nose close to the window. It was hard to see through it because of the reflections and condensation. Again he rubbed a clear place to look through.

'I will help you,' said Loiseau.

She cleared her own little portion of glass and peered along the waterfront. 'He's a damn long time with that coffee,' said Loiseau.

'There's the Englishman,' said Maria, 'and Datt.'

'Well I'm damned,' said Loiseau. 'He's brought him.'

Datt's voice echoed down the corridor as the hut door swung open. 'This is it,' he said excitedly. 'All my documents. Colour seals denote year, index letters code names.' He tapped the boxes proudly. 'Where is Loiseau?' he asked the Englishman as he walked slowly down the rank of stacked tins and boxes, stroking them as he read the code letters.

'The second door,' said the Englishman, easing his way past the boxes.

Maria knew exactly what she had to do. Jean-Paul said she'd never made one real decision in her life. It was not hysteria, nor heightened emotion. Her father stood in the doorway, tins of documents in his arms, nursing them as though they were a newly-born child. He smiled the smile she remembered from her childhood. His body was poised like that of a tightrope walker about to step off the platform. This time his powers of persuasion and manipulation were about to be tried to the utmost, but she had no doubt that he would succeed. Not even Loiseau was proof against the smooth cool method of Datt, her puppet-master. She knew Datt's mind and could predict the weapons he would use: he would use the fact that he was her father and the grandfather of Loiseau's child. He would use the hold he had over so many important people. He would use everything he had and he would win.

Datt smiled and extended a hand. 'Chief Inspector Loiseau,' he said. 'I think I can be of immeasurable help to you – and to France.'

She had her handbag open now. No one looked at her.

Loiseau motioned towards a chair. The Englishman moved aside and glanced quickly around the room. Her hand was around the butt by now, the safety catch slid down noiselessly. She let go of her handbag and it sat upon the gun like a tea cosy.

'The ship's position,' said Datt, 'is clearly marked upon this chart. It seemed my duty to pretend to help them.'

'Just a moment,' said Loiseau wearily.

The Englishman saw what was happening. He punched towards the handbag. And then Datt realized, just as the pistol went off. She pulled the trigger again as fast as she could. Loiseau grabbed her by the neck and the Englishman punched her arm. She dropped the bag. Datt was through the door fumbling with the lock to prevent them from chasing him. He couldn't operate the lock and ran down the corridor. There was the sound of the outer door opening. Maria wrenched herself free and ran after Datt, the gun still in her hand. Everyone was shouting. Behind her she heard Loiseau call, 'Lieutenant, stop that man.'

The soldier with the tray of coffee may have heard Loiseau's shout or he may have seen Maria or the Englishman brandishing a pistol. Whatever it was that prompted him, he threw the tray of coffee aside. He swung the rifle around his neck like a hula-hoop. The stock slammed into his hand and a burst of fire echoed across the waterfront almost simultaneously with the sound of the coffee cups smashing. From all over the waterfront shots were fired; Maria's bullets must have made very little difference.

You can recognize a head shot by a high-velocity weapon; a cloud of blood particles appeared like vapour in the air above him as Datt and his armful of tapes, film and papers was punched off the waterfront like a golf ball.

'There,' called Loiseau. The high-power lamps operated by the soldiers probed the spreading tangle of recording tapes and films that covered the water like a Sargasso Sea. A great bubble of air rose to the surface and a cluster of pornographic photos slid apart and drifted away. Datt was in there amongst it and for a moment it looked as though he was still alive as he turned in the water very slowly and laboriously, his stiff arm clawing out through the air like a swimmer doing the crawl. For a moment it seemed as if he stared at us. The tapes caught in his fingers and the soldiers flinched. 'He's turning over, that's all,' said Loiseau. 'Men float face down, women

242

face up. Get the hook under his collar. He's not a ghost man, just a corpse, a criminal corpse.'

A soldier tried to reach him with a fixed bayonet, but the lieutenant stopped him. 'They'll say we did it, if the body is full of bayonet wounds. They'll say we tortured him.' Loiseau turned to me and passed me a small reel of tape in a tin. 'This is yours,' he said. 'Your confession, I believe, although I haven't played it.'

'Thanks,' I said.

'That was the agreement,' said Loiseau.

'Yes,' I said, 'that was the agreement.'

Datt's body floated deeper now, even more entangled in the endless tape and film.

Maria had hidden the gun, or perhaps she'd thrown it away. Loiseau didn't look at her. He was concerned with the body of Datt – too concerned with it, in fact, to be convincing.

I said, 'Is that your ambulance, Maria?' She nodded; Loiseau was listening but he didn't turn round.

'That's a silly place to leave it. It's a terrible obstruction; you'll have to move it.' I turned to the Belgian para officer. 'Let her move it,' I said.

Loiseau nodded.

'How far?' said the officer. He had a mind like Loiseau's. Perhaps Loiseau read my thoughts. He grinned.

'It's all right,' said Loiseau. 'The woman can go.' The lieutenant was relieved to get a direct order. 'Yes sir,' he said and saluted Loiseau gravely. He walked towards the ambulance.

Maria touched Loiseau's arm. 'I'll go to my mother's. I'll go to the boy,' she said. He nodded. Her face looked strange, for only one eye was made up. She smiled and followed the officer.

'Why did you do that?' Loiseau asked.

'I couldn't risk you doing it,' I said. 'You'd never forgive yourself.'

It was light now. The sea had taken on a dawn-fresh sparkle and the birds began to think about food. Along the shore herring gulls probed for tiny shellfish left by the tide. They carried them high above the dunes and dropped them upon the concrete blockhouses. Some fell to safety in the sand, some hit the ancient gun emplacements and cracked open, some fell on to the concrete but did not crack; these last were retrieved by the herring gulls and then dropped again and again. The tops of the blockhouses were covered in tiny fragments of shell, for eventually each shell cracked. Very high, one bird flew purposefully and alone on a course as straight as a light beam. Farther along the shore, in and out of the dunes, a hedgehog wandered aimlessly sniffing and scratching at the colourless grass and watching the gulls at their game. The hedgehog would fly higher and stronger than any of the birds, if only he knew how.

BLOOD ROCK

Also by James Jackson

Dead Headers

Cold Cut

The Reaper

The Counter-Terrorist Handbook

BLOOD
ROCK

JAMES JACKSON

JOHN MURRAY

A CIP catalogue record for this title is available from the British Library

ISBN 978-0-7195-6983-8

Typeset in 12.5/15.5 Monotype Bembo by Servis Filmsetting Ltd, Manchester

Printed and bound by Clays Ltd, St Ives plc

Hodder Headline's policy is to use papers that are natural, renewable and recyclable products and
made from wood grown in sustainable forests. The logging and manufacturing processes are
expected to conform to the environmental regulations of the country of origin.

John Murray (Publishers)
338 Euston Road
London NW1 3BH

For Lucy, my mother –
with love and gratitude

A small island, an epic siege, and the future course of world history hangs in the balance . . .

In 1530 the Hospitaller Knights of St John, last of the great surviving Christian military orders from the Crusades, made their home on the Mediterranean island of Malta. Expelled from Rhodes eight years previously by Suleiman the Magnificent, greatest of the Ottoman emperors, the Knights were an unpopular and piratical anachronism, a relic in an age of sixteenth-century nation-states. Dedicated to ongoing religious conflict against the Islamic and heathen world, and depending for their prosperity on harassing Ottoman trade routes along the North African coast, the Knights inevitably provoked wrath and outrage in Constantinople. The patience of the Sultan would not last. In 1565 – over forty years since he first engaged the Order of St John in battle – Suleiman again dispatched his army. This time, there would be no mistake or clemency. Total victory and annihilation were demanded. What followed was to become for ever known as the Great Siege.

Many of the events described are documented historical fact.

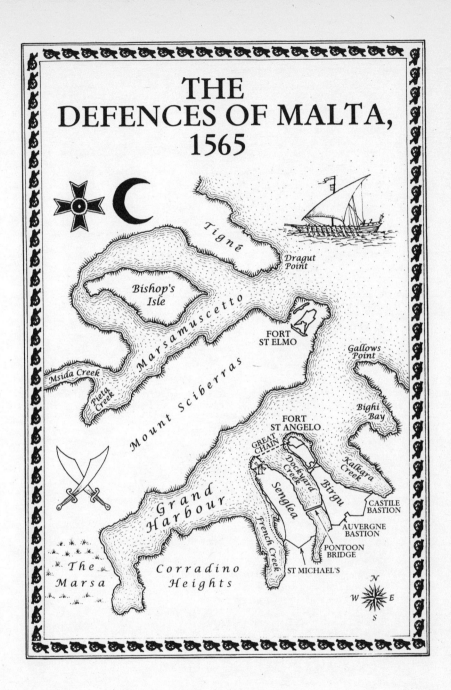

THE
DEFENCES OF MALTA,
1565

Tigné

Dragut
Point

*Bishop's
Isle*

FORT
ST ELMO

Gallows
Point

Msida Creek

Marsamuscetto

*Piota
Creek*

Mount Sciberras

Bighi
Bay

FORT
ST ANGELO

GREAT
CHAIN

*Dockyard
Creek*

*Kalkara
Creek*

Senglea

Birgu

CASTILE
BASTION

*Grand
Harbour*

French Creek

AUVERGNE
BASTION

PONTOON
BRIDGE

*The
Marsa*

*Corradino
Heights*

ST MICHAEL'S

N
W   E
S

Beginning

The vice-regent of God on earth looked out upon the still and glittering waters of the Golden Horn and saw that it was good. For he was Suleiman the Magnificent, Sultan of the Ottoman Empire, King of Kings, Lord of the Lords of the World, Emperor of the East and West, Possessor of Men's Necks. And before him lay his navy, a fleet of some two hundred ships, a vast armada ready to sail at his bidding, to seize and conquer in his name. By land and sea, his was the greatest military power, the furthest-flung empire, the world had ever seen. From the gates of Vienna to the gardens of Babylon, from the port of Aden to the city of Budapest, his writ and influence were all. But he was not yet done. It was late March 1565. An auspicous time to launch invasion and soak the earth in Christian blood.

He felt the incisor-bite of gout feeding on his leg. Aged seventy-one, he was falling prey to the vicissitudes of fate and the frailties of humankind. Pain could make a man cry out, could make a man cruel. Nothing, however, would disturb the aura of imperial majesty, at least not in public. The rages could wait for the inner courtyards, the gem-encrusted chambers, the hidden rose-gardens and scented pathways of the Grand Seraglio palace. Here he was the living embodiment of divine authority. And here he was a ruler aloof on his dais, resplendent in silk robes and ermine-trimmed gown, a jewelled scimitar at his side, a turban with diamond clasp and aigrette of peacock feathers poised on his head. All who surveyed him would tremble. He was giver of life and bringer of death.

His bead-black eyes flickered to watch the rich and thronging multitude of his court. They were thousands strong, a kaleidoscope of magnificent hues. There were the green silks of his ministers and viziers, the blue of the sheikhs, the gold and scarlet of the ambassadors, the white of the muftis. Each had his role, knew his place. Close by was the bejewelled presence of the Grand Vizier and his retinue. Near also was the Chief Black Eunuch – the Kislar Aga – a bloated grotesque in flower-patterned silks and tall sugarloaf headdress. Around them were others: the Chief Armourer, the Chief Huntsman, the Chief Astronomer, the Chief Keeper of the Hummingbirds, the Custodian of the Heron Plume, the Masters of the Keys, the Stirrup, the Turbans, the Perfumes – rival factions and fawning alliances, bound up and bedecked in sable and precious stones. Constantinople's finest. They were come to pay homage to their Sultan, to greet, preen, jostle and flaunt. They were come to observe the vast Turkish fleet depart for war.

Emperor of the East and West. Suleiman could taste the salt in the air, could hear the undulating rhythm of the drums, the crash of cymbals, the blast of horns and trumpets, the shrill whistle-calls of the galley masters. There was nothing like it. It was the hypnotic throb of conquest, of past and promised victory. And it would freeze the blood of his enemies. A gust of wind tugged at the hem of his robe, carried the brass and rolling notes of a Janissary band. Ah, his Janissaries, his Invincible Ones, his spearhead aimed at the convulsing heart of the foe. They were readying. Their emperor and commander had found them a fresh target.

To the untutored eye, the small Mediterranean island and archipelago to which he was sending his forces was of supreme insignificance. But he, Suleiman the First, the Magnificent, was not untutored. Nor was this cursed rock, this barren pile of limestone, at all insignificant. As grit in the eye could vex a giant, so too the lifeless speck of Malta could discomfort and plague the body and well-being of the Turks. That was its value. Positioned in the straits between Sicily and North Africa, it divided the eastern from the western parts of the Mediterranean, hung poised above the exposed throat of the Ottoman trade routes. An uncomfortable situation for Suleiman, which had become increasingly intolerable. In 1522 he had invaded the island of Rhodes and banished for ever those Christian warriors, those zealot Knights of the noble Order of St John of Jerusalem. There was nothing noble about them. They were pirates, fanatics who had dedicated themselves to waging war against the one True Faith, thieves who preyed on his merchantmen, raided his ports, chained his subjects in stinking dungeons or as slaves to the oars of their privateer galleys. Within eight years of their departure from Rhodes they had regrouped and resettled, choosing Malta as their home. It offered anchorage. It offered a fortress from which to sally forth and strike at the Islamic world. Outrage followed outrage, humiliation piled upon insult. Even the trading ship of the Kislar Aga himself had been seized by the marauding Knights while bound for Constantinople and sailing near the island of Zante. Nowhere was safe from them. Until this moment. His mistake had been to show mercy, to have allowed them to escape Rhodes alive. Their mistake was to have again incurred his anger. He would crush them.

Another fanfare, and the two military leaders of the expedition approached to bow low and long. Suleiman waited while they abased themselves. Absolute rule had its own tempo. Before him was Mustapha Pasha, commander-in-chief of the land invasion force, a celebrated and ruthless veteran of the Persian and Hungarian campaigns, a descendant of Ben Welid, standard-bearer to the Prophet Mohammed. He had been there at Rhodes, and in Malta would finish the project. Beside the General stood Admiral Piali, commander of the galleys, influential, well connected, son-in-law of the Sultan's heir, Selim, and at thirty-five years of age already a renowned scourge of the Italian coast. Co-commanders, reliable men, committed to sweeping the Christians from the Mediterranean and the Knights of St John from their island redoubt. They would be joined by others in the pantheon and diaspora of Islam, of course – by those who owed allegiance, who craved the honour of serving the Sultan. El Louck Aly, the doughty governor of Alexandria; Hassem, governor of Algiers; Salih, the Rais of Salik; Aly Fartax, the most feared Turkish pirate in the Aegean. And, above them, Dragut – the Drawn Sword of Islam – legendary corsair and governor of Tripoli. Holy war, the projection of power, the extension of empire. Everything was prepared.

Suleiman stroked the white tresses of his long moustache and forked beard. 'You are ready to punish the infidel?'

'Some forty thousand troops are embarked, Divine Majesty.' Deference and solemnity sat heavy on Mustapha Pasha. 'An invincible army. It shall not be long before we smoke the vipers from their nest.'

'It shall not be long before we strike off their heads.'

'They are weak and low in number, Divine Majesty.'

'While we have the power of God, the weight and strength of our siege cannons and arquebusiers, the superiority of our Janissaries, victors of Buda, to annihilate them all.'

'They shall be as chaff, Divine Majesty. A few hundred Christian Knights, several thousand Spanish troops, a collection of native islanders, simple peasants and fishermen.'

'Fishermen to pull the bodies of their infidel own from the sea.'

'The defenders cower in their forts, tremble before Your Divine Majesty and the glory of all Islam.'

The Sultan nodded. 'Already they have been deserted, cast to their fate by the princes of Europe. No relief army has been sent, no reinforcements arrived from Rome or Spain, from Austria or the German lands. Even the Viceroy of Sicily hesitates, denies succour or aid to the Grand Master and his troops. And yet these pirates on Malta continue to prepare.'

'To no avail, Divine Majesty.'

'The occasion of their destruction will be a historic and propitious day for our cause.'

'An anchorage, an island, a stepping-stone into the underbelly of Europe, Divine Majesty. Nothing will save them.'

Indeed, nothing would, reflected Suleiman. He had toured the dockyards and armouries, the barracks and powder-mills, had witnessed the war-machine of his Ottoman empire build towards this moment, aim itself at that outcrop in the Mediterranean Sea. Almost one hundred thousand rounds of cannon shot and fifteen thousand quintals of gunpowder were stowed aboard the galleys and galleases. Some seven thousand Janissaries, nine thousand black-plumed Spahi cavalry troops, four thousand Iayalars, ten thousand levies and volunteers, assembled, paraded, embarked, to be joined by the corsairs and cut-throats of North Africa. Thus had the materiel and manpower of conquest been gathered. The island would be his. Beyond it, the rest of the unbeliever domain lay ripe and exposed for the taking. *Suleiman the First, Lord of the Lords of the World.* Malta the anvil on which he would break the back of Christendom.

He turned to Piali. 'And you, Admiral? Your fleet will carry a blood tide across the waters?'

'Hear the sound, Divine Majesty.' The ambitious and calculating eyes of the naval commander shone bright as he gestured towards the fleet. 'It is the noise of one hundred and thirty galleys and almost seventy transports, of heavenly prophecy, of your sacred and imperial supremacy.'

'Then I entrust you both with the will of God, to do His bidding and my purpose.'

Their faces sank deep in loyal reverence. They were powerful men rendered powerless at the feet of their master. Status, position, the attachment of heads to necks, all were insecure in the cloistered world of the Grand Seraglio. All could be granted or removed at the whim, at a nod, of the Sultan. The neck was vulnerable to the silk bow-strings of the five deaf-mute assassins maintained by Suleiman. The head could end blackening on a spike above the turret gateway to the Second Court. It was considered a high honour. Mustapha Pasha and Admiral Piali preferred to avoid such reward.

Their emperor beckoned them closer. 'Who is the warrior of the Mediterranean I most admire?'

'Dragut, Divine Majesty.' Their response came in unison.

'That is so. The Drawn Sword of Islam. The greatest seafarer of our age, the finest siege tactician in our kingdom. Confer with him, heed his advice.'

Mustapha Pasha nodded eagerly. 'As you command, Divine Majesty.'

'It will be done, Divine Majesty.' Piali was no less fervent.

'Go to your galleys. You shall not fail.'

With due ceremony and the timpani-clamour of vested authority, general and admiral departed for their ships. Suleiman stood awhile, tall, expressionless, before processing the richly carpeted and halberdier-flanked route to the portals of the imperial tents ranged above the foreshore.

It was cavernous within, a fusion and vision of untrammelled wealth and unsurpassed power. Lamps glowed, their soft radiance shimmering from walls hung with pearls and cloth of gold, stretching across floors swathed in silver-threaded silks. On low tables of precious metal and rare marble were set the malachite incense burners, the diamond-crusted hookahs and candleholders, the cascades of emerald and ruby. Everywhere opulence, everything to excess. It meant little to the jaded palate of Suleiman the Magnificent.

He settled himself on a couch and breathed deep, allowed the heavy pungence of musk, rose and frankincense to filter through to his senses. Attendants brought platters heaped with dates and prunes from Egypt, grapes from Smyrna and Trebizond, the fruits of empire. He waved them away. The smell of roses had provoked memories. They were of his queen, his beloved odalisque, his Roxelana, the slave-girl who had seized his heart and dominated his harem, who had walked in his private gardens and in his soul, who had been dead these seven years. His companions now were old age, gout and rage. Mere mortals would not comprehend true loss, real bitterness.

His mood swung, mercurial and restless with the pang of grief. Perhaps a sorbet would rebalance his humours. On a single command, the tray of sherbets was proffered, the ices perfumed with Candia honey and the exotic trace of amber, violets and water-lilies. The ice had been carried as snow in felt saddlebags from the slopes of Mount Olympus. Nothing was too much for the Sultan, nowhere too far from his reach. The small gathering of Hospitaller Knights and their ageing Grand Master on the doomed island would shortly find this out. Suleiman selected and sipped from the cup. The melt-water trickled cool and soothing at the back of his throat. His two captives would be ingesting something a little less chilled. It was time.

A clap of his hands, and the prisoners were dragged mewling and struggling to his presence. The audience would be of limited duration. Suleiman continued to drink his sherbet, his eyes peering dispassionate above the gold rim of his cup. The men were Genoese traders, spies, had been found observing the fleet, noting its strength, writing coded messages in invisible ink on parchment bound for Malta. Letters rendered in lemon-juice revealed themselves when warmed above a candle flame. Foreign agents in the guise of merchants revealed themselves when exposed to the persistent charms of the torturer. Their suffering was of no consequence. The aftertaste of violets was sharp in his mouth. Like all things Ottoman, all forms of Turkish execution, it was an acquired taste. The prisoners were on their knees, beseeching, shaking in their chains. They had served the wrong master, were prostrate before the wrong imperial throne. Sentence had been passed.

The curtain was drawn back, a theatrical flourish intended to give first sight of awaiting punishment. Molten lead. Yet the unbelievers could not quite comprehend. Suleiman sat perfectly still. It was how he had attended the murder of his first son, had watched as the deaf mutes fought to apply the bow-string to his neck. A lengthy struggle. Liquidation of condemned agents posed fewer complications. The two captives appeared finally to notice and to understand. It might have been the vapour fumes, the proximity of the heat. It might have been the manner in which their heads were wrenched back, their mouths forced open. The better to scream and to drink.

As the choking, screeching finale played out, Suleiman pondered on the irony. These servants of the Christian dogs were breathing their last, but he too could engage in subterfuge and espionage. At the heart of the Knights of St John, close to their Grand Master, Jean Parisot de La Valette, was a traitor, a spy. He had already identified every defensive position, passed on details of cannons and manpower, morale and deployment. Soon he would bring the rock crashing down about his brethren, would deliver up the prize to the Ottoman overlord. God wished it so. God favoured the true believer. Suleiman drained his cup and patted dry his thin, mirthless lips.

Leaving behind the minarets, domes and cypress-clad hills of Constantinople, the arrowhead of the naval formation moved on along the coast. Oars dipped and rose, lateen sails filled with breeze, and fishing caiques flitted at the periphery as the great invasion fleet passed by. It was an awesome sight. In the vanguard were the vessels of the commanders: the gilded and carved fig-wood galley of Mustapha Pasha; the majestic sixty-eight-oared leviathan carrying Admiral Piali. Above the stern of the Admiral's ship flew the standard of the Grand Turk, its horsehair plume billowing from the golden orb and crescent. It signalled the beginning, signified the preordained end. The Sultan had decreed and would prevail.

Chapter 1

Fear spread across the island of Malta. It came on the dust and the wind, with whispers, with the crack of whips and the creak of donkey-carts. Occasionally the distant boom of cannon, the deeper crump of explosion swelled and drifted in the air. Gunnery practice was under way; buildings beyond the walled confines of the Grand Harbour villages of Senglea and Birgu were being razed. It all added to the tension, increased the scurrying pace. These were hardy folk, toughened by subsistence, inured to the raids and slave-gathering expeditions of the Barbary Coast pirates. But this was different. Possessions were bundled, children hurried, livestock driven onward, the scattered groups of refugees heading inland for Mdina passing scrabble fields already deserted and harvested of their early crop. They would leave nothing but scorched earth and strewn stone for the enemy. By order of Grand Master La Valette and his Knights of the Order of St John. Mid-May 1565. Invasion imminent.

A large steel-grey Andalusian stallion trotted fast along a coastal track on the eastern edge of the island. Its rider carried a sword at his side, a bow and a quiver of arrows on his back. Yet there was no conventional armour, no indication of status or rank. The high boots were frayed, the brigantine jacket faded, its crimson velvet front scoured by the sea, its internal steel plates and gilded brass rivets distressed by skirmish and wear. He was a young man, tall, strong, strikingly handsome, at ease in the saddle, his eyes blue and sharp, his features north-European, his jaw-line set with the confidence of a veteran. To the side of his brow, the trace wound from a musket shot told of battles won, of a life almost lost. His name was Christian Hardy.

It was a ride of several miles, a mission to ensure that the fishing-villages were cleared, the proclamation of the Grand Master enforced. Helios, his horse, needed the ride. When invasion came, there might be little chance for such freedom. The sole certainty was that a conflict of historic import and unparalleled ferocity lay close. Many would perish. Perhaps he too would lie among the slain. The thought barely troubled him.

Fate was always capricious, death usually cruel in his profession. It had been fate that brought the corsairs from their Mediterranean lair to maul the southern coast of England, death that was visited upon his family and the Dorset village of his birth. He had been only a boy – a boy of ten years who had witnessed his father cut down while defending the home, who had heard his mother and sisters cry out from the flames as their dwelling burned. His revenge had been brief. In blind rage, he had attacked, hacking at the pirates with a billhook, gutting one, near-beheading another. It had won him his life, had earned him passage as trophy to the palm-fringed abattoir of the Barbary Coast. Again he endured, learning fast, growing strong, fighting with a knife in the alleyways of Algiers and Bougie, wrestling on the beaches of Djerba, stealing from the markets of Tripoli. He showed promise. A Turkish officer pronounced him a fine specimen, a candidate for the harsh rigours of the Janissary training-schools of the Sultan. The corsairs demurred. They had taken him from his land, now took him as their own. He could outride their champions, could read the stars and waves with their best, could board a slow merchantman out of Naples with the agility and viciousness of a dervish. His companions marvelled, applauded. Dragut himself paid tribute. And on a silent and moonless night Christian Hardy had taken a small open boat and slipped away to the north.

Helios snorted, wanted to stretch into a canter. Hardy allowed him his head. They were old companions, the horse the product of an evening of dice and gaming with a nobleman in the court of Don Garcia de Toledo, Viceroy of Sicily. A fine stallion, bred for hunting and war, maturing to the colour of white marble. Naturally, the Grand Master had disapproved. Eventually the Grand Master had conceded. While he was no Knight, was certainly low-born, the Order of St John had use for Christian Hardy. He knew the enemy like no other, had lived among them, inhabited their minds, understood their ways and cunning, could trace them to their anchorages. Some thought him brash, impetuous. Others believed him an adventurer without principle, an outsider and apostate stray devoid of the Religion. No matter. He enjoyed the patronage of La Valette. Malta was his shelter, protecting it his duty. Perhaps one day he would return to England and kneel at the untended gravesides of his family. It would be some time yet. There was work to do, redemption to be earned at the point of a sword.

The boy appeared from between the rocks, running breathless and frantic towards him. He was accompanied by a dog, a mongrel as unkempt and wild as its owner. Hardy reined in Helios and sat to watch. His horse could kill with its hooves on command.

'Boy, you are either pursued or possessed.'

'The enemy. I have seen them.' The report was delivered in short, panting gasps. 'Come, seigneur. You must follow me.'

Hardy swung himself to the ground. 'You have a name?'

'It is Luqa.'

'Well, Master Luqa, we have patrols along the coast, watchtowers manned on every clifftop. They have yet to see the Turkish fleet.'

'No fleet. But men. They are Mohammedans, they speak their tongue. They hide in an abandoned shelter close to the creek. You must hurry.'

Hardy considered the boy, could sense the truth in his urgency. The eyes were suffused with the fierce and feral independence of survival; the body was sturdy and carried the weathered scars of abandonment. He would have been about thirteen years of age.

'Where are your mother and father, Luqa?'

'They were taken by corsairs from Gozo many years ago.'

'Then we each have argument with the Saracen.'

Hardy was reaching into a saddlebag, extracting the tools of his trade. If he were to be outnumbered, he would employ the trickery and articles supplied by his friend the black Moor.

The boy was shifting excitedly on his feet. 'I will help you, seigneur.'

'You should be making for Mdina, where you will be safe.'

'I wish to fight.'

'What of your friend?' Hardy indicated the dog. It slunk back, its ears flattening, its teeth bared.

'He too will fight.'

'Then we are almost an army. The enemy strength?'

'I heard two, seigneur.'

'You saw a boat?'

'Nothing.'

It could be that the landing-party came by night, that they scuttled their craft in anticipation of a longer stay. They might be heavily armed, might be more numerous than the estimate. Or they were figments of imagination. A boy who dwelt too long upon a shore, who spent his days spearing fish, his nights prizing open sea-urchins, could become unbalanced of mind and judgement. Hardy would perform his own reconnaissance.

He slapped Helios affectionately on the flank and gestured to the boy. 'Very well. Let us take battle to our opponents.'

'I will not let you down, seigneur.'

'Neither will you put yourself in danger or provoke rescue. You will obey me at all times.'

'That I will do.'

The shelter was low-built and derelict, an abandoned structure completed for forgotten reasons and decaying into the surrounding coastal rock. It was the kind of place a boy and his mongrel dog might seek rest or shelter. Few others would care to visit. Yet someone had.

Hardy lay on his belly and watched the entrance, the razor touch of the grey rocks hard against his skin, the needle-prick of tension jabbing in his spine. The interior of the shelter was dark. No sign of habitation, no indication of sentries. But he knew the boy Luqa was right. Years in the company of corsairs heightened the senses, alerted the nerves to a hostile presence. A sound, a smell, a taste in the air. The sea swell continued as it had; the clouds maintained their gossamer course. Yet atmosphere had altered. The Turk was here.

Luqa had again appeared, monkey-scrambling on to the broken limestone roof of the refuge, an earthenware sphere grasped in his hand. It was a smokepot, its fuse alight and sputtering. For a moment the boy paused, balancing to savour his role, before stooping to drop his ordnance through an opening. Just as he had been instructed. The space below him erupted in spumes of sulphurous fog, choking, blinding, turpentine-fuelled. With it came the Turks. They cascaded into the light, coughing for air, clutching at their eyes. The boy had miscounted.

Five men were stumbling into the open. One was in flames, his arms flapping wildly at his clothing as the fire caught and climbed. He was the first to drop. An arrow from Hardy's composite bow pierced him in the chest, ending the frenzied movement, cutting off the screams. A second arrow-shaft protruded from the body of a large man flailing sightless with a drawn scimitar. The barb had bitten deep, and the victim pitched forward.

Hardy rose and drew his sword. He had faced worse, was evening the odds, but the shock effect was dissipating and the Turks left alive were advancing fast. They spread into a concave skirmish-line. The flanks were circling, closing, the sun catching on curved blades and short stabbing-swords. He saw the faces, felt the focus of their intensity. There was no time for a further launch of arrows. He adjusted his footing, waited for contact.

Then there were two. The crack of pebble impacting on skull shattered the prelude. Eyes wobbled upward, and the central figure in the group sank slowly to his knees. Behind was Luqa on his rooftop, his sling raised in triumph, his feet dancing a victory jig. Aim had been true. In those seconds, while the survivors faltered, as the left-field turned to confront an additional threat, Hardy pressed home.

Steel clashed. He danced back, coaxing, chiding. Enraged, the Turk came in pursuit, striking out, forgetting himself, his eyes and muscles straining with exertion and ferocity. He had been cut from the herd for a reason. Hardy feinted, parried and lunged. The Turk blocked with a flick of his wrist and a circling of his blade. He was good. But the best could prove flawed, could stumble when blinded by sand and kicked in the groin. He was no alley-fighter. He was an Ottoman soldier out on a scouting mission, out of his depth. The man was attempting to wipe the sand from his face, shouting with rage, staggering forward. He overreached. With a deft sidestep, Hardy let him pass, aided his journey with a dagger-thrust to the stomach, a beheading while he fell.

Howling with desperation and a strange dogged fatalism, the surviving Turk did not give up. He was crouching low, prancing in defence. It was the choreography of last resort. Hardy wiped his sword cursorily on the canvas breeches of his headless victim and tested the grip in his palm. Toledo steel possessed an appetite. He smiled respectfully at his opponent and spoke to him in his native tongue.

'Your companions are dead. Surrender or join them.'

His offer was spurned, its rejection accompanied by darting eyes and a frenzied sword. The quarry was at bay; the quarry was small and wiry, quick and restless on his feet. Hardy studied him. A Turk far from Constantinople. It was merely a few steps to the killing-circle. But the dog had reached it first, was snapping and snarling, chasing round to disorientate its adversary and attack from behind. The Turk swung, his scimitar descending and deflecting from rock. Already the dog had leaped back, scurrying on, was moving in once more. Turk-baiting, Turk-worrying. With a growl, it pounced, seizing a hamstring, its jaws locking deep, its muzzle and body shaking with the effort.

The screams were high-pitched. Losing his balance, floundering in pain, the Turk scrabbled untidily on the ground. He had lost his sword, was twisting to kick away the canine savaging his lower leg. It was too late. Hardy dispatched him with a single blow as the man pulled a knife from its metal sheath. All five down.

He was patting the bodies, searching for valuables, when Luqa joined him. 'You did well with your sling.'

'I kill seabirds for food. A man makes an easy target.'

'He may often make a monied corpse.' Hardy cut the strings to a purse and emptied its contents into his palm. 'Silver pieces intended to buy the loyalty and silence of islanders. The harvest of battle. You shall have half.'

'I thank you, seigneur.'

'And I thank you, Luqa. Without your eye and your hound, I faced a treacherous foe.'

Grinning pleasure wreathed the boy's face. 'I am a soldier now. A rich one.'

'Serving a noble cause. If you are not to travel to Mdina, you should return with me to Grand Harbour. A fishing-family will care for you.'

'I care for myself, seigneur.' The boy was stripping a corpse of a waistcoat and overjacket.

'In the open you will be caught, Luqa.'

'In the open I am free.'

'For how long? Until the Turks and corsairs seize the island; until they find you, flay you alive, cut you into a thousand pieces for their sport? Remember your parents, Luqa.'

The boy stood, diminished in the outsize clothing of the Turk. His dog continued to gnaw on the leg-joint. 'I cannot leave my friend.'

'He will fill his belly on the carcasses soon to strew Malta. He will be content enough.'

'He will die if I go.'

'You will die if you remain.'

They busied themselves in silence until it was time to depart. Finally, Hardy climbed the rocky cliff path to the coastal track and his horse, stowed his possessions, and prepared to mount. Helios snorted at the smell of blood. He comprehended – always did.

With a nodded farewell to the boy, the soldier lifted himself fluidly into the saddle and walked the stallion on. He had spilled first blood, taken first spoils. Luqa watched, his face neutral, his dog seated at his side.

'*Wait.*'

The boy ran to catch up, his legs pumping, his movements clumsy in the Moslem garb. Christian Hardy neither turned his head nor slowed. He lowered an arm, hoisted the youth aloft and behind him. Luqa clenched his fist and saluted the sky. A bond had been forged, a friendship struck. He looked back only once. The dog whined, its head and ears cocked, before it sloped away to investigate the cadavers. Helios quickened his pace. They were bound for Grand Harbour and the fortress of the Knights.

Around Grand Harbour the tempo of preparation was feverish and unremitting, the claustrophobia of impending siege increasing. For thirty-five years the Knights had found anchorage and safe haven there. They had built their home, constructed forts, erected their hospital, their Conventual Church, their chapels of devotion, their auberges in which to quarter the sons of the great Christian houses of Europe. A south-east corner of a diminutive island, and all was under threat.

Open boats overloaded with supplies and reinforcements were

shuttling across the harbour mouth to the small star-shaped fort of St Elmo commanding its northern side. Perched on a rock outcrop at the foot of Mount Sciberras, it was a vulnerable and isolated position, but a strategic one. For it both dominated the entrance to Grand Harbour and the opening to a second bay, Marsamuscetto, beyond. The Knights had every reason to send more troops. Sweeping away from this headland, along the western shore of Grand Harbour, was the low ground of the Marsa. The plain had already been emptied, its meagre population moved on and away. In their place were forage parties, foot soldiers picking over rubble, horsemen poisoning wells and springs with flax and bitter herbs. Little would be left to chance, nothing left for the Turk. And at the southern reaches of the Marsa, jutting on their paired peninsulas from the bottom edge of the bay, were the fortified villages of Senglea and Birgu. On its landward side, the narrow neck of Senglea was guarded by the fort of St Michael. Birgu was further on, protected by twin and monumental bastions set into high and dense walls almost two miles round. A formidable defence, a menacing and imposing sight. It was in Birgu that the Knights of St John had made their redoubt. It was at the tip of Birgu, holding sway above the harbour, looking out towards St Elmo, that the brooding and heavy mass of a third fort could be seen. Fort St Angelo, headquarters of the Order.

In the Council Chamber of the palace atop the main keep, a meeting of the Sacro Consiglio – the Supreme Council – was under way. Seated on benches along its blazoned walls were the men who led the Order. The Bishop, the deans, the priors, the conventual bailiffs, the Knights Grand Cross, the heads of each of the national *langues*, all present, every one of them garbed in the black vestments of office and wearing the eight-pointed cross of St John. These were the Hospitallers. They were a brotherhood of warrior-priests, inheritors of a cause stretching back to the Crusades, when their founders had first nursed sick pilgrims to the Holy Land and then taken up arms to defend them. The fighting and nursing skills remained. Each of the brother members had taken a vow of chastity, poverty and obedience; each had pledged himself to serve the Pope and to wage war ceaselessly until death against the Moslem infidel. They were a living embodiment of history, a foreign legion of combative Christianity, an incongruity in an era of sixteenth-century city- and nation-statehood. The last of their kind. At their head, sitting stern but serene on the throne of the Council Chamber, was Grand Master Jean Parisot de La Valette.

He listened as the latest communication from Messina was read aloud to the assembly. More weasel words from the Viceroy of Sicily, more hollow promises, more delay. Yet La Valette remained unmoved and unmoving, a still presence radiating calm and authority while those about him argued. The news had provoked consternation, was bound to. By the hour, extinction was graduating from possibility to probability.

Voices climbed in discord. A senior officer of the military Knights of Justice had the floor. 'I say again, my brethren, King Philip of Spain and his viceroy in Sicily abandon us in our hour. King Francis of the French turns his back. The Emperor of Germany campaigns elsewhere. The heretic Queen Elizabeth of England will not come to the aid of Catholics. What do we owe these princes? For what reason do we guard their bloated underbelly?'

'For the reason that we took a solemn oath before God.' The Bishop had risen to respond. 'For the reason that when Emperor Charles V ceded Malta to our keeping he charged us with fighting the perfidious enemies of our Holy Faith.'

'And with what should we fight, Brother Bishop? Even His Holiness the Pope appears deaf to our plight.'

'His Holiness is our patron, our overlord.'

'Yet in place of soldiers he sends his platitudes and goodwill. We are but seven hundred Knights, have but four thousand Spanish troops and four thousand Maltese irregulars under arms.'

'They are also under God. With His mercy, we shall prevail.'

'Against thirty thousand of the enemy? Forty thousand?'

'Against the strength of a million heathen.'

Another Knight stood. 'Nine thousand of us garrisoned behind high walls. At Rhodes we withstood the Turk for six months.'

'Quite so.' The Bishop nodded. 'In Malta we shall once again withstand them.'

A conventual bailiff interrupted. 'But for no more than a few weeks. The fort of St Elmo is overlooked by Mount Sciberras, our walls here overlooked by the heights of Corradino. When the Turks seize such ground, their cannon will pound us to dust.'

'Then to dust we shall return. The cause is noble.'

'While we remain, the Religion and cause are doomed.'

'What would you have us do?' Enraged, the Knight Grand Cross Lacroix had jumped to his feet. 'Cower as fools? Run as frightened beasts? Surrender as whipped dogs?'

'Repair to Sicily. Station our forces where they may be supplied, joined with ease by the combined armies of Christendom.'

'You would bow before the Turk.'

'I believe our brother bailiff bows only to God, Brother Grand Cross.'

De Pontieux, Magisterial Knight and Knight of Justice, spoke in soft and emollient tones. But his eyes were sly, baleful, staring uncompromising at his old foe Lacroix. He had his followers, was playing to them. There was more to say.

'Like our brother bailiff, I too propose not surrender but retreat. Retreat, and we avoid extinction. Retreat, and we live to fight the heathen Turk on better terms, on grounds of our choosing.'

'We have made our choice. It is Malta.'

'A dry rock of little merit.'

'A dry rock which has been our home for near forty years.' Lacroix glared at de Pontieux. 'When Suleiman forced us from our beloved Rhodes, we wandered as Israelites for eight years. For how long would you have us wander again? Eighty? Eight hundred?'

'The Grand Cross Lacroix plays with figures.'

'While you play with the future of the Religion, the destiny of our noble Order.'

Prior Garza, a Spaniard and ally of de Pontieux, jabbed his finger towards Lacroix. 'Within days, the Mohammedans will hold this Christian island, will have taken the city of Mdina, occupied the isle of Gozo, cut off our escape to the north. Our sole recourse is to parley with the Turk, to negotiate a truce and safe passage.'

'I cannot hear such things.'

'Nor can you feel the noose tightening about our necks.'

The Bishop slumped back in his pew. 'We see clearly, Brother Prior.'

'We seek merely to save the Religion.' Again it was de Pontieux, soothing, serpentine.

Lacroix shook his head, his face mottled with animosity. 'You seek merely to save yourselves.'

Argument flowed, The currents of dissent were strong, national differences and personal enmities, alliances and interests emerging or fragmenting as the officers squabbled. Threat could ever divide. Finally the Grand Master rose to his feet and walked to an open window. He appeared lost in thought, perhaps listening to the distant sounds from the narrow streets of Birgu or dwelling on the nearer debate. Talk subsided. The Council members watched him, suddenly mute, aware and ashamed of their own foolishness before their leader. His was a commanding presence.

'My brethren.'

He turned to face them, a tall man of seventy years with the military bearing of a general, the gravity and dignity of a priest. The beard was grey, the skin roughened by a life of battle. But the eyes of Jean Parisot de La Valette shone with a vehemence and certainty that held others in thrall. His nature, his standing, his steel will were forged from elements that induced others to follow. His audience were rapt.

'I stand before you, the forty-eighth Grand Master of this Order. An Order which has outlived the Templars and the Teutons, which has survived the ravages of time, the horrors of siege, the trials of men, and the tribulations of exodus. I was with the Knights when they left the island of Rhodes, forced out by the very Sultan who now sends his fleet against us.' La Valette looked about him, the intensity of his gaze raking the room. 'Some of you would have us hide. Others of you would have us reach accord with the heathen Turk. To what end? To our destruction, to our eternal shame and damnation, to the breaching of every sacred covenant we struck as hospitallers and warriors in the Holy Land. We may be few in number, but we are strong at heart. We may lack the mighty walls of Rhodes, but we have provisions and powder aplenty, and the Holy Spirit to guide us. Brother Knights, there is no more glorious thing than to seek death in the service of the Religion. Our Lord suffered and died for us on the bare rock of Golgotha. And for His sake, and in His name, we will find salvation on ours. I shall not be the last Grand Master. So make your peace. We stay and we endure.'

His statement was complete. It had served its purpose, had calmed doubt, quelled disunity. There would be no further discussion. It was time for prayer and reflection, for the commanders to make their final dispositions. The Castilian Knights would hold one of the great bastions of Birgu, the Knights of Auvergne, Provence and France would man the landward walls beside them. Arrayed elsewhere were the Knights of the German *langue* and those of Aragon, and the fighting squads of Sir Oliver Starkey, Englishman and Latin secretary to La Valette. They would protect the curtain walls leading up to Fort St Angelo. The heart of the Order, shielded by stone, secured with steel. From here on it would beat faster.

★

Unfortunate fools, mused the traitor. Neither their God nor their Grand Master could save them. Beyond the horizon, nosing its way westward across the Ionian and Mediterranean seas, was a vast and oncoming armada of Ottoman ships. Beyond this conclave of noblemen, of prelates and knights, were matters of state and politics, machinations to change the world. It could not be left to the clash of arms alone. He was present to see that unfair play was done. Where there was hope, he would bring discord and doubt. Where there was light, he would spread darkness. Malta was to be sacrificed. The traitor stared at his companions, future victims of his game and vision. They would surely die. By his hand, through his design.

The great door to the Council Chamber sounded to the knock of a stave. A page entered, bowing to the Grand Master and approaching to speak in a whisper. News had come. No other reason would warrant such interruption. The members of the Sacro Consiglio muttered in anticipation, straining to divine nuance, to read expression. It could be the Viceroy of Sicily sending word of reinforcements, might be a swift Christian galley reporting sightings of the enemy. Impending battle always bred tension.

La Valette nodded, and, while his page retreated to perform his duties, once more addressed the gathering. 'My brethren, it seems that contact with the enemy has been made. Their armies will yet be close behind.'

A collective frown creased the features of the assembled as Christian Hardy set foot inside the room and acknowledged them with a token dip of his head. He rarely stood on ceremony, barely recognized the mannered formalities of courtliness. It had not endeared him.

'Your Highness, members of the Supreme Council, I should report to you an action with the Turk on the east coast not six miles hence.'

'The nature of this action?' It was a conventual bailiff who asked.

'Five Mohammedans. Hiding in a shelter, scouting ahead of the main force.'

Grand Cross Lacroix peered at him. 'They are dead?'

'Indeed, sir.'

'We congratulate you.'

'And are there others of their kind?' It was the turn of de Pontieux to interject.

'I know not, sir.'

'For you failed to take captives, failed to ask questions.' His manner was wrapped in sarcasm and veiled hostility. 'And you have left us blind.'

'I have left myself alive.'

'For the present, no crime. But it would be of greater benefit to learn the opinions of the Turk.'

'They made their opinions clear, sir.'

Prior Garza joined his ally in the attack. 'Five are discovered and are now no more. Where is proof?'

'My word is proof.'

'The word of a commoner counts for little before the Sacro Consiglio.'

Lacroix slapped the side of his bench. 'To our besieged Order, the word of a fighting-man is everything.' Around him there were low murmurs of agreement.

Hardy slipped the linen pouch from his belt and threw it to the flagstoned ground. He stared at de Pontieux and Prior Garza. 'Proof, noble sirs. Within are five left ears from five dead souls.'

'A dagger or two would have sufficed.' De Pontieux smiled at the laughter he had generated. 'Besides, the heathen has no soul.'

The Grand Master raised his hand, and the chamber fell silent. It might have been a glint of humour in his eye, could have been paternal benevolence or patrician disapproval. The face remained closed. Hardy understood. For La Valette had once been a captive of the corsairs, had toiled and suffered as a slave on the rowing-bench of a galley. It changed men, hardened them, set them apart. He and La Valette occupied the remoter parts of the same realm.

'Urgency is upon us. These Saracen spies made landfall, and their fleet is behind. One day, two at most. At where will the Turk strike, Monsieur Hardy?'

'Towards us, Your Highness. Their spies were landed on the eastern side, I believe were headed south.'

'Marsamuscetto.'

'None other, Your Highness. The Turk is arrogant and full of confidence. He requires shelter for his galleys, will want quick victory for his Sultan.'

'I am of similar mind.'

'Then Fort St Elmo is the key, Your Highness.'

'The key to everything, Monsieur Hardy – to our triumph or defeat. Unlock St Elmo, they gain an anchorage. Gain the anchorage, they have access to every point, will invest Grand Harbour, hit us from all quarters. One by one, they will roll up our fortifications, crush us at their leisure.'

'We shall confound them, Your Highness.'

'That is our intent.' La Valette ran his fingers along his chain of office, traced the edges of the cross of St John. 'Make haste. Take my nephew, the Chevalier Henri de La Valette, ride for Mdina and instruct Governor Mesquita to return his infantry to these walls. It is here in Grand Harbour that the hammer-blow will fall.'

Christian Hardy bowed respectfully. The Grand Master was risking much, leaving Mdina vulnerable on the strength of his instinct. But the Maltese capital was expendable. It was in the forts of St Elmo, St Angelo and St Michael that the Knights would cluster to meet the foe and create their destiny. The Council Chamber was still hushed when Hardy left.

✳

Chapter 2

A hand clamped firm on his shoulder. 'You have the balls of a lion, the head of a bull, the ears of several dead Turk. A singular combination, young Hardy.'

It was Grand Cross Lacroix, his gruff voice and grizzled features emerging behind in the candlelit gloom of the corridor. Hardy turned to greet him,

'I am indebted to you for your assistance before the Sacro Consiglio, sir.'

'And I to you for your tenacity.' The veteran Knight smiled, his face wrinkling in admiration. 'Your example is one our greener brethren should hold to their hearts.'

'Many of your Council would disagree.'

'Let them. No Council ever charged the enemy, took a ship, thrust a blade in the throat of the heathen. In this hour of war, it is the gladiator, not the priest or politician, who is master.'

'You are yourself a venerated survivor of battle.'

'I am an old man, nothing more. But old men see things. Old men hear things.' He patted Hardy on the arm, fell into step as he resumed his walk. 'On what four principles, the arms of our cross, is the Order of St John established?'

'Prudence, temperance, fortitude and justice.'

'We have among us men who have forsaken these, officers who weaken as the Turk draws near.'

'Faith may renew itself in danger.'

'Or the spirit can be broken. Enmities flare, rivalries flourish. You have created adversaries of your own, young Hardy.'

'Prior Garza?'

'A snake.'

'De Pontieux?'

'A scorpion mated with a snake. He is calculating, ruthless, resentful of our sojourn on this island. Until Grand Master La Valette banished duelling, de Pontieux inflicted many wounds.'

'A character of several parts.'

'Most of them dangerous.' Lacroix halted, his perambulation done. 'Watch yourself, young Hardy. Watch others. You are favoured, well liked, by the Grand Master. Sometimes it is not enough.'

Hardy continued alone, his thoughts travelling to different matters, his steady pace carrying him on through hallways and passages. He was not a man to dwell on warnings, on the intrigue of the Supreme Council. A snake could be avoided, a scorpion ignored. He descended the stairway taking him from a cloistered twilight to the opening brightness of the lower gun-terrace. Below the serried muzzles of cannon, Grand Harbour stretched out languid and blue, its waters lapping at the base of the solitary St Elmo resting on its promontory above the north shore. A gull wheeled and screamed.

He reacted fast, intercepting the flung canister with an out-stretched hand. 'You play with fire, Moor.'

'While you play in the lion den of the Supreme Council, Christian Hardy.'

'Is there anything of which you are not informed?'

His friend had returned to crimping a wire. 'A black skin is a fine cloak for the blacker arts. I am poet and philosopher, eaves-dropper, gossip, studier of humankind, your guide and counsel.'

'I see today you are alchemist of war.'

Dressed in a white turban and long robe, the Moor sat cross-legged and content among the implements of his craft. Strewn about were clay pots and coils of fuse-string, jars of pitch and black powder, the constituents of incendiaries, the components for explosive. Arranged against a rampart wall were readied bundles of trumps, their hollowed wooden tubes filled with turpentine and linseed oil formulated to spew flame to fifteen feet or more. Beside them were fire-hoops, dipped and redipped in brandy, saltpetre, gunpowder and pitch, wrapped with cotton, saturated in oil, designed to catch enemies in their burning embrace. The black Moor was a perfectionist.

Hardy turned the sealed vessel in his palm, peering at the gummed lengths of string wrapped around its shallow neck. A simple object, and deadly. 'Your fire-grenade is a diabolic thing.'

'No mere fire, Christian Hardy. Wildfire. The best in either East or West. Saltpetre, pitch, sulphur, resin, salts of ammonia, and turpentine. A magic blend handed down from my ancestors.'

'The piss is all yours.'

'It may yet save these forts.' The Moor bent to apply sealing-wax to a completed piece of ordnance. 'My smokepot functioned?'

'The Turkish spies were more than a little cured.'

'What you see here will roast them. To where do you now travel?'

'Mdina. On errand for the Grand Master.'

'On command of your passions and your prick. The Lady Maria dwells in the city.'

'You tread dangerously, Moor.'

'You also. She is a Mediterranean beauty, the daughter of Maltese nobility. A Maltese nobility which resents the Order.'

'There was no resentment in her eye when she smiled at me in the groves of Naxxar.'

'Issues of war are more pressing.'

'They do not engage the heart.'

'So engage your head. There will be tens of thousands of enemy scaling these walls for the purpose of butchery.'

Hardy vaulted on to a ledge to scan the panorama. 'All in the name of God.'

'The name of God?' The Moor shook his head and quietly laughed. 'When a ruler commits his armies to battle it is for profit and gain, for lands, for gold, for trade, for power. If he does so in the name of God, he is thus a blasphemer and a liar.'

'The men who soldier for him?'

'Fools.'

'What are you and I?'

'Greater fools. For we do not belong. You are attached to the Service Brothers, employed as hired sword, I am a Moor, a despised Mohammedan, present for I was chained with La Valette at the oar of a galley belonging to corsair Abd-ur-Rahman Kust.'

'You saved the life of the Grand Master.'

'It is no guarantor of survival, no shield against all threat. Be careful, Christian Hardy.'

The encroaching atmosphere of siege was touching minds, affecting reason, Hardy decided. First Lacroix, then the Moor, advising caution, expressing concern. They minded too much. With a shout, he hailed the two figures approaching across the fortress esplanade. The comrades he had been awaiting.

'Henri, we must away to Mdina. The horses are saddled.'

'My uncle has requested we take Hubert. We are to convince the turbulent hermit-priest Fra Roberto to return to the confines of Birgu.'

Hubert smiled ruefully. 'A challenging undertaking.'

'While you, Henri, must convince the Maltese nobles in Mdina they have nothing to fear in the loss of our infantry.'

The smile from Henri de La Valette was weaker. Like his uncle the Grand Master, he was tall and solemn, a brave Hospitaller with a caring heart, a learned head and a serious disposition. Hardy had accompanied him often on caravan. He had initiated the young nobleman into the fighting ways of the Order, had parried scimitar-thrusts for him, had taken enemy galleys with him. Yet Henri sought God and texts, forever carried a devotional book of hours. In place of the killing-ground, he preferred the contemplation of the convent, the peace of the hospital. A true Knight. Hubert was different. At eighteen years of age, slight of build and unworldly in manner, he was a probationer, a conventual chaplain with a ready laugh and an optimistic outlook. Perhaps too decent by nature, too trusting for the cloth, he had arrived in the Order by chance, remained there almost by coincidence. The Chevalier Henri, the Chaplain Hubert, the Service Brother Christian. A trinity of comradeship.

'Observe.'

To the touch of a lit taper, the fire-hoop ignited. The Moor held it aloft in a pair of giant tongs, watching the fire race and explode on its inner frame. It was a fearsome sight. With a heave, the Moor launched it over the ramparts, the wheel spinning, tumbling, in its own raging incandescence towards the foot of St Angelo. The three friends craned to study its descent. In a pool of light, the hoop detonated and kept burning.

The Moor nodded in satisfaction. 'The next time, it will have its victims.'

From his vantage on the higher defences, the traitor watched the spiralling disc curve and disappear like a falling sun. Such instruments of war were of no consequence. They were hopeless measures undertaken by desperate men. Nothing would change. He had incendiary ideas of his own.

Astride their mounts, the three friends picked their way through the thronging alleyways of Birgu. The influx of refugees had swelled the population, the chatter of anxious voices, the press of bodies welling between the flat-roofed houses. From every quarter came a torrent of ceaseless sound. The rumble of carts, the neighing of horses, the ring and tap of blacksmith hammers and stonemason mallets, beating out time, counting down. There was armour to modify, chain-mail to repair, horseshoes to fit. In the main square, a squad of Maltese auxiliaries practised fighting hand to hand. In cellars and courtyards, barrels were stowed, swords and pikes stockpiled. Among it all trudged the gangs of captive slaves, hauling, ferrying, forced on by the lash.

The boy Luqa dodged a blizzard of escaping chickens and trotted to keep pace with Helios.

'Seigneur.' He called frantically to Hardy. 'I will ride with you.'

'Battle will not commence this day, Luqa. Stay with your people. They have need of you.'

'I wish to kill the Turk.'

'Ensure he does not kill you first. Build the defences.'

'Where, seigneur? How, seigneur?'

'Visit the powder-mills and carry the gunpowder. Visit the smithies and polish the steel. Visit my friend the Moor and cut fuses, fill the pots.'

'Dull work for a soldier, seigneur.'

'It may save a life. That life may save yours.'

They left Luqa in the dusty street and made for the central gate between the bastions. The Castilian Knights were already taking up position, cleaning guns, heaving cannon-shot in hessian nets towards the battlements. Shouts of salutation and encouragement were exchanged as the horsemen passed by. Henri de La Valette gazed silently upward at the murder-holes of the stone passage-way. Such moments could put a man in reflective mood.

The drawbridge was down. They crossed it in single file, their attention drawn by the sights and sounds, by the light playing off the bastion walls, by the lines of Moslem slaves labouring to deepen the defensive ditchwork. The last details were being finessed, the final unpleasant surprises incorporated for the invader. There would before long be further Mohammedans struggling in the ditch, Christian Hardy thought to himself. He nudged Helios with his feet, and felt the stallion accelerate into the gallop. Behind, Hubert was whooping, giving chase, forgetting dignity and horsemanship in favour of exuberance. Henri followed more soberly. It would have been unseemly for a nobleman, a Knight Commander, nephew to the Grand Master, to appear uncontrolled. In this fashion, and in a travelling cloud of dust, they advanced towards Mdina.

On the rising escarpment leading to the ridge-line and the walled city of Mdina, teams of Maltese were filling clay bottles with spring water for transport to Birgu. Water elsewhere was scarce – in the Grand Harbour home of the Knights was almost entirely absent. This was the answer. The population had given their menfolk to the militia; now they gave the lifeblood of their aquifers and streams. And there among the women and children, barefoot, smiling, laughing, her long dark hair tied back in a simple kerchief, her arms splashed wet, was Maria.

'Henri, continue to the Governor. Hubert, go find your priest. I shall attend later.'

The young La Valette halted alongside and shaded his eyes. 'Chastity and obedience, the foundations of our Order.'

'They will not crumble with mere conversation.'

'Christian, the enemy lies over the horizon.'

'The more reason to still the soul, to find peace and comfort in one's heart.'

'Reason? She is a noblewoman, you are no Knight.'

'You sound as the Moor.'

'The Moor is wise.'

'I may dream, Henri.'

'You may also pay your respects to Governor Mesquita, conduct with me the business on which we are sent.'

'In good time.'

He spurred Helios on to the rocky incline, heard the sigh of acceptance from Henri, the suppressed mirth of Hubert. Maria had lifted her head, had become aware of him. She straightened, observed his oncoming with the elegant insouciance of superiority. But her eyes. They were warm-brown and deep, and danced with a spirit independent of breeding or accident of birth. He was held by them. Helios nodded, walking carefully on uneven ground.

'My lady.' He slid from his saddle and bowed extravagantly before her.

'A visitor with the manners of a gentleman yet the clothing of a corsair. I am curious.'

'I too, my lady. A noblewoman who toils barefoot in a stream.'

'It is my duty.'

'You make merry while you work.'

'There will be days enough to weep, Monsieur Hardy.'

'You know my name?'

'Your reputation also.'

'It disturbs you, my lady?'

'It does not. Yet your presence disrupts.' Her lips parted in a half-smile, the bottle in her hand spilling its contents. 'There are a thousand vessels to fill – ten thousand.'

'I would glad go without water for this moment, my lady.'

'My father would be happy to see you thirst.'

'Our argument is with the Turk.'

'And for the Turk he roundly blames you. He has no love for the Order of St John. Nor have the other ruling families of this city. They condemn the Knights for the woes befalling us. They rail against your piracy which has so enraged the Ottoman Sultan.'

'The message we bring today will not improve their temper.'

'One cannot reason with them.'

'Yet you, my lady, stand with fellow citizens beyond the walls and collect water for us.'

Her eyes acquired the lustre of defiance. 'Your religion is our religion. Your enemies are our enemies.'

'Our island is your island.'

'It will for ever be our island.' Whether you remain or go, her inflection suggested.

He would remain, he decided. 'The enterprise will be bloody, my lady. Why did you not depart for the safety of Sicily?'

'Why not you, Monsieur Hardy?'

'I am a soldier.'

'I am the daughter of one of the oldest houses. My brother and widowed father stay. I will abide with them, with the people and defenders of Malta.'

He was grateful for that, appreciative too for the stolen glimpses and occasional glances exchanged among the groves and physic herbs of nearby villages. She was no mirage, but flesh and blood, a composite of inner light and outward perfection. It was beguiling; it was breathtaking.

Crouching, he took a bottle and filled it from the spring. An excuse to tarry, to extend the moment. She looked on, teasing. 'The fighting cock on his knees. A rare sight.'

'To become rarer.' He presented her with the flask. 'I am late for matters with the Governor.'

'You will find him with my father.'

'Then it is a day for family business.' He bowed and put his lips to her proffered hand.

'My father is no ogre, Monsieur Hardy. He cares for his island and his city.'

'As do I.' He swung himself on to Helios and wheeled the horse. 'I trust to see you again, my lady.'

'I have no doubt you shall.'

With a shake of the mane and flick of the tail, the stallion headed for the gates of Mdina. Hardy glanced back along the slope. Maria was staring after him.

'The tide has brought us further driftwood.'

It was a barbed remark, intended to sting. An old man inconvenienced, an aged bystander witnessing the ruin of his home, Maria's father scowled at him. Gone were the aspects of Mdina which had earned it the sobriquet of the Silent City. Like Birgu, it was pregnant with the noise of influx and activity; as in Birgu, the shaded streets played host to preparations for combat. But in the coolness of this palace courtyard only Governor Mesquita of the Order of St John, Henri de La Valette and the late-arrived Christian Hardy were present to endure the wrath of a lame Maltese nobleman.

Hardy maintained his poise. 'I, driftwood? Even driftwood may be salvaged, sir.'

'Or it may end rotting and despoiling on the shore. Like the rest of you. Like every Knight who sets foot upon our island.' The elderly aristocrat pounded his walking-cane on the cobbles. 'What have you done for us? What do you now bring down upon our heads?'

Henri was grave. 'We defend the Religion, sir.'

'You defend your privileges, your forts, your positions at Grand Harbour. We are left with women and children to guard the walls of Mdina.'

'The Grand Master believes the blow will fall elsewhere.'

'How convenient for La Valette. And if he is mistaken? If the Turk should choose to devour us here?'

'We are all in the hands of God.'

'I trust He will show more mercy and wisdom than the Order in whose care we have rested these thirty-five years long.'

'There are some four thousand Maltese militia, monsieur.' Colour spots of exasperation had developed in the Governor's cheeks. 'They stand beside the Knights on the walls of Senglea and Birgu, believe in the justness of the cause.'

'Justness? Where is justness when disaster is upon us?'

'We face the same invader.'

'You, a Portuguese Knight from an alien Order, presume to speak of invasion. It seems one invader begets another.' The rheumy and baleful gaze returned to Henri. 'And you, a nephew of La Valette who acts as messenger and executioner, who strips our city of its infantry.'

'I do my duty.'

'As I do mine. I have a son and daughter. Are they to die for naught, my people to perish or be carried to slavery on account of the vanity and pride of forgotten Crusaders?'

'Be careful of what you say, sir.' Governor Mesquita had been goaded enough.

'I will not.' The old man spat his contempt. 'You even bring this Englishman, this wildcat who leads charges against Ottoman ships, who goads the Sultan to unholy war. He is the architect of our damnation.'

'You credit me with much.' Hardy bowed.

'I damn you with every thought, with every fibre of my soul.'

Even driftwood may be salvaged. He should thank this old man with the hate-filled face, be grateful for the gift of his daughter. While others dwelt on coming battle, he could think of her. She was further reason to stand and fight.

There was commotion, the ordered tension in the courtyard broken by distant tumult. Shouts echoed from the street. Behind came the murmured outrage and excitement of a crowd, the protest of guards, the crash of doors.

The Governor rolled his eyes. 'It will be Fra Roberto.'

In confirmation, Hubert appeared, running, gasping to catch his breath, to deliver his news in wheezing panic. 'Christian, Henri. The priest is in Mdina. He is beyond control.'

'He is ever beyond control.' The Governor smiled a thin and tired smile. 'I wish you luck, gentlemen.'

Henri bowed. 'We are three in number to return him to Birgu, Governor Mesquita.'

'Return? First you must apprehend him.'

Maria's father was shaking his head, his expression framed in accusation. 'See! Your priests offend and transgress our codes. What hope for the remainder of your Order?'

Hardy answered. 'They will show themselves in combat, sir.'

Fra Roberto was in town. A bearded giant of a man in tattered robes, he was fighting, was plainly fighting drunk. Two soldiers crashed against a water-butt, a third collided with a wall. It was an unequal contest, and the victor strutted and paraded, beat his

chest, and gaped with pleasure at his bemused audience. A pair of
burly locals threw themselves at him, were cast aside. A man with
a club rushed him, was punched flat. He received a blessing on
the way. The priest continued his unpredictable circuit, roaring
his challenge, muttering oaths, offering up prayers. Occasionally
he stumbled, but recovery was swift. At other times he was light
on his feet, weaving and dodging, shadow-boxing and prancing.
All comers were welcome. He seemed impervious to attack.

'*Enough.*'

He whirled to meet the provocation, received the water full in
the face. Confused, he blinked, wiping his streaming eyes, shaking
his clinging hair. The tip of a sword was held towards him.

'You would strike down a holy man?'

Henri did not flinch. 'Holy men do not brawl. Brothers of our
Order do not bring it into disrepute.' Beside him, Hardy carried
the emptied bucket.

'Whom is it I have the pleasure of addressing?'

'Chevalier Henri de La Valette. Nephew to the Grand Master.'

'You honour me.' The priest lifted his robe and sank deep into
an ironic and ungainly curtsy.

'I prefer you on your feet, Fra Roberto.'

'A disciplinarian like your uncle.' Wincing, he struggled
upright. 'And who is your companion, the pretty milkmaid with
her pail?'

'Christian Hardy.'

An eyebrow raised. 'I have heard tell of you. A fine soldier,
accomplished with sword, bow and water-pitcher. How are you
with fists?' The priest raised his balled hands and began to sway.

Henri maintained his guard. 'Save your energies for the Turk.'

'Save your breath for those who care. Leave me to my life of
quiet contemplation.'

'It is neither quiet nor contemplative. Why come to Mdina?'

'Rumours of war, a desire to test myself among the populace
of Sodom and Gomorrah, a necessity for victuals.'

'Are locusts and wild honey not enough for the hermit?'

'I have a body to nourish.'

'A habit to feed. You are drunk.'

The priest shrugged and belched. 'The rocks and caves are no judge of sobriety, young Chevalier La Valette.'

'Our court will judge more harshly. You will return with us this hour to Birgu.'

'To reacquaint myself with old friends? How is that shit Prior Garza?'

'He remains a loyal brother to our Order.'

'Brother? You wish to hear of brothers?' The finger wagged. 'Garza has a twin, a Franciscan in the employ of the Spanish Inquisition. A charmer, by all accounts. Good with his hands. They call him the spit-boy for his efforts in burning heretics.'

'Auto-da-fé and the practices of the Inquisition are not our concern, Fra Roberto.'

'De Pontieux, a shit thrice over. What of he?'

'Our forts and our Order are imperilled. You are obliged to join us.'

'If I should refuse?'

'We shall carry you in chains.'

'An escort for my procession?' Fra Robert gave a happy smile. 'The Grand Master has need of me.'

'He requests your presence. Nothing more.'

The priest nodded and sauntered to the water-butt. Without a word, he plunged his head deep inside. When satisfied, and again soaked, he emerged and ambled back to deliver his verdict.

'As brother chaplain, as true servant to the Religion, as former secretary to the Sacro Consiglio, I will follow the Word of God and obey the command of Jean Parisot de La Valette. We go.'

The deal was done. Hubert approached with caution, emerging from his refuge among the thinning crowd of onlookers. He was greeted with a bellow of approval and enveloped in a bear-embrace. The probationer had acted as a lowly messenger, a go-between for the Order and its volatile and wayward son. Friendship had developed. But Hubert was right to be wary, to tiptoe as lightly as would a keeper around a barely tamed beast.

Eventually, with the mission complete, a horse and cart requisitioned, and the afternoon light fading towards early dusk, the four men were ready to depart. Fra Roberto clambered aboard the wagon and took the reins.

'So this is how I am to travel to hell.'

Astride his horse, Henri moved into position alongside. 'Only the infidels will journey that way. We seek paradise.'

'Perhaps, Brother Chevalier, we each shall find it.'

Their small caravan jolted into movement, joining the flow of others heading for Grand Harbour. Above the walls of Mdina, construction was under way. They were building gallows in anticipation of their first Turkish prisoners. As Fra Roberto slapped the reins and the pace quickened, the sky was seeping pink in the west and blood-dark shadows stretched across the fields of purple clover.

Dressed in steel cuirass and holding a two-handed longsword, Grand Master de La Valette stood aloft on a trestle platform. Behind was the towering edifice of Fort St Angelo. To his front were the massed and armoured ranks of his garrisons. Not a whisper could be heard, not a man shuffled or moved, coughed or created sound. They gazed up at their leader. He was transfigured, an ancient warrior before battle, Charlemagne resurrected, a general imbued with the Holy Spirit and communicating the Word of God. The sermon came.

'My brothers, the hour of darkness is at hand, and the struggle between the Cross and Koran begins. It is on us that the forces of the infidel will fall. It is on us that the future destiny of Europe and civilization rests. Should we fail, all Christian nations will follow into the fiery pit, and the banner of the heathen crescent will fly above every city across our ancient lands. We are few in number. But few in history have been honoured,

blessed, with such vocation. Look not to others for your deliverance. Look to yourselves, and to God. For we are the chosen soldiers of the Cross. And if heaven demands the sacrifice of our lives, there can be no better occasion, no finer position, than this. It is our duty. It is our calling. It is our time. Let us break bread as Our Lord broke bread. Let us renew our vows through the Holy Sacrament. Let the sword be our cross. Be steadfast in the Religion and stand fast at your posts. Have faith. Embrace death. Exult in bloodshed. At the Day of Judgement, we shall be counted · among the saved. Thus will we walk with saints, thus are we rendered invincible. Prepare.'

Trumpets blew, drums rolled, and La Valette led his men in solemn procession through the streets of Birgu to the Conventual Church. There they prayed to the Lord of Mercies, prostrated themselves before the crucified Christ and the jewelled reliquary containing the hand of St John the Baptist. Outside, the pace of the slave-gangs did not slacken. A giant chain some two hundred yards in length, forged by the smithies of Venice, supported by rafts, was raised by capstan below St Angelo to seal the channel entrance between Birgu and Senglea. In the sea-moat behind the fort, the galleys were secured. And over at Fort St Elmo on the north side of Grand Harbour the work crews continued to labour, to strengthen the earthworks of the outer ravelin, to build up the stone blocks of the inner walls.

The bell of the Conventual Church tolled. In their tunnels and cellars, the people huddled and waited. On the ramparts, singing hymns and saying prayers, the Knights of the Order of St John of Jerusalem stepped up to their positions.

Above the earth hillock at the spur end of Senglea, the sails of two windmills turned on the easterly breeze. It was the same favourable wind that carried the Turk.

Chapter 3

'*F*etch others! Sound the alert!*'

It was the morning of Friday 18 May 1565. The lookouts had seen something. In the dawn mist, the shapes were vague, ghostly smudges emerging and dematerializing on the far horizon. On the high cavalier towers of St Elmo and St Angelo, eyes strained. False alarms were not uncommon. Nerves could conjure illusion from the air. But the apparitions stayed, solidifying into the form of ships, growing in number until they colonized the entire north-eastern skyline. As the haze lifted, the warning cannon of St Elmo boomed. It was answered by three blasts from St Angelo, repeated from the walls of Mdina, carried to the citadel on the island of Gozo. There was no mistake. Beacons flared. From battlements and coastal watchtowers, pinpricks of light blazed their story, tracing the eighteen-mile length and nine-mile breadth of Malta. The massed invasion fleet of Suleiman the Magnificent had arrived.

Christian Hardy sat in the saddle and walked Helios on. They had joined the cavalry detail tracking the fleet, and watched as the armada turned south and processed down the coast. A breathtaking sight, the squadrons of galleys under sail and oar, gliding in long gilded formation less than half a mile from the horsemen on their clifftop trail. Hours passed. The fleet never paused or diverted. Delimara Point, Marsasirocco Bay, the fishing-village of Zurrieq, the islet of Filfla. Places bypassed, landing-sites ignored. Occasionally an object splashed soundless in the water, another body of a galley slave discarded overboard. Those who slackened at a rowing-bench were beaten to death where they sat. The law of the sea, the way of the Ottoman. Everything was designed to terrify. It was a victory parade before the final surrender had been taken or the first shot fired. The Turk had every reason to be confident.

Nightfall. All day the horsemen had stalked the ships, had observed the pilot tending his depth-line in the lead galliot, had picked out the majestic shapes of the galleys ferrying Mustapha Pasha and Admiral Piali. The stroke-beat of the drums went on, the cry of the mullahs calling for blood and holy triumph gusted on the breeze. It gave the defenders time to ponder, provided them reason to weaken with fear. Now the enemy were anchored. Wrapped in a cloak, Hardy rested against the warm and sleeping form of Helios and gazed out from the cliffs of Ghain Tuffieha. Below, the light from a thousand lanterns sparkled on the dark waters like fallen stars. He could almost smell the galley interiors, could imagine the stench of suffering and decay, invoke the sights, the sounds, of chained humanity bleeding in its own filth. They were the memories of North Africa.

He would remain awake. Perhaps he had been wrong – the Grand Master too. It was conceivable the Turk would make landing here on the west side of the island, would march inland to take Mdina, the interior, to impose a slow death on the Knights. But it was unlikely. This was a ruse. The enemy needed shelter, a harbour, water for their army, the glory of direct attack, and that was to the east. He could wait. In these early hours, he would maintain vigil, keep company with his thoughts, feel the steady rise and fall of Helios breathing. Some men trembled at proximity to the foe. Not he. He was fascinated by their strength and presence, drawn to the echoes of his youth. His fellow soldiers might test their faith. He would test himself. The skirmishes, the boarding-parties, the raids on Moslem towns, they were merely preludes to this moment. On the cliffs above the Turkish navy, life had purpose.

As the day brightened to a new morn, the ships weighed anchor and began to retrace their passage southward around the island.

He had been right. Ottoman soldiers were streaming ashore at Marsasirocco, fanning outward, spreading inland and heading for the bleak and undulating approaches to Grand Harbour. At the abandoned village of Zeitun, a party of Janissaries and support levies foraged for food. But the livestock had gone, the fields were bare and the dwellings emptied of vegetables or grain. Even goat dung had been removed as potential fuel for fires; even drystone walls had been carried off to prevent their use as shelter. The imprint of La Valette was here, the effects of his edict everywhere. A Janissary officer spat with disgust at the barren earth.

Helios whinnied and bucked his head. He had seen the aim-point. Along the line of cavalry, raw anticipation of the kill was infecting spirits, affecting all. Hardy steadied the stallion. Beside him, bridles jangled, horses snorted, and the rasp and clatter of armour, lances and unsheathed swords sounded harsh, forbidding, in the midday sun. They were a hundred strong, a cavalry detachment sent out on sweeping patrol. Targets of opportunity were to be engaged, unprotected infantry would be cut down. Emerging from dead ground, they had found what they were looking for. Contact was made.

'*For God and the Religion. Charge!*'

The torrent moved, and Hardy rode the surge. It was uncontrolled, visceral, a rage that descended in a thundering acceleration of hooves and howling men. Helios foamed at the mouth, his eyes rolling, his ears flattening. He was part of the stampede. Hardy leaned low against his neck, exultant, shouting his euphoria. The red haze settled. Individual acts slowed into a collective madness. Turks ran or fell, stood to fire arquebuses, knelt to elevate pikes. To no avail. They were hacked down or impaled. Hardy watched his sword-arm reach out, a head lift from its neck, the fountain-gush

44

of blood. The vignette passed at the gallop. Another took its place, soundless, wordless, the slaughter distant.

A Knight somersaulted dead from his horse, his face shot away. Hardy recognized the heraldic badge. It belonged to Mesquita, a young Portuguese probationer and nephew of the Governor of Mdina. The first of the European nobility to die. Hardy swerved Helios into a turn and rode down a shrieking levy who had abandoned his weapon, surrendered all hope. The man floundered. Hardy leaned from the saddle and cut clean through his spine. One convulsion, and movement ceased. A trio of Spahis had joined the grim confusion, their plumed Arab horses circling for an arrow sight-line, then chasing in at speed. Helios shook with delight. He met the lead head on, rearing, biting, his raking hooves unseating the rider as he tried to raise a steel mace. Hanging from his stirrup, the Moslem presented himself for butchering. The blade went in.

'Kill me! Brothers, kill me!'

Held by the arms, a wounded Knight was being born away between the two remaining Spahi horsemen. He screamed and struggled as he went, his legs kicking. The grip of his captors was unrelenting. They would retrieve some honour, a single prize, from this debacle. Not without a chase. Hardy spurred Helios in pursuit, but a musket-ball gouging leather from his jacket warned of other threats, of infantry to his flank. He slashed with his sword at an arquebusier fumbling to reload. Blade and hilt reddened. Another Turk challenged in vain, the butt of his musket raised to strike. Hardy lunged, Helios completed. The Spahis and their prisoner were gone.

There would be no loitering. Hit and run, strike and hide did not allow for a gentle survey of the battle aftermath. More Spahis might appear, a regiment of Janissaries march into view. It was time to withdraw. The wounded were counted, enemy weapons collected, the corpse of young Mesquita roped across his horse, and the heads of the Moslem slain struck from their bodies. Hardy wiped the sweat from his eyes and returned the congratulatory salute of the commander. The killings were the start. They would be forgotten in the brutality to come.

Two days after the initial sighting of the Turkish fleet, Mustapha Pasha came ashore. Mounted on a white Arab charger, accompanied by his war council, the commander-in-chief of the Ottoman army made his way in grand review to the tented encampment near the shore. He could permit himself a small inward smile, allow himself the indulgence of a military parade. It felt right to be on Malta. It was good to be at the beginning of a campaign that would praise God, glorify Suleiman, nourish this rock desert with the blood and entrails of Christians. Trappings of pomp and pageant merely confirmed the might of empire. Formed-up ranks of Janissaries, their scimitars drawn and gleaming, the heron plumes of their headdress waving, only confirmed the speed at which victory would be achieved. The war was already won.

In a blaze of gaudy silks, and to the sound of trumpets, the senior officers reached their temporary quarters. Tomorrow or the next day they would move, would take up residence at the command posts overlooking Grand Harbour. At this very moment their forces were pushing past Zabban, making for the terrain above Birgu. Soon the first banner would crest the hill-line to strike terror in the hearts of the Knights. Soon too the entire weight of the Turkish war-machine would smash the walls of the infidel redoubts. Things would come to pass. The officers could afford to rest after their long voyage. They would drink their sherbets, smoke hashish, consort with their prostitutes. Anything to pass time before they counted the plunder of conquest.

Mustapha Pasha glared at Admiral Piali. He had known it was a bad mix, the capricious Sultan unwise to impose dual command on a key expedition. Pure delusion, total absurdity. It set his fire against Piali's coolness, his experience against Piali's exaggeration, his land campaigns against Piali's token naval raids. Mustapha

Pasha: feared and fearless general. Admiral Piali: pampered court favourite and political manipulator of the harem. The Sultan believed them complementary. A nagging ache was never complementary.

'You have made it to land, Admiral Piali.'

'I am as comfortable here as at sea.'

But not as welcome. Mustapha Pasha seated himself on a silk cushion. 'At the least your precious galleys are secure.'

'Galleys which have transported your men, your horses, your munitions these many miles. Without my fleet, you would have no invasion.'

'Without my army, you would have no impending annihilation of the Knights, no reason to return to Constantinople in triumph.'

'It appears we are wedded to the same goal, Mustapha Pasha.'

'Chained to the same oar, Piali.'

The Admiral smiled. 'A fascinating dilemma. One which I am sure we may overcome with tact and patience.'

'I have shown patience, Piali. For no other reason did I accept your plan to assault these southern parts of Malta.'

'It is where the Knights reside, Mustapha Pasha.'

'And to the north is where danger lies. If Christian reinforcements should arrive from Sicily? If a relief army establishes itself on the coast or takes shelter in Mdina?'

'Achieve quick victory, they will be of no concern.'

'The view of an admiral.'

'Of a tactician and leader. My ships require anchorage. The Knights control it.'

'We are safe enough here.'

'Until the winds come, the gales blow. I need Marsamuscetto, the harbour guarded by Fort St Elmo, the harbour that leads us to Grand Harbour.'

'Dragut will disagree.'

'Dragut is not married to the daughter of the heir to the

Ottoman throne.' It was a warning shot, a pointed reminder of where real power lay.

Mustapha Pasha did not rise to the insult. He was artful enough to recognize the manoeuvrings, to have the measure of his rival. Certainly, Piali had his naval fleet. He enjoyed strong factional support. But he would overplay his hand, as the arrogant and uninitiated always did. Besides, the infidel would be defeated on land, and that was an army matter, his own domain, the realm of the siege-engineer, the gunner, the sharpshooter, the soldier with the sword. For the sake of expediency and shallow unity, Mustapha Pasha would swallow his contempt.

There were ways to vent anger, to work through frustration. He entered the interrogation tent and ordered the torturers to leave. They had been busy. Outstretched and manacled on the plank-wood table was the naked and fractured body of a man. Mustapha Pasha drew close. The sight of such living remnants did not disturb him. Fingers and toes were missing, the right leg was broken, the skin was livid with welts and burns. Yet it was a thing of monstrous beauty. For here was a near-mythic creature, a wounded Knight of St John, a repository of information. And it sobbed and prayed in its own tongue.

'War is a bloody affair.' Speaking Italian, the General chewed contemplatively on a piece of Turkish delight. 'You are Adrien de La Rivière?'

'I am.' The words issued slow and painful between cracked lips.

'A noble name for such an ignoble fate.'

Silence followed. The captive might have fainted, might have let his concentration lapse. Mustapha took another bite of *rahat lokum* and drew up a stool, the easier to observe, to converse. Sweetness trickled in the back of his throat.

'You were foolish to mount a cavalry charge, Adrien de La Rivière.'

'It was my given task.'

'To squander your life on meaningless gesture?'

'I suffer as my Lord Jesus suffered.'

'You will suffer many times worse.' Mustapha Pasha leaned close, could smell the sweat and blood, see the shallow rise and fall of the chest. 'Where is your God, Adrien de La Rivière?'

'He is with me.'

'I am with you, infidel whore. How you live is at my determination. How you die is with my judgement.'

'I have my faith.'

'You have fear.'

It was well justified. The General watched the travelling shudder vibrate along the torso. Such encounters rarely differed. Captives could be strong or weak, brave or cowardly, contemptuous or craven. But they were all afraid. They all opened up to the pliers and the branding-iron. He had seen it Austria and Hungary, had witnessed it in Persia. Varied languages, the same result. Chevalier La Rivière was an unexceptional find.

'Tell me, Knight. Survivors of your action speak of a fighting-man on a grey steed, a fighting-man dressed as common corsair who kills like a devil.'

'Christian Hardy. An Englishman.'

'Your Grand Master draws widely for his pirates. None will survive.'

'They will be exalted in the Kingdom of Heaven.'

'They shall enter it as butchered meat. For tomorrow our armies descend on their fortifications. Tomorrow we find if you told the truth of flaws in their defence.'

'I did not lie.'

'You inform us that the walls of Birgu are weak, that the Castilian Knights in its great bastion are few in number.'

'We are spread thin. Grand Master de La Valette has sent them elsewhere.'

Mustapha Pasha struck the broken shin-bone of the man with a metal baton, and with force. The screams lasted a long while, the captured Knight wrenching and animated in his restraints.

49

Eventually the noise subsided to an extended groan. Mustapha gripped the distorted face between his thumb and forefinger.

'Do not trifle with me, infidel dog. You say again the Castile bastion is frail?'

'Yes . . . yes.' The answer was faint, came in a line of dribbled wretchedness.

'If you deceive, I will have you bastinadoed before the ramparts.'

'I have told of everything.'

'Then I too shall share a secret.'

He bent close to the ear of the stricken French Knight and spoke softly of the spy at the heart of the Order of St John. That spy would make contact, would ensure the destruction of the Knights from within. La Rivière whimpered. Revelation could be an unkind thing. As Jesus had been betrayed by Judas, so La Valette and his armed disciples would be undermined. Betrayal, integral to the Christian narrative, would become central to the unfolding siege. There was no harm in confiding to a condemned man. The Knight was a captive audience.

His tale complete, Mustapha Pasha rose to take his leave. He had much to oversee for the following day. In one morning he would test the mettle of these cornered Knights. In a headlong charge he might topple them from their ramparts. Only if it failed would he turn his attention to St Elmo, comply with the wishes of the irrepressible Admiral. Point-scoring never came cheap. He would reward La Rivière with an expedited death. Would that it were Piali stretched out upon the slab. The Turkish general spat full in the face of the prone chevalier and departed.

They were a multitude, an insect swarm of bright colours and exotic display rolling from the south. Monday 21 May 1565, and the Turks were pushing forward, probing the Christian front. Their intention was to kill. From the landward walls of Birgu and Senglea, the call to arms rang out. Men crouched low or crowded to see, gunners primed their cannons. It was their hour. Across the uneven plain, the triangular banners and clashing music of the Ottoman came on, the ground trembling, the skyline shimmering, the air awash with menace and moment. Far off, the Christian cavalry could be seen, circling and darting in, dashing itself without effect against the onward enemy advance. Nothing would slow the attack.

On the crenellated heights of the Castile bastion, Grand Master La Valette stood with his senior officers. He waited and watched. The foe would soon be within range of the guns. Yet the Turks had prepared no bombardment of their own. Mustapha Pasha could absorb casualties, was indifferent to loss of life. It was a statement. He squandered manpower simply to awe the defenders and pinpoint weakness. A costly approach.

'An immense sight, Your Highness.'

La Valette gazed ahead. 'The Greeks repulsed the armies of Xerxes. With God's great mercy, we shall do the same.'

'The cavalry acquit themselves well.'

'They perform in the manner expected.'

The Knight de Pontieux cleared his throat. 'They take many casualties, Your Highness.'

'It is the nature of war, Brother Chevalier.'

De Pontieux squinted at the distant scene. 'There are a number of young Knights eager to join them in the fray.'

'We shall conserve their vigour within these defences. Our numbers are too few to waste beyond the walls.'

'Too late, Your Highness.'

The Knight pointed. Below, streaming on foot across the draw-bridge, hundreds of defenders were rushing to confront the enemy. They carried battleaxes and pikes, longswords and maces, their Christian banners fluttering in challenge to the Moslem horde, their chants of defiance rising to the ears of La Valette and his lieutenants. To the right and left, musketeers loaded their weapons; in front, crossbowmen knelt to unleash their bolts.

Grand Cross Lacroix turned from his observation point, his face crumpled with rage and concern. 'It is madness, Your Highness. They will be slain. I shall order recall.'

'No.' La Valette paused, his manner unruffled. 'Let us turn the madness to advantage.'

'Our men have disobeyed orders, Your Highness. They lack discipline.'

'Yet they have zeal.'

'It will not suffice against such weight. You cautioned yourself against this action.'

'Indeed, not a minute past, Brother Grand Cross. But a situation may change in that minute; a war may be won or lost in that minute.'

'Permit me to join our young brethren in the field, Your Highness.' It was de Pontieux seizing back the moment. 'They will require the counsel of older heads.'

'I too require the counsel of older heads. Events shall proceed as they are. We will blood our young Knights, demonstrate to the infidel Turk the qualities of our fighting spirit. Then neither side may doubt the nature of the battle to come.'

There could be no doubt. With a swelling roar, the massed Ottoman army threw itself against the defenders, concentrating its force on the bastion of Castile. Above, La Valette was onlooker to the shuddering tableau. He ordered the cannons to fire, their muzzles belching, smoke and flame lancing from platforms and towers, shot tearing wide and ragged wounds in the body of the enemy ranks. Gaps filled, the Turk drove on. The fronts met in a clawing impact, the haphazard butchery rendered almost orderly at a distance. But the shouts and cries, the ring and clash of steel, the stuttering ripple of arquebus reports could only mean killing.

In a tide of coloured silk and lamellar plate, the Turks charged the ditch, were repelled, and tried again. A Knight in gleaming silver armour led a counter-charge, his sword held high. He faltered as though stunned and disappeared, consumed beneath stampeding feet and hacking blades. Surrounded and cut off, a squad of Christian arquebusiers fumbled to reload. They were too slow. In another pocket, an armoured phalanx of defenders cut a swathe for others to follow. The dead mounted, and the Turks pressed in.

Without uttering a sound, a Spanish soldier dropped dead at the feet of La Valette. His eye had become an entry wound.

The Grand Master glanced down. 'I must commend the Turk on his marksmanship. It far surpasses our own.'

A second musket-ball found its mark, a page screeching in pain and clutching at his neck.

'Your Highness, it becomes too dangerous for you here.'

'What of down there?' La Valette nodded at the tumult below. 'Would you have me desert them? Would you have me cower from my fate?'

'At least pull back behind the curtain wall, sir. The bastion is exposed.'

'Then we are all equally in the hands of God.'

He was an example to them all, the traitor mused, a mighty oak standing proud against the storm. But how easily trees could be felled, their limbs removed, their trunks chopped, their roots poisoned. Planning had taken time, and execution was in train. It depended on this moment, on the arrival of the Turks. Slowly the defenders were being forced back, crushed by numerical strength. La Valette would have little choice but to sound the retreat. The traitor felt the ricochet of a musket-ball pass hot and hissing near his cheek. He edged back. Others were better placed to play the role of victim.

Battle was done. It had been six hours of hard fighting, had cost the lives of some twenty-one Knights. But the enemy dead littered the ground in their hundreds, bloodied piles chewed up by cannon-shot or cut down with sword and halberd. Perhaps

Mustapha Pasha had learned a lesson. Or possibly he had delivered one, was demonstrating his contempt for the encircled garrisons. Wearily, the defenders staggered back through the streets of Birgu. Some were elated, others dulled by shock, the able-bodied carrying the wounded or lending shoulders to the lame. All would give thanks in the Conventual Church for their initial survival and early success.

'Seigneur, where is Helios your horse?' The boy Luqa had been awaiting his return.

Hardy tossed him a gold-and-gem-set ornament and continued to guide an injured soldier.

'We cannot have a horse share in the plunder. I sent him to Mdina with the rest of the cavalry.'

'You do not go with him?'

'My place is here.'

'Mine also, seigneur. I have been carrying powder from the mills to the guns, filling ordnance pots for the Moor.'

'We rely on you, Luqa.'

'How many infidel did you kill this time, seigneur?'

'Enough.' He rattled the looted bracelets on his forearm.

'They are precious?'

'They are Turkish and won in holy struggle. It puts them beyond price.'

The boy seemed happy with the news. He kept pace, asking questions, demanding detail. Answers were relayed on, feeding the rumours and the mood of celebration. Fra Roberto strode by and winked, a dead Knight in full armour slung across his shoulder. The priest appeared oblivious to the weight. It would have been close to three hundred pounds. Behind, Hubert carried the steel helmet of the Knight and a linen shroud. They were bound for a chapel, and the first of several funerals.

Knight Grand Cross Lacroix was emerging from the doorway to a storehouse. 'A tough contest, young Hardy.'

'There will be tougher to come, sir.'

'You are already acclaimed as a champion. The Grand Master and his war council observed your horsemanship from their position on the bastion.'

'Fighting in the breach requires no horsemanship, sir. It requires brave friends such as these.'

Lacroix smiled at the wounded soldier supported by the Englishman. 'You are right. We are all now infantrymen. But I must not delay your progress to the infirmary.'

'I thank you, sir.'

'I thank you. At least this day we blood the infidel.'

The old Grand Cross walked on, a senior Knight with the weight of the garrison and the well-being of the men on his mind and shoulders. Hardy rejoined the battle-damaged procession. He could hear the cheers, the calls of recognition to soldiers glad to be alive, the weeping intensity of those who mourned. War was a strange place.

She appeared before him, strip bandages in one hand, a bowl of herb poultice in the other. He blinked, uncertain at the vision. 'My lady.'

'Monsieur Hardy.'

'Birgu is not a usual destination for a noblewoman.'

Maria held his gaze. 'Because it is a fishing-village and home to the Knights? Or because battle is joined?'

'Hospitals are no respecter of rank.'

'Nor, it seems, are you, Monsieur Hardy.'

'We face siege, my lady.'

'The island faces siege. I can neither ignore it nor refuse my service where it is required.'

'Your father, your brother, your families of high birth are in Mdina.'

'The greater need is here.' She gestured to the rows of cots and litters spread through the vaulted chambers. 'These beds will fill soon enough.'

'They will carry terrible sights, my lady.'

'Conscience and imagination carry worse. You think I am weak? You believe a maiden of my age and virtue may not tend the sick, cannot rise to occasion when demanded?'

'I believed you content with springs and water vessels.'

'Your belief was wrong, Monsieur Hardy.'

'I am corrected.' Hardy let suggestion roll on his tongue, longing emit from his eyes.

She showed no displeasure. 'I drove a cart with supplies from the city. Now I find myself trapped and all escape closed.'

'Happy coincidence in unhappy times.'

He wanted to place his arms around her, to shield her, to hear her ask for his succour and protection. Again, he found himself hesitate. The certainties of combat were easier to negotiate than the uncertainties of feeling. She hinted at a smile. It was that look – part knowing, part questioning – that drew him in, took him back to those first sightings as she rode near Naxxar, to their first conversation on the slopes of Mdina. He could imagine dying for her. More importantly, he would be willing to kill for her.

'My lady, it is not too late to sail for Sicily. Grand Master La Valette continues to send message by small boat at night to the Viceroy.'

'I have little to add to his message, Monsieur Hardy.'

'Distance would ensure your safety.'

'Would England not provide you with yours?'

Hardy walked to a trestle table and rolled out two parallel bandages. 'The peninsulas of Birgu and Senglea. Around them, the sea and the Turk fleet. At the landward end, the Turk army against our bastions and walls. Their trenches will spread and deepen, their confidence grow. And with it the ferocity of their attack.'

'It seems that flight is on neither of our minds.'

'What is, my lady?'

They smiled at each other. He was twenty-two years of age, she eighteen. Events had brought them close; attraction could bring them closer. Her eyes dipped. It was sudden shyness or brief submission, a lowering of her defence. The signal he desired.

More casualties were arriving. 'Forgive me, Monsieur Hardy. I must look to the injured.'

'And I to military affairs, my lady.'

He took his leave, warmed by the conviction she had travelled to Birgu to find him. His departure from England, his life with the corsairs, his flight from North Africa had come to this point, this threatened enclave. To her. It was confluence and destiny. His wandering was over.

In the balmy night air, a different sound had joined the soft moans, the prayers and pleas, of the dying, gusting faint from the deserted battlefield. Sentries on the landward walls of Birgu strained to hear. It was a thin, high-pitched scream which came to them. Mustapha Pasha had kept his promise. For behind a screen of earth and brushwood the captured Knight Adrien de La Rivière was suffering for his lie, was bleeding from every orifice. His torturers had become his executioners. They beat him with wooden batons, at first on the soles of his feet, and then on his limbs, his stomach, his chest. Practised hands, methodical work. Bastinado did not come more savage. Before dawn, the Knight expired. His internal organs had been pulped, his blood vessels rupturing in endless haemorrhage. A stillness followed, yet the echoing cries of La Rivière appeared to haunt on. He had left his beleaguered brethren in no doubt of Turkish commitment.

Chapter 4

Siege-cannon were on the move. Picked out by the sporadic flame of burning torches, accompanied by the ever-present crack of whips, the long and lumbering trains of harnessed slaves and yoked oxen struggled onward in the darkness. Dragged behind, seated in their wood limbers, were the guns. There were the eighty-pounders, the smaller culverins, the immense basilisks capable of demolishing fortifications with their two-hundred-pound loads of iron, marble and stone. Little could withstand them. Less would remain standing. These were the weapons which had brought cities to their knees, castles to surrender. They were on their way to St Elmo.

Closeted in his small audience chamber in the fort of St Angelo, Grand Master La Valette was engaged in sending a friend to his death. The man was Pierre de Massuez, known to all as Colonel Mas, a soldier of note, a popular officer and, like La Valette himself, a seasoned Knight from Provence. Both knew the odds. Neither would shy from them.

'I ask much of you, Pierre.'

'No more than you ask of yourself or any other Knight, Jean Parisot. I go willingly and with my trust in God.'

'You shall take two hundred Spanish troops with you to St Elmo. I will spare whatever else I can.'

'Do not weaken yourself here.'

'It is the Turk I intend to weaken. The longer you stand at St Elmo, the more they are likely to buckle. Their casualties will

58

grow, their resolve will suffer, the strength of their eventual attack on Birgu and Senglea will lose its potency.'

'Then I am glad for my circumstance.'

'Make every moment, every life, every musket-ball count. Expend the energies of the heathen; grind him down as he intends to grind down the walls of the fort.'

'Our spirits will not falter, Jean Parisot. You have my word.'

'While you have the chance to make the name of the Order live for ever.'

'St Elmo has food, water and fifteen hundred men. With the lifeblood of reinforcements, the fervour of our Religion, we will give good account of ourselves.'

'I have no doubt.'

'You honour me, Jean Parisot.'

'I rely on you. Deliverance will come, yet will take time. You shall create it. Every day the infidels fight is a summer day vanished. Every week they are denied victory is a week closer to the autumn storms when their galleys must depart.'

'They will find St Elmo the prickliest of fruits.'

'May they choke on it.'

Colonel Mas nodded. 'Broglio as fort commander, de Guaras as deputy, the flower of Europe alongside. We are unconquerable.'

'The boats await to carry you.' La Valette rose. 'We shall meet again, Pierre.'

'Perhaps in paradise.'

'Be resolute, my friend.'

The Knight knelt on one knee and kissed the proffered hand. 'Pray for our souls, Jean Parisot.'

With Colonel Mas departed, La Valette sat alone to peruse again the latest communication from the Viceroy of Sicily. Courageous Maltese fishermen had risked their lives to bring this letter. They had wasted their effort. Don Garcia de Toledo was stalling, was citing difficulties in raising troops. He had no intention of saving Malta. There were his own affairs to consider, his own skin to preserve, his own island to defend. Why, he had even suggested the Order give up its remaining galleys for the greater good. The coward, the imbecile. La Valette held the document to the hearth and watched it shrivel in the flame. Malta was condemned.

A page interrupted his ruminations, entering the room to announce the presence of visitors. He would see them.

'Monsieur Hardy, the Moor and my own nephew Henri. A fearsome sight.' The three bowed. 'I trust there is urgency to your mission.'

Hardy answered for them. 'The hours of darkness make it so, Your Highness.'

'Speak of it.'

'The Turk axe is to fall on St Elmo. It is our duty and intent to blunt it.'

'You have an army?'

'A plan, Your Highness.'

Hardy gestured to the Moor, who removed from a canvas bag a small ordnance device with attached copper cone. It was presented to La Valette for inspection.

'An improvement on severed infidel ears, Monsieur Hardy. The Moor has a habit of drawing on his dark imagination to create the most pernicious inventions of war.'

'Placed in the body of a cannon, it will serve to split it asunder, Your Highness.'

'Is this true?'

The Moor was grave. 'I hope with my heart, Your Highness. The intensity of explosion will be directed not from the cannon mouths, but at their sides. They will fracture to the blow.'

'If they do not?'

'We will spike them with nails, will set ablaze the wood cradles on which these guns stand, on which at this very moment they proceed for Mount Sciberras.'

Henri spoke. 'The enemy have armourers, but cannot recast

cannon. They have carpenters, but cannot create gun-platforms where there is scarce any wood.'

'They will consume their galleys for the purpose.'

'At the least it will slow them. Is that not what the defenders of Fort St Elmo desire, sir?'

'You think you shall go undetected?'

'Night is our ally.' Hardy sensed the anticipation behind the deadpan of the Grand Master. 'Ten cowled riders, ten black horses with muffled hooves. The enemy intends the movement of cannon to go unseen. It will work to our favour.'

'Your men are ready?'

'The volunteers are found.'

'And you, Henri?'

'With your permission, sir, I will ride with Christian.'

La Valette did not hesitate. 'I cannot command others to do what I would deny my nephew to perform. You have my blessing.'

'We give you our loyalty and thanks, sir.'

'Do what you must to punish these guns.'

To Christian Hardy and Henri de La Valette, he made the sign of the cross. They went, not in the way of peace, but for the purpose of war.

'*Who comes?*'

The traitor also had his reasons and method. Out on the land-ward walls of Birgu, the sentry would not suspect his own, would never stand a chance. No lanterns were carried, no candle allowed to draw the attention of a Turkish marksman. It helped. He identified himself. Such acts could lull, could encourage the right mood, foster the appropriate response. The man seemed genuinely impressed by his presence.

'All is well?'

'No movement among the heathen, sir.'

'They will be tending their wounds, praying for their dead. We gave them a fight they will not forget.'

'We bested them in fair combat, sir.'

'What is fair? What counts as combat?'

The soldier seemed puzzled. As though it mattered, the traitor thought. Inconsequential conversation was merely an interval for positioning, for stepping close.

'The nature of your armour?'

'A casque and chain-mail, sir.'

'Your weapon?'

'A pike, sir.'

'We carry what is necessary for our task. Some of us have different edge to our purpose, to meet the challenge of the moment. You are vigilant on your watch?'

'I am, sir.'

'Then you may assist.'

'In what manner, sir?'

The sentry stood rigid and awkward. He was ill-prepared to respond. Without warning, the traitor moved in, clasped the head, and thrust the stiletto-blade upward. The knife buried itself vertically beneath the jaw, driving up through the soft palate, the tongue, the roof of the mouth. It was easier when one could not see the expression change. He worked the steel spike, could feel the limbs shake, the body spasm as the brain of the sentry died. With fluid ease, he walked the corpse backwards to the embrasure and pitched it cleanly into the void. It was risk-reduction, one less defender to challenge the Turks when they again appeared.

Quickly, the traitor unslung his recurved bow and fitted the arrow. He would aim high, shoot blind, let the shaft travel to join the Ottoman dead beyond the ditch. His message would be found. He drew the string and angled his shoulder. Release; the arrow flew. Satisfied, the traitor arranged his weapons and continued on his round. The game was in play. Contact had been made.

'Would that I rode with you, Christian.'

'Hubert, to bless us is sufficient.'

Hardy adjusted the harness of his borrowed black steed, bent again to check its saddle-straps, the cloth coverings muffling its hooves. Around him, Henri and the volunteers did the same. They were making ready for the night raid. Brass had been dulled, armour discarded, faces and bodies shrouded. Until they struck, they would be silent wraiths on the field.

The young priest Hubert looked on. 'You do battle without Helios. He will not thank you.'

'His pale skin would soon show itself to the enemy. It is as well he is at Mdina. Tonight we bring terror without him.'

'While your friend Hubert hides away.'

Hardy turned and placed a hand on his shoulder. 'Know thyself, as the great Socrates said. Your place is at the altar.'

'He is right, Hubert.' Henri had joined them, held up a rosary between his fingers. 'We are nothing without you, have no strength that is not the strength of God.'

'Return safe, my brothers.'

The troop were assembled. They were made to jump and run on the spot as Hardy and Henri de La Valette walked among them, listening for noise, removing objects which might jar or betray. In open country, sound would travel, give away their presence.

'Each man of you knows his function.' Hardy stood before them, his black hood thrown back. 'Remember that neither you nor your horse wears armour. Be swift and be brutal, and break where encirclement threatens. God be with you. Mount up.'

Hubert whispered to him as he placed his foot in the stirrup. 'You wish to make confession, Christian?'

'I am comfortable in my sin.' He swung himself up into the saddle.

A soft and solitary hand-clap could be heard. From the flickering shadow, de Pontieux appeared, his thin face white above the darkness of his military cloak.

'Why, it is a band of Black Friars. I am intrigued.'

Hardy held his horse steady. 'We are to frustrate the enemy and their guns before they reach St Elmo.'

'A stirring sight. Yet you waste your effort. The fort is doomed.'

'It will defend itself well.'

'As did you before the Supreme Council.' The tone was gently chiding, the eyes vulpine. 'Was this the idea of the Grand Cross Lacroix?'

'Of ourselves, sir.' Henri had drawn up beside his friend.

'Ah, the cherished nephew of our Grand Master. I assume your uncle Jean Parisot sanctions such escapade?'

'He does.'

'A selfless act free of preference or sentiment.'

'We fight the same enemy for the same cause.'

'But not all of us consenting to be led by a paid and hired hand, Chevalier La Valette.'

Hardy backed his mount away. 'We leave.'

'Follow your calling as I do mine. I bid you adieu.'

Silhouetted briefly against the flare of a torch-brand, the mounted Turk sentry patrolled the flank. He was having an easier time of it than the slaves. Occasionally a man would scream, would flounder in his task or sink beneath the weight of blows. At other moments, protesting oxen would charge from their path, dragging handlers, crushing porters. But order was always restored, the pace never changed. The sentry turned his horse and peered into the blue-black gloom. Ahead and behind, comparable scenes were replicating and unfolding. Everywhere, progress was under way, the army on the move. If Mustapha Pasha wished for mountains to be moved, the Ottoman army would see it done. Their commander was the representative of the Sultan, their Sultan the designate and deputy of God on earth. The Christians stood no chance.

With a near-soundless exhalation, the sentry fell dead from his steed. Along the line, more guards were dying, picked off, brought down without display or alarm. Random noise would not be noticed; the occasional disturbance was unlikely to provoke interest. The teams sweated on. Up on Mount Sciberras, the Turk labour corps were preparing the ground, excavating trenches and gun-pits, creating protective berms with sacks of earth brought from the galleys. Inhospitable terrain. Yet they worked in the certainty that the fort of St Elmo below was staring at defeat, that its defenders would shortly be staring direct into the mouths of Ottoman guns.

Not all those guns would reach their destination. In a sudden sleet of arrows, Turkish overseers collapsed where they stood. A horse walked on, its rider slumped in the saddle with an arrow bisecting his neck. Another reared and galloped away, its officer catapulted to the ground. The man landed hard. Dazed, he stumbled to his feet, shouting vainly, attempting to make sense of enveloping chaos. He could see shapes, the shadows of dark horsemen cutting down resistance, leaning to insert packages in the maw of the basilisk, reaching to empty leather bladders of liquid on to the great gun-pallet. They were creating a funeral pyre. Men were fleeing and crying out; burning torches were snatched and thrown. Flames arced and travelled. Then the detonations, the crash of splintered iron, the pyrotechnic brilliance of inferno. In the distance, a team of panicked oxen dragged their burning limber waywardly for a hidden objective. Closer, slaves tumbled free of their harnesses or caught alight in their chains. The Turk officer watched. He mouthed a prayer and reached for his sword. A lance pierced him through.

'*Christian, to your back!*'

It was Henri de La Valette who had cried the warning. Hardy saw the threat, a turbaned levy rushing from behind with a pike. Helios would have back-kicked, would have knocked the Turk spinning. But this horse was an unknown. A second and third Ottoman soldier were closing, the tips of their spears glinting orange in the flame and jabbing near. The stallion could feel the heat, sense the predators and its own predicament. It was cornered.

Hardy spurred it ferociously, dropping low and parrying the spear, running his sword along the haft until it met and entered the body. Momentum carried him on, taking him past, ripping the blade up and through the gut until the Turk fell away. Focused on the plight of their comrade, the remaining levies failed to notice Henri bearing down.

'Henri, my thanks. It is time to retreat, brother.'

'The Turk thinks otherwise, Christian. See!'

Spahis. The alarm had been sounded and illumination rockets sent skyward. In a dazzling instant, the world became shadowless-white, had the bright intensity of an electric storm. Hardy shielded his eyes. On the horizon was a moving ripple of black. It was the Turkish cavalry, incoming, trotting fast, awaiting the order to charge.

Henri stood in his stirrups to watch the sight. 'A trap, Christian.'

'Aiming to take us in the side.' He motioned to his troop. 'Do not linger. Follow me, divide right and left only when they are upon us.'

'*For St John!*'

They broke into a thundering gallop, whooping and howling, racing for the narrowing gap as the Spahis hastened to close it. The higher-pitched ululation of the Turks swung in behind. A horse stumbled, threw its rider, and continued on in gathering terror. Hardy had seen. He judged the moment, nudging the steed aside, seizing the reins and coaxing it round in a widening circle to gather up its discarded load. The soldier remounted. But time had been lost. Before them, the black-plumed forest of enemy horsemen had drawn up, its ranks impenetrable, its fighting formation inescapable.

'We are surrounded, Christian.'

'Let us hope that our brothers reach safety, that we have diverted the enemy flood.'

'For what do these infidels wait?'

'Their moment.' Hardy threw aside his black cloak, rested his sword against his boot.

'Why do they not take us with arrows?'

'It would ruin their sport. They prefer to carve us with knives.'

'You should not have returned for me, Christian.'

'And miss this combat?' He turned and smiled at the soldier. 'They might sing of us one day.'

Another firework-illumination burst and showered its light across the plain. The Turks remained motionless, awaiting a command or an instant when tension broke and action began. An unequal face-off.

'Are you prepared to close with the enemy?'

The man vomited, wiping his mouth with the back of a gauntleted hand. 'I am afraid, Christian.'

'Fear only for your reputation or soul. Both are secure.'

'It is a privilege to serve and die with you, Christian.'

'If we are to die, it shall be as men.' Hardy lifted his sword. 'Ready yourself.'

There was no need. A storm front broke. It arrived with the call of a horn, hurled itself upon the Ottoman flank with a fury which shuddered along the line. Marshal Copier's cavalry had swept down from Mdina.

'Our chance. Death or glory, my friend.'

Both men flung their horses forward, aiming for a fracture opening in the ranks. They went into the breach.

'You are wounded.'

'Those left standing do not count as wounded.'

Maria led him to a bench and brought a bowl of warmed water. She placed it down, began to sponge and clean the long cut across the back of his hand.

'It is not deep. You have luck, Monsieur Hardy.'

He said nothing, but agreed. It was the first time they had touched this way, a moment of formal tenderness, minutes for him to observe the tilt of her neck, the flick of her eyelashes, the work of her hands. She blushed, compensating with a rush of words.

'How did you come by such injury?'

'My lady does not wish to hear of these things.'

'Oblige me, monsieur.'

'My gauntlet was torn away in our escape. A Turk struck at me with a scimitar.'

'You parried with your hand?'

'Better a hand than a head.'

'My skill at medicine would have been tested, Monsieur Hardy.'

'I would have prevailed upon you to try.'

'Without stinting.' She had dried the wound, was binding it with dressing. 'My preference is you avoid the Turkish scimitar.'

'My profession would disappoint your preference.'

'Then it is a foolish profession.'

'Yet a worthy preference.'

She flushed again, at ease with his presence, uncertain of herself. He closed his fingers lightly on her hand. She did not flinch or pull away. A noblewoman could have screamed, might have called for the guard. But Maria was staring into his eyes.

'You work late, my lady.'

'Casualties may arrive at any hour.'

He was grateful to be among them, surprised to have lived through a night that had seen the ground populated with the fallen cannon and still or twitching shapes of Turks.

It was approaching dawn as he left for his quarters. He needed sleep, but would fail to find it. For a while, he stood outside the Sacred Infirmary, watched the sky brighten behind the dark mass of Fort St Angelo. Maria had claimed he had luck. Yet there was little luck to discovering love in the midst of war, the shadow of siege.

'Again outwitting the Turk, Hardy.'

The greeting was not one of friendship, the encounter probably not one of coincidence. Prior Garza had sidled into view. He was short and corpulent, had the round face of a glutton, prehensile lips that fed several appetites. Godliness appeared at odds with his countenance. A high-pitched voice and air of effeminacy sat more oddly still. He came to stand beside the Englishman.

'A word, if it pleases you.'

'I have no other company, Prior.'

'It is short of the truth. A noble lady, although Maltese, and a man of poor stock. At this hour.'

'There were wounds to dress.'

'Rather there were urges to meet. It is unseemly.'

'As it is unseemly for a prior to pry.'

'The Order does not allow for such union.'

'You impugn her honour and my motive.'

'Your motive?' The glance was long, was at once salacious and disapproving. 'You bedeck yourself with the bangles and baubles of fallen Turks. You revel in difference, in your contrary position. You believe yourself outside our laws.'

'I think myself to be in a besieged village.'

'You have few allies, Hardy.'

'I have enough.'

'His Highness the Grand Master will not live for ever.'

'Immortality is granted to few of us, Prior.'

'A new Grand Master will show scant benevolence to you. You offend, you ignore our ways, you disregard our code.'

'Yet I fight for this Order. I am a soldier, nothing more.'

'And I am a prior. Remember it.'

'It is difficult to forget. The Lord does indeed move in mysterious ways.'

Prior Garza contemplated him, his mouth pursed, his small

69

eyes glistening. He was almost as dangerous as de Pontieux. Even in war there were agendas, subtle undercurrents which could hide lust or hatred, allegiance or betrayal.

'You make enemies of the wrong kind, Hardy.' The Prior mopped at the perspiration sheen on his face. 'Choose your side with care.'

Audience was over. Garza, the scorpion, scuttled away.

At dawn on Thursday 24 May 1565, four days after Mustapha Pasha had set foot on Malta, the bombardment of St Elmo began. The night raid had scarcely caused the build-up to miss a beat. From every ridge-line of Mount Sciberras, cannons thundered. Their shot screamed into limestone walls, ricocheted over ramparts, plunged into the sea beyond. The fort and its rock foundations shook. Within an hour, a yellow-brown cloud of dust hung above the peninsula. Within two, blocks were crashing from the walls. Disintegration was under way. Behind the crumbling ramparts, the defenders cowered or sought frantically to rebuild their cover. There would be no respite.

Each day, the intensity of the barrage grew. Beneath its fire, the slaves and engineers of the Turkish labour corps pushed their way forward. They built up parapets, erected fascines, edged their attack trenches towards the earthwork ring of outer defences. With them came the sharpshooters. Hidden by screens of brush-wood, they picked off the Christian sentries until none dared to show, infiltrating along the shore of Marsamuscetto harbour to bracket the seaward walls with musket-shot. Every side was covered. The gunners of St Elmo fought back, sending round upon round into the Ottoman lines, demolishing positions, throwing up bodies and showers of stone. Without pause, the Turks rolled their dead into the construction and progressed on.

The circle was tightening about St Elmo. From the cavalier tower of Fort St Angelo, La Valette looked out across Grand Harbour and watched the walls corrupt, the smoke rise, the shivering images of concussive impact. It was his agony, his slow death. He was asking the impossible of his besieged brethren, demanding their sacrifice for the sake of the Order. Their duty was to withstand the onslaught, to hold the Turk until the last Knight drew breath and the final grain of gunpowder was expended. By night, he would send the small boats to ferry in volunteers, carry away the dead and injured. That too would be closed down, interdicted by the enemy. And the sun climbed and the summer heat intensified.

'Uncle, my apologies.'

'Your interruption will have its reason.'

The Grand Master stirred and lifted his eyes. It was the early hours, the final week of May, and he had been in prayer. Sleep was for younger men. For him, refuge lay in the Cross, solace was to be found in communing with God. Now Henri had intruded, was dragging him back to earthly affairs, to the incessant hammering of the guns, to the torment of Fort St Elmo.

He rose from his knees. 'There is news from across the harbour?'

'A sortie, Uncle.'

'Of what kind?'

'Dramatic and bold. It appears our Knights have ventured to attack in strength and under cover of darkness.'

'How does the Turk respond?'

'The sound is of flight and consternation. It is why I sought to find you, Uncle.'

'I thank you for it, Henri. If it is as you say, it will gladden the hearts of every Christian here. We shall watch for ourselves.'

Accompanied by Henri, and pausing only to don a cloak against the night chill, La Valette made his way along the ramparts to the roof of the cavalier. Already he could hear the ringing clash of battle, the snap and whicker of swords, the pepper-volleys of musketry. Around him, the garrison was waking. Men were stumbling to the battlements, drowsily staring to pick out detail, to make sense of turmoil. The sights and the sounds were extraordinary, were almost beyond belief. Turks were in headlong retreat.

It was Colonel Mas. As the Grand Master viewed the brightening scene from his high vantage, the effect of the raid by the defenders of St Elmo rippled outward from the small fortress. The Knight had made his move. He had led his men silently across the wooden bridge, attacking without warning, falling upon the gangs of Turk labourers while they excavated in the dark. Picks and bars were no match for arquebuses and steel blades, for the trained ferocity of the Order. The Turks broke and ran. Their rout had become infectious, spreading panic, spilling down the slopes of Mount Sciberras until even the main encampments on the Marsa were contaminated with disarray. Nothing seemed to stem the flow. The impregnable Turk was undone. Dawn glimmered in the east, and on the ramparts of St Angelo the watchers cheered.

'*Janissaries forward! Kill them all. Spare no-one!*'

It had been arrogant and misguided of the Christians to presume they had advantage. Of course they had unleashed a surprise, had inflicted embarrassment and not a few casualties. But they would pay. Mustapha Pasha did not appreciate humiliation. Roused from his tent, he was leading the counter-charge, riding his white stallion, advancing up the escarpment with his jewelled sabre raised. With him came the Janissaries. Ordinary soldiers stood aside, fleeing engineers halted. For these were the Invincible Ones, the spartan elite with their heron-plumed helmets, drawn scimitars and engraved muskets. These were the fanatical Moslem killers, born to Christians, taken by the empire, moulded and bent to the way of war and total obedience to the Sultan. They were bred to slaughter infidels.

'*See the Janissaries! Follow them! Fight as they fight, you whores! Or I shall have every one of you stoned to death!*'

Mustapha Pasha slashed at a running labourer, splitting turban and head in a single stroke. Butchery could act as a form of instruction and encouragement. Levies faltered. He curved the blade across the throat of another, saw the blood-stripe widen, the man stagger and fall.

'*Now seek paradise! Massacre the infidel for the dignity of your souls!*'

The moment turned. In a howling rage of shouts and battle-cries, the Janissaries tore into the Knights. Some Turks fell to the cannon of St Elmo, others to the longer-range shot from the high guns of St Angelo. Yet they pushed on. Combat could pivot on an individual action, outcome depend on the effect of a few seconds. These were the seconds. What had been a Christian advance was now a haphazard withdrawal. The Knights were overstretched, vulnerable. The line wavered. As daylight streamed across the peninsula and burnt off the north-easterly sirocco haze, the banners of the Janissary corps fluttered on the defensive counterscarp leading to the earthwork ravelin. Bodies lay everywhere. But the Turks had moved closer to the fort, and the cheering from the ramparts of St Angelo had changed to cheerless silence.

A single galley. It had appeared from the south in the late afternoon, was making fast for Grand Harbour. Perhaps it carried a message for the Turks from the Barbary Coast, was a forward unit of the corsairs. On the ramparts of St Angelo, the defenders watched. At first they could distinguish only the outline, the moving banks of oars, the bow wave as the ship ploughed on towards them. Sharper focus came. The pennants and flags could be seen, the cross of St John, the standard of Knight Commander St Aubin. One of their own.

It was madness. He was aiming at a harbour entrance crowded with Turkish vessels, was attempting to penetrate to the safety of the waters behind St Angelo and a berth in the moat. Always the daredevil, St Aubin was testing, goading. He might just as well have stirred up a nest of vengeful hornets. From the Ottoman fleet, six galleys peeled away to confront and take the intruder. St Aubin fired his bow-chasers and backwatered his starboard oars. His galley spun. The chase was under way. Along the curtain walls of St Angelo, the Christians were shouting, yelling encouragement, invoking the power of God. Here was one Christian galley running before the Turk colossus. Here were their hopes, their faith, their abject fear summarized in an act of supreme defiance and nautical skill.

The Christian galley was pulling away. Five Turkish vessels fell back, their pace ebbing, their strength spent in the headlong pursuit. One clung on. There was always the wrath of Admiral Piali to consider, the pride of the Ottoman empire at stake. It could stiffen the resolve of any captain, strengthen the whip-hand of any slave overseer. The Turkish galley was overhauling the Knight Commander. From Fort St Angelo the shouts were frenzied. If St Aubin and his men were caught, there would be no mercy or restraint from the Turk. The consequences were almost too appalling to consider, the developing scene almost too unbearable to watch. Distance closed to several hundred feet.

But the Turks had not considered the nature of Knight Commander St Aubin, had forgotten that the Order of St John were the masters of the sea. Piracy was in their blood, the daring sleight of hand an article of their profession. With another manoeuvre, the Christian galley feinted and came about. It pointed directly at its Turkish adversary and began to move towards it. Onlookers held their breath. St Aubin was attacking. St Aubin had turned his reconnaissance mission to North Africa into a flirtation with disaster, was transforming close encounter into a bravura display of seamanship. With the Christian on its tail, the Turkish galley was in furious retreat.

Celebration was muted. On the heights of St Angelo, Knights and soldiers saw the Turk vessel rejoin the rest, the Christian ship at last veer away to head for the north and Sicily. They were alone again, the isolation more profound than ever. The gun barrage on the far side of Grand Harbour was unrelenting. St Elmo appeared to be sinking into its own grave of dust.

Other ships did come. It was in the closing part of May that a flotilla of galleys appeared off the southern coast. The arrival was marked by a grand expression of Ottoman might, by the entire Turkish fleet forming up in line astern to bombard St Elmo from the sea. Such a parade was appropriate. For the legendary Dragut, the Drawn Sword of Islam, had finally reached the island.

Chapter 5

'You die, Henri.'

'For a fourth time in as many minutes, alas.'

The young Knight went to retrieve the sword struck from his grasp by Christian Hardy. They had been duelling hard, finessing the base tricks and low cunning that made the Englishman master, his friend the disciple.

'Again, Henri.'

'You have murdered me enough, brother.' Henri panted, his pale features flushed from exertion. 'Even my reputation shrivels at such a beating.'

'Yet your learning improves.'

'I do not deny it, Christian. Though I declare you three parts devil, magician and alley-cat.'

'A tutor requires few other faculties in these days.'

Hardy juggled and spun his sword in virtuoso display, catching it in his scabbard. His audience applauded. Before him sat Maria, Hubert and Luqa, and lounging at further distance the Spanish and Maltese volunteers who had accompanied him on the night raid against the Turk guns. Allies, comrades, present to gain insight from the peerless.

'To you all, I say this. Be simple in your moves, quick on your feet, and clever with your minds. Out-think the foe. Be aware of where you are, where you mean to be.'

A Spaniard called out. 'None among us mean to end at your feet. Yet it occurs.'

'Better to end alive at my feet than dead at those of a Janissary.'
He raised a hand. 'You have two of these. Use both to effect.
Where one carries a sword, find employment for the other. It can
parry or strike, be clenched as a fist, hold a mattock, cudgel or
dagger, may seed confusion or throw dirt and sand.'

'You are no gentleman, Christian Hardy.'

'Manners are for funerals. Here we fight. Hubert, stand.'

'Christian?'

'It is your chance to find glory.'

'You wish me to challenge?'

'I intend you to learn.'

The novice priest rose, at once uncertain yet pleased at his
sudden elevation, his face framed in schoolboy eagerness.

Hardy tossed him the wood facsimile of a knife. 'Our exhibition demands you do not bleed.'

'What do we exhibit?'

'The natural laws of combat. Who do you despise beyond all,
Hubert?'

'The Ottoman Sultan.'

'Who besides?'

'Prior Garza.' The soldiers enjoyed the joke.

'He will do. Imagine I am he, that I threaten all you hold dear.
Come at me.'

Hubert obeyed, was sent sprawling into a bale of straw.
Winded, he lay still, resembling not so much a young and skinny
priest as a skeleton in a sack. As he rolled on his back, the sword
was at his throat.

'The first law of combat. To fall is to die.' Hardy proffered his
hand and pulled him upward.

'The second?'

'Come at me once more.'

Hubert performed the run-in, again went airborne, his arms
and legs flailing.

'The second law of combat. Expect what is unexpected.'

With a groan, the student reclaimed his wooden dagger and staggered unsteadily to his feet. There were good-natured cheers and catcalls from his audience, to which he responded with an ironic bow. His smile remained.

'I suspect there is a third law, Christian.'

'And others to follow.'

'Cruel fate.' He began his attack.

The third law: do not raise the arm and expose the body to counter-strike. The fourth: present the flank to an opponent instead of the front. Each lesson was taught, absorbed, concluded with impact and a simulated sword-thrust. Bruised but cheerful, Hubert accepted his acrobatic lot.

Another display completed, he lay gasping in pained mirth on the ground. 'My lady, gentlemen, the show is ended.'

'You study well, Hubert.'

'Every bone tells me so, Christian. I am not fit for this task.'

'Then you discover for yourself the final law of combat.'

'I do?'

'Never perform what is beyond your reach.'

'I take it with me to an early grave.'

He crawled to his seat aided by Maria, whose face showed concern and gaiety in equal measure. She comprehended the value of the teaching.

It did not prevent her tender admonition. 'You inflict much hurt on him, Monsieur Hardy.'

'The corsairs of Dragut would inflict worse, my lady.'

'How would you teach a feeble woman to protect herself from these pirate beasts?'

'With consideration for her sex; with close regard to her need.'

'Am I also to fall?'

'Depending on circumstance, my lady.' He held out his hand and smiled as she stepped forward to oblige. 'The primary rule. To disarm the adversary.'

'You will find me a diligent pupil, Monsieur Hardy.'

'I suggest the pavanne.'

'Let class commence.'

It was a courtly dance, slow and formal, conducted to the respectful delight of the onlookers. He had wooed and seduced many a fine lady of Messina or Naples to its rhythm. As the noise of cannon backwashed across Grand Harbour, here was confirmation of life, of spirit. The pair moved unhurried and composed. Yet Hardy felt the jolt of energy, the same pulsing magnetism that had drawn them close as she bound his injured hand. The others would not see through the playfulness, the teasing correctness of the steps. He could; she did. Courtship and desire lay there.

She held his gaze. 'What should I learn, Monsieur Hardy?'

'That to lose is to perish, my lady.'

'I perish a little, then.'

'And what have you lost?'

'Nothing which may ever be replaced, Monsieur Hardy.'

'Perhaps you shall be stronger for it.'

'Yet I find myself growing weak.'

They continued to dance, their fingers lightly touching. When it was done, he bowed to her, she curtsied in reply. It did not do justice to his thoughts.

'I am certain the Drawn Sword of Islam will be frightened of us, Monsieur Hardy.'

'Together we shall see to it, my lady.'

He straightened, detected the amusement in her eyes, in those of the assembled. The blow came from behind. It struck at the knee, carried the force of a charging boy, and toppled him in an inglorious heap with his assailant.

Luqa had triumphed. Rowdily encouraged, he sat astride his victim's chest and punched the air.

'The second law of combat, seigneur.'

'Quite so.' Hardy whipped his legs into the vertical, caught the boy by the shoulders, and rolled him away into instant surrender. 'Expect what is unexpected.'

He stood, brushing himself down, observing Maria observe him. She was in on the jest. But her look communicated other things.

'Master Luqa shows us the importance of trust. He will show us anew.'

'I will, seigneur?'

'Take your sling. Choose shot for it.'

'You have the target, seigneur?'

Hardy strode to a weathered pile of discarded clay jars and amphoras and made his selection. With a cracked vessel in either hand he paced out the distance, steadied one on a sandstone buttress to his side, balanced the other on his head.

Alarmed, Maria spoke out with quiet emotion. 'Is this wise, monsieur?'

'It is no more foolish than war itself.'

'But you have no quarrel with the boy.'

'What I have is the bond of faith and fellowship.' He glanced at the thirteen-year-old. 'The field is yours, Luqa.'

The sling whirred, the pebble flew, and the clay beneath his hand shattered. Luqa reloaded. He sized the next object, squinting nerveless to judge distance and trajectory. To miss was to kill. It did not seem to enter his calculation. Around him, the adults had grown silent, willing success, aware of the implication. Hardy was an unconventional teacher.

For a second time the sling spun and a stone hurtled for its mark. Impact achieved. With a splintering crack, the pot erupted and showered Hardy in its wreckage. There were whoops of relief and astonishment from among the spectators.

Hardy held up a fragment of broken pottery. 'Each of us is dependent on the other. Remember it, or we break apart like this clay.'

He was content. His friends were with him. Maria cared for him.

★

80

Dragut was everywhere. Garbed in brilliant silks, resplendent with gemstones, the pirate king toured the battlefield. He was eighty years of age, his beard white, his features storm-weathered, but his energy unquenchable. On the slopes of Mount Sciberras he studied maps, observed St Elmo, and picked out sites for further gun-emplacements. At the water's edge he surveyed Grand Harbour, instructed labour gangs, supervised construction. Wherever he went, the tempo increased, the rate of fire soared.

This was the greatest seafarer of his age, the most feared Moslem warrior in the Mediterranean. As the Knights of St John had harassed the trade routes of the Sultan, so Dragut had visited terror upon the Christians. He had eluded the famed Genoese admiral Andrea Doria at Djerba by transporting his galleys over-land, had captured and sacked towns the length of Italy, had enslaved and carried off entire populations. Tens of thousands of galley slaves owed their hellish existence to him. Malta itself had been subjected to his forays, seen the inhabitants of Gozo killed or herded away. The Drawn Sword of Islam had returned, and the Knights and the islanders had every reason to anticipate catastrophe.

In the perfumed interior of the command-tent, the three men sat in conference. Mustapha Pasha puffed contemplatively on a hookah, Admiral Piali sipped coffee, Dragut remained abstemious and aloof on a high divan. They were generals thrown together by circumstance and common cause, by service to the Sultan. But the corsair was a breed apart, a leader with scant regard for indolence or inertia.

'I land in Malta and find you engaged in a pageant around St Elmo.'

Piali lowered his coffee glass. 'It is important we take the fort.'

'It is a waste. Of men, of cannon-shot, of time. What of the northern parts of the island, Admiral?'

'What of them?'

'Only this morning the Christian cavalry rode out from Mdina and cut down two hundred of your troops searching around Dingli. If these were not mere cavalry, but a relief army from Spain or Sicily? If these were not a few hundred enemy, but several thousand?'

'Conjecture.'

'Possibility. You have left your position here exposed, Admiral.'

'I have left myself with the freedom to take action where it is needed. My galleys require safe anchorage; the harbour of Marsamuscetto will provide it. St Elmo is the key.'

'St Elmo is irrelevant.' Dragut leaned forward, his gold-hoop earrings framing his scarred features. 'I have sailed these waters for over sixty years, have raided Malta on countless occasions. There are no summer storms to speak of, no winds that could wreck your precious fleet in its current berth.'

'It is indeed precious, Dragut. I am its guardian and its commander.'

The old man snorted his derision. 'I hear you command six galleys that failed to capture a lone Christian pigeon flying north. Your efforts would be better directed in patrolling near Gozo, in guarding the approaches against an infidel fleet.'

'You worry, Dragut.'

'The very reason why I reach this age, why I am governor of Tripoli, why the Sultan calls me to his war.'

'To assist and advise.'

'Heed that advice, Admiral.'

'St Elmo will quickly succumb The Grand Master and his Knights will follow.'

'Do not underestimate La Valette. I met him when he was a galley slave, met him again when I was captured and set to a Christian oar. He is a remarkable man.'

'An infidel at the head of a condemned Order.'

'They will fight to the end, Admiral.'

'That end shall be soon.'

'Very well.' Dragut sat back, his face a mask of resignation and stern resolve. 'If this is your design. I will place a battery of cannon on Tigné Point to assail St Elmo from the sea. I will add a further fifty guns on Mount Sciberras to pound it from the land. I will site yet more cannon at the mouth of Grand Harbour on Gallows Point to prevent reinforcements crossing from St Angelo.'

'I am impressed, Dragut.'

'We have started the business, so let us finish it. There will be no slowing until the deed is done.'

Mustapha Pasha reclined against the cushions. There was purpose in his silence, advantage to be gained in allowing Piali and Dragut their disagreement. The trying admiral was already a laughing-stock. How he had vented his rage, had spat abuse at his torpid captain left behind by the escaping Christian galley. Now it was the turn of Dragut to encounter the arrogance and stupidity. It would quickly bring the veteran corsair into the camp of the army commander.

He drew on his pipe, let the hashish smoke drift from his nostrils. 'The infidel Knights are beyond rescue, Governor Dragut. A source at their very heart informs us the Viceroy of Sicily does not intend to send an army. They are ours for the taking.'

'Let us hope so, Mustapha Pasha.'

'In the meanwhile, I will see you escorted to your quarters.'

'My quarters are with my men among the trenches on Mount Sciberras.'

'Then I pray you are not exposed to gunfire from the Admiral's ships.' It was an easy gibe, for a number of cannonballs fired by the fleet had overshot St Elmo and landed in the Turkish lines. Mustapha Pasha was not about to let the matter pass.

'My corsairs are immune to cannon.' Dragut stood, an ancient warrior more at ease in the face of battle than in the perfume-scented confines of deliberation and debate. 'In my last raid on these islands I lost a brother. I am back for blood.'

★

Early June, the second week of invasion, and that blood would flow. From every point, iron and stone balls were flung against the erupting walls of St Elmo. From hour to hour the casualties among the defenders grew. *There will be no slowing*. Dragut would keep his word. The earth reverberated to a constant quake, the air was laden with dust, and the siege wore on and bore down. Even the peninsulas of Birgu and Senglea were not immune, were punished day and night by Turkish batteries established on the high ground. Everything was to be softened up; each edifice was to be blasted.

A small trickle of masonry powder fell from the ceiling of the Council Chamber in Fort St Angelo. Beneath it sat La Valette and his war council. It was late at night, the room lit by candles and the sheet-lightning flicker of artillery, and they listened as a Spanish Knight related news from St Elmo.

'Your Highness, noble lords.' The Knight was ashen-grey beneath the blistering of the sun, his eyes hollowed, his body still trembling to the cannon-shot. 'You will have witnessed the trials of our small fort. Daily we count six thousand cannon-rounds or more striking our walls. Hourly we see those walls vanish. As fast as we seek to rebuild our defence, it is shot away. As fast as we place sentries, they are felled. Our dead and injured litter the ground.'

La Valette stared at the man. 'It is the nature of siege.'

'There is nothing natural in this, sir. The breaches grow wide, invite immediate attack from the massed ranks of the Ottoman.'

'You will meet it when it comes.'

'We cannot hold, sir.'

'You must. You have your obligation to the Faith. You have food and water, a garrison of fifteen hundred men.'

'Fifteen hundred who bleed, who tire, who are racked by the merciless attention of the heathen.'

'We send you reinforcements.'

'For how long, sir? The Turk commits boats to intercept our

nightly resupply, builds a protective wall for marksmen along the shore, begins emplacing a battery of cannon on Gallows Point to compound our isolation.'

'The actions of Dragut.'

'Actions which destroy us.'

'We shall deal with the battery. As for your isolation, use it to concentrate your minds, to steel your nerve, to render yourselves to God.'

'It is an honour to die in His name and for the Order, sir. But to do so at St Elmo is to cast aside our lives without reason on an indefensible place.'

'God provides reason. I decide what is indefensible.'

'I beg that Your Highness might consider evacuation.'

'Before you have yet spent a week under siege? Before the Turk has reached your walls?'

'There will soon be no walls.'

'And how many think as you? How many talk as you?'

'Numerous among the younger Knights, sir.'

'But few among the older. Follow instead their example, take their counsel. Acquire the courage and reason of Colonel Mas. They have endured many battles with the infidel. Endure with them.'

'You ask the impossible, sir.'

'I demand no more than Our Lord required of St Peter or St Paul.'

'They spread the Gospel, established the Church. We sit and wait for slaughter.'

'You will fight without question as you have never fought. You will establish our Church, our Religion, our Order for a thousand millennia with what you do.'

'St Elmo is a solitary and shattered fort, sir.'

'St Elmo is a beacon. Would you have me come with volunteers to rekindle its flame?' The Knight lowered his face before the level gaze and measured tone. La Valette walked to a plain wood crucifix attached to the wall and placed his hand on the pinned feet of the Christ. 'Lift up your eyes, Chevalier. Martyrdom is a noble thing. Now leave us. Return to St Elmo. Tell our brothers they shall have my reply by tomorrow night.'

'Mutiny.'

It was de Pontieux who spoke in the echoing aftermath filled only by the distant thunder of cannon.

La Valette sat composed. 'It is no mutiny, brother. It is the anxieties of brave men we have sent away to die.'

'Brave men who are in haste to retreat.'

'I recollect you were among those who advocated withdrawal from the fort, flight from this island.'

'Before we committed to its defence, Your Highness.' De Pontieux offered up a thin and lipless smile. 'Before I was persuaded by your argument. I believe now our gallant brethren should remain at St Elmo.'

'They must challenge the infidel for every stone.'

'Surely you do not intend to go yourself, sir?'

'I made no pledge, but merely suggested I journey to their side. It will cool their temper for a while.'

'What of the reply you give tomorrow night, sir?'

Grand Cross Lacroix rose heavily in his cuirass. 'I will be that reply, Your Highness.'

'You honour me, Brother Grand Cross.'

'I was with you when Grand Master de L'Isle-Adam led the Order out of Rhodes, sir. This old dog will teach the fretful youths in St Elmo the meaning of siege and fortitude.'

'I shall not lose you yet.' La Valette motioned Lacroix to sit. 'There will come the moment to expend my close advisers in open combat.'

De Pontieux bowed fractionally towards his rival. 'As is his custom, the Brother Grand Cross makes a generous offer. My solution would be at lesser cost.'

'You proffer a solution?'

'If your desire is to invigorate or shame the Knights at St Elmo into fighting to the last, it requires no intervention by either Grand Master or Knight Grand Cross.'

'How would you proceed?'

'With younger blood, sir. A hothead, a warrior, a boy who has proven his mettle, who may inspire through sacrifice.'

'Monsieur Hardy.'

'He is neither Knight nor nobleman, sir. To send him is to show we place more worth in a common adventurer, a Service Brother hireling, than in our own Knightly convent.'

Lacroix was on his feet. 'It is a senseless conceit.'

'It is a perfect settlement.'

'To what end and for whose benefit, de Pontieux? Matters of petty spite and vengeance?'

'Considerations of urgency and conflict. The defenders of St Elmo cry out for direction, Brother Grand Cross. We may provide it by dint of a pirate wanderer.'

Debate still sounded as La Valette retired to his private audience chamber. Food had been left for him – a lump of bread, a bowl of goat stew, a flagon of wine. But a sudden wave of nausea made him retch and sit panting for a while. He had not been feeling well of late. It might have been fatigue, the strain of command, the constant fears for his brothers and the Religion. Yet his creeping sickness paled against the onslaught of the Turk. It was nothing that faith and iron self-control could not hide or conquer. He steadied himself, readying for the conversation.

'Your Highness.' Christian Hardy was ushered in by a page. 'I hope I do not trouble you at this hour.'

'The waking state is better than the sleeping, Monsieur Hardy.'

'Few of us sleep, sir. The Turk cannon must wake the inhabitants of Sicily.'

'Letters from the Viceroy confirm as much.'

'Is there news of the relief force?'

'We need no relief to determine our fate. We alone are arbiters of it.'

'Then I come with proposal for a fresh attack upon the Turk.'

'Gallows Point?'

'Their guns have been landed; their preparations are advanced.'

'I have no doubt they plan to sever our links with St Elmo.'

'Permit me to confound them, sir.'

'I cannot.'

'Two boatloads of men would suffice, sir. Our brothers at St Elmo depend on it.'

'They may yet come to depend on you.' The eyes of La Valette were understanding, their gentleness at odds with the severity of his features. 'Spirit appears low among some at the fort. It is suggested we place more steel to their backbone, greater fire in their bellies.'

'With your guidance, they will have it, sir.'

'Or with your presence, Monsieur Hardy.'

The Englishman neither blinked nor hesitated. 'When do you wish my departure, sir?'

'Tomorrow night.' La Valette paused. 'I will not order you to this task.'

'What is a soldier if he does not seek out combat, sir?'

'St Elmo is not combat. It is death, Monsieur Hardy.'

'I go as willing as the other volunteers.'

'You will take with you the two hundred remaining Spanish infantry of Colonel Mas. And you shall carry our thanks and prayers.'

Sentence had been passed. Hardy bowed and took his leave. There were farewells to make.

Seems and not seems. The traitor held the small ceramic bottle between his thumb and forefinger. It contained arsenic, his poison of choice, the odourless, colourless, tasteless substance which acted as primer, initiated the first stage in the eventual demise of the Grand Master. None would suspect; no one could trace the gradual disintegration of the man to him. Death had to appear natural, a tragic yet ordinary consequence of a life brought down by old age, the travails of office, the pressures of siege. If the technique was subtle enough for the Borgias, it should be subtle enough to fool the Knights. Arsenic provoked many symptoms – stomach cramps, constipation, vomiting, terrible thirst, hair-loss, fatigue, and burning sensations throughout the body – all elusive, all likely to prompt treatment for each complaint. It was these cures that would kill. In his weakened state, La Valette would ingest medication designed to remedy, but which combined would conspire to slay. Without knowing it, the Hospitallers were themselves the chosen murderers. There was a certain symmetry to it all, a logic. Smiling to himself, the traitor placed the phial in a hidden pocket close to his skin. The world of the Order was beginning to implode.

Luqa had found new friends, was running and throwing stones for a pair of hunting-dogs. The hounds leaped playfully at the boy, laughter and barks mingling in the dusty street. A happy scene. Hardy watched them, loath to intrude, to bear tidings that would puncture the moment, bring an end to the mirth. It would have been easier to slip away, less cruel had he never brought the boy to Birgu. The thirteen-year-old relied on him, believed in him. He was here to breach that trust.

The boy saw him. He must have sensed, for he stilled the dogs and stood motionless as Hardy approached.

'Your face is sad, seigneur.'

'I have much to think upon.'

'You plan to leave.'

It was said with the bluntness and honesty of a child, a direct-ness which adults rarely mastered. Luqa glared accusingly at him.

'I go to St Elmo, Luqa.'

'You go to your death, seigneur.'

'Perhaps a glorious one. You too are a soldier, a comrade-in-arms. We have a duty to fight.'

'I saved your life.'

'In journeying to the fort, I have chance to save many more.'

'You lie.'

'Would I lie to a friend? Would I discard my life for naught?'

'No friend would abandon me, seigneur.'

'They need me, Luqa.'

'I need you. The Moor needs you. Chevalier Henri, Hubert, the Lady Maria need you.'

'They will understand, Luqa. So must you.'

'I understand.' The boy was using rage to blanket his grief. 'I understand that I should have remained on the shore with my dog. I understand that you do not care.'

'If I did not care, I would not be before you now.'

'Who will look after Helios?'

'I leave him to Henri. My gold I leave to you.'

'Gold is not company, seigneur. Gold cannot laugh, cannot teach me archery or swordsmanship, cannot play chequers or balle.'

'These things we will do if God is kind.'

'If He is not? Why did you come, seigneur?'

Luqa had turned his head away, ashamed at the tears beginning to stream warm on his face. It was the struggle of wanting to stay, of intending to run, of wishing both to strike out at and to hold on to this man he hated, the soldier he worshipped.

'Look at me, Luqa.' Hardy gently prized the face around, holding it between his hands, wiping at the eyes with his thumbs. 'A man must have dry eyes to bid adieu to another.'

'So he may pretend there is no pain?'

'There is pain, Luqa. But there is also war. We are not the masters of our fate.'

'You choose to fight the Turk at St Elmo.'

'We engage them where we must. Which heathen corsair arrived with fanfare these few days past?'

'Dragut.'

'The Drawn Sword himself, the commander who raided these islands when you were newborn, who visited fire upon Gozo. Were you older, you would have stood and challenged like your father.' Hardy gazed at his face, at the raw and wavering emotion. 'It is my turn to stand and challenge.'

'Then I will lose you as I lost my father.'

'I will remember you, Luqa. I ask you to remember me.'

'It is better we forget, seigneur.'

'I cannot. You are my son and my brother combined. You will be strong. You will live. You will guard the Lady Maria. You will rebuild and claim your island. Promise me this.'

Instead, Luqa bolted, racing for a flight of stone steps that would take him to the walled ramparts, carry him from the truth. The dogs rose to give chase, but decided against it. There was no more merriment, nothing more to say. Just a frightened boy deserted. Hardy waited until he had disappeared from view, then went on his way. It would be one of many sorrows.

'I know why you are come.'

'News travels fast in these streets, my lady.'

'Intuition is faster.'

Maria was pale, her skin translucent with exhaustion and concern. Each night, the boats brought back more casualties from St Elmo; each night, she would dress the wounds, attempt to ease the suffering. In peacetime the hospitalized would eat off silver salvers, restore their strength in the quiet and ordered confines of their Order. In war they lay on rush mats, groaning, coughing up blood, as priests walked among them praying and administering rites. It was a disturbing scene, a grimly evolving one.

'I leave for St Elmo this night, my lady.'

'It grieves me.'

'You do not flee as the boy Luqa fled; you do not condemn or berate me for my mission.'

'A noblewoman esteems duty, Monsieur Hardy. I could not

condemn you. Yet it is a pity we have not exchanged more words.'

'Words do not encompass all, my lady.'

'At Mdina I filled clay bottles with water. In Birgu I fill clay bottles with ointments and unctions. We part as we met.'

'Though not as strangers.'

His gaze travelled with hers, watched as an orderly mopped the brow of an injured Knight babbling in his delirium. Pity overcame her, and she averted her eyes.

'They have such bravery.'

'It is why I must join them at the fort.'

'St Elmo will be the better for it. I the poorer.'

'I will endeavour to remain safe.'

Her eyes shone with quiet desperation. 'We know it shall not be. I wish that I were with you, Monsieur Hardy.'

'You will be here, my lady.' He touched his forehead. 'And here.' He touched his heart.

'Take this.' On impulse, she removed the silver cross from her neck and placed it about his.

'I am your servant, my lady.'

'You are more than a servant, Monsieur Hardy.'

'It gladdens me.' He reached out and took her hand. 'I live on with Henri and Hubert, with the boy Luqa. Have regard and love for them. Allow them to care for you.'

'I shall try.'

The conversation and courtship were a dance, and the dance was drawing to a close. He bent to put his lips to her fingers.

'Think of me, my lady.'

'Always, Christian.'

Christian. She had spoken his name for the first time, probably for the last. It was worth celebrating, worth weeping for. The image of the beautiful girl amid the horrors of the dying would stay with him as vivid as the face of the Virgin Mary now gazing on him in the intimate gloom of the Conventual Church. Such a smile, such sweetness, such warm acceptance. He knelt before the cross. The smell of incense soothed the brain; the sound of cannon receded. He rarely prayed, was uncertain if he should petition the God of Forgiveness or the God of War. It was ungallant to think of himself. Instead, he would dwell on his friends, on their lives and coming death, on Grand Master La Valette, on the black Moor, on his beloved Maria. Have mercy upon them. He began to whisper, began to recite the *De profundis*. It was only slowly that he became aware of a presence, that others had taken up position beside him. Henri de La Valette and Hubert were kneeling in silent support, in a simple act of fellowship and valediction.

Darkness had fallen, and the small boats were drawn up below St Angelo ready for embarkation. The glow and flicker of the night salvos from Mount Sciberras lent definition to the distance. But here it was shadow, the whispers of comrades saying goodbye, of men asking for wills and last wishes to be executed. There was no ceremony, no chance that any of these souls would be seen alive or uninjured again. Grand Harbour was the Styx. St Elmo was the other side.

The Moor was already at the water edge. He had supervised the loading of his precious incendiaries, in his low rumbling baritone was giving instruction on their handling. Hardy knew where to find him.

'I see you are more concerned with the safe passage of your infernal devices than of myself.'

'You will not break in the crossing, Christian Hardy.'

'I will never break, Moor.'

'I know this is true. Your Order is fortunate to have you as a soldier. I am fortunate to have you as a friend.'

'I too am fortunate.'

They embraced. 'May your God go with you and help you.'

'*A Christian gaining succour from a Mohammedan. An uncommon thing.*'

'A turd wrapped in the cloth is less uncommon, Prior Garza.'

Hardy turned to face the voice and shaded figure of the Prior. There might be several reasons for his presence, and not one would be charitable.

'I see you volunteer for damnation, Hardy.'

'Fighting for Christ is to be blessed, Prior.'

'Do you fight for any but yourself?'

'Do you visit for any reason but to gloat?'

'I am here to give absolution to my Spanish countrymen and the brethren of my *langue*.'

'Then I thank God I am an Englishman.'

'You will thank no one when the Turk has you on his blade.'

'*Prior Garza. The learned churchman I seek.*' It was Fra Roberto, his mass looming vast but near-invisible behind the Prior. From the squeal of pain and protest, he must have seized the senior prelate in a tight and friendly grip. 'Let us walk awhile, you and I.'

'Unhand me, you dolt.'

'Dolt? I was clever enough to live in the north away from you these many years.'

'Consider your position, Fra Roberto.'

'I am happy to consider yours. Now come away.'

Protesting, struggling, his high-pitched voice rising higher, the Prior was led from the scene.

The Moor held Hardy by his shoulders. 'You exchange one madness for another.'

'I leave behind many I love.'

Oars dipped, their blades puddling green in the phosphorescence as the boats pulled away towards the open water. Sanctuary was gone. In its place were the rhythmic efforts of the oarsmen, the scampering heartbeat and shallow breath of scared men, the powder mists around the lone fort on its peninsula. Even here they could taste the battle, smell the sweet geranium-stench of corpses travelling on the air. An unsettling state.

The whisper was urgent. 'Christian, a light on the St Angelo cavalier.'

Hardy had been concentrating ahead, focused on the ethereal image of St Elmo. He squinted back towards their former home, looking up towards the hidden tower. Nothing. He peered again. It was there, a small pinprick, a lamp, blinking periodically in the black, unlikely to be seen by any but the most dedicated.

'What does it mean, Christian? A signal?'

'Look to your forward. That is where the threat will lie.'

He had no real answer. The illumination on the tower could be an oversight or lack of discipline, a sentry pausing with a lantern or igniting a linen wick. It was not his responsibility. Uncertainty nagged. He expelled it from his mind, leaned to stare ahead as the boats glided on. They were drawing closer to the fort.

A shot was followed by another, a fusillade of arquebus-fire ripping up the silence, tearing at their sides. The Turks had come to intercept. There were shouts, screams, returning volleys, the crash of splintering wood as boats met and blind skirmishing escalated. The man beside Hardy sighed and slumped. Beyond him, a Spanish musketeer stood to take aim and was launched overboard by the impact of lead.

'Brace yourselves. Lower your pikes.'

Preparations were rapid, almost too late. A Turkish boat struck, the vessels locking, the naval melee taking the form of sightless savagery and instinct. One on one. Hardy ducked. The blade-stroke went wide, and he did not give the attacker a second chance. An arquebus discharged nearby. Deafened, almost blinded, he had glimpsed a round shield and pressed home below it. The Turk staggered backwards, toppling, unbalancing a comrade who fell on a body. Within seconds the Ottoman boat capsized.

Now it was sport of a different kind, apple-bobbing, the piercing of floundering and water-logged humans with spear and sword. The Christians killed until there was no further movement. Surviving Turks had fled, their frantic oar-splashes interrupted and pursued by triumphant salvos. A small win of sorts. But the Christians could not afford to give chase or rest, had no remit to delay their harsher destiny. They rowed on across the harbour.

✳

Chapter 6

'You carry the response of the Grand Master to our petition?' They crowded round, young Knights anxious for news, eager to be evacuated to the better climes of St Angelo. Hardy pushed his way through. Before him, the light from pitch torches picked out the devastation, the blitzed ruins of what had once been St Elmo. The defenders had become troglodytes, gaunt-faced denizens of tunnels and shallow scrapes, of temporary barricades of stone and bedding. They were brave men. But below their feet the ground shook; about them the melting walls had lost all form and any height. Breaking-point, and they had every reason to reach it. So this was where he had come to die.

He leaped on to a block of limestone and faced them. 'You desire an answer to your pleas. I am that answer.'

There was puzzlement, shock, rebellious murmuring among the assembled.

One called out, 'What is this? A trick? A play of words?'

'Neither.'

'We wish to return to St Angelo.'

'Then do so. The Grand Master has provided boats for the occasion. Fill them. Go back to your *langues*; explain to them the circumstance of your desertion.'

'Desertion?' A furious face thrust close towards him. 'Look about you. There is nothing to desert, nothing left but a worthless pile of brick.'

'Brick that is given value by the spirit of the defence.'

'Defence cannot be spirited if it is squandered, if we are crushed by the weight of enemy shot.

We would be of greater service were we to charge at the infidel naked and unarmed.'

'Instead, you choose to slip away.'

'You, a mercenary to the Service Brothers, would lecture us?'

'True, we are different. I will stand and fight. What you do as noble Knights is for your own conscience.'

'Presume not to question our allegiance to the Religion and the Order.'

'How could I, noble brothers?' Hardy watched their faces, saw his words bite deep. 'You have endured more than is reasonable for any man. You have striven as hard in battle as could any true Christian. You have taken upon yourselves the burdens and hopes of the Order and Christendom itself. Grand Master La Valette recognizes he asks too much.'

'You twist our thoughts.'

'I understand them. Hurry to the boats. You will be replaced by volunteers collecting at this moment in their hundreds at St Angelo.'

They shifted uneasily, were moving ground. 'Does Grand Master La Valette condemn us as cowards, as traitors?'

'He does not. You are his brethren. But he begs that you should pass your weapons to those who will use them to greater effect here at St Elmo.'

'Surrender up our swords, our muskets?'

'While those of us who remain have breath, limbs, and steel or powder to hand, we will stand to the last.'

'*I shall stay.*'

'*As will I.*'

'*Listen to Christian Hardy. If he and two hundred Spanish troops can fight, so may we.*'

'*Were we lowly soldiers, we would be hanged for this.*'

'*We cannot face our brothers in Birgu in the knowledge we have left others to die.*'

'*We cannot face God.*'

Hardy left them to their argument. Shame would inspire them, would evaporate dissent. They would rather chain themselves to their positions than be marked or exiled as fainthearts. He walked through the wrecked body of the fort to the seaward side, heading for the drawbridge that led to the cavalier tower. The smell of decay lessened out there. Behind him, a basilisk-ball erupted through a rubble mound of sandstone, its arrival pulverizing the rock, shredding a group of the newly arrived Spaniards sheltering close by. Another breach made.

He stepped on to the drawbridge and found Colonel Mas waiting for him. The Knight saluted.

'Welcome to your mausoleum, Christian.'

To the landward side of St Elmo was a deep ditch protected by the high earthwork walls of the ravelin. This was no ordinary embankment. It was a formidable obstacle, reinforced with trees cut and brought from the Sicilian forests, and it constituted the main outer defence of the fortress. The Turks had reached it. Try as they might, they had failed to penetrate its monumental construction. Bombard as they might, their shot could damage but not destroy. And behind its parapet the Knights patrolled, keeping watch, staying ready, linked to the relative sanctuary of the fort by a narrow plank-bridge running between the base of the earth barrier and the main portcullis gate. A waiting game.

It was before dawn on Sunday 3 June 1565, St Elmo's Day in the Christian calendar. The fifteenth day of invasion. For defender and attacker alike, it would doubtless be a day like any other: the constant blast of cannon, the patter of arquebus-shot, the holding-off of final assault until the walls and spirit of the Christians were broken. Dragut was no fool. The king of the corsairs would not commit, could not countenance a frontal charge, unless all factors pointed to victory. Today, another of those factors would be brought to bear: the opening salvos fired by the new battery on Tigné Point. In the meantime, the engineers would go forward to inspect the walls and search for weakness. Surgical operations required initial exploration.

The small party of Turks crept to the bottom of the ravelin. At any moment they might be challenged, could be met with a line of arquebus muzzles spitting flame and lead in their direction. They were right to be cautious. The Christians enjoyed their little tricks and ambushes. Previous scouting and sapper patrols had found themselves overwhelmed in seconds. So far, not a sound. The Turk officer laid his ear against the earth berm and listened. The clink of mail, the rasp of a sword, the scrape and flare of a lighting taper, all could be preludes to aggression. He pressed his head closer. Yet silence like this was puzzling. With the squeeze of an arm, he indicated that a soldier should climb on to the shoulders of another and observe through an unguarded embrasure to the ground beyond. Having come this far, they would push their luck and the boundaries of their reconnaissance. The men obeyed and the scout was lifted upward. It did not take long. He slithered down and made his report, his body vibrating with tension, his whispers breathless in excitement. The infidels were asleep. There were no sentries, no patrolling guards, no Knights making their inspections from the fort. God was truly smiling on the Sultan and his armies. Now was the moment to strike.

Hurriedly, the Turk officer led his squad away, the engineers retracing their steps through the trenches and troop positions towards the command-tents. Dragut and Mustapha Pasha would know what to do.

Habit was difficult to shed. For most of his life, dawn had carried the threat of an enemy assault or involved preparations for a raid. In St Elmo that expectation, preoccupation, was stronger still. Hardy buckled on his sword and took up a heavy partisan spear before making for the portcullis entrance. Around him, exhausted men slept, their snores and shell-shocked nightmares floating eerily from behind fire-points and random stones. Each was alone with his demons, his own thoughts of death. He let them be, would conduct his rounds without commotion or attendants. Any later, the cannon-shot would begin to fall, the arquebusiers would find their aim. Better to slip out to the forward posts before daylight and the inferno it would bring.

He nudged the portcullis guards with his foot. 'Raise your gate enough to let me through. Watch the approaches.'

Grumbling, they obeyed, their sleep-starved minds barely registering the command. Iron slid from its grooves, the grating creak of a capstan sounded, and the portcullis lifted a fraction. He slid beneath. There was a certain freedom to escaping beyond the stone confines, a thrill to walking a perilous route separated from the enemy only by a mud wall. The suicide watch. He strolled slowly on the narrow wood bridge, careful with his footing, his eyes glancing to left and right. One wrong step and he would be pitched headlong into the deep ditch below. If the fall did not kill him, the excreta-covered stakes set into the bottom surely would. He shuffled forward again, the partisan employed as an improvised staff. His sight would adapt eventually to the dark and grainy image.

Quietness blanketed the scene. After the night bombardment, the brief respite compounded the stillness. It was a mystery how the volunteers manning the ravelin could find rest in these hours. Yet they appeared to be slumbering, seemed to be content to lie huddled around the base of the looming wall. Hardy stared around. Something pricked at his instinct. It was imperceptible, a feeling grasping for a reason. But he had trusted it before, and it had saved his life. He swung the partisan down and held it forward in his hands. In the dimness, the sentries would be watching. Perchance they too were dozing, or were already dead. Hardy swept his gaze along the length of the wall. The picture had changed, the top of the ravelin was moving.

'*Turks! Sound the alarm! Sound the alarm!*'

He was shouting as the first musket-balls flicked overhead, as the enemy swarmed up their scaling-ladders and over the summit. Scimitars hacked remorselessly. A few defenders survived the initial wave, running for their lives and for the bridge while Hardy guarded their flight. He jabbed with the partisan, stepping back, giving ground, feeling his way. One on one, he might hold them for a while, give his companions time to rally and man the walls. A balancing act. He had to prevent the Ottomans from crossing the bridge, had to stall them in reaching the portcullis.

The storm broke against him. He ran a Janissary through, cutting off the high-pitched war cry. Another came forward, his round shield parrying the spear, his scimitar carving the air. Hardy stabbed at his lower legs. With a shriek, the Turk tripped and toppled into the ditch, floundering and dying on impact. His replacement was in position. Hardy gripped the partisan diagonally across his chest, whipping it round to confuse and knock flat. Three down, several thousand more coming on behind.

'*Retire, Christian! You must withdraw!*' His friends were calling him, urging him back.

'*Christian, we will hold them with cannon! Your situation is without hope!*'

He shouted back. 'There is ever hope! Destroy the bridge! You must destroy the bridge!'

'*There is no time! Come away, Christian!*'

His feet slithered on the planking. He was nearing the portcullis, fending off the jostling horde. Their weight pressed in, their howling noise climbing. They could scent the kill. Above, the Christian muskets were popping, finding their targets. But the Janissaries remorselessly pushed on, dragging masts, beginning to attempt new crossings of the ditch.

A piteous cry, and a Knight fell past Hardy into the trench. He would be lost among the later press of dead.

'*The trump! Christian, take the trump!*'

It had been quick thinking by a guardian angel on the walls. With an upward glance, he caught the long wooden shaft of the incendiary and swept it in a fiery arc towards the advancing enemy.

The muzzle snorted, spitting flame, igniting a swathe of robed Turks. In seconds they were indistinct shapes writhing in a sea of fire, some staggering among their brethren, spreading the conflagration, others dropping like wax candles to burn in the ditch below. A figure stripped of life and flesh collapsed in molten incandescence on the bridge. Wood smouldered. Hardy moved forward, catching a trio of kneeling arquebusiers as they sought to take aim. They erupted into individual pyres, their powder-horns detonating and blowing away body parts. The foe were edging away.

Gradually the blazing tongue of the trump weakened. It sputtered, its bellow growing asthmatic and thin. The Turks pushed in. A large Janissary smiled as he inched forward, signalling to the arquebusiers beside him to lower their weapons. The infidel would be his, was there for the taking and the trophy head.

'You stare at death, unbeliever.'

Hardy did not move. 'I stare at mere Turk.'

'A Janissary, an Invincible One.'

'None are invincible.' He watched as the flame from the trump died. 'You are a clown bedecked in heron plumes.'

'I am a soldier of the Sultan and the Crescent who will drink your blood.'

'For that you will need a mouth and a stomach.'

It was the black Moor who had modified the trump, who had placed inside its hollow tube a brass canister full of musket-balls. These now discharged. In a ripple-explosion, they tore through the Turkish ranks, winnowing, flattening, driving back. Men clutched at faces which had ceased to be, clasped at bellies that spilled their contents. The upper torso of the Janissary had vanished.

Chased by the splintering impact of arquebus-rounds, Hardy raced over the bridge and dived beneath the portcullis. It dropped as he rolled clear, as the cannons above it opened fire direct into the oncoming force. Hardy slithered to cover. One Turk had almost caught him, was himself pinioned by the full load of the portcullis descending through his backbone. Bug-eyed and frantic, the soldier struggled for a time.

In frenzied and collective rage, the vanguard hit the portcullis, firing through to the interior passage, hacking at the steel grille and soft limestone surround. Access was their aim, dismantling their chosen course. Behind them, the rest of the Janissary corps poured over the ravelin, sustaining the momentum, ignoring casualties, hurling themselves across the ditch with grapple-hooks and makeshift ladders. Many died. Yet death held no fear, offered no excuse to lessen the pace. A deceased Janissary could be as useful as a living one, was a stepping-stone, a building-block, a filler for a ditch.

'*Over here, Christian.*'

Hardy moved around the subsiding ramparts, clearing embrasures of Turks, throwing back Janissaries and levies from smoking breaches. An Ottoman soldier clung to a crenellation until his hands were shorn off and he fell away. A brace of combatants emerged over a battlement and were promptly disembowelled with the cutting edge of a glaive. Even the stones seemed to leak blood. Where heads were removed, their replacements appeared; where Moslem attackers were repulsed, more returned. It was a moment of last resort, and of wildfire.

Holocaust burst upon the enemy. The attackers were ill-prepared, unprotected, against the hail of clay pots shattering among them. Fire spewed, burning through cloth, clinging to skin and chain-mail, cascading in a brilliant waterfall down the sides of the fort. Turks combusted, plummeted, windmilling in their descent, catching others, adding to the erupting hell of the ditch. Then came the fire-hoops, spiralling down to circle and entangle groups of escalading Janissaries. Robes became sheets of flame; humans became glowing embers leaping and dancing from the walls. The Christians watched them go.

It was no longer a man, but a furnace which had climbed above the rampart to seize and embrace a Spanish soldier too slow, too astonished, to respond. The pair toppled backwards and disappeared. A Knight tottered, arquebus-rounds striking and flashing on his armour, before he fumbled the wildfire and was quickly engulfed. He stood rooted, trapped within a one-twenty-pound roasting-oven, expecting to be cooked, waiting to die. It did not happen. Hardy propelled him with a kick towards a water barrel and extinguished the flames with immersion.

'*Christian, to your left!*'

'*Over here, Christian!*'

'*Christian, they try again!*'

They fought into the afternoon, the attackers battering against the walls in wave upon wave, the defenders replying with blocks of stone, with cauldrons of burning pitch, with trumps, wildfire and hoops. There was no give, no respite. The ditch blazed with corpses, incinerating the wrecked detritus of spars and lateen-masts. Above it hung a black and heavy pall of smoke and the sick-sweet smell of charred flesh.

Without a sound, the Knight slumped heavily to the ground. It was Bridiers de La Gardampe, an Auvergne nobleman who had battled hard throughout the day, had shown himself too long in the sights of the Janissary sharpshooters. A musket-ball must have penetrated. Hardy crawled across the open breach towards him, staying low, threading his way between puffs of dust thrown up by striking rounds.

'Keep away, my brother.' The Knight motioned feebly at him, a line of bloody sputum trickling from his mouth. 'I am among the dead. Spend your time with those who live.'

A section of wall collapsed. Hardy struggled free and found himself at close quarters with an oncoming band of Janissaries.

They never learned, rarely abandoned their position at the point of the spearhead. That could be of benefit. He studied them as they rushed him, admiring their focus, their nerve, their single-minded commitment to the kill. All they would see was a lone infidel blocking their path. What he could see was a bunched group of assassins without depth of vision or awareness of miscalculation.

At the last moment, he sidestepped behind a slab of limestone. In his place, facing the Turks, was the muzzle of an anti-personnel gun. The weapon had been removed from a galley, transported to the fort, and filled with the gunpowder and scrap metal which made it so deadly at sea. It was equally lethal on land. With a roar, the blast came and the image which had existed reddened and dissolved.

In the early evening the defenders of St Elmo went to their chapel to give thanks. Against the odds and overwhelming numbers, the fort had held. For fewer than a hundred Christians slain, the Ottoman forces had lost thousands. Enemy casualties littered the field, carpeted the protecting ditch. A high price, but one that would be absorbed, which had stripped the fortress of its ravelin and carried the crescent banners to the foot of the besieged bastion. Turk cannons could fire point-blank; Turk snipers could pick off targets at will; Turk onslaughts could be launched without warning. The Knights had merely won an extension of time, a prolonging of their agony. And stretched out dead before the altar in the small chapel was the Auvergne Knight Bridiers de La Gardampe. Mortally wounded, he had dragged himself there to meet his God. His comrades were readying to do the same.

'I cannot bring them back, Henri.'

'It is why I do not ask, Uncle.'

'Would that more in the Sacro Consiglio thought as you. Each day they petition me to abandon the position.'

From a window in the cavalier of St Angelo, the Grand Master and his nephew watched. Half a mile distant – the harbour mouth and a world away – another Turk attack was going in. The scorched heap of St Elmo shook, belching flame, shedding stone, unrecognizable and collapsed beyond its former contours. Even here in St Angelo, they could feel the shock waves, the flaring temperature of conflict above the summer heat. It was a wonder anything could survive, a greater miracle that anyone still fought.

'Mustapha Pasha and Dragut seem resolved to raze the entire headland, Uncle.'

'I have no doubt they will achieve it.'

'Is there no more we can do?'

'We may pray and send token assistance. We may urge them to stand until the end.'

'I should be with them, Uncle.'

'They have their part as you have yours.'

'None complain, even when they are brought to the infirmary and are near to death.'

'We are all of us near to death, Henri. It is what gives us our purpose, our belief in defending the Religion.'

'I cannot forget they hold fast for us.'

'While they bleed, the heathen bleeds worse. It is the sole comfort we may take from their plight.'

'You think it will be long, Uncle?'

'The ravelin and the ditch are taken, the walls sink, the defences are beset. At the most, it will be days.'

The battle was unfolding as it had before, with the Turks scrambling up a ditch made ever-shallower by the rubble of the fortress walls and the exertions of the Ottoman labour corps. With each assault, the Turks were forced back by steel, lead-shot and fire. Yet with each assault, too, another breach appeared, a further toll was taken of the diminishing Christian garrison.

La Valette placed a hand on his nephew's shoulder. 'Monsieur Hardy gives good account of himself, Henri.'

'I have heard from among the injured. They say he has turned the fortune of combat on many occasion.'

'It will not change the fate of St Elmo.' The Grand Master brushed away the fine layer of dust blown from the ruined fortress and gathering on his doublet. 'The infidels have built a mound outside the ravelin, will command every aspect of the fort with cannon and musket. Our brothers will perish as their sport.'

'Christian will offer them a more challenging game.'

'He has shown so far the wit to escape serious ill.'

But wit had little to do with situations of chance. Neither Hardy nor a fresh commitment of troops would alter the predicted course. All would be consumed. La Valette closed his eyes and sniffed the battle-tainted air. There was no other way, no comforting outcome. The Viceroy of Sicily had again written, lied anew, had promised to send relief by the end of the month. They were empty words, the lines of a politician bidding farewell.

'You wondered if there was more we might do, Henri.'

'Whatever is demanded will be performed, Uncle.'

'Then look to Gallows Point. What do you see?'

'The completed battery of Dragut.'

'One which achieves the encirclement of St Elmo, which will engage our boats at night, ensure we can neither send reinforcements in nor bring casualties out.'

'Allow me to lead a raid, Uncle.'

'Monsieur Hardy came to me with suggestion for attack. We are without him, and those guns remain. Take whoever you require for the assault.'

'I will not let you down, Uncle.'

La Valette contemplated him fondly. 'Whatever happened to my nephew who was satisfied with books, content in the gentler arts of the hospital?'

'He fell into the company of Christian Hardy, encountered the Turk.'

'Each in itself an education and a baptism.'

Henri looked away, his attention drawn back to St Elmo, to the assigned resting-place and purgatory of his friend and mentor Christian. Nothing had to be said. The Englishman was a professional soldier, had forbidden his companions to mourn. It did not make it easier to be left behind.

The movement beside him intruded. He turned to find the Grand Master hunched over, leaning on the balustrade, a spasm of pain creasing his face.

'Uncle, you are hurt?'

'A complaint of old age. It is little more.'

'Not so, Uncle. You must come at once to the physician.'

'I will not.' La Valette straightened and glared direct into the eyes of the younger man. 'On your life, and as my closest blood, you will listen and you will vow. You never witnessed this incident. You have no knowledge of my state. The Order and the outcome of this siege will depend on it.'

'Sworn to God, you have my word, Uncle.'

'So we are agreed to forget.'

Henri de La Valette nodded, another doubt added to a sea of concern.

They had brought Luigi Broglia, commander of St Elmo, to the Sacred Infirmary. His bones fractured, his face torn and burnt, he lay stoic and silent as the medics tended his wounds. He was one among many. At his bedside, his old friend Knight Grand Cross Lacroix kept vigil, talking of former days, recounting the escapades of youth, of Rhodes, of better times. But neither could dismiss the reality of these darkened wards.

Maria flinched at the echo of the gun salvo. It was another cannon aimed at St Elmo, another iron ball sent hurtling towards Christian. She whispered a prayer, and bent to apply warmed stones to the infected leg of a victim. The man cried out.

'I apologize, monsieur. It is done to draw the poison.'

She repeated the procedure, heard the sharp intake of breath, the swallowed sob. Hers was a token act. Within a day he would be delirious, within two would lose the limb, within three would be dead. There was a grinding predictability to it all. She could read the future in their eyes, could tell with a touch the difference between a night chill and the cold of dying.

Blood dripped loud into a bowl as a medic opened the vein of a prone Knight. Enough had been shed on the battlefield. She moved on to the next alcove, setting down her lamp and stooping to inspect a dressing. The maggots were feeding, had consumed much of the rotten flesh.

'Take heart, monsieur. You revive well.'

'Do not be deceived, my lady. St Elmo has done for me.'

'Its spirit will endure and inspire.'

'When its commander himself lies wounded here, there is no doubt as to the end.'

'God may yet intervene.' Her hands trembled as she applied the bandage.

The soldier gripped her fingers. 'If you visited, my lady, you would see that God has long since abandoned the post.'

A voice was calling out for water. She hurried away, anxious to leave the conversation, to avoid betraying emotion and the start of tears welling in her eyes. Weeping was for the privacy of her own bedchamber. There were sights and sounds which in the rarefied cage of Mdina she had never encountered, extremes of courage and conflict she had never before thought possible. She ached with pity for these broken men. But she was also jealous, for their recent proximity to Christian Hardy, for sharing a danger that to her was denied. It was absurd and selfish, a feeling she would work hard to quell. And yet. The voice pleaded again for water.

Hubert had completed his prayer. He rose from the foot of the bed and found Maria waiting for him.

'I trust I do not intrude, Hubert.'

He blushed deep-red, self-conscious and conscious of her aura. 'My task is not an urgent one, my lady.'

'Entreaties to God are as pressing as any. We each do what we may.'

'I am humbled by their actions, my lady. They are the bravest of warriors, I the merest of novice chaplains.'

'Without chaplains there would be no Religion, no future to the Order, no Hubert to apply a spiritual salve in time of need.'

He grinned. 'You say kind things, my lady.'

'I say the truth. How would these souls or any of us fare were your friendship and concern to be absent?'

'In part I am here through friendship and concern for Christian.'

'I too, sweet Hubert.'

'While he does not lie on these litters, he may yet be alive.'

'And while you aid his stricken companions, you will be assisting him.'

'Then there is some comfort, my lady.'

She hesitated, uncertain whether to speak her thoughts, if it were wrong to involve an innocent in her cause. The young priest might seek to dissuade her. Or he would comply, ever anxious to help a human in need. Whichever his response, she was imposing on his goodness.

His eyes were bright and understanding. 'My lady, you wish to go to St Elmo.'

He was dreaming. It was a peaceful place, a sunlit valley reaching to the sea and bounded by rolling hills, and he was riding Helios. In the distance he could see peasants gathering in the harvest, beyond them a whitewashed cottage he knew to be home. As he drew near, Helios reared and shied, unwilling to go on. He tried to calm the stallion, struggled to control him. The horse resisted. Then the reason became clear. It was no simple valley, but a trap, the sea a mirage, the hills around him the covered outline of a fortress. Now the peasants had formed into ranks, their faces distended and blackened like those of dead Turks, their hands gripping arquebuses and scimitars instead of sickles and hoes. He had been a fool to be so easily tricked. The signs were there all along, the seasonal crop of severed heads and limbs so neatly stacked, the snatches of country song which had turned suddenly to the battle-chants of Janissaries. The cottage began to burn. Still Helios refused to move. And above the rising din was something else, a sound that made him fear as only a child could fear. His mother and sisters were screaming.

Another presence floated calm into his fevered trance. She was cradling his head, caressing him, holding water to his cracked lips and letting it spill on his dust-hardened beard. Maria had come to him. He reached out, asking for her blessing and forgiveness.

She stroked his head. 'Do not be angry that I am here, Christian.'

'Maria? It is you?' He struggled upright, met and answered her loving kiss. 'It cannot be, it cannot.'

'My lord, it is so.'

'But it is madness, Maria.'

'One we may share for a while until the boats depart.'

'The boats? How was this possible?'

'A simple matter of Henri destroying Dragut's battery on Gallows Point, of Hubert and Fra Roberto smuggling me in a chaplain's cowl aboard the night flotilla.'

'You take such risk, Maria.'

'How could I not? We left so much unsaid when last we parted.'

'Yet I fear for you here. It is a place of death, not of assignation.'

'For a moment we may change it.' They kissed again, holding each other in the fetid night air. 'You wear my silver cross?'

'Beside my heart.'

'It is where I wish to be.'

He nuzzled her neck, whispered in her ear, smelled and touched her skin. 'We have lost all reason.'

'We have found each other.'

'A wonder in the midst of Hades.'

'There is no love that is not worth danger, no joy that is not enhanced by proximity to despair.'

'You have visited me in my dreams. I have thought of you, ached for you, at every moment.'

'Put thought aside, Christian.'

They sank back together, losing themselves, forgetting in their intensity the powdering stones, the closeness of decay, the immediacy of destruction. Out here on the wasted rampart, the insanity made sense. They were fumbling, rolling, tearing at clothing, groping at flesh. Lips and tongues coupled, probing, a precursor to the coming act. There was so little time. A lifespan was being mapped, a passion consummated, the torment of simultaneous discovery and loss becoming exposed. Something to celebrate and to mourn. She opened to him, let him slide inside, taking him deep with a shuddering whimper. They were slick with sweat, moving slow and fast, feeling their way, each other, fire-shivering with momentum. He was burying himself and his memories, giving himself up to carnality and worship. She received him, consumed him. An altered state. They bucked, fused and shifting, groaning and growing, the energy raw, affirming, building to climax. It was love besieged by hate, sexual congress bounded by the stench of mortality. Two people devoted. No experience could matter more, be so fierce or so tender. Nothing would ever replicate it.

She had gone. He was alone, asleep again, when the Turkish flare burst high above the fort. Its brilliance hurt his eyes. He thought it must be dawn and the arrival of another tortured day. But it remained night – one that threw sudden shadows, which came alive with a shower-fall of shot, the shouts of men, the staccato trumpet-blast of a call to arms. The Ottomans were attacking.

They carried flaming torches, were streaming from Mount Sciberras in an endless lava-flow that washed up to St Elmo. So beautiful, so deadly. Hardy slithered forward. Caught in the open, ambushed in the act of pushing a block of stone across a gaping rift, a Spanish sentry recoiled and fell to the impact of arquebus-rounds. Blood pumped, and the ground puddled black at his feet. The musket-balls continued to strike. Distance was closing. Hardy listened to the cries of the Janissaries, could hear the mullahs call out to the faithful, to the lions of Islam, to those chosen to slaughter the last offending remnants of the infidel. He would have to disoblige.

The advance troops hit, throwing their *sachetti* fire-grenades, leaping forward with their scimitars raised. Hardy bludgeoned a shield aside with his war-club and lunged with his sword. Another kill. Flames danced around him, the acrid smoke filling his nostrils and searing his eyes. He did not notice. His focus was on annihilation, on ensuring that as few of the enemy as possible remained standing and able to mount a challenge to the walls of Birgu. That would be his legacy, his dying gift to Maria. He could taste her in his mouth, scent her lingering sweetness, feel her long dark hair brush soft against his face. The murder zone enveloped him, and the dream of the burning cottage returned.

Chapter 7

'I have heard Piali nurses a splinter-wound.'

'He nurses his shame, Dragut.' Mustapha Pasha scowled behind his moustaches. 'It was the Admiral who urged us to attack St Elmo, who insisted it would fall within three days. Look below you, Dragut. Three weeks, and the ground is still held by the infidel.'

'Yet it does not much resemble a fort.'

'Even termites can defend their pile of earth.'

The army commander and the old corsair sat on their horses and stared down from the summit of Mount Sciberras upon the blistered remains of St Elmo. Again the guns had opened up, atomizing what had already been destroyed, adding to the dust haze clouding the peninsula. It was almost beyond belief that such a corpse could continue to fight.

Dragut shook his head. 'I have rarely seen such resistance.'

'Five thousand of my men already lost in combat, the cream of my Janissaries slaughtered, fifteen hundred of them in the night attack alone. Further thousands lie dead or dying from sickness.'

'We will crush St Elmo.'

'We have no choice, Dragut. It is a matter of honour and reputation, the dignity of the Sultan at stake.'

'All of which are threatened by the bastard upstart Piali.'

'A bastard upstart with influence in the harem and the ear of Suleiman. We can but solve the problem through total victory here.'

'It will be done, Mustapha Pasha, I have rebuilt and reinforced the battery destroyed by the infidel raid on Gallows Point. My cannoneers have brought to bear their heaviest guns. Four thousand arquebusiers ring the fort, guard-posts line the shore. Not a swallow could reach the position.'

'Their confidence and fighting spirit remain.'

'Neither will count when they are buried where they lie.'

'While our troops lie sprawled on the open mounds where they fall.' Mustapha Pasha peered down the slope, followed the curve of a cannonball until its impact in an angry puff of smoke. 'But perhaps you are right, Dragut. Perhaps the enemy will soon break.'

'The fort is at the limit of its perseverance.'

'My patience is strained in similar measure. A Spaniard defecting from their ranks informs me there are those among them who would seek to parley, who would withdraw to Birgu if offered the occasion.'

'You believe him, Mustapha Pasha?'

'I believe he will suffer the slowest and most terrible of deaths if he lies.'

'How should we respond to his advice?'

'With caution, with tactics to divide those infidel who persist. I will send to St Elmo a messenger carrying peace terms, extending final chance to leave the fort alive.'

'Why not also use the Spaniard? He will serve as living proof to its defenders of the advantage in submission.'

'I will ponder it, Dragut. Though I confess I would prefer to drown this base coward in a vat of sulphur.'

'Let us first employ him.'

'One thing he has confirmed. The cavalryman who engaged and slew our forage party at Zeitun is the infidel who held our forces when we took the outer ravelin. His name is Christian Hardy. He is still within St Elmo.'

'Vengeance will be the sweeter when it comes.'

'To this end, I will provide any man who brings him to me alive or dead his weight in gold and gemstones.'

'Your soldiers will find competition from my corsairs.'

'None have known you to reach Tripoli empty-handed, Dragut.'

'I have doubt I shall ever see my lands again.'

Maybe the aged pirate had premonition of his own death. It was conceivable he forecast a future role as governor of Malta. Whatever these musings, Mustapha Pasha had other concerns. His forces were hungry and sickening, grumbling and dying. He had sent supply-ships to North Africa, but they had yet to return. Morale was poor, victuals low; quick victory had changed to bloody attrition. Because of one damned admiral; because of one cursed fort. The real challenge, the battle for Senglea and Birgu, for the fort of St Michael and the mighty parapets of St Angelo, was to come. Nothing was assured. He would be needing the spy.

He spat the dust from his throat, but the bitter taste clung. His horse swayed as another Ottoman barrage shook the ground. They were remarkable people, these Knights. He might once have respected them had not issues of power and faith and all-consuming hatred intervened. It would be a pleasure beyond compare to cut their throats.

A cannon-round was incoming the thousand yards from St Angelo. It appeared to drift lazily across the water, hanging aimless, before closing and accelerating fast. The army chief and the corsair tracked it. In a whistling shriek it dropped, clawing for distance, reaching for a knot of senior officers gathered on a ridge-line. A long shot, and it found its mark. Rock fractured, Turks flew ragged in the air, and the pulped remnants of the Lieutenant Aga of the Janissaries slammed shapeless in a heap of broken bone and ruined plumage. Mustapha Pasha and Dragut viewed the spectacle in silence before turning their horses and riding away.

★

Piali was indeed nursing a splinter-wound. His arm in a sling, he lounged on cushions in his grand tent on the Marsa. There were better things to do than join his rivals in the sport of artillery-spotting, than to put himself once more in danger. Out there he would be forced to endure the smell of disease and decay, suffer the indignity of sideways glances and sly comment. In here he was immune, away from Mustapha Pasha and that ancient mariner Dragut. Rosewater could be sipped, incense breathed, the cooler air enjoyed. Campaigning had its delights.

He viewed one of them now. 'You are a prize I did not expect.'

'War holds many surprises.'

'A Maltese girl who speaks the tongues of both France and Italy. You are a noblewoman.' He studied her face, observed her blank defiance. 'It is rare to see such beauty.'

'While I encounter only ugliness.'

'Careful, my lady. Days spent tied to a mast in the sun will soon spoil your features and complexion.'

'Do what you will. I have seen of what you are capable, how the other captives from my boat fared.'

'They were surplus to my need.'

'Essential to your blood-lust.'

'The hand of the Ottoman is guided by God.'

'You are wrong.' Her face wrinkled in contempt. 'It is controlled by the most base of instincts.'

'Be certain the same punishment will be meted to the satanic dogs which guard St Elmo.'

'I have no doubt they will visit harsher punishment on you.'

Maria had struck a blow, hit a nerve. She saw the perfumed savage bridle at her remark. That was one advantage to being held in chains and brought to his tent. She wanted to tear at his face and gouge out his eyes, wanted to scream, to weep for the man she had left behind, for those from the open boat she had lost. They had been captured with ease in the mouth of Grand Harbour, had failed to outrun the sudden pursuit. This monster in his silks and gold thread had strangled or clubbed each of her companions in turn. She heard their cries still, could smell their terror.

He approached and touched her face. 'A branding-iron should tame you. Or perhaps I will throw you to our army as a working whore, or make gift of you to the Sultan for his harem.' The Admiral walked around her, admiring her form. 'But I am intrigued. A flawless pearl disguised, returning by small boat from a condemned fortress. Such daring.'

'I care for the injured.'

'They are Hospitallers. They care for themselves.'

'At present they fight.'

'At present you lie.' She stood rigid, her eyes fixed ahead, as he came close, sniffed at her skin. 'Should I have you beaten to find the truth?'

'You have the truth. It is no secret that the defenders of St Elmo suffer, that you rain down stone and iron upon them. I could not deny them my help.'

'Your mercy is beguiling.' He licked her ear, slow, deliberate, lapping down to her neck.

'For an officer, you behave with the manners of a gutter rat.'

He gripped her throat, a flash of chill rage bursting through the calm masquerade. 'Do not goad me.'

'You wish to bruise me before I reach the Sultan?'

'Womanhood may be broken in several ways.' His finger traced a descent from her breasts to her pubis, jabbed deep.

She thought of Christian, of how he might have avenged her, would have exacted retribution for her misery and degradation. It was unjust that he should die while men such as Piali lived. She had few weapons with which to resist. Her guile against his desire, her femininity against his hatred. Of a single fact she had become certain. She would not remain in his charge for long.

The dark eyes of the Admiral were engaged, questing. 'Tell me your name.'

'It is Maria.'

'Then prepare, Maria. Your new life is with the Ottoman.'

The arrangement would be temporary, she decided. She would take no instructions from a heathen, obey no vile creature such as this. Preening self-regard was there to play on, libidinous cravings to take advantage of. She owed it to Christian. It was the Admiral who should prepare.

One could die for any reason. It might be the collapse of a battered wall, the ricochet of a musket-round, the presence of a human target indicated to Turk gunners by the column of flies loitering above a defecating soldier. Damn flies. They hatched in the shit and danced on the graves. Christian Hardy swatted the insects away and felt for a pulse. Heatstroke had done for the Portuguese Knight. He had toppled without a word, lay encased in his broiling steel, his eyes bulging and tongue swollen, his face a mottled tone of purple. Not quite the warrior's passing. A quick prayer would suffice and the corpse would begin its short, yard-long, cortège to a surface grave and the other fallen. There it would moulder into the afterlife and ether. Hardy replaced the helmet and slammed shut the visor. Friends rarely went far. They merely lingered, adding to the atmosphere.

Colonel Mas was pepper-potting his way across, his progress marked by the dirt-spouts of Ottoman shot.

He leaned panting against a boulder. 'You have checked for gold, Christian?'

'I test for signs of life, Colonel.'

'A waste of effort in St Elmo.' The officer laughed harshly at his own joke and wiped the sweat from his eyes. 'As for precious metal, no amount will buy us from this impasse.'

'How fare you on the far side of the fort?'

'As poor as in any place. Our position is indefensible, my sentries are shot before they raise their heads, the open space is denied us, our sole shelter is the chapel, and my troops talk of desertion.'

'So all is well.'

'I cannot complain.'

'That is for lesser men.'

'And for those who abandon their posts. Already I have lost one officer in flight to the enemy.'

'We are fortunate it is not a hundred.'

They sat in silence for a while, observing the debris-field of their surroundings, the prone or limping figures of the Knights. Some shook as if afflicted by the palsy. Others babbled incomprehensibly, their bowels voiding through shock and fright. Most were wounded, their ravaged forms bent, disfigured, bandaged. A skeleton crew.

'Look at them, Christian. Our populace of lame beggars and scarecrows.'

'They will find salvation.'

'Not in this world.'

'The next will suffice for all of us, Colonel. It shall not be long.'

'I am glad the Grand Master sends to us no further reserves.'

'He would be unable to. Dragut prevents it with his strengthened battery on Gallows Point, Piali patrols with small boats, Mustapha Pasha directs his men to fortify the shoreline.'

'Thus are we penned in for the kill, the flies our mourners and our pall-bearers.'

'You are a Knight of St John. You have your seat in heaven.'

The Frenchman grimaced, watching as a cannonball rent a heap of loose stones and skipped across the pitted courtyard. 'My seat is well kicked and truly bruised on earth.'

Conversation was interrupted. St Elmo convulsed, was gripped and shaken by the powerful and sudden hand of a full artillery earthquake. Men tumbled, stone shattered. In an instant, nothing could be heard but the scream and crash of ordnance, nothing was felt but the oscillation of the ground and sky. Colonel Mas was running, stumbling, vanishing into the smoke. Hardy lay flat and covered his ears. The rock chippings were again beginning to cover him.

It lasted all day and into the night, the Turkish fleet joining in, fanning out around the peninsula to pump iron rounds into the fort. They were going to it with a vengeance, with a message. The Knights would find peace only if they capitulated or died. It was the heaviest bombardment so far. The batteries on Mount Sciberras, on Tigné and Gallows Point, all were firing, all were obliterating. There were boundaries to the endurance of men, limits on the commitment of God.

Silence that was no silence. It reverberated as an aftershock, deafening, threatening, a ringing stillness which carried devastation, an absence which promised worse. Those who remained alive waited.

A shout. '*Christians, defenders of St Elmo, I bear a message from the merciful one, our commander Mustapha Pasha.*'

'Why so? Do you seek to surrender?' The voice of de Guaras, deputy commander of the fort, sounded as dry as a cicada-call in the night air.

Falteringly, the messenger tried once more. '*I come in peace.*'

'You may go to hell.'

'*Mustapha Pasha is willing to discuss terms.*'

'We are not.'

'*He offers clemency, will show leniency to every man in the fort.*'

'If he forgives so much, let him take his armies from our island.'

'*Any among you who wish to leave for Birgu may do so without fear of harm.*'

'It is a decision for the Grand Master of our Order, not for any heathen.'

'*Mustapha Pasha promises safe passage.*'

'While we promise him many thousands more of his finest troops lying crumpled and bloodied before our walls.'

'*You have no walls, no future, no fortress. Your position is without hope.*'

'Our hearts are filled with the spirit and power of the Lord.'

'*Mustapha Pasha asks that you see reason.*'

'We see only God.'

A second voice rang out, Spanish instead of French. '*Chevalier de Guaras. It is Captain Alvarez.*'

'You are held against your will?'

'*I am not.*'

'Then you are a traitor to the Religion and to your men, and you will die.'

'*Some length of time after you, Commander. Hear me, countrymen.*' The words were insistent, hung seductive in the charred darkness. '*To what end do you struggle? To what benefit do you resist? Is your pay good? Are your conditions pleasing? Why should you suffer and die for this, for a Grand Master who deserts you, for an Order which cares nothing for you? The Turks give their word.*'

'And we give ours.'

Volleys of musket-fire erupted along the line, accompanied by cheers and catcalls, by the anger of men bent on achieving a single kill. They were aiming blind, unlikely to hit a target in rapid and unseemly retreat. Yet it was essential to try. The Spanish captain was one of their number, had been drawn to the Turk, lured to Satan in his wilderness, through cowardice and personal failing. He was the final insult, the spear in the side of the crucified Christ. They would not forgive.

Within minutes, the Turks responded to the decision of the besieged defenders. Basilisk-shot sledgehammered home into the ruins, culverin-balls careered murderously among the craters and recesses. A dying, disintegrating netherworld. It was not yet over – not by far. Only when dawn came did the barrage ease, did the flicker of the Turkish cannons trail off into an unsettled interlude. The night watch was through. Slowly the sounds of the coming day supplanted it, the tempo of the Ottoman drumbeat and clamour of tambourines and cymbals rose, as an army prepared for attack. Saturday 16 June 1565. The twenty-eighth day of invasion.

In the broken husk of St Elmo, men were emerging to shake stone wreckage from their bodies and armour. They were more ghostly than ever, their eyes peering bloodshot from faces masked and mired in grime. But they held their swords and their pikes, carried the few remaining incendiaries, hobbled to take their positions. Some gathered in the gloom near the former site of the main portcullis gate.

'What is this?' De Guaras, the deputy commander, confronted them.

'It is as you see, Brother Chevalier. We intend to charge the enemy.'

'You have no authority.'

'We have our duty as Christian Knights and warriors, are entrusted to kill the infidel. It is what we shall do.'

'At the cost of St Elmo.'

'To the glory of God. Better to die of our choosing than to tarry and be torn apart by heathen cannon.'

De Guaras raised his sword. 'You will first encounter my blade.'

'Lower it, Brother Chevalier.' Weapons and the rage of desperation jostled in a crowded space.

'I will not.'

'Noble brothers.' Hardy and Colonel Mas stepped in to flank de Guaras. The Englishman held his weapons at his side. 'The enemy is outside the breach.'

'We head that way.'

'You, my brothers, are the gallants and braves. It is why I joined you from St Angelo, why so many volunteer to stand with you in this endeavour.'

'The moment for speeches is past, Monsieur Hardy.'

'But not the moment to inflict loss upon the Turk. You have held this ground, this holy soil, for three long and bloody weeks. Do not abandon it now.'

'Stand aside.'

Hardy dropped his mace and sword and folded his arms. 'Stay with me, brothers. We shall perform such feat of arms that none may match.'

'*Hark! The noise of the Turk!*'

They had not heard it before. It was a strange and ominous sound, a welling and droning of flies busying themselves behind the background wail of trumpets. Hardy knew. He gathered his weaponry and moved fast to his chosen redoubt. Behind him, the rebels too were racing to their stations.

He shouted after them. 'You have your battle. Now perform your act of faith.'

'*Allah! Allah! Allah! Allah! Allah! Allah!*'

The flies became human, the sound had turned to voices. Iayalars had been unleashed. On their lips was only one word, in their minds was a single thought. They existed to kill the unbeliever. There would be no tactics, no finesse, no quarter given. These were the berserker fanatics of the East, maddened and demon-eyed with hashish, clothed in the skins of wild animals, sent to rip the stomachs and drink the blood of the enemy infidel. To massacre for their Sultan was a privilege. To die in armed struggle and in the name of Allah was their ultimate desire.

They threw themselves at the defenders in a raging pulse of ferocity, round shields bearing religious text held before them, their scimitars slashing at any resistance. It was the sharp end of holy war. Grapple-hooks were thrown, arcing over the burst ramparts, taking hold, pulling Iayalars behind. Even as a hidden battery of Christian guns tore holes in their ranks, they did not pause. They thronged, pushing forward through the charnel-piles, treading down corpses, oblivious to anything but their reward.

A hook caught a Knight at the back of his head and dragged him screeching into the teeming pit. In the opening that was left, an Iayalar balanced on a crag, his eyes crazed beneath his gilded helmet, his sword poised. He wobbled as musket-balls hit. With a smile, he regained his footing, discarded his weapon, and leaped at a soldier. The duel was as unequal as it was unconventional. It took a battleaxe between the shoulder-blades to finish off the Turk. By then he had bitten out the throat of the infantryman.

Hardy ran an Iayalar through, watched as the pin-prick pupils of the man focused on the impaling, waited as the hands clenched the blade and pulled it deeper. He kicked the body off. In a shower of sparks, he parried a scimitar-thrust, feinted, and side-stabbed an Iayalar through the ribs. The man did not fall at once. He began to weave an unsteady path, a strange figure garbed in the head and fur of a bear, performing a dance, playing to a baying crowd. Act over, the bear dropped. Behind him, a dervish was whirling in a trance, speaking in tongues, calling to his friends to seek death and eternity. Hardy facilitated, beating him down with a discarded shield. It would be a long and bloody morning, a longer and bloodier day.

There was something unearthly in the light. The fortress glowed with the dying embers of a garrison, St Elmo's fire. By night and day the assaults went in, the carpet of Turk bodies gaining fresh layers beyond the perimeter. Still the occupants of the ruins held. Yet their time was short and borrowed, their ability to man breaches subsided into chasms was ever diminishing. From the walls of Birgu and its stronghold of St Angelo, the Knights and their followers could only bear passive witness.

In his audience chamber, Grand Master La Valette listened intently to a report. His visitor was a Maltese soldier, a swimmer who had braved the hostile waters of Grand Harbour to bring news of St Elmo. Any dispatch was likely to be grim. It could not have been worse.

La Valette sat upright, his eyes questioning. 'You say de Medran and Pepe di Ruvo are killed?'

'Along with so many, Your Highness.'

'I demanded much of them.'

'They served with joy and willingness, sir.'

'We are in their debt. Those who survive?'

'Almost all are wounded, sir. The Chevalier Miranda is close to death from musketry, Colonel Mas sustains terrible burns, Chevalier de Guaras is cut to the bone by scimitar.'

'Our fighters such as Christian Hardy?'

'He also is injured, sir. Yet he continues in the fray.'

'It is the nature of St Elmo and its men. The scene would move any mortal.'

'They ask that none should grieve, and wish all to know they feel blessed in their calling. It is their intention to keep aloft the colours of the Order until torn down by the Turk.'

'Each will find a place in heaven. They have shown us how to fight and how to die. We commend their souls to God.'

La Valette was alone again when he permitted himself the indulgence of tears. He wept for the brethren he had lost, for the Knights and soldiers he had consigned to St Elmo and their deaths. Fine men, pilgrims of war. Perhaps it was best this way. A heroic conflagration was the manner in which an ancient and crusading religious brotherhood should take its bow from the world. Things had changed. From the princely courts of Europe to the Grand Seraglio of Suleiman the Magnificent, the name of the noble Order of St John would be expunged. Grand Master Jean Parisot de La Valette the Last.

'Uncle, you weep.'

'A moment of frailty, Henri.' La Valette looked up at his nephew. 'I am a foolish old man.'

'You are touched by neither age nor simple mind, Uncle.'

'Yet I cry as a child.'

'It is appropriate to the moment.'

'Though not befitting to leadership.' Emotional austerity reasserted itself. 'A messenger has brought final word from St Elmo. It grows more perilous by the minute. Most are wounded or are dead. A true miracle they persist at all.'

'Should we not send further volunteers?'

'The gesture would bring scant reward.'

'Reward has many parts, Uncle.'

'Failure only one. I see no advantage in squandering our lifeblood on a fort which is lost.'

'They have honoured us with their sacrifice, Uncle. Perhaps it is our turn now to honour them.'

'Their dying wish is to be left, to avoid us frittering ourselves on what in a week will become memory.'

'The memory is one I cherish.'

'You think I would not put myself in their place, Henri? You think I would not row alone to be at their side if I believed it was to some avail?'

'Forgive my own moment of frailty, Uncle.'

'On whose behalf do you petition?'

'My heart, my soul, a thousand others who stand ready to board the small boats and venture across Grand Harbour.'

'They have lost all reason. I have not.'

'Faith and common cause outweigh reason, Uncle.'

'While Turk cannon again installed on Gallows Point, Turk arquebuses along the Mount Sciberras foreshore will outweigh attempt at landing.'

'Few would be daunted.'

'Fewer would return.' La Valette sat back and wearily rubbed his brow. 'To take one's own life for naught is sin, Henri.'

'To avoid placing it in danger for God is another.'

The Grand Master stared at the ceiling, listened to the eddying crack and roll of the guns, absorbed each impact and announcement of a coming end. It was the darkest of funeral dirges. He rose slowly to his feet.

'I too hear the cannon, Henri. I too hear the cheers of the martyrs of St Elmo when again they beat back the heathen, when again the Turk trumpet sounds recall. I will allow a final act of gratitude.'

'In what form, Uncle?'

'Token. Five boats may attempt a landing. They will be led by

Chevalier de Romegas, filled with any volunteer expecting to die.'

'I would gladly be with them, Uncle.'

'I lose enough that is dear and trusted, Henri. I will not lightly discard my own blood and confidant.'

'This confidant has led attack on Gallows Point, charged Turk gun-limbers on the Marsa.'

'You serve me well by living, by standing with me when true battle comes. Guide the flock, accompany Romegas, but leave others to go ashore.'

Henri bowed. 'It will be so, Uncle.'

'Go, before a wiser mind counsels me against it.'

His nephew departed, La Valette rested his head against the cool stone of the wall and let out a sob of pain. The cursed malady was upon him again, consuming him, setting him afire. He had to be strong, had to prevent knowledge of his affliction from reaching the Knights. A single whisper would precipitate disaster. As he weakened, so the Order would become enfeebled; as he withered, so the resistance would shrivel. He prayed, his breath fast and shallow. The Lord could not desert him.

He had recovered by the time he entered the Council Chamber. For the moment, argument abated as the members of the Sacro Consiglio stood and he walked to his gilded chair. At each session they expected revelation, details from Sicily. He could offer them only leadership and will.

'Brothers, St Elmo carries on its defiance and its guardianship of our faith.'

Knight Grand Cross Lacroix frowned. 'Have we news, Your Highness?'

'A Maltese soldier has spoken of how they suffer and fight. We expect the fort to fall within hours or days.'

'We have thought it before, sir. They confound expectation each time.'

'No longer, Brother Grand Cross. They are depleted to the point of collapse.'

'Then there is nothing we may do but pray.'

'And give thanks. The heathen have spent themselves against those walls. It is our duty to attempt one final supply of men.'

'May I lead them, sir?'

'Your place is taken by others. We who remain must concern ourselves with the living garrison here.'

'We are ready, sir.'

'Be more so. Drill your men, husband your supplies, and harness the energies of the women and children. The smallest hand may shift fate, stitch cloth, carry bread, collect musket-balls.'

'Your Highness.' De Pontieux spoke up, his words silk-smooth. 'Is there word from Don Garcia de Toledo?'

'None that does not offer false hope. His Excellency the Viceroy remains committed to wishing us well.'

'He might have committed troops had we courted him more assiduously.'

The latent fury of Lacroix erupted. 'Would you have kissed his rear, provided him our galleys?'

'Brother Grand Cross, I do not recall Jesus in Gethsemane treating his disciples in such fashion.'

'Of what are you a disciple, de Pontieux?'

La Valette raised a hand, and the room fell silent. 'While our brothers labour and die not half a mile hence, we can brook no division. Your loyalty is to the Order and not to yourselves. Concentrate your energies here.'

The members of the Supreme Council slapped their benches in approval. Their Grand Master was right: strength lay in unity, in hunkering down for siege and the weeks that lay ahead. It would soon be the ramparts of Birgu and Senglea which crumbled, the sacred heart of their Order which bore the full force of the Turkish guns. Feuding was inappropriate, dangerous.

Prior Garza prayerfully clasped his hands together. 'Brothers, our holy mission to secure these walls falls at auspicious time. We are close on one of the great mysteries of the Religion, the Feast of Corpus Christi. For the memory of His sacrifice, we must labour for His blessing and do His bidding.'

'The sentiment of our Brother Prior is correct,' La Valette acknowledged with a nod. 'We shall greet our festival with wonderment and gladness. We shall ask for atonement and the gift of victory. We shall harden ourselves for the trial ahead. Do your rounds; go make your inspections.'

His Highness was looking somewhat careworn, a little sicklier of late, the traitor thought. Poison could wreck a man. But there were other pressing considerations to fill both time and mind. He was content to leave behind the suffocating ruminations of the Council, to walk on the battlements of St Angelo and hear the deafening barrage from across Grand Harbour. Music to his ears. The unwitting fools of the Sacro Consiglio forever sought God, yet would never glimpse the truth. It would be too distressing. They talked, while he acted. They asked for deliverance, while he wrung their necks. *The Feast of Corpus Christi*. If it were mystery and wonderment they required, he could provide. A final and reckless attempt to resupply St Elmo would shortly ensue, and he would notify the Turk as he had done before. The signal-lamp was all it took. A sustained attack on Birgu would flow from the demise of the fort. He was best placed to ensure its success. So easy, so necessary.

He reached the narrow flight of steps leading down into the powder-mill. The sentry drew to attention, anxious to prove alert. A kind word put him at his ease. The traitor proceeded inside. Just doing his rounds, making his inspection.

Chapter 8

'Steady, men! Hold them!'
Hardy was shouting, plunging into the chaos of the falling and the flailing. His blade and sword-arm were slick with blood, his face and plated jacket caked in body matter. He did not let up. They were not fighting for their lives or for St Elmo, as both were finished. It was something more desperate. An ecstasy had come upon them, a crazed joyfulness that conclusion was within their grasp, that they might at last find peace and sleep among the slain.

Endgame: the long and weary days of June that had followed the Iayalar assault, that counted down to finale. They were fighting hand to hand, living hand to mouth, expecting at any moment the Ottoman tide to consume them and roll on to Birgu and Senglea.

The Turkish skirmish-party retreated. More would come, probing for weakness, corroding the defence. It was not far for them to travel. And, as they departed, in their wake would be a few more Christian stragglers cut down, a few more huddled soldiers overwhelmed and taken to pieces. Not a sight for the squeamish or the sane.

A toppled cannon had become the rendezvous for one of the battered clumps of survivors. They lay or crouched beside their weapons, binding wounds, whispering prayers, blistering beneath the midday sun. Remnants surrounded by remnants. Here a Knight hammered vainly to straighten the dented nosepiece of a Venetian *salade* before discarding it. There a soldier tried to grip a needle in his torn hands to stitch a leather jerkin. Hardy was kneeling beside the blackened grotesque of Colonel Mas, holding a water-gourd to what had previously been a mouth.

'Drink, my friend. You must drink.'

'Why, Christian? You fear I may die of thirst?' There was still humour where there was no face, a bond born of proximity to death. 'Do not concern yourself with this piece of charcoal.'

'I am no sight for a lady either, Colonel.'

'Yet I see you acquire more gold, wear more trophies and trinkets. It will draw the wrath and fire of the Turk.'

'My intention, Colonel.' Hardy raised his arm and let the precious metal glitter through the gore. 'They come for me as flies to honey.'

'Such sweetness does not suit.'

'It appears to kill them.'

The Colonel coughed a cinder-dry laugh, his body racked by a convulsion of pain. He lay gasping for a while, his breath shallow, his eyes staring fixed through burnt-out eyelids. Hardy uncapped a small brass flask.

'Opiates, Colonel. Another gift of the infidels. A few drops will dull the pain.'

A hand waved it away. 'I stand before the gates, Christian. I will not pass through delirious.'

'You shall pass through accompanied by us all.'

'I can think of no greater honour.' The voice drifted to guttural silence before reviving. 'We have done well, Christian.'

'We have done what was asked of us.'

'More so.'

'Rest and be at peace, my friend.'

An infantryman was jogging over to bring a report from a section commander. It was a formality, and a wasted one. As he halted, a musket-round struck the back of his head, jettisoning the interior through his mouth, ears and nose. A strange and vivid sight. Before the gathered company could respond, another was felled. He quivered, kicking up dust, clutching for a dropped Bible, and expired on the second shot.

'*They are behind us! They are in the cavalier!*'

Nothing was beyond their reach. From the ruined and abandoned stump of the seaward tower, Janissary snipers had taken up position and were firing on the unprotected defenders. They must have scaled the outer defences during the night, made good their hold. And their aim was true.

'Arquebusiers, follow me.'

Hardy weaved towards the threat, shouting commands, urging his men to spread out in a fighting-line. He could hear the alarm trumpet sound. The Ottoman army was moving on the landward side again. Caught and constricted between it and the marksmen were the weakening occupants. A rock and a hard, merciless place.

He reached the embrasures close to the drawbridge, the site where he had first been greeted by Colonel Mas. *Welcome to your mausoleum, Christian.*

'Sustain your fire. The only agreeable heathen head is one which carries a hole.'

'They fight fierce, Christian.'

'We fight foul.'

Musket-rounds skimmed his shoulder, brushed his cheek. He ignored them, dragging aside a dead artilleryman from a cannon, applying the powder charge, ramming home the ball. Bar-shot should shake the perch.

'To me. I need hands.' The barrel was trained, the pitch taper applied. Discharge came with a shattering roar. 'Again.'

Janissaries, or at least their constituent parts, were airborne. Dislodged from the cavalier, they showered down, each cannon-ball impact accompanied by crashing stone and the cheers of the defenders. Contest was over; the cannon had won. The leaning tower had again become no man's territory.

Celebration was premature and short-lived. On the south-west side, the clash of arms was climbing in a hollering din, consuming men, spitting out their remains. A new sound permeated. It was an explosion, a detonation pulsing from across Grand Harbour, rising in a smoke plume above the ramparts of Fort St Angelo. Somewhere within the walls, a mill producing gunpowder had been set off. The turn of the Turks to applaud.

Death throes had a particular rhythm, a wavering beat all of their own. Dragut had supervised enough sieges to recognize the change. It could have been in the sporadic arquebus fire of the St Elmo defenders, the way in which the exhausted Knights seemed slower to respond, the less forceful rebound of the Turkish line. The signs were never wrong. He could see, taste, smell the finish. To an old corsair, it was the very essence of life. For a true believer, it was to walk before God on a carpet of enemy slain. An honour, a pathway to perfection. The Drawn Sword of Islam would complete his task, was still training the guns, giving orders to his lieutenants. Monday 18 June 1565. The thirtieth day of invasion.

'Invest forward a further two thousand arquebusiers. We have the infidels on their knees.'

'And yet they have no time to pray.'

Dragut laughed. 'These dogs have given us a fight. For that I respect them. For that we will widen their smiles with our scimitars.'

'Almost four weeks they have defied us, Dragut Rais.'

'Blame it on that perfumed trifler Admiral Piali. I want more cannon played against the southern remnants. The enemy possess hidden guns that must be tamed.'

'There will scarce be a gold piece or galley slave for the taking once we seize the ground, Dragut Rais.'

'Consider it a pilgrimage. This day Malta, then later Venice, Naples, Genoa or the southern lands of Spain. You will find gold and slaves aplenty there.'

Friendship among thieves. They were fearless and proud men, wore the finery of princes, had the mindset of raiders. There was one true God, and one true privateer-servant of God. They would follow Dragut anywhere, would be loyal unto death. This was to be their last meeting with the hated Knights. A final settling of historic scores.

Dragut strode down the slope, his officers in close attendance. 'Hear the gunfire, my brothers. The sweetest and most sacred of music.'

'Are we not the finest musicians, Dragut Rais?'

'Masters of every note. Without us, Mustapha Pasha and Piali are lost, would be content to grow roses for their Sultan in the loam of Turk corpses.'

He was shouting instructions to his gunners when the cannon-round from St Angelo flew overhead. Impervious to danger, his officers continued to confer. But the iron ball had glanced off rock, thrown up splinters, and a fragment had found its target. Dragut lay on his face, the right side of his turban a bloodied tangle. The body of the old man was still. His companions gathered round, silent and stupefied in their trauma, unwilling to display grief. They would not defile the memory of their leader with girlish weeping. The code of the corsair was an unsentimental one.

'He is dead?' The Turkish commander-in-chief had ridden up on his Arab charger.

'We believe so, Mustapha Pasha.'

'It is the will of God. Cover his face. I do not wish my troops to see him at this moment. Take him to the command-tents on the Marsa.'

They bore him away, a famed veteran who had become another casualty, a further corpse to be carried from the field. Yet he was not dead. That would take time. For seafarers were tough, and the ancient Dragut toughest of them all. Mortally wounded and unable to communicate, he would inhabit a twilight, linger for days. A grim and gradual fade – everything a pirate hated. Siege warfare had many twists.

★

Wednesday 20 June 1565, the Feast of Corpus Christi. The thirty-second day of invasion. In a solemn and winding procession, led by their Grand Master, Jean Parisot de La Valette, the Knights made their way through the narrow streets of Birgu to give praise in the Conventual Church. For this great moment they had put aside their weapons and armour, wearing the long black vestments of the Religion adorned with the white eight-pointed cross. War would not intrude upon their honouring of the Eucharist. Over centuries, they had performed the same ritual, escorted the Holy Host, paraded by as devout onlookers bowed or knelt along the route. God was with them. There was nobody else.

The traitor stared ahead, playing his part with accustomed ease. He enjoyed the role. It was faith and it was theatre; it was a cry to heaven which would go unanswered. In the background was the thudding beat of the Turk cannon on Mount Sciberras and Tigné Point, the swelling sound of St Elmo's obliteration. Well might his fellow Knights and the foolish populace pray. They were next. In days, when the small star-shaped fort had become a memory, when only a blackened crater remained on the far promontory, the full weight of enemy fire would descend here. He entered the church behind the Grand Master and genuflected reverentially to the cross. A pity to have to end the calm.

Hue and cry had broken out, the clamour of angry men demanding justice and bent on punishment. It was an ugly sound. They came into view, a crowd of Knights half-dragging their prisoner, their faces contorted in rage, their frenzy suggesting a lynching. A criminal had been caught. At their head were de Pontieux and Prior Garza. And at their feet the black Moor.

The Grand Master appeared, a lone figure unmoved before the mob. 'This is a day of renewed faith and celebration, not one of ferocity and retribution.'

'We have found a traitor.'

'You have found my friend, stumbled upon your own fears and weakness. Remove his chains.'

'Your Highness, he is a vile heathen.'

'A dangerous one, sir.' Prior Garza was quick to second the opinion.

La Valette did not flinch. 'I too may be dangerous. Raise him up and release him.'

'Sir, it is a matter of our security, a moment of revelation.'

'It is a moment of madness. If you apprehend him, you must also fetter me. Do as I command. Abandon the irons.'

It was done and the Moor stood, a hated outcast at bay before a hostile population. He was too dignified to plead, too proud to show apprehension. His tormentors, once comrades, were restless.

De Pontieux performed as spokesman. 'We act through necessity and with sorrow, Your Highness.'

'You act in haste.'

'The Moor is condemned by his deeds.'

'I see none.'

'For none were designed to be seen, sir. He is clever, as cunning as a serpent.'

'Yet you capture him, Brother Chevalier.'

'A consequence of diligence and kind fate. He is the demon who initiated fire in a powder-mill here in St Angelo – a fire which caused explosion and the deaths of eight good men.'

'Where is your proof?'

'It lies with the possessions of the deceased uncovered in his chamber, in his stores of powder, in his observed movement prior to the conflagration.'

'Conjecture, Brother Chevalier.'

'Evidence, Your Highness.' The tone was measured, supported by the jeers and calls of the men-at-arms behind.

'This is the man who created incendiaries for our brothers at St Elmo, the trumps, the wildfire, the hoops.'

'All the better to deceive us, to disguise his true intent.'

'All the better to kill the enemy and defend our territory.'

'He is a Mohammedan, sir.'

'Ally of our Order and no accomplice to the Turk.'

'You would have us count on his word, Your Highness?'

'And would you have me incarcerate an innocent?'

De Pontieux smiled modestly. 'We ask you to put him to death, sir.'

'I will not.'

'It cannot be wise to see him walk free beyond a dungeon and the confines of a noose, sir.'

'How wise is it to be trapped within the rigid confines of your mind, Brother Chevalier?' La Valette frowned, his brow furrowed above brooding eyes. 'At the galley bench, the Moor was my brother.'

'In St Angelo, we are your brothers.'

'You have never experienced living death at an oar, never known how it bares the soul. The Moor and I have shared the lash and our last scraps of food and breath, shared the same endless furlong of torment. I tell you again, he is no betrayer of us.'

'A common past as galley slave, sir? It is a peerless way to plant a Saracen spy, for an adversary to worm his way deep into our flesh.'

'Brothers, it is not justice to behave in this fashion.'

'Conflict does not embrace justice, sir. It involves our continuation.'

'I see only decay.' The words of La Valette were slow and cold.

Prior Garza moved closer to de Pontieux. 'We have the truth, Your Highness.'

'You have a scapegoat.'

'The heathen is the foe that tramples our brothers in St Elmo. The Moor is a heathen.'

'You blacken his name as surely as his face is black.'

'We protect the garrison and Religion.'

'At what cost, Brother Prior?' La Valette turned to address the throng. 'Step away. I would speak with the Moor alone.'

'He is an assassin, Your Highness. He may carry a stiletto-knife or silk cord.'

'It is the lesser danger to insurrection and disobedience.'

They moved back, temporarily chastened before the authority of their commander. Together, La Valette and the Moor climbed a flight of steps to a flagstoned terrace. There they could talk, could be watched at a distance.

The Moor slapped at the dust on his robes. 'Do not be sorrowful, Jean Parisot.'

'I will not allow harm to befall you.'

'Such things are a matter for God.'

'These men invoke God to suit their ends, use war to justify their contempt. As Grand Master, I cannot permit the rule of the mob.'

'As Grand Master, you must bend to prevailing will. Prior Garza and Chevalier de Pontieux are no mere rabble.'

'That is the misfortune. They have influence, carry others with them.'

'They might yet carry the day, Jean Parisot.'

'I will thwart such moves, dismantle any gallows.'

'Are you able to prevent murder in the night, the sword-thrust to the back, the fire in the sleeping-straw?' The Moor looked searchingly at his friend. 'Whoever placed the damning articles in my chamber, whoever spreads malicious rumour of my treachery, intends me ill.'

'A hearing before the Sacro Consiglio would banish idea of your disloyalty.'

'It will confirm division, invite discord.'

'The risk is one I am prepared to take.'

'One that would provoke other risks.'

'You expect me to behave as Pilate, to wash my hands, to throw you on their harsh mercies?'

'I expect you to let fate run its course, Jean Parisot. I expect you to unite your Order.'

'How may it unite around lies and false accusation?'

'Many nations have shown it to be possible. Give the garrison what it wants. Banish me to the dungeons, consign me to be with the galley slaves quartered deep in the tunnels beneath this fort.'

'You are not deserving of it, Moor.'

'It will show you as strong, remove me from sight. That may assuage their demands, secure the position of us both.'

La Valette considered the advice, a wise man in company with another. The vultures remained below. There was advantage in spiriting the Moor from their grasp, in placing him in forgotten isolation. But there was disadvantage also: the loss of trusted counsel, the insidious rise of the reptiles and the diplomats, of Knights such as de Pontieux and prelates such as Garza. Old soldiers like Grand Cross Lacroix, tyros like nephew Henri were no match.

The Moor reached out and gently plucked a hair from La Valette's beard. 'See how easy it comes away, Jean Parisot. Be certain to keep any enemy and ailment under inquiry. Your cause, and life itself, depend on it.'

'I will be vigilant.'

'We share the God of Abraham and the common bond of friendship.'

'I acknowledge it by delivering you into subjugation and captivity.'

'I go willingly, Jean Parisot.' The Moor tilted his head towards the noise of St Elmo. 'Against the forfeiture of such noble souls, the sacrifice of my liberty counts for little.'

'It means much.'

'Save your energies for the fight ahead, your grief for our lost and dying comrades, for the likes of Christian Hardy. I will while time to emerge renewed from the tunnels. The men of St Elmo will never return.'

The two stood in silent communion, the Grand Master and a casualty of his war. They had anticipated such events, had understood that a brotherhood besieged could turn on itself or tear others to pieces. For the sake of the Order and the course of battle, the Moor was being consigned underground. It was an unhappy moment in a dismal time. And it was the art of survival.

It had followed the customary pattern: the dawn bombardment trailing off to allow the Janissary charges and the rampage and carnage of close-quarter combat. For six hours the Turks and the defenders of St Elmo had battled, each assault met and beaten back, every clash leaving strewn viscera and more dead. A last section of wall had collapsed, burying hundreds from either side. Musket-rounds and longswords shredded flesh. The Christians had held, cheering again as the enemy withdrew. But the day was different, was to be the last. The evening of Friday 22 June 1565, the thirty-fourth day of invasion. As the light subsided across their outpost, the survivors gathered in preparation for the end. Their struggle was almost over. They had done enough, accomplished what they could. Tomorrow would bring the coldest of dawns, the *coup de grâce*.

Now it was dark, and the open boats set out from the wharf below Fort St Angelo. They carried men committed to die, dedicated to joining their brethren in the final stand. A wasted gesture, an empty mission. Yet religious impulse required no sense. Even Jews were among the company of the Knights and their cohorts on board, had been inspired by the images of heroism, were driven to volunteer. It was the motliest of suicide squads.

Henri de La Valette, nephew of the Grand Master, sat low in the prow of the second craft. He could make out the diminished and broken outline of the fort ahead, the crumpled mass that resembled nothing more than a haphazard pile of gravestones. A terrible place. On it or beneath it his friend Christian would be lying, half-alive or wholly dead, resolute and courageous to the finish. The substance of legend, the nature of tragedy. What he would give to be with him, to face the foe with his warrior-brother, his guide. Yet he would obey his uncle and return to St Angelo.

The boat glided through the splintered gloom, the troops silent, the oarsmen bending and rising in their task. Each man carried his own thoughts, cloaked his own dread. However committed, none on board could fail to tremble at the prospect or deny the imminence of execution. On the horizon, a flare burst and dimmed. The soldiers shrank from it. They were almost at their destination, pulling softly towards the landing-stage at the bottom of the cliff. An ambush would be costly. Pikes and arquebuses were gripped more firmly, last prayers were whispered beneath shallow breaths. They were here for God, and would find Him soon.

'*Back! Back! They wait for us!*'

In a flurry of oars and panic-strokes, the first boat was turning. Beyond it, the initial flash of musketry burst along the shoreline, revealed the truth and a trap. The Turks had been expecting them. Lead rounds triangulated on the flotilla, flattening on wood, throwing up debris. Henri ducked. He was shouting, urging his men into retreat, calling to the accompanying vessels to spread out and race for their lives. They should have known, should have appreciated that quiet was a prelude, that absence of cannon-shot was a forerunner to this. At the landing-platform, shrapnel-guns were firing, filling the air with metal shards, illuminating the waterfront and assembled enemy. The plot laid bare.

Admiral Piali was not finished. The waterborne attack came, converging on the fleeing boats, attempting to pick them off while they manoeuvred and dispersed. They ran them close. A chase and musket-duel ensued, the pop and patter of rival volleys, the screams of the injured, the splash of bodies echoing in the harbour mouth. The small boats of the Order hauled clear. But it was temporary respite. In a shattering cacophony, the resting cannons of Dragut's battery on Gallows Point unleashed their opening salvo. Solid balls of shot skimmed and leaped across the water, ranging overhead, passing between the straining crews. And men sobbed, desolate at failure. St Elmo was gone, and their brethren were left to die alone.

'Pray for us sinners now, and at the hour of our death . . .'
Calm had settled upon the fort and the few hundred souls who remained alive within it. There was little to do but wait, attend to devotional duties, receive absolution and the Holy Sacrament from the two chaplains who had refused to depart. In the flame-hued murk, men embraced and said farewell. So many had gone before them. One by one, or in great swathes, they had been scythed down, blown apart, transformed into shapeless scraps. For their sake, these stubborn fragments of a former garrison would resist. They had seen the small boats scurry back to St Angelo, could feel the poised and pressing weight of the Turk. A lively show was promised.

Hardy belly-crawled among the outer positions, sharing a word, giving encouragement, distributing bread soaked in wine and water. Their Last Supper.

A wounded soldier muttered his thanks. 'God bless you, Christian.'

'Rest, my friend. You will need your strength this morrow.'

'Depend on it, I shall take a dozen infidel when I go.'

'No idle boast. The ground is strewn with your work.'

'And the air tainted with it.' The man chuckled heartily at the thought. 'Breathe deep, Christian. Rotting Turk. It is a sacred odour.'

'That we have created it is no mean feat.'

'That we have endured too, for so long withstood the hellish heathen might, will be talked of in a hundred or five hundred years.'

'To be talked of in the Grand Seraglio of Constantinople is triumph enough. Suleiman the Shamed they will call him.'

'I have names to call him of my own.'

They conversed softly, spoke of friends departed, of heroic acts, of the coming hour. St Elmo was the home and grave they knew, a place of comforting and familiar horrors.

The soldier reached out and gripped his hand. 'I thank you, Christian. You have been first in the fray, the most courageous among us.'

'I had many beside me.'

'The many now are few. The few will become dust.'

'Even dust may prick the eye of the Turk. We dispatched near two thousand of them this last fight.'

'We shall match it in the next.'

'Wreak your worst, soldier. We will rush the gates of paradise together.'

He took his leave, continued his slow and methodical circuit. It was a pilgrimage of sorts, a last chance to touch the stones, to traverse the bloodied ground where his comrades had fallen. Occasionally a musket-round would flick overhead. He admired the persistence of the enemy marksmen, had grown accustomed to their ways. Only hours remained until the end of courtship and the start of grisly consummation.

'Christian, it is time.'

The chaplain Pierre Vigneron beckoned towards the chapel, a glimmer of candlelight glowing from the door recess behind. Hardy followed him inside. Nothing was sacred. The smell of death was as strong here, the walls lined with the mortally wounded, the floor wet with blood. Already men were taking down tapestries and paintings, pulling up flagstones to bury relics and the precious treasures of the Faith. Part of the final rites. An icon of the Virgin Mary was handed round to kiss.

Hardy joined the band of Knights and began to break up the altar and drag furniture to the courtyard. No Turk would have the pleasure of gaining such booty. They would find only a heap of ash, would curse at the price paid for inheriting a blighted spot populated by corpses.

A Portuguese Knight walked by, a rolled tapestry on his shoulder. 'I trust the Lord will forgive us this desecration.'

'We have defended his Religion. He would forgive us any sin.'

'Yet a sad thing to see such objects destroyed.'

'You should rejoice. We snatch them from the grasp of the enemy.'

'I will be snatched soon enough.'

When it was done and the pyre complete, they set a torch to it, standing back as the flames caught and leaped. They were silent, absorbed in the image of the funnelling blaze and thoughts of death. A point had been reached, a moment poised between earth and heaven, mortality and oblivion. They would never gather again. At first a solo voice rang out, clear and steady against the roaring fire. Others joined, the sound of the hymn swelling until it became a shouted chant of defiance, a choral blast of celebration. The bell of the chapel tolled. It was marking time, announcing to the night and to those who listened that the defenders were composed and in the presence of God.

Luqa, the boy, stood on the ramparts and shivered at each distant peal of the bell. He could see the fire, the last glow of life and warmth from St Elmo. His friend Seigneur Hardy was there, his mentor and protector, whom he had betrayed by failing to keep a promise in allowing the Lady Maria to disappear on her ill-fated expedition. He could not forgive himself. Men of honour did not behave in such a fashion. Now it was too late to make amends, too late to ask forgiveness, too late to bid proper farewell without juvenile tears or rage.

The fire seemed to fade. It could have been the cooling heart of the fortress itself. Luqa balled his fists and lowered his face. He wanted to be brave, to be present for the Order, for his country-men, for the English warrior he loved as his brother and father and soul. Beside him, Hubert stepped up and placed a shielding arm across his shoulders. Together they watched, bearing witness, paying silent tribute.

✳

Chapter 9

'I come to die.'

'It is the place for it, boy.'

The crippled sentry seemed unsurprised at the apparition of Luqa emerging in the gloom. He had seen enough insanity not to question the motives of others. The youngster was soaked, half-naked, exhausted by a swim which had brought him the distance from St Angelo. He had dodged the roving Turk patrols to be here, had crept past arquebusiers lying in wait, had climbed the cliff path to this benighted position. That was commitment. Maybe it was sickness of the mind. At this hour, in this situation, nobody cared.

'You may pass. But you will not thank God or yourself for the privilege.'

For a moment, Luqa felt his legs give, his stomach and throat convulse at the stench. Foulness and death were everywhere. He stared at it, stood on it, breathed and absorbed it. Nothing had prepared him. In the twilight greyness, creatures hobbled or dragged themselves about, easing themselves into crannies, helping each other towards the breaches in which they had chosen to die. Every man for himself and his Order. Propped on a line of chairs, the contorted figures of injured Knights bent low over their weapons behind the cover of a makeshift rampart. They would not be spared, could not have excused themselves from the closing act. Luqa peered about him, repelled and drawn to the nightmare vision.

'Take this if you wish to fight.'

He accepted the heavy pike that was thrust in his hands, continued to stand and observe a scene of which he had already become part. It was strange to have been absorbed so rapidly into their host.

'Luqa.'

It had the voice but not the face of Christian Hardy. The features were scarred and bruised, the nose broken, the cheek split by a wound that ran from ear to chin. A blood-soaked bandage wrapped the forehead.

'Can it be you, seigneur?'

'If my memory is not confused.'

Hardy stooped and enveloped Luqa in his arms, the boy clutching him tight, burying his head in his shoulder. Finally, the Englishman spoke.

'A poor time for reunion, Luqa.'

'Yet good for combat, seigneur.'

Hardy crouched to face him. 'Go back. You are not ready for this butchery.'

'I am ever prepared, seigneur. When first we met, I slew an infidel with my sling. What is one more?'

'It will be the death of you as it is of me. You are young. Live out your years, enjoy what God has granted you.'

'He grants me your friendship and chance to fight.'

'This is no chance, no mere skirmish. They will roast you on a spit for their amusement.'

'I will kill them for mine.'

'You speak of our friendship. Respect it and return.'

'I have no right, seigneur. The Lady Maria is dead.'

They looked at each other, the impact of the telling and receiving translated into silence.

'How?'

'Her boat did not return from St Elmo. The enemy attacked while she crossed the water.'

'I was unaware.' His voice was low, his eyes clouded. 'It is greater reason for you to leave, Luqa. I cannot die knowing you too are lost.'

'I am not lost. I am at your side, seigneur. And there is nothing for me in Birgu. Even the Moor has left me.'

'The Moor?'

'He is accused of treachery, of causing destruction to a powder-mill, the deaths of eight men.'

'A false accusation.'

'One that has seen him imprisoned, sent to the tunnel dungeons beneath St Angelo.'

'It is folly.'

'You wish me to withdraw to a place of folly, seigneur?'

No reason would penetrate, no argument prevail. Hardy searched the face of the boy for signs of weakness or misgiving, for paling resolution. There were none. He could not condemn him for that, would not judge such aberration when surrounded by madness.

He pulled an emptied hessian sack from the roof of a shelter, fashioned it with a knife, and offered it to the boy. 'You cannot fight without clothing.'

It was quickly donned. 'I will be a lion, seigneur.'

'A lion without armour or mail. You will stay back, away from the arquebuses and the scimitars. Do not confront or engage direct. Challenge from afar and be light on your feet.'

'I will do as you say, seigneur.'

'I am doubtful of it. Yet if you are to be a soldier, be a wise one.'

A pair of Maltese padded by bearing Colonel Mas on a litter. The Knight lay prone, his skin carbonized, his sword held ready on his chest. Like the rest of them, it would be his concluding journey. His eyes flickered, focusing on Hardy. They still carried the devil in them, the recognition of one soldier for another, the flame of expectation for the fray.

'View him well, Luqa. He is the most gallant of our kind.'

The boy was scavenging ammunition for his sling.

Piali's galleys broke through into Marsamuscetto harbour at first light. Each fired its bow-chaser cannon at St Elmo as it passed, each paraded between the fort and Tigné Point in glittering review. Death deserved its pageant. Then the Turkish army descended upon the outpost. It came in headlong rush, a deluge that raged and curled in a white-robed crest above the razed defences. Janissaries, levies, dervishes, Iayalars, all were in the tumult, all throwing themselves without tactics or heed at the loathed Christian foe. They sought blood, and today would find it. St Elmo began to break.

'*They are through!*'

A detachment of Turkish troops blossomed into an empty space, fanning out inside the breach. They were met, cut down, their reinforcements beaten back. But more Knights had fallen, were falling still.

'We are a mere hundred left, Christian.'

'A hundred who will each take a hundred!' Hardy clambered over rubble to kick a sprawling dervish in the face, cutting his throat as he rolled away. 'Fight on!'

They did, foraying in ebbing strength and diminishing numbers to stem the flow. Wielding a longsword, Hardy braced himself against a tumbled gun-position, rendering a Janissary in half, beheading two more in a single sweep. Bodies slumped in a semi-circle around him. It was an Iayalar who approached next, running at him with the name of Allah on his lips, dying with the same. Others followed, three closing in, the first disembowelled, the second sectioned with a blow to the side, the third knocked unconscious with the pommel and finished by the sword-thrust of a Maltese soldier.

Hardy shouted his thanks. 'It is a kill to you.'

The man did not reply, could not. A musket-round had lodged

at the back of his throat. He appeared to cough, crossed himself, and slid to the ground. Beyond him, a squad of Janissaries were lopping pieces from Colonel Mas, their high-pitched cries keening with excitement. The Knights were fading. They had no reservoir of power, no reserves of any kind. The Ottomans drew in.

It took an hour before the defence yielded. The collapse was sudden. In a maelstrom of rushing figures and waving scimitars, Turks poured through. There were many last stands, undignified and unequal affairs forgotten in the torrent. De Guaras, the wounded deputy, was hurled from his chair. He seized a pike, tried vainly to resist, and was decapitated for his efforts. Beside him, the Knight Miranda lolled transfixed in his seat, a spear protruding at front and back. Cornered in a gully, abandoning both nerve and weapon, a young German rushed to and fro before the jeering, jabbing mob. He was screaming loudly, leaking blood, scrabbling in animal desperation as his flesh was pierced. Minutes passed before he stilled. Few would go quietly. Grim pictures played out, men kneeling, scattering, simply disappearing.

'To the chapel.' Hardy leaped from his position, felt a stone from Luqa's sling speed by to strike between the eyes of a Turk. He called to whoever would listen. 'All those who can, retreat! We shall regroup and charge again!'

The words had little effect, scant meaning. There was no one left to regroup. Outside the entrance to the chapel, he found the Italian Paolo Avogardo, resplendent in gilded armour, waiting for his moment.

'Who is within, Paolo?'

'The chaplains at prayer.'

'Then let us extend their time.'

The Knight smiled. 'I can think of no finer reason to use this sword, Christian.'

'It may yet gain us our place among the saints.'

'We are few enough to enter unnoticed.'

'The boy Luqa go unnoticed?' Hardy indicated the youngster wielding his sling and darting for cover. 'We are outshone by youth.'

'Bless all who labour against the heathen.'

'They are upon us. Farewell, my brother.'

Fatigue and pain had departed. He was in a place where steel blades could not reach him, where blood did not course in rivulets on his face. At some stage Avogardo staggered and fell, vomiting redness and curses behind his visor. In another instant, Hardy was using an arquebus to stove in the head of a Janissary, stabbing at a dismounted Spahi with the hilt of a broken dagger. He was killing for his mother, his father, his sisters, avenging Maria.

The signal was prearranged, a beacon lit by a remaining defender to inform the Grand Master that St Elmo was lost. La Valette would need no telling. The Turk infested every corner of the fort, hunting down, finishing off. There was nowhere to run or hide. A trio of Maltese soldiers were dismembered where they stood, a Portuguese Knight was castrated and fed his own testicles, a Spaniard was impaled on a grapple-hook and dragged in celebration through the dust. Images so vivid they merged and became indistinct.

Cornered, outnumbered, Hardy fought on. He glimpsed Luqa to his side. The boy now carried a sword. 'Luqa, we are finished. Make quick your escape.'

The boy could not hear him, but shook his head anyway. He mouthed the words 'I stay.'

'Take this, Luqa.' Hardy ripped the silver crucifix from his throat and flung it to him. 'It belongs with the living. Carry it to safety. Take yourself with it.'

Luqa reached for the cross. A foot had stamped down on it, a dervish claiming possession for himself. The man was laughing, dancing, readying himself with a whirling scimitar to claim the scalp of the impudent Maltese pup. He underestimated. Luqa ran him through, seizing the cross and backing away as the bearded figure embarked on new and faltering footwork.

'I have it, seigneur.'

'Tell them how we fought, Luqa. Tell them.'

It was a moment of parting and understanding, the coming to an end. In a blast of black and orange flame, a grenade-pot exploded, the enclosed world of Christian Hardy fragmenting in a million particles. He was aware of a dark and descending mist, of shadows racing through it to find the praying chaplains, of a looming presence rising up grey before him. God or Satan. He wished they could be more distinct.

With a triumphant howl, the Janissary arced his blade towards the prone defender. He would carve a name for himself, mutilate the corpse beyond recognition. Another scimitar parried the blow.

'Step aside.' The Janissary hissed his anger at the interloper. 'The prize is mine.'

'Then you will contest it with over ten of my men.'

'I am an Invincible One, an officer from the corps of Janissaries.'

'You will prove less invincible should you fail to give up the spoils.'

'Offend me and you affront the Sultan.'

'Oppose me and you provoke the wrath of the corsairs.'

At a hand gesture, a dozen blades lifted towards the throat of the Janissary. He spat at the ground, dismissive of their cheap theatrics. They were a stinking rabble, a bunch of cut-throats and simpletons devoid of honour or discipline. Thieves by nature, hired executioners from birth. It was part of the problem. He despised them, could take several with him. Yet they would prevail. Let them have their small and stolen victory.

'You waste effort on the corpse of an unbeliever.'

'A fair trade for your life, Janissary. Find other pickings.'

Without a word, the officer retreated, his expression fixed in assumed indifference, his swagger disguising lost authority. The corsairs gathered round their human bounty. Some prodded the body with their feet, others picked at the singed brigantine jacket in search of precious stones and gold. It was he, the Englishman who fitted the description, who wore the crimson velvet. A privateer like themselves. Alive or dead, the infidel was to be delivered to their master, ransomed to Mustapha Pasha for a tidy sum. There was profit even in the driest of bones. A wooden spar was brought, the carcass tied and slung, and the pole shouldered between two pirates for transportation. Possession had passed.

For Luqa, a different journey was in train. He was darting among the confusion, clambering across corpses and broken rock, slipping across open ground and through gaping breaches. Bad sights and terrible sounds encroached. He tried to exclude them from his thoughts, attempted to hum a folk-song his English friend had taught him. It amplified his terror. He no longer wished to die, no longer wanted to remain in this place, share in its darkness. The panic was choking him. He had witnessed the detonation, seen the bright percussive halo about the head of Christian Hardy as he dropped. A good man had died. There was not yet time to grieve, might yet be no time for escape. Turkish marksmen were tracking his progress. He shied as limestone billowed to the strike of a musket-round, was sliding into a steep descent, tearing at the rock with his hands and feet. Everyone he knew vanished, everything he touched turned to dust.

Two levies were waiting for him. They held arquebuses across their chests, had been stationed to prevent a breakout, to ensure that annihilation was complete. A boy posed few challenges. One of the men winked at him. It was to put him at ease before the murder act. Luqa panted. They did not seem to comprehend he had changed his mind, intended to survive. Behind them, Fort St Angelo beckoned.

It was unfortunate that they blocked his route, more unfortunate that they could not swim. He hit them low and hard, carrying them back, propelling them from their post in a tangle of thrashing limbs and expelled air. Surprise and suddenness provided advantage. In a ragged spray, they collided with the water, Luqa kicking away, the two Turks floundering. He was free of them. A hand clutched at his ankle, gaining purchase, pulling him back. He twisted, but the grip tightened. A face appeared, then another, drowning men unwilling to sink, desperate for air. Hatred and blind fear filled their eyes. Luqa struggled, went under. Fingers were clawing for his neck, the weight of bodies bearing down. He bit, tasted blood, felt the reflex. There was give. He kicked again, made connection, drove his heel direct into an exposed throat. As the man gagged and wallowed, he slipped clear.

The noise had subsided, replaced by the sound of his own heartbeat and the rush of water in his ears. Occasionally a musket-ball would pock the surface. He would dive, swim submerged until his lungs gave out. But the enemy aim was erratic and half-hearted, the rate of fire desultory. They had more meaningful slaughter to attend. Eventually, his limbs heavy, his body water-logged, he slowed, turning on his back to float and view St Elmo. It was already in the past. Smoke drifted from every quarter, Ottoman banners hung from every crumpled vantage. He had merely been a visitor. At least he knew the nature of the coming devastation, had abandoned one fire in order to enter a furnace. With a final glance, he resumed his stroke, pulling and pushing himself wearily towards Birgu. The small silver cross remained clenched as talisman and keepsake in his hand.

'Send word to Dragut. St Elmo is taken.'

Accompanied by a clique of officers, Mustapha Pasha made stately passage across the debris-filled ditch into what had once been a fort. So this was what it was about, what had cost him some eight thousand Turkish lives. Bodies and body parts were everywhere strewn among the blackened ruins. Discarded and broken weapons vied for space with coagulated blood and hewn pieces of flesh. The aftertaste of battle and bitter victory was ever thus. He paused to survey the scene. A splintered row of chairs appeared to have been crushed where it stood, the occupants flung aside or torn to pieces. It marked the start-line, the beginning of the piled death within.

'Piali cannot complain. He has his anchorage, I have the remains of this fort.'

'A high price for the sheltering of galleys from a sea breeze, Mustapha Pasha.'

'The role of our army was ever to protect the timid and effete members of the navy.' The officers chortled at the gibe. 'You have identified the corpses of the senior Knights?'

'We have, Mustapha Pasha.'

'Remove their heads to spikes facing St Angelo. I want La Valette and his Order to stare at their own destinies.'

'Their spirit appears strong.'

'It is the bravery of the cornered, the defiance of the condemned.' The commander-in-chief was gazing at a blood pattern spread across a fall of rock. 'We shall terrorize them. We will play the full weight of our artillery against their walls, deploy the skill of our engineers to undermine their position. This time we wage a different and more subtle war.'

He travelled on, passing through the wreckage of a thirty-day battle. *Thirty days.* God had sore tested him, had allowed these stubborn defenders to fight on, to reap a glittering harvest. The Master of the Turkish Ordnance, the Lieutenant Aga of the Janissaries, Dragut the Drawn Sword of Islam, all had succumbed to Christian shot. The aged corsair still lingered, of course, unyielding to the end in his deathbed trance. Informing him of victory at St Elmo was mere formality. And Mustapha Pasha was tired of formality, weary of convention, of protocol, of Piali, of Malta, of Grand Master La Valette and his satanic followers. His anger climbed, bitter and vengeful.

'Where is the fighter they call Christian Hardy?'

'Taken by the corsairs as prize, Mustapha Pasha.'

'Recover him. He is the vilest of canker, will suffer every agony devised.'

'He may yet be dead, Mustapha Pasha.'

'We shall desecrate him all the same, display him in a manner that will make the unbelievers quake.'

'Others remain alive and closer for the purpose of your retribution, Mustapha Pasha.'

'Show them to me.'

They were a small and wretched band, scarce alive, barely comprehending the horrors of their plight. Had they surrendered early, accepted the terms offered, they might have won concessions, reprieve, been consigned as slaves to the galleys. No longer. They had resisted to the end, killed thousands, broken every tenet of the honour code. For this they would perish. Mustapha Pasha was of a creative bent.

He approached, drawing his scimitar and holding it to the throat of a prone and injured Knight. The infidel refused to flinch or cower.

'Your name?'

'Chevalier Alessandro San Giorgio.'

'San Giorgio? Your saints appear to have deserted you.'

'I think not. Look closer at these ruins.'

'Ruins they may be, occupied by your slain.'

'And by yours. You sent your best against us. They lie in the ditch, buried by our walls, charred by our wildfire. Is that victory?'

'It is I who hold the sword.'

'I who go with joy to my Maker. You inherit a desolate and blighted place. I will inhabit a place of everlasting life.'

'The moment will be of my choosing.'

'You expect me to fear your blade when I have parried so many, stared at death so oft?'

'You are aware of who I am?'

'Heathen.'

There was an intake of breath among the Turkish officers, a collective tremor of anticipation. A nerve tugged beside the eye of their commander-in-chief.

'I am Mustapha Pasha, head of the Ottoman army. I shall have your submission, infidel.'

'You cannot touch me.'

'A brave man and a fool. I will mark you in ways you have not dreamt.'

'Your worst does not trouble me. You will never take the other forts, never pluck the heart from our Order.'

'It is as well I have yours to seize.'

The struggle was brief but unpleasant. Mustapha Pasha did not delegate. He cut the man open with a single deft stroke, left him alive long enough to reach inside and liberate the warm and beating heart. A magical moment, the summit of raw authority.

'Where is your joy now, Knight?' He turned to his aides, held the dripping organ in his palm. 'I will do likewise to those among you who show hesitation or pity.'

'We shall obey any command, Mustapha Pasha.'

'You shall bring a deeper dread to these obstinate Christians. Fetch wood and nails. The defenders of Birgu must recognize the foolhardiness of resistance.'

In the background, Turkish soldiers played kick-ball with a severed head while others drowned the second of the two chaplains in the water-cistern. They would be allowed their games, their respite. Mustapha Pasha led his gathering to the ramparts overlooking Grand Harbour, mounted the steps to observe the future jewel of his endeavours. It would be the last time that Birgu and its fortress bastion of St Angelo looked so pristine and impregnable. He would reduce them to nothing, would stand like Rameses and watch the rule of this vestige Order melt into the sea.

Alongside him, the reclaimed heads of the officers of St Elmo began to rise on a plantation of lances. They faced their brethren across the water, a united front, an expression of intent. Saturday 23 June 1565, the day St Elmo fell. Mustapha Pasha nodded his approval. In campaigns of terror, a brutal deed always spoke more eloquently than any word.

A runner had arrived breathless from the conquered fort. He stood before the recumbent figure of Dragut, uncertain at approaching, hesitant in his speech. Even in the throes of death, the Drawn Sword could inspire awe. In the distance, Turkish guns boomed in celebration. But here there was no cheer, no sound save the shallow pant of an old man approaching his final hours.

'I bring news, Dragut Rais.' There was no response from the wax-grey effigy. 'Mustapha Pasha commands me inform you that St Elmo is taken, our banners fly above it.'

The messenger paused. It might have been imagination, a trick of his nerves and the moment, yet he thought he detected a sigh.

Encouraged, he continued. 'Mustapha Pasha will for ever be thankful for your counsel and leadership, Dragut Rais. Your name will be honoured, you will be acclaimed as a great servant of the One God and our True Religion. Praise be to Him.'

The hand raised briefly from the silk covers, the mouth agitating as if to reply. Dying energy, fading as quickly as it had emerged. Unsettled, the herald drew back. He had done as bidden, had entered this perfumed tent and tomb to deliver the victory tidings. It was never pleasant to see greatness brought low, a legend reduced to this. A pitiful state. Even Dragut's servants and slaves had abandoned him in favour of the living.

Bowing dutifully, the messenger took his leave. Dragut breathed on, alone again, one casualty in a tented settlement, stretching over the plain, filling inexorably with the victims of disease and combat. There were many who would not be participating in the festivities.

'The mighty Dragut. Could this be the great corsair, the governor of Tripoli?'

Dressed in the uniform of an Ottoman soldier, staying close to the shadows and protection of the walls, Maria crouched low. She spoke softly in the Italian tongue.

'A destroyer of all that is good is himself destroyed. Some would consider it justice. I would call it past due.' She had things to say, would talk as alternative to plunging in a knife. 'I should kill you myself, Dragut Rais. For the times you have raided these islands, carried away the men, women and children. For the fear you have sown about the Mediterranean, and the suffering you brought to St Elmo.'

She listened as the carnival rites of the Turkish army carried from the vanquished fort. They seemed to prompt her words and trembling ire. 'It is the way of decent Christians to forgive. Yet I cannot forgive you the loss of my Christian. He escaped the evils of your Barbary Coast to have those evils catch him here – your pirates, your guns, your Ottoman allies convey him to his grave.'

Cautious, but determined, she went forward to whisper in his ear. Lest he forget, or failed to hear through his stricken slumber.

'I vow that I will find freedom, will witness the defeat of the Saracen armies. I vow that your life will be forgotten, that your death is in vain.'

The Drawn Sword of Islam was shaking uncontrollably, his face mobile with the spectre of wrath and desperation. No one was present to notice.

They had both been startled, for a moment the slave cowering, Maria searching for escape. The man might raise the alarm, could run shouting for assistance. It would earn him the thanks and silver of his masters. But he remained where he was, his eyes intelligent and appraising, his expression as closed as that of any who served the cruel and capricious Turk. She put her finger to her lips. Still he did not move or make a sound, the jar of camphor-oil held beneath his arm, his gnarled body obstructing her direction of travel. A tented corridor and nowhere for either to go.

She whispered to him. 'I too am a captive.'

'Only briefly did I believe you to be a levy.' He replied in lightly accented Italian, his speech educated, his demeanour careful. 'You choose your time well for escape.'

'Behind me is a guard too drunk to stand and now bound with whatever I could find. Ahead is the entire encampment.'

'There are means of passing through it.'

'You will not betray me?'

'I am Armenian. I do not serve the Mohammedans by choice, do not count my daily blessings that I live and travel in their company.'

'Then come away with me. You will find haven with the Knights.'

He shook his head. 'Here I fill the lamps, suffer occasional beating. I am too old and cowardly to exchange it for the punishment of cannon and arquebus fire.'

'I do not condemn you for it.'

'I condemn myself. But there are other ways to resist the Ottoman. Keep close and I will prove it.'

She followed him because she had no choice, because she was already committed to flight. Each had made their calculation. They were enslaved within an empire built on slavery. Even the Sultan was born of a slave-girl, the Janissaries of subjugated Christians, Piali of Bulgarian ones. The system bred compliance, reinforced control. But here, ducking through the entrance to a tent of whores, working their way along the edge of a row of guard positions, was defiance in motion. He helped her; perhaps in some small way she was helping him.

He was unfolding lengths of black cloth pilfered en route. 'We enter the area of the fever and dysentery tents. Few dare to travel here that are not already sick. Those who do are shrouded against disease, veil their faces from the odour. We shall be among them.'

'I adopt the guise that is of most effect.' She wrapped the proffered material about her head and upper body.

'Take my arm. Become the ailing Turk to my escorting presence.'

In this fashion they stumbled on, hearing the cries and whimpers, the sounds of dying men vomiting their last. Occasionally they caught a glimpse of the rows of prone and stricken soldiers, of wild and staring eyes before the fade. She had seen it before in the Sacred Infirmary of the Order. Her pity welled. Such waste, such shattered consequence of the affairs of men. She thought again of her beloved Christian.

'State your business or you die!'

She noted the unsheathed sword, heard distantly the suspicion and hatred in the challenge of the officer. He swung the blade closer. Opiates or betrayal – either could have created this moment. She tried to steady her nerves. The Armenian was explaining from beneath his mask, his words rapid, becoming frantic. His audience did not listen. With a sudden spasm, his energy and delirium spent, the Turk stiffened and collapsed into unconsciousness or death. A further victim had been claimed. Maria and her ally continued.

'This is where I must leave you.'

They knelt beside a mound of broken kegs and discarded galley spars, the heaped flotsam of the Marsa camp. Beyond it were the shuddering thud of hooves and chattering yips of mounted Spahis, the promise of open ground and freedom.

She rested her hand on his shoulder. 'I have no means to repay your courage and kindness.'

'Find your liberty, return to your people. It will be my reward.'

'You have yet to tell me your name.'

'Perhaps that is the way intended in war. I wish you well.'

Consciousness returned, arrived with the cold and sudden impact of seawater to his face. Hardy groaned. He was aware that he still lived, lay chained and naked on a plank deck, was among the company of corsairs once more. Full circle. He opened his eyes, slowly focused. A figure dressed in white stood over him, part holy man, part demon, unusually austere for a pirate. His hair and beard were black and unkempt, his face gaunt, his eyes deep-set and brooding behind heavy lids. El Louck Aly Fartax. An arresting sight, which boded ill.

'An exquisite if damaged specimen.' The eyes and mouth remained unsmiling. 'I know who you are, Christian Hardy.'

'I know you also.'

He had learned too much. The corsair captain was the scourge of the Aegean, infamous for meting terrible punishment on his men and captives alike. Few would have guessed he had once been a Dominican brother, a *Domini canis*, a savage hound for the Lord and the papacy. Old fanaticism had been redirected to a new profession and creed. These days he slit throats, burned towns in the service of Islam.

El Louck knelt beside him. 'You are well informed, Christian Hardy.'

'Reputation and rumour travel fast in war.'

'We both have earned our standing. I a corsair, you a soldier of rare distinction, a collectable, an item to be bartered for his own weight in gold and gemstones.'

'Is this why I live?'

'You live at my direction and for my pleasure.' El Louck allowed his stare to drift along his captive's torso. 'We shall fatten you for the scales, present you to Mustapha Pasha in exchange for his reward. He intends to flay off your skin, place your head on the prow of his galley.'

'I accept my fate as any soldier must.'

A finger traced his chest and abdomen. 'In my opinion, a waste of your qualities. You have such strength, Christian Hardy.'

'The easier to fight, El Louck.'

'Bears may be caged, lions rendered pliant when their teeth and claws are pulled.'

'Corsairs may be hunted down.'

'Not by you, Christian Hardy, nor by the Hospitaller Knights. Your Order is condemned.'

'You forget, Birgu and Senglea still stand.'

'They have no relevance.' El Louck bent close, his words becoming hushed. 'We have a spy in the Sacro Consiglio, an agent of destruction who stands close and venomous to the Grand Master, adds poisons to his repast. La Valette and his defences will decay from within, will fall away even as our cannon besiege him from without.'

Hardy lay motionless. A light flickered in his memory, a signal-lamp blinking from the cavalier tower of St Angelo as he took his troops by night across Grand Harbour. They were betrayed, undone. Against all reason, perhaps this corsair captain spoke the truth. *An agent of destruction.* He tried to clear his mind, to make sense of the absurd. The enemy ambushes on the relief supplies and reinforcements to the fort, the explosion at the powder-mill, the denunciation and imprisonment of the Moor. Separate events, a single goal. Everywhere, victims fell to the intrigue. Maria too was gone. La Valette would follow – a Grand Master isolated and unprotected, ailing, taking the hand which proffered help but administered toxin.

'I believe you not, corsair.'

'Your eyes tell different. You are vexed, my pretty thing.'

'I am wounded.'

'Wounds are for dressing, splinters for removing. When you are cured, I will play with you awhile.'

'When I am cured I will kill you.'

El Louck ignored the riposte, stretching to probe a cluster of shrapnel lacerations. Hardy winced. The corsair was licking blood from his fingers.

'What we will do to the Hospitaller Knights cannot be remedied by ointment and bandaging, Christian Hardy.' Madness and mysticism shone in his eyes. 'They will never see the death which stalks them, never hear warning of it from you. But console your-self. Remember your brothers who died at St Elmo.'

He would – would carry the blood-drenched images to meld with those of a more distant past. They would feed his rage, drive him on, compel him to find redress, exact reprisal against the cor-sairs, the Turks, the deceiver lodged at the centre of the Order. He had to reach La Valette.

It was a bleak irony that St Elmo fell on the eve of the Feast of St John, patron saint of the Order. In the Conventual Church, the Grand Master and his Knights had gathered, kneeling in prayer and silent vigil before the reliquary containing the sacred hand of the Baptist. A different kind of baptism was soon to be upon them. They had seen the death agony of St Elmo, the heads of their deceased and gallant brethren appear on the tips of pitched spears. They had witnessed the night fires spread in jubilation across the Turkish camp. Well might the heathen carouse. All that were left to the defenders were the power of faith, the strength of their walls and resolve.

La Valette bent his head and worked the rosary. Against the searing scenes of that day, his sickness was as nothing. He thought of the beacon that had heralded the close, the Maltese survivors who described it, the young boy Luqa who told in low and colourless whisper of Christian Hardy, the wailing cry of the Janissaries, the subsequent massacre. He had demanded so much of these men. Their departure would not go wasted or unavenged.

Midnight passed and the early hours of Sunday progressed towards dawn. Still the senior ranks of the Order knelt in their pews. It might be their last chance to find solace before battle, their final act of devotion while breath and life remained. The traitor sat with them, marking time, observing the ritual. He was grati-fied they drew comfort from such enduring custom. It meant their minds were on higher things while he contented himself with the low. Transformation was in prospect.

Henri de La Valette entered the church as silently as his armour would allow, genuflected to the altar, and approached his uncle. Ordinarily, interruption was prohibited, the intrusion of weaponry into the holy place forbidden. There was little ordinary during siege. The Grand Master leaned to hear as Henri spoke softly in his ear, rising at once to follow. Others stood. But La Valette motioned them back, accepting only Knight Grand Cross Lacroix as companion. The rest would discover later. It was for their good that they remained to concentrate on their faith.

On the shoreline below the walls of Birgu, La Valette found the reason for disruption to his worship. Crucifixes, four of them, bobbed in the shallows. Already Henri and the old veteran Lacroix were thigh-deep in the water, manhandling the objects, hauling them to land. An unconventional catch, for nailed to each cross was the headless torso of a Knight. The Grand Master watched, his back straight, his expression unchanged. He would not bend in such circumstance. At a glance he had identified the tunic heraldry of the corpses, taken in the symbol of the cross carved mockingly on their chests. The Turks were ill-advised in their taunting.

He lifted his eyes towards the grey and shattered remnants of St Elmo. 'Mustapha Pasha has delivered his message. We are obliged to respond.'

Chapter 10

Nightfall brought its own sounds: the wail of horns, the merrymaking of Turks at play in the aftermath of victory. Forgotten now were past losses and future clashes, the dead on the battlefield and the dying in their tents. For a few days the troops could dance and sing. They deserved such reward. On Mount Sciberras the slaves were being shackled again, yoked to the gun-cradles for onward passage to the heights of Corradino and its elevated positions overlooking Birgu and Senglea. The Christians would cease to be. But the moment could wait.

Few paid attention to the echoing fire of the unbeliever cannons. The Knights and their beleaguered garrisons could not be blamed for feeling sour and begrudging the Ottomans their entertainment, for loosing off some spoiling shot. Men joked and laughed or failed to notice.

The Janissary captain walked the lines, inspecting the guard and examining the trenches. He would not underestimate the enemy. They could fight – had proved so at St Elmo – were resourceful and cunning enough to initiate surprise attack. None of his men had anticipated such resistance. They had left Constantinople with a song on their lips and the expectation of an easy kill in their hearts. Nothing was easy. It was the scorched remains of their comrades that populated the landscape before the captured fort, their putrefaction which befouled the air. Not for them, or for him, the sweet-scented luxury and silk-lined certainties of the generals. Harsh times, bitter thoughts.

He paused and ducked at the scudding rush of air, the sweep-ing sigh of incoming ordnance. Typical of the infidels to ruin the party. Quickly, he took cover, throwing himself behind a shallow parapet as a second and then a third object bounded past. He cursed. The enemy gunners had altitude and reach, were plainly intent on bracketing the camp, scoring a few random casualties. He would not be among them. Another item landed, spinning awkwardly, leaping obstacles, spotting the ground. It rolled to the edge of the hollow and dropped beside him. Tentatively, he reached to touch it, instinctively knowing what it was, hoping it was not. His fingers withdrew. They had made contact with an unwelcome visitor.

'Dragut is dead.'

Mustapha Pasha looked about him at the war council. The faces were neutral, belonged to seasoned campaigners who rarely showed empathy, never displayed fragility. It was the will of God that the famed corsair had suffered his fate. They would simply move to the next item, the ensuing stage of their campaign. The commander-in-chief eyed Piali. With Dragut gone, there was no peacemaker left, no wise arbitrator to smooth tensions and ease hostility. Only rivalry and open hatred remained. Mustapha Pasha met the reflected gaze. He could yet outmanoeuvre this unctuous and loathsome turd of a court servant.

'Admiral Piali, you now have your base of Marsamuscetto harbour. How will you intend to use it?'

'To the disadvantage of La Valette and his Knights.'

'At the price we paid for St Elmo and your mooring, it is as well you serve in the interest of our cause.'

'I serve in the interest of the Sultan.'

'You disguise it.'

'My vessels patrol this coast, guard your flanks, carried your army. Do not make light of it, Mustapha Pasha.'

'It is my artillery which will raze Birgu and Senglea, my men who will storm their ramparts, fly our crescent flags above St Angelo.'

Piali toyed with a platter of dates. 'And those are my galleys placed on rollers, pulled by slaves around the foot of Mount Sciberras towards Grand Harbour. They will attack the very walls your guns cannot reach.'

'I welcome you to the fight.' Mustapha Pasha turned back to his generals. 'Fight it shall be. Our informant within the Knights advises that La Valette has stored some three thousand bushels of barley, eight thousand bushels of wheat. Scarcity of troops rather than coming starvation is their weakness.'

'They counter it with their aggression, their appetite for war.' It was the Governor of Alexandria who ventured his opinion.

'You lose your nerve?'

'I speak my mind. Even the common and untrained Maltese stood their ground against your levies at St Elmo.'

'They died nonetheless.'

'As did your men in large number, Mustapha Pasha.'

'I do not recall your Egyptians and corsairs playing so great a part.'

'You shall witness them soon. Yet their skills will not be misused, their energies not expended on armoured Knights who wait to meet them on their terms.'

'It is on our terms we shall challenge. The infidels will be stripped first of their defensive walls and then of their Grand Master. Our decisive blow will fall within a month.'

'A month?' Piali raised an eyebrow, another piece of fruit at his lips. 'Such delay will lead us towards autumn.'

'If we must winter here, so be it. I shall complete the mission.'

'My galleys cannot. They will be endangered by storm.'

'Admiral, I have yet to see them endangered by anything.'

The officers laughed, onlookers to animosity. St Elmo had reminded them that success was not foreordained. It had to be fought for, argued over. Setback too required anticipation and planning. Which way to jump, where to hide, who to blame or to join. Everyone watched each other, indulged in the game of uncivil relations. Their lives might depend on it.

Mustapha Pasha spat a prune-stone to his side. 'El Louck Aly Fartax, you reserve your comment. Are you fatigued from tending your prisoners?'

'I listen, Mustapha Pasha. My tastes are simple, my intent to serve.'

'Your intent is to swell your coffers. You stole captives from my Janissaries.'

'What is done in battle is often hard to judge, Mustapha Pasha.'

'You ask for ransom?'

'You offered reward.'

'Bring Hardy to me alive and I will pay, El Louck.'

Conversation went no further. The commander-in-chief had sensed something, a change in the ambient murmur of the camp, in the bursting of fireworks and the pop of enemy cannon. He was brushing past aides and servants, hurrying for the gold-embroidered doorway.

Mood and tempo had altered, shouts carried dismay instead of jubilation. Among the dotted fires, figures were rushing, eager to get away, to find shelter. Yet no trumpet sounded alarm. Mustapha Pasha squinted into the darkness, unable to focus above the glare of the flames, confused by the formless articles hurtling in through the night sky. Surely his encampments were beyond the range of the infidel guns.

'Mustapha Pasha, I beg to report.'

He stared at the Janissary captain and at the objects held in either hand. 'Explain what occurs.'

'Heads, Mustapha Pasha.' Both packages were placed down before him. 'The sky is raining heads.'

Across the Marsa, hundreds of them were landing in salvos fired from the Christian cannons. They flew well, travelled far. Each belonged to a Turkish captive taken prisoner in the first clash or some later skirmish, every last one of whom had been executed by order of the Grand Master. La Valette had given his reply.

Hardy shivered. Sleep was impossible when the mind raced and the wounds ached, when the faces of the dead haunted as though they lived. He thought of Colonel Mas burnt beyond recognition, of de Guaras in his chair, of the men he had shared bread and laughter with now buried beneath the stones of St Elmo. At least it was over for them. For him it was the beginning – of his capture, his torture, his end. In the glow-worm dimness of the galley lamps, he could see the piled remains of his recent past, his brigantine jacket and boots. Beyond them, the ladder leading to the oar-deck, the filth-smeared bodies of the slaves. What a place; what misadventure.

Movement betrayed their presence before the sound. A struggle was under way, subsided as quickly as it had started. Hardy peered towards the lower deck, but the silk hangings, the lack of light, the resistance of his chains impeded his view. He tugged at his shackles. In ordinary circumstance there would be the shrill call of the whistle, angry cries, the flinch-inducing blows of the whip. Nothing; a return to calm. He was not fooled. They had chosen well their time to strike.

A lantern was held to his face, a voice whispering in perfect French. 'You are Christian Hardy?'

'It is I.'

'We come from Mdina, have watched the Saracens rejoicing at the fall of the fort, their few prisoners taken aboard the galleys.'

'Why elect upon the vessel of El Louck?'

'It invited our attention, is abandoned by its crew, who make merry ashore.'

'I am grateful for it. But I cannot leave without the fate of the poor souls below determined. El Louck will soon return, accompanied from conference with Mustapha Pasha. He will seek revenge for my escape.'

'We will await him.'

'How many do you number?'

'Five, all quick up an anchor-chain and trained with the knife.'

'You may add over two hundred and fifty men from the rowing-benches.'

'An army.' The face came closer, was that of a young man with dark eyes and familiar features.

'One which will open up an unexpected front. Your name, friend?'

'Antonio, brother of Maria.'

They worked fast, releasing manacles, briefing the oarsmen. Many had not been free of their chains in years. Hardy moved among them. Some wept, others sat confused at the prospect of liberty, their horizons and hopes confined by the limits of their stinking pen. Most could not swim; none would find safety on the island. There were other ways to gain freedom.

It was late when El Louck Aly Fartax and his senior lieutenants arrived back on board. They were in high spirits, had dined and drunk well, were not averse to selecting from their captives for the purposes of entertainment. It would be as the mood took them. Hardy played dumb, stayed low, remained naked and chained at the stern.

'My prize and my treasure.' El Louck crouched down, his eyes hidden in their recesses, his presence redolent with hashish. 'You have waited for me.'

'I have no choice.'

'It would suit you to struggle. I like to smell the sweat and hopelessness in a captured man.'

'I am never wanting of hope.'

'You inhabit a world in which there is none. Your Grand Master sends the heads of our brothers by cannon into camp. It will not go unanswered.'

'Horror begets horror. It is the way of war.'

'I will show you the way of the corsair.' El Louck leaned and kissed him gently on the crown of his head.

Hardy remained still, anticipating brutality, the flurry of blows that would follow the tenderness. He had heard of the young men brought before El Louck, the tales of their torment and demise.

'You are rare indeed.' The pirate captain caressed his face. 'It saddens me to lose something so exquisite.'

'Who knows what we may lose, El Louck?'

'I have agreed your sale to Mustapha Pasha. Your future is over.'

His future was far from over — would embrace the destinies of Birgu, of La Valette, of his old ally Grand Cross Lacroix, of Henri and Hubert, of Luqa and the Moor. Again he thought of Maria, felt the creeping sickness at her loss. She had died for him, on account of him. It was bitter chance he should be saved by her brother, the man to whom he would have to confess, from whom he would need to ask forgiveness. He listened to El Louck, to the drifting sounds of the Turks on the water. The blocks groaned, the cordage creaked on the lateen masts. Events were moving.

'El Louck, the men we left have vanished from the *rambades*.'

'You are drunk. Check the platform again. They are asleep.'

'We have searched every inch of the prow. The gunners, the overseers, all have disappeared.'

'Do as I command, or it will be you who disappears.'

The crew-member retreated, anxious to obey, apprehensive at the prospect of chastisement. El Louck walked to the edge of the poop deck and scanned the huddled banks of slaves ranged below. One hundred and eighty feet of galley, of undiluted misery. He enjoyed being master, the unforgiving lord of darkness.

'You have found them?'

The corsair called back. 'We have not, El Louck. I suggest they have gone ashore.'

'I suggest you scourge the truth from a slave. Pick one.'

Without hesitation, the cord lash was applied to the back and shoulders of the nearest unfortunate. He was possibly the wrong choice. The pirate expected the slave to scream, to bleed and whimper in his bindings. Instead, the sinewed giant rose free, seized the whip, and wrapped it around the neck of his assailant. Arms made powerful at the oar bulged with exertion. The feet of the Arab kicked wildly, lifting from the deck.

'Castrate every man on that bench.' El Louck was shouting to his officers. 'We shall see how these vermin take to mutiny.'

They were taking to it well. As a corsair raced to aid his companion, his head split to the impact of a wood block. Another fell writhing, a ship-hook lodged in his eye. From beneath the sheepskin covers of the benches, weapons liberated from the armoury emerged, knives and cutlasses brandished and used by a mob intent on retribution. El Louck viewed the massacre, the takeover of his command. He regretted allowing shore-leave to his crew. The rebels were coming for him.

Or he would go to them. Hardy was behind him, a knife in his hand, Antonio at his side. 'You wished me to struggle, El Louck. Is this struggle enough?'

A foot to the small of his back propelled the captain into flight. He landed hard and did not rise, was obscured and overcome in the thrashing torrent of limbs and blades.

Antonio shook his head. 'It seems he is become the woman he wished to be.'

'The briefest of experiences.'

'His galley has new ownership. We should leave for Mdina before discovery is made.'

'You are right, Antonio. These men will take their chances as we take ours.'

'I shall gift them a pilot to navigate passage to the north. From henceforth they bend to their oars with freedom and impunity.'

'They do so for their lives.'

★

News of the sudden night departure of El Louck Aly Fartax and his corsairs was eventually to reach Mustapha Pasha and spread throughout the Turkish lines. The rage of the commander-in-chief knew few bounds. He had been betrayed, tricked, his Sultan dishonoured, his coalition wounded by the spiteful cowardice of a weak, self-serving pirate. The man had simply run from battle, carried off his spoils. And that man, he promised, would one day pay in blood.

'Your return is most welcome, Monsieur Hardy.'

Governor Mesquita had aged in the brief interim, was already careworn through responsibility for guarding a city deprived of resources and manpower. Yet his greeting was warm and dignified.

Hardy, dressed again in battle-stained boots, hose and brigantine jacket, bowed to him. 'I thank you for sending young Antonio and his party.'

'Their reconnaissance has been of much value. They inform on targets for our cavalry, reported each night on the plight of St Elmo.'

'You will have heard of how it fell.'

'I have grieved long over every detail, each fragment we have gleaned from defectors and spies. How the heathen snatched the ravelin, how you held the portcullis bridge, how so many of our gallant brethren met their end.'

'It was my privilege to serve with them.'

'I will not ask you to recount the tales or revisit those scenes, Monsieur Hardy. Your scars speak eloquently of the fight.'

'We all have made sacrifices, Governor Mesquita. I offer my condolence for the loss of your nephew. He was with me in the skirmish charge at Zeitun when struck by musket-ball. A courageous man.'

'The bravest. Yet there are too many for whom to weep; battles yet to come, the nobility of our cause, bid us dry our eyes.' Mesquita unbuckled his sword and presented it to the

Englishman. 'I thought one day I would pass this to my nephew. Now it is yours.'

'I am undeserving.'

'You survived St Elmo through the intervention of God. I can think of none more rightful.'

'I will put it to use, Governor Mesquita. You have my word.'

'Perhaps such employment is close.' The Knight was watching Hardy's face, choosing his words. 'On the very day that your fort was vanquished, a small relief force led by Chevalier de Robles landed from Sicily.'

'Its size?'

'A mere forty-eight Knights, accompanied by a hundred or so gunners and volunteers and six hundred imperial Spanish infantry.'

'Better than an empty promise.'

'Less than a true army.'

Hardy was weighing the new weapon in his hand. 'We showed at St Elmo what may be accomplished with skilled swordsmanship and a few stout hearts.'

'Would that they came to Mdina. But the Grand Master has the greater need.'

'It is why I must take my leave and rejoin the defenders of Birgu.'

'What of your wounds?'

'They will heal with time and through the aid of the hospital. The relief force requires escort, and I shall provide it.'

'You must go where your duty takes you. Yet remain as my guest while we make preparation for the rendezvous.'

'There are those to whom I must first speak, Governor Mesquita.'

It was approaching dawn as Hardy slipped from the Governor's residence and padded through the dirt streets. He had not yet slept, in part through the energy-elation of his escape, in part through the knowledge that rest would bring too deep a slumber.

Weariness dragged at his heels, weighed on his shoulders. He would not be diverted. A spy was poisoning La Valette, betraying the Order, throwing wide the gates to the Turkish flood. He had to return and meet the threat. His mission, his secret.

Helios was expecting him, must have recognized his footfall, picked out his scent. Equine intuition. The stallion snorted and whinnied, his hooves stamping restless in his stall as he tried to reach his master.

'You have waited for me, Helios.' Hardy went to him and placed his arms about his neck, pressed his face into his nose. The horse sniffed him, the ears pricked, the eyes enquiring. 'I have missed you, my friend.'

There was understanding and complete communication in the moment, the love of a brother for a brother, the respect of a soldier for a fellow soldier. No treason here, no confusion, no motive but loyalty and the common bond of war. Hardy stroked and patted the steed, spoke gently to him. They would lie together in the straw. Old times.

'Christian.'

Morning seeped through, hours had passed, and Antonio stood before them. Hardy rose stiffly to greet him.

'After the privations of a corsair galley, the stable is a palace. I owe you my life, Antonio.'

'You owe me nothing, though I will accept your friendship.' The young Maltese noble extended a hand.

'Your hostility is what I merit.'

'I know Maria to be dead.' Tears pricked in Antonio's eyes. 'I know too she loved you, Christian. There is no blame in it.'

'I should have safeguarded her.'

'Could I prevent her from leaving Mdina for Birgu? Could you forestall her journeying from Birgu to St Elmo? She was a free spirit, a wondrous sister, the sweetest and most headstrong of her sex. We honour her by fighting on.'

'I must visit your father.'

'He is unaware of her fate, will remain so until the outcome of this siege is decided. Revelation would destroy him.'

'Then I shall respect your wishes, Antonio.'

'Come, brother. We have your expedition to prepare.'

Together the two men made their way back towards the Governor's palace. A skirmish-troop of cavalry trotted by, calling their salutations to Hardy as they passed. Night pickings had been average. Slung across the backs of two horses were Turkish sentries seized as they patrolled their outer defences. They would join the list of those destined for the gallows on Mdina's city walls.

Outside the cathedral, a squad of Maltese civilians was formed up with their pikes. A Spanish officer berated them.

'*Slope arms! You are to look like soldiers, like fighting men able to counter a charging rank of Janissaries. Do you understand?*'

'Methinks *I* do, Captain Alvarez.'

The Spaniard swivelled slowly on his heel, his colour draining, recognition and dread flaring in his eyes. He had seen a ghost, a survivor from St Elmo, an event he had not foreseen when offering himself to the Turk, in striving to persuade his countrymen to desert. Guilty by expression.

Hardy stepped forward, his sword already drawn. 'Will you stand beyond these walls at night as you did at St Elmo? Will you betray these citizens as you did your brothers?'

'I was captured.'

'You left your post, crossed the lines by cover of darkness. You sought to bring us down.'

'It was not I.'

'Become a man and speak the truth. You planned to save yourself, to find favour with Mustapha Pasha. You attacked us with serpent words to cajole soldiers from the fort.'

'I beg you, sir.'

'Beggars beg. Traitors face punishment.'

'I am no traitor. You mistake my motive.'

'Do not mistake mine.' Hardy was sheathing his sword. 'Yet I would not waste noble steel on your hide.'

Babbling now in fear and justification, the officer threw himself on the mercy of the gathering crowd. There was none. He tried to explain, attempted to tell how the Turks had coerced him. Finally, gradually, the excuses dissolved into weeping confession and acceptance. He had been sent away by a Turkish commander-in-chief contemptuous of his weakness. His exploits were now at an end.

Hardy and Antonio left them. The pikemen were dragging their captive into a courtyard for summary and public execution. With a frenzied roar from the mob, the first stone was cast, the initial blow struck. Little would remain of the Spanish captain.

'*Halt.*'

Arquebuses pointed, and the landscape became alive with the emerging forms of Christian soldiers. The forward detachment of the relief army had been found. Hardy raised his hand in greeting, Antonio and a cavalry detachment coming to a halt behind.

'We come from Mdina.'

'Your appearance would suggest you come from hell, Christian Hardy.'

It was the Knight de Robles of the Order of Santiago, the tough and pugilistic commander who led from the front, who would have enjoyed nothing more than to encounter a live Turk patrol and tear it to pieces with his bare hands. He sounded disappointed.

'My apologies we are not the enemy, Chevalier.'

The Knight shrugged. 'In good time, Christian. You intend to join us in our quest to reach the Grand Master?'

'If there is room in your column.'

'I would have room for twenty thousand if the Viceroy of Sicily allowed it.'

'He continues to vacillate?'

'Vacillate?' De Robles grimaced in disgust. 'He hides beneath his bedclothes. I disobeyed his orders in bringing my force ashore.'

'Your dissent is our benefit.'

'And my pleasure. The stalwart defence of St Elmo has fired our zeal, excited our imaginations.'

'My own imagination is somewhat spent.'

'The coming battle will rekindle it. We have need of you to guide us to the fight.'

Hardy turned in his saddle to Antonio. 'Ride swift for Mdina, my brother, and guard it well. I will make atonement for Maria.'

'God speed and keep you safe, Christian.'

That night the small relief force continued on its way down the western edge of the island. Since the lightning raids conducted from Mdina by the cavalry of Marshal Copier, the enemy had become more circumspect, had reduced their presence. Occasionally the faint proximity of mounted Spahis could be heard, the glimmer of shaded torches detected. The Knights and their infantry crept on.

They were drawing close. Over the following two days and nights they would hide up, move again, swing inland to bypass the main Ottoman camp laid out across the Marsa. A perilous operation, but any move neighbouring the Turk, nearing the traitor at the shoulder of La Valette, carried its risk. Hardy would confide what he knew to no one. He would wait and watch, would prevent word of their mission from reaching the Grand Master. To inform him early was to alert the betrayer, invite ambush. For now, he would rest until evening faded to dusk and the seven hundred men started on their onward trail.

'Christian, we have a Turkish prisoner. Your attendance is requested.'

His musings had been interrupted, his preparations for the

march put aside. The man might carry information. As soldier and linguist, with knife or words, Hardy could be trusted to prompt the memory, provide translation for any faltering prose.

He entered the cave, peered into the grey shadows thrown by a diminishing sun. No guards were present.

'Chevalier de Robles has been kind enough to spare my life.'

'Maria.'

She emerged from behind a screen of boulders, an indistinct figure still cloaked in the military uniform of her escape. Even in the semi-gloom, even as a Turkish levy, she radiated grace and beauty. They stumbled towards each other, meeting, enfolding, speechless in the moment. Miracles required few words.

He kissed her, felt the give and her response. 'My perfect Maria. It cannot be you.'

'My Christian.'

'How came you here? At this hour, this place?'

'Wandering, or the will of God – there is no easy explanation. I merely left the clutches of the barbarian Piali and headed for the safety of the west.'

Her tale came in a rush, incidents and vignettes linked by chance, propelled by accident. A drunken guard she had left naked and bound, an Armenian slave who had discovered then aided her flight, a tent of whores she had passed through in disguise. Each step had led her to the boundary of the Marsa camp. It was unwise of the Spahi cavalrymen to have dismounted where they did, to have abandoned their horses in haste to reach the celebrations at St Elmo.

Hardy shook his head in wonderment. 'Against it, my story may wait.'

'It seems we both have had adventure.'

'From henceforth they combine.' He pressed his lips to hers, to her ear, her cheek, her neck, smoothing her hair, touching her skin. 'I have encountered many Turk levies these past weeks. I vouch none as pretty or compassionate as you.'

She laughed between her coursing tears, tracing her fingers lightly on the cuts to his face. 'My poor Christian. You carry such wounds.'

'They would be worse but for your brother Antonio coming to my aid, swimming to the corsair galley.'

'Antonio?'

'He is become the eyes and ears of Mdina, spying on the Turk, confounding their every turn. He grieves for you, believes you dead.'

'Like you, I live. With you, I return to Birgu.'

'It is full of hazard.'

'I care not, Christian. We face it together.'

They held each other in silence and in love, reunited in temporary happiness, alone as they had been that night on the collapsing ramparts of St Elmo. It was a week previous, and yet it was a lifetime. The Turk remained in Malta, was descending on the very point for which they aimed.

They were killing the dogs in Birgu. It would reduce the number of mouths to feed, provide meat if supplies dwindled and starvation loomed. Everywhere, Knights and soldiers patrolled the streets and searched the houses. They were taking food too, paying fair price at the insistence of La Valette, carrying off grain and produce to the general store. It was for the greater good, for the purpose of survival. The Grand Master moved among the populace, counselling the fearful, inspiring the weak to be strong. They looked to him. He urged them to look to God.

Luqa hid in the cellar of the merchant house. He had made it his home, used it as refuge for himself and the two hounds. If invasion had destroyed his friend the Englishman, seen the disappearance of the Lady Maria, consigned the good Moor to a dungeon, no smiling divinity existed. Nor was there adult justice or happy ending. He had survived well enough on his own by the sea, just he and his canine companions. As it should be; as it would be.

The door creaked open to the weight of a man, the light of a lantern swinging in behind. A face appeared, disturbing in the glow. It was the Knight de Pontieux.

'I have come for the dogs, boy.'

'You will leave without them.'

'You would defy the wishes, the command, of the war council?'

'They mean nothing to me.'

'Then you are a fool.'

'And you a liar.'

'Dogs bark, will interrupt the night-rest of our men. Dogs eat, will consume provisions for our people.'

'Men eat more food than women. Would you kill them? Cannon make greater noise than dogs. Would you dismantle them?'

'The laws of the Order prevail, even over the will of a native idiot. Hand me the hounds.'

'Never.' Luqa pulled a knife, held it to his front, the blade pointing at the Knight.

'A trying one.' De Pontieux could afford to be almost congenial. 'I tremble at the threat.'

'My friend would cut you to pieces.'

'Christian Hardy? It is as well I am in luck and he is no more.'

'I can defend myself.'

'Desist from idle boasts. I will be forced to harm you.'

'I may harm you first.'

Keeping his gaze on the boy, de Pontieux drew and raised his sword. 'Enough insolence and delay, bastard child. You will pass the hounds to me for quick dispatch.'

'I shall not desert them.'

'Were they not mere creatures, I would think you admirable. Instead, you are a clown.'

'A clown with a knife.'

The tip of the sword moved. 'Therefore in much danger. Do not oppose me.'

'Stay away.' Luqa crouched, ready to give fight.

'Three dogs, all for the same blade. None will question why you were stuck through. None outside will hear.'

'*Except I.*'

De Pontieux felt the steel to his neck, turned his eyes to glimpse what he had already appreciated. 'I see the cherished prodigal is returned.'

'Lower your sword, de Pontieux.'

'You would challenge a Knight, a member of the Sacro Consiglio?'

'You would menace a boy?'

'Simple discourse and quiet argument.'

Hardy flexed his sword-hand. 'I will give you argument. Put up the weapon.'

'There is the matter of the dogs.'

'A lesser matter than your life. Leave us, before you make it forfeit.'

'It is considered treasonable to defy a Knight Commander.'

'It is considered prudent to retreat while able.'

'This is not the end, Monsieur Hardy.'

'Why? You intend to cry to the Grand Master? I have brought to him some seven hundred extra troops.'

'Bravo.' De Pontieux smiled. 'You are quite the champion to us all. Though still mortal.'

'Perhaps you and Prior Garza could pray for me.'

'The least we may do for your miraculous restoration to our side.'

'I am obliged.' Hardy bowed, standing aside as de Pontieux glanced coolly at Luqa and turned to leave.

'Be in no doubt, Christian Hardy. When next our swords cross, it will be to the death.'

'Yours, Chevalier.'

The Knight stalked from the room. Cautiously, Luqa rose and stepped forward. He pressed the small silver cross into the palm of his friend, repeated the words he had heard in the final moments of St Elmo.

'It belongs with the living.'

Chapter 11

'Hang him.'

La Valette stared without pity at the elderly Greek slave. The man had been sent by Mustapha Pasha under flag of truce to offer terms, to persuade the defenders of Birgu and Senglea that resistance was futile, surrender more appropriate. There was no need for further bloodshed. The Knights and their followers could leave the island with their dignity intact, their lives spared and their stand made. St Elmo had reminded all of their fighting prowess and unquenchable spirit. Its destruction had also shown the inevitability of total obliteration. That was the message. But the Grand Master too could play psychological games.

In abject terror, the Greek dropped to his knees. He had already fouled his undergarments.

'Your Highness, I am but a poor Greek, a messenger.'

'A poor Greek in service to the wrong cause, a messenger who bears the lies and double-meaning of the heathen Antichrist.'

'I was born no infidel, Your Highness.'

'Thus you have still less reason to whore yourself in their name.'

'Your Highness, I am old.'

'As am I. Yet I do not find my will failing with the years. I do not discover treachery in my heart.'

'I am present under flag of truce, Your Highness.'

'You are not present as our friend. Therefore you are the enemy, and will find appointment with our gallows.'

The ancient was vibrating in his wretchedness, his face wet, his sobs loud. 'I throw myself on your mercy, Your Highness.'

'I lost all mercy when the Turk invaded my island, when they dismembered my Knights and men on the far side of Grand Harbour. You will suffer for it.'

'Your Highness, I was tasked with bringing you word from Mustapha Pasha. I have done so.'

'Then you presume.'

'It was on pain of death, Your Highness.'

'So death it shall be.'

The Grand Master walked an unhurried circuit of the room. He was in no rush, was content to prolong the agony and the moment. Fear, imagination would exaggerate the encounter in the mind of the weeping Greek, would engrave it on his soul. By the time he reached the Turkish lines, he would believe in dragons and monsters and tell of an invincible defence.

'St Elmo did not surrender.' La Valette turned back to the cowering slave. 'Its troops fought for each stone, every inch. They left Turk dead to fester in their thousands. And Mustapha Pasha believes I would abdicate my responsibility, abandon Malta to his grasp?'

'He deemed you would see reason, Your Highness.'

'What I see is past history and future glory. What I see is the enemy weaken, his army bleed into the rock.'

'The Turk claims advantage in number.'

'We shall see how we are matched. I am no Grand Master de L'Isle-Adam taking the Knights of St John from Rhodes. I am Grand Master Jean Parisot de La Valette. Negotiation and retreat will not be countenanced.'

'Your Highness, I was raised a good Christian.' The Greek wrung his hands, his voice tremulous. 'I ask you to look upon this simple man with charity and understanding.'

'I look upon you with scorn.'

'Your Highness, I must take opinion to Mustapha Pasha.'

'It may be delivered from the mouth of a cannon.'

The pleading was frantic. 'I do not want to hang, Your Highness. I do not wish to die.'

'A pity this world is cruel and a slave has no right to wish. Guards, bind his eyes.'

Soldiers stepped forward and seized the man. Roughly, they wound the bandaging tight, ignoring the cries, eventually throwing their victim trussed and sightless to the ground. He lay writhing in his misery, his moans soft and persistent. It was how La Valette left him.

'You stink, slave.'

Another presence, a different voice, had entered the room. It seemed to be unaccompanied, had insinuated itself like a chill into the enveloping quiet. The Greek drew up his legs, tried to curl more tightly into a protective ball. It had little effect. The hidden spectre remained close, watchful, talking in riddle.

'Can you find no dignity, Greek?'

'My employment is not as a fighter, sir.'

'Your forebears were warriors. You stain their memory as you sully your breeches.'

'I am destined for the gallows, sir.'

'Is that so?'

'I know not the crime I commit. Yet Grand Master La Valette has ordained it.'

'He is hard to sway when his mind is set.'

'My entreaties mean nothing. None care for a mere carrier of news, for an old man who may be executed without reason.'

'War does not favour reason.'

The traitor was silent for a while, observing the whining and piteous creature. He was content to let the old fool agonize and wallow in his own shit, to believe what his thoughts desired him to believe. The more terrified, the more pliant he would be. There was craft in manipulating another human.

'You brought word from Mustapha Pasha, slave. What say you to taking word back?'

'I face death.'

'La Valette trifles with you. To preserve our security, your eyes were covered when first you entered Birgu. Would we take such measure did we not intend to return you to the Turk?'

'I cannot say.'

'I, however, can. I will keep you alive if you listen well and learn fast, if you are willing to repeat to Mustapha Pasha the detail of my disclosure.'

'How should I know this is no trap, no trick designed to ensnare me?'

'A simple matter of trust. Should I lie, and La Valette tell the truth, then you are already ensnared, already at the foot of the scaffold. Better to seize the moment, the hand that proffers aid.'

'Your identity is hidden, the provenance of your words a mystery.'

'It will remain so. What I tell you is for the ears of the Turk commander alone. You understand?'

'I do, sir.' The slave was nodding furiously, clutching at hope, constrained by circumstance and rope-ties.

'We have little time. Let us begin.'

It was later that the Greek messenger was led out blindfold into the scouring light and heat of the summer day. He was taken back through the streets of Birgu, a small man jeered onward by a crowd, accompanied by the beat of a single drum. His hosts were not about to abandon their performance. Only when they came to the walls did the procession pause, was the covering removed. The slave blinked. His limited horizons had opened to a new and more generous vista. Before him, and to either side, ranks of soldiers stood to attention in full armour and in depth. Menacing types, the troops of Provence and Auvergne.

'Regard these men.' La Valette called from a stone balcony set above the scene. 'And as you leave our gate, observe the ditch beyond these walls. Inform your master Mustapha Pasha it is the sole portion of our territory we will permit his forces to inhabit.'

For a second time, the quaking visitor released the contents of his bowels.

Mustapha Pasha reacted poorly to the rejection of his offer. The bombardment of Birgu and Senglea opened in the first week of July, the crossfire of eighty and then a hundred cannon blazing from Gallows Point, Mount Sciberras and the high ground of Corradino, and was joined by the galleys of Pilali that had been dragged overland from Marsamuscetto into the waters of Grand Harbour. Everywhere was encompassed by fire. There would be no respite, no let-up in the day-and-night barrage that crashed against the walls of the two fortified peninsulas. And inexorably the Turkish entrenchments spread, blocking reinforcement, shutting off escape. The circle had been closed.

In the slave-tunnels beneath St Angelo, the sounds echoed and distorted in the Stygian darkness. If it was hell for the defenders above, down here it was beyond the wildest of nightmares. Yet the Moor seemed indifferent. He sat cross-legged in the straw, dignified and unperturbed in his captivity, a figure dressed in white and holding court behind bars. Hardy was with him.

'You frequent the darkest of places, Moor.'

'Speaks one who was at St Elmo.'

The Englishman grimaced. 'I would rather be with a sword in my hand than in a cell.'

'And miss the noble and illustrious company I keep? In the next dungeon is the distinguished Sanjak of Alexandria. Beyond him, the officers of the merchant ship you captured from the Sultan's chief eunuch. Across the way, the aged nurse of Suleiman's daughter Mihrma.'

'They must wish they had been ransomed.'

'The loudness of the tumult informs me the time for bargaining is past.'

'Beasts would not tolerate such conditions.'

'It is what I call my home, what five hundred galley slaves look upon as dry land and safe lodging.'

'You have been wronged, Moor.'

'A man may grow accustomed to circumstance.'

'Even though he is innocent?' Hardy leaned forward. 'This is no position for a friend of mine, no situation for a loyal servant to the Order.'

'Tell it to de Pontieux and Prior Garza. Tell it to the hidden forces that conspired to have me caught, sentenced and hanged.'

'You are needed by the Grand Master.'

'I do better to stay away. Here I find invisibility and a certain solace, a platform from which to observe.'

'And what do you see?'

'Two powers collide on a limestone rock, the destruction consuming, the fragments scattering. Much is at stake.'

'The Grand Master is being poisoned, Moor.'

There was no surprise shown. Acceptance of fate was part of his creed, part of the age. Life was tenuous, open to violent chance, in a world of siege and battle. Like the soldier or sailor, like Hardy, the Moor comprehended his place, embraced his lot. *Fragments scattering*. An accurate assessment. Much was at stake.

As the jarring notes of gunfire eased, the Moor spoke again. 'Dwell upon the fate of the other military Orders of Christendom. The Templars gone, crushed by avarice and imperial design over two hundred years since. The Teutons no more, dying out after defeat at their Battle of Tannenberg in the year of 1410. Their moment has passed.'

'Enemies exist among us who would seek to speed the passing-moment of the Hospitallers.'

'I judge it true, Christian Hardy. Invasion by the Turk is their cover and excuse. Without the Grand Master, the Order is nothing, the voices of doubt and capitulation, of retreat and downfall, would soon hold sway.'

'A shrewd game.'

'We all are at risk in it. Whoever poisons La Valette is close to him, undermines our foundations, confounds our defence.'

'Consigning you and me to places from which we were intended never to return.'

'God is merciful.'

'He also grants us insight. We know of a traitor, and the traitor is unaware of it.'

'Use the knowledge to advantage. Be cautious and move slow. To alert the betrayer is to compel him to act, to dispatch La Valette to his death in haste.'

'Should we not warn the Grand Master?'

The Moor shook his head. 'He would not listen or carry himself from danger, would not countenance suspicion of his brethren.'

'I am myself hard put to recognize the fact.'

'There are other ways to thwart a foe.' The Moor waited as another barrage passed, as sand chippings crumbled from the walls. 'The conspirator uses arsenic, I am sure of it. It will go unnoticed, will corrupt the body, usurp the health of La Valette through seeming natural cause.'

'We must discover him.'

'Or remove La Valette from his St Angelo domain. Speak with young Henri. Together, compose excuse to persuade his uncle to reside with the wider populace of Birgu.'

'It would indeed render him a harder target.'

'That is my instinct and intent.'

'What of you, Moor?'

'The fingers of the traitor reach even into these tunnels. I have seen their shadow, have smelled the Ottoman.'

'You sit beside them, Moor. Slaves fill every corner, are chained throughout these burrows.'

'Rebellion is close, Christian Hardy.'

'It will come to naught. They are manacled hand and foot, have heard of how the heads of Turk captives flew so well from our cannons.'

'It shall not prevent their armed revolt. The traitor and his masters prepare for it. They find access through the sewer sluice, send spies by night to study the approach and foment their plans. It is the stench of the cesspool I detect, the whisper of a plot I hear.'

'Surprise attack?'

'A further front opened with a ready army.'

'And mounted from within St Angelo itself. It could break us.'

'You may depend on it.'

'As I may depend on you, Moor.' The two friends stood and embraced. 'It seems we are besieged from every side.'

'We will hold the enemy yet, will hold the betrayer to account.'

'I must first find our reinforcements.'

'Trust few, Christian Hardy.'

He picked his way across the pontoon bridge carried on small boats floating between Birgu and Senglea. It had been constructed by command of the Grand Master, a means of rapid reinforcement, of sharing resources among the sparsely manned walls and fortifications. Another detail, another manifestation of siege. Hardy felt the gentle give of the planks beneath his feet, remembered the narrow bridge above the ravelin ditch at St Elmo, the crowding faces of the Janissaries, the blizzard of flesh as the trump had detonated. He could not escape the images, could not avoid those to come.

Senglea, a ghost enclave, contained its own particular horrors. A three-hundred-pound basilisk-ball cut through a stone rampart and plunged to demolish a flat-roofed dwelling. Close behind came its twin, levelling houses, crushing inhabitants. An inhospitable location. It was bearing the brunt of the Turkish cannonades, appearing deserted but for the occasional scream and the shouts of men ferrying the wounded and rebuilding buttresses.

Familiar scenes. How it had begun and how St Elmo had died, reflected Hardy.

'A cruel night, Christian.'

'I have lost ability to judge.'

Henri de La Valette was on the foreshore of Senglea, the overseer to construction of a wood palisade that reached the entire length of the waterfront. Around him, gangs of Maltese volunteers worked in the darkness to carry the sharpened stakes, to embed them in the shallows and secure them with metal hoops and chains. An immense and urgent undertaking. At best it would prevent beach landing by Turkish swimmers or boats; at worst would hinder and throw further hazard in the path of the adversary.

'The most impressive stockade I have yet seen, Henri.' Hardy slapped his friend on the back. 'Mustapha Pasha and his Sultan will rue the day they brought war against the family La Valette.'

'They must rue the day Christian Hardy slipped their grasp at St Elmo. It is good to have you again beside me, brother.'

'There were moments I believed the impossibility of such event.'

'Many times, I wager. But now we are to stand together once more.'

'A privilege, Henri.'

'An epic endeavour. I do not doubt that few of us will remain when it is done.'

'Then we must ensure we are among those few.'

'I shall leave it to God.'

'While I shall leave it to my sword and my wits, to the keen eyes of my companions.'

'I will for ever seek to protect you, Christian.'

'And I you, Henri. It is how we have come to live this long.'

'Is that so?' There was humour in his seriousness. 'Confess you have sought to kill me with every one of your adventures.'

'I cannot deny that death accompanied most of them.'

'Yet my uncle considers you fine example, the best among our kind.'

'He knows well I am not of your kind.'

'While he is the rarest of his.'

Hardy turned towards the young Knight. He had heard the worry defined in the words. The Grand Master was being poisoned, and his nephew suspected it.

'Your uncle sickens, Henri.'

'I cannot say.'

'Will not say. For you wish to guard him as you would guard me, have pledged to him your silence.'

'Do not ask, Christian.'

'I will speak instead. Listen to me, Henri. The Grand Master is in the gravest of danger.'

'More so than the rest?'

'The Saracens have a spy within our midst. He poisons your uncle, plots each stage of his affliction as he does each step of our demise.'

'How came you by such knowledge?'

'Prisoners of corsairs are privy to the strangest of truths.' Hardy let the silence lag. 'I am right in this, Henri.'

'I have seldom known you wrong.'

'Evil is afoot, and our duty is to counter it. We do so through pretence, by adopting a manner of calm inscrutability.'

'And meanwhile?'

'We engage in subterfuge, pluck the Grand Master from the traitor's lair in St Angelo, set our bloodhounds on the scent.'

'Uncovering a demon within our walls might destroy the Order, Christian.'

'Failure to find him would be certain to.'

They were interrupted by the large and moonlit shape of Fra Roberto, his habit knotted at his thighs, lumbering in their direction. The priest had assigned himself to the work detail, had immersed himself in both the water and his labours. Now he

196

bore a new and lightly carried load to place at the feet of the two men. It was Hubert.

The priest seemed aggrieved. 'You brought me from Mdina to haul logs and ferry simpletons?'

'Are you not a fisher of men, Fra Roberto?'

'It appears I am become a saviour of drowning fools.' He prodded the novice cleric, who retched a stream of seawater. 'His enthusiasm is greater than his ability to swim.'

'We give thanks for his deliverance.'

'The Maltese give thanks I pulled him from their palisade.'

Hubert was panting for air. 'I intended to help, Fra Roberto.'

'Instead, you thrash and flounder as a stranded eel.'

'My apologies.'

'Think nothing more.' The colossus stooped and smacked him fondly on the head. 'Give me your word you will not venture so close again to the sea.'

'You have it.'

'As I have witnesses. Stay with them, Hubert. Too much laughter in a night is distraction to our effort.'

The young probationer climbed unsteadily to his feet. 'My theatre is over, Fra Roberto. From henceforth, I remain in infirmary or church.'

'We may all sleep more sound.'

With a chuckle, the priest shouldered a log and headed for the sound of the work-gangs. Hardy and his two companions remained, listening to the straining men, the tap of hammers, the rattle of chain. Already the last defenders of St Elmo had been dead a fortnight. War moved on; new imperatives crowded in.

Henri watched Fra Roberto recede into the gloom. 'The man is an entire crew in himself, Christian.'

'He is an army.'

'One I am pleased was to hand when I slipped beneath the water.' There was a ruefulness in Hubert's tone.

'Go dry yourself, brother.' Hardy took his shoulder and gently propelled him towards the ladder on the seaward wall. 'You will be of no use should you catch a chill.'

'I have no use save as a jester.'

'The Turk will make work for all of us.'

They waited until he was gone and they were alone with talk of conspiracy and betrayal. In erecting a palisade they were keeping one enemy at bay while locking another inside. It was hard to tell which posed the greater threat.

Hardy spoke his thought aloud. 'We have found our blood-hound, Henri.'

Turk swimmers appeared. They had entered the waters below Corradino, came armed with knives and hatchets and intent to dismantle the palisade. Mustapha Pasha could not allow the structure to stand. His men fanned out, moving purposefully across the few hundred feet of water, homing on the sections that appeared the weakest. Given time and effort, it could be reduced to kindling.

But they were met. Streaming from cover, clambering and sliding naked down the rocks, knives clenched between their teeth, the defenders threw themselves into the sea. They were fishermen, expert divers, adept with the blade. It was these skills which now were put to use. In a tumbling and water-deluged frenzy, the opposing forces clashed. Limbs beat among the sail-yards, bodies kicked and twisted, faces rose and sank. They were desperate scenes of foundering death. A Turk was gutted with a shellfish knife and rolled away, his place taken by another wielding an axe. He too was felled, disappearing to a blade-strike through the temple. Behind them a stricken comrade splashed erratically to make poor his escape. He was seen. A Maltese dived after him, gaining, catching, taking him down in a welter of blows, a pink flurry of choking screams.

Brandishing a hatchet, Luqa sat astride a spar and chopped gaily at the foe. Occasionally he would scramble along the palisade to reach and dispatch an injured or exhausted invader. At other moments he plunged into the water to pick off stragglers or join a hunting-pack.

He found the swimmer cowering and entangled in loose rigging. 'You are caught, Turk?'

The man did not understand, but spoke anyway, his eyes pleading, his hands raised in capitulation. He need not have bothered. Luqa struck him between the eyes.

There were many targets. A blood-slick covered the surface of French Creek and trailed into Grand Harbour. Corpses floated among the thrashing figures; men clawed and stabbed and struggled to flee. It was hand to hand, feet stamping into faces, mouths tearing at flesh. The Turks were weakening.

'*Boats!*'

From the enemy shoreline, vessels were bringing reinforcements. Already arquebusiers were firing at the Maltese racing to withdraw, sailors in the prow swinging grapple-irons and man-handling hawsers in preparation for their act of demolition. Where the swimmers had failed, they would succeed. Under a fusillade of covering fire, the cables were attached, the oar-strokes reversed, the lines carried back to capstans mounted on the Ottoman beach. The order was given, and shoulders set to their task. Frantically, as sections of palisade began to collapse, the Maltese regrouped and counter-attacked. Some sat astride the cables and cut at them with their knives, others swam out to sever them offshore. The Turkish boats moved in.

Pierced by an arrow at the very moment of raising his spear to run a defender through, an Ottoman levy somersaulted into the water. It left the soldier behind exposed. He too fell, struck by a succeeding shaft which flew fast, aimed true. The man slumped, staring dumbfounded at the feathered flight protruding from his abdomen.

'Fine shooting, young Hardy.'

Hardy reached into his quiver, strung another arrow, found a target, and let fly. 'The enemy places himself well, sir.'

'Permit me to join you in the sport.'

Knight Grand Cross Lacroix unslung his recurved bow and took up position beside him. The old warrior was quick and fluid, had the sureness and accuracy of experienced hands.

'To your right, sir.'

'Take him. He is yours.'

They talked as they worked, conceding or accepting points, remarking on the fight. Battles were curious affairs, could be both distant and intimate, dispassionate yet bloody. The two men were like grandfather and grandson enjoying a common pursuit.

'Nothing can match the bow, young Hardy.'

'Save for an arquebus.'

Lacroix snorted. 'Firearms are for donkeys.' He released his bow-fingers and watched the dart speed the distance. 'There is no artistry in gunpowder and lead.'

'Yet therein rests the fate of our Order.'

'Today we guard it with our archery.'

'And tomorrow?' It was the turn of Hardy to loose a steel-barbed shaft. 'I saw what the Turk gunners and arquebusiers exacted at St Elmo. I see what they already do here.'

'We shall best them as we best them now.'

'Or we shall die in our attempt.'

The Grand Cross glanced across and smiled. 'A splendid prospect for soldiers.'

'It holds no terror.'

'When is one more alive or pure than in facing death? Where is one closer to God than in confronting Satan?'

When holding Maria; when discovering something rather to live for than to die for. Hardy unleashed a brace of arrows in rapid succession. Each achieved a kill.

'You have not lost your eye or instinct, young Hardy.'

'Nor you, sir.'

'An old dog may yet retain its bite. I was your age when I slew the heathen at Rhodes. What I learned then I carry to this day.'

'Harsh lessons, I venture.'

'Never surrender or retreat. Never listen to the timid. Never show your back to an enemy.'

'The very code I embrace.'

'We are as one, young Hardy. Let us trust the remainder in our garrison are with us.'

'You have your doubts?'

'This siege will make either heroes or cowards of us all.' The old Knight lowered his bow. 'We have won the bout. The boats begin to depart.'

Abandoning their assault, the Turks were pulling back in frantic and churning haste. The Maltese pursued them, clinging to oars, hurling themselves or their projectiles at any craft too slow and burdened to withdraw. Luqa was with them. As a Turk leaned to bail water from a sinking stern, the boy surfaced and plucked him overboard. Crewmen tried to fend the boy off, but the threat had shifted, Luqa darting beneath the hull to rise and strike at arms, backs and hamstrings. He moved away, circling and treading water, shouting his defiance.

Lacroix pointed. 'A fiery spirit.'

'It will need be. When next the Turk comes, it will be to take our walls.'

They returned across the pontoon bridge to Birgu, Hardy in the lead, Luqa and Grand Cross Lacroix behind. The boy talked, the men listened. A successful skirmish encouraged high spirits, demanded its participants recount the details, relive the minutes. Luqa deserved praise. He had beamed as Hardy joined in ovation, had shrugged at warning of the risks. A survivor of the final scenes at St Elmo required no instruction.

On the far bank, de Pontieux waited to puncture the mood. 'Monsieur Hardy, I see again you are the champion of our hour.'

'Were you present at the fight, you would witness many champions.'

'Alas, there are callings on my time.'

'None of which place you in the way of harm.'

'I do not seek it out as you.' The gaze was smooth and level. 'Friend to children and to hounds, and a visitor even to the black and vile Moor in jail, I hear.'

'He is a comrade and an ally.'

'Not so to our Order and Religion.'

'You forget he served well the Grand Master and the interests of the Knights. You forget too his incendiaries on daily occasion repelled attack at St Elmo.'

'I forget nothing, Hardy.'

Lacroix had stepped ashore. 'Except honour and conduct, Chevalier.'

'It seems your own conduct is fed by anger, Brother Grand Cross.'

'Believe it.'

'Is it infirmity of age or bitterness at the steady slide of power?'

'You goad me.'

'So muster your support, Brother Grand Cross. A mercenary and low-born English pirate, a native boy in loincloth, a few clinging relics on the benches of the Sacro Consiglio. These do not suffice to mount a challenge.'

'You would call yourself a Knight? A man who wears full armour yet keeps from the shore, stays remote from battle.'

'I anticipate worthier foes.'

'Consider me among them. You shall never be Grand Master, Chevalier de Pontieux.'

'Succession is a capricious thing.'

'You shall find it so.'

'And you shall find I have the vote of many, the efforts of Prior Garza, the influence of the princes of Europe.'

'An unreliable measure. Your confidence is misplaced.'

'Learn judgement, Brother Grand Cross.'

'Acquire loyalty, Chevalier. For, as I have breath, I will obstruct any move you undertake.'

'It would be to the loss of the Order and yourself.'

'A threat?'

'Mere observation.'

Lacroix growled his contempt. 'Had I not spent my arrows, I would spare one for you.'

'You were spent long past, Brother Grand Cross.'

Maria kissed him deep. She tasted of love and longing, of open sky, of places far from war. He could lose himself in the moment, believe in the illusion of peace and magic. Here among the apothecary bottles the Turk was far away, the din of cannon a distant rumour. Hardy held her close. It seemed strange, a miracle, that the girl he had so formally courted should transmute into his lover and his life. The Maltese noblewoman had become Maria. Maria in turn was become his reason.

His lips wandered on her face. 'It is a kinder welcome than that I received from de Pontieux.'

'A soldier cannot be liked by all.'

'With events at the palisade, I suspect my friendship with Mustapha Pasha too is at an end.'

'We know it to be finished long since.' Her body trembled with tenderness. 'I would ask you to take care, but it would be to no avail.'

'I am not born to hide, and I am poor at making tapestry.'

'Shoeing horses?'

'My skill is worse.'

'Baking?'

'More dangerous than soldiery.' He rested his chin on her shoulder. 'Baker or blacksmith, each one of them faces combat. Even priests and children needs must fight to rescue these ramparts.'

'I thank God for the time we have had, the moments we may yet have.'

'I trust He will smile on a noble lady and a poor English

traveller in the storeroom of an infirmary in a besieged Maltese village.'

'If not smile, at least forgive.'

Hardy loosened his undershirt to reveal the silver cross at his throat. 'I wear your love and His devotion. I am double blessed.'

'I a hundredfold.' She slipped her hands beneath the garment and ran her fingers across his naked skin. 'Your wounds heal well, my lord.'

'Parts remain inflamed, my lady.'

'We shall together find a cure.'

She bit at his ear, her breathing losing its rhythm, her body rubbing against his. He responded, easing his hands to the small of her back and pulling her forward. She groaned, her fingers tightening, her pelvis rocking. The descent into full immersion. If this were sinful, there was no better wrong, no more pleasing way to enter perdition. Tautness crawled from his balls to his brain. He would find release in her. It was a slow and frantic madness, anticipation building, clothes shedding. He could weep for its intensity. Sounds were guttural and unearthly, movement instinctive. This was more primal than lovemaking. It was need.

They were on the floor, rolling and moaning among the sacks of herbs and earthenware jars. Out there, men lay dying on their litters and mattresses of straw. In here, two people were living, dedicating themselves to each other. He lay beneath her, held her hips as she moved above him.

'You conquer me, my lady.'

'It is I who bow before you.'

'There is fight yet left in both of us.'

She laughed and panted, leaning over him, letting her hair tumble across his face. The mannered lady of Mdina was gone, replaced by an island girl with carnal eyes and consuming passion. Her haunches took the strain. He lifted her, allowed her to ride, rose to greet and caress her breasts, her lips, her being. In this time of pulsing ecstasy, they had travelled from lust to sacredness, transcended coupling to become one. He gasped. A soldier could have religious experience after all.

Still exhilarated by victory at the palisade, Luqa gripped a loaf of bread and headed for his cellar home. No spite-filled words of Knights such as de Pontieux could diminish the achievement. No fatigue could lessen the sense of satisfaction. He was thirteen years old and yet a man – a man who had brawled with the Turk and won; a man who had chased the enemy swimmers back across the water. Alas, there had been neither precious charms nor fat purses full of gold for the taking. Next time, perhaps. His friend the Englishman had congratulated him, and that was what mattered. They were a fine team, brothers-in-arms, had worked well together at St Elmo and at the Senglea palisade. It was good to be wanted.

He descended the steps, accustomed to the sudden coolness, the sound of his bare feet on the stone. The two hounds would welcome him back, would sit and wait patiently for their share. Everything was as it should be. Yet someone had visited.

With a stuttering heart and the beginning of panic, he leaped the final steps and pushed his way through. Light filtered past a basement grille, petered to a gloomy vagueness within. It was enough. Scattered about, hewn pieces of dog lay discarded on the ground. A comprehensive exercise – one designed to teach a lesson.

✠

Chapter 12

It had taken only a small amount of powder to blow the lock.
The black Moor had inserted into the opening the wadded
contents of his metal clasp, unravelled the fuse-string from the
lining of his robe, and extracted the striking-flint from a sandal.
He rarely went anywhere without the tricks of his profession. It
was a method of survival, a habit inherited from his days as a galley
slave. As the noise from the Turk bombardment reached a climax,
he had struck the spark that lit the flame that travelled to initiate
the small explosive report. Iron pieces fell away. Now he waited.

No jailer would visit in the small hours. Yet the whispered
restlessness of the slaves, the tempo-change from slumber to
expectation, swelled in the tunnels. The Turk scout picked his way
through in the darkness. He knew the route, had visited before.
And his Moslem brothers welcomed him, listened as he murmured his instruction and told of the raiding party closing fast to
release and arm them for the fray. They would teach the Knights
a lesson in tactical surprise from which they would not recover.

The sewer-stench came with him. At some stage the gate to
the outlet flow had been loosened. At another, news of the sluice
passage had reached Mustapha Pasha, intelligence on the guard
detail been provided. Such things did not concern the scout. His
role was to secure the approach, to unreel the guide-string along
the path he took. He did not anticipate any trouble.

Nor had he predicted the Moor. There was scarcely a sound as
the weighted end of an uncoiled turban flew outward and

wrapped around the neck. Wrenched backwards, the Turk clutched at his throat, his mouth gaping in wonderment and air-deprivation. It was all over bar the shuddering. The Moor dragged the corpse into his cell and went to retrieve the spindle of string.

No doubt about it, the scout was in position and had given his cue. The Janissary officer felt the sharp tugging on the cord. He smiled. The infidels would be caught as they slept, overrun before they could gauge the direction of the threat or the magnitude of their calamity. Seven open boats had slipped from among the Turkish fleet and headed for the shore. They would go unnoticed, would not be challenged by the opiate-drugged sentries stationed on the beach. Unknown friends had seen to it. Grand Master La Valette was about to receive the most unpleasant shock of his life. It would almost certainly count as one of the last.

Weapons were passed upward, tied to ropes and hauled behind the first climbers. All was going to plan. More men followed, creeping forward, some baulking and vomiting at the latrine foulness, each in turn disappearing into the sluice. The only shits ever to flow upstream, mused the officer. He took his place and groped his way for the outlet. The things one did for God and His Sultan. It was an uneventful journey, a fitful and malodorous voyage conducted on all fours, bounded by slime-decked walls and the sliding shapes of Ottoman soldiers. They were a sorry sight. By all things human, a far worse smell. But they would kill, would lead the breakout. That made their cruel induction into this world of excreta entirely worthwhile.

Breath and discipline held. They berthed at their destination as sodden and disgusting clumps, scraping and shaking themselves down, moving off in file to trace the prepared course and their own scent. Around them, the soft clink of chains and tap of hammers proved that escape was in train. In wordless gratitude, galley slaves received their weapons, falling in with the formation, pushing on among an ever-growing company. It was their duty as true believers to join this holy enterprise, their pleasure to exact revenge on their captors and masters. Most had once served as soldiers and sailors of the Crescent. Their chance was come to enlist again.

Crouching low, the Turkish officer crept into the turn. There had been no interruptions, not a single flaw in the smooth unfolding of the plan. His army was now several hundred strong, a force bearing pitch torches, equipped with scimitars and pikes, muskets and bows. It would be unstoppable. He could sense the energy, the press of men behind. In minutes they would be spreading through the streets of Birgu, putting Knights and civilians alike to the sword, throwing lighted brands into their powder-stores. Few ever gained the chance to outwit a foe as wily and deadly as the Order of St John. How fate could change on the throw of dice, the word of a spy, the command of Mustapha Pasha.

Or it could turn on the skittering movement of a ceramic sphere landing at the officer's feet. It broke as he opened his mouth to scream a warning, its flame burning away his face, its smoke spewing thick and choking to fill the cavern. Blinded, the herd became directionless. Some pushed forward, others fell back, their clamour and apprehension rising. They were caught. Behind the fog, a section of wall collapsed, the wide muzzle of a cannon rolling out to fill the breach. In their confusion, the Turks failed to notice. It was point-blank, the targets confined, and grapeshot had been selected. Firing was commenced.

'A bloody business, Christian Hardy.'

'None bloodier, Moor.' Hardy squinted into the sunlight. 'Yet a small price to prove your innocence and commitment to our cause.'

'The unseen traitor will not think it so. We are marked men.'

'That is to the good. He is but one and we are several. Before long, he will overplay his hand, overreach his balance.'

'Should he invent further tricks as we have witnessed, it may be we who topple first.'

'Today we outfox him. We shall do so again.'

'Mere skirmish is no conclusion. Do not relax your guard, Christian Hardy.'

An expectorating cough came from behind, and Henri emerged from the mouth of the tunnel, his eyes streaming, his chain-mail discoloured with blood. Wisps of smoke followed him out. He and a handful of chosen men had initially checked, then counter-attacked and finally demolished the covert enemy advance. Not so much a battle hard fought as an exercise in threshing humans. What cannon, sword and shrapnel-pot had failed to complete, stampede and asphyxiation had finished. The sewer flow was running red.

Henri removed his gauntlets and flexed fingers stiff from combat. 'I spend my days with books seeking glimpses of paradise. You, Christian, offer me visions of hell.'

'You will not learn survival from books alone, my brother.'

'I will not discover humanity from wading in blood. War makes fiends of us all.'

'It is the profession I choose.'

'And you, Moor?'

The Moor was absorbed in his freedom, gazing intently at the sky. 'Perhaps two civilizations of law and learning which quarrel at present in underground caves may yet sit together in harmony and peace.'

'A lamb may lie down with the lion.'

'For the purpose of our siege, we shall each play the lion.'

It was the Grand Master who spoke. Accompanied by a page, he had descended a flight of steps from St Angelo above, and stood to review the aftermath of the subterranean battle. His eyes missed nothing. The men bowed, aware that their actions had constituted either insubordination or initiative, that La Valette would make analysis of his own. They noticed too he leaned a little too heavily on his sword.

'You have a nose for the enemy, Monsieur Hardy.'

'It is the instinct of a soldier, Your Highness.'

'Correct, as it has proved. Yet you kept the threat from me, informed neither a member of the war council nor the bailiff of St Angelo.'

'I had no wish to trouble you with faint suspicion, sir.'

'Enough suspicion to raise your men, deploy your band of brothers?'

'They are accustomed to my ways, sir.'

'I am surprised they are not weary of them. And you, Moor? Are you responsible in this?'

'My fears incited their preparation, Jean Parisot.'

'A motley alliance indeed.' La Valette surveyed the group. 'A Moor, a nephew of mine and a Service Brother with his hench-men. How many lie dead?'

'Hundreds of the enemy, sir. Most from among our galley slaves.'

'It is fortunate we have no oars for them to work, and happy eventuality you reduce the number of bellies we must feed.'

Henri cleared his throat. 'You are not angry, sir?'

'I am resigned to your eagerness, Henri.'

He did not favour them with a smile, but his stern authority had dissipated, his cool aloofness warmed to tepid approachability. It was akin to being blessed. Hardy saw the glimmer in La Valette's eye. It communicated amused forbearance, the same wry benevolence he had always shown. They had his forgiveness. Matters might yet go their way, if the Grand Master survived, escaped the poison clutches of the betrayer.

'The foe tries every artifice and turn, Your Highness.'

'We have countered them thus far, Monsieur Hardy. At the palisade, in these tunnels. One wonders what next they may attempt.'

Your death, Hardy reflected. 'Whatever challenge, we shall meet it, sir.'

'So I observe. But the Turk learns. He will prick us, bleed us, pound us with his cannon, will abstain from full engagement until we crawl in the dust.'

'His patience will dry.'

'And when it does, he will come against us with every battalion and every infernal machine of war.' La Valette seemed to stare momentarily into his own internal distance. 'Perhaps you advise me well, Henri. I should place my command within the heart of Birgu.'

'The people would welcome it, sir.'

'It shall be. Make ready, gentlemen. We have further labours ahead.'

Grand Master and page departed. There was something in the gait of La Valette which suggested the dragging weariness of decay, a hint of concealed pain. The arsenic was doing its worst. Hardy caught the gaze of Henri and the Moor. Without proof they were mere scaremongers in search of ghosts, liable either to be laughed at or locked away. In the present, under such conditions, talk of treachery could itself be ruled treasonable.

'You heard your uncle, Henri. He moves to Birgu. It will extend his life and the period for our investigation.'

'Or time will expire for both.'

Prior Garza was praying and bleeding. He scourged himself hard, murmuring the Latin verse, shuddering with agony and pleasure at each stroke of the knotted lash. It was not a pretty sight, not one for the eyes of others. For self-flagellation was a very private affair. The cord bit deep and a new cut opened. It was atonement, a chance to suffer as Christ had suffered, to banish impure thought, to whip corrupted flesh and dwell on the divine.

Corpulence created its own particular sound when hit. Hubert winced. It was unnerving to be in these further reaches of St Angelo, to be tiptoeing through the inner sanctum and temporary quarters of the leadership. Another strike, another snatch of Latin. '*Petra mea, ne surdus fueris mihi, ne, si non audieris me, similis fiam descendentibus in foveam.'* Dear God, he thought, and then crossed himself at the blasphemy. He was not meant to be here, to pry and peep, to rummage about on behalf of his friends. A novice priest should know his place, then keep to it. Still, there was an attraction to it all. He, Hubert, could at last be of use; he, the weakling, the innocent, the butt of good-natured jokes, could prove himself to Christian, might yet foil a plot and save the Order. His was the perfect disguise. Happy-go-lucky Hubert, happy to go looking.

He moved on into an adjoining cell. It was bare but for a simple mattress of horsehair and a crucifix nailed to the wall. He glanced about. The only thing suspicious in this space was himself. But he had his instructions, began his fingertip search of the doorway, beneath the stone bench, around the Norman window. As in the other chambers he had visited, there was nothing beyond the commonplace, nothing that jarred in his consciousness.

The brick gave a fraction. It had not drawn him in any way, yet responded to the press of his hand close to the archway casement. These walls were several feet thick, could hide valuables, parchment, a multitude of secrets. He worked his fingers deep into the cracks and pulled. The stone came away, rested heavy in his grasp. Without hesitating, he placed it down and reached inside, probing a cavity deeper than that suggested by its cover. Excited, Hubert extended his arm to full stretch. Connection made. Carefully, almost losing it from his grip, he withdrew the small pewter flask to uncork it and hold to his nostrils. He sniffed.

Calomel. Damnation, the hollow was little more than a disused medicine cabinet, the foul-smelling potion the oft-used constipation cure of mercury chloride. It was barely worthy of his interest. He felt cheated; his spirits ebbed. For centuries the Hospitallers had documented, prepared and applied these basic components of their nursing craft. They understood the healing properties of the rarest plant, could mix minerals and restoratives that would bring the sickest of pilgrims and patients back to health. And he had unearthed a pot of crap-generator. How his comrades would laugh.

Beginning to see the humour of it, he smiled resignedly, replaced the bottle, and levered the stone back into position. There were other rooms to examine, different bricks and flag-stones to tap or prod. A laborious undertaking. Yet important too. He would not let his companions down. Cautiously, he slunk from the spartan bedchamber and made his way silently towards a suite reserved for the clergy, refugees from their battered homes close to the Birgu walls. He had failed to notice the piece of silk thread dislodged by his inspection and now lying on the floor.

A steel blade swept up to block his progress, was held an inch from his throat. 'An impostor, no less.'

'No impostor, sir.'

'Then a rabbit caught among a field of cabbage.'

It was de Pontieux, his sword teasingly steady.

Hubert backed against a wall, the cutting edge following him. 'I am on errand, Chevalier.'

'Your own?'

'For the Order.' Hubert gulped, his speech rapid and breath shallow. 'The Grand Master moves his command into Birgu. I come to aid and attend those who would go with him.'

'A useful rabbit.'

'I try to be of service, Chevalier.'

'How so? Your shoulders are narrow, your arms are as string. I surmise a bag of grain, a flagon of wine, would crush you.'

'Do not be deceived, Chevalier de Pontieux.'

'It is rare that I am.' The Knight had yet to lower his sword. 'Which brothers do you find to help?'

'I remain to hand.'

'You shall be thanked, though many of us are ready stationed to repel the heathen on the walls of Senglea and Birgu.'

'I may not have the prowess to fight, but I endeavour to stand with them.'

'It reassures me. Some of more questioning bent might suggest your presence is to inquire and explore.'

'To what end, Chevalier?'

'The question would be better answered by yourself, novice Hubert.'

'I hide nothing.'

'Such noble sentiment from one allied with such ignoble friends.'

Interrogation was interrupted by the hollow clanging of a bell. De Pontieux allowed his sword to drift to his side. An emergency was unfolding. There were further peals and the relay call of trumpets, the shouts of soldiers lumbering armoured to their stations.

The Knight paused, his ear cocked, his gaze remaining on Hubert. 'Senglea.'

Then he was striding fast down the passageway, the cornered novice forgotten, a new challenge found. Shaken, Hubert leaned against the wall and breathed deep. For the moment he was at liberty. Yet he felt marked, had gained the distinct impression he was unfinished business that would keep. In his chamber, the Prior continued to flog himself.

On the spur bastion of Senglea, it had been not so much a false alarm as an overreading of events. The man had given little impression of what he planned. He was dressed as a Turkish officer, had appeared at the Marsa shoreline waving for all the world, and certainly for the Christian sentries, to see. Bizarre enough; and what followed was stranger still. Halting only to discard his turban and his silk pelisse, he plunged into the water, was plainly struggling to keep afloat, desperate to reach the walls of the defence. A defection of sorts was under way; the Turks moved to intercept.

'*He is unable to swim!*'

'*The heathen will catch him.*'

'*Or he will sink.*'

'*They give chase, send their swimmers.*'

'*We must counter them with our own! Launch the boats!*'

It was a matter of principle and of pride, a question of reaching the floundering man before he drowned. Already the enemy were swarming on the shore, their arquebusiers and archers kneeling or standing for a steady aim. But they held fire, waiting as swimmers dived to claim the prize, to drag the tormented deserter back to land. It made no sense he should seek refuge in an infidel garrison doomed to fall. Perchance he had lost all reason, been driven mad by the heat and the bloodshed, by the incessant guns and the spreading sickness. The torturers would discover the truth soon enough. He was dead, whatever the outcome.

The Christians reached him first. Spurred on by gathering shouts of encouragement, covered by cannon-rounds crashing among the Moslems, a brace of rescuers fought to keep the man alive. A rowing-gig pulled alongside and he was manhandled aboard. Another race ensued, against time, against the oncoming shoal of Ottoman swimmers and their support. Spectators on either side hurled abuse and loosed off weapons. They were too far away to have effect.

'I thank you.' Coughing water, his robes clinging sodden and cumbersome to his frame, the officer stumbled from the boat.

'Your Italian is excellent, Turk.'

'I am no Turk, but a Bulgar holding senior rank in their employ.'

'You have found sanctuary, my friend.'

'No.' His tone was emphatic, his eyes restless and determined. 'We are all of us far from sanctuary. I know things. You must take me at once to your Grand Master.'

'It is for the Grand Master himself to decide.'

'It is for Grand Master La Valette to die. I must speak with him.'

'As you wish. The manner of your journey attests to its urgency.'

'Believe it. And guard me well. Not for my own sake, but for that of your Order.'

'I and my brothers are pledged to your safety.'

A promise almost instantly undermined. As the Knight clapped a sympathetic hand on his arm, a musket-ball struck the renegade in the head. In the confusion that reigned, shots were exchanged with Turks drawing near by boat, an artillery duel flared inter-mittently between opposing lines. None would remember the exact details of the clash, of how the right temple of the victim had crumpled to the impact of lead. Nor would any see the long and smoking barrel of the rifled arquebus withdraw from a castel-lated nook on the Christian ramparts. Accidents happened. There was much gunfire around that day.

As dawn broke on 15 July 1565, the fifty-seventh day of invasion, the corsairs attacked. Accustomed to quick victory, disdainful of Turkish inability to achieve it, the pirate lords of the Barbary Coast were bent on conquest. Their target was Senglea, least-well defended of the peninsulas. With the sun brightening on the waters of Grand Harbour, a fleet of small boats sailed in formation along the Marsa and headed for the palisade. In the leading vessels were dark-robed imams chanting Koranic verse. Behind came the chiefs, dressed in jewelled turbans and golden silks, their men clutching scimitars and muskets and crouched expectantly for the fray. These were the legendary fighters of Algiers and Tripoli, allies and followers of the late Dragut, sworn enemies to the Order. They would show Mustapha Pasha what it was to kill infidels.

The boats hit the palisade, but failed to break through. Men jumped into the water, wading, and clambered ashore, their shields raised above their heads against the desperate volleys of shot flurrying from the ramparts. Forming up, their assault ladders at the ready, they charged.

On the landward side at the same moment, the corsairs began their advance on Fort St Michael. Heedless of loss, they surged forward, some blown apart by cannon-fire, others dropping to the pelting lead of muskets, the mass growing faster and gaining in strength as it closed. It was not so much an army as a running, howling freak of nature, a travelling force of will. Few could oppose it. Firing on the move, scything aside the defence, the mob escaladed the walls and fell upon the Knights. Within minutes, Moslem banners hung above the walls, the Christians locked in deadly struggle for every inch given, each life taken. Men toppled, were hacked, impaled, split asunder. At this range, with so much at stake, there were no rules and nothing but bloodshed.

Explosion ripped without warning through the low seaward wall. An ordnance store had blown, tearing a ragged breach around which the invaders now clustered. Blinded, deafened, the defenders rushed through the choking smoke and searing flame to meet the threat. But more boats were disgorging the enemy, sending corsair reinforcements to push onward, drive upward. The Christians were being overwhelmed.

Sweat-stained and breathless, a runner bowed to deliver his report to the Grand Master and his war council stationed atop an observation point on St Angelo.

'Your Highness, the heathen press in from every aspect. At the seaward side, they already gain foothold in the breach.'

'A breach we may be certain the Moor did not cause.' La Valette aimed a glance at de Pontieux before returning to the messenger. 'I see infidel pennants cresting St Michael. What news?'

'None that is not bad, sir. Chevalier de Robles leads the counter-charge, but the enemy seem oblivious to the damage we inflict.'

'They are corsairs. We must expect it.'

'Our positions in Senglea will fail if reinforcements are not sent, Your Highness.'

'Is this your considered opinion?'

'The opinion of every soldier manning the walls, the opinion of every Maltese woman and child who hurries to join them.'

'We all are obliged to make sacrifice. Go tell them I will spare from Birgu what I can. Give assurance God is with them in their hour.'

Grateful for such encouragement, the messenger backed away and headed for the pontoon bridge. On its far side, Senglea was immersed in battle, the violence raging like a firestorm, swallowing the peninsula.

La Valette watched. 'I advise our men that God is with them. Yet what I witness would challenge such notion.'

'They stand with the Spirit of the Lord within them, sir.' Knight Grand Cross Lacroix nodded towards the chaos.

'Not a single foot of wall must be surrendered. Pray they fight the infidel to impasse.'

'Where are the princes of Europe now? Playing quoits? Dancing the gavotte and the galliard while we hark to the sounds of war?'

'We are troublemakers, Brother Grand Cross. They will not come to our aid. But as the enemy sends corsairs against us, so we shall unleash our own.' La Valette had made his decision. 'Draw near, Monsieur Hardy.'

Hardy broke from his squad and jogged across swiftly to report. 'I am at your command, Your Highness.'

'While we continue in your debt. Take your skirmish-party to Senglea without delay. Stall the heathen; stiffen the seaward defence and hold the breach.'

'We shall drive the enemy back from whence he came, sir.'

'Hell would be too near.'

Hell would be too good for Christian Hardy, the traitor mused. He studied the receding form of the Englishman with a mixture of admiration and hate. Such a fine specimen. Such perseverance. Such sound luck. It was remarkable he had survived the annihilation of St Elmo, the rigours of captivity with the Aegean pirate El Louck Aly Fartax. He had returned to haunt Birgu, to serve La

Valette once more, to upset outcomes which had been minutely planned. Why, it was Hardy who had foiled the Turk incursion into the tunnels below this fort, Hardy who had assigned his friend and infant-cleric Hubert to pry into matters outside his concern. Curiosity could kill. The novice priest would discover little until it was too late, until the point of a dagger penetrated his scrawny throat. Aimless dolts. They scratched for clues as chickens scratched for grain, had barely marked the surface. One manoeuvre had been blocked, that was all. There were many ways remaining to achieve the desired goal. And Hardy would be unable to prevent it, as he had proved unable to thwart the shooting of the Turk defector, the detonation in the Senglea arsenal, the silencing of the rampart mortar-gunners. That detonation, initiated by a length of slow-burn fuse, had created the breach; that silencing of the mortar-gunners had allowed the corsairs to storm ashore without great loss. The varied ways of treachery. It left La Valette to be dealt with.

The Grand Master was so gaunt, so ashen grey. It was possible he had moved his command-post into Birgu for reasons other than those stated. Perhaps he suspected, had been warned of a poisoning plot by the meddling Christian Hardy and his friends. It would not save him. Of course the arsenic would be harder to dispense, but it had already done its work, produced the required degeneration and malaise. There was little doubt the old man sickened, had responded with practice customary for the age. He plainly dosed himself with purgatives to vomit the bad humours and expel the illness. An ill-judged move. For the favoured medicine was tartar emetic, and tartar emetic was antimony potassium tartrate. The apparent cure would in fact progress the decline. La Valette could heave up all he liked, believe he was cleansed and improving. He had no insight into the true effect, would not see how his stomach-lining was becoming dissolved, was being prepared to absorb the next cocktail of poison. If arsenic was the primer, tartar emetic was the enabler. It was a means to speed delivery and demise, to reduce the chance of regurgitating future toxins and prevent La Valette from escape. The terminal phase.

As the battle raged, the traitor could afford an inward and self-congratulatory smile. He was merely the firestarter, an initiator of events at whose conclusion he would still appear the innocent. Without even knowing it, the Knights of St John were hammering the last nails into the coffin of their own Order, administering the potions of death to their own Grand Master. There was nothing quite like having a clean pair of hands.

'They break through! Take them down!'

Hardy led his men at a run. Already the corsairs were washing over and through the seaward wall, at first dashing against, then crashing above the weakening ranks of the defence. So like St Elmo, he thought. The same oppressive clamour, the same blurred images of faceless, nameless people rising and falling in an endless screaming torrent.

He focused. The corsair confronted him, his shield raised, his short stabbing-blade thrusting forward. Enthusiastic, but poorly timed. Hardy flipped the shield, let the man rush in, circled his sword, and drove it deep beneath the armpit. The Algerian sagged and dropped. In a fluid instant, Hardy had reversed his pommel, was mashing it into the face of another threat, returning with a backhand to sever head and hands as the pirate clutched at the damage. Hardy moved on, cut through. The old man faced him, cursing loudly, spitting insults. No contest. The Englishman divided him vertically to his neck, watching the shocked eyes part wide to view him at an angle.

Move, dodge, kick, parry, strike, move . . . It had a simplicity about it, a rhythm, a single and defining end. Beside him, his men performed as they were trained. Slowly they were forcing the attackers back, turning the offensive into grudging, inadvertent retreat.

'*Isra'el!*'

The cry had emanated from a young North African bedecked

in gold and refusing to yield. He stood proud and bare-chested among the slain, his scimitar mired in blood to its hilt, his eyes directing their challenge straight at Hardy. Again the shout, '*Isra'el!*' – the angel of death. Hardy paused. He had been recognized, had not heard the name in many years, since he was raised with these boys, sailed with them, galloped their horses in reckless pursuit along the warm sands of the Barbary Coast. Friendship had moved on. He lunged. His past, and the man, fell away.

Quickly, he mounted the steps to the ramparts. Here the pirates continued to cascade into view, were thrown back only to rally and return again. Above them, women and children laboured frantically to load muskets, to fling whatever came to mind or hand down upon the foe. Two middle-aged matrons eased a limestone block over the lip of the parapet and watched as it shed corsairs in a human slough from their ladder. A young girl drove a metal spike through the eye of a rearing face, let her brother complete the task. Everyone was engaged in the murderous free-for-all.

Fra Roberto was not one to miss such opportunity. The front of his habit flecked with blood, he dominated the shallow battlements, a broadsword in one hand, a large wooden cross in the other. Both were tools of his trade; each was employed as a weapon. It was a fearsome sight and combination. Woven into his tousled hair were lit tapers, and through their smoke peered the face of an enraged giant, a man of God intent on performing unholy deeds.

He bludgeoned a corsair to the ground with his crucifix. 'Now do you recognize the power of the Cross?' A downward stamp silenced the screaming man. 'Your muskets from Fez, your Damascene scimitars, are as naught against the majesty of His armies.'

A bandit swung at him, his blade carving close. Fra Roberto caught him behind the neck with a cross-beam, fixed him in position, and ran him through. Next, a scarred and leather-faced veteran was hooked with a side-sweep and sent spinning over the edge.

'Tremble at the might of the Lord! For ye are as chaff before His whirlwind!'

Dashing to kill a corsair leaning to throw a javelin, Hardy shouted a warning. 'Take care, Fra Roberto.'

'I care not for care, friend Christian.' The priest cleanly disembowelled a fast-moving pirate, swivelled neatly to parry a down-thrust, and rammed home his point. 'We all must stand and perish for the Religion.'

In confirmation, a figure in brilliant silver stepped back from the line. It was the Knight Zanoguerra, tall and imposing, a natural leader, and his features had been shot away. For seconds he hung motionless and upright, supported by his armour. Then he crashed face down.

'There are others who need you, Christian.' Fra Roberto motioned along the teeming fortifications. 'Every citizen is here. You will find Lady Maria and the boy Luqa snapping at the heathen dogs.'

Hardy was sprinting, weaving through the deadly gauntlet to reach them. A boy lay limp in an embrasure. He pulled him away, ducked as a musket-ball cracked against the stone. It was not Luqa. He let the corpse go, pushed on, rolled beneath a ship's spar being used to batter enemy from a fighting platform, and punched his blade into the back of a sheikh. The man screeched once and died. Thirsty and bloody toil. He deadheaded as he went, taking lives, meeting threats, searching in the throng. Rarely had he felt this way, known the nausea-creep of dread, the tightening knot of powerlessness. Not since that childhood day when the corsairs came to Dorset.

He found them. They were kneeling beside a steaming cauldron, releasing boiling water into the upturned faces of an ascending crowd of pirates.

'Maria . . . Luqa.' He loped across. 'Pull away from the wall.'

They retrieved the empty vessel and crouched low as the scalded features of a raider emerged above the edge. Hardy dealt with it, his spiked warclub flying fast to strike the forehead. He moved forward and twisted the embedded weapon free.

'Water is not sufficient. Luqa. Hand to me the wildfire.'

The pots were ignited and thrown, flames and screams billowing skyward up the twenty-five-foot incline. For a moment the threat eased. It would erupt again as replacements queued to fill the void. But Luqa breathed, Maria was still safe.

He turned and caught her gaze. This was no place for her. She was so fragile here, so close to oblivion. And it filled him with terror and agonizing love, with a savage need to protect.

'Maria, be my wife.' He whisper-shouted in her ear. 'Marry me, my lady.'

She mouthed her assent, her words scurrying into the tumult.

One made allowances for disappointment. Perched on a high ridge of Corradino, Mustapha Pasha eased himself back into the padded comfort of his chair and viewed the catastrophe developing below. Two thousand dead, three thousand — the reported estimates of casualties were vague but climbing. Now the vagabonds of the Barbary Coast were in headlong retreat, were being pursued and torn apart by the victorious Christians flooding from the smoking mound of St Michael. A high price for impetuosity and arrogance; an error of judgement, fatal as it proved. The corsairs should not have ignored military logic, should not have believed they could succeed where the Ottoman army had failed.

Yet it had started so well. Even he, siege-master and seasoned general, had been mildly surprised at the dramatic early gains. They had compensated for the calamitous excursion into the tunnels beneath St Angelo, had stilled his nagging doubts over the efficacy and loyalty of the spy in the midst of the Order. That spy had done well, had created a breach in the Senglea wall, silenced artillery-pieces overlooking the landing. But victory had not emerged. Six hours of battle and these feared Arab warrior-sailors of North Africa had seen their attack blunted, their colourful gesture sink into grisly quagmire.

He began to think idly of the one thousand Janissaries he had sent in ten large boats to mount a flanking assault on the northern tip of Senglea. They had been his personal contribution. After all, the defenders were close to collapse, were busy on the western side. Turkish shock troops appearing elsewhere, striking at the unmanned walls, would surely tilt the fight in favour of the Moslem. But they had not. His intervention had made no difference, and, worse, his Invincible Ones had failed to reappear. It was time to return to his tent. Tomorrow the bombardment of Birgu and Senglea would recommence.

Out in Grand Harbour, the first bodies of the Janissaries drifted gently into view. They had achieved their landing, coming ashore apparently unseen and wholly unopposed beneath the walls of the Senglea spur. It was the briefest of successes. For, unknown to them, their chosen site directly faced a battery of five hidden cannon nestling two hundred yards distant at the base of the cliff on which St Angelo perched. Its gunners were alert, its commander urgently whispering his order to load stones, grapeshot, steel fléchettes and chain. A devastating combination. The Turks were tightly packed, their boats closely grouped. They had been unprepared when, from behind, the concealing boulders rolled aside and gun-muzzles gaped through. Massacre had awaited.

Chapter 13

His name was Simon de Sousa, a senior Knight of the Portugues *langue*, and his head had just been removed by a Turk cannonball. Craning to direct counter-fire, Chevalier de Robles, the Knight of Santiago who had led the small relief force to Malta, catapulted backwards, a hole drilled through his chain-mail below his armoured neck-gorget. It was how many Christians died during these hot and closing days of July.

The *Collachio* area of Birgu was being dismantled. Close to the landward walls, it contained the auberges and palaces which had housed the Knights for over thirty years. Now it shook and crumbled to the avalanche of enemy shot. In its alleyways and narrow streets, gangs of slaves were driven on by the lash to construct barriers and slow the path of the travelling death. A dangerous place to be. Entire columns of men disappeared in clouds of blood and smoke, the maimed and limbless writhing where they fell or crawling off to die. None could save them; none would bother. The rest toiled on. Until it was their turn to be consumed.

A slave, his ears cropped for an earlier misdemeanour, broke from the pack and ran aimless and screaming for imagined safety. He did not get far. With the downward sweep of a steel club, an Austrian enforcer dashed out his brains. It was his third scalp of the day. There would be no easing of the pace, no allowance for mutiny or refusal in the besieged kingdom of the Order.

*

The Knights could also kill their own. In an interior yard of the magisterial courts, four prisoners were being led from surrounding cells to their execution. Before them was the gallows, a mast laid horizontal between two frames, the rope nooses strung only a few inches above their heads. Held by guards, each man stood before his appointed mounting-block.

De Pontieux observed proceedings, his ally Prior Garza at his side. 'Like the killing of the hounds, it will liberate provisions for more worthy mouths.'

'I concur, brother.' The Prior mopped sweat from his rubicund face. 'Yet your sentencing of a Calabrian Knight is not without drawback.'

'The Italians respond better to harsh treatment than they do to reason.'

'There is rumour of ill-feeling.'

'So they are displeased. This condemned creature is a sodomite, was granted opportunity to fight, to find redemption with sixty other prisoners at St Elmo. He refused. Now he dies.'

'A fitting end for them all.'

'For any who defy our code, who besmirch the sacred name of St John.'

'Who raise a sword-point to your throat?' The Prior arched an eyebrow.

'I hazard the pirate Christian Hardy will not outlive this siege.' De Pontieux was concentrating on the scene before him. 'Entertainment begins.'

As the prisoners were forced to step up, the nooses were tugged over their heads and placed about their necks. Prior Garza approached the first.

'You have anything to say?'

Chattering teeth and a rambling stream of prayer and terror were the response.

The Prior gazed blankly at the individual. 'You are condemned for the sin of cowardice and desertion. May God have mercy upon you.'

He made the sign of the cross and nodded to the executioner. The stone was removed, the sound cutting instantly to a glottal stop, the legs of the doomed captive beginning their wild aerial gyration.

Prior Garza moved to the next. 'Another to die for dereliction of his duty. You disobeyed orders, murdered a sergeant-at-arms.'

'Please, I will fight.'

'Solely for your breath. You have placed yourself here through your action.'

'I will face any danger, any heathen.'

'You will face judgement at the heavenly gates. May God have mercy upon you.'

Again the stone was withdrawn, and the violent shaking on the rope added to vibrations along the mast.

The third man, the Calabrian, went quickly. Finally the Prior stood opposite the fourth.

'The final element of our quartet.'

'Rot in hell, Garza. And you, de Pontieux. You are devils, not Christians.'

'We have your confession. It is you who sides with Satan.'

'Mohammedans are at our walls, and you make space for execution, find time to employ the pliers and branding-iron against believers in Christ.'

'A heretic, a Lutheran spy who seeks to subvert the very rock on which our Church is built.'

'And what became of our forgiving God?'

'Forgiveness has no part in holy war.'

'War you inflict on your own civilization as against the Saracen. War which stains the cause for which you fight, the virtues for which you stand.'

'You are no judge of virtue.'

'Nor you, Garza. A lackey of the Inquisition, a shit-carrying fly from the court of Spain.'

'Curb your tongue, heretic. Or we shall extract it.'

'I am beyond your machinations, Garza. And yours, de Pontieux. You kill me for no reason other than I oppose you, I threaten your ascendancy.'

'It is motive enough.'

'I pray that if the Order should survive, you will not inherit.'

'Make your prayers swift.'

A glance from the Prior sufficed. The stone came away, the body spasmed, the legs kicked. Garza rejoined de Pontieux to view the spectacle.

'They dance well, Prior.'

'With some encouragement.'

'A pity we are constrained by edict of the Grand Master, his wish to conserve manpower for the fight.'

'La Valette is sentimental as he is foolish, brother.'

'He is also old. Circumstance is against him. We are against him.'

Prior Garza indicated the four corpses twitching on their lengths of rope. 'Today we outflank further enemies, brother.'

'Be sure, they are not the last.'

Emerging through a shower of falling stone, Hardy vaulted a barricade and picked his way through the smoking streets. He could think of more tranquil places. It was merely another day following another night, a thicker powder-haze enveloping the crumpling walls of Birgu and Senglea. The sights, the sounds did not bode well. Round every corner he anticipated a squad of yelling Janissaries. On every rampart he expected to see the waving banners of the Ottoman crescent. It would not be long.

He heard the whistle of incoming shot and crouched in a demolished entrance as it bounded past. Nearby, a goat scavenged hungrily for weeds. Life and death went on. He resumed his journey, his ears tuned, his eyes searching, his sixth sense reaching ahead and pricking at danger. That was the problem. The shot, the blade, the detonation could come from anywhere or anyone. Hubert had found nothing. A few medicines perhaps, the odd and unexplained absence or presence of a senior Knight. But no treachery, no poisoner. Aside from the Grand Master, there were nineteen members of the Sacro Consiglio, nineteen interests, nineteen factions, nineteen possibilities. The Judas might not even be one of these. War had once been so much simpler than politics.

'Fra Roberto, you are drunk.'

'You wake me to provide such intelligence?'

'I wake you for other purpose.'

'None which may not wait.' The priest remained horizontal, his eyelids closed. 'It is a place of exquisite beauty I inhabit.'

'For those within earshot, a place of raucous thunder.'

'Do not deride my quest for peace.'

'You are at peace only in the midst of battle.'

'A condition we share.' He cocked an eye half open. 'You know what I observed this morning? A horse, a chestnut steed without its rider, in full and glorious gallop along the length of the Birgu waterfront.'

'Some parable of yours?'

'Mere perception. Unchecked, the beast ran in trepidation from the noise of arms, reached the edge, and jumped straight without pause to the water and its death. Thus, you see, rats and European princes are not alone in deserting us.'

'They determine we are doomed.'

'I do not reproach them for it. Yet I blame you for wrenching me from sweet slumber and the pressing arms of mistress drink.'

'I have my reason.'

'It will be sound, or I shall snap off the foot which goaded me. You discover our traitor?'

'We persist.'

'Could it be de Pontieux, or Prior Garza, his bloated Spanish accessory? Or the haughty Admiral Piro del Monte? The great Marshal Copier of the cavalry? The meek and humble Filippo Pilli, prior of Capua? Perhaps the learned confidant and Latin secretary Sir Oliver Starkey? The noble warrior Louis Dupont or the combative Bailiff of Eagle? Their allies, John de Montagut and Lieutenant of the Grand Conservator Mateo Ferer?'

'For the moment, I do not know.'

'While, for the moment, I do not care.' Fra Roberto rolled and settled massive on his side. 'Find the motive, you might find the man.'

'I would ask your assistance, Fra Roberto.'

'If it may be delivered from the recline, you shall have it.'

'I seek to wed the Lady Maria.'

The priest was sitting upright. 'Wed? Lady Maria? You will not outlive the nuptials.'

'The more reason to hasten our vows.'

'Have you consent of her father?'

'We have eloped.'

'Have you the blessing of the Grand Master?'

'We shall wed in secret.'

'Have you noble lineage? Lands? A future in a European court?'

'What future we have we will share.'

'It is contrary to every tenet of the Order. It goes against the grain of heritage and titled blood.'

'Jesus was a carpenter, Fra Roberto.'

'And you are a pirate, Christian. A rebel, a seducer, a wanderer, a soldier, a man whose purse grows fat with gold prised from Barbary corpses.'

'So you will consecrate our union?'

'Without hesitation or delay.' The priest allowed himself to break wind. 'Should you live together as well as you fight on the ramparts side by side together, few will pull you asunder.'

'None shall.'

'Go make your preparations. You and Maria of Mdina will be man and wife.'

Hardy had struck the deal he came for. By the time he left the smouldering annex of the Bishop's palace, Fra Roberto had again slipped into deep and contented sleep.

It was no sight for the faint-hearted. On the far side of Grand Harbour, the blackened and distorted heads of the defenders of St Elmo still sat on spears above the remnants of their wrecked fort. La Valette studied them for a while from the window of his audience chamber. Such loss, such sacrifice. A thousand yards and over a month distant. His heart grew heavy, his eyes misted, with recollection and regret. He was here to pay tribute, to bid farewell as their commander and friend, as forty-eighth and probably final Grand Master of the noble and ancient Order of St John. Tomorrow, or in a week, he too might end with his head on a spike or his body hung in chains. For Mustapha Pasha had plans, had an army at the gates. Unless victorious, he, Jean Parisot de La Valette, would not gaze again from this point, would never return to this palace on the roof of the inner keep of St Angelo. Birgu was now his home.

He turned away and walked silently through the empty chambers of his former residence. So much history, so much argument, so much cajoling and pleading with the emissaries and ambassadors from the courts of Europe. It had come to this, had been of no avail. He stood in the doorway to the Council Chamber, looked about him at the tapestries, the heraldry, the half-timbered ceiling. Familiar scenes; the ghostly fragments of remembered debate. He nodded to himself. These last months, his most frequent companions had become doubt and near-despair.

The summer heat, the noise of cannon billowed in his face as he stepped on to the flagstones of the inner ward. Up here, in his private garden, with his own thoughts, he had once found solace and sanctuary. In their place were questions, commands, decisions. And sickness – always the sickness. He loitered, surveying the enclosure, the pleasure-grounds that gave no pleasure, the formerly diverting features blighted by war. Even the nymphaeum, the cooling grotto that had provided rest from the midday sun, was become a store for cannon-shot. Artillery had been hauled on to platforms erected around the perimeter, an encampment was established over the area reserved for boule. Nothing remained as it was. Everything came to an end.

The Chapel of the Epiphany. This was his core, the spiritual kernel of the Religion. A dark and solemn place. Grand Master de L'Isle-Adam had built it when he brought the Knights to Malta in 1530; the remains of the old man were interred beneath a marble slab before the altar. Another old man might not share the honour, La Valette reflected. He had stood with de L'Isle-Adam when they began their retreat from Rhodes, now stood with him again in the present. There would be no further withdrawal, no exodus to a land of milk and honey, to a new Rhodes, to one more Malta. His Hospitallers, his Order founded by the blessed Gérard in the year 1099, militarized by its second rector, Brother Pascal, had suffered much and endured beyond compare. They had been threatened before, had teetered many times on a precipice-edge. In 1291 only seven Knights of St John, their Grand Master among them, had escaped the carnage of Acre and made it from the Holy Land. Fighting was in their blood; survival was their legacy. He would not squander it.

Reverentially, he knelt and kissed the tomb of his predecessor. Then he rose and placed his lips to the foot of the gilt Messiah nailed to the cross. The torment of Christ made his own crucifixion bearable. He retched, coughing blood into his balled fist, leaning for support against the pink-granite column to his side. He and the pillar shared history, for the stone too had been transported from Rhodes. An additional comrade to take leave of.

He was buckling on his sword as he greeted Knight Grand

Cross Lacroix at the base of the fort. 'You show patience, my brother.'

'Even a Grand Master is permitted time alone with his prayers and demons.'

'I attend to both.'

'A committed army of Christians is present and God is at hand.'

'We must hope they are enough for victory. My orders are acted on?'

'With expedition, Jean Parisot.'

'Then we are done here. Let us make our stand and find our immortality.'

Leaving the great fort of St Angelo behind, the pair walked across the drawbridge and headed for the Conventual Church and the sound of guns. The final station of their cross.

There was a moment when the barrage ceased. In the trembling silence, the forces of Christendom crouched massed and low behind their tottering castellations. Along the landward walls, from the two immense and jutting bastions of Birgu to St Michael, the stub tower-fort of Senglea, they waited. Morions and burgonet helmets glittered; armour-plate and cuirasses gleamed. There were the musketeers and skirmish-arquebusiers with their matchlocks and wheel-locks, the pike-soldiers in their leather jerkins and carrying fifteen-foot spears tipped with spiked, partisan, glaive and billhook *ronca* blades. There were the specialists from Germany and Italy wielding double-handed longswords, the mercenaries and adventurers dressed in vests of chain-mail and brandishing rapiers and battle-hammers. And the Knights. In the rising temperature of the day, and for the coming heat of combat, they wore only their upper *corsaletto* armour. Below the thigh they were unprotected. But it gave them freedom to move, to leap and run, to apply the skills learned during countless years of caravan aboard their galleys.

All had donned the mantle of their faith, the red surcoat

adorned with a large white Latin cross. It was a rallying-sign, a symbol of recognition and their crusade. The lowliest of infantrymen and most conceited of Knights had a common cause, a single enemy. That enemy stood poised on the slopes of Corradino and in the approaches from the Marsa. The plumes and pennants fluttered in the warming air. The sharp edges of scimitars caught the light. The tension-noise and tempo of kettledrums climbed. A throbbing, intimidating scene. Thursday 2 August 1565, the seventy-fifth day of invasion, and Mustapha Pasha was readying to commit. He expected conclusion.

On the harsh command of a trumpet, the Ottoman army moved. It came forward in a headlong rush, its spearheads aiming straight for the open breaches, its assault troops protected by arquebusiers, and pushing hard against walls with masts and scaling-ladders. Hit by rifle-fire, defenders plummeted past them. The corsairs had visited before, but their numbers had been fewer, their ascent unaided by the shattering precursor of a hundred firing siege-guns. This was a shock wave of different dimension.

As footholds were gained and ground taken, Turk sappers placed charges to widen entry points, grenade-throwers held off counter-attacks, and Janissaries swept through. Their advance could not be checked. Atop the summit of St Michael, Christian gunners repeatedly discharged their shrapnel loads point-blank into the incoming horde. Each time, it reformed and returned, covering the distance, howling in rage, propelling itself over the blood smears and body parts to again reach its target. The Knights were staring into the faces of the infidel, at the crushing presence of defeat.

At his command-post before the doors of the Conventual Church, La Valette was in conference.

'Yes, I have reserves. Of Maltese women and children; of goats and chickens.'

'Sir, our bastion is threatened.'

'What bastion is not? Which section of wall does not see heathen battering at its rampart?' The Grand Master frowned at the Knight. 'The defence is one less because you are here, Chevalier. Return to your station. Stand firm or die there.'

'We have need of infantry, sir.'

'You have need of faith. I am no conjuror.'

'I meant no disrespect, Your Highness.'

'I am Grand Master of an Order destined to fight alone. Go now, be cheerful in your task. Spread word that he who falls in action will receive papal indulgence, shall enter the hereafter free of any sin.'

'We are blessed, Your Highness.'

The Knight saluted and jogged away in the direction of battle. La Valette beckoned his Latin secretary, Sir Oliver Starkey, and Lacroix to his side.

'It appears we are beaten down.'

'A dog may turn, sir.'

'With no teeth to bare, we rely on our spirit alone. What news from Sicily, Sir Oliver?'

'The latest is not good, sir.'

'Was it ever?'

'His Excellency the Viceroy pledges a relief army this very month.'

Lacroix scowled. 'He claimed the same for the month of June.'

'Our survival may be measured in a matter of hours – days if fate smiles.' La Valette watched a plume of black smoke rise above a storehouse. 'Though it seems that little smiles.'

'You wish to dispatch fresh letters, sir?'

'It would be abandoning our duty not to do so. Don Garcia de Toledo must be informed, must be shamed into decisive commitment.'

'Decisive, he?' The lip of the Knight Grand Cross curled with contempt.

'Do not forget he left his son to our charge, as sign of intent, as hostage to fortune. That son perished to a corsair blade but two weeks past.'

'The less reason for the Viceroy to send troops, sir.'

'Knights from our furthest points are come to Sicily, will be raising men, agitating to assist.'

'They must be quick. I detect no equal urgency from His Holiness in Rome or His Imperial Majesty in Spain.'

'We shall see, my brothers.'

Or we shall die. There could be no misapprehension of the truth, no illusion that the defence was not rupturing. A garrison of a mere seven hundred Knights, eight thousand men, had lost fifteen hundred souls at St Elmo and several hundred since. With each attacking wave, each cannon-round, each musket-shot, fewer would remain. The Turks were assaulting the landward side of the two peninsulas. They had yet to strike at the rest.

Another messenger staggered bleeding and breathless towards him. 'Your Highness.'

'You come from Senglea?'

'Fort St Michael itself, sir. It is at final gasp.'

'It will be so when a heathen scimitar cuts air from the last Christian throat.'

'We cannot hold them, sir. We have repulsed them from our heights thrice this morn alone.'

'You will do it again.'

'Your Highness, I must ask . . .'

'And I must refuse. The bastions of Birgu make similar plea. Stand fast. We offer every man the prayers of His Holiness and cancellation of all sin.'

Glass-eyed and grey through loss of blood, the man collapsed in a faint to the ground. La Valette motioned to a soldier.

'Carry him to the infirmary. See that his wounds are dressed, his enfeebled state tended. Then restore him to St Michael.'

Knight Grand Cross Lacroix slapped the pommel of his sword. 'No idler will escape punishment or damnation.'

'Perchance we too will not escape, my brother.' The Grand Master watched as his order was obeyed. 'Perchance it will fall upon the frail city of Mdina to wage the last desperate fight of this island and our Order. Where is Monsieur Hardy?'

'*Heave . . . again.*'

With a final pull, and in concert with his crew of volunteers, Christian Hardy levered a limestone block into position. Stripped to the waist, caked in dust, and resembling a statue freed from its plinth, he did not slacken the pace. They were erecting a rampart. As the walls of Birgu shuddered and slid, so a new one, an inner skin, was rising to take its place behind. None could afford to rest. Above their heads, all around, the solid and consuming noise of combat raged. The cries, the shouts, the report of muskets, the clash of steel had lost distinctiveness, melded into a single and terrifying whole. Along the line, the work-gangs of men, women and children toiled, their ramps and rope-ladders lengthening. The enemy was close, becoming closer.

Others also laboured. Seated on a cart filled with wooden kegs and clay pots, the black Moor poured, measured and spliced as the heap of finished products collected at his side. His was a mobile workshop, and the objects were incendiaries. Luqa appeared. The boy began to take the devices and lay them carefully in canvas bags. His load complete, with a cheerful wave he was away, scampering up and over the rim of the swelling construction and ascending the steps to the melee beyond. Wares delivered, he would soon be back.

'Playing with sandcastles, Monsieur Hardy?'

'I am certain you will come to hide behind them, Chevalier.'

De Pontieux stood, his sword drawn, a look of mocking amusement on his face. 'I released two of our jailed to your employ.'

'We accept any man adept with pick or sword.'

'You should grow accustomed to sharing space with prisoners.'

'While you should be at ease with any structure resembling the scaffold.'

Hardy indicated a wooden spar being used to winch up stone. He would not delay for conversation.

'*Keep it steady, men! Add more hands to the rope!*'

The Knight remained where he was, observing as the Englishman bent to lift a rock to his shoulder. 'Your effort could be to little purpose.'

'To greater effect than your words, de Pontieux.'

'A Knight is a man of his word.'

'He should further be a man of valour, a man seen fighting at the rampart.'

'I have done my share.'

'I believed you too busy hanging and quartering your own brethren.'

'Without discipline we are lost. Remember it well, Hardy.'

'I forget nothing.'

He started to climb a ladder to the summit of a wall section. Beyond him, on the flight of steps leading from the Castile bastion, a soldier stumbled clutching at his shoulder. His arm had been neatly severed.

'Christian . . .'

Hardy jumped down and lifted another stone. 'One man attend to the wounded. The remainder continue at your task.'

'You have the bearing of an officer.' De Pontieux had not moved. 'Yet the breeding of a bastard commoner.'

'It is the common man who protects your walls, who loses limb and life for your benefit and Religion.'

'God will thank him.'

'Will you?'

'Know your position, Hardy.'

'Know yours, de Pontieux. I am among friends.'

'You reside in the home of the Knights.'

'Put your hands to rope or block. Or make your departure.'

'Such work is not for nobles.'

'Is it not, Brother Chevalier?' Henri de La Valette, his face and torso encrusted in sweat-mingled powder, emerged from the labour-gang. 'It seems fitting for any man concerned with defence of our cause.'

'I will leave you to your judgement.'

'Fare you well, Brother Chevalier.'

A flash, a burst of green smoke and flame, and a pyrotechnic detonated beside de Pontieux. Reflexively, the Knight threw himself down. He recovered fast, but by then the spectators had laughed, the damage to dignity was done.

Hardy called back as he tossed rope to a militiaman. 'Not the response of a nobleman, I venture.'

The eyes of de Pontieux were chill as they absorbed the scene, sweeping from the Moor on his cart to the returning Luqa and on to Hardy. Wordless, he strode away.

'Christian, you play dice with the Devil.'

'I play at nothing, Henri. We have a wall to build.'

He had marriage to prepare.

Night that was no night, an overheated darkness that had come alive to the heaviest of Turk bombardments. The assault might have been called off, but cannon-fire substituted for the volleys of Ottoman muskets, the whining path of solid shot replaced the battle-wail of Janissaries. Defences split, defenders cowered. The peninsulas seemed on fire. Wedding night.

'It is not the customary peal of bells.'

Fra Roberto ushered them both into the small chapel. It was lit by three candles, their weak glow casting shadows, shuddering to the distant impacts. An icon glistened. Like the chapel itself, it appeared out of place and time in this theatre of war.

The priest sensed the incongruity. 'We are gathered together in the sight of God. Yet God Himself would be wise to flee.'

'He has already answered our prayers, Fra Roberto.' Maria

clutched Hardy to her side. 'He smiled on us, brought us to each other.'

'He has yet to bring you to your senses, my lady.'

She laughed. 'These weeks past, I have seen enough sadness and precious little sanctity of life. We seek only minutes of happiness in the face of death.'

'You cannot wait?'

'Time does not.'

Hardy took her hand in his and looked at the priest. 'This very eve, I go on errand for the Grand Master to Mdina.'

'La Valette will have his reasons.'

'He believes Birgu and Senglea will not hold, intends the old city to take its place as bulwark against the Turk.'

'Bulwark? The walls are ancient and unmanned, the populace ill-prepared. It will drop without argument into the palm of Mustapha Pasha.'

'Nowhere is its fate written.'

'I have read it for myself, seen it in the stones, in the smattering of aged cannon. Why, with no effort, I oft broke through its defence.'

'You are more fearsome than any heathen aggressor.'

'What am I to think, Christian? You charm me. You marry your Maria. You desert us both.'

'No desertion, Fra Roberto. A chance to sting the rump of the Turk, to turn his head, draw him out.'

'Such confidence.'

'Bred of despération. In St Elmo we cost the Ottoman dear. In Mdina we may do the same once more.'

'What if you should fail – if we should fall?'

'You shall at least greet your Maker with a sword in your hand, a curse for the infidel on your lips.'

'And you?'

'I will have the thing I most desire, will be wed to my beloved.'

'The madness of youth.'

Maria went to him and placed her hand lightly on his mountainous shoulder. 'Our madness befits the moment, Fra Roberto. Even among the cracked and blistered stones of St Elmo, our love flowered.'

'I am in part to blame for such enterprise.' The priest shook his head. 'Whether circled by peace or conflict, sweetness or sorrow, you will be joined.'

'Passion shall survive all siege, will outlive us.'

'Then in spirit of joy, and on summer night hotter than a furnace in hell, we witness union between pirate prince and noble lady.'

'We are ready.'

'I shall return, Moor.'

His friend was silent, standing beside the capstan-deck at the foot of St Angelo. There was a certain freedom, an obvious danger, to being out here beyond the giant chain stretched protectively between the fort and Senglea. This was the outer limit of the kingdom of the Knights. Every few seconds, crossfire from the Turk batteries on Mount Sciberras and Gallows Point would fizz overhead. Occasionally the ambient light of a fire or flare would catch the shape of galleys prowling Grand Harbour. Hardy was heading into their domain.

'Be of good cheer for me, friend.'

'If you would be careful, Christian Hardy.'

'I am new-wed a mere hour, Moor. My inclination is to live.'

'Yet you are bound for open water in a small boat of ox-hide. Turk vessels are plentiful. You are but one.'

'It is our strength and our disguise. We are a craft among many, ferrying loads for the galleys, jostling among the throng. If Piali and his fleet are deficient in daylight, at night they are no match.'

'I trust you are right.' The Moor stooped to retrieve a basket and stepped forward to present it. 'These will sow confusion, bedazzle the foe, should you be wrong.'

'Your incendiaries have saved me before.'

'May do so again. They are the brightest of my wares, will tear the clouds asunder. To look is to be blinded.'

'Think too of yourself, Moor. We have each stirred enmity, provoked the hatred of a few. Among them is a traitor intent on murdering La Valette and yielding up his garrison. He will not hesitate to slay you.'

'I am aware of it.'

'It is not too late to join our expedition, to come away to Mdina.'

'My duty is with the Grand Master.'

'Then be watchful, and be armed.'

Hardy stowed the supplies, working quickly with his two Maltese companions. The Moor did not intrude. In place of conversation was the bond of fellowship and accepted fate. They might not meet again, might yet witness the destruction of their worlds, of Birgu, Senglea, Mdina, the end of days. So be it. The Englishman had already peered at the abyss, danced along its edge. The small boat floated free of the platform.

'May the God of Abraham be with you.'

'With you also, Moor.'

Retracing his steps, the Moor crossed the drawbridge of the fort back into the warren streets of Birgu. There would be little sleep and no rest for its wearied inhabitants. Walls demanded repair; steel plate needed restoration; weapons required service, And the Sacred Infirmary filled with the wounded and the dying, the quicklime pits with those already dead.

The Moor reached the bottom of the stepped alleyway which led to his lodgings. It was sheltered here, a fishing district beyond the *Collachio* of the Knights, a neighbourhood whose menfolk guarded the ramparts, whose women and children laboured and died alongside. No one was immune or innocent in siege. He paused and listened. Against the storm rumble of cannon he could hear the hammering of armourer mallets, the knock of stonemason chisels. Somewhere, the higher pitch of weeping broke through. So much grief. He made to move, but halted again, aware of a hinted presence, of his own apprehension. Then he comprehended. A blade was being drawn from its scabbard.

Out on the earth mound at the tip of Senglea, slowly and in flames, like outsize Catherine wheels, the great canvas sails of the two windmills revolved until they disintegrated.

✳

Chapter 14

'Where are my merchantmen?'

The incendiary rage of Mustapha Pasha had ignited. He had already beaten a slave, kicked a prone officer from his tent, hurled goblets and invective at members of his war council. For victory still eluded him. The proud army which had paraded ashore in late May was now a diseased and disheartened remnant more inclined to mutiny than to battle. Provisions had not arrived, ships had sailed without returning, allies had parted company. Even Janissaries were known to have stowed aboard vessels and fled the island. They left behind the putrid corpses of their comrades, the pall of sickness, the sullen despair of starvation. And pigs.

How the Christians taunted them, worsened their gnawing hunger with the release of these unclean beasts to the Turkish lines. Such insult to the Faith would not go unanswered. He threw another artefact at a pearl-inlaid chest. The object shattered in a spray of glass and precious stones. But only butchery would improve his mood – the slow impaling of the Knights, the sound of their screams, the sight of their faces contorting at the pain. He would prove the whispers and his own doubts wrong. Grand Master La Valette and his pirate crew could not oppose for ever the might of the Ottoman. They too weakened, saw their walls soften to the consistency of curd, their numbers dwindle to the point of nothing. He would take them yet. Because autumn storms threatened and Admiral Piali fretted to be away; because otherwise his head would be insecure in the presence of a vengeful and unforgiving Sultan.

'Send for Piali.'

'He visits his galleys on patrol to the north of the island, Mustapha Pasha.'

'For what purpose? To plot with his captains their early flight from Malta? To arrange excuse for his failure? To reach Constantinople and prepare the ground for his laying of blame?'

'I am not privy to his thoughts, Mustapha Pasha.' The aide shrank involuntarily from his commander's stare.

'Yet I may guess at their blackness. He avoids me, sends runners to represent him. I am minded to return these worthless fools as diced meat. Now fetch him.'

'As you command, Mustapha Pasha.'

'My Master Engineer also. I trust he has not boarded ship to make good his escape?'

'He is at present close with his officers, Mustapha Pasha.'

'They should know I will have any who display weakness or irresolution nailed by their balls to a mast.'

The aide bowed and retreated; the Master Engineer was fetched. Mustapha Pasha observed him from his divan of silken cushions, allowed his gaze and silence to linger. The man was an Egyptian, the best that money and vocation could breed.

'A difficult time.'

'None we may not overcome with dedication and forethought, Mustapha Pasha.' Unwittingly, he had just saved his testes.

'Continue.'

'While we speak, our mining teams prepare to burrow from the ditch into the rock foundations beneath the bastion walls of Birgu. Within three weeks the minehead will be secure.'

'Two weeks.'

'As you desire, Mustapha Pasha.' The engineer bowed low.

'What I desire is for the unbelievers to be fed to the crows, for each of them to suffer a thousand agonies upon a thousand.'

'I will endeavour to achieve it, Mustapha Pasha.'

'Our other instruments? Our siege-engines?'

'Rising as the tallest of towers.' The Master Engineer smiled with the self-congratulation of success. 'Over seventy feet in height, they will be pulled to the edge of the protective ditch of Birgu, will give access to bastion walls which climb above a hundred feet from their base.'

'We shall see of what they and you are capable.'

The old general sat and stroked his beard, content with the unease his authority and silence provoked. These machines of war, this vaulting over or tunnelling below the Christian defence, could yet be unnecessary. The walls were filling the ditch as they had done at St Elmo; the breaches gaped. Another push might be all it took. He would assign Piali to command the next offensive on Birgu, while he himself focused on Senglea. It was spreading the risk, sharing the load, ensuring that if the Sultan executed one he would be bound to execute the other. The possibility of failure could bring out the politician in any soldier.

'Mustapha Pasha, there is the matter of Mdina.' The Master Engineer sounded almost apologetic.

'What do you discover?'

'That its walls are as old and weak as we believed. Our scouts confirm its southern face alone may be taken. The rest is inaccessible, perched as the city is high on its cliff.'

'We know the Knights have drained it of troops for defence of Grand Harbour. We know we may take it whenever we please.' The spy in the Order had told him so.

'The cavalry remains, Mustapha Pasha.'

'Its attacks diminish; its losses mount. Such raids are of no significance.'

'Mdina will be yours, Mustapha Pasha.'

'Malta will be mine.'

He would keep the ancient capital in mind, would retain it as fallback, as winter refuge, in event of military reverse or catastrophic delay. The real prize was here. He had the Order within his grasp, would pluck out the hearts of the Knights as he had done with their stubborn brethren in the first of their forts to succumb. La Valette, for the moment, he would keep alive. Suleiman the Magnificent would be sure to decree something most particular for the former Grand Master of the Knights of St John.

Close to the Conventual Church, in the small Chapel of the Madonna of Damascus, Jean Parisot de La Valette gave prayer and thanks for another day survived. He had asked for feats of unimaginable bravery and resilience from his dwindling garrison. And they had responded to his call and to the Word of God. It was a miracle. One that would need to be repeated.

'Uncle.'

Henri had entered the chapel, closing the door softly behind him. Without turning, La Valette lowered his head. The hesitancy in his nephew's voice, its controlled anguish, had already informed him.

'The Moor.'

'Cut to pieces, Uncle. By assassins unknown.'

'I have lost a rare friend – one I trusted with my life.'

'One who was willing to forfeit his own for yours. He wished to remain in Birgu when Christian offered him passage to Mdina.'

'He should have left.'

'His duty was to you, Uncle. He saw danger about you, your enemies draw in.'

'They reached him first. How could I have placed him in the path of such great threat? How could I have mistreated him so, committed him to the dungeon?'

'He requested you did so.'

'And then he saved us from the Turk. I will miss his counsel, Henri. I will suffer for its loss.' The shoulders of the Grand Master drooped, his voice raw with sorrow.

'You may yet gain from it, Uncle.'

'I see no gain.'

'Without his death, you would not believe. Without his sacrifice, you would not act.'

La Valette swung his head slowly round. 'Speak your thoughts.'

'A plot is afoot – one that would see you poisoned unto death, the Order betrayed to the heathen from within.'

'Our men lie as corpses on the ramparts, as wounded in the Sacred Infirmary. And you talk of betrayal.'

'Among your court is one who wishes you ill.'

'Your mind plays tricks, Henri.'

'Treachery not trickery killed the Moor. It may yet do for us all. The corsair captain El Louck Aly Fartax revealed to Christian the presence and purpose of a renegade in your Council.'

'You take the word of a corsair?'

'Who is it that directed the Turk to the tunnels? Who is it that ignited a powder-mill in St Angelo, an ordnance store in Senglea? Who is it that allowed the corsairs to land unharried by our mortars along the Senglea shore? Who is it that poisons you?'

La Valette rose and faced his nephew. 'You vowed on oath not to speak of my malaise.'

'To none have I done so, Uncle. Nor have I directed any to such conclusion.'

'What is your reason for hiding these facts from me?'

'The same reason I suggested you move to Birgu, Uncle. For your safety. We must not alert the betrayer, alarm him to rash and sudden move.'

'Yet you inform me now.'

'Our loyal Moor encouraged me to wait until his death. He studied your signs, adjudged your body to be imbued with arsenic.'

'His own is rent by blades.'

'Thus does he warn you. This evil is not through, Uncle.'

'We shall see if it is the Turk that completes it.'

As though in confirmation, the enemy guns opened up as one, their sound ripping the air, shaking the earth. It would create another dust storm, send a further length of wall crashing to the ditch. Conversation between uncle and nephew ceased. There was understanding between them, recognition that the calm was over, that a larger tempest was about to break.

It came on Tuesday 7 August 1565, the eightieth day of invasion, and five days after the initial mass Turk assault on the two peninsulas. Prepared, yet wholly unready for what they faced, the defenders fought doggedly to hold their evaporating line, to stem the killing torrent in spate at their feet. Their grip was loosening. Ragged clumps of them were overwhelmed, incendiaries flew more sporadic, the aim of muskets grew more wild. Out on a parapet, a Knight slashed desperately with his sword. Outflanked and doomed, he was mere residue. The shot took him in the groin, fired by an arquebusier with orders to target below the armour. Clutching feverishly at the gushing wound, the Knight dropped to his knees and then to his front. Mopping up. The Turks moved on.

Hubert was changed. Gone were his innocence, his customary lightness and easy laughter. In their place was something different, darker, a pair of trauma-strained eyes set in features sapped of everything but resolve.

Outside the infirmary, where the wounded lay heaped and waiting to die, he held water to the lips of a soldier propped against a wall.

'Hubert, save the gourd for another.' Maria called gently to him as she rigged a canvas sail for shade. 'He is gone.'

'They handle weapons while I handle pots. They die for the Religion while I count the slain.'

'We each do what we may.'

'Is what I do enough, my lady?'

'In the eyes of God and your companions you cannot be faulted, Hubert.'

'Neither should I be thanked. It is these brothers we must cherish, those martyred on the ramparts to whom we owe our gratitude.'

'An army has many trades, an Order many aspects.'

'Some more worthy than others.'

'Yet all part of the whole.' She approached him while he knelt to sponge water on the face of a soldier quietly dying from an abdominal wound. 'They need you, Hubert. Can you not see?'

'I see myself, my lady. I care not for the sight.'

'What is the more courageous? To strike with sword at the enemy in rush of blood and temper, or to hold fast and give comfort in the very moment of despair?'

'Forgive my selfish pity.'

'It is the meaning of humanity. We are not all of us warriors.'

'Christian is, my lady.'

She smiled, her eyes cut with pain. 'Yet men such as Christian are not present as you to brighten the darkness.'

They were instead spread around as cadavers or crying out for water, for absolution, for the swift and sweet onset of death. A hospital was the worst place to be in battle. She headed inside for the overcrowded wards. Hubert remained behind, coping, praying, holding compresses to injuries, closing eyelids.

'Another for your care, friend Hubert.' Fra Roberto unslung a musketeer punctured by two arrowheads. 'It is the foulest of squalls out there.'

'I behold its effects wherever I look.'

'Arm yourself, for it comes this way. Everywhere, the heathen are upon us. At the bastions of Birgu they swarm unchecked. At St Michael the situation is so perilous La Valette himself prepares to lead the counter-charge.'

'We must pray for a miracle.'

'We must fight as rabid dogs, acquire the spirit and ferocity of your pirate Englishman.'

'He would revel in such occasion.'

'Sweet Jesu, we need him now.' The priest back-wiped the sweat from his forehead. It left behind a red smear.

'Fra Roberto, you bleed.'

'Christ bled. It is the business of our Order to do the same for Him.'

'Some follow a divergent path.'

Fra Roberto lowered his voice. 'You discover its course, the identity of its traveller, our traitor?'

'I search. Yet what I find are routines of war, the predictable habits of Knights, their hidden stores of calomel.'

'Calomel?' The priest grinned at the thought of the laxative potion. 'Is there no end to which you do not stoop?'

'No matter, Fra Roberto. It seems conspiracy is overtaken by events.'

'Reminding me that we are near overtaken by the infidel. Fare you well, Hubert.'

'God smile on you, brother.'

They embraced, the titan enfolding the probationer in a mighty hug.

'Choose your moment to die and make it count. And be cautious of the traitor, Hubert. The Moor is already his victim.'

Whistling tunefully, Fra Roberto strode towards the rolling crescendo of conflict. Hubert whispered a quiet plea heavenward and returned to winding a bandage.

'They are through!'

It was a shout that gave voice to the obvious. As the defenders broke, so the Turks came after them, hundreds of their number disgorging into the interior of the breach. This was the moment for which they had waited and suffered, for which they had gone without food or comfort. Thousands had been sacrificed to reach such a point. They would not delay, would press home the attack until the streets of Birgu were awash with infidel blood.

Ottomans crowded, fired by their religion, driven on by the imminence of victory, by the crazed stampede of combat. Knights and soldiers fell, crushed beneath the weight of the advance. They had proved unable to escape, incapable of pulling back from the onrush. The day belonged to Admiral Piali. His was the responsibility for Birgu, and he would use it well, would seize the peninsula beneath the very nose of Mustapha Pasha. There was no stopping his men.

Except for the inner wall. Recognition of a trap took time to absorb, still longer to articulate and pass back. In those seconds, more troops had passed through the breach, aggravating the press of bodies, adding to the confusion. Instead of alleyways leading to the interior, they found their path blocked by an improvised rampart. They were chanelled, pinned in a corridor bounded to one side by the fortifications, on the other by limestone blocks erected by Christian Hardy and his crews. Men began to crowd and shout, to flee for openings which did not exist. Nowhere to go. And others were funnelling in.

'*They are above us!*'

'*Incendiaries!*'

'*There, you fool! Shoot him!*'

'*They surround us!*'

'*Get back! Get back! We are dead if we stay!*'

Few listened. Even with comprehension dawning, it was too late to respond or escape. On every flank, silhouetted against the cerulean sky, the defenders reappeared. They threw javelins, discharged their muskets, dropped sulphurous pots of pitch and wildfire. How quickly fortune could turn, a narrow space become a killing-zone without compare. Turks screamed, fought each other to retreat. Their efforts and shouts were in vain. The Christians did not relent, firing again and again into the searing furnace that they had created and continued to fuel. At their feet, flaming wraiths ricocheted, trampled and fell. Yet it was not the end. That came as the survivors staggered for the breach, joined the tumbling exodus spilling back into the ditch. Behind them, the defenders leaped from their retrenchments and hacked at the jabbering throng with swords, pikes and axes. It was the worst of scenes, the best of triumphs. The Knights and their infantry found rich and easy pickings.

Celebration was premature, for in Senglea the Turks were in the ascendant. By now they had the keep of St Michael, their banners and troops pouring into the vacuum left by the retreating Knights. Force of arms, density of numbers would prevail. Here a squad of Christian arquebusiers were overwhelmed as they struggled to reload; there a troop of Spanish infantry were annihilated where they stood. Wherever the eye looked, wherever Turk engaged Christian, defence and fighting withdrawal had dissolved into scrabbling chaos.

The pivot point had been reached, the critical instant for which every army trained, for which every commander planned and hoped. Mustapha Pasha would snatch back the initiative from both the infidel and Admiral Piali. Each needed to be taught a lesson. It would be one written in blood, delivered with a final and all-conquering effort. Within an hour Senglea would be his. By day-end the Order would have capitulated, its brethren lie dismembered and forgotten among the ruins. The choking air smelled sweet; the cries of men were as heavenly choirs. He would lead.

Accompanied by his Janissary bodyguards, his scimitar drawn, the seventy-year-old general moved forward. 'With me, my troops, my brothers! Bleed the unbelievers! The day is ours!'

Over one hundred and fifty cavalry lances locked into their breastplate brackets and swung down to the horizontal. The mounted detachments of Mdina had arrived. A small force, the vestige of a unit once some three-hundred-strong, though since reduced by charge and skirmish. But it had a mission to which it would commit its all. Before it lay the Turkish camp on the Marsa, a vista of silk and canvas tents, of tethered horses, of piled stores and dotted armouries. It was a magnificent and terrifying sight. And almost unguarded. For the Ottomans were engaged at the front, were consumed with the task of burying Grand Master La Valette and his Knights once and for all. Events in the rear were incidental to their victory.

Hardy sat astride Helios and felt the horse tremble with excitement. It had been over two months since last they galloped together down upon the Turk. This was the pair of them reacquainted, rediscovering the thrill of the chase, the meaning of existence at the blade-edge. There were few better places. He touched a gauntleted hand to his throat and the site of the silver crucifix hidden behind the velvet-clad plates of his brigantine jacket. His other hand turned and flicked the grip of a long cavalry sword. Beside him, Antonio, brother of Maria, made the sign of the cross and whispered a prayer.

'Stay close, Antonio. I do not intend to lose you.'

'Whatever is ordained, Christian.'

'The Turk would have us believe the Order is condemned this day to oblivion. They are themselves condemned by their own conceit.'

'We are few.'

'As they are unwary. We will not find better chance.'

'You are master of it, Christian. Without your urging, Governor Mesquita would not have settled on so great a venture.'

'I trust that I was right to urge, that he was right to accede.'

'We shall discover.'

A hand-signal from Chevalier de Lugny and the whole force began to advance in line abreast. On the wing, Hardy and his Maltese squadron aimed for the serried rows of hospital tents. It was a different kind of nursing care the Hospitallers and islanders intended to mete out. Walk turned to trot, trot to canter, canter exploded into a frenzied gallop which marked the last two hundred yards and the point of no return.

In a fury of hooves and dust, to the inconsequential shots of startled sentries, the attackers fell on the camp. Steel blades raced along the lines, severing throats and guy-ropes, collapsing tents, butchering oxen and livestock wherever they were found. Burning brands were tossed. The tents caught fire easily, their inhabitants, the sick and wounded, consumed and writhing within. Some crawled free. They were already in flames, blindly crawling or staggering until stilled by arquebus-round or steel tip. Encircled by horsemen, a plump administrator tried to run in gaudy robes and impractical slippers. He was impaled between the shoulders and deposited screaming on a pyre. Many would be joining him.

'Head for the command-tents!'

Against sunlight blackened by dust and soot, and to the deathly shrieks of animals and humans, the cavalry wheeled. Everything in its path was to be obliterated. Hardy saw a figure spring from its hiding-place and race for the cover of a smoke-bank. The freedom bid was short-lived. On the lightest command Helios went in pursuit, his whinnying rage travelling on and over the hapless fugitive. Another down.

'Christian, an archer to your left!'

'I have him, Antonio.'

The arrow was in flight, was caught on the shield by the young Maltese nobleman. Fumbling for a second arrow, the Turkish bowman found his pair of targets growing larger, descending fast. They struck simultaneously, carving through and on.

'Resistance at last, Antonio.'

Hardy pointed to a stricken group of wounded Janissaries forming up in final defence of their hospital tent. It was a piteous sight. Some had suffered hideous burns in previous action; others were missing limbs. All now held scimitars and pikes, were defiantly singing a Janissary song. It ended abruptly and to the dazzle-flash of an incendiary pot. The Moor had performed his magic. Blinded, the Janissaries staggered back. Before they had recovered, they were surrounded by whirling and stabbing cavalry, consigned to ash.

'I beg you, do not kill this horse.'

'You would place its life above your own?'

'Would not you?'

The Turkish youth, a comfort-boy or stable-hand, peered at him with resigned and doleful eyes. He held the bridle of a white Arab stallion, the prized mount of Mustapha Pasha. Hardy stood before them, his sword at his side, Helios snorting impatiently behind.

'He is magnificent.'

'A gift from Sultan Suleiman himself.'

'Tell Mustapha Pasha his Arab joins the stable of Christian Hardy.'

'I thank you for sparing one.'

'Would that we had need of them all. Yet we have no choice but to sever them from their Spahi riders.'

'As you have no choice but to run me through.'

'We conduct business and not a duel, my friend. Lie with the dead. They shall see you safe.'

Antonio was calling to him. He took the harness and walked the horse away. Around him the massacre was ebbing to its untidy conclusion, the last escapee rounded up, the final store set ablaze. He climbed into his saddle and scanned the devastation. The Marsa had become a tar-pit of blood and heat.

'Christian, we have done well.'

'Or our worst.'

A cavalryman spurred past. '*The heathen abandons his attack!*'

It had worked.

For a while, the sight rendered Mustapha Pasha speechless. He wandered among the burning wreckage, lost in thought and the magnitude of disaster. Occasionally he would pause to inspect the carcasses of oxen, the mutilated and hamstrung horses, the glowing embers from a row of tents. Nemesis indeed followed hubris. He had been so close, had tasted mastery, had ascended the ruptured tower of St Michael to gloat upon the other side. It was within his grasp, sat in his open palm. Then fate and the infidel cavalry conspired to snatch it away. Instead of the corpses of the garrison at Senglea, he was inhaling the singed foulness of his camp. In place of flames lapping at the heels of Christians, they cooked-off his gunpowder, devoured his sick and wounded. Last gasp for the unbeliever. It was he who found difficulty in breathing.

'Blame this on Piali! All of it!' He stamped his foot through the carbonized remains of a wheel. 'Witness it and curse him! It was he who insisted on anchorage at Marsamuscetto, on taking St Elmo! It was he who ignored the threat from Mdina!'

He approached an officer. 'You have Spahis?'

'Many have lost their mounts, Mustapha Pasha.'

'Others have not. Send them out, scour the island, cut off the escape of these bandits.'

'We shall catch them, Mustapha Pasha.'

'It will not suffice. We shall take Mdina.'

'Have we the men, the cannon, the supplies?' It was the quartermaster who spoke. He did not anticipate the backhanded blow to his face.

Mustapha Pasha peered into the watering eyes. 'Your comments are ill-judged.'

'My concern was to advise, Mustapha Pasha.'

'Yet you fail to please. Find what we require or you will be shot from a basilisk gun.'

'You have my loyalty, Mustapha Pasha.'

'I need your ability to muster and equip. Mdina will fall without struggle. It possesses neither infantry nor defence of any kind. What it has aplenty are food and water, provisions to replenish those lost here, shelter to house an army robbed of its tents.'

'How great should be our force, Mustapha Pasha?'

'Four thousand men, no more. Leave siege-guns behind. It is our speed and vengeful intent that will overcome their walls.'

Something caught on his barbed gaze. He strode towards it, pausing before a semicircle of dead horses and the site of his ruined private quarters.

'Stand.'

The young man rose from a bed of equine entrails and bowed. 'My master.'

'My horse, my white Arab, is not present.'

'He was seized by the unbeliever, my master.'

'You live.'

'By the grace of God Most Merciful.'

'As proof of your own cowardice. You did not fight.'

'I was unarmed, my master.'

'Not a scratch, not a wound afflicts you. You hid, cowered as my charger was stolen from me. Who took him? Who?'

He started to beat the boy, at first with his fists and then with the gilt riding-quirt looped at his waist. The intensity of his blows grew; the blood-flow increased. It was one way to work off tension.

The boy was screaming. 'Christian Hardy . . . My master, his name was Christian Hardy.'

'He wore long boots and crimson brigantine jacket, had piercing eyes of blue, the swagger and bearing of a pirate?'

'The same, my master.'

'And you saw fit to offer up my stallion to this devil, this thief?' His whip rose and fell.

'What could I do, my master?'

'What can you now do? With no horses to tend, no hands with which to tend them?'

'My master?'

Mustapha Pasha turned away. 'He is in league with an infidel corsair. Remove his hands.'

While sentence was executed, the General roamed on. Fresh

thoughts had entered his mind, reported sightings, fragments of memory. *Christian Hardy*. He had heard the name, received the description, so often. The killer on a steel-grey horse who had routed his forage troops at Zeitun. The fearless defender who had held the narrow plank-bridge across the ditch of St Elmo. The prisoner who had disappeared aboard the galley of El Louck Aly Fartax before payment and exchange were concluded. He was risen again, was back from the dead. Mustapha Pasha hawked a ball of grimed phlegm to the ground. He had acquired new reason to capture and raze the walled citadel of Mdina.

With a prayer and a heave, another member of European nobility was rolled unceremoniously into the mass grave. Losses were too numerous to mourn, the heat too strong to allow for delay. Hubert stood back and wiped sweat from his shrunken features. It seemed as though the entire world were decomposing.

Fra Roberto muttered a line in Latin and sent a corpse tumbling. 'We are become an Order of grave-diggers, Hubert.'

'If distinction remains between victory and defeat, I no longer see it.'

'It is a question of at which level we populate this ditch.'

'I begin to envy those already there.'

'Christian would not wish to hear you speak so. I vouch it was our friend who saved our hides.'

'There are those in Senglea who believe the sound of Turkish recall was the trumpet of God Himself.'

'They may be right, Hubert. It was miracle that the heathen scourge melted at the very moment of their success.'

'They will be back.'

'We shall await them.'

'*Hubert, Hubert . . .*' Luqa had appeared, was gesturing excitedly at the novice priest to follow.

Fra Roberto shrugged. 'Go, Hubert. You will have no peace until you do.'

'I should stay.'

'Your patients here are beyond all remedy. I will see they are put to bed.'

Hubert trailed as the youngster ran ahead. Like Christian, the boy appeared to thrive among the blighted ruins. They were of a kind, were suited to the harshness. He merely tried to keep up or emulate. Attempted to stay sane.

There, Hubert. Place your ear to the ground.'

The two had descended into the deep cellar depths beneath the Castile bastion. It smelled of decay and hewn rock, of the breath and sweat of human confinement. Others stood with them, everyone silent. They were closer to the enemy here, thrust out on their underground peninsula far beyond the Birgu walls. A stone sarcophagus, a listening-post.

Tap . . . tap . . . tap . . . It was the trace sound of a hammer-strike muffled and distant through the foundations. Unmistakable, and unmistakably heading their way. No explanation was required. For it confirmed only one thing, presented a single and terrifying truth to those who heard it in the darkness. The Turks had opened a new front. They were beginning to mine below the ramparts.

Quietly, the traitor emerged in the gloom and knelt to whisper in the ear of the probationer chaplain.

'We seek volunteers to blunt such excavation, Brother Hubert. The Maltese cannot bear the burden alone. You are slight of build, have the wit and bravery. I am certain also the inclination. It is your time.'

✠

Chapter 15

Spahis were hunting. On the rising ground towards Mdina, among the olive-groves and terraced fields, the nodding plumes of horses and riders indicated their progress. Their prey was the fragmented cavalry of the Knights, and they were closing, killing. Individually or in small groups, Christians were flushed out and cut down. Some bolted, urging their wearied mounts to final effort, leaping walls and banks of prickly-pear in desperate flight. Others turned to face their pursuers, galloping at them with hate-filled eyes and weapons raised. Each action ended with the trajectory of an arrow or the downward sweep of a scimitar. A running battle, and the cavalry of Marshal Copier was being run to ground.

'When, Christian?'

'Hold fast, Antonio. I shall give the word.'

'Your judgement I trust, brother. It is enemy steel I do not.'

'You brought me safe from corsair galley. My intent is to return such favour.'

'Do it soon.'

They crouched low beside their horses, both men peering through openings in the tumbled stonework. It was no place for fugitives. At any moment they would be discovered, already seemed to be outflanked. Horsemen combed the area, their swords threshing, their cries changing pitch as they made discovery or gave chase.

Hooves thudded in the dust. A lone and cornered cavalier had pre-empted discovery by emerging in a charge from a cactus thicket. The suicidal sortie of one was opportunity for another. Attention swung.

'Now, Antonio!'

On a hissed command, the pair ran out their horses and leaped into their saddles. There was no easy way to break cover, no tested method of outpacing a superior force. They would rely on surprise and daring. Beside them, held on a long rein, the white Arab of Mustapha Pasha joined their dash.

Shouts erupted, the confusion of men torn by priorities and different targets. Hardy and Antonio took the irrigation ditch together. Helios was straining, his sinews and breath working to open the distance, to carry his master away.

'They are on us, Christian.'

'Advantage is not ours to keep.'

An arrow flew overhead. It was quickly followed by a second, a third. Antonio leaned against the neck of his stallion, willing it on, attempting to match the speed of his companion. His burgonet helmet was gone, his broken lance discarded. This required no weapons. It needed luck, and the undivided focus of the enemy.

Letting the reins drop, trusting Helios to himself and the Arab to herd instinct, Hardy reached into the padded saddlebags. Spahis were fine horsemen and warriors, but they and their mounts were no match for the truly unexpected. He would give them it. With a backwards heave, he tossed two flash-pots high into the air. They detonated on impact, their brilliant glare casting shadows forward, sowing instant disarray and blindness in those behind. Horses shied and threw riders, steel blades clattered earthward as men shielded their faces. All about, the petrified whinnying and screams gave witness to turmoil. The quarry had escaped.

Only as they approached within cannon-range of Mdina did they slow. Slick with sweat, moulded with dust to their saddles, they gasped with post-trauma delight. Hardy leaned and gripped the hand of the young Maltese noble.

'I could not wish for better company in these ventures, Antonio.'

'Nor I, Christian. Your reputation as warrior is well deserved.'

'Yet we present the sorriest of sights.'

'To be alive is enough.'

'We have lost many this day among our mounted squadrons. More, I have no doubt, in Birgu and Senglea.' He walked Helios and the begrimed Arab prize over to a spring and let them drink. 'We must hope our endeavour was to some avail.'

'You saw the recall of the Turk, how they deserted the attack and hastened to their camp.'

'It feels good to singe the beard of Mustapha Pasha.'

'We may yet burn off his face.'

One raid from Mdina, and they had seized jewels, taken horses, destroyed stores, created a bonfire at the very heart of the invasion army. It might divert or provoke, weaken or enrage. But it had won more time for Grand Master La Valette.

Somewhere in the fields, the Spahis had caught the fleeing Maltese cavalrymen.

'A fine bounty you gain, Monsieur Hardy.'

'Mustapha Pasha is in generous mood.'

Hardy slid from Helios and greeted Governor Mesquita with a salute. Around them in the small square before the main portcullis gate, exhausted men and horses lay at water-troughs or limped away to find stabling. They were the survivors, and they were few.

'How many, Governor Mesquita?'

'We count some forty safe returned.'

'Heavy toll of one hundred and fifty who set forth.'

'Yet worthy exchange for what was achieved.' Mesquita paused at the guttural sounds and branding hiss of a cavalryman receiving cauterizing treatment for his wounds 'Signal shots from the petard mortars of Birgu and Senglea confirm both continue to stand.'

'Their respite will be brief.'

'I have little doubt the Grand Master will use it well. As for ourselves, I fear that, since the hornets are disturbed, they will turn their wrath against a weaker beast.'

'We will draw their sting, Governor Mesquita.'

'If God so wills. And if it takes the loss of Mdina to save the Religion, I am willing to attempt it.'

'There is still fight in us.'

'As befits a Christian and military Order. Though I wish on occasion we possessed a thousand of your kind with which to oppose the foe.'

'War makes each of us a brigand. Even Antonio here.' Hardy clapped his comrade on the shoulder. 'Look at these men, sir. At the sound of a trumpet, all would again ride out.'

'For which I owe them gratitude.' Mesquita summoned a tired smile.

'The Turk weakens and sickens. He fights, but I have felt his pulse, observed the doubt in his eye. The Janissary, the Iayalar, the dervish, the levy – they expected easy victory, suffer erosion, cremation, of their confidence.'

'At what point will they break, Monsieur Hardy?'

'Pray it precedes us.'

An alarm sounded, the rocket bursting high above the walls, activity stilling then accelerating in sudden energy. The Turks were coming. Accompanied by Hardy and Antonio, Mesquita made for the high ramparts. Messengers were running, each fragment of news confirming the last, each step taken encountering greater dread. It was rare that a city populace retained its dignity in the face of imminent slaughter.

'*Save us!*'

'*God have mercy on us!*'

'*What can be done? We have no soldiers!*'

'*Can the walls hold them? Are we to perish?*'

Mournful faces and beseeching cries pursued them on their

route. There was no simple answer – probably no answer at all. The Ottomans had decided to attack Mdina. And, as the Governor and his retinue crested the rampart and looked towards the south-east, the cause of anguish and fear was plain. Rolling out from the Marsa, the customary cloud of sand and limestone dust hanging over Grand Harbour was thickening and moving. Through it came the glint of light catching on helmets and beaten steel, the throb of drums.

Mesquita shaded his eyes. 'Our hornets, Monsieur Hardy.'

'We have succeeded in attracting them.'

'Can we further succeed in defeating them?'

'They wish to put consternation in our hearts with this display. Let us instead place it in theirs.'

'With women, children, a handful of cannon?'

'The stuff of great illusion. Blow horns, beat drums, line these ramparts with any who may wear a helmet and carry a pike. For the cannons, fire them long before the enemy is within range.'

'To what end, Monsieur Hardy?'

'That of our survival. To the heathen we will appear impregnable, a fortress filled to its towers with purpose and armed troops, able to expend powder and shot from infinite reserves.'

'It is a desperate measure.'

'Born of dangerous times. We have little to lose but our city and our lives.'

'Perhaps there is method to such insanity.' Mesquita turned to his attendants. 'Rouse the populace, open the armouries. I want a show of might to make a sultan quake. I want these stones topped with morions and spears at least ten deep.'

Antonio stepped forward. 'I will assist, sir.'

'Quick now. We cannot delay. If theatre is to be our shield, we must create the deception for benefit of their forward scouts.'

'*What rank folly is this?*'

The aged father of Maria and Antonio confronted them. He was shaking with rage, the prince of an island annexed by

Knights, beset with Turks. Powerless, provoked, his hostility towards the occupier had reached its zenith.

He pointed at Hardy. 'Curse you, Englishman. I espied you riding out, taking the cavalry on fruitless expedition to the Turk. Now the enemy comes hither, will show us no mercy.'

'So we fight.'

'With illusion? With tricks of magic?'

'It is all we have.'

'What we had was a peaceful life, an island of commerce and tranquillity.'

'There is more to life than commerce.'

'And you have condemned us with yours.' Disgust creased the face of the old nobleman. 'Your kind has brought us woe, enticed the wolf to our door.'

Antonio interjected. 'How would you have us behave, Father?'

'*Us?* It is not our battle.'

'Yet these are our walls the heathen threatens, our citizens who will be sacrificed. Your opprobrium will not save a single one of us.'

'Nor your desertion of your filial duties.'

'My duty is to our cause, to the honour of our name, to the defeat of our common foe.'

'All is lost. And you align yourself with those who lose it.'

'I am more content to fight and die than to avert my eyes or seek solace in senseless dreams of parley and surrender.'

'I am your father, your lord. Speak not this way to me.'

'Why so? You would draw your sword against me? Save your spleen for the Turk.'

'These devil Knights, this pirate Englishman have usurped your judgement.'

'Arrogance and infirmity have warped yours.'

'You are fools, each and every man among you. Let the matter of this war be decided around Grand Harbour. I shall myself ride out and conduct negotiation with the Turk. Diplomacy, not fire, will free us yet.'

Governor Mesquita rounded on him. 'Put your talk and timidity aside, or you will venture beyond these walls only at the end of a rope.'

'You would dare do this to me?'

'I am governor of Mdina.'

'I the head of its most ancient and illustrious house.'

'Do not forget, Grand Master La Valette hanged a councillor of this city for simple complaint against us to the King of Spain.'

'Know that I am no mere councillor.'

'We know you to be subject to the direction of our Order.'

'They are the laws of an occupier.'

'From which you have profited and gained. Now is the moment to pay your due.'

'I find myself unable to serve.'

'Not so. You may don the morion and coloured mantle, patrol the ramparts with the rest.'

'You take from me my son, my daughter, and on this day my standing.'

'We return to you your dignity.'

'Should I refuse, Mesquita?'

'There will be appointment with the hangman.'

It was piteous to see pride buckle before authority, the ungainly climbdown of a patriarch from the high ground of confrontation. The old man was handed the spear and rudimentary armour of a common soldier and sent on his way. He did not look at his son, did not speak another word. In the distance, the swelling bank of dust came on.

Word and whisper had reached the rear of the column. It was unsettling news, the kind that spread like infection, that caused men to doubt and falter. *Mdina was defended.* Officers had begun to use their whips, their threats and curses mingling with the ever-louder prayers of the imams. Always a bad sign. But the troops needed steadying. They had come to respect these once-despised

Christians, had grown to fear their incendiaries, their pikes, their longswords, the insane bravery of their resistance. The soft target of the capital appeared suddenly to have hardened.

A scout galloped his horse up to the commander-in-chief. 'I come in haste from my forward position, Mustapha Pasha.'

'Make your report.'

'The capital is awash with soldiers. Its walls groan beneath their weight, its rallying trumpets sound from every quarter.'

'You lie.'

'Neither my tongue nor my eyes and ears deceive, Mustapha Pasha. Others witness the same.'

'Then you are informed more by hashish than by reason.'

'Would that it were so, Mustapha Pasha. Would that these infidel dogs were not howling their scorn upon us.'

'They will sing a different tune when I flay off their skin.'

He signalled to his mounted staff to follow and cantered up the line. The guns of Mdina were firing. Strange how in the hour of their obliteration the inhabitants could be so defiant. Their self-belief was misplaced. It was bravado, an act, a mirage summoned from the thinnest of air. He stared ahead. Here the questioning mood of his troops was more pronounced, the murmur of their dissent louder as he passed. He would show them. They served to die for their Sultan, not to hesitate.

His journey ended abruptly as he reined back his horse and peered at the near horizon. For the love of God, there was no explanation. The scout had been right, the spy at the heart of the Knights so very wrong. It was plain to see, engraved along the skyline were the bristling tips of spears, around them the flash and echo-boom of cannon.

'Tell me. How can this be?'

An officer shifted nervous in his saddle. 'They have reserves of which we were unaware, Mustapha Pasha.'

'Impossible. And yet I observe it.'

'Their defence seems powerful, Mustapha Pasha.'

'Fort St Elmo seemed weak. It cost us many thousand lives.'

'You deem this a worse portent, Mustapha Pasha?'

'I deem it a steel-plated rock against which we may dash our brains, a destination of fatal consequence for our army.'

'They taunt us.'

'Their faith is well-placed. I begin to believe their cavalry was sent to our Marsa camp to lure us into reckless attack upon these city walls. They strive for greater reward, for the longevity of the Grand Master and his Knights.'

Leaving his lieutenants, he walked his horse on a few hundred paces. Alone, he could brood, could study the rising edifice of the city looming on its hillside. What had once been so weak had since become so strong. Unexpected, inexplicable. He leaned forward in his saddle, processing the image, scarce able to breathe with the fury of his disappointment. The chance to save his neck, to salvage something from the wreckage of the campaign, was gone. He wanted Mdina, needed Mdina. And yet it stood. He had been betrayed, lied to, conspired against – by the Admiral, by the spy, by the fates. The only blood shed was that which he tasted in his mouth. It would not do at all.

'*Quiet* . . .'

They paused and listened, their fear and the closeness of the tunnel walls pressing in on their position. Counter-mining, the sharp end. Hubert wiped the sweat and dust from his eyes and nose and tried to breathe. It was difficult not to panic, hard not to scream when limestone cascaded, when the enemy were near, when the tap and scrape of their tools acted in concert with one's own. They sought to chip away at his very mind. He would not let them, would not permit their minehead to reach beneath the Castile bastion. That was the promise he had made to himself and to God. He owed it to his friends, his faith, his Order, owed it to Christian Hardy, to the deceased Moor, to put aside selfish terrors and childish things and become a man. A rope tugged on his foot. He could continue.

Naked and prone, he wriggled forward in the darkness and placed the chisel to the wall. Another strike of the hammer, another lungful of powder. Occasionally the rock would tremble to a detonation or conduct a trace-noise of shouts and screams. It could be the start of a roof collapse, the breakthrough of an opposing shaft, the initiation of battle below ground. Scenes of hellish nature were playing out in the subterranean labyrinth.

'Back, my friends! Get back!'

His warning was cut short, immersed in a crashing deluge of rock and filings. It needed no explanation. A tunnel had collapsed, its roof pushing down, its sides tumbling and covering those who burrowed. He kicked, struggling to break loose. But he was held, crushed by the crawling pressure, his mouth and nostrils filling with debris. To think he had wanted to make a difference, and now it made no difference. Each movement earned further downpour, each choking breath brought certainty that death was with him. On his head be it. He was entombed.

A blacker darkness had descended. He was aware of his own prayers, the subsiding of his dread. It was best to lie still and to wait for the coming light.

'You are with the living, Hubert.'

He was on all fours, hacking up powder residue from his lungs, his mortal flesh bruised and pummelled through extraction. The voice, rudely and reassuringly familiar, was correct. He was not yet in the presence of saints and angels. Far from it.

Fra Roberto landed another blow between his shoulder-blades with an oversized fist. 'I pluck you first from the sea and now from a ditch. Is this how we train our novice priests?'

'Again, I am indebted.'

'Save your breath for other than speech, young Hubert. Besides, few would thank a man for returning them to the bleakness of our current plight.'

'I do, Fra Roberto. Our Lord has spared me this one time more.'

'He is a kind and misguided God.'

'For His glory, I will rededicate myself and redouble my effort.'

'Then I shall place mine own self on alert.'

A rare grin, reminiscent of former days, split the features of the young probationer. 'To die would be to miss the derision of my friends.'

'We shall not let you go until we are done, Hubert.'

'I am the luckier for it.' He rose unsteadily and began to brush himself down. 'What news of Christian?'

'He has yet to be restored to us. But the heathen gathers and will not be diverted.'

'They will come at us with everything, Fra Roberto.'

'And we shall reply. That they turned back from Mdina shows they are not the proud force of old, nor an invincible army able to take whichever rampart they choose. We have wounded them, Hubert.'

'Goaded them, Fra Roberto.'

'The finer sport for it. We have Henri de La Valette, Luqa with his slingshot, the Grand Master, the devout manning the walls, the legendary Hubert guarding our cellars.'

'When the sounds of the infidel hammers cease and their powder is placed beneath us, what then?'

'We pray and fight the harder.'

Hubert reached for a pick. 'You may depend on it, Fra Roberto.'

In the small square before the Conventual Church, the Grand Master stood in conclave with his war council. They were a stained and battle-wearied group, subdued in the gravity of the moment and the acceptance of their fate. The garrison was in its final days. No amount of religious fervour, no appeals to God, to the crowned heads of Europe, to the Viceroy of Sicily, would stave off the end. Yet they could still argue and politic, still press their own factional or personal cases. It was how condemned men often acted. At their centre, La Valette listened and presided as he had always done. His body seemed weaker. But his eyes were fierce-bright, his aura undiminished.

De Pontieux was agitating. 'You reject my counsel, Your Highness?'

'I consider it in equal measure with the rest.'

'Forgive my insolence, sir. I do not question your authority.'

'Yet you question my judgement.'

'I seek merely to inform it. Our forces are dead, dying, or soon destined to die. Surely it is better to husband our resource, to withdraw to St Angelo and from there make our final stand.'

'That stand would be hastened by such action. If we retreat from the walls of Senglea and Birgu we surrender the very ground we have shed blood to defend, cede territory from which we will be pounded to submission.'

'We cannot defend the entire length of our walls, sir.'

'Under which section of our code is this ordained, Chevalier?'

'Military reason decrees it, sir.'

'How does your military reason protect the Maltese populace we would be forced to abandon? How does your military reason permit us to fight on from an isolated fort besieged on all sides?'

'Sir, we are already besieged, from above ground and below it. We hold the line with ramparts which daily dissolve, with a garrison which daily declines.'

'Your solution is to betray the Maltese.'

'They may fend for themselves. It is the Order to which we devote our lives and our faith.'

'We are as much Knights of this island as of St John. There is no Order without our survival, no survival without inclusion of the citizens of our kingdom.'

'Brave words, sir. No doubt brave people. But neither will stem the Turk when next he assails us.'

The old soldier Lacroix glowered at de Pontieux. 'Heed what His Highness says. Stay with what you know. And what you know is the enacting of law, the passing of sentence, and the hanging of prisoners.'

'You may become more acquainted in time with my practice, Brother Grand Cross.'

'I am all too acquainted with your perfidy.'

'Age and resentment cloud your judgement.'

'Clarity is my friend in any duel.'

Lacroix rested his hand on the pommel of his sheathed sword, a veteran goaded and rising to the bait. De Pontieux smiled. There was no fool like an ageing combatant, a warrior whose day had been, whose slippered retirement beckoned. Avowed rivalry could so easily degenerate to open hostility. Career endings could be so precipitous.

An explosion blurted into the rumbling backdrop of cannon-fire. It came from an odd direction, from the tip of Birgu and St Angelo itself. Heads turned, expressions on faces at once alarmed and confused. Another powder-mill perhaps, another stray spark igniting an ordnance store and sending part of the fort crashing to the sea. The senior commanders looked at their Grand Master. He was composed, appeared resigned to this latest blow.

'Your Highness . . .'

'Be calm, my brothers. It is not unexpected.'

'You have answer for it?'

'I have reply to many of your doubts and questions. That sound was the demolition of the drawbridge to St Angelo.'

'At whose behest, Your Highness?'

'Mine alone. The fort is cut off, will provide its cannon-fire to the very end. As for ourselves, there is no retreat, no alternative path or temptation to faint-heartedness. Now is the moment for every man, be he Knight or infantry, to remain at his post and render himself unto God.'

'What have you done, sir?' De Pontieux was incredulous.

'It is what I have prevented us from doing, Brother Chevalier. We shall abide with our Conventual Church, with our sacred relics, with the twin peninsulas that have been our home these thirty years past. If these should fall, we will follow, and the Religion perish.'

'We sabotage our own redoubt, sir.'

'Our hearts provide it. Men are the steadier where denied leave of their posts'.

'Some would suggest we take leave or our senses.'

'The future will tell.'

'It may yet condemn us.'

The meeting broke up and the noblemen went their separate ways to make final preparation. Few orders needed to be given, and there were too few troops remaining to receive them. Stand and perish. That was the simple message, the stark truth proffered by Jean Parisot de La Valette.

De Pontieux walked back to his quarters in the magistral buildings. It had brought a certain satisfaction to see the antipathy in the eyes of Lacroix and his allies, to stir the simmering tensions between the clans. The world was closing in; there was little else to do. His feet made puddle tracks on the shaking and cindered ground. Everything was turning to ash. It must have been similar for the citizens of Pompeii and Herculaneum before Vesuvius blew, before the molten rock extinguished their civilization. As for them, there was nowhere to run or regroup. Because La Valette had ordained it, had caused the drawbridge-crossing to St Angelo to be destroyed.

He splashed water from the stone wash-butt into his stinging eyes. At least here in the cool gloom of his chambers he could escape the clinging heat, the abrasive stench of death, the pervading torment of the carrion flies. He cupped the water in his hands and let it trickle down his face. A pity the trappings of office were gone and his private staff lay dismembered and rotting on the Birgu walls.

The punch to his kidney was hard, well aimed. He might have screamed, might have twisted to fend off attack. But exhalation had become a submerged bubble of escaping air, resistance was nothing more than reflexive thrashing of his limbs. He was being drowned. Powerful hands gripped him, thrust his head deeper into the cistern. He was losing reason and consciousness, scrabbling to return, floating away.

His face rose, his mouth vomiting water and contorting for air. The voice of Christian Hardy intruded.

'My apologies for such disturbance, Chevalier.'

'You . . .'

'I cannot deny it. Floated back to Birgu with the aid of pig-bladders. You appear less at ease with water than I.'

'Unhand me.'

'I am not so unwise.'

'There is no wisdom here.' Saturated lungs heaved. 'You make grave error, Englishman.'

'Crécy, Poitiers, Agincourt. Most French Knights have claimed such things before defeat.'

'Consider what you do.'

'Very well.'

Immersion again, the short plunge into blackness. De Pontieux fought, his struggle foaming on the surface, his legs kicking aimless. It was half a minute before he won reprieve.

'I land you again, Chevalier. A slippery catch.'

'*Murder . . .*' The word emerged weak and sodden.

'Justice. For my friend the Moor, whose life you ripped away, whose body you took apart with your sword.'

'*Justice? This?*'

'You were executioner. I will be the same.'

'The Order will see you hanged.'

'While I shall see you drowned.'

Hardy forced the head of de Pontieux down, overcoming resistance, tipping his body into the narrow opening. He had enjoyed demolishing the bridge to St Angelo on secret instruction of the Grand Master. But this was more rewarding, and it was freelance, personal. The Knight slid in, his feet protruding comical from his baptism.

'Christian, if truly we are brothers you must desist.'

'Do not ask it of me, Henri.'

'I beg.'

The young La Valette stood in the doorway, his stance careful, his voice resolute yet calm. He peered at his friend.

'There are ways to confront the adversary, Christian.'

'This is mine.'

'Arbitrary sentence? Sating a vengeful and ravenous temper?'

'Your uncle fires heads from cannon.'

'They were heathen.'

'De Pontieux a villain, a devil who shed the blood of a good man, who inflicts wounds upon the Order.'

'We have no proof.'

'He sinks. It is proof enough. So let him bathe awhile.'

'I took oath to protect all Christians.'

'I to kill all enemies.'

'Thus are you soldier and no judge.' Henri nodded at the upturned and quivering feet. 'Whether he be assassin of the Moor or poisoner of the Grand Master will be decided in time, by others. Release him, Christian. He is not the sole suspect.'

Hardy paused, considering the request, weighing the competing calls on his conscience. His fire had been dampened, his pirate instincts tempered by reason. Against the quiet advocacy of his friend, he had little option but to concede.

With a sigh, he began to haul the submerged de Pontieux from his water-hole. It took effort, rolling the sodden and near-unconscious form on to the flagstones and rekindling movement with a kick. The Knight convulsed, liquid gushing from his mouth and nostrils.

'I will leave you to your conversation, Henri. Fellow Knights must have their room to fraternize.'

'My thanks, Christian.'

'We may yet learn if such generosity is advantage or flaw.'

He bowed and sauntered from the chamber. There would be no ill-will between them. It was merely a matter of judgement, a difference in approach. Henri would make a fine Grand Master. If the Order endured; if any survived.

Alone with de Pontieux, the younger Knight waited and watched as life and breath returned to his charge. The process was slow and loud. Finally, the dripping face swivelled round, the voice barely audible or more than a pained croak.

'As you are my witness, Brother Chevalier, the Englishman will stand in chains before the Sacro Consiglio for his crime.'

Henri gave a rare and slight smile. 'I saw nothing, Chevalier.'

He was better at reading the growl of the cannon than a seer was in divining the runes. The Turks had increased the tempo of their fire, were building to the climax of an attack. It would happen soon. Tomorrow at dawn, maybe. And here was he, worrying at the discomfort of his constipation. Grand Master La Valette brought the spoonful of calomel to his lips and swallowed. He winced. The taste of the liquid was more bitter than any discord between his Knights. He hoped its effects were more beneficial. At least it was not poison, was delivered by his own hand. That hand was given to trembling, was grey with the paralysing sickness which clung to him still. Surely the killer who stalked him had not the opportunity to plant more arsenic. He had ensured he remained on the move, ate with his men, switched platters of food to confound his foe. But age, or nerves, or the crabbing pain of the toxins, remained to enfeeble him. Jean Parisot de La Valette, the nobleman, the warrior, the Grand Master, the cripple who could not shit. They were all doomed anyway.

Beginning at dawn on Saturday 18 August 1565, the ninety-first day of invasion, the Ottomans launched their crushing attack on Senglea. It was a battle without precedent, an endless screaming wave of Iayalars and Janissaries, of levies and dismounted Spahis, sent crashing against the vanishing defences. This time there would be no diversion caused by Christian cavalry, no pause allowed in the annihilation of the pockets of resistance. Defining moments rarely came sweeter or more bloody.

It was a feint. Designed to draw the forces of the Order away from Birgu, where the main thrust of the assault had yet to be unleashed. For, beneath the Castile bastion, the Turk mine was complete. The shaft ran deep, its cramped passageway a conduit for barrels of gunpowder moving steadily towards the tunnel head. Shuttered lanterns jolted along the trail, casting shadows, catching their light on bodies pearled with sweat. The sappers had every reason to strain at their task, to fear. They were about to create an explosion that would rip apart the fortifications and the final shield of the Knights.

Another fall of rock. With an eruction of sound and dust, the ceiling burst inward. It was no ordinary collapse. Through the swirling debris, a naked Hubert, knife in hand, slashed the throat of a Turk engineer and scrambled to confront the next. There were warning cries, the conflicting yells of men pulling back or surging forward to confront. The enemy had landed in their midst.

The novice priest lunged and drove his blade deep through the eye of the cowering labourer. He could not afford to pause, could not let the lethargy of his own terror pin him down. Nothing was more noble. He had dreamt of this kill, had dragged himself blind through the nightmare maze to challenge and defeat the heathen. They were scared, should be. He had righteousness and God, surprise and tactical advantage on his side. No more poor Hubert the malnourished probationer with the cheerful outlook and easy nature. Siege had changed him. He could stand tall or crouch low with the best, fight as they fought, experience what they experienced. Hubert, saviour of the Castile bastion. He had arrived.

Random illumination from a fallen lantern revealed the long stretch of tunnel. At its furthest reach was a hollowed chamber, and arrayed within it the stacked mass of powder-kegs. Hubert blinked. The semi-light could play tricks. He became aware of figures crawling and scurrying like roaches through the haze, picked out details he had not seen before. The Turks were departing. And there it was. He should have known it was too late, should have guessed self-delusion could not save either the bastion or himself. They would tease him mercilessly for this. Before him, the trail of black powder had caught, was racing in a fiery trail for the main charge. God give him strength to die like a man. God protect and preserve the Order and Religion. God help his friends. He headed to intercept the burning course of the powder.

✱

Chapter 16

Cataclysm arrived with an apocalyptic blast which stripped the walls of men and the Castile bastion of its walls. Blocks of limestone fell in a storm of hail; a tar-black cloud corkscrewed a thousand feet. They were the lesser manifestations. For, as the smoke shifted across the charred ruins, a gaping breach had appeared. It was what the forces of Admiral Piali had been mustered for, why the assault by Mustapha Pasha on Senglea had been launched. The Turkish army descended from the high ground.

In Birgu, the Christians were streaming from the infirmary. The sick and the injured, some hobbling on makeshift crutches, others crawling as their bandages unwound behind, dragged themselves towards the threat. The oddest of parades. Yet these were the sole reserves. None intended to die in their cots, to lie mute and passive as the heathen passed along their wards. Their wish was to end gloriously, their sacred vow to do so in the service of the Order and the Lord. Desperate men in a desperate hour. Clutching pikes and swords, they set to their task.

At the pontoon bridge, Hardy counted his troops as they stepped up to make the crossing to Senglea. Too few, and a fraction remaining from his original force. Those with whom he had ridden out to spike the Turkish siege-guns, gone. Those who had first accompanied him to Senglea and driven back the corsairs, lost. Those who had laboured alongside him in building the inner wall of Birgu, buried. The able-bodied had been replaced by the barely able.

He reached out and held Luqa by the shoulder. 'The landward walls are no place for slingshot.'

'Where there is fighting there is Luqa, seigneur.'

You are without sword, mail or armour. Obey me this once.'

'I will cross.'

'My words are wasted. I should have isolated you in St Angelo when I blew the drawbridge.'

The boy grinned. 'We stand together, seigneur.'

'Perhaps we shall fall together.'

They embraced, and Luqa climbed on to the planking to follow the soldiers. One boy, and the sins of religion, invasion and adulthood were heaped upon his shoulders. Hardy stifled the acid pang of remorse. He should never have brought him to Birgu, never have taken him from his life of hunting gulls and scooping shellfish on the shore. His brother, his son, his shadow was heading for battle. The youngster walked on.

'You have employ for further infantry?'

Maria had appeared at the rear of the column. Dressed in leather jerkin and the red-and-white mantle, she held a Turkish arquebus.

He cupped her face in his hands and leaned to kiss her. 'I already lose too much.'

'We may yet lose all.'

'Hubert lies now beneath yon coiling smoke and Castile bastion, Luqa trips merry towards the guns, the black Moor was hacked asunder by sword unknown. Must I see everyone I cherish torn from me?'

'The only death I fear is one apart from you.'

'Long ago I failed to save my mother and my sisters. What if I should fail with my wife?'

'Christian, even the most afflicted depart the infirmary for combat. It is my duty also. I am ready for the fray.'

'My pure, sweet Maria. No mere lady of medicine and poultice.'

He stroked her hair before moving to select a morion from a piled heap of armour. Returning, he placed it gently on her head. 'There are kinder ways to crown our love.'

'None more befitting, Christian.'

'I trusted the silver cross about my neck sufficed.'

'Advance, commander. We go to war.'

That war was not hard to find. The southern boundary of the Senglea peninsula was alive with the sulphurous eruption of battle, men rushing and screaming, falling and dying. Into it, his sword working, his crimson brigantine jacket at the leading point of the formation, Hardy led his unit. They cleared a Turkish salient and discovered another, retook a fighting platform and saw the Moslem banner rise above its neighbour. Around, noise and shapeless anarchy prevailed. Yet through it came the clarity of a single truth. The Christians were being overwhelmed.

'Christian, we must fall back. The position will not hold.'

'The more reason to remain.'

'Their jaws close on us.'

'So become to them ill-flavoured.'

The soldier would not get the opportunity. A musket-ball removed his lower mandible and the rear of his head. Few noticed in the rolling uproar. A round shield clenched forward in his left hand, Hardy butted aside the strike of a scimitar and cut upwards into the abdomen of a levy. He would let the man writhe a little, would allow him to savour the agony of demise. Only the rich were finished off, only those with a jewelled charm or golden amulet to snatch.

Before him, an Iayalar snarled glass-eyed. Old friends. Hardy crouched and swung his sword. The fanatic lost his footing, then his feet, rocking forward and splitting open on a rising blade. But his supporters had arrived.

'Make quick! Lock shields and sweep the foe to your front!'

Steel and leather overlapped at his command, pressing in

against the Turks. The Iayalars responded, dashing themselves in shrieking efforts on the moving wall. They were quickly dispatched, the single chant of '*Allah!*' still playing on their lips.

'More return, Christian.'

'We will greet them the same. Watch to your flank.'

'Their numbers are too great.'

'Our fleetness will challenge them yet. We are not undone till the crescent flag is driven through our hearts.'

Another man dropped, his chest peeled open by a Janissary axe. The killer staggered backwards. A hole had replaced much of his face. Hardy glanced to his side. Maria was kneeling to reload her arquebus, tipping the powder-horn for the main charge, ramming home the ball, applying the primer. Infirmary or battle-front, her calm dexterity was the same. He despaired for the coming loss. What a place to be in love; what surroundings into which to bring his wife.

Like shingle sliding on a beach, the Christians were washed back from their decayed ramparts. The Ottomans were confident, had every reason to be. Outcome was predestined. It was written by the will of God, could be read in the eyes of the stumbling defenders, in their fading resistance, in the way that some threw down their weapons and ran while others knelt to receive the scimitar edge. All would eventually succumb.

Whispers of a sighting spread. '*The Sanjak Cheder is here.*' There could be no greater symbol of impending finale. He was the most feted warrior in the Turkish army, an aged veteran of countless battles, a taker of lives without compare. He was present for he smelled the blood. Attended by his bodyguards, dressed in the finery of a potentate, he pointed his jewelled scimitar forward and led the Janissaries in frontal charge towards St Michael. Little opposed them. They killed as they moved, annexing ground, populating the undulating remnants of the fort with a baying horde intent on conquest.

'*Invincible Ones, we shall take St Michael or we shall die!*'

Fate obliged. He was shot through the breastplate and heart by a musket-round. Stupefied, his followers hesitated, their attack blunted, their rapturous momentum converted to despair. The Knights counter-attacked.

'Why do we not join the pursuit, Christian?'

'We are needed most in defence.' Hardy turned to congratulate a nearby sharpshooter. 'Chevalier Pessoa, I believe we owe to you our deliverance from the Cheder.'

'You honour me, Monsieur Hardy.'

'Senglea or Birgu, such skill is required this day.'

'If for a second it confounds the heathen, I am glad to serve among your ranks.'

'As we are blessed to have you.'

Luqa was struggling to raise a discarded Moslem pennant. 'I will bear it as trophy to the Conventual Church, seigneur.'

'A waving standard may draw eye and lead. Take care you are not mistaken for the foe.'

'I am too quick for any musketeer, seigneur.'

He released his grip with a yell as splinters flew from the staff and a tight grouping of shot punched through the waving silk above his head.

'None may outrun black powder, Luqa. Follow me or you shall be interred in your flag.'

Hardy took his troop along the stricken front, lending assistance, joining in skirmishes, shoring and suppressing the firefights that billowed around the enclave. A losing contest. More of his men fell, more failed to return from each engagement. It was a diminished and wearied band which completed its tour of the landward boundary. No respite was offered.

'Christian, look!' Maria pointed.

He had already seen it, was tracking the object as it bounced and rolled in wayward descent towards a sheltering group of Knights and men. They too had noticed, were attempting to scatter from its path. It would be in vain. The thing gathered speed, its immense barrel-shape chasing across the rubble. Attached to it was a lit fuse. Decimation was the aim.

Motioning for his section to lie flat, Hardy moved to intercept. He heard their calls, ignored them, was running straight for the danger. The bomb had come to rest.

Two Knights peered at him from a rock scrape. 'Keep from it, Monsieur Hardy. 'Tis a diabolic and infernal machine.'

'There is flaw in the Turk plan.'

'Also in yours. You will be killed.'

'A prouder death than with my face in the dirt.'

'Madness.'

'Where do you not find madness in this hour?'

'It soon ignites. Get from it.'

'Observe the fuse. We have fleeting moment to turn fate. Join me, brothers.' He put his shoulder to the device. It shifted a fraction, its fuse bright and shortening.

'Your folly inspires, Monsieur Hardy.'

The Knights were beside him, pushing in unison, heaving the iron-hooped load to an opposite course. More hands pressed against its side. Maria and Luqa were there, their feet seeking purchase, their bodies forcing the device higher up the incline.

'Again, more quick.'

'Hear us, O Lord. Deliver us from evil.'

'Deliver it to the heathen.'

There were shouts and oaths, the prayers and frantic tenacity of pilgrims dedicated to a single purpose. It might have been a religious festival, the time-honoured practice of townsfolk conducting an ancient rite. But it was deadly pursuit. Hardy felt Maria close, the fingertip touch of her hand. She was once a girl filling clay bottles from a freshwater spring near Mdina. The slow fuse spluttered, the bomb climbed.

Massed in the approaches to the Senglea rampart, the Turks waited for explosion. Their specialists had gone forward under cover of the last assault, had transferred their live and devastating invention direct into the belly of the Christian defence. Possession was yielded, and it would do grievous harm. Filled with gunpowder and shot, nails and chain, its detonation was designed to paralyse and to finish. They would find little left of the infidels when they stormed through the smouldering aftermath. It was worth enjoying, would reward their patience.

The tell-tale shape bounded once on the debris-pile of the ditch, flew high, and ignited. Nothing would have prepared the Christians; nothing could protect the Turks. In a single instant, hundreds died, burnt and clawed apart in a shrapnel storm. Some who lived were blinded, others mutilated with innumerable embedded fragments. Military reversal had been swift. None were ready for the Knights who had been their intended victims, who now slithered down the bank intent on exacting revenge. The Order would not pass quietly into the chronicles.

In Birgu, the bell of the Conventual Church was tolling. It was not a celebratory peal, but a message to the inhabitants that the Ottomans had broken through. By way of the mine breach they came, forcing their way to the interior, pushing the defenders back into the narrow village alleyways. Yet more streamed on to the standing ramparts of the Castile bastion across a drawbridge lowered from the towering siege-engine drawn up by slaves and horses. The twin torrents converged. Never had the Knights faced such menace; never had the Turks been so close to victory.

As a dervish screamed in tongues and rushed along a street bordered by flame, he was impaled on a long battle-fork, lifted from the ground, and pitched headlong through a window into the fire. Fra Roberto had scored another success.

He crouched as low as his size would allow. 'Musketeers, let loose!'

The volley burst above his head, and the forward ranks of the enemy crumpled. Behind them, the second wave faltered, their momentum slowed, their way obstructed by Christians and fallen comrades. They had failed to scan the roof-line. The Maltese appeared, chanting phantoms glimpsed in smoke and funnelling flame, their rocks and spears hurtling down upon the foe.

'Arise, my brothers! Smite the heathen dogs with all your might!'

Lumbering into a charge, the prongs of his fork probing for fresh meat, Fra Roberto led the advance. He caught a retreating levy and pierced him through, stamping on his head before driving on.

'They are in flight, Fra Roberto.'

'God smiles. Do not slacken in your task.' He lunged at a Turk officer, pinning him through his brightly-coloured pantaloons and holding him to roast above the blaze. 'They burst if first their skins are not pricked.'

'We have them trapped.'

'You are contradicted by events. It is they who have us caught.'

He ducked again, the muskets discharging into the fleeing crowd. One skirmish did not make triumph. It was going badly, going the way of Mustapha Pasha. In other streets, resistance had already been overwhelmed.

'Reckoning is upon us. And if I am to die this day, it will be as common soldier among my brethren.'

Dressed as a lowly infantryman, a plain steel morion upon his head, Grand Master La Valette surveyed his gathering of senior Knights. Their eyes reflected the moment, the comprehension that all that they stood for and the Religion for which they strived had reached the final act.

Knight Grand Cross Lacroix leaned on his longsword. 'Whatever our fate, we stand beside you, sir.' There were murmurs of assent.

A bailiff spoke. 'The hour is more glorious than bleak. We seek what our brothers at St Elmo have found. We go where they are gone.'

'It is our privilege.'

'Our duty.'

'A destiny which will test us, which will see us judged and measured against the saints.'

'His Holiness has blessed us.'

'Heaven awaits us.'

'We are prepared and are strong in the Faith.'

La Valette nodded. His disciples were ready, were heading from a command-post that had little remaining to command. About them in the square, both day and battle were drawing in. Yet they would turn their faces to God, ply their swords against the enemy, set example for Europe and Christendom to follow.

'Well may our flesh become spirit, my brothers. We are the few, the elect, the last of our kind. Behind us is our church, the baptismal hand and sacred relic of St John. Before us is the Saracen. Embrace this chance to purify yourselves in infidel blood, to be martyrs in Christ.'

'Amen.' They bowed their heads and crossed themselves.

'My nephew Henri, you shall take the Turk siege-engine which now looms above the Castile bastion.'

'When I am done, it shall lie in splintered ruin.'

'Chevalier de Montagut will rally the Aragon bastion, Chevalier Salzedo will hold our Conventual Church to the end.' La Valette swept them with his solemn gaze. 'Brothers, the remainder of you shall make deployment where you will.'

'You have no further instruction, Your Highness?' It was de Pontieux.

'From here on, it is God alone who instructs.'

'Then we must bid each farewell.'

'Praise be to Him, and good chance to you all.'

They adjusted armour and collected weapons, every Knight choosing his path and fighting-companions. The square was emptying. Grasping a partisan spear and accompanied by his loyal retinue, La Valette made for a flight of steps and the direction of combat. He paused.

'You join us, Brother Prior?'

Prior Garza was sickly pale, the front of his mantle stained with vomit. 'Alas, I am no fighter, Your Highness.'

'Nor are the women and children who are so staunch in our defence, who soak with their blood our hallowed ground.'

'They are to be commended to God.'

'And you derided by your fellow men. Are we not all of us soldiers of the Cross?'

'He calls me instead to prayer.'

'I, your commander, call you to arms.' The Grand Master seized a second pike and thrust it into the trembling hands of the churchman. 'Sloth and gluttony are mortal sin, Brother Prior. Atone for them. Serve in our ranks; feel the joyous heat of the fray.'

'I cannot.' The words were falsetto-weak with terror.

'You shall. Or it is the dungeon and later judgement to which you will be consigned.'

With his newest recruit in reluctant attendance, La Valette resumed his mission. He led his men on, moving against the tide of withdrawal, encouraging others to stand fast and trust in fate. Numbers swelled, mood turned. Their Grand Master was come among them. He was the quiet eye of the storm, the one they admired and to whom they had pledged their allegiance. Why, he had fought off the Turk these months past, would surely do so again. They could not betray him now.

The enemy was encountered. In a headlong charge, La Valette and his ragged battalion hit the lead elements, turning their advance, forcing them back. Another strike, the violent momentum travelling as a shock wave through the Ottoman ranks. Pressure points, fault lines. The Turkish monolith fractured. In the whirling smoke, the Christians chased the enemy down, their hatred unbridled, their confidence and impetus gaining. Each step was contested, every street cleared through barricades of the slain. Adherents multiplied from stream to flood. Fra Roberto was with them, preaching loud, killing freely, his laughter ringing as he jabbed at cleric and sheikh alike. Knight fought alongside citizen, noble aided peasant, chaplain wielded battleaxe and sword. The brotherhood swept on. And at its head, Jean Parisot de La Valette.

How circumstance could change, the traitor thought. One moment the heathen were in the ascendant, the Order on its knees; the next, it was the army of the Sultan that reeled from the hammer-blow. The course of battle was forever in flux and never preordained. Like love, like loyalty, like diplomatic alliance. It was wise to plan for all occasions. La Valette and his men strove hard in their pursuit, were pushing the Turk back into the breach. A Herculean effort. To no avail. The Grand Master was a spectre in the gaping fissure of the walls, a commanding presence, an infantry-man at the very tip of the Christian lance. So courageous, so exposed. Things could happen, go desperately wrong, among such confusion. Occasionally, poison was too slow and difficult to apply.

'*He is down!*'

True enough. A grenade-pot had landed close to where the Grand Master stood, its trajectory and source unseen. In a flurry-blaze of shrapnel, La Valette stumbled and fell. He was instantly surrounded, shielded by companions intent on dragging him clear, on saving the day. La Valette shook them off. He appeared to rise, clambering to his feet with the aid of his partisan. Old men could be stubborn. They could also be frail. The traitor watched. There was no doubt La Valette was injured, his wounds deep, possibly fatal. Yet he insisted on remaining, on being, on setting example as last and most poignant of the Grand Masters. He slumped again, then revived. No longer so inspiring, the traitor reflected. Through the vortex, the Turks gathered to retake the breach.

Henri wondered what Christian would do. His friend might be dead as Hubert was, as the Moor was, lost like so many to this accursed conflict. He himself faced its latest manifestation. A siege-engine, soaring, its sides clad in water-drenched ox-hide against the wildfire, its levels invested with Janissary snipers, its drawbridge down and spewing forth Turks straight on to the worn ramparts. The menace, the immediacy, the task of its destruction helped quell the pain of grief. Henri knelt behind a limestone boulder and stared. He was far from the solitude he craved, the library and apothecary rooms he loved. Close by, another defender rolled in his final throes.

The young Chevalier Polasstron called across from his cover of stones. 'We are prepared, Henri.'

'Then we must strike.'

'You wear no surcoat. Armour of a Knight draws attention of their marksmen.'

'I am beheld by the Lord. Their arquebus hold no fear for me.'

'We follow you unto death.'

'It is the light we seek. Ready yourselves.'

As a squad of levies blundered into a fusillade of musket-fire, Henri lifted his sword. There would be no turning back, no redemption if he failed his brother Knights, his uncle, his Order. '*Hail Mary* . . .' He whispered a prayer and rose.

'Set for me a candle should I fall.'

'Salvation is upon us.'

'Forward, my brothers.'

He ran towards the enemy drawbridge. Its mouth was open, its sides speckling with the flash of muskets. A visitation, an image of the Beast. He could see himself from afar, was transported to the days of caravan when he and Christian stormed galleys and merchantmen, carried the points of their swords to the throat of the infidel. The Englishman had taught him well.

Someone was hit, musket-balls raking through armour, legs beginning to buckle. He was aware of a pressure in his chest, of the sensation of falling. Hands were trying to drag him. Strange to be part of a battle and yet not a part. The Turks were attempting to claim him as their prize, to take him and his gilded armour into their tower. His comrades would put up a fight. There was such noise – cries he could identify, the words of the enemy he could not. He was dying.

'I am with you my brother.'

'Christian?'

'Returned from Senglea. I could not let you confront alone the heathen.'

'The caravan once more . . .'

His words choked on a bubble of blood, his eyes open and searching, his fingers clutching for support. He was entering a dream. It was a landscape of brown fields and purple clover, of sharp limestone washed by the salt Mediterranean breeze. He was riding towards Mdina, his companions at his side.

'Stay with me, Christian.'

'I will take you to the gates, my brother.'

'The infidel . . . they seize my shoes.'

'We shall struggle afresh to win them back.'

'You do it without me.'

The voice trailed, the body shuddered on a concluding breath. Henri de La Valette was gone. Turks were emerging from the brooding tower; musket-rounds danced around. Hardy cradled the corpse in his arms and closed its eyes.

'Go to Him, Henri. Walk with Him, my brother.'

Into the night the attack continued. The illumination flares of the Turks streaked the sky; the clash of arms reverberated beneath them. No section of the landward walls escaped assault; no inhabitant was spared the fight. The dying were left or piled on those already dead. And in the Sacred Infirmary the next wave of injured were littering the corridors and halls. Grand Master La Valette was among them.

He was stoic as the fungal poultice was applied, as his leg wounds were bound. It was not until the hours of darkness that he had agreed to pull back from the contested breach. There were too many pressing concerns – briefings from messengers, the needs of other casualties – to have regard for himself. But the weariness showed; the gravity of the moment shadowed his calm.

Motioning away the Hospitaller medic, he rose from the operating-trestle and limped across the crowded flagstones to a straw litter lodged in a far corner. Even in the guttering gloom of candlelight, he had noticed its occupant. The Knight Grand Cross Lacroix.

'How fare you, brother?'

'Well enough, Jean Parisot.' The old campaigner, his face part-obscured by bloody bandage, his left arm carried in a sling, pointed to the room. 'I merely catch my breath. Yet in these halls I see more tragedy and pathos than ever I did on the ramparts.'

'When with sword, we are blind to consequence.'

'So give me the heat of battle.' Lacroix broke a piece of bread from a platter at his side, folded it into his mouth, and gestured to La Valette to do the same.

The Grand Master soaked his morsel in a goblet of wine and ate. 'Perhaps our own last supper, brother.'

'I am glad I share it with you, to have been apostle for the Religion. We stood together even at Rhodes.'

'Served together these forty-three years since.'

'Again now the sour breath of the heathen is upon us.'

'Behind it, the sweeter breath and promise of life eternal.' La Valette seated himself at the bedside and took another bite of bread.

'Will they salute us in Rome, throughout the princely courts of Europe, as champions and martyrs of Christ? Or will they mock the conceit of our defence?'

'Praise from God is sufficient.'

Lacroix leaned back, his visible eye closing, a black bloodstain leaking across his chest. His breathing was shallow, each intake vibrating with pain.

'You wish for herb or wine, brother?'

'Your company and prayer instead, Jean Parisot.' He turned his face away as La Valette proffered the goblet. 'Drink, for you have more use of sustenance.'

La Valette complied. 'I must soon to the walls.'

'While I will join you in slower time.'

'Rest, brother.'

'We defy the infidel Sultan. What luck and pleasure to be a Knight, to be at such a fulcrum of history.'

'What honour to be your Grand Master.'

'My brother.' The eye of the Knight Grand Cross opened, and he reached to grasp the hand of his friend.

They were in silent prayer when Maria found them, her face blackened with gun-smoke, her clothes and skin roughened by the rigours of combat.

'Your Highness.'

'Lady Maria.' La Valette stood in greeting. 'I judge from appearance you have been in thick of battle.'

'It is inescapable, sir. As is my fate to bear the worst of tidings.'

'Unless the Turk triumphs, there is none such.'

'Your nephew Henri.'

Nephew Henri. There was an inflection he hoped he would never hear, a message which drew him in faltering haste towards the Conventual Church. He had to see for himself. For a moment, for the brief journey lit by the glare of war, he experienced loneliness which travelled far beyond the realm of leadership into that of total loss.

Christian Hardy waited for him before the altar. The body of Henri de La Valette lay on a bier.

The Grand Master inclined his head. 'Then it is true.'

'I would not send word with false pretence, sir.'

'He died well?'

'A credit to the Order and to your noble name, sir.'

'Then we have no reason for bitterness or regret.'

'There is ever reason for regret, sir. I loved him as my brother.'

'I as my son. Yet he is blessed in the sight of God, goes before us to a better and less troubled place.'

'Soldiering is my calling, sir. But Henri was of gentler, kinder and more worthy disposition. He did not deserve to perish.'

La Valette looked upward at the barrel-vaulting, at the Turkish banners hung as trophies. 'See what we take from the heathen.'

'See what they take from us.'

'The perfect death for a perfect Knight. My nephew Henri would not have wished it other.'

'Those who are left wish it for him.'

'You did your most to protect him, Monsieur Hardy. You fought valiantly at St Elmo, brought relief to Birgu, helped save Mdina, warned me of poison. I owe you my thanks.'

'Your Highness.' Hardy bowed.

The two men stood before the corpse, the older and younger paying homage, remembering, dwelling on their own mortality. It was the wordless communion of participants in war. A bond, a controlled anguish. A sharing.

'You do not weep, sir.'

'I cannot mourn for Henri more than I do for others slain in our vocation. They are all sons of light, all glorious in their sacrifice.'

'Sacrifice we squander if we break.'

'What is squandered, Monsieur Hardy? An island, a patch of barren earth, a few thousand living beings of flesh, blood and sinew? Our gain is greater. We have stood alone against the wrath of Satan and the baneful empire of his minions. We have restored to Christendom its dignity and pride, its power to send the heathen to the bottomless pit.'

'For the sake of Henri, I shall inflict the same upon their siege-engine.'

'The roving adventurer washed ashore is become our most valued asset. My trust is in you, Monsieur Hardy.'

'I carry it to the rampart.'

His men were already well advanced in their task. Above, the enemy continued to surge across the lowered drawbridge of their tower. They pushed on or fell back, absorbed into the ceaseless noise and seamless chaos of the conflict. But at the base of the Castile bastion, hidden within its walls, the work detail of Christian Hardy sweated for a different reason. Another lever was applied, men strained. The stone gave.

'We are close to the outside, Christian.'

'Ready the cannon with bar-shot.'

This was how he preferred to fight, with the lowest tricks played against a backdrop of the highest stakes. It was the way of the corsair. Rope and tackle took the weight, and the last block of limestone fell away.

'Run out the gun! Fire at will!'

He was bringing the Turk back down to earth. In a raw and spitting fury that mirrored his own, the cannon vented itself through the narrow opening. Rocking back, it was reloaded and pushed forward, the process repeated, the smoke and flame rolling into the confines. Oblivious, possessed, Hardy and his crew worked on. They did not hear the iron shot cutting through the structure, did not see the collapsing spars, the imams, the dervishes, the Janissaries tumbling as their tower shook. A further blast, the crash of critical damage. Flying splinters became falling beams, supports protested and were sheared away. Gravity triumphed. In a shrieking plunge, shedding itself, the giant siege-engine lurched into its terminal and accelerating descent.

'Finish the beast.'

They obeyed his command, switching to grapeshot, loosing their volleys direct into the black and billowing geyser. Within it, the remains of the tower and its complement of Ottoman troops lay burning in the ditch.

At the Conventual Church, the Grand Master maintained his vigil at the side of his dead nephew. The young man was at peace, was at last far from the mortal strife and woe of the world. That strife haunted every scene, pervaded every sense. Dawn would soon arrive. More attacks, more teetering on the very edge of destruction. La Valette stirred. The pain was clawing at his gut, emerging to climb and flay his body from within. His bones and flesh were afire. He clutched at his stomach, attempted to shout. What came was no voice, no running of his pages and assistants to attend to his distress. But blood, thick and dark, choking him, smearing the flagstones on which he crawled.

✠

Chapter 17

Late August, and the heavy-humid winds of the tramontara had brought rain. Water teemed over Turk and Christian alike, filling trenches, coursing through tents and shelters, enveloping all in the sodden misery of downpour. Fighting stalled. It was a matter of necessity, as soaking haze rendered gunpowder unusable and slithering purchase on rubble almost unattainable. The defenders huddled and prayed, waited for judgement beneath the swollen clouds. Another day, a further hour. And the stench of death and putrefaction climbed. These seemed to be the final moments of the Order of St John. For Mustapha Pasha, they provided opportunity.

As fresh deluge came, the shock troops of the Ottomans moved forward. There would be no blast of infidel cannon, no ripple-fire of muskets to winnow the levies while they escaladed the ramparts across the wreckage-strewn ditch. The scimitar would prevail. In hand-to-hand combat, numbers were what counted. A few hundred Christians stood no chance. Indeed, they barely stood at all. Their drenched and redundant marksmen would be cut to ribbons, their rusting Knights would be torn apart. The Turks began their ascent.

Optimism and misjudgement had combined. The Moslems were not to know that La Valette had anticipated such possibility, that in the months preceding invasion he had ordered the repair and reconditioning of every crossbow in his arsenal. These were now deployed. In a silent gale of steel, barbed and shard-nosed quarrels ripped into the approaching line. Officers were felled first, then their men, their bodies snapping forward or thrown backwards in a mass exhalation of screams. More bolts thudded through silk and light armour. The tip of each had been treated, dipped in dung, pig fat or carrion, to add injury and insult, to carry disease straight into the Turkish ranks. A little something for the heathen to enjoy, to stretch the resources of their physicians. It was no surprise the Turks broke and ran.

'One hundred days we have existed on this hellish island.'

Mustapha Pasha stared from his tent at the drifting rain. His mood was as dark as the sky; his sullen despondency matched the leaden drops streaming across the Marsa. Hope was drowning. And behind him Admiral Piali sat on a divan, a rival trapped with him by fate, searching for escape.

'You hear what they say throughout the camp, Mustapha Pasha?'

'I am all too aware of what *you* say, of how you usurp and plot, machinate against my land campaign.'

'They speak of God willing our defeat, intending our departure.'

'Are we now to abandon holy war, the instruction of the Sultan?'

'There is nothing holy in dysentery and disease, in the ague, in the calamitous cracking of near half our guns, in the fruitless application of our dwindling force.'

'We persevere, Admiral.'

'With what? Which regiment remains effective? Which mine or siege-engine have we not employed? Which devilish trick or combination have we not attempted?'

'Our spy tells us the Grand Master sickens unto death.'

'The same spy who spoke of access through tunnels beneath St Angelo, of quick victory at Mdina.'

'It is lack of supplies that thwarts our effort.'

'Look to your own failure, Mustapha Pasha. Look to the turning of the wind and weather.'

The old general glowered at Piali. This popinjay admiral provoked him with his calm acceptance of potential defeat. The world might collapse, the campaign wither, but the friend of royal circles would always save himself, ever use the debris as stepping-stones to advancement. He would see about that. Endgames could be vicious, their results startling.

He spoke slowly. 'A mere one hundred and eighty miles from Djerba and your navy cannot replenish our stores. It would suit your design to have us starved from Malta.'

'You pluck conspiracy from the air, Mustapha Pasha.'

'I see the truth writ plain.'

'My object is no more than preservation of the fleet.'

'Or saving of your hide.' The army commander spat the words. 'My own quest was to win. And you have brought it low, damaged us with insistence on anchorage at Marsamuscetto, with needless assault upon St Elmo.'

'Take care, General. I am close to the harem and the imperial family.'

'I closer to the hilt of my scimitar.'

Piali rose, squaring up, facing down. 'You threaten me?'

'If my neck is to fall to vengeful diktat of Suleiman, be assured yours will follow.'

'Dangerous days, Mustapha Pasha.'

'Better to succeed, to snatch victory from these closing moments.'

'My galleys cannot tarry. They have no shelter from the autumn tempest, no provision for refit or repair.'

'They stay. Or I will kill you here.'

'You have a week – two at most.'

Obsession and hatred welled in Mustapha Pasha. He had never been known to fail or retreat, never suffered the indignity, the shame, of returning to Constantinople as pariah and laughing-stock. Death held no fears. It was the breaking of his oath to the Sultan, the sullying of his reputation, the role he had played in military climbdown that made him tremble. To think that a forebear had carried the banner of the Prophet Mohammed, that he himself had fumbled and dropped it. Ignominy, the damaged offspring of pride and former glory.

'I am not yet done, Piali.' He stalked from the tent into the gusting rain.

Dawn clawed pink across the still-dark sky, and Hardy was awake to greet it. Saturday 1 September 1565. A new month, and the one-hundred-and-fifth day of invasion. It felt similar to the rest, neither good nor bad to be alive, but a twilight in which he killed Turks and loved Maria. She slept on beside him, the outline of her naked form unfolded on the straw. Such moments helped soften the trauma of combat. Up here on the flat roof, he could imagine existence beyond the rotting stench, distance himself from the bundled corpses scattered down below. Yet he could not forget. His friends were gone, the ailing Grand Master slipped towards death, and the waves of enemy continued to crash against a splintered resistance. No situation for newly-weds.

He climbed to his feet and stretched, splashed his face and torso from the rain-butt to rid himself of sleep and sweat. The morn was starting tranquil enough. It might be his last, could end with little incident or great consequence, the Ottomans breaking through or suffering reverse. Any outcome was possible. The pirate boy from England, Isra'el the angel of death, was ready for it.

'Christian?'

It was while he gazed blinking towards the ramparts that she called to him.

'You awake, my Maria?'

'I do not slumber well in this ponderous heat.'

'So let us embrace the day and each other.'

She held her arms towards him as he went to her. 'Should we not feel guilt at this share of happiness?'

'Would you feel guilt at discovering the most perfect of flowers in a desert?'

'Friends die around us, Christian.'

'The more reason to find humanity and solace, to hold what is precious.'

'So many gone. So many with whom we broke bread, with whom we shared laugher and jest, devoured by this darkness.'

'Honour their memory; think on them without regret.'

'So speaks a soldier, Christian.'

'A lover.'

They sat entwined, overshadowed by history and cannon, excluding all but the moment and the tenderness. This was what mattered. It was survival and need, the simplest of instincts. And it was how man and woman endured the ravages of war.

'Is it life or death we await, Christian?'

'There is ever life.'

'Even here? Even when encircled by the heathen?'

'The more so.' He pulled her closer, felt the press of her breasts, the radiated warmth of her body. 'Be trusting and untroubled, my sweetest wife.'

'My gentlest of warriors.'

'Hospitaller Knights may defend their Religion. It is you I defend.'

'You bear the wounds for it, Christian.'

'I would forfeit my life for it.'

'That I know.'

He grazed on her neck and mouth. 'Do you know too it is the first I have fought for more than glory or gold?'

'I am complimented.'

'While I am made whole.'

'No soldier should go naked in the furnace of battle.' Her hands toured his chest and stomach.

'It is different fire I have.'

'Your sword? Your brigantine jacket?'

'Put aside.'

He responded to her touch, the silver cross at his neck held by their union. In her arms he could believe that his companions survived and La Valette would persist, could dream that relief and resolution would come by ship from Sicily. Stubbornness was his chosen course. He was a fool to consider it would alter the outcome.

Her warm and soft tears coursed on his shoulder.

'You weep, Maria.'

'For those we lose and have yet to lose. For the time dissipated before we met, the little remaining ere we must part.'

'Lock away such sorrows.'

'I am no infantryman able to stow grief.'

'Yet no finer arquebusier have I seen, or greater carer for the injured, or braver ally in rolling back a murderous Turkish barrel.'

'And the slaughter continues.'

'By implication, our defence still holds.' He whispered to her, caressed her head against his neck.

'What would you ask of me, Christian?'

'That you rest, that you outlive this siege, that you one day will travel with me to every point of the compass.'

'It requires you besides to emerge unharmed.'

Wordlessly, he lowered her to the straw bedding.

She was asleep again as he dressed, her head resting on a rolled cavalry cloak, her body glistening in the humid dew. It was an image he could watch without pause, one he would take with him. He shrugged on the armoured heaviness of his jacket, its steel plates dented and uncovered beneath the threadbare velvet. Combat was no respecter of style. After three months of fighting, he was barely sightlier.

On the heights of Corradino the Turk fires were winking. Sound came behind. They were the batteries opening up, the early call of the enemy to a garrison which had slept fitfully, which scarcely now existed. The alarm trumpet blew. The Ottomans would be hitting hard.

Fewer souls raced to man the slumped ramparts these days. Most who once had were dead. Hardy moved through alleyways demolished by cannonball, flame, and cannibalization for stone. Contemplative piety was gone; the sounds of fishermen or laughing children had been replaced by grim and dusty dereliction. He pushed on. Somewhere a mine exploded, a section of wall sending high a plume of smoke. The usual clamour, the customary patterns. He expected to see the Moor amble into view, anticipated a cheerful shout as Henri and Hubert strode towards him. Instead, this: ghosts, animal and human remains, a propped and rusting suit of fluted Maximilian armour hosting a ball of maggots where once a face had been.

'War conjures much piteous spectacle.'

'None more so than yourself, de Pontieux.'

The Knight remained in his path, superiority and confidence playing on his features. They suggested ambush.

'A man who makes light of his circumstance is either a clown or worthy of our respect, Monsieur Hardy.'

'You have never commanded the respect of any.'

'While those who lauded you are dead.'

'I do not recall you counter-mining against the Turk, taking arms against their siege-engine.'

'Responsibility takes many forms.'

'For what are you responsible, de Pontieux?'

'Careful of your tongue, *mercenaire*.'

'Or you will rebuke me, traitor?'

De Pontieux studied him, maintained his still and watchful poise. 'Power shifts, Hardy. The old man declines; new authority is in the ascent.'

'Our walls are breached; our troops perish. And you speak of authority and ascent.'

'There is no better time.'

'I have no time for your scheming.'

'Yet you comprehend the exercise of influence. You under-stand that you are alone, your support ebbs, your beloved Grand Master is not present to advise clemency or restraint.'

'State your purpose, de Pontieux.'

'Is it not evident? I neither forgive insult nor forget your attempt at murder.'

'It was justly deserved.'

'And you make accusation of treachery.' De Pontieux stepped closer. 'In this world, popular repute and affection, a handsome visage, are no surety of survival.'

'Your own longevity will be reduced by ill-thought move.'

'Can it be more ill-thought than habiting on a rooftop with a Maltese whore?'

Hardy drew his sword. His rival pricked him for a reason, would not challenge from position of weakness. He tested his footing, gauged the distance, exercised his grip. Swordsmanship was more than a skill. It was extension of his soul. He could be certain of a kill.

'I will not be bested in single combat, de Pontieux.'

'Single?'

There was a casualness to the delivery, an insouciance that suggested tactics were rehearsed. Hardy turned. Behind him were others, their expressions hostile, their pikes and muskets lowered to the horizontal. Prior Garza was in the forefront. They advanced.

Hardy edged on to a block of stone, gaining height and time. 'Brothers, is this the moment for private feud and petty duel?'

'It is to my word they answer, Hardy.' De Pontieux was coolly triumphant. 'They are good men of Provence or well-paid sol-diers of Spain.'

'Aside from Judas silver, what is it they find in you?'

'Mettle, strength, the future of our Order.'

'You endanger that future with your tricks.'

'No mere tricks, Hardy. The succession is what I seek.'

'My death little aids your cause.'

'It gives plenty to my peace of mind. One more body lying broken among so many. A brave defender trampled, lost, forgotten in the fray.'

'What of you, Prior?' Hardy swung his focus to Garza. 'Are you to waste your strength, apply your paltry skill with a partisan to committing against a fellow Christian?'

The churchman scowled. 'You are Christian in name alone.'

'Yet by deed I defend the Faith, guard the walls of your Religion, have stood these more than a hundred days against the heathen foe.'

'This day we stand you down.'

'Question your action, my brothers.'

'They are vexed by different question. Whether to behead, hang or burn you.'

The crowd pressed in, those same who had excited for arrest of the Moor, who owed fealty to the richest patron, to the faction of Chevalier de Pontieux. Appeals to reason would be in vain.

De Pontieux had unsheathed his own sword. 'We are tossed about by fate, are we not?'

'On occasion manipulated by members of the Sacro Consiglio.'

'No rules pertain to a pirate.'

'I should have drowned you, de Pontieux.'

'Such chance is gone, and with it your life.' The Knight raised his blade. 'I warned when next our swords crossed it would be to the death.'

'I pledged it would be yours.'

'In the circumstance, an idle promise.'

His sentence ended on a screech of pain, the sword sent spinning from his grasp. He was clutching his hand, searching for the source of the hazard. Luqa crouched at a distance on a building.

'Your native imp spots well, Hardy. Let him try our response.' De Pontieux snarled an order to his men. 'Aim true and bring him down.'

'*Obey him and you all shall drop.*'

None could mistake the identity of the caller. They shuffled to see, swivelling to repel the danger at their rear. Fra Roberto offered up his beaming countenance. He leaned idly on his battle-fork, his wooden cross resting on his shoulder, a host of combatants gathering at his side.

Hardy addressed de Pontieux. 'It seems we are more even matched.'

'A disordered rabble, a smattering of Maltese with knives, is no match.'

'Are your men so sure of your judgement? Are they to test it?'

'They will obey.'

'Through willingness or your compulsion?' Hardy raised his voice to the crowd. 'Have we not spilt enough of our precious blood? Should we not save it for continuing endeavour against the avenging Turk?'

'Your pretty speech fails to move, Hardy.'

The pronged steel of Fra Roberto swung downward. 'Perhaps I may reinforce it. I have long wished to toast the Prior on my fork, to visit on him the burning methods of his Inquisitor blood-line.'

'While I in person will deal with de Pontieux.' Hardy gestured at the Knight.

Initiative had been snatched away. Prior Garza looked sick. Without support, he was no more than a rubicund weakling, his impotence exposed, his authority confronted, beaten, by stronger will. Shame-faced and silent, his men deserted. Flustered, without a choice, he soon followed.

No more needed to be said, no second glance needed to be given. As de Pontieux stood aside, Hardy and Fra Roberto led their formation past. There were greater imperatives. The alarm trumpet had ceased, had been replaced by the howl of the Turkish onslaught.

'They bring a new siege-engine, seigneur.'

'I note it well, Luqa.'

In the weary morning light, the dark presence of the tower hung immense above the bastion walls. The enemy learned well from their mistakes. There would be no running out of the cannon and systematic demolition of the whole. This time the base of the engine was protected by a barrier of earth and stone. Nothing would break through. Within, dominating the strewn and wasted Christian lines, the Janissary sharpshooters were already finding their mark. Knights and soldiers flattened. The beginning of the next few hours.

'We are pinned by them, seigneur.' The boy squinted uncertainly at the edifice.

'Even the loftiest giant may fall.'

'How so, seigneur? You have an idea?'

'Always, Luqa.' He forced the head of the youngster back into cover. 'We stay low and retreat. We return to our earlier excavation.'

With that, he slithered into reverse, backing sinuously away while musket-shot embedded itself around. Luqa joined him, snaking on his belly, crawling fast into a gully and disappearing into the descent. Little wonder he had eluded the Turk at St Elmo, the Englishman mused. He levered himself over in pursuit.

His squad were assembled beside the temporary gun-port reopened in the wall.

'We again tunnel through, Christian.'

'Your effort is not wasted.'

'There is no remedy for such stout construction. They counter bar-shot with earth and rock.'

'Then we shall counter them.'

'With what, Christian?'

'Something befitting that they least suspect.'

'Send to them our Fra Roberto.'

The priest laughed heartily at the joke. Around him, the ragged band of defenders checked their muskets, stropped blades on whetstones, or bent their heads in prayer. Dulled resignation had replaced fervour. They knew what they faced – had faced it too long.

'I ask for men who are keen of eye and fleet of foot.'

'We all would volunteer.'

'Eight will suffice, with further eight to guard our progress.'

'Progress, Christian? You mean to launch attack?'

'Through this very portal.'

'Impossible.'

'Each day we prove naught is beyond the possible.' Hardy collected his firearms. 'We take the tower.'

'I am with you, Christian.'

'I also.'

'I too will carry fight to the heart of the heathen.' Soldiers crowded round.

Hardy raised his hand. 'I thank you, my brothers. Make quick. Form on Knight Commander Claramont and Chevalier de Pereira.'

'Which weapons shall we choose?'

'Two arquebus apiece. There will be scant time to reload in the thick of it.'

'Incendiaries?'

'None. We seize the monster, and turn it with cannon and musket against its creators.'

'The remainder of us, Christian? Are we to keep watch for your return?'

'Replace the stones once we are through; attend us at its summit. We either scale the ladders, secure each floor, or we are dead in our attempt.'

Last preparations were made, final farewells and entreaties to God offered up. Fra Roberto delivered his blessing.

'Travel well and kill in rage, you fearsome dogs. Whatever medicine you deliver, it will contain the fire of the Lord, shall burn out their throats and bellies.'

'The cure may yet kill us all, Fra Roberto.'

With a nod to his men, Hardy ducked into the opening. In seconds he was through, part-crawling and part-sprinting for the target. The raiding-party were behind, fanning out for skirmish across the unevenness of rock-fall and ditch, closing on the parapets. They were over. In the midst of battle, no one had noticed their arrival, none would pick out figures dodging low through the flame and mist.

Hardy moulded himself against a rough wooden beam. This close, the tower blocked the light, could steal the breath and courage from a man. He looked back along the cracked Birgu walls, saw only smoke, the struggling mass of the Turk climbing and falling. At least they were diverted. For a brief period the siege-engine was oasis, an object ignored, a fire platform keeping the heads of the Knights down and the eyes of its Janissary residents trained.

'We are visitors they do not foresee. Let us pay our respects.'

'Pay them with God and gunpowder and steel.'

The ascent began.

Luqa had attempted to join the mission. As the end detail slipped into the opening, he stepped forward with a short stabbing-sword in his hand. Perhaps with luck he could avoid attention, provide reinforcement wherever the enemy proved too stubborn. His friends trusted him, needed him. He got no further. The broad and fatherly arm of Fra Roberto encircled him in its restraining grip.

'I am too large for their venture. You are too small.'

The youngster resisted. 'I have fought everywhere, will fight now.'

'Know the limit to your strength, boy.'

'Keen of eye and fleet of foot. That is I.'

'You have many qualities, yet discernment is not among them.'

'I will have my day.'

'It is not this one.'

'Release me, seigneur priest. God wills me to action.'

'He wills me to bind you here until you speak sense.'

'I must go.'

'You shall stay.'

Luqa was kicking, his desperation growing, his feet drumming powerlessly against the sides of his captor. The priest was not for moving.

'Impatience is no virtue, boy.'

'I am a soldier. You have no right.'

'You have no say. I am Fra Roberto.'

The hole through which Hardy and his troops had passed was being sealed. Luqa whimpered, his disconsolate fury complete.

'Why, seigneur priest? Why deny my chance to kill infidels, to support my comrades in this hour?'

'And I ask you, Why does Christian Hardy succeed? Because, for all his skill and daring, he thinks. Do the same, Luqa.'

'I think I like you not, old priest.'

Fra Roberto cuffed him and relinquished his hold. 'Reflect harder.'

A reluctant smile glimmered on the face of the boy. Beneath his dejection was recognition. To be a man was to put aside petty sentiment. To be a soldier was to do more than wield slingshot or blade.

'Forgive me, seigneur priest.'

Fra Roberto took and clasped the proffered hand. 'Amity is restored. But there is yet work and trial ahead. We must repair to the subsided roof of this bastion and await emergence of our brothers from the heathen nest.'

'What does the seigneur Hardy plan?'

'Devilment, you may be sure of it.'

He stood for a while, listening to the hue and din of surrounding battle, pondering the departure of Christian Hardy and his meagre brood. *The cure may yet kill us, Fra Roberto . . . The cure may yet kill.* Concern tugged at his subconscious, different thoughts worrying at his mind. Images of the black Moor, of Hubert, of the Grand Master appeared and would not leave. Arsenic had poisoned La Valette, had frayed his beard, had brought the great man crashing to his knees. And the scrawny novice priest had discovered calomel, the common bowel-encouragement of no importance. Illness brought medicine, ointments and tartar emetic; treatment could beget illness. Everything overlooked, designed to go ignored. The traitor had been clever.

'You are troubled, seigneur priest?'

'I find confluence and connection.'

'Both summer and Turk fade, Jean Parisot.'

'I fear I do the same.'

Knight Grand Cross Lacroix sponged water on the forehead of the Grand Master. Still convalescing, he had answered the call, had emerged from the infirmary to nurse dutifully his commander and friend. These were grim and desolate days. Fever and delirium alternated with lucidity; calm repose was interspersed with violent spasm. La Valette weakened. His fiefdom fared no better. Beyond his sickbed in the dark confines of the Conventual Church, his surviving apostles clung on, held out. Thursday 6 September 1565, the one-hundred-and-tenth day of invasion. The margins of existence.

'We Grand Crosses and Knights Commander who remain would urge your remove to St Angelo, Jean Parisot.'

'I destroyed its drawbridge for sound reason. While I breathe, I breathe here.'

'With traitor loose, it is something you breathe at all.'

'Can a renegade harm me worse than surgeon with knife and bleeding-bowl? I take my chances with the rest.'

'I take none. Guards are posted at door of this church; your page is commanded to pour water from sealed vessel. Each morsel you eat will first be tasted.'

'And you declare surprise I did not acquaint you of the threat sooner?' If La Valette joked, it was lost in a shuddering cough. 'I need no guards against my brethren. Send them to the walls, where they have use.'

'I crave forgiveness for my countermand.'

'Perhaps our villain is no more, is counted among our thousands slain.'

'I say again, I take no chance.'

'For seasoned warrior, you fret so.'

'It is no more than I owe to my Order and Grand Master.'

'Each is thankful. Yet I was protected well by Monsieur Hardy and my late nephew Henri, was kept a step ahead of the assassin.'

'You lie now enfeebled.'

'Is it poison or natural infirmity, my wounds or the frailties of advanced age? How may we determine reason for my plight?'

'I should have been informed, Jean Parisot.'

'I saw no need.'

'Young Hardy is a fine soldier, has elan and abilities which rouse our defence and rekindle our spirit. To you and me he is son and brother, has an aspect in which we see our youthful selves. But he is not from among the Knights, neither watches nor comprehends the plots and machination of the Sacro Consiglio. Villainy is afoot. That is the need, Jean Parisot.'

La Valette rested a hand on that of his friend. 'My life is unimportant against survival of the Religion. Monsieur Hardy captured the heathen siege-tower, placed in its scaffold heights our cannon to assail them from fresh vantage. My infirmity may grow. Theirs will yet outpace me.'

'I hope with my heart it is so, Jean Parisot.'

'The enemy fleet will be lashed by storms, its army by coming plague. They will escape neither if they remain.'

'It is we who will not escape if they remain.'

'However it is ordained, I shall stay at my post.'

A signal petard sounded, its mortar-shells bursting high and loud above the Birgu walls. Three distinct detonations. They came in response to message from Mdina, were answered again, replied in kind. No mistake. The Grand Master struggled to sit upright, his body and face contorting with spent effort. Outside there were shouts, thin pockets of cheering and musket-volleys drifting from the margins. The sound of angels.

Forgetting convention and himself, a herald threw wide the doors and rushed inside.

'Your Highness, there are ships! Relief is at hand!'

La Valette was slumped on his pillow.

Men and horses streamed ashore. The sea mist clung, the waters rolled heavy, but in the northern bays of Mgarr and Mellieha there would be no slowing in the landings. Emerging through the shallows, cavalry and infantry spread out to guard the beachhead and prevent Turk attack. Don Garcia de Toledo, Viceroy of Sicily, favoured caution, had proved it through months of prevarication and excuse. He need not have worried. The despondent forces of Mustapha Pasha remained festering on the Marsa; the fearful navy of Admiral Piali was barricaded at its moorings of Marsamuscetto and Marsasirocco. It was the perfect moment for invasion.

Quickly the Christian troops marched inland for Mdina and its adjoining village of Rabat. There they would quarter, prepare their ground, await the expected enemy counterstroke. Two hundred Knights and eight thousand infantry. A small force, a fraction of what had been promised. But they were on holy mission to avenge, to show that they too could acquit themselves with honour and panache. Don Garcia was the laggard, not they.

Messages were relayed by signal-gun and Maltese swimmer-couriers to the dying garrison of Birgu and Senglea. Word came back. Scarcely several hundred remained alive, few of them unwounded, and all would succumb in further Ottoman assault. Urgency was vital. The newcomers deliberated. They intended to act, understood the entreaties for immediate campaign on the enemy encampment. Yet they were few in number, might over-reach and risk defeat. The veteran leader of the Knights, Ascanio de la Corna, preached wariness. His second-in-command, Alvareze de Sandé, in charge of the Spanish regiment of Naples, advocated night attack. And Vincenti Vitelli, officer heading a force of Italian adventurers and European mercenaries, advised killing any infidel who moved. The result was stalemate. For the present they would consolidate their position on the high ground.

Mustapha Pasha was far from consolidating. He had already seen too much, had witnessed the galleys of Don Garcia diverting unopposed past Grand Harbour to offer encouragement and salute the populace of those besieged peninsulas. It was almost too much to bear, certainly too great a risk to remain on Malta. Christendom had landed with a vengeance and in force. There was little point in challenging the inevitable, in confronting the dark forces of the unbeliever. They might be twenty thousand strong or more – fresh troops restless to do battle, aching to extinguish every trace of the Turk. He could not match them. His men had battered themselves to inertia, scarce had the energy to drag themselves to the boats for embarkation. If only Piali had allowed him to take the north of the island. If only Piali had secured the approaches. If only Piali had attacked the relief army at sea. He knew who to blame, comprehended the scale of fiasco. The order was given.

✳

Chapter 18

Bewildered by the suddenness of silence, stupefied at the lifting of their torment, the survivors straggled from the smoking ruins. Tentatively, like skeletons emerging from a tomb, they picked their way across the deserted enemy lines. They expected a trap, the appearance of Spahis cresting the slopes of Corradino, a formation of Janissaries rising from cover. But there was nothing. Camp had been struck; the Turk was gone. Where the banners had flown and the guns had thundered was blackened desolation. Rotting carcasses of horses mingled with rat-eaten human remains; cooking-pots and weapons lay scattered as ungathered harvest. What had once been trenches were now hastily filled mass graves. The night sounds of creaking gun-carts, the flickering lines of Ottoman torches and illumination flares, had not lied. Exodus was complete. The air smelled of decay and victory.

Scouts were sent forward to Mount Sciberras. They reported back that the enemy were embarking in haste, the troops clambering to board galleys or being ferried out to waiting merchantmen. Everywhere was crowded confusion. Summary executions had been observed, officers attempting to restore order and imbue discipline where both had fled. Evacuation rarely conjured scenes of regulated calm.

The mounted reconnaissance moved on, navigating the craters and fire-positions, making their way down the hillside spine for the abandoned and blasted shell of St Elmo. There they raised the flag of St John, let the eight-pointed cross of their Order fly high above the vanquished heathen. Saturday 8 September 1565. The Feast of the Nativity of the Virgin. Christendom had won, and the bell of the Conventual Church rang out. The Great Siege was over.

Hardy cantered his borrowed steed towards Mdina. He had news and instruction for the relief force, had resisted temptation to stay and forage for jewels and booty. There was time enough for that, years in which to build a life, a family, with Maria. Unfinished labours remained, could divert him from plunder a while longer. They allowed him to ignore the searing pain in his thigh caused by a javelin-thrust, to delay grieving for his departed friends. Safety was in avoidance.

Steel glinted on the ridge-line, quickening his pulse, marking the location of the arrived army. A proud sight of fluttering pennants and gilded crests. So bright, so different to the dulled and dented armour, the limestone dust and grim coagulations of blood that infested his world. He was free. If there was to be action against the fleeing Turk, he would be in the vanguard. Astride Helios, he would gallop with the chevaliers, charge down the foe as he had at Zeitun, as he had on the Marsa. It was who he was. He craved a proper ending and the peacefulness of combat, not the disappointment of gentle and stuttering comple-tion.

'Christian.'

He recognized the voice and roguish smile, dismounted to greet his old gaming and sparring partner Vincenti Vitelli.

'You are late for the fray as ever, Vincenti.'

The Italian adventurer shrugged. 'A viceroy averse to danger, a storm that scattered our ships and near drowned us all. Yet we are here.'

'We are grateful, old friend.'

'And you, Christian?'

'Alive for the present.'

'In Sicily we heard tell of your deeds. You have suffered for them.'

'My brothers in Birgu, Senglea and St Elmo suffered more.'

'Such pluck and valour.' Pity and admiration filled his eyes as he surveyed the wounds and battle-scars. 'There shall be time yet for stories. What of the Grand Master?'

'He is well,' Hardy lied.

'His garrison?'

'Most are dead, decaying behind walls that have ceased to be.'

'We feared so. The fury of the Turk, the thunder of the cannon, carried far to us on the wind.'

'It did not hasten you to our shore.'

Another grin. 'And yet without us your haggard band wins full victory.'

'Victory is incomplete. The enemy withdraw in disarray to their galleys; we send up guns to harry them from Mount Sciberras. It is your turn to give chase.'

'They flee. Let us celebrate for it.'

'No, Vincenti.' Hardy placed a hand on his shoulder and stared in his eyes. 'La Valette bids you descend upon the foe, strike them in the hour of their departure.'

'Would that I might.'

'You arrive equipped for war, not to stand idle on this hillside.'

'Look at them, Christian. Each would dear wish to plunge into the heathen, to find redress, to search for golden prize. But, while the will is strong, our commanders are opposed, our ranks are sparse.'

'Sparse may do much.'

'It may also be frittered on costly venture.'

'You speak to me of cost, Vincenti?'

'I speak to you as brother, as warrior, as seer of truth. Stay with me here. Together we shall witness events.'

'I cannot be content with mere observation.'

'Then busy yourself with preparation.'

He would do that, would saddle up Helios and sharpen his sword, would reconnoitre forward to the edge of the receding Ottomans. Perhaps he should accept it, should watch the Turkish fleet pull away as he had once watched it sail in. The relief army was right to hold the high ground. He was happier in descending to the low.

Antonio was advancing on him, his joy uncontained. 'Our island is saved, Christian.'

'Able now to feast and entertain our courtly visitors from the north.' Hardy glanced at Vincenti before embracing the young Maltese noble. 'We are instructed to abide till the hateful Saracen is gone.'

'For our island nation, I must thank you, Christian.'

'What regard is owed to me that is not due us all? I recall it was you who brought me safe from capture aboard the corsair galley, you who rode with me in sally against the Turk encampment.'

'I would do so a thousandfold, Christian.'

'That is good, for we are now the two of us tied. Maria is my wife.'

Delight flared anew on Antonio's face. 'I am overjoyed, my brother.'

'Your father would hold opinion of a different hue.'

'He is disgraced; his comments stand for naught.'

'Yet he is still your father. When all is done, I shall seek reconciliation and his blessing.'

'You may count on mine.'

'*Monsieur Hardy, ever thus the vagabond.*'

Ascanio de la Corna, wise, respected, appeared with a gaggle of his captains. He was a strong advocate of tradition, a rigorous enforcer for the Religion and its code.

'I approve of neither your morals nor your outlook, Englishman. But I travel here with Vincenti Vitelli. It breeds pliancy and acceptance in a man.'

'We prove our worth in many ways, sir.'

'You fight hard in defence of the Order. For it I salute you, and will find you employ.'

'I remain servant of the Grand Master.'

'You become attendant to our wider cause.'

Hardy bowed. Others were converging, crowding for news, gathering to touch the hem and hear the words of a hero of the battle. They urged him to talk of the final stand at St Elmo, of the months beneath the Turkish guns, of the last valiant moments of their friends and compatriots. He could not explain. And they could not know the bloody ecstasy and rush, would not grasp the sorrow and rapture, the drudgery of survival or the thrill of death. Making excuse, and with Antonio at his side, he made for the main gate of the city. Helios would be waiting.

Another member of the Birgu garrison was undertaking a journey. From the rocky slopes of Mount Sciberras, the traitor watched the activities of the Turks in Marsamuscetto harbour. They had not ventured across the seas for this; he had not striven and murdered and poisoned in order that they should turn tail. Mustapha Pasha had been duped. At each turn, with every tactic, he had seen his efforts thwarted, his troops slaughtered, and the Knights succeed. Now, unsettled by sightings of Christian reinforcements, the Turk general was loading his spent and defeated force for passage home. A little premature. The traitor scanned the pulsing throng, listened to the frantic shouts and bustling commotion. He had once held such high hopes. Disappointment could be a positive impulse, would outweigh the risk.

'An infidel! Kill him!'

'He carries flag of truce.'

'It is a trick. We cannot trust the unbeliever.'

'Then trust instead to reason. One man alone is no army.'

'Satan travels in any guise.'

Arquebuses were trained, debate continued as the startled pickets viewed the spectre emerging from the scree. He was cowled, unarmed, his step assured and slow. It could foster confidence or breed nervousness.

'I come to parley.'

'We sail. There is no virtue in discussion.'

The visitor held the man in a steady gaze. 'Let Mustapha Pasha be the judge.'

'What is your identity?'

'None that is concern to mere sentry.'

'You are unwise to scorn those who may slay you.'

'I believe it the less wise to threaten one who may save you.'

'Save us? Your venture is misguided.'

'Shoot me and you will never know.'

The stranger spoke their tongue, was measured and untroubled in a manner distinct from average herald or usual deserter. He was probably a senior Knight, possibly the Devil himself. They would seek out an officer for advice.

Conferring and decision took time. The traitor was patient, as he had been throughout. He saw messengers set out and return, the deliberations of juniors with their seniors, of seniors with their equals. His arrival had plainly caused disturbance in what was already disordered. The Moslems had set their minds and hearts on withdrawal. His mission was to turn them back.

He was escorted through, taken as guest or prisoner deeper into the moving host. The stench of defeat assailed him. But he was closer to where he wished to be, travelling up the chain of command. The harbour-front, a gangplank, the poop deck of a magnificent galley. Mustapha Pasha faced him.

'Is this madness which brings you hither?'

'Common purpose.'

'Infidel, I could command your most uncommon death.'

'The chance I take bears witness to the greatness of the reward.'

'To be cut into a thousand pieces, to have flesh seared from the bones is no reward.'

'Yet destruction of the Christians is, Mustapha Pasha.'

The General observed him for a moment, his dark eyes small and dangerous. 'You are the spy?'

'That has been my duty and my calling.'

'You fail.'

'Harsh verdict on one whose loyalty has served you well.'

'Who achieves nothing.' Mustapha Pasha stared at the man. 'You pledged to bring low the garrison from within. It is we who retreat.'

'What will they say of you in Constantinople? That you were weak, a coward, a commander in his dotage who ran when challenged?'

'Vultures will soon pick out your eyes and tongue, infidel.'

'Then we share equal fate. Let us use our time.'

'I have no time for riddles, as you have none to live.'

'You scamper for your boats, fear the relief force of the Christians will any instant be upon you. Rest awhile. Ask how it could be, if the enemy is so mighty, it hesitates, draws back, does not descend on you as vengeful wolf upon the fold.'

'They have their reason.'

'Weakness is chief cause. They number as few as eight thousand men, were carried in mere twenty-eight vessels.'

'My scouts estimate more formidable foe.'

'A matter of deception and rumour, its purpose to vex and put you to flight.'

'Yours is the act of deception, infidel. Am I to believe your lies, to endanger my army on the word of a spy, a traitor to his own cause, a deficiency to mine?'

'I endanger myself to reach you.'

Mustapha Pasha began to pace the deck, his eyes darting, his mind diverted. Around him, the hollering of soldiers and stevedores, the crack of rawhide lashes across the naked backs of slaves swelled in orchestrated unison. Galleys were casting off; momentum climbed. Beyond them, the Mediterranean. They were approaching the point of no return.

'You advised from the beginning the Viceroy of Sicily would send no reinforcement, infidel.'

'It was the belief of the Grand Master himself.'

'A Grand Master destined to be poisoned by you, intended to be ripped from the bosom of his Knights.'

'He is, as I speak, in final throes of his demise.'

'Promise upon undelivered promise. You gave notice that the capital, Mdina, lay defenceless, would succumb to the slightest skirmish.'

'What you saw was more illusion and trickery, the artful placing of women and children in armour on its walls.' The traitor was emollient and calm. 'No fault or artifice of mine has caused you ill, Mustapha Pasha.'

'Yet somehow I feel it.'

'Regard how I signalled by lamp the passage of reinforcements to St Elmo. Consider how I used fire and fuse to dismantle powder-mill in St Angelo, ordnance store in Senglea.'

'I cannot deny, of some advantage.'

'Of critical import.'

'Set against it your rash counsel to commit my men into the tunnels below St Angelo. It cost me dear.'

'Which war is not of some expense, Mustapha Pasha?'

'One where I am offered victory by stealth and secret agent, by guaranteed annihilation of Grand Master La Valette.'

'I have stripped him of his allies, neutered his guards and confidants. Now I take him to the threshold.'

'As we depart.'

'Rescind your order. It is not too late.'

'More speech, duplicity, from an infidel stranger I trust not.'

'Do you trust your Sultan to display clemency, your people to show you understanding?'

'Concern yourself with your own short future.'

'I concern myself with what we may yet attain. Triumph, Mustapha Pasha. Leave, and you walk from history, abandon this single chance to remedy ill, to erase the Order, to write yourself into the annals of Ottoman renown.'

The words were hypnotic, plucked at the Turk's vanity, played on his doubts. To be defeated was one thing, to be foiled by dissimulation another. There was reason to retreat and incentive to stay. Mustapha Pasha turned back to the spy.

'What of the man they call Christian Hardy?'

'Sent with dispatch to the relief force. You will find him there.'

'He took my finest Arab stallion, spirited away my corsair captain El Louck Aly Fartax.'

'Through luck he has thwarted our many ploys, both yours and mine. The plank bridge of St Elmo and slave tunnels of St Angelo, the infernal machine delivered to St Michael, the siege-engines drawn up beside the Castile bastion.'

'Some fighter.'

'An impudent rogue, Mustapha Pasha. One who, through his friends, warned La Valette of attempt on his life.'

'Yet the Englishman is human, susceptible to fate.'

'Vulnerable to the vicissitude of war, to the force of your advancing army.'

'He taunts us.'

'They all of them do so, Mustapha Pasha. Each surviving Knight, each soldier arrived from Sicily, each Maltese noble or peasant who breathes within Birgu, Senglea or Mdina.'

A decision had been taken. It showed in the cruel blankness, in the set of the face and the tilt of the beard, in the way fingers caressed the jewelled hilt of a scimitar. Mustapha Pasha was returning to battle.

He peered at the spy. 'Go now. I have campaign to end. You have Grand Master to finish.'

'What is it we seek, Fra Roberto?'

'I know not until we find it.'

The priest turned another page and continued to study the Latin text. Maria watched him, a bundle of documents in her arms. For so large a man, he approached his task with surprising care. It was fortunate he had once been secretary to the Supreme Council. He frowned and put the book aside.

'Hours spent and volumes read, and still I discern nothing.'

'There is much to peruse.'

'We shall dwell on papers and parchment that come from Rome, those collected by the Order while in exile.'

'Why Rome, Fra Roberto?'

'The darkest of arts have been practised and find nexus there, are born and nurtured within the papacy, the great families and the city states.'

'Murder?'

'Every wile and crime imagined, my lady.' He cleared room for the fresh documents.

'They would not by necessity be written down.'

'We must pray they are.'

'Yet which Hospitaller is versed in these bloodthirsty ways?'

'Blood is our creed. We drink that of Christ; we shed it of the Moslem heathen.'

'You are Knights and brothers.'

'It is merely our vestments and cross which divide us from the savage beast or most barbarous of corsair.'

'Noble and holy cause lends righteousness to your acts.'

Fra Roberto shook his head. 'An ancient Order is sum of many parts and nations, of dim and hidden recesses. Hearts and minds are not always so virtuous or pure as our sacred vows purport. In skilful hands, medicine may become poison, cure may act as curse.'

'The Grand Master falls prey to such plot?'

'I believe it so, my lady. And I vouch we must find with haste the culprit and his method.'

He returned to his research, his skilled hands and expert eyes working through the scripts. It was not a silent affair. He would sigh and nod, puff out his cheeks, talk to himself or shout aloud. But they would not be interrupted. In the closing hours of this conflict, men and women were giving thanks or scouring for treasure. And in the darkness of the conventual Church the life of the victorious La Valette hovered. The medical library was a place few Hospitallers would be visiting.

Frustrated, the priest slammed shut the tome. 'A is for arsenic, and I have yet to reach the beginning.'

'The assassin has yet to achieve result.'

'His outlook is long.'

'Too long, Fra Roberto. The Turk leaves and we are delivered.'

'True, I grant you.'

'Then our traitor is beaten.'

'It is possible. Yet La Valette still wanes.' The priest rocked back in his seat. 'A chain of events gives birth to sequence of medicine. Arsenic engenders sickness; sickness encourages purge.'

'What follows purge?'

'Greater sickness, for tartar emetic is no remedy for symptoms of arsenic.'

'Which symptoms are these?'

'Among them, the burning flux, raging thirst, blockage to passing of the stool. La Valette is given potion for each, and they combine to kill him.'

'Such circuitous route to death.'

'Designed to seem of natural cause. And Christian slowed it – with Henri, persuaded Jean Parisot to reside among his men in Birgu.'

'He did not confide it in me.'

'For your safety. The Moor was felled by hand unseen, perhaps others beside. There is danger in knowledge.'

'Concealed purpose in every quarter.'

'Some wish to replace La Valette, to speed his journey. Others have wider ambition: to erase the Religion. De Pontieux or Prior Garza, Knights who sought withdrawal to Sicily or retreat to St Angelo, mutinous souls among the Spanish infantry.' Fra Roberto reached for a bundle of parchment. 'All of them or none. We maintain our effort.'

A sound of scampering feet, and the worried face of Luqa appeared. He was in haste to report, sending the printed piles tumbling.

'My lady . . . seigneur priest.'

'Panting interruption bodes not well.' Fra Roberto pointed to the purse tied at the boy's waist. 'The magpie of Malta has busied himself with his collecting.'

'I have news.'

'You achieve a fine haul. Deliver up your purse for my inspection.'

'I make my report.'

'Obey me, boy.'

Reluctantly, Luqa complied, tipping the glittering contents of the bag out on to the table. They were gemstones and charms, the harvest of adroit grazing on Turkish dead. Luqa flushed, ashamed, as Fra Roberto pinched an emerald between thumb and forefinger and held it to the window light.

'What wondrous lustre. You went beyond the walls?'

'I did.'

'Ignoring strict instruction to tarry beside the Conventual Church, to watch and listen, to warn us of any happening.'

'I warn you now, seigneur priest. His Highness the Grand Master La Valette is borne away to St Angelo.'

'On whose authority?'

'That of his most senior Knights.'

Fra Roberto was scooping up books and loose pages, packing them into a piece of sackcloth. Mystified, Maria looked on.

'La Valette is carried back to his palace, Fra Roberto. What is its meaning?'

'Its meaning?' The priest did not pause. 'He is taken home to die. Our traitor is unleashed.'

Luqa was frantically gathering up his trophies.

And so it had come to pass. The Grand Master was returned to St Angelo where he belonged, where he would be tended, cared for and finally killed. Kindness and charity could do that. The traitor observed the scene through the doorway to the chamber. How the servants fretted, how the few remaining allies and companions strove to make the old man comfortable in his decline. They were wasting their time, and his. La Valette died of his infected wounds, they would say. It did not matter what they said. The Grand Master of the Hospital had become a patient, was about to become a corpse. Hardly a victorious homecoming.

He watched a page dampen the dry lips and withered face with water. Such little dignity in these closing stages. La Valette might have been remembered as one of the greats, yet now was unlikely to be remembered at all. They would weep and process through the streets, deliver fine eulogy. Their triumphant celebrations would be tempered with pathos and tragedy. The bitter-sweetness, the farce. It was to be cut short. For at any hour the Turk would relaunch attack and rout the Christian army at Mdina, would return to Birgu and complete the task. Unaware, La Valette took another sip. So he lingered, murmuring prayers, a Bible in one hand, the book of hours belonging to his late nephew Henri resting in the other.

Water would not slake his raging thirst. Nor could it save him. There would come a time when they brought orgeat, the quenching drink of orange-juice and oil of bitter almonds. How thoughtful of them, and how careless. Bitter almonds contained prussic acid, which, when combined with calomel, the mercury-chloride cure for constipation and stomach cramp, reacted to produce something rather special. *Mercury cyanide*. La Valette could not vomit it out; the tartar emetic had seen to that. His body could not fight it, for the long-term arsenic poisoning had weakened him so. The result would be massive swelling of the pylorus muscle, the rapid onset of paralysis, then unconsciousness and death. Everything disguised, every step explained away. His masters had much to thank him for.

The Christians had been quick to bring up their cannons to St Elmo. It was mostly bravado, a parting shot to the enemy as its troops struggled to embark and break free of the crowded Marsamuscetto waters. Each booming report strengthened the sense of defeat, each round that struck was reminder of the cost and waste in taking the fort. But the defenders above detected change. Boats were again landing, soldiers were being ferried and marshalled ashore. It could not be. A blast of trumpets informed them it was.

In a command-tent pitched hastily on a rock shelf, Mustapha Pasha and Admiral Piali faced each other.

'Can you not see the madness in your action, Mustapha Pasha?'

'What I see is chance to redeem ourselves. What I see is your betrayal, your failure to intercept the infidels when at sea.'

'You will not sully me with such accusation.'

'It may wait, Piali. For the present, I have appointment with a different foe.'

'Your men are faint and disheartened.'

'I am not.'

'They are scarce ready to crawl to their berths, and you ask that they fight?'

'It is the duty of imperial soldiers to serve well their Sultan.'

'The obligation of commanders-in-chief to show wisdom.'

'Have you that quality?'

Piali balled his fists, his spine stiffening. The old cur should know better than to insult him, to have spent the dreary months of summer taunting and mocking. The Admiral had plans for Mustapha Pasha. He would ensure close encounter with assassin or executioner upon return to Constantinople. Before rumour spread, before reputation was irretrievably blackened.

He found himself thinking of the Maltese girl brought to his quarters, of her rare beauty and obvious breeding. She had managed to flee, had slipped his grasp as surely as her island nation too had done. So much had been lost. Her image faded, was replaced by that of the General.

'Take your galleys seven miles hence to the bay of St Paul's. Attend me there, Piali.'

'While you join battle with enemy whose strength you make light of.'

'I never misjudge an adversary. And I have my army.'

'Army?' Piali pulled aside the drapes of the tent. 'A rabble; a collection of sick and dying. How do you propose to rouse them to combat, to commit them to the front?'

'A naval whore who hides his fleet, who prefers wine and indolence to the rigours of war, presumes to question me?'

'You head for disaster.'

'Better noble disaster than ignoble disgrace. In three months I have lost near thirty thousand men, have buried the legend Dragut, the Lieutenant Aga of Janissaries, the Master of Ordnance. What do we gain for it?'

'We are weak, Mustapha Pasha.'

'They the weaker. Scarce but a handful stand at Birgu and Senglea.'

'More on the ridges before Mdina.'

'The very reason I march.'

'I cannot countenance it, Mustapha Pasha.'

'You . . . cannot . . . countenance it?'

The old soldier repeated the words, slow, venomous. His battle was not simply with the infidel. It was with this languid jester, this unfit admiral beyond his depth, at sea when called upon to fight. He was a product of court, and the royal court had grown soft and effete. It would be left to real generalship to restore the glory of the Ottoman.

'Where there is enemy army there is hostile fleet, Mustapha Pasha.'

'Perhaps you should seek it out as I do that army.'

'Don Garcia de Toledo will come again from Sicily. We shall be trapped.'

'Your fleet will wait on station as ordered.'

'I am no handmaiden to your misadventure. My ships leave for Turkey.'

Mustapha Pasha was upon him, slapping and raking his face, ripping jewels from his gown and turban. He was a powerful man, and age did not diminish his fury. Piali attempted to protect himself. But the blows broke through, producing blood and garbled pleas as the General warmed to his theme.

'I will not be cheated of my prize, will not have this island snatched from my grasp.' Mustapha Pasha had drawn his dagger, pressed its curved blade to the throat of the cowering Admiral. 'Remain at St Paul's, or by the beard of the Prophet you will die on this ledge.'

He took the nod as acquiescence and rose to his feet. There would be no further argument, no delay to the ongoing campaign. All that mattered was mustering his troops. By day-end they would be standing on the bleeding remains of another batch of presumptuous Knights.

Without turning to view the prone Piali, he strode from the tent. Before him was the agreeable sight of an expanse of troops reassembling, of muskets being checked, of Spahis exercising their mounts. The moments before expedition. His men would rise to his demands. Their complaints meant nothing; their hunger, their wounds, their sickness paled against the call of empire and the radiance of its Sultan.

The enemy gunners found their target. In a spray of blood and bone-marrow, a solid ball of iron completed its trajectory among a squad of waiting levies. It could not be helped. Mustapha Pasha swung himself heavily into the saddle of a nearby horse. He was ready to move out.

✠

Chapter 19

'Here is the conclusion you seek, Christian.'
Vincenti Vitelli pointed. It was as though a discoloured fog had settled around Marsamuscetto, its radius spreading. Somewhere within was a Turkish army. It was travelling fast, heading north-west for Mdina. Mustapha Pasha was in a hurry to finish what he had begun. The newcomers had been misguided in their hopes of uncontested victory, were wrong to believe he would simply weigh anchor and sail. He relished the prospect of open fight. There would be no walls to climb, no ditches to negotiate, no incendiaries to overcome. He was settling scores, setting straight the historical record.

Helios quivered, skittish with anticipation, his nostrils flaring, his hooves stamping at the ground. Hardy steadied him. The vibration-thrill of impending combat affected everyone. To one side, Vitelli shaded his eyes and watched the oncoming cloud, his soldiers of fortune gathered behind. To the other, Antonio was adjusting his steel burgonet, the remnants of the Mdina cavalry clustered with him.

'They are the open jaws of hell itself.'

'The easier to plunge in the lance, Antonio.'

'We have no artifice to use this time, no women and children bearing pikes to unnerve the foe.'

'We will shake them enough.' Hardy leaned forward in his saddle, tried to distinguish the enemy formation. 'I am uncertain whether to applaud their daring or deride their folly.'

'Their commander is not one to quit.'

'Nor we, Antonio. It is the makings of fine battle.'

Across the climbing plain, rising on the slack and heavy air, the wail of Moslem horns, the crash of kettledrums and cymbals pulsed their war rhythm. It carried a message. The glory of Suleiman was untrammelled. Malta would yet fall.

A soldier muttered in the background. 'Is it not how the last trumpet shall sound, how the final battle twixt good and evil shall begin?'

'You are fortunate to be on the side of good.'

Vitelli shouted to his men. 'In God we place our trust.'

'*Praise be to Him!*' The chorus response was strong.

Hardy petted the neck of Helios and whispered in his ear. It was their usual communion before the charge. Others might put their faith in the Lord, but his own resided with his Andalusian mount, with his sword-arm, with Maria, with her brother at his side.

He looked along the ridge-line at the front ranks, at the waving pennants and the nodding heads of horses. The hopes of Europe, of the island, of the survivors at Grand Harbour rested with them and on this moment. Eight thousand men. They were a match for any Turks. There were Knights of St John in their battle surcoats, Knights of St Stephen wearing the red eight-pointed cross, Knights of Santiago with their symbol of paired and inverted fleur-de-lis swords. All sought to prove themselves equal to La Valette and his proud garrison.

'Heed my words, brother Knights and soldiers.' Ascanio de la Corna rode along the line. 'We hold the high ground. Do not forfeit it with rash and emboldened onslaught upon the heathen.'

'You expect us to whistle tunes and whittle wood?'

'I count on you to obey commands and maintain order. Conserve your force until required.'

'It is required now.'

'If one of us should break rank, the entire army may fold. The future is at stake.'

'Our future lies before us.'

'Rein in your eagerness and your mounts.' De la Corna raised his hand, addressed the growling throng. 'We are a military Order. We will not preserve the Religion through ill-judged escapade.'

'For too long did we sit on Sicily and listen to Don Garcia. For too long do we sit as statues astride our steeds.'

'Patience, brothers.'

'God wills us to act.'

'He commands you submit your hot tempers to our noble cause. You are the army of Christ, directed by His Holiness and the King of Spain. Led by me.'

The horse pranced and carried Ascanio de la Corna on. Behind came a page, a flag-bearer, a priest offering his benediction.

Vitelli snorted with mirth. 'Such pretty ritual for the slaughter that is to follow.'

'Enjoy while it lasts, Vincenti.'

'Perverse is it not, Christian? We create magnificent spectacle only for purpose of war. And only for purpose of war do we then smash it to a thousand pieces.'

'Man is a contrary beast.'

'Created in the image of his Maker. He must be a sour and bellicose God.'

'Whatever His nature, I credit He favours us this day.'

'You are sure of it, Christian?'

'I am versed in the Turk. They have vigour in the attack, but lack in the defence. Turn them, bewilder them, throw them from their path, and we have them routed.'

Vitelli grasped his hand. 'You may count on me.'

'On me also, Christian.' Antonio added his own gauntleted palm.

'So, brothers, we watch fate unfold and wait to ride.'

He could see them, the Christian relief grouped on the skyline, dominating the escarpment over which they looked. Mustapha

Pasha rode at the head of his column and kept his gaze on the spectacle. He had called their bluff. They did not appreciate that he knew, did not recognize he would soon expose their lie with total obliteration. They were straw men, hollow men, an itinerant mob of thrill-seekers and boastful drunks. And he had their measure.

'Cavalry will move to left and right flanks. Infantry will advance to the centre.'

His orders were relayed, the force ripple-spreading like the giant opening of petals. The flower of Turkey. So they were tired and hungry, injured and diseased. They were still the pre-eminent troops of their age, hardened by experience, imbued with holy zeal. A standing army. It would leave none standing.

From his saddle, an emir spat in the dust. 'I like it not that the infidel commands the heights, Mustapha Pasha.'

'We shall entice them down.'

'What then? The full velocity of their charge will strike and fracture us.'

'That is not my intent. They are nothing against our arquebusiers and horsemen, will shatter on the steel of our blades.'

'Their troops are fresh, Mustapha Pasha.'

'Ours have experience.'

'Yet I hear their complaints, sense the diminishing of their passions.'

'Fire rekindles itself in heat of battle.' The commander-in-chief nodded towards the enemy. 'See these unbelievers. They are thieves, brigands, consumed with greed and made of nothing. Devoid of ramparts, without stratagem or control, they will crumble to our touch.'

'They put on fine display.'

'It is pretence before the fall.'

He twisted to watch his units move up, the Spahis galloping out in heady exhibition. How he would regale the Sultan with memories of this moment, as one soldier to another. Piali could doubt.

Piali could conspire. Piali could sit trembling aboard his galley. It would be recorded that the Admiral played no part in this victory.

'We take prisoner an enemy scout, Mustapha Pasha.'

'Bring him before me.'

The Spahi officer wheeled his horse and quickened away to join his men in the outlying fields. He was just one of many, another figure moving within greater movement, lost among the forces forming up for battle. Mustapha Pasha stared at the enemy. Not long now before he broke them; not long before he passed through the smouldering ruins of Birgu to examine the mortal remains of former Grand Master Jean Parisot de La Valette.

'Behold the captive, Mustapha Pasha.'

It hardly merited his attention. The native was bleeding, a Maltese horseman bound and thrown at his feet, angular with pain and trepidation.

'Raise him.' He would speak Italian. 'You are unfortunate indeed to fall into our hands. What did you seek to find?'

'Information.'

'I will gladly provide it, will demonstrate to your masters the error of their plan.'

'You will be defeated.'

'A slave who finds both courage and voice. The Knights are no friend of your island.'

'Nor is the Turk who comes with armada and cannon.'

'To save your souls, to wrest this rock from the grasp of the infidel occupier.' Mustapha Pasha raised his arm towards Mdina. 'Even your walled and ancient city was once built by Moslem traders. We are your people and brothers, share common heritage.'

'Yet you fight us.'

'What has value that is not worth shedding blood for?'

'It is your blood that will be spilt. You will not hold back the tide, cannot deflect the coming judgement.'

'A general as well as mere scout.'

'An islander defending his home.'

'You wish to pass message to your commanders and country-men?'

'If that is your will and my fate.'

Mustapha Pasha drew his scimitar and flicked its blade to catch the light. The captive understood. They were the common rules of engagement, eternal laws which deemed the lowliest of no worth and the likeliest to die. For a local primitive he took it well, as a man, received the eviscerating blow from his chestbone to his pelvis. Fleetingly, he glanced down at the flooding wound. His expression changed and he dropped.

'First blood is to the army of the Grand Turk. Send him on his way.'

'A scout with the Devil on his tail.'

The horse carried its rider in frantic flight up the incline, its mane and tail streaming with panicked abandon. It was only as it drew close, stampeded along the Christian line, that the reason for its wayward ascent became clear. The horseman would not be reporting. His eyes were gouged out, his tongue removed, his belly slit open.

'Thus do we bait and tease before our worlds collide.' Antonio viewed the passing image and crossed himself.

Hardy was studying the Turks below. 'More terrible sights will yet appear. See how their commander makes his dispositions.'

'They spread across a wide front.'

'Permitting us to find their weakest join, to exploit the fading eagerness of their force.'

'Mustapha Pasha is a man possessed.'

'His troops are possessed of nothing but desire to flee. Constantinople beckons. We must ensure they first reach Purgatory.'

'Why is he so reckless, Christian? Why does he gamble his fortunes in this way?'

337

'He is a general who knows only the offensive, a soldier whose chief adviser is his God.'

'Powerful motive, Christian.'

'Or calamitous mistake.'

'*Who is with me? Who will confront and slay the cursed heathen?*'

Vincenti Vitelli stood in the stirrups of his rearing horse and waved his sword. The Italian was not about to abide by any rule, had no intention of being denied the sweet discovery of fame, gemstones and soft infidel throats awaiting on the plain.

He shouted to his men. 'To trounce the foe we must meet him, while to rest is a sin! Will you deliberate and debate while there is work to do? Will you stand by when your brothers have battled without pause these hundred days and twelve? Our time is here!'

With that he spun his mount and charged. His horsemen followed, Knights too, lost to the frenzy of the moment, focused only on the need to close with and kill the enemy. They surged over the lip of the ridge, gathering momentum that drew others behind.

'They must sound the general charge, Christian.'

'We cannot wait for it, Antonio. And I cannot hold Helios.'

Hardy and the young Maltese noble spurred into the chase. The rest of the Mdina cavalry was with them, disobeying orders which were already forgotten. Alongside were the officers of de la Corna, abandoning their posts, heading for blood and glory. It was a vibration that grew to a thundering roar. The trumpet call came, whether for recall or advance it made no difference. Along the entire length of the line, the army of the Christians was descending on the Turk.

A rhythmic beat had started in his head, the drumming of hooves, the pulse of his heart. It hypnotized, stilled time. He saw the enemy unfurled and anonymous before him, saw the rushing forms of men and horses glide in for the attack. In places, infantry soldiers hung between war-horses in their haste to reach the front.

Everyone was caught in the madness, hurtled with joy into the waiting host.

'To the right, Antonio! Let us loose our havoc!'

They struck, their energy travelling on, rippling through. Noise and fury detonated. Helios did as he was trained or bidden, back-kicking an Iayalar, forward-stamping a dismounted Spahi. Above, Hardy engaged in his own battle, exploiting confusion, searching for opportunity. A Janissary approached, his skirmish-axe raised. It was too little, and Hardy felled him with a single curving blow. On his right, a levy jabbed at him with a pike, but was run through from behind. Beside him, a cavalryman took an arrow and fell screaming to merge with the writhing ground.

'With me, brothers! The Spahis must be countered!'

He led a troop through, their horses wading in the human mire as they sought to find their darting quarry. The black plumes of the Turk riders were circling. The enemy were picking off Knights, loosing their arrows, moving in to isolate and kill. But they would not go uncontested. Hardy and his force were upon them, pursuing them with lances, bringing them down with swords and battle-hammers. The threat was neutralized; others appeared.

Battle had fragmented into a thousand separate shards of incident and horror. German mercenaries, wielding great *Zweihänder* swords about their heads, cut bloody channels through the enemy ranks. In one strike, a seven-foot blade removed five heads; in another, a pair of peacock officers were sheared in half. Then came the Spaniards, their pikes and rapiers bristling, and the Italians, hacking aside resistance with their scythes and billhooks. Mob rule, and this mob thirsted.

A sudden squall of musket-shot buffeted the formation.

Antonio called, reining round his horse. 'Christian, they have the tower and train their marksmen upon us!'

'We shall reclaim it! Keep with me and call infantry!'

His friend did not answer. Within seconds, he had been

surrounded by a group of Janissaries, was slashing with his sabre, struggling to remain upright and in possession of his scalp. Armour-plate rang to the impact of their blows. They would reach him eventually, would inevitably bring him down. Their cries grew more excitable. Yet they had not counted on Helios, were not prepared for the blur of crimson-red which announced arrival of an English pirate in brigantine jacket and reaping with his sword. The Janissaries scattered.

Together they cleared a passage. It was a rampaging procession of split faces and unholy wails, of surging torsos and trampled limbs. Somewhere, the banner of Ascanio de la Corna flew deep within the uproar. Somewhere, Vincenti Vitelli gave a cheery wave and returned to his carving. Somewhere, a bolting horse dragged its unseated and headless owner for the ridge, the entrails pulled behind like a limp flag in the dust.

The stone observation tower was taken, cleansed of its Turk sharpshooters. Around, the fight whirled with cavalry charge and counter-thrust, with the crashing riot of those with lives to play for and an island to lose. It became a physical reverberation that made the air sing and the earth quake. All-consuming and consuming all. At times, Hardy found himself caught behind the enemy, forgotten in the wider scheme. Or he would be in the vanguard, urging on, driving in. His sword and Helios were his protectors, delivering him safe, giving physical form to his conviction that the Ottomans would break, their troops run.

Instincts were correct and the collapse rapid. As their flank was turned by renewed assault of mounted Knights, the Turks crumpled. Wherever they faced, there were the serried ranks of spear-tips, the raking fire of muskets and crossbows, the barbarous shapes of lancers. They had been content to sail before, were desperate to quit now. Only two miles to the east lay salvation and the fleet of Piali. A small gap in the low hills, a wide valley beyond, and they would be on their way. Anguished shouts grew to a chorus. Stand and they would perish. They should never have disembarked, should never have come to Malta. Their campaign was done.

'The beast is wounded, Christian.'

'It prepares to escape. Their soldiers discard weapons, abandon hope and reason.'

'We shall harry them without pause.'

'I once took you as a placid fellow, Antonio.'

'In truth, this is a less than placid place.'

The Englishman wiped his blade on his saddlecloth. 'Helios is deprived of real pursuit. Now he has full rein.'

'Why do you block my path?'

'We are directed by command of the war council, Fra Roberto.'

The priest faced the two sentries guarding access to the temporary bridge of galley-masts laid across the sea-moat to St Angelo. On the fortress side, two more watched casually, complacent in their position of strength. They were the foot soldiers of de Pontieux. How power shifted; how deliberately the Grand Master had been spirited away and his succession arranged.

Fra Roberto raised an eyebrow. 'Am I not a brother of our Order?'

'Indeed you are, Fra Roberto. Yet you will not pass.'

'Will not? The most precise of terms.'

'Step away from the bridge. You have no place here.'

'But I am called by God to the side of my friend, our Grand Master, Jean Parisot de La Valette.'

'He is well attended.'

The face of the priest puckered as he scrutinized the pair. 'Our relief army engages in mortal battle a few miles hence. What if it should lose? What if the Turk should assail again our devastated walls?'

'These matters are for the Council.'

'They are for you. You have no right to stand idle in ceremony and display when the threat is not here, when the threat is not I.'

'Return to your quarters, priest.'

They were anxious, intimidated by his presence and proximity, by his physical size. Uneasiness was catching. The hafts of their pikes crossed, their grip changing from one hand to two, challenging. Alerted, the other sentries placed themselves in ready reserve. Fra Roberto twisted the wooden crucifix at his side, passing time, making comment.

'You take arms against one who has fought for the Religion, who has bled the heathen in the name of St John?'

'Our role is to protect.'

Fra Roberto sighed. 'Then it is settled.'

'Do not test our patience, priest.'

'I shall test instead your strength.'

In a single move, the crucifix came down on the crossed pikes, knocking them away, rendering the guards unarmed. Fra Roberto was in no mind to negotiate. He swept aside resistance, punching flat the one sentry, swatting the second over the lip of the moat.

He peered over. 'Learn from your baptism, you woeful sinner.'

Turning, he whistled, summoning his waiting band of volunteers. They joined him at the edge of the mast walkway, their expressions set, their glaives and crossbows levelled towards the two remaining pickets. Fra Roberto called across.

'Would you deny the plea of a humble priest to pray at the bedside of his Grand Master?'

Plainly, they would not. Leaving his troop to take possession of the bridge, the priest continued unopposed and alone. He strode along the parade dominated by the brute mass of the fortress walls, overshadowed by the tiered parapets of the gun-ramps. The sea breeze had done little to disperse the bitter taint of powder smoke. And war might yet return, the Turkish fleet round the headland to Grand Harbour.

It was Prior Garza who met him.

'Though solitary hermit, you seem intent to insinuate yourself deep within the bosom of our Order, Fra Roberto.'

'For one most average, you achieve the highest of office, Brother Prior.'

'I serve the Religion.'

'You benefit yourself.'

'Not so, Fra Roberto. Everything I do is for the glory of the Lord and survival of our brotherhood.'

'What of the survival of Grand Master La Valette?'

'He weakens.'

'I have no doubt, left to your kind mercies, that he does. Why was he brought from the Conventual Church?'

'We wished to lend him dignity in his descent.'

'Against his wishes, Brother Prior.'

'A command-post means nothing when there is no command-er and nothing to command.'

'So you retreat to St Angelo, barricade yourselves within its keep?'

'It is the heart of our Order.'

'The heart is to be found in those who fight, those who con-tinue to man our walls.'

'Then carry your crucifix and be with them. You will find in their company Knight Grand Cross Lacroix.' The smile was pink and gleeful, the eyes dead and pig-like.

'I will first see the Grand Master.'

'On whose authority?'

'That of a brother who will break you in twain should you not accede.'

'I am sure we may reach accommodation.'

Maria reached for a third bundle of parchment and untied the ribbons. More documents purloined from the library by Fra Roberto, business dealings and family letters full of detail and signifying little. She paused and rubbed her eyes. It was hard to concentrate when Christian was in the midst of battle, when that battle raged within distant earshot of the walls. Every air current brought the stammering noise of killing; any glimpse of movement or shadow or light produced fresh rumour. The tension made men weep and the misery of survival worse. She had so much yet to tell her love, so much she had left unsaid.

'I will seek news.' Luqa jumped up from where he had been squatting on his haunches.

'Be still, I beg you, Luqa. Outcome will neither alter nor advance through your action.'

'I do not read, am of no use here.'

'You are my company and my friend. It is of much value to me.'

'I should accompany the seigneur priest.'

'Fra Roberto is of size to finish matters by himself. Besides, he commands us remain, to study these papers he acquired.'

'What are papers when there is war, my lady?'

'There are many kinds of conflict. The course of the enemy may lie within these pages.'

'It is not yet found.'

'Patience, Luqa.' She held out her arms, let him come to her. 'You suffer, I know it. Victory postponed is more cruel than victory snatched away. But Christian will be with us safe.'

'I trust it is so, my lady.'

Her gaze alighted on the documents, on the family crests emblazoned on their vellum face. The usual litany of clan feuds and petty histories. She would go through the motions, would scan and arrange them to create diversion for her troubled mind. The Borgias. It was a symbol she recognized. She stared at the page, lifted another, and began to read. Luqa looked on, forgotten, quizzical, standing back to observe her renewed concentration. Five minutes, ten, and her head lifted, the excitement luminous in her features.

'Prepare for our adversary, Luqa. We make discovery.'

★

Retreat had widened into rout, the Turks tumbling pell-mell through the breach in the ridge to a false freedom beyond. Order was gone; weapons had been discarded. The Moslems were in a broad valley, making for the coast, pursued from behind, harried from all sides. Around them, the Christian horsemen looped and charged. More Turks fell. At the rear, squads of Janissary musketeers put up a defence, tried to screen the haphazard exodus. They were soon overwhelmed, their battle-cries dwindling as those of the Christians rose. Blood was in the nostrils, gun-smoke in the eyes. They were chased onward, staggering blind. Another outpost of resistance gave. A feeding frenzy, and the Ottomans were the prey.

'On, on . . .'

Mustapha Pasha waved his scimitar, urging his stumbling troops to greater effort. They were on their knees, lowing with dumb fear and heedless exhaustion. But he drove them forward, dragging, herding, guiding his second mount back into the fight. His first horse had already been shot from under him. It did not matter. He was oblivious to the danger, aware only of the need to save his army, to salvage something from defeat. A scrap of honour, the battle-standard of the Grand Turk, a troop of levies. He might reach the ships with these, might not reach the ships at all.

They had found the coast, were going north, for a mile on would be St Paul's Bay and the fleet of Piali. Bitterness sat solid like a cancer. The Admiral had been right, that timid, pitiful creature could crow and fawn at the feet of his Sultan. It was not he who had taken the risks, who had devised ingenious strategies, who had gambled life and limb and reputation to win or lose the blood rock. The thought made Mustapha Pasha spur his whinnying horse into the gallop.

'Their cavalry keep pace, Mustapha Pasha.'

'They overreach.'

'Yet they cut us down from every quarter.'

'With the sea to our right, they cannot manoeuvre. Without infantry, they cannot build on any gain.'

'You have orders, Mustapha Pasha?'

'To quicken your pace, to still wound the infidels.'

He rode on to the next group of officers, their coloured silks tattered and grey with dust.

'Command the Janissaries to intervene, to mount staged defence of our withdrawal.'

'We have done so, Mustapha Pasha.'

'Aim for the infidel horses. The foe is nothing when brought to earth.' He called to a mounted captain threading through the shifting scenes. 'Where are the Spahis?'

'Gone.' The man did not pause.

Mustapha Pasha spied an officer without his sword and trotted alongside. 'You have abandoned your weapon.'

'It was torn from my grasp in earlier engagement, Mustapha Pasha.'

'Your hand survives. Either it is slothful or you avoid battle.'

'We all escape, Mustapha Pasha.'

'You shall take your chance by foot.'

He tipped the hapless rider from his saddle and snatched up the reins. At random, he offered the charger to a bemused foot soldier. Such were the accidents of war.

'Do not slacken, you dogs! The bay of St Paul and the fleet of Piali are close! Maintain your march; revel in this instant to test your courage!'

Few responded to his exhortations; fewer had time for exhibition of nerve. They kept their heads bowed, not pausing to aid those cut off or mown down along the barren route. Every man was for himself, lost it seemed in a private race from death. Their tormentors came back.

The sharp prows and squat masts of galleys peppered the horizon. They might have given hope were the sights around not so grisly, the situation so desperate. Mustapha Pasha attempted to rally the rear and intercept pursuit, was sacrificing his units in last and lonely stands against the onrush. It was for the greater good and to small avail. From the low crests and undulations ahead, the marksmen of Hassem, governor of Algiers, took up their firing-positions. Without them, the departing Turks would be overrun.

'Fire now!'

A downward sweep of his scimitar and Mustapha Pasha brought forth a volley of Janisssary fire upon the approaching cavalry. The Christian line fractured, Knights and horses bucking and flailing in the haze. The musketeers reloaded, aimed, and discharged a second time. The Christians reeled. But they reformed fast, their aggression unchecked, their war-yelps and outstretched swords cutting through the smoke. Among them was the figure of a warrior in crimson brigantine jacket, dominant, eager, bearing down astride a steel-grey stallion. There could be only one possibility as to his identity.

It was Satan himself who plunged from his horse. Hardy saw the animal stumble and die, the descent of its master as he fell hard and floundered on the limestone track. The commander-in-chief was down. Mustapha Pasha had lost the campaign, was about to lose his life. Hardy stared at the Turk. The man had butchered so many, had reduced St Elmo to powdered ruin and the garrisons of Birgu and Senglea to a few scattered remnants. He would pay, would forfeit his existence for those he had snatched away, for the torture and suffering, for the one hundred and twelve days he had spent on this island. Hardy pressed his heels, and Helios surged forward.

Their gaze held. There was recognition in the eyes of Mustapha Pasha. And hatred – of the English pirate who had resisted his troops at St Elmo, who had outwitted the corsair El Louck Aly Fartax, who had taken his beloved Arab steed from his camp on the Marsa and tricked him at Mdina. A meeting of equals, a moment to appreciate. Hardy leaned against the neck of Helios as he had done so often, the thudding hooves, the pounding equine muscularity pulling him in, forcing him on. Distance closed and he stretched out the point of his blade, aiming straight, willing it to slice through the guts and chest.

Helios must have sensed, must have known it was the fragile instant before the squad of Janissaries again loosed their shot. He never wavered. It was instinctive, the loyalty of a friend, the duty of a horse who had carried his lord unscathed through peace and combat. Now was his time. Uncommanded, he reared and took the strike of musket-lead deep into his underside. Hardy felt the shuddering impact, the sliding and dying energy, the slipping of Helios towards the ground. He rolled away and knelt beside him, holding him, burying his face against the warm coat. They were sharing a stable again at Mdina. They were galloping free and unburdened across the island. They were resting at night above the cliffs to observe the glow of lamps from the enemy fleet. The intelligent eyes watched him and slowly glazed, and the heart stilled. And Hardy screamed at the sky, howled for his loss. Certainty was gone, the Moor, Hubert and Henri were gone, and Helios was gone. In this barren place he had broken his soul, was losing his mind. The battle curled about him, and he did not care.

Chapter 20

'They say the waters of St Paul's run red, that several thousand Turk bodies float within the bay.'

'The greater pity it is that any escape.'

'Mustapha Pasha was among the last to reach the safety of the galleys.'

'Then we are rid of him, and our great siege is concluded.'

Conversation was subdued, the senior Knights aware that solemnity was more fitting than euphoria, that while they spoke La Valette lay stricken. Perhaps they had asked too much of God. He had delivered to them an epic victory, seemed resolved to call back to His side its architect and champion. A fair exchange; a bitterly sweet occasion. Their Grand Master would for ever be remembered and honoured in their prayers.

De Pontieux surveyed them as he entered the chamber. 'Such long and dejected faces, my brothers.'

'Have you further news of His Highness?'

'He is unchanged from the last. We must wait, and we must ask for intercession of our patron saint.'

'Our cries have been answered before.'

'They may be rejoined again. Yet I must confess Jean Parisot de La Valette does not respond to the medicines and care to which we expose him.'

'Is there nothing more we may do?'

'Embrace the will of God'. The tone of de Pontieux was

measured. 'His Highness is old, enfeebled and made sick by the trials of war and burden of office.'

'Yet he is our Grand Master.'

'I do not deny it. But consider how diminished is he in his powers, how his strength wanes since wounding to his leg.'

'Brother de Pontieux is right. We should prepare for the worse.'

De Pontieux raised a hand. 'Not so, my brother chevaliers. We should prepare for the peace.'

'You make suggestion?'

'I offer solution. We send for guidance to His Holiness in Rome; we begin election for new Grand Master.'

'I accord with Brother de Pontieux.'

'I also.' Others murmured in agreement.'

'While I do not.'

'Sir Oliver Starkey?' De Pontieux narrowed his eyes. 'Your position as Latin secretary to La Valette gives you no say on the Sacro Consiglio.'

'I am his counsel and his friend.'

'We are his brothers.'

'Behave as such. He has led you, stood with you, fought against the heathen with you.'

'It is for his sake we act.'

'There are those who believe it is for personal ambition.'

'They may speak in Council, may challenge on every count. I will not be found wanting.'

'Your conduct is already found wanting.'

'Why is it the English try me so?' De Pontieux raised an eyebrow, drew laughter from the assembled. 'Remember, it is I who administer justice and apportion penalty, Sir Oliver.'

'Are you to imprison me as you have Fra Roberto?'

'We keep the peace, we defend ourselves, we contain endangerment to our Order.'

'Fra Roberto is no threat.'

'He is of a fractious and defiant disposition.'

Who next? Myself? Grand Cross Lacroix? Any who displease you?'

'That will be determined.'

A chaplain approached, and de Pontieux turned towards him, secure in his authority, confident he had neutralized any lingering challenge. Soon the victorious relief army would be marching for Birgu, would bring to a close this chapter in the history of the Hospitaller Knights. La Valette had served his purpose.

The cleric was sombre. 'His skin is fevered, his thirst worsens, Brother Chevalier.'

'You find remedy?'

'We try.'

'Extend your efforts. I shall myself impel the apothecary and physician in their tasks.'

He swept through the open doorway, heading with urgency for the suite of palace rooms reserved for the Grand Master. The situation demanded an energetic reponse. It also warranted drama, a playing to his submissive audience. La Valette might be ill, but life went on, the business of acquiring influence and arranging for succession continued.

'What do you provide him?' He delivered his question as accusation.'

The medic frowned. 'Water and a little goat milk, Brother Chevalier.'

'It is not sufficient.'

'He imbibes near to nothing, Brother Chevalier.'

'That is still something. Squeeze oranges, prepare the bowl. Find too the oil of bitter almonds.'

'You wish to make orgeat?'

'I can think of no better solution to stave his thirst, to bring relief and moisture to a parched throat.' He took the ingredients, pressing, mixing, adding drops of oil to the final blend. Sipping the concoction, he nodded. 'His Highness will be grateful for our exertion.'

Decanting the liquid into a silver goblet, he carried it through to the anteroom, a small retinue of supporters falling in behind. They were the new Order, a changing of the guard. He walked on, focused on his mission, certain of the future. A page bowed and prepared to throw wide the entrance to the bedchamber.

It was as the oak door swung open that the sword descended. A masterful stroke. The blade arced near-invisible, sending the chalice spinning away, rising to greet the throat of its bearer. Christian Hardy stood in the way.

De Pontieux spoke, his breath tight, his voice controlled. 'The meaning of this?'

'You are aware of its meaning, understanding of its effect.'

'I provide the Grand Master with drink.'

'Of what kind, de Pontieux?'

'That which would meet a thirst.'

'And that would kill.'

'You lie.'

'As you poison.'

'Poison? I have myself consumed of this cup.'

'Part of the conspiracy, a fraction of your deceit and disguise.'

'Your imaginings do you no credit, Hardy.'

'Yet I hold sword to your throat, would pin you as though you were an insect.'

'For which you would thus hang.'

'It holds no fear for me, de Pontieux.' The sword pressed closer. 'Do you fear? Do you wonder at the turn of events, at how lives betrayed return to haunt you?'

'As God is my judge, I do no wrong.'

'I, not God, shall be your judge. What liquid rested in the goblet?'

'Orgeat, nothing more.'

'And nothing less. Orgeat, with its oil of bitter almonds. Orgeat, which would worm its cyanide way into a body defiled by arsenic, into a stomach weakened by emetic purge. Orgeat, which will combine with cure of calomel to render dead its victim.'

'You bewilder with such accusation, confuse me for the lowest knave.'

'I see you as you are, de Pontieux.'

'A Knight Commander of St John, loyal servant to the Religion.'

'An assassin.'

'Such falsehood.'

'How may you deny your eye is on the prize, your fingers close about the palace keys?'

'I am no murderer, Hardy.'

'Yet I have inclination to be.'

'You intend to cut from me confession?'

'I intend to tear from you your life.' Hardy lowered his blade towards the chest, allowed seconds to pass and de Pontieux to sweat. 'For those you have wronged and killed, I bring retribution. We fight to the death as once we swore.'

'The Grand Master forbids duelling.'

'He revokes his stricture for our occasion.'

'Then let us take our places.'

'In the courtyard beyond these palace walls, on the roof of this great keep.'

'A fine place to learn your lesson.'

'I have learned enough, de Pontieux. There is no escape. Fra Roberto is released from the cell to which you sent him. My men hold the approaches to St Angelo. Our stage is set.'

'Your final act begins.'

There was no festivity of the joust, just dull expectation and a collection of Knights and churchmen present to bear witness. Weapons had been chosen. It would be a contest of rapiers and daggers, fought without armour or interruption, spanning the flagstones until one man fell. Simple rules for the most basic of tasks. The opponents circled, testing the ground, eyeing each other to gauge mind and moment.

Hardy shifted his grip, altered his balance. He was content to eke out these minutes, to watch de Pontieux pace and fret and feel. The conclusion was not in doubt. He would finish the Knight when ready, when he had unnerved him sufficiently with his wait.

De Pontieux rushed him. It was a brief clash, the easiest of parries. The Knight retreated, was plainly summoning his strength, inciting himself to commit. Hardy peered at him. The swordplay of a nobleman was no match for the cunning of a common brawler, a natural pirate. But reptiles could acquire skills.

'Your friend the heathen Moor died as loud as a stuck boar, Hardy.'

'What noise will you make?'

'He was slit from end to end, scarce comprehended his grim fate.'

'Be not deluded of your own.'

'You are confident, Hardy.'

'A blade to the back is easy done. The truer test is to face your foe.'

'I am prepared.'

'So bid yourself farewell.' Swords touched and steel scraped.

'No hired hand, no military whore, may overcome a Knight.'

'Put conjecture to the trial.'

A fresh attempt, the scream of effort, the secondary cry of an inflicted wound. De Pontieux backed away, his dagger discarded. Blood was streaming from his arm.

'You surprise me, de Pontieux. It is blood and not venom you leak.'

Enraged, the Knight struck again. Hardy danced back, flicking his sword playfully, goading as he went.

'I am pleased I did not drown you, de Pontieux.'

'Your pleasure will be brief.'

Rapier points flashed. It was now Hardy who moved forward, who forced his adversary across the stones. There was desperation in the eyes of de Pontieux, the fixed intensity of a man fighting for his reputation, his honour and his life. Something else glimmered. Hardy had witnessed it in enemy and friend, encountered it on garrison walls and the decks of ships. Fear could not be hidden.

Prior Garza broke first, seizing a javelin from an infantryman and charging forward with intent to plunge it into the exposed back of the Englishman. It was on an impulse, and deadly meant. Fat churchmen could be quick, could respond to the call of an ally in need. But he was too slow for Fra Roberto. From beneath the voluminous folds of his habit and cloak, the priest raised a cocked and loaded crossbow. Without pausing, seemingly without aiming, he fired.

The bolt flew the distance, impacting with a heavy-wet blow, its twin-pronged head bisecting the spine of the travelling cleric. His scream was piercing and short. Hardy did not turn to view the crumpled form. He bore down on de Pontieux, probing his weakness, dismissing his rallies with a rotation of the wrist and a whip-like response. The Knight was staring at death, had the corpse of a comrade framed in his sight. It could not have improved his morale. Hardy was remorseless and steady. He pushed de Pontieux back, removing his freedom, reversing him towards the curving elegance of the nymphaeum. In this small grotto, La Valette would once have sat and meditated, found shelter from wind and sun in the cool shade of its barrel-vaulting. De Pontieux was seeking refuge from different forces.

He slipped, was kicked for his trouble, came too close, was pierced through his shoulder. Weakening, sobbing with the rawness of pain and inevitability, he gave more ground. It was a tactical error. Beneath the lip of the coffered ceiling, he was in shadow, blinking into the light. Hardy was there. His outline loomed, his blade teased.

'Are you willing to submit, de Pontieux?'

'To a bastard vagabond, to offspring of a harlot? Never.' He thrust at the target, was answered with a flat-stroke to his knee. It shattered.

'I cause you discomfort?'

Between panting yips of agony, the Knight shook his head. 'You will not bring me low.'

'My work is incomplete.'

Hardy lunged and gouged the other knee. Bone and ligament separated. De Pontieux was crawling, scrambling to withdraw, reaching for purchase on statues and urns. He made it to the fountain and clawed his way up.

'I have no sword, Hardy.'

'You keep your tongue.'

'What is to be gained in this? What is there that cannot be pursued with reason?'

'Some things are beyond reason.'

'You would be a common murderer, an outcast of the Order?'

'I will be true to myself, shall do as you did to the Moor.' He planted both sword and dagger through the chest.

Walking slowly, he emerged from the nymphaeum to the waiting ranks of silent faces. Behind him, the traitor was dead, enthroned as a comic grotesque on the marble water-pan of the cooling spring. It was an image that Hardy put behind him. No more would he take up the sword or wear the brigantine, defend ramparts or lead armed sorties. The infection and ecstasy of war were gone, and in their place was grief, the heavy tiredness of a tainted core. He wanted to sleep. He wanted forgiveness. He wanted the solace of Maria and her arms about him.

'It is complete.'

'You are wrong, Monsieur Hardy.'

La Valette was stooped over the entrance balustrade, a Lazarus not quite fully risen. He was cadaver-pale, his eyes sunken, his skin drawn tight across his skull. But unaided he stood, alive, present, observing the scene. It was effort to speak. Each word and gesture tested his resilience, tapped his reserves. Yet he would be heard.

He went on. 'The strewn bodies of a Knight and of a prior are testament to the follies of men, to pride and perfidy, to ambition and greed. Look long upon them, brothers. They are flesh, and they are we. Their sin is as old as Creation itself. Guarding against it will never be complete.'

'You confront it without me, Your Highness.'

'That is your choosing, Monsieur Hardy, and we do not condemn you. You earn our gratitude and respect.' La Valette returned to his audience. 'Mighty accomplishment is achieved this day. The heathen is gone, and we that are left must praise the Lord, should consign our sorrow and dead to earth, and will rebuild our walls and auberges. The Mohammedan survives, and may come again. For our war is eternal, our hatred unbounded. There is no love between our tribes, no peace betwixt Cross and Crescent. And wheresoever we shall meet, it will be in enmity and holy combat.'

It was summary of present purpose and statement of future intent. Nothing changed. Hardy let them be, let them savour the precious respite. Their Grand Master was saved, their Order preserved, their island, their ways, their existence secured. He could not begrudge them. But he would not be part of it. His was a separate journey, a renewal, a path that required no eight-pointed cross. He reached the steps of the keep and descended.

She was there, worry and then relief etched in her features. They met as he climbed from his horse, holding each other in silent embrace, her tears mingling with his kisses. There was much to celebrate and remember, and too much to say. The Turk was vanished, the Great Siege already history. And it had left them alive, wed, able to do as normal folk did, to greet the morrow as citizens and not as combatants.

She whispered to him, toyed with the silver crucifix at his throat. 'You have vanquished evil, Christian.'

'My sweet Maria, without you I would be too late.'

'The Grand Master lives?'

'He does, and the Order gives thanks for it. De Pontieux and Prior Garza are no more.'

'Then we each have done our duty.'

'You far beyond that which is expected of a noble lady.'

'I am your wife, Christian.'

'A wife who wields an arquebus, who rains fire and boiling water upon the foe, who rolls explosive barrel back into their line.'

'We did as were obliged.'

'There are men who see this day because you bound their wounds and tended them. There is Grand Master La Valette, who leads his Knights because you read correspondence of the Borgias, learned of their foul wiles of poisoning and murder.'

'It was Fra Roberto who suspected the truth and began the quest.'

'What strange conjuncture of persons and events.'

'They lead us here, Christian.'

'For which I give praise.'

He rested his head on her shoulder, lost himself in the smell of her skin. It brought memories: of the night she had visited and lain with him at St Elmo, of their comfort and closeness in the cave near the shore. She was imprinted on his soul. Her presence banished the dark, ushered in peace.

'Why did Chevalier de Pontieux plot so, Christian?'

'Is there explanation for why man is filled with lust for power?'

'And yet there has been here such heroism and sacrifice.'

'It will ever counter the blackness.'

'I hope with all my heart it will.'

'While the Viceroy of Sicily wrung his hands and the princes of Europe stood by, mere mortals altered destiny. It can be done.'

'Though I weep for those who are lost in trying.'

'They would be happy we live to speak of them, that some of us remain. The Moor, with his solemnity and incendiaries, his friendship and devotion. Hubert, his courage burning through timidity, his gentle heart too large for such small frame. And Henri, the sweet scholar and Hospitaller who took up sword because he must.'

'Are we worthy of their destruction?'

'I know not.' He looked into her eyes. 'Yet they fought so we need fight no more. We owe to them our everything.'

'We three.'

Her smile flittered through the clouded emotion, widening as his own expression changed. She took his hand and placed it on her belly.

'You carry our child, Maria?'

'You said mere mortals can alter destiny.'

'We change our own for ever.'

'Out of war is come tranquillity; from the death of comrades is come hope. We shall not waste it.'

Slowly, he sank to his knees and kissed her abdomen. It was a simple act of veneration. He was giving thanks to her, to their child, to God, for his salvation and his future. The boy who had lived among corsairs, landed on Malta, borne arms for the Knights was dead. His successor knelt in the dust before this woman and the unborn he loved.

Islanders would be watching from the shore, nervous as the fleet passed. They need not fear. Mustapha Pasha gazed from the stern at the departing horizon, listened to the beat of the drum, to the groans of slaves and creak of oars. The imams kept silent. There was little left for them to say, too few men to hear them say it. This was how holy war ended when God did not favour the faithful. Navarino, Koron, Cape Matapan, the Cape of Malia, Andros, Saniz, waypoints to Malta, return markers to Constantinople.

They were limping home, riding before the storms, not with the swagger of conquest, but with the grey melancholy of failure.

He spat over the gilded rail. It was hard to expel the sour taste in his mouth, harder to erase the searing flashes of memory from his thoughts. The final moments haunted him. There had been so many bodies in the water, struggling, dying or dead, a human mass in pitched and drenched battle. In all his life he had encountered nothing like it. Yet somehow his small boat had picked its way through, had navigated the steel reefs of jabbing blades, dodged the darting shoals of arrow and lead-shot. He had reached his galley. The slow were abandoned to their fate, St Paul's Bay to their screams.

Crimson red dripped into his conscousness. It was the colour of the shallows he had fled, the colour of the brigantine jacket worn by Christian Hardy. He had seen the magnificent grey stallion fall and the young English pirate sink down beside it. Such a human response in the midst of war. It provoked in him only rage. He had intended to run forward, to wash his blade in the viscera of this demon. But a Janissary bodyguard had ushered him away. A wise precaution, for the enemy cavalry had pounded forward again, overwhelming his marksmen, outpacing his stumbling retreat. Some opportunities simply slipped from the grasp.

The wind gusted stronger, and he braced himself against the deepening swell. Were he to be lucky, the ship would broach and sink and his body disappear. It would not happen. He was destined to appear before his Sultan, to throw himself at the feet and upon the mercy of an old unforgiving tyrant. Absolute calamity rarely found preference with an absolute ruler. Mustapha Pasha grimaced at the chasing, blackening clouds. He felt the limestone rock in his palm, the keepsake he had unthinkingly seized while scrabbling in the dirt once he fell. Miles travelled, tens of thousands slain, and his sole prize was a lump of stone. It had cost him everything. With a snarl, he hurled it into the waves and saw it swallowed in an instant. His dream was over and Malta was gone.

★

Far off in Constantinople, an aged Sultan waited. His deaf mutes attended, as ever at the ready.

Across the Marsa, the strain of trumpets, the roll of cannons and drums indicated the arrival of the relief army in Birgu. The new-comers were in for a shock, They would find smouldering ruin, the broken and emaciated forms of humans clinging to existence among a cratered wilderness. It had been a close-run thing. Christian galleys floated in the harbour, their stores shuttled ashore, their presence a comfort to veterans of siege who had come to expect reversal of fortune and Turkish ruse. Soon the Viceroy of Sicily himself would appear, providing assurance, making excuse. Blame and recrimination could be banished by festivity.

Hardy left the noise behind, trotted his horse towards St Elmo. It was his final mission. He was on pilgrimage to his recent past, paying homage to the brothers with whom he had shared those strange and deathly weeks and hours. Their spirits were with him, their voices loud in his ear.

He dismounted at the crumbling line of the ravelin and made his way across the remnants of the ditch. Desolation and memory infested his senses, as choking as the ash kicked up at his feet. Such scorched and punished stones, such wide and empty breaches, each representing a skirmish, a charge, a respite won, a life lost. Here he had stood with a trump and held at bay the first attack. And there had been the chairs on which the wounded de Guaras and his Knights had crouched waiting for the inevitable, resisting until the end. *Sleep in peace, my brothers . . .*

A rat hauled itself from cover and paraded fat and self-satisfied along a tumble of brick. More recollection, more overlaid scenes of suffering and endeavour. He had stood on that broken cannon to rally his men, had shattered that cavalier tower while ridding it of Janissaries. The outpost where he had illicit congress with Maria, the collapsed stonework where again and again he had

361

beaten back the Turks, the entrance to the chapel where finally they reached him.

The rodent had disappeared from view. Hardy let his sight drift across the ploughed wreckage of the courtyard, placed his fingers into the scars and indentations of the limestone. This was how the clash of powers looked, the sum achievement of militant religion and opposing creeds, of what man could do in anger. Everything silent and blighted. He found steps and climbed them to the rampart.

'The slumber of the dead and the guilt of the living.'

Knight Grand Cross Lacroix stood behind him, a pistol in each hand, the distance no more than six feet. He would not miss.

Hardy swivelled slow to face him. 'I see no guilt in your eyes.'

'Nor shall you.'

'You stand where the heads of my commanders and friends were placed on spikes.'

'They were not wise heads.'

'Yet they were brave and noble ones.' Hardy squinted at the gun muzzles. 'What is the meaning of these weapons?'

'Your execution.'

'Then de Pontieux was not the betrayer we sought.'

'Chevalier de Pontieux is no loss. He and Prior Garza served their purpose and did not know it. They created tension and diversion, enmities which cloaked my actions and deeper intent.'

'You unmask yourself.'

'At place and time of my choosing, and your death.'

'Such effort is squandered. The Order is saved, the Turk sails.'

'Suleiman will not accept setback of this nature. In a year, his armies will return invigorated. The walls of Birgu and Senglea are destroyed, the Knights decimated, and you and La Valette shall dwell in a different realm.'

'It is a long game you play.'

'What other exists?'

'One of honour and service, of loyal devotion and not deceit.'

'So speaks a scavenger, a jackal who follows the lion pride, who feeds on the bones and misery of others, who cracks the marrowbone that is left for him.'

'Traitor.'

'Not I, and not to my sovereign state.'

'You consort with the enemy.'

'Turkey is ally of France, France a foe to pirates who would threaten trade and harmony, who would bring down upon our shores the wrath of the Sultan.'

'The Order defends Europe and Christendom.'

'It defends itself, grows rich on its raiding at expense of the whole.'

'And you have been brother to La Valette, constant at his side, a Knight who fought through Rhodes and brought with him the banner of St John to Malta.'

'A man may learn, may grow to understand his wider duty.'

'I vouch it has a price.'

'As the Templars outlived their use, so in 1307 King Philip the Fourth of France ordered their destruction. In similar fashion, by order of King Francis the First, the Knights of the Hospital are damned, are come to their natural end.'

'You believe the Sultan will refrain from further conquest and ambition, will safeguard the boundaries of France?'

'We have arrangement.'

'You sup with Satan.'

'It is our way, young Hardy.'

The barrels of the pistols drooped. They were long, heavy, would need shortly to be rested or used. Hardy studied the face of the old Knight, searching for clues, attempting to make sense, to match this blank innocence to the confession. Murder and manipulation were skilfully hid.

'Your wounds recover well, Lacroix.'

'They were cosmetic and self-inflicted, designed to gain entry to the infirmary and win reprieve from battle.'

'There you met La Valette.'

'The easier to break bread with him, drink wine with him. To poison him anew.'

'You took vow to protect the Order and Religion.'

'Harsher realities befit our age and shape our actions. Malta is Spanish possession, guarded for papal advantage. It serves no interest of my country. Thus I gift it to the Turk that we may live and thrive.'

'Thousands die, Lacroix.'

'War and cruelty are oft paired.'

'You have no remorse?'

'That I did not kill you earlier; that you snatched La Valette from my grasp, thwarted my intent on so many occasion.'

'The signals to the Turk of reinforcement to St Elmo? Explosion in our powder-stores? Janissaries in the tunnels beneath St Angelo?'

'Much more beside.'

'Fra Roberto warned if I should find the motive, I would discover the felon.'

'He is wise for a drunk. Quick too, I hear, with crossbow.'

'You are beneath all contempt.'

'While your friend Hubert resides below ground. He was so open to suggestion.'

'Loose your pistols, Lacroix. I have no desire for your company.'

'This mortal coil grows weary of yours.'

Lacroix sighed, reason and reasonableness in his voice, acceptance in his eyes. Dispatching an opponent was mere afterthought, a tying of loose ends. Unwavering, Hardy faced him. He thought of the dead and of the living, of Maria and the child he would not know. At least they would live; at least he had endured to witness victory and hear the celebration bell of the Conventual Church. There was no fear. The screams of his mother and sisters were stilled, the humble dwelling of his youth and dreams no longer burned. Quietness settled. He had made his peace. Twenty-two years were over.

'Whether from God or man, you will not escape justice, Lacroix.'

'I shall witness triumph that you delayed. Begin your prayer.'

'Our Father, Which art in heaven . . . '

The pistols fired.

Lacroix stood and viewed the corpse awhile. The Englishman had been worthy quarry, had died as expected, with the calm dignity and defiant indifference of the breed. He could respect him for that. His killing was not personal, was nothing more than the defence of a position, the outflanking of a threat. Vulnerability had been removed, certainty restored. But there was work to do. He would be paying a visit to Jean Parisot de La Valette to assess the progress in his recovery.

He retraced his steps through the fortress, had no interest in loitering, in dwelling on the stories and sentimentality associated with its ruins. The fading past could not compete with a rewritten future. He looked back once before taking the reins and rising into the saddle. Hardy was where he should have stayed earlier, had gone to join his brethren. In the frayed aftermath of conflict, none would ask or pry, would seek out Knight Grand Cross Lacroix. Life went on. The cause, the aims of his homeland, continued.

It was as he turned his mount that the slingshot struck. Lacroix stiffened, his eyes fixed in trauma, a thin line of blood coursing between them, before he plunged. Luqa ran past. He hurried through the fort, calling, searching, his shouts and footfall deadened by the ruptured limestone, until he reached the steps. Instinct drew him upward. He found the body with ease, saw the gaping wounds. No breath, no flicker of life. Hardy lay sprawled on his side, his face to the sea, an arm flung out towards St Angelo. The boy knelt reverentially beside him, leaning to close his eyes, to touch his head. A final farewell. Gently, he kissed the forehead of Christian Hardy and removed the silver cross to place about his own neck. It belonged with the living.

End

She soared, found an updraught, and spiralled higher, a gyrfalcon–barbary cross climbing towards nine hundred feet. There she would wait, hanging in the thermals, circling, hunting. La Valette shaded his eyes. The stoop, the kill, would come, when this diminished speck of sharp-set ferocity dropped to punch its prey from the sky. Even in level flight she could overhaul the fastest pigeon, would bind on and bring it down. An awesome display. It reminded him of the chasing prows of his galleys, of the lightning raids, of the dash and aggression of his Knights. The bird of prey was dominant in its kingdom. He was master in his.

July 1568. Three years had passed since the Turk left. It was a time of renewal and rebuilding, of creating a magnificent walled city, Valletta, on the barren slopes of Mount Sciberras. Eight thousand slaves and labourers toiling on a single project. Out of ordeal and Ottoman defeat was come glorious beginning. The Order was rich. Princes paid homage, bishops paid money. Coffers filled, palaces rose, honours were given, and tale and song of that brave defence thrilled every court in Christendom. Why, the Pope had offered to create him cardinal.

It made no difference. He was old and frail, felt the weight of office, the heavy hand of his years. Ghosts were his companions. Their names and faces visited him in his dreams, conjured those terrible months of three summers past. He had rid himself of the poison, ordered destruction of all record. But the melancholy stayed, the grieving went on, hidden behind prayer and pageant, by the legend of the bold Order and its mighty Grand Master La Valette. A quarter of his Knights dead, almost his entire garrison slaughtered. Yet he had won great victory. Suleiman the Magnificent never again sent invasion force to those shores. The Sultan was too busy, committed elsewhere, engaged in military campaigns in Hungary, in managing his fractious and far-flung empire. It was just as well, an added benefit, he had died a year after his island venture, on 5 September 1566.

The falcon had found her target. She plummeted with the sound of tearing canvas, diving vertically to break the back of a gull and knock it to the ground. It was a clean kill. La Valette motioned to his falconers to go forward with their wooden cadges, to retrieve her before her natural greed and wild instinct encouraged her to desertion. She was no easy charge.

Another sight drew his eye, a young woman on horseback leading by rein a pony on which sat her infant son.

Maria smiled as he approached. 'Your Highness. I trust we do not intrude.'

'My hunting is done, my lady.'

'I see she flies better than any saker or lanner.'

'Yet she is capricious, will guard and mantle over the kill, will bate on each occasion on my hand.'

'She is right to be versed in combat, vested with fighting spirit.'

'And your boy?' Valette nodded to the child who beamed in return. 'He sits well in the saddle.'

'A soldier in heart and soul.'

So like his father, La Valette mused. A two-year-old with more than mere resemblance. The same directness in the blue eyes, the same grin, the same restless vigour. He was a son of war, of Christian Hardy. It would bring both comfort and anguish to his mother. *A soldier in heart and soul.* Perhaps he would hear one day of the Great Siege, might learn of the exploits of his father. Who knew if he would understand. Few ever did.

'We should away, Your Highness.'

'As I must to my falcon.' He adjusted his pigskin glove and inclined gravely to them both.

The boy bowed from his pony and laughed delighted.

'Come now, Christian. We travel on.'

La Valette watched them go, suddenly wistful at recollection of bygone childhood, of promise yet to be discovered. He had been young, had once faced the world with eagerness and optimism. It was the lot of mortals to crumble into dust, the fate of all Grand Masters to decline on a whimper. He should be content. There would always be the likes of Christian Hardy, of Henri and young Hubert and the Moor, willing to fight for what they believed or to fight because it was there. The future of the Religion was secure.

That afternoon, having returned to Grand Harbour from his hunting expedition, the Grand Master suffered a stroke. His Knights bore him to a room in the Magisterial Palace, where he lingered part-paralysed, semi-conscious, for some weeks. Surrounded by his loyal brethren, he prayed, dictated his final testament, and prepared for the end. It came in the early hours of a fetid summer morning. The life of Jean Parisot de La Valette, forty-eighth Grand Master of the Knights of St John of Jerusalem, saviour of Malta, champion of Europe, was over.

Acknowledgements

Thanks are due to the following for contributing in so many ways to the completion of this book: Ram, Nick and Lizzy for accompanying me and steering me in my research; Nancy Calamatta, Michael Stroud and Fra John Critien for their valuable time and welcome insights; Stephen C. Spiteri and the late Ernle Brandford for their respective books, *The Great Siege: Anatomy of a Hospitaller Victory* and *The Great Siege: Malta 1565*, which have so inspired and informed; Eugenie Furniss, my agent, and Kate Parkin, my editor, for their input, patience and friendship; the people of Malta, for an island whose history and character held me spellbound as a child.